THE VIKING PORTABLE LIBRARY

Edgar Allan Poe

Edgar Allan Poe was born in Boston in 1809, the son of itinerant actors. Both his parents died within two years of his birth. Edgar was taken into the home of a Richmond merchant, John Allan, although he was never legally adopted. Poe's relationship with his foster-father was not good and was further strained when he was forced to withdraw from the University of Virginia because Allan refused to finance him. After a reconciliation, Poe entered the Military Academy at West Point in 1830; he was dishonorably discharged in January 1831. His early work as a writer went unrecognized and he was forced to earn his living on newspapers, working as an editor in Richmond, Philadelphia, and New York. He achieved respect as a literary critic but it was not until the publication of *The Raven and Other Poems* in 1845 that he gained success as a writer. And, despite his increasing fame, Poe remained in the same poverty which characterized most of his life. In 1836 he married his cousin, Virginia, who was then fourteen; she died eleven years later of tuberculosis. Poe died a few years later in 1849 and was buried in Baltimore beside his wife.

Philip Van Doren Stern (1900–1984) compiled and edited many volumes and wrote many others, the latter including *The Man Who Killed Lincoln*.

Each volume in The Viking Portable Library either presents a representative selection from the works of a single outstanding writer or offers a comprehensive anthology on a special subject. Averaging 700 pages in length and designed for compactness and readability, these books fill a need not met by other compilations. All are edited by distinguished authorities, who have written introductory essays and included much other helpful material.

D1016160

The Portable

Edgar Allan Poe

*Selected and Edited, with an Introduction
and Notes, by*

PHILIP VAN DOREN STERN

PENGUIN BOOKS

PENGUIN BOOKS

Published by the Penguin Group

Penguin Group (USA) Inc., 375 Hudson Street, New York, New York 10014, U.S.A.

Penguin Group (Canada), 90 Eglinton Avenue East, Suite 700, Toronto,
Ontario, Canada M4P 2Y3 (a division of Pearson Penguin Canada Inc.)

Penguin Books Ltd, 80 Strand, London WC2R 0RL, England

Penguin Ireland, 25 St Stephen's Green, Dublin 2, Ireland (a division of Penguin Books Ltd)

Penguin Group (Australia), 250 Camberwell Road, Camberwell,
Victoria 3124, Australia (a division of Pearson Australia Group Pty Ltd)

Penguin Books India Pvt Ltd, 11 Community Centre, Panchsheel Park, New Delhi – 110 017, India

Penguin Group (NZ), cnr Airborne and Rosedale Roads,
Albany, Auckland 1310, New Zealand (a division of Pearson New Zealand Ltd)

Penguin Books (South Africa) (Pty) Ltd, 24 Sturdee Avenue,
Rosebank, Johannesburg 2196, South Africa

Penguin Books Ltd, Registered Offices: 80 Strand, London WC2R 0RL, England

**First published in the United States of America
by Viking Penguin Inc. 1945
Paperbound edition published 1957
Reprinted 1959, 1960 (twice), 1961 (twice), 1962 (twice),
1963, 1964, 1965 (twice), 1966, 1967, 1968, 1969 (twice),
1971 (twice), 1972 (twice), 1973, 1974, 1976
Published in Penguin Books 1977**

40 39 38 37 36

Copyright 1945 by Philip van Doren Stern
Copyright © renewed Philip Van Doren Stern 1973
All rights reserved

LIBRARY OF CONGRESS CATALOGING IN PUBLICATION DATA
Poe, Edgar Allan, 1809–1849.
The portable Edgar Allan Poe.
Reprint of the 1945 ed. published by Viking Press,
New York under title: Edgar Allan Poe, issued in series:
The Viking portable library.
I. Stern, Philip Van Doren, 1900–   II. Title.
PS2602.s68   1977   818′.3′09   76-54888
ISBN 0 14 015.012 9

Printed in the United States of America
Set in Linotype Caledonia

Some of the material in this volume is reprinted by
permission of the holders of copyright and
publication rights. Acknowledgments will be found on page x.

CONTENTS

TALES

OF FANTASY

OF TERROR

OF DEATH

OPINIONS

ACKNOWLEDGMENTS

The editor wishes to express his appreciation to the following for the use of copyrighted material:

To Mr. Richard H. Hart of the Enoch Pratt Library, Baltimore, for two letters to Mrs. Clemm printed in *Edgar Allan Poe Letters and Documents,* 1941.

To the Valentine Museum, Richmond, for four letters to John Allan printed in *Edgar Allan Poe Letters . . . In the Valentine Museum,* Lippincott, 1925.

To the Houghton Mifflin Co., Boston, for the letters to James Russell Lowell and to Mary Louise Shew printed in *The Life of Edgar Allan Poe* by George Woodberry, 1909.

To Dean James Southall Wilson of the University of Virginia, Charlottesville, for the letter to Mrs. Nancy L. H. Richmond.

To Charles Scribner's Sons, New York, for the two letters to Sarah Helen Whitman printed in *Poe's Helen* by Caroline Ticknor, 1916.

To Major Howard Haycraft and the D. Appleton-Century Company, Inc., for the paragraph quoted from *Murder for Pleasure,* 1941

And especially to Thomas Y. Crowell and Co., New York, for their gracious permission to draw freely from their seventeen-volume "Virginia" edition of *The Complete Works of Edgar Allan Poe,* edited by James A. Harrison, to provide the basic text used in this volume.

CHRONOLOGY

1809 JANUARY 19. Edgar Poe born in Boston, Mass.

1811 DECEMBER 8. Elizabeth Arnold Hopkins Poe, his mother, dies in Richmond, Va. Poe is adopted a few days later by Mr. & Mrs. John Allan of Richmond.

1815 JULY 28. The Allans and their adopted son arrive in England.

1818-1820 Poe attends the Manor House School at Stoke Newington, near London.

1820 JULY 21. The Allans and Poe arrive in New York. They reach Richmond on August 2 and reside with Charles Ellis, Allan's partner.

1821 They move to Fifth Street between Marshall and Clay. Poe attends the Clarke School until December 1822.

1823 APRIL 1. He enters William Burke's school.

1825 June 28. John Allan purchases a house at Fifth and Main Streets, Richmond.

1826 FEBRUARY 14. Poe enters the University of Virginia, Charlottesville.

DECEMBER 15. The term ends, and John Allan removes Poe from the University.

1827 MARCH 24. Poe leaves Richmond and goes to Boston, where he arrives on April 7.

MAY 26. He enlists as a private in the U. S. Army under the name of Edgar A. Perry and is stationed at Fort Independence in Boston Harbor.

Tamerlane and Other Poems is published in Boston.

NOVEMBER 8-18. En route with his battery of artillery to Fort Moultrie, Charleston, S. C.

1828 DECEMBER 11-15. En route to Fortress Monroe, Va.

1829 JANUARY 1. He is promoted to the rank of Sergeant Major.

FEBRUARY 29. Frances Allan, Poe's foster mother, dies in Richmond.

APRIL 15. Poe is honorably discharged from the Army and goes to Washington to seek an appointment at West Point.

AUTUMN. He stays in Baltimore, perhaps with his aunt, Mrs. Maria Clemm, and her daughter Virginia.

DECEMBER. *Al Aaraaf, Tamerlane, and Minor Poems* is published in Baltimore.

1830 JUNE. At the U. S. Military Academy at West Point, N. Y.

1831 FEBRUARY 19. He leaves West Point.

APRIL (?) *Poems by Edgar A. Poe, Second Edition* is published in New York.

SUMMER. He again takes up residence with his aunt, Mrs. Clemm, in Baltimore.

1832 *The Philadelphia Saturday Courier* publishes five of Poe's tales.

1833 OCTOBER 12. His *Ms Found in a Bottle* wins first prize in a contest in *The Baltimore Saturday Visiter*.

1834 MARCH 27. John Allan, Poe's wealthy foster father, dies in Richmond, leaving Poe nothing.

1835 *The Southern Literary Messenger* of Richmond publishes four of Poe's tales.

AUGUST. Poe leaves Baltimore and goes to Richmond to become an assistant editor of *The Southern Literary Messenger*.

OCTOBER 3. Mrs. Clemm and Virginia join him in Richmond.

1836 MAY 16. Poe marries Virginia, who is not yet fourteen years old. (She was born on August 15, 1822.)

1837 JANUARY 3. He leaves the *Messenger*, and, in February, goes to New York, where he and his family live at Sixth Avenue and Waverly Place and then at 113½ Carmine Street.

1838 JULY. *The Narrative of Arthur Gordon Pym* is published in New York.

SUMMER. Poe moves to Philadelphia.

1839 *The Conchologist's First Book* is published in Philadelphia.

JUNE. Poe becomes assistant editor of Burton's *Gentleman's Magazine*.

1840 *Tales of the Grotesque and Arabesque* is published in Philadelphia. Poe leaves Burton and in April 1841 becomes editor of *Graham's Magazine*.

1841 JULY. He attempts—unsuccessfully—to get a position as a clerk in the Treasury Department in Washington.

1842 JANUARY. Virginia breaks a blood vessel while singing.

MAY. He leaves *Graham's Magazine.*

1843 *The Prose Romances of Edgar A. Poe* is published in Philadelphia.

1844 APRIL 7. Poe moves to New York and settles near 84th Street and Broadway.

1845 JANUARY 29. First printing of "The Raven" in the New York *Evening Mirror,* on which he serves as assistant editor.

MARCH 8. He becomes one of the editors of the *Broadway Journal.*

MAY (?). Poe moves to 195 East Broadway, New York.

SUMMER. *Tales* by Edgar A. Poe is published in New York.

OCTOBER 24 He becomes the proprietor of *The Broadway Journal.*

NOVEMBER. *The Raven and Other Poems* is published in New York.

WINTER. He moves to 85 Amity Street, New York.

1846 JANUARY 3. He loses control of *The Broadway Journal,* and it ceases publication.

MAY (?). He moves to a cottage in Fordham, then thirteen miles from the city.

1847 JANUARY 30. Virginia dies there.

1848 FEBRUARY 3. Poe reads *Eureka* to an audience at the New York Society Library.

JUNE (?). *Eureka* is published in New York. He plans to write a book entitled *Literary America.*

JUNE 10. He lectures at Lowell, Mass., and meets Mrs. Nancy Locke Heywood Richmond ("Annie") there.

JULY 17. He goes to Richmond, Va., and remains there "horribly drunk and discoursing *Eureka* to the audiences of the Bar Rooms."

SEPTEMBER 21. He goes to Providence, R. I., to meet Mrs. Sarah Helen Whitman and proposes marriage to her.

NOVEMBER 2 (?). He again goes to Providence to persuade Mrs. Whitman but goes on to Boston and takes laudanum in an attempt to commit suicide.

DECEMBER 20. He lectures in Providence. A marriage agreement is drawn up on DECEMBER 22, and a marriage is planned for a few days later. Then the engagement is suddenly broken.

1849 SPRING. Poe makes an attempt to interest E. H. N. Patterson of Oquawka, Ill., in starting a new magazine. JUNE 30. He leaves New York for Richmond to promote his plans for a magazine.

JULY 2 (?). He arrives at the home of John Sartain in Philadelphia in a state of delirium.

JULY 13. He leaves Philadelphia for Richmond and there meets Sarah Elmira Royster with whom he had been in love many years before. He plans to marry her.

AUGUST 17. He lectures in Richmond on "The Poetic Principle" and repeats the lecture in Norfolk on SEPTEMBER 14 and in Richmond on SEPTEMBER 24.

SEPTEMBER 27. He leaves Richmond, intending to return to New York.

OCTOBER 3. He is found in Baltimore, unconscious, and "rather the worse for wear," and is taken to the Washington College Hospital, where he never fully regains consciousness.

OCTOBER 7. At five o'clock on Sunday morning he dies.

INTRODUCTION

THERE is a ghost haunting America—a forlorn ghost who wanders at night through the older sections of some of our Eastern seaboard cities. In Boston, long after the theatre crowds have gone home, his slight, dark figure may occasionally be seen in the vicinity of Washington and State Streets. There an obscure print shop once stood—a print shop that is remembered only because it issued a thin little pamphlet of poetry which now brings the price of a country estate. It brought our ghost nothing—except disappointment, but then neither did any of his other books, for they were all unprofitable to their author.

In Providence, where he met one of the emotional crises of his life, his black-cloaked form may sometimes be glimpsed under the Doric portico of the Athenæum on College Hill. In New York, far uptown in Fordham, there is a tiny cottage much visited by sightseers during the day and by our errant ghost at night. Philadelphia, too, is one of his cities. There he haunts a small brick house near Spring Garden Street where roses once grew. In Baltimore (where his mortal remains are buried) his ghost frequents an unpretentious little house on Amity Street, for he dwelt in poverty nearly all his life, and most of his associations are with mean streets and small houses that could be rented cheaply. Only in Richmond did he ever know affluence and even then it was short-lived. The great house where he lived during his adolescence is gone, but his name is well remembered in that city. He returned there again and again, not to luxury but to river-front taverns and to rented rooms in shabby boardinghouses. In Charlottesville, the room he occupied in the West Range of the University of Virginia is still proudly pointed out, but he was unhappy during the short time he lived there, and he can hardly be expected to revisit it often. Charleston also knew him for a short while, especially the sea beach on Sullivan's Island, about which he wrote one of his most celebrated stories.

Except for five years of his childhood, which were spent in England, he dwelt all his life in these cities, and he is intimately associated with them. In his odd way he was as American as Irving or Cooper or Bryant —his contemporaries—and, despite his fame abroad, it is only as an American author that he can be understood. He lived in the age of antimacassars and slavery, of lace valentines and covered wagons, of old-fashioned chivalry and new-fangled railroads. He helped to shape the literature that was just beginning to win cultural independence of England—and he in turn was shaped by it. He gave us much and received pathetically little in return, for he was all his life a starveling poet and a miserably paid writer for ephemeral magazines. It is a final irony that his letters and manuscripts have become the most valuable of all American writers'.

He is the most often read of all his contemporaries, but this is no accident, for this neurotic and unhappy artist is strangely modern, oddly in keeping with our own neurotic and unhappy age. He knew what the death wish was long before Freud defined it. He was in love with violence half a century before Hemingway was born; he knew how to create suspense before the psycho-thriller was thought of; he used the theme of the double self before the term "split-personality" was invented. And, most important of all, he was endlessly concerned with inner conflict—the major theme of present-day literature. But it was his misfortune to have been born in this country at a time when its cultural development was just beginning. His ideas were far in advance of his age; his contempt for the mediocre work which was then receiving high praise made enemies for him in literary circles; and his personal habits shocked the people of his day.

Yet it is his eccentricities that have caused him to be remembered while most of his soberer contemporaries are forgotten. Of all American writers' lives, his is the most fascinating. He was the great romantic, the man who burned himself out in a blaze of tragic glory. He paid dearly for immortality, gave his whole life to attain it. But in his terms it was probably worth the cost.

He was born in Boston of wandering actor parents; his English mother, Elizabeth Arnold Hopkins, was the typical talented and beautiful lady of the stage, while his Irish father, David Poe, was the equally typical young ne'er-do-well who incurred his family's displeasure by entering the theatrical profession. He was apparently rash, impetuous, and addicted to alcohol. He and his wife quarreled and parted while their son was still an infant, and he then disappeared so completely that no record of his death is known.

He left three young children for whom his wife attempted to earn a living by travelling from city to city as theatrical engagements were offered. She was in Richmond toward the end of 1811, and there she fell ill and died. Her children were promptly adopted; the one named Edgar was taken into the home of a well-to-do merchant, John Allan, and was given his name— a name of which he afterwards had so little reason to be proud that he nearly always signed himself simply Edgar A. Poe.

As the child grew up in ante-bellum Richmond he

had every reason to believe that he would someday in-
herit his foster father's estate. When he was six years
old, the family went to England to remain there for
five years. The boy was sent to private school; his education as a gentleman had begun. After the Allans
returned to Richmond, their adopted son continued his
education at some of the local schools. It was at this
time, too, that he first fell in love—with the mother of
one of his playmates. Her name was Jane Stith Stanard,
and she was only one of the many women whose names
were to be saved from oblivion through their connection with Poe. She died shortly after he met her—the
first of several beautiful women in his life who were to
die young. It was to her that he addressed one of his
finest lyrics, the brief poem entitled "To Helen."

At the age of seventeen Poe was sent to the University of Virginia, and the happy years of his youth ended.
During his stay at the University, his foster father
treated him in a niggardly fashion, giving him just
enough money to live on. The young lad, who had been
brought up to believe that he was a Virginia gentleman,
was thrown into the company of the sons of wealthy
planters. With them he took to gambling to make up for
his insufficient funds. What happened was to be expected—he lost and gambled again to recoup his losses.
And then, of course, he lost and gambled still more. He
took to drink, too, and soon found that liquor had a
peculiarly unfortunate effect on him. One glass of wine
went to his head; very little more than that made him
drunk. Alcohol was a dangerous stimulant for him—
one that was eventually to bring about his ruin. But it
had a peculiar fascination, so that he returned to it
again and again, sometimes after long periods of ab-
stention. Apologists have tried to show that alcohol was
something to which he resorted only occasionally and

then under stress of circumstance. This is true, but there were many such occasions, and circumstance nearly always worked against him. He did, however, try to fight off the hold that alcohol had on him. His letters speak poignantly of his attempts to free himself from it, but there is no doubt that it had him in its thrall. Again and again, after the best of intentions, he relapsed. Anyone who knows the alcoholic as a type will recognize in Poe the familiar pattern—the resolution to renounce drinking, the urge to take "just one small one," and then the nightmarish descent into temporary oblivion.

No man drinks without cause. In Poe's case the causes are not difficult to determine. He was a sensitive and neurotic child, orphaned at an early age, who was unable to find in the Allan home the feeling of security every young person needs. As a result, his dead mother came to represent the maternal protection he was so desperately seeking. All the women in his life were substitutes for her, and poor substitutes they must have been for an idealized creature who never existed and never could exist. The unstable element in Poe kept twisting him farther and farther from the norm, and every disaster in his ill-starred life contributed to the warping. To him the real world was intolerable, and he sought escape from it in his writing, in his sexless quest for the perfect woman, and in alcohol. The fact that he happened to be a poor drinker is immaterial. Alcohol gave him surcease from his troubles, and he took to it as a drug-addict takes to opium. Insanity lay close beneath the surface, and he knew how near it was. In fact he once complained that his "enemies referred the insanity to the drink rather than the drink to the insanity." Toward the end of his life he said: "I have absolutely no pleasure in the stimulants in which I sometimes so madly indulge. It has not been in pursuit of pleasure that I have periled life and reputation and reason. It has been in the desperate attempt to escape from torturing memories, from a sense of insupportable loneliness, and a dread of some strange impending doom."

However, he was not all dreamer and escapist; underneath was a hard core of practicality that expressed itself in unceasing labor and that is best seen in his critical and analytical work. Because of it he was able to preserve his sanity for most of his life and accomplish so much. Toward the end, when his wife died and his household seemed threatened, he went to pieces and sought refuge in alcohol, in narcotics, and finally in death.

What happened at the University of Virginia set the pattern for the rest of Poe's life. Before he went there he was still a child—then he suddenly had to grow up. He did not become emotionally mature during that time or ever, but the problems he had to face thereafter were adult problems, not childish ones. It was there that the first break with his foster father came— and it was then that he first sought escape in drinking. The greatest misfortune in his career occurred when John Allan, presumably out of some sense of pity or charity, took him into his home. Two more dissimilar people would be hard to find. The boy was imaginative, romantic, and desperately in need of affection; the foster father was a dour Scotsman, realistic, eminently practical, and as undemonstrative as a wooden Indian. Oddly enough, Allan's correspondence shows that he too had once had ambitions to write. But this did not work in Poe's favor. Disappointed authors often get a grim satisfaction in placing obstacles in the way of young men who possess the talent they themselves lack.

At any rate, Allan was parsimonious in doling out

funds to his adopted son, and then, hearing of the debts
Poe had incurred, he removed him from the University
after less than a year's attendance there.

Poe returned to Richmond, where the misunderstand-
ing between him and his foster father deepened. Allan
had at least one mistress who bore him several illegitimate children. His adopted son, who adored his foster
mother, may have heard something of Allan's sexual
irregularities and perhaps threatened to expose him.
Before Poe had left for the University he had fallen in
love with—and perhaps had become engaged to—a
young Richmond girl, Sarah Elmira Royster. During
his absence, his letters to her had been intercepted by
her father, and now Poe found out that she was about
to marry another man. Less than three months after
his return from the University, he abruptly left his
foster father's home and went to Boston.

There he met a young printer, Calvin Thomas, who
undertook the publication of a slender pamphlet entitled *Tamerlane and Other Poems,* "by a Bostonian"—
probably so signed because Poe may have thought that
the city of his birth would receive the work more favor-
ably if it were known that it had been written by a
native. The printing was small; the price was twelve
and a half cents; but the book did not sell, nor did it
get much critical notice.

The young poet, penniless and without friends, enlisted in the Army, where he was to spend most of his
time during the next four years. He used the name
Edgar A. Perry, which was only one of the assumed
names he adopted on various occasions; Henri le
Rennet and Edward S. T. Grey were others. Apparently
he was ashamed of being an enlisted man, for he afterwards spun an elaborate tissue of lies to conceal this
phase of his career. He accounted for the time spent

in the Army by saying that he had gone abroad to fight in the Greek war of independence and had been in Russia. He even permitted such statements to appear in biographical data printed about him.

He must have made a fairly good soldier, however, for he was promoted to the rank of Sergeant Major—the highest noncommissioned rank possible—after only a year and a half of service. Shortly thereafter his foster mother died. Poe succeeded in getting leave to go to Richmond, where he arrived the day after her funeral. He was then honorably discharged from the Army, but as usual he was without funds, nor could he depend on his foster father for much help.

He went to Baltimore, where he managed to get his second volume of poems published under the title *Al Aaraaf, Tamerlane, and Minor Poems.* He probably stayed, for a while at least, at the home of his aunt, Mrs. Maria Clemm, who was living there with her seven-year-old daughter, Virginia. In the same household was William Henry Poe, Edgar Poe's elder brother, who was then slowly dying of tuberculosis and chronic alcoholism. The sister, Rosalie, who had been adopted by a Richmond family, was also a pathetic figure, not actually moronic, but of less than normal intelligence. Poe was unfortunate in his family, and the spectres of his father, his brother, and his sister must have tortured him all his life.

Through John Allan's influence he obtained an appointment to the United States Military Academy at West Point, where he went when he was twenty-one years old. Although he was evidently a good student, he soon tired of the rigidly disciplined life at the Academy and purposely absented himself from parades, classes, and chapel in order to get himself dismissed. He was court-martialed for neglect of duty and left the

Point in the early spring of 1831. He went to New York and there succeeded in finding another publisher who issued a little volume entitled *Poems by Edgar A. Poe, Second Edition*. Shortly thereafter, he returned to Baltimore to rejoin his aunt's household. His brother died soon after his arrival.

Poe then for the first time took up the writing of prose fiction, turning out five stories in rapid succession. In 1833 he won the first prize offered by *The Baltimore Saturday Visiter* with his "MS Found in a Bottle."

John Allan died on March 27, 1834. His will provided for his legitimate and illegitimate children but ignored his adopted son. Poe was on his own, and he knew that he would somehow have to earn a living. Fortunately he had served his apprenticeship; as a professional writer he would need a regular outlet for his work.

He left the little household in Baltimore and went to Richmond to become assistant editor of *The Southern Literary Messenger*. For a while he lived there alone, desperately unhappy, and suffering from long-continued depression that drove him to drink and thoughts of suicide. He must have visited Baltimore on September 22, 1835, for on that day he took out a license to marry his cousin Virginia, who was then just one month more than thirteen years old. She and her mother joined Poe in Richmond, where they all lived in a boardinghouse on the young editor's salary of fifteen dollars a week. The next spring, on May 26, 1836, he married Virginia.

Poe's relationship to his child wife has been the subject of much controversy. There can be no doubt that he loved her—his letters show that. But he alludes to her nearly always as "Sis," and it is possible that he married her just to keep Mrs. Clemm near him, for he had found in his mother-in-law the maternal image he had been seeking all his life. He was always dependent upon female companionship; he needed the security of a home, the assurance that came from having loving women near him. It has been hinted that his marriage to Virginia was never actually consummated, but that, of course, is merely speculation. Poe's unstable temperament, his neurotic compulsion toward drink and self-destruction indicate that he may have been sexually abnormal, but there is no way of proving it.

In January 1837 he severed his connection with *The Southern Literary Messenger* and the next month took his family to New York. There he succeeded in finding a publisher for his only book-length story, *The Narrative of Arthur Gordon Pym*, a pseudo-real account of mutiny, shipwreck, and adventure on the high seas. Like nearly all Poe's work that was published in his lifetime, it did not sell.

A year later, the restless wanderer moved his family to Philadelphia. There he undertook a piece of hack work which has brought more discredit upon his name than anything else he ever did. A Philadelphia publisher, who wanted to issue a textbook on Conchology, employed Poe to write an introduction and lend his name to the project. The book was based—without any credit—upon an earlier treatise published in Scotland. In his introduction, Poe borrowed heavily from the original work, in some cases hardly even bothering to change the phrasing. This was not the only instance of plagiarism in Poe's life. His critical theories on poetry derive from Coleridge, and in some instances follow Coleridge's text word for word. It is characteristic that Poe was ever ready to charge others with plagiarism, once accusing Longfellow of the same kind of literary theft of which he himself was guilty.

After a year of precarious free-lance work, Poe obtained a position as assistant editor on Burton's *Gentle-man's Magazine.* "The Fall of the House of Usher," and "William Wilson," were printed in this publication, but Poe's connection with it lasted for less than a year. During this time he arranged with Lea and Blanchard of Philadelphia to issue his collected stories as a two-volume work entitled *"Tales of the Grotesque and Arabesque."* A few free copies for distribution to his friends were his only compensation.

The great ambition that dominated him for the rest of his life was to have his own magazine. He drew up and circulated a prospectus for it but was unable to raise the necessary funds. Meanwhile he obtained a position with *Graham's Magazine,* which in April 1841 published his first story of ratiocination, "The Murders in the Rue Morgue." Its appearance marked the birth of the detective story, and its central character, C. Auguste Dupin, was the precursor of a long line of fictional sleuths. Howard Haycraft has said of it in his critique of detective literature, *Murder for Pleasure:*

In the very first tale he proceeded to lay down the two great concepts upon which all fictional detection worth the name has been based: (1) That the solvability of a case varies in proportion to its outré character. (2) The famous dictum-by-inference (as best phrased by Dorothy Sayers) that "when you have eliminated all the impossibilities, then, whatever remains, however improbable, must be the truth," which has been relied on and often re-stated by all the better sleuths in the decades that have followed. As for the almost infinite minutiæ, time-hallowed today, which Poe created virtually with a single stroke of the pen, only a suggestive catalogue need be given. The transcendent and eccentric detective; the admiring and slightly stupid foil; the well-intentioned blundering and unimaginativeness of the official guardians of the law; the locked-room convention; the pointing finger of unjust suspicion; the solution by surprise; deduction by putting one's self in another's position (now called psychology); concealment by means of the ultra-obvious; the staged ruse to force the culprit's hand; even the expansive and condescending explanation when the chase is done; all these sprang full-panoplied from the buzzing brain and lofty brow of the Philadelphia editor. In fact, it is not too much to say—except, possibly, for the influence of latter-day science—that nothing really primary has been added either to the framework of the detective story or to its internals since Poe completed his trilogy.

The next issue of *Graham's* contained "A Descent into the Maelström"; subsequent numbers marked the first appearance of "The Masque of the Red Death," several pieces on Cryptography and Autography, and a number of important critical articles. Poe was at his best at this time, living in what was perhaps the only happy period of his adult life. *Graham's* circulation increased enormously during the next two years; its editor's salary, to be sure, remained fixed at only $800 per annum, but that was probably as much as Poe ever made in any one year of his life.

This brief interlude of happiness came abruptly to an end. In January 1842 Virginia ruptured a blood vessel while singing. Her husband wrote of it six years later:

Her life was despaired of. I took leave of her forever and underwent all the agonies of her death.

She recovered partially and again I hoped. At the end of a year the vessel broke again. . . . Then again—again—again and even once again. . . . I became insane, with long intervals of horrible sanity. During these fits of absolute unconsciousness I drank, God only knows how often or how much.

Despite his anguish, Poe worked on, turning out some of his greatest masterpieces, among them his second story of ratiocination, "The Mystery of Marie Rogêt," as well as "The Pit and the Pendulum," "The Tell-Tale Heart," "The Gold-Bug," and "The Black Cat." He left *Graham's Magazine* but still kept trying to obtain funds to launch a periodical of his own. He succeeded in persuading a Philadelphia publisher to issue a paper-bound volume of his tales entitled *The Prose Romances of Edgar A. Poe.* This little volume, originally priced at twelve and a half cents, has become the rarest of all Poeiana. Its very scarcity, however, is testimony to the fact that it did not sell, and that its author, as usual, probably made little or nothing from its publication.

In April 1844, perhaps hoping that he could find a backer for his projected magazine there and so improve his fortune, he moved again to New York. Virginia and he went on ahead, leaving Mrs. Clemm to follow. A few days after his arrival he sold the *Sun* a hoax story dealing with the supposed crossing of the Atlantic by a passenger balloon. Its publication created a sensation; premium prices were paid for a copy of the newspaper, and the issue was so quickly sold out that Poe was unable to obtain a copy for himself. But, again, very little money for the author was involved.

A short time afterwards, Poe found lodgings for his

family in a frame house on the Bloomingdale Road near what is now Broadway and 84th Street. This house, long since demolished, would be famous if it were still standing, for it was there that Poe wrote his most celebrated poem, "The Raven." Its publication, early in 1845, attracted more attention than anything he had written. Poe obtained a minor position on *The Evening Mirror*, which had first printed the poem, but again he did not hold the post very long. After a few months he left to join *The Broadway Journal*, a newly founded paper on which he doubtless thought he would have a better chance to exercise his talents. It soon got into financial difficulties; by summer, Poe was its editor—the only time he was ever to hold such a position. By autumn, he was the sole proprietor of a journal that was in serious financial straits, and he was fighting a desperate battle to keep the paper alive. He lost, and by the end of the year his brief, inglorious career as a publisher was over.

Nevertheless, it had been an outstanding year of achievement. During it he had published a new collection of his tales and a volume entitled *The Raven and Other Poems*. He had won some fame and proved —to himself at least—that he could edit a magazine single-handed. But he was as poor as ever; his wife needed medical care; he worked long hours and poured everything into what he did, yet the reputation he had won was of little help in getting better prices for his writing.

The year 1845 was the highest peak; the next four years were to be a slow descent into Avernus. In 1846 he got into a bitter quarrel with Thomas Dunn English because of a satiric portrait in a series of sketches he had written under the title "The Literati." English retaliated with an attack on Poe in *The Evening Mirror*. The language he used was so intemperate that Poe brought a suit for libel against the proprietors of the *Mirror* and was awarded $225 as damages. The resultant publicity, however, did him a great deal of harm.

In the early summer of 1846 he moved his family to a cottage in Fordham, which was then far out in the country. He was ill and Virginia was dying, so that he was in no condition to do much work. As a result, their meagre income vanished; when winter came they even lacked money to buy fuel. A friend who visited the cottage wrote a description of Virginia's plight:

> There was no clothing on the bed . . . but a snow white spread and sheets. The weather was cold, and the sick lady had the dreadful chills that accompany the hectic fever of consumption. She lay on the straw bed, wrapped in her husband's greatcoat, with a large tortoise-shell cat on her bosom. The wonderful cat seemed conscious of her great usefulness. The coat and the cat were the sufferer's only means of warmth. . . .

A public appeal for funds was made in the newspapers—an act which Poe, of course, resented. But Virginia was beyond all human aid. She died on January 30, 1847, and her death marked the end of the sanest period in her husband's life. He plunged into the writing of a book-length mystical and pseudo-scientific work entitled *Eureka*, in which he set forth his theories of the universe. He intended it as a prose poem, and as such it should be judged, rather than as a scientific explanation of matters beyond its author's ken.

It was at this time that Poe wrote two of his most celebrated poems, the darkly brooding "Ulalume" and the onomatopoetic "The Bells." There was little creative energy left in him, however, and he had taken to drink again. During the summer of 1848 he went to Richmond for a brief visit. Not much is known about what he did there, but one witness said that "he remained about three weeks, horribly drunk and discoursing *Eureka* every night to the audiences of the Bar Rooms."

After his return to New York the strangest and most involved period in his tangled career began. In 1845, during a visit to Providence, he had seen but not met Mrs. Sarah Helen Whitman, a widow six years his senior, who wrote poetry, was interested in literature, and had some private means. They addressed poems to each other, which they both published, and then in September 1848 Poe went to Providence to persuade Mrs. Whitman to marry him. His reputation was hardly of the sort to appeal to a middle-aged lady who had been brought up in an ultra-conventional environment, and her family was violently opposed to the match. Poe persisted, although the uncertainty kept him on edge. He saw Mrs. Whitman again in October, and then, in November, he went to Providence, suddenly bought some laudanum there, proceeded to Boston and tried to commit suicide. But he took an overdose of the drug, so that it did not kill him but simply made him violently ill. After he recovered, he met Mrs. Whitman at the Athenæum in Providence, where she showed him some of the denunciatory letters she had received about him. He promised to forego all hope of marriage but appeared at her house on the following day in a terrible state of agitation. Thinking perhaps that she could reform him, Mrs. Whitman promised to marry him if he would refrain from drinking. He readily agreed, of course, and to please her family he also consented to relinquish any claim on her estate. When he returned to Providence on December 20 to lecture, final arrangements were made for the wedding ceremony. Before it could be performed, however, Poe met some young men of the town who got him drunk and he appeared at his fiancée's home in an intoxicated condition. This apparently was forgiven, but pressure was brought on Mrs. Whitman to call off the marriage. She spoke to Poe, and then her mother summoned him to the house, where a scene took place which sounds as though it had been borrowed from a Victorian melodrama. After a tearful interview, Mrs. Whitman fell back, half-fainting, on a couch, and pressing to her mouth a handkerchief soaked in ether. Her mother took charge and broke off the engagement. Poe got the next train to New York, and the affair was over.

But complicated as his relations to Mrs. Whitman are, they are still further complicated by the fact that while he was trying to marry her he was at the same time making wild protestations of love to another woman, Mrs. Nancy Richmond ("Annie"), who was married and living with her husband in Lowell. Poe confided to her the most intimate details of his engagement to Mrs. Whitman. As soon as it was over he wrote her that he would henceforth "shun the pestilential society of literary women."

He did not keep his promise. He paid court to Mrs. Sarah Anna Lewis ("Stella"), a Brooklyn poetess whose husband employed Poe to "correct" his wife's verses. And there were still other women. Poe's association with them all was probably on an asexual basis, but he craved their companionship, for Virginia's death had left a void which he had to fill.

The one thing he never abandoned was his ambition

to own a magazine. In the summer of 1849 he went to Richmond, presumably to try to raise funds for its publication.

By the time he had gotten as far as Philadelphia he was in the midst of a serious mental breakdown. He managed to get in touch with a friend, to whom he kept babbling a wildly improbable story about some men on the train who were planning to kill him; then he rambled on about having been arrested and confined in Moyamensing Prison, where he had seen visions and heard voices. It was two weeks before he was in condition to proceed to Richmond. He wrote to Mrs. Clemm about his experiences:

> For more than ten days I was totally deranged, although I was drinking not one drop; and during this interval I imagined the most horrible calamities. All was hallucination, arising from an attack which I had never before experienced—an attack of *mania-à-potu.*

Frightened as he undoubtedly was by this temporary loss of sanity, he nevertheless could not resist temptation when acquaintances in Richmond offered him the alcohol that was literally poison to him. A doctor there warned him that another attack would be fatal. Poe officially took the temperance pledge, but, despite his best intentions, he was unable to keep it.

He continued his attempts to raise money for his projected magazine; he lectured in Richmond and then in Norfolk, always feeling that he was at last on the verge of making money and achieving everything that had so long been denied him. Most important of all, he met his boyhood sweetheart, Mrs. Sarah Elmira Royster Shelton, who was now a widow. Again he began to woo, and this time he was successful, for Mrs.

Shelton promised to marry him. She had some money, so she would be able to look after him and perhaps help finance his magazine. All his problems suddenly seemed solved.

On September 27 he took the boat to Baltimore to return to New York and make preparations for the wedding. What happened during the next few days is unknown and will probably always have to remain so. But on October 3 (an election day in Baltimore) Dr. Snodgrass, a physician Poe knew, received a brief note which read:

> There is a gentleman, rather the worse for wear, at Ryan's 4th ward polls, who goes under the cognomen of Edgar A. Poe, and who appears in great distress, and says he is acquainted with you, and I assure you he is in need of immediate assistance.

Because Poe had been found at a polling place the story sprang up that he had been made drunk and used as a repeater in fraudulent voting. The story may or may not be true; there is no way of proving or disproving it. When found, he was unconscious, dirty, dressed in clothing that was not his own, and very near death. He was removed to the Washington College Hospital. There he remained unconscious for a while; when he came to, he talked vacantly "to spectral and imaginary objects on the walls" and was unable to tell what had happened to him. This was succeeded by a state of violent delirium; after which he became exhausted and seemed to rest. For four days he struggled on the edge of death. Then, at five o'clock in the morning of October 7, he cried out, "God help my poor soul!" and at last found the escape he had so long been seeking.

He was as unlucky in death as he had been in life. In

1841 he had met an influential editor named Rufus W. Griswold, who made an excellent living from various literary enterprises. Poe, who was a poor judge of character, was incautious enough to appoint Griswold as his literary executor. Actually he could not have made a worse choice, for Griswold hated him, perhaps because Poe possessed the genius that Griswold himself lacked.

Two days after Poe's death, there appeared in *The New York Tribune* a memorial article signed "Ludwig" but written by Griswold. It was a bitter attack, filled with innuendo and actual falsehood. Nor did Griswold stop there. He proceeded to edit Poe's work, which was published in four volumes; in the third volume he inserted a memoir of Poe that was even worse than the "Ludwig" article. He also "re-wrote" some of Poe's letters and probably forged others entirely.

A number of people came to the defense of Poe's reputation, N. P. Willis, Mrs. Whitman, and George Graham among them, but the damage had been done, especially in England, where Griswold's interpretation was accepted for many years because of his position as the authorized editor of Poe's work. In France, however, Baudelaire espoused Poe's cause, translated his writings, and wrote a memorable essay on him.

As a result of Baudelaire's sponsorship, Poe became a major influence in French literature, particularly upon Mallarmé, Verlaine, Rimbaud, and others of the Symbolist school. His fame spread throughout Europe, so that today he is probably better known there than any other American writer.

He was, of course, one of the leading exponents of romanticism, and his work must be considered as a part of the great tradition established by Byron, Keats, Shelley, Coleridge, De Quincey, Scott, and the German writers who made so profound an impression upon early nineteenth-century literature. He belongs, too, to the aristocratic school of writing. As a Southerner who felt himself—despite his poverty—allied with the slave· owning class of wealthy planters, it was inevitable that he should have become what he did, for the South was both aristocratic and romantic. Like his compatriots, he was confessedly anti-democratic, once referring to the government of his own country as "the most odious and insupportable despotism . . . upon the face of the earth," the usurping tyrant of which he designated as "Mob."

Most of his stories and poems have a European, Oriental, or purely imaginative setting but his criticism deals almost exclusively with the literature of his day and is concerned largely with American books and American authors. As a practicing editor writing for a popular audience he had to deal with current issues, so that it would be a mistake to think of him as an unworldly creature who had no connection with the life of his time. It is, however, his imaginative writing that has caused him to be remembered, and it is that part of his work which will interest most modern readers.

His stories and poems are timeless, and they gain in timelessness through the very fact that they are so divorced from reality, so little concerned with actual places, with lifelike characters, or with situations that could conceivably happen in this world. In that respect they are like poetry; some of them, like "The Masque of the Red Death" and "Eleonora," are definitely poetic in concept and language, and at least two of them, "Silence" and "Shadow," are so close to poetry that they have been arranged in this volume in free-verse form.

Both the stories and the poems have a narrow range of subject. Through nearly all of them runs the same sombre leitmotif—the omnipresence of death and the corruption that awaits the flesh. In most of them there are only two characters—Poe himself and the death-doomed or already dead mother-wife. No matter how protean the characters may appear to be, they are basically always the same. The self may be called William Wilson, Roderick Usher, or even C. Auguste Dupin, but it is inevitably some phase of the author that is being projected. Even the despised and crippled dwarf, Hop-Frog, is Poe vicariously taking revenge on those who had hurt him. And the women in his stories and poems are all symbols of the mother-wife in her two aspects—the ideal, beautiful maiden, doomed to die at an early age (Eleonora, Helen, Annabel Lee, Lenore, Eulalie, etc.), or the dreadful revenant whose flesh has been ravaged by the conqueror worm (Berenice, Morella, Ligeia, Madeline Usher, etc.).

Poe's life must have been a nightmare, more horrible even than his stories or letters indicate. His writings are a reflection of the inner turmoil that was destroying him, and the fact that pain, cruelty, premature burial, and the corruption of the grave (all expressions of the death wish) were an obsession with him, shows how strong was the hold that the desire for self-destruction had upon him. His mind turned inward and slowly devoured itself, until the very act of living grew unbearable. The sensitive and introspective child became an egocentric adult, who developed into an egomaniac, until Poe came as near to being the complete solipsist as one can be and still remain a part of this world. He once said that he could not conceive of any being superior to himself; despite his poverty and rejection, he was fiercely proud and difficult to deal with. He had no close friends, and as he grew older there was no one with whom he could associate on equal terms. He complained of his loneliness, but he did not try to alleviate it except by a frantic seeking for feminine companionship, and in that he was limited by the fatal mother-image which beclouded all his relations with women. He was condemned in early childhood to probable unhappiness; the circumstances of his life made that probability a certainty, for he was both unlucky and self-destructive. Defeat engendered further defeat, until his whole life became a slow suicide.

Frustration fosters fantasy; the man who cannot get what he wants will conjure up images of his desire. Out of Poe's misery came the stuff of his dreams and the materials for his poems and his stories. He enriched posterity at the cost of his personal happiness and—eventually—of his sanity and his life. The force that drove him to create also drove him mad.

As a child he was motherless and set apart from other children; as an adolescent he was humiliated and thrust out into a hostile world; as a man he met continual disappointment and was denied the recognition he felt he deserved. There have been many such ill-starred creatures, and most of them have gone down forgotten into their graves. But Poe did not merely take refuge in his fantasies; he turned them to account, setting down in prose and poetry the dark spectres that thronged his unhappy, tortured mind.

The fantasy images of the human brain are not subject to control; they rise unbidden from the subconscious mind and are the most original of man's concepts. They are part of the creative faculty, closely connected with the power that enables man to conceive new ideas, invent new machines, and devise new ways of living. From them art and literature spring into being; through them one can get a glimpse into the deep substrata where lie the roots that bind together all mankind.

Poe wrote of elemental things—of love and hate, of fear and death, of the mysteries beyond life, and of the mutability and brevity of human existence. He explored the universe in an attempt to force an understanding of man's origin and ultimate destiny; he dwelt with Death as a close companion in an effort to find out the secrets of the grave. He was ever the eager seeker, the innovator who marked out new areas in the *terra incognita* of the mind and drove back some of the darkness from man's understanding of himself.

Charlatan, plagiarist, pathological liar, egomaniac, whimpering child, braggart, and irresponsible drunkard, he did what few American writers had even tried to do before: he tapped the rich reservoir of the subconscious mind to set free the strange and terrible images which had seldom been allowed to stalk the printed page until he introduced them into his work. He was one of the first to establish the dark tradition in American literature, a tradition carried on by Hawthorne, Melville, Bierce, and Faulkner among others. His work—and theirs—shows that the American mind is not all optimism and easy confidence. The great spaces, the lonely forests, the lurking savage enemies, the sullen sea-girt coasts, and the ever-present threat of sudden death left their impress upon the men who settled this continent. Even in America the sun shines only for half the day; after it comes the night—black, menacing, and given over to dreams and phantoms. There are ghosts among us even now, and one of them still haunts our memory and our literature.

—PHILIP VAN DOREN STERN

May 8, 1945

LETTERS

TO JOHN ALLAN

[After the death of John Allan, his widow gave a number of letters from Poe to his foster father to a relative who turned them over in 1882 to Mann S. Valentine, the founder of the Valentine Museum in Richmond. They were then kept locked away for nearly half a century and were not published until 1925, when they were brought out in a volume entitled *Edgar Allan Poe Letters Till Now Unpublished*. These first four letters come from that volume and are reproduced with permission.

The first two letters were written about three months after Allan had refused to let Poe return to the University of Virginia. They reflect the quarrel which must have taken place between them and show Poe's determination to leave his foster father's home. He sailed from Richmond on March 24 to go to Boston, where he published *Tamerlane* and enlisted in the army.

The third letter was written after the death of Poe's beloved foster mother and after Allan had remarried. The Sergt. Graves to whom Poe refers was his substitute when Poe was released from the army as an enlisted man. The letter Poe admits having written to him was about money owed to Graves, money which Poe tried to get his foster father to pay. In that letter Poe had said that Allan was "not often very sober," a statement which had naturally angered his foster father. On the back of this letter Allan wrote: "I do not think the boy has one good quality."

The fourth letter is the last one Poe is known to have written to John Allan. (Allan died less than a year later.) It is a cry for help, which, so far as is known, went unanswered.]

Richmond, Monday [March 19, 1827]

Sɪʀ,

After my treatment on yesterday and what passed between us this morning, I can hardly think you will be surprised at the contents of this letter. My determination is at length taken to leave your house and

1

endeavour to find some place in this wide world, where I will be treated—not as you have treated me. This is not a hurried determination, but one on which I have long considered—and having so considered my resolution is unalterable. You may perhaps think that I have flown off in a passion, & that I am already wishing to return; But not so—I will give you the reasons which have actuated me, and then judge—

Since I have been able to think on any subject, my thoughts have aspired, and they have been taught by you to aspire, to eminence in public life—this cannot be attained without a good Education, such a one I cannot obtain at a Primary school—

A collegiate Education therefore was what I most ardently desired, and I had been led to expect that it would at some future time be granted—but in a moment of caprice you have blasted my hope—because forsooth I disagreed with you in an opinion, which opinion I was forced to express—

Again, I have heard you say (when you little thought I was listening and therefore must have said it in earnest) that you had no affection for me—

You have moreover ordered me to quit your house, and are continually upbraiding me with eating the bread of idleness, when you yourself were the only person to remedy the evil by placing me to some business—

You take delight in exposing me before those whom you think likely to advance my interest in this world—

You suffer me to be subjected to the whims & caprice, not only of your white family, but the complete authority of the blacks—these grievances I could not submit to; and I am gone—

I request that you will send me my trunk containing my clothes & books—and if you still have the least affection for me, as the last call I shall make on your bounty, to prevent the fulfilment of the Prediction you this morning expressed—send me as much money as will defray the expences of my passage to some of the Northern cities & then support me for one month, by which time I shall be enabled to place myself in some situation where I may not only obtain a livelihood, but lay by a sum which one day or another will support me at the University. Send my trunk &c. to the Court-House Tavern. Send me I entreat you some money immediately, as I am in the greatest necessity. If you fail to comply with my request—I tremble for the consequence.

Yours, &c.

EDGAR. A. POE

It depends upon yourself if hereafter you see or hear from me.

EDGAR. A. POE

TO JOHN ALLAN

Richmond, Tuesday [March 20, 1827]

DEAR SIR,

Be so good as to send me my trunk with my clothes. I wrote you on yesterday explaining my reasons for leaving. I suppose by my not receiving either my trunk, or an answer to my letter, that you did not receive it. I am in the greatest necessity, not having tasted food since yesterday morning. I have no where to sleep at night, but roam about the streets. I am nearly exhausted —I beseech you as you wish not your prediction concerning me to be fulfilled—to send me without delay my trunk containing my clothes, and to lend if you will not give me as much money as will defray the expence of my passage to Boston ($12) and a little to support

me there untill I shall be enabled to engage in some
business. I sail on Saturday. A letter will be received by
me at the Court House Tavern, where be so good as to
send my trunk.

Give my love to all
at home

I am yours, &c
EDGAR. A. POE
I have not one cent in the
world to provide any food.

TO JOHN ALLAN

West Point, Jan'y 3d, 1831 [Misdated 1830]

SIR,

I suppose, (altho' you desire no further communication with yourself, on my part,) that your restriction
does not extend to my answering your final letter.

Did I, when an infant, sollicit your charity and protection, or was it of your own free will, that you volunteered your services in my behalf? It is well known
to respectable individuals in Baltimore, and elsewhere,
that my Grandfather (my natural protector at the time
you interposed) was wealthy, and that I was his favourite grand-child. But the promises of adoption, and
liberal education which you held forth to him in a
letter which is now in possession of my family, induced
him to resign all care of me into your hands. Under
such circumstances, can it be said that I have no right
to expect anything at your hands? You may probably
urge that you have given me a liberal education. I will
leave the decision of that question to those who know
how far liberal educations can be obtained in 8 months
at the University of Va. Here you will say that it was
my own fault that I did not return. You would not let
me return because bills were presented you for pay-

ment which I never wished nor desired you to pay. Had you let me return, my reformation had been sure— as my conduct the last 3 months gave every reason to believe—and you would never have heard more of my extravagances. But I am not about to proclaim myself guilty of all that has been alledged against me, and which I have hitherto endured, simply because I was too proud to reply. I will boldly say that it was wholly and entirely your own mistaken parsimony that caused all the difficulties in which I was involved while at Charlottesville. The expenses of the institution at the lowest estimate were $350 per annum. You sent me there with $110. Of this $50 were to be paid immediately for board—$60 for attendance upon 2 professors—and you even then did not miss the opportunity of abusing me because I did not attend 3. Then $15 more were to be paid in advance with $110—$12 more for a bed—and $12 more for room furniture. I had of course, the mortification of running in debt for public property—against the known rules of the institution, and was immediately regarded in the light of a beggar. You will remember that in a week after my arrival I wrote to you for some more money, and for books. You replied in terms of the utmost abuse—if I had been the vilest wretch on earth you could not have been more abusive than you were because I could not continue to pay $150 with $110.

I had enclosed to you in my letter (according to your express commands) an account of the expenses incured amounting to $149—the balance to be paid was $39—you enclosed me $40, leaving me one dollar in pocket. In a short time afterwards, I received a packet of books consisting of *Gil Blas,* and the Cambridge *Mathematics* in 2 vols: books for which I had no earthly use since I had no means of attending the mathe-

matical lectures. But books must be had, if I intended
to remain at the institution—and they were bought accordingly upon credit. In this manner debts were ac-
cumulated, and money borrowed of Jews in Charlottesville at extravagant interest—for I was obliged to hire
a servant, to pay for wood, for washing, and a thousand
other necessaries. It was then that I became dissolute,
for how could it be otherwise? I could associate with
no students, except those who were in a similar situation with myself—altho' from different causes—they
from drunkenness, and extravagance—I, because it was
my crime to have no one on Earth who cared for me, or
loved me. I call God to witness that I have never loved
dissipation. Those who know me know that my pur-
suits and habits are very far from anything of the kind.
But I was drawn into it by my companions. Even their
professions of friendship—hollow as they were—were
a relief. Towards the close of the session you sent me
$100—but it was too late—to be of any service in
extricating me from my difficulties. I kept it for some
time—thinking that if I could obtain more I could yet
retrieve my character. I applied to James Galt—but
he, I believe, from the best of motives refused to lend
me any. I then became desperate and gambled—until
I finally involved myself irretrievably. If I have been to
blame in all this—place yourself in my situation, and
tell me if you would not have been equally so. But
these circumstances were all unknown to my friends
when I returned home. They knew that I had been
extravagant—but that was all. I had no hope of returning to Charlottesville, and I waited in vain in expectation that you would, at least, obtain me some employment. I saw no prospect of this—and I could endure it
no longer. Every day threatened with a warrant &c.
I left home—and after nearly 2 years conduct with

which no fault could be found—in the army, as a common soldier—I earned, myself, by the most humiliating privations—a Cadet's warrant which you could have obtained at any time for asking. It was then that I thought I might venture to sollicit your assistance in giving me an outfit. I came home, you will remember, the night after the burial. If she had not have died while I was away there would have been nothing for me to regret. Your love I never valued—but she I believe loved me as her own child. You promised me to forgive all—but you soon forgot your promise. You sent me to W. Point like a beggar. The same difficulties are threatening me as before at Charlottesville—and I must resign.

As to your injunction not to trouble you with further communication, rest assured, Sir, that I will most religiously observe it. When I parted from you—at the steam-boat—I knew that I should never see you again. As regards Sergt. Graves—I did write him that letter. As to the truth of its contents, I leave it to God, and your own conscience.—The Time in which I wrote it was within a half hour after you had embittered every feeling of my heart against you by your abuse of my family, and myself, under your own roof—and at a time when you knew that my heart was almost breaking.

I have no more to say—except that my future life (which thank God will not endure long) must be passed in indigence and sickness. I have no energy left, nor health. If it was possible to put up with the fatigues of this place, and the inconveniences which my absolute want of necessaries subject me to, and as I mentioned before it is my intention to resign—For this end it will be necessary that you (as my nominal guardian) enclose me your written permission. It will be useless to refuse me this last request—for I can leave the place without any permission—your refusal would only deprive me of the little pay which is now due as mileage.

From the time of this writing I shall neglect my studies and duties at the institution. If I do not receive your answer in 10 days, I will leave the Point without —for otherwise I should subject myself to dismission.

E. A. Poe

TO JOHN ALLAN

Baltimore, April 12th, 1833

It has now been more than two years since you have assisted me, and more than three since you have spoken to me. I feel little hope that you will pay any regard to this letter, but still I cannot refrain from making one more attempt to interest you in my behalf. If you will only consider in what a situation I am placed you will surely pity me—without friends, without any means, consequently of obtaining employment, I am perishing —absolutely perishing for want of aid. And yet I am not idle—nor addicted to any vice—nor have I committed any offence against society which would render me deserving of so hard a fate. For God's sake pity me, and save me from destruction.

E. A. Poe

TO WILLIAM POE

[This letter is interesting for its family history and for Poe's own account of his early years and his relationship to John Allan. Poe says here that no will was found among Allan's papers. Allan did, however, leave a will—which made no mention of Poe—but Poe may not have known about it at this time.]

Richmond, Aug: 20, 1835

DEAR SIR,—I received your very kind and compli-
mentary letter only a few minutes ago, and hasten to
reply.

I have been long aware that a connection existed
between us—without knowing precisely in what manner. Your letter however has satisfied me that we are
second cousins. I will briefly relate to you what little
I have been able to ascertain, or rather to remember, in
relation to our families. That I know but little on this
head will not appear so singular to you when I relate the
circumstances connected with my own particular history. But to return. My paternal grandfather was Gen.
David Poe of Baltimore—originally of Ireland. I know
that he had brothers—two I believe. But my knowledge extends only to one, Mr. George Poe. My grandfather married, when very young, a Miss Elizabeth
Carnes of Lancaster, Pa., by whom he had 5 sons—
viz: George (who died while an infant), John, William,
David, and Samuel; also two daughters, Maria and
Eliza. Of the sons none married with the exception of
David. He married a Mrs. Elizabeth Hopkins, an English lady, by whom he had 3 children, Henry, myself,
and Rosalie. Henry died about 4 years ago—Rosalie and
myself remain. The daughters of Gen. David Poe, Maria
and Eliza, both married young. Maria married Mr. Wm.
Clemm, a gentleman of high standing and some property in Baltimore. He was a widower with 5 children
—and had after his marriage to Maria Poe 3 others—
viz: 2 girls and a boy, of which a girl Virginia, and a
boy Henry are still living. Mr. Clemm died about 9 years
ago without any property whatever, leaving his widow
desolate, and unprotected, and little likely to receive
protection or assistance from the relatives of her husband—most of whom were opposed to the marriage in

the first instance—and whose opposition was no doubt aggravated by the petty quarrels frequently occurring between Maria's children, and Mr. C's children by his former wife. This Maria is the one of whom you speak, and to whom I will allude again presently. Eliza the second daughter of the General, married a Mr. Henry Herring of Baltimore, . . . by whom she had several children. She is now dead, and Mr. Herring, having married again ceased communication with the family of his wife's sister. Mrs. Poe the widow of General D. Poe, and the mother of Maria, died only [illegible] ago, at the age of 79. She had for the last 8 years of her life been confined entirely to bed—never, in any instance, leaving it during that time. She had been paralyzed and suffered from many other complaints—her daughter Maria attending her during her long & tedious illness with a Christian and martyr-like fortitude, and with a constancy of attention, and unremitting affection, which must exalt her character in the eyes of all who know her. Maria is now the only survivor of my grandfather's family.

In relation to my grandfather's brother George, I know but little. Jacob Poe of Fredericktown, Maryland, is his son—also George Poe of Mobile—and I presume your father Wm. Poe. Jacob Poe has two sons, Neilson and George—also one daughter Amelia.

My father David died when I was in the second year of my age, and when my sister Rosalie was an infant in arms. Our mother died a few weeks before him. Thus we were left orphans at an age when the hand of a parent is so peculiarly requisite. At this period my grandfather's circumstances were at a low ebb, he from great wealth having been reduced to poverty. It was therefore in his power to do little for us. My brother Henry he took however under his charge, while myself and Rosalie were adopted by gentlemen in Richmond, where we were at the period of our parents' death I was adopted by Mr. Jno. Allan of Richmond, Va., and she by Mr. Wm. McKenzie of the same place. Rosalie is still living at Mr. McK* still unmarried, and is treated as one of the family, being a favorite with all. I accompanied Mr. Allan to England in my 7th year, and remained there at school 5 years, since which I resided with Mr. A. until a few years ago. The first Mrs. A. having died, and Mr. A. having married again I found my situation not so comfortable as before, and obtained a Cadet's appointment at W. Point. During my stay there Mr. A. died suddenly, and left me— nothing. No will was found among his papers. I have accordingly been thrown entirely upon my own resources. Brought up to no profession, and educated in the expectation of an immense fortune (Mr. A. having been worth $750,000) the blow has been a heavy one, and I had nearly succumbed to its influence, and yielded to despair. But by the exertion of much resolution I am now beginning to look upon the matter in a less serious light, and although struggling still with many embarrassments, am enabled to keep up my spirits. I have lately obtained the Editorship of the *Southern Messenger*, and may probably yet do well.

Mrs. Thompson, your Aunt, is still living in Baltimore. George Poe of Baltimore allows her a small income.

In conclusion, I beg leave to assure you that whatever aid you may have it in your power to bestow upon Mrs. Clemm will be given to one who well deserves every kindness and attention. Would to God that I could at this moment aid her. She is now, while I write, struggling without friends, without money, and without health to support herself and 2 children. I sincerely pray God that the words which I am writing may be the means of inducing you to unite with your brothers and friends, and send her that *immediate* relief which is *utterly* out of my power to give her just now, and which, unless it reach her soon will, I am afraid, reach her too late. Entreating your attention to this subject I remain,

Yours very truly & affectionately,

EDGAR A. POE

TO MRS. MARIA CLEMM

[Poe wrote this letter shortly after he had left Mrs. Clemm's house in Baltimore to go to Richmond to work on *The Southern Literary Messenger*. Evidently Neilson Poe, who had married Virginia's half sister, had offered to take Virginia into his home and educate her. Poe writes to protest and to declare his love for Virginia, who was then just thirteen. White is Thomas Willis White, a Richmond printer who had begun publishing the *Messenger* just a year before. It is interesting to note that when Poe addresses Virginia directly in his postscript he calls her "Sissy, my darling little wifey."]

Aug: 29th 1835

MY DEAREST AUNTY,

I am blinded with tears while writing this letter—I have no wish to live another hour. Amid sorrow, and the deepest anxiety your letter reached—and you well know how little I am able to bear up under the pressure of grief— My bitterest enemy would pity me could he now read my heart— My last my last my only hold on life is cruelly torn away— I have no desire to live and *will not* But let my duty be done. I love, *you know* I love Virginia passionately devotedly. I cannot express in words the fervent devotion I feel towards my dear little cousin—my own darling. But what can [I] say. Oh think for me for I am incapable of thinking. Al [l my] thoughts are occupied with the supposition that both you & she will prefer to go with N[eilson] Poe; I do sincerely believe that your *comforts* will for the present be secured—I cannot speak as regards your peace— your happiness. You have both tender hearts—and you will always have the reflection that my agony is more than I can bear—that you have driven me to the grave —for love like mine can never be gotten over. It is use- less to disguise the truth that when Virginia goes with N.P. that I shall never behold her again—that is ab- solutely sure. Pity me, my dear Aunty, pity me. I have no one now to fly to—I am among strangers, and my wretchedness is more than I can bear. It is useless to expect advice from me—what can I say? Can I, in honour & in truth say—Virginia! do not go! do not go where you can be comfortable & perhaps happy—and on the other hand can I calmly resign my—life itself[?] If she had truly loved me would she not have rejected the offer with scorn? Oh God have mercy on me! If she goes with N.P. what are you to do, my own Aunty,?

I had procured a sweet little house in a retired situa- tion on Church hill—newly done up and with a large garden and [ever]y convenience—at only $5 month. I have been dreaming every day & night since of the rapture I should feel in [havin]g my only friends—all I love on Earth with me there, [and] the pride I would take in making you both comfor[table] & in calling her my wife— But the dream is over [Oh G]od have mercy on me. What have I *to live for?* Among strangers with *not one soul to love me.*

The situation has this morning been conferred upon another. Branch T. Saunders. But White has engaged to make my salary $60 a month, and we could live in

comparative comfort & happiness—even the $4 a week
I am now paying for board would support us all—but
I shall have $15 a week. & what need would we have
of more? I had thought to send you on a little money
every week until you could either hear from Hall or
Wm. Poe, and then we could get a [little] furniture for
a start—for White will not be able [to a]dvance any.
After that all would go well—or I would make a desperate exertion & try to borrow enough for that purpose.
There is little danger of the house being taken immediately. I would send you on $5 now—for White paid
me the $8 2 days since—but you appear not to have
received my last letter and I am afraid to trust it to the
mail, as the letters are continually robbed. I have it
for you & will keep it until I hear from you when I
will send it & more if I get any in the meantime. I
wrote you that Wm. Poe had written to me concerning
you & has offered to assist you asking me questions concerning you which I answered. He will beyond doubt
aid you shortly & with an effectual aid. Trust in God.

The tone of your letter wounds me to the soul. Oh
Aunty, Aunty you loved me once—how can you be so
cruel now? You speak of Virginia acquiring accom-
plishments, and entering into society—you speak in
so *worldly* a tone. Are you sure she would be more
happy. Do you think any one could love her more
dearly than I[?] She will have far—very far better opportunities of entering into society here than with N.P.
Every one here receives me with open arms.

Adieu my dear Aunty. I *cannot advise you.* Ask Virginia. Leave it to her. Let me have, under her own hand,
a letter, bidding me *good bye*—forever—and I may
die—my heart will break—but I will say no more.

EAP

Kiss her for me—a million times

For Virginia,

My love, my own sweetest Sissy, my darling little
wifey, think well before you break the heart of your
Cousin, Eddy.

I open this letter to enclose the 5$—I have just re-
ceived another letter from you announcing the rect. of
mine. My heart bleeds for you. Dearest Aunty, consider
my happiness while you are thinking about your own.
I am saving all I can. The only money I have yet spent
is 50cts for washing—I have now $2.25. left. I will
shortly send you more. Write immediately. I shall be all
anxiety & dread until I hear from you. Try and convince
my dear Virga. how devotedly I love her. I wish you
would get me the *Republican wh:* noticed the *Messenger* & send it on immediately by mail. God bless &
protect you both.

FROM A LETTER
TO DR. J. E. SNODGRASS

[This is an extract from a long letter which Poe wrote to
Snodgrass about Burton after he had left Burton's *Gentleman's Magazine*. The letter deals mostly with the quarrel between the two men, but the pertinent part of it, which is
Poe's explanation to a physician of his drinking habits, is reproduced here.]

Philadelphia, April 1, 1841

You are a physician, and I presume no physician can
have difficulty in detecting the *drunkard* at a glance.
You are, moreover, a literary man, well read in morals.
You will never be brought to believe that I could write
what I daily write, as I write it, were I as this villain
would induce those who know me not, to believe. In

fine, I pledge you, before God, the solemn word of a gentleman, that I am temperate even to rigor. From the hour in which I first saw this basest of calumniators to the hour in which I retired from his office in uncontrollable disgust at his chicanery, arrogance, ignorance, and brutality, *nothing stronger than water ever passed my lips.*

At no period of my life was I ever what men call intemperate. I never was in the *habit* of intoxication. I never drunk drams, &c. But, for a brief period, while I resided in Richmond, and edited the *Messenger* I certainly did give way, at long intervals, to the temptation held out on all sides by the spirit of Southern conviviality. My sensitive temperament could not stand an excitement which was an everyday matter to my companions. In short, it sometimes happened that I was completely intoxicated. For some days after each excess I was invariably confined to bed. But it is now quite four years since I have abandoned every kind of alcoholic drink—four years, with the exception of a single deviation, which occurred shortly *after* my leaving Burton, and when I was induced to resort to the occasional use of *cider,* with the hope of relieving a nervous attack. . . .

I have now only to repeat to you, in general, my solemn assurance that my habits are as far removed from intemperance as the day from the night. My sole drink is water.

Will you do me the kindness to repeat this assurance to such of your own friends as happen to speak of me in your hearing?

Yours most cordially,

EDGAR A. POE

TO LEA & BLANCHARD

[This business letter has implications which make it one of the most pathetic of all Poe documents. Lea and Blanchard, Philadelphia publishers, had issued his *Tales of the Grotesque and Arabesque* in two volumes in 1840. In their agreement to publish they had said to Poe: "We will at our own risque and expense print a Small Ed. say 1750 copies. This sum—if sold—will pay but a small profit which if realized is to be ours— The copyright will remain with you, and when ready 'a few copies for distribution among your friends will be at your Service." Poe writes here, proposing a new and expanded edition which would contain some of his greatest stories, and for which he asks only for the same terms he had been given on the previous collection. The publishers took only three days to reject his offer, saying that they had not yet sold all the copies of the first collection. The final ironic touch took place in 1944, when the original of the letter printed here was sold at auction for $3000.]

Philadelphia, August 13, 1841

MESS. LEA & BLANCHARD

GENTLEMEN,—I wish to publish a new collection of my prose Tales with some such title as this—

"The Prose Tales of Edgar A. Poe, Including 'The Murders in the Rue Morgue.' The 'Descent into the Maelström,' and all his later pieces, with a second edition of the 'Tales of the Grotesque and Arabesque.'"

The "later pieces" will be eight in number, making the entire collection thirty-three—which would occupy two *thick* novel volumes.

I am anxious that your firm should continue to be my publishers, and, if you would be willing to bring out the book, I should be glad to accept the terms which you allowed me before—that is—you receive all profits, and allow me twenty copies for distribution to friends.

Will you be kind enough to give me an early reply to this letter, and believe me

Yours very resp.

EDGAR A. POE

TO MRS. MARIA CLEMM

[Of all the known Poe letters this one gives the most intimate glimpse of his family life. It was written to his mother-
in-law the day after he and Virginia had arrived in New York
to settle there. The house at 130 Greenwich Street, which
Poe called old a century ago, is still standing, although it has
been somewhat altered. Catterina was the tortoise-shell cat
which stayed with the Poes until after Virginia's death. The
signature on the second page of the original letter has been
cut out by some thoughtless autograph seeker, thus mutilat-
ing part of the text.]

New York, Sunday Morning,
April 7, [1844] just after breakfast

MY DEAR MUDDY,—We have just this minute done
breakfast, and I now sit down to write you about everything. I can't pay for the letter, because the P. O. won't
be open to-day.—In the first place, we arrived safe at
Walnut S^t. wharf. The driver wanted to make me pay a
dollar, but I wouldn't. Then I had to pay a boy a levy
to put the trunks in the baggage car. In the meantime I
took Sis in the Depôt Hotel. It was only a quarter past
6, and we had to wait till 7. We saw the *Ledger* &
Times—nothing in either—a few words of no account
in the *Chronicle*.—We started in good spirits, but did
not get here until nearly 3 o'clock. We went in the cars
to Amboy about 40 miles from N. York, and then took
the steamboat the rest of the way.—Sissy coughed none
at all. When we got to the wharf it was raining hard.
I left her on board the boat, after putting the trunks in
the Ladies' Cabin, and set off to buy an umbrella and
look for a boarding-house. I met a man selling umbrellas
and bought one for 62 cents. Then I went up Greenwich St. and soon found a boarding-house. It is just
before you get to Cedar S^t. on the West side going up—
the left hand side. It has brown stone steps with a porch

with brown pillars. "Morrison" is the name on the door. I made a bargain in a few minutes and then got a hack and went for Sis. I was not gone more than ½ an hour, and she was quite astonished to see me back so soon. She didn't expect me for an hour. There were 2 other ladies waiting on board—so she was n't very lonely.— When we got to the house we had to wait about ½ an hour before the room was ready. The house is old & looks buggy. [Part of letter missing.]

The cheapest board I ever knew, taking into consideration the central situation and the *living*. I wish Kate could see it—she would faint. Last night, for supper, we had the nicest tea you ever drank, strong & hot —wheat bread & rye bread—cheese—tea-cakes (elegant) a great dish (2 dishes) of elegant ham, and 2 of cold veal, piled up like a mountain and large slices—3 dishes of the cakes, and every thing in the greatest profusion. No fear of starving here. The landlady seemed as if she could n't press us enough, and we were at home directly. Her husband is living with her—a fat good-natured old soul. There are 8 or 10 boarders—2 or 3 of them ladies—2 servants.—For breakfast we had excellent-flavored coffee, hot & strong—not very clear & no great deal of cream—veal cutlets, elegant ham & eggs & nice bread and butter. I never sat down to a more plentiful or a nicer breakfast. I wish you could have seen the eggs—and the great dishes of meat. I ate the first hearty breakfast I have eaten since we left our little home. Sis is delighted, and we are both in excellent spirits. She has coughed hardly any and had no night sweat. She is now busy mending my pants which I tore against a nail. I went out last night and bought a skein of silk, a skein of thread, 2 buttons a pair of slippers & a tin pan for the stove. The fire kept in all night— We have now got $4 and a half left. To-morrow

I am going to try & borrow $3—so that I may have a fortnight to go upon. I feel in excellent spirits & have n't drank a drop—so that I hope to get out of trouble. The very instant I scrape together enough money I will send it on. You can't imagine how much we both do miss you. Sissy had a hearty cry last night—, because you and Catterina weren't here. We are resolved to get 2 rooms the first moment we can. In the meantime it is impossible we could be more comfortable or more at home than we are.—It looks as if it was going to clear up now.—Be sure and go to the P. O. & have my letters forwarded. As soon as I write Lowell's article, I will send it to you, & get you to get the money from Graham. Give our best loves to Catterina. . . .

　　　　　　　　　　　　　　　　　　[Signature cut out]

　Be sure & take home the *Messenger*. . . .
　We hope to send for you *very* soon.

TO JAMES RUSSELL LOWELL

[This is a letter from a writer to a writer. Lowell had asked Poe for "a spiritual autobiography," which he wanted to use in the preparation of a short biography of Poe for *Graham's Magazine*. Poe's reply is a long, self-analytical letter of great importance. Hirst's article, to which Poe refers, was a biographical piece that had appeared in the Philadelphia *Sunday Museum* on February 25, 1843.]

　　　　　　　　　　　　　　　　　New York, July 2, '44
MY DEAR MR. LOWELL,
　I can feel for the "constitutional indolence" of which you complain—for it is one of my own besetting sins. I am excessively slothful and wonderfully industrious —by fits. There are epochs when any kind of mental

exercise is torture, and when nothing yields me pleasure but solitary communion with the "mountains and the woods,"—the "altars" of Byron. I have thus rambled and dreamed away whole months, and awake, at last, to a sort of mania for composition. Then I scribble all day, and read all night, so long as the disease endures. This is also the temperament of P. P. Cooke, of Virginia, the author of "Florence Vane," "Young Rosalie Lee," and some other sweet poems—and I should not be surprised if it were your own. Cooke writes and thinks as you—and I have been told that you resemble him personally.

I am not ambitious—unless negatively. I now and then feel stirred up to excel a fool, merely because I hate to let a fool imagine that he may excell me. Beyond this I feel nothing of ambition. I really perceive that vanity about which most men merely prate,—the vanity of the human or temporal life. I live continually in a reverie of the future. I have no faith in human perfectibility. I think that human exertion will have no appreciable effect upon humanity. Man is now only more active—not more happy—nor more wise, than he was 6000 years ago. The result will never vary—and to suppose that it will, is to suppose that the foregone man has lived in vain—that the foregone time is but the rudiment of the future—that the myriads who have perished have not been upon equal footing with ourselves—nor are we with our posterity. I cannot agree to lose sight of man the individual in man the mass. I have no belief in spirituality. I think the word a mere word. No one has really a conception of spirit. We cannot imagine what is not. We deceive ourselves by the idea of infinitely rarefied matter. Matter escapes the senses by degrees—a stone—a metal—a liquid—the atmosphere—a gas—the luminiferous ether. Beyond this there are other modifications more rare. But to all we attach the notion of a constitution of particles—atomic composition. For this reason only we think spirit different; for spirit, we say, is unparticled, and therefore is not matter. But it is clear that if we proceed sufficiently far in our ideas of rarefaction, we shall arrive at a point where the particles coalesce; for, although the particles be infinite, the infinity of littleness in the spaces between them is an absurdity. The unparticled matter, permeating and impelling all things, is God. Its activity is the thought of God—which creates. Man, and other thinking beings, are individualizations of the unparticled matter. Man exists as a "person," by being clothed with matter (the particled matter) which individualizes him. Thus habited, his life is rudimental. What we call "death" is the painful metamorphosis. The stars are the habitations of rudimental beings. But for the necessity of the rudimental life, there would have been no worlds. At death, the worm is the butterfly—still material, but of a matter unrecognized by our organs—recognized occasionally, perhaps, by the sleep-walker directly— without organs—through the mesmeric medium. Thus a sleep-walker may see ghosts. Divested of the rudimental covering, the being inhabits space,—what we suppose to be the immaterial universe,—passing everywhere, and acting all things, by mere volition, cognizant of all secrets but that of the nature of God's volition,—the motion, or activity, of the unparticled matter.

You speak of "an estimate of my life,"—and, from what I have already said, you will see that I have none to give. I have been too deeply conscious of the mutability and evanescence of temporal things to give any continuous effort to anything—to be consistent in anything. My life has been whim—impulse—passion—a longing for solitude—a scorn of all things present, in an earnest desire for the future.

I am profoundly excited by music, and by some poems,—those of Tennyson especially—whom, with Keats, Shelley, Coleridge (occasionally), and a few others of like thought and expression, I regard as the *sole* poets Music is the perfection of the soul, or idea, of Poetry. The *vagueness* of exaltation aroused by a sweet air (which should be strictly indefinite and never too strongly suggestive) is precisely what we should aim at in poetry. Affectation, within bounds, is thus no blemish.

I still adhere to Dickens as either author, or dictator, of the review. My reasons would convince you, could I give them to you, but I have left myself no space. I had two long interviews with Mr. D. when here. Nearly everything in the critique, I heard from him, or suggested to him, personally. The poem of Emerson I read to him.

I have been so negligent as not to preserve copies of any of my volumes of poems—nor was either worthy of preservation. The best passages were culled in Hirst's article. I think my best poems "The Sleeper," "The Conqueror Worm," "The Haunted Palace," "Lenore," "Dreamland," and the "Coliseum,"—but all have been hurried and unconsidered. My best tales are "Ligeia," the "Gold-Bug," the "Murders in the Rue Morgue," "The Fall of the House of Usher," the "Tell-tale Heart," the "Black Cat," "William Wilson," and "The Descent into the Maelström." "The Purloined Letter," forthcoming in the "Gift," is perhaps the best of my tales of ratiocination. I have lately written for Godey "The Oblong Box" and "Thou are the Man,"—as yet unpublished. With this I mail you the "Gold-Bug," which is the only one of my tales I have on hand

Graham has had, for nine months, a review of mine on Longfellow's "Spanish Student," which I have "used up," and in which I have exposed some of the grossest plagiarisms ever perpetrated. I can't tell why he does not publish it.—I believe G. intends my Life for the September number, which will be made up by the 10th August. Your article should be on hand as soon as convenient.

Believe me your true friend,

E. A. POE

FROM A LETTER
TO E. A. DUYCKINCK

[Poe had become the editor and proprietor of *The Broadway Journal,* but the paper was in bad shape financially. He writes here to Evert A. Duyckinck, a successful New York editor who is best known for his monumental *Cyclopaedia of American Literature,* which he edited with his brother George. Virginia was ailing; Poe had been depressed and ill; and he was on the point of losing the *Journal.* Whether Duyckinck came to his aid or not is unknown. At any rate, he lost the paper by the end of the year.]

[November 13, 1845?]
85 Amity St., [N. Y.]

MY DEAR MR DUYCKINCK,—For the first time during two months I find myself entirely myself—dreadfully sick and depressed, but still myself. I seem to have just awakened from some horrible dream, in which all was confusion, and suffering—relieved only by the constant sense of your kindness, and that of one or two other considerate friends. I really believe that I have been mad—but indeed I have had abundant reason to be so. I have made up my mind to a step which will preserve me, for

the future, from at least the greater portion of the
troubles which have beset me. In the meantime, I have
need of the most active exertion to extricate myself from
the embarrassments into which I have already fallen—
and my object in writing you this note is, (once again)
to beg your aid. Of course I need not say to you that my
most urgent trouble is the want of ready money. I find
that what I said to you about the prospects of the
B.[roadway] J.[ournal] is strictly correct. The most
trifling immediate relief would put it on an excellent
footing. All that I want is time in which to look about
me; and I think that it is in your power to afford me
this.

Please send your answer to 85 Amity St. and believe
me—with the most sincere friendship and ardent gratitude

Yours
Edgar A. Poe

TO VIRGINIA POE

[This, except for the brief postscript in his letter written to
Mrs. Clemm on August 29, 1835 (q.v.). is the only known
message that Poe addressed to his wife. His references to a
promised interview and a recent disappointment cannot be
identified. The peaceful summer which he prays for was the
last summer he was to spend with Virginia. She died the next
January.]

June 12, 1846

My dear Heart—my dear Virginia,—Our mother
will explain to you why I stay away from you this night.
I trust the interview I am promised will result in some
substantial good for me—for your dear sake and hers
—keep up your heart in all hopefulness, and trust yet

a little longer. On my last great disappointment I should have lost my courage *but for you*—my little darling wife. You are my *greatest* and *only* stimulus now, to battle with this uncongenial, unsatisfactory, and ungrateful life.

I shall be with you to-morrow . . . P. M., and be assured until I see you I will keep in *loving remembrance* your *last words*, and your fervent prayer!

Sleep well, and may God grant you a peaceful summer with your devoted

EDGAR

TO N. P. WILLIS

[Virginia was dying, and Poe was destitute and half out of his mind. A notice appeared in a New York paper asking his friends to come to his assistance; a similar notice appeared in Philadelphia which said that Poe was "without money and without friends." Poe was furious. His friend Willis wrote a kindly editorial in *The Home Journal*, in which, under pretext of proposing "a retreat for disabled labourers with the brain," he subtly brought Poe's case to public attention This is Poe's comment on the situation.]

December 30, 1846 [?]

MY DEAR WILLIS,—The paragraph which has been put in circulation respecting my wife's illness, my own, my poverty, etc., is now lying before me; together with the beautiful lines by Mrs. Locke and those by Mrs. ———, to which the paragraph has given rise, as well as your kind and manly comments in *The Home Journal*. The motive of the paragraph I leave to the conscience of him or her who wrote it or suggested it. Since the thing is done, however, and since the concerns of my family are thus pitilessly thrust before the public, I perceive no mode of escape from a public statement of what is true and what erroneous in the report alluded to. That my wife is ill, then, is true; and you may imagine with what feelings I add that this illness, hopeless from the first, has been heightened and precipitated by her reception at two different periods, of anonymous letters, —one enclosing the paragraph now in question; the other, those published calumnies of Messrs. ———, for which I yet hope to find redress in a court of justice.

Of the facts, that I myself have been long and dangerously ill, and that my illness has been a well understood thing among my brethren of the press, the best evidence is afforded by the innumerable paragraphs of personal and of literary abuse with which I have been latterly assailed. This matter, however, will remedy itself. At the very first blush of my new prosperity, the gentlemen who toadied me in the old, will recollect themselves and toady me again. You, who know me, will comprehend that I speak of these things only as having served, in a measure, to lighten the gloom of unhappiness, by a gentle and not unpleasant sentiment of mingled pity, merriment and contempt. That, as the inevitable consequence of so long an illness, I have been in want of money, it would be folly in me to deny—but that I have ever materially suffered from privation, beyond the extent of my capacity for suffering, is not altogether true. That I am "without friends" is a gross calumny, which I am sure *you* never could have believed, and which a thousand noble-hearted men would have good right never to forgive me for permitting to pass unnoticed and undenied. Even in the city of New York I could have no difficulty in naming a hundred persons, to each of whom—when the hour for speaking had arrived—I could and would have applied for aid with unbounded confidence, and with absolutely *no* sense of humiliation. I do not think, my dear Willis, that there is any need of my saying more. I am getting better, and may add—if it be any comfort to my enemies—that I have little fear of getting worse. The truth is, I have a great deal to do; and I have made up my mind not to die till it is done.

Sincerely yours,

EDGAR A. POE

TO MRS. MARY LOUISE SHEW

[This brief, anguished note was written the day before Virginia died. Mrs. Shew was a friend of the family, a woman who had had some practical medical training. It was at her house in New York, after Virginia's death, that Poe wrote "The Bells," supposedly inspired by the chimes of near-by Grace Church.]

Fordham, January 29, 1847

KINDEST, DEAREST FRIEND,

My poor Virginia still lives, although failing fast and now suffering much pain. May God grant her life until she sees you and thanks you once again! Her bosom is full to overflowing—like my own—with a boundless, inexpressible gratitude to you. Lest she may never see you more—she bids me say that she sends you her sweetest kiss of love and will die blessing you. But come—oh, come to-morrow! Yes, I will be calm—everything you so nobly wish to see me. My mother sends you, also, her "warmest love and thanks." She begs me to ask you, if possible, to make arrangements at home so that you may stay with us to-morrow night. I enclose the order to the Postmaster.

Heaven bless you and farewell!

EDGAR A. POE

FROM A LETTER
TO GEORGE EVELETH

[The following two letters deal with Poe's drinking habits; together they form a remarkable confessional. Eveleth lived in Phillips, Maine, and was an admirer of Poe's work. It is remarkable that Poe should have been so frank to a man he hardly knew, but he may have felt freer in writing to Eveleth than to a person who knew him better.]

Jan. 4, 1848

You say, "Can you *hint* to me what was the 'terrible evil' which caused the 'irregularities' so profoundly lamented?" Yes, I can do more than hint. This "evil" was the greatest which can befall a man. Six years ago, a wife, whom I loved as no man ever loved before, ruptured a blood-vessel in singing. Her life was despaired of. I took leave of her forever, and underwent all the agonies of her death. She recovered partially, and I again hoped. At the end of a year, the vessel broke again. I went through precisely the same scene. Again in about a year afterward. Then again—again—again—and even once again, at varying intervals. Each time I felt all the agonies of her death—and at each accession of the disorder I loved her more dearly and clung to her life with more desperate pertinacity. But I am constitutionally sensitive—nervous in a very unusual degree. I became insane, with long intervals of horrible sanity. During these fits of absolute unconsciousness, I drank—God only knows how often or how much. As a matter of course, my enemies referred the insanity to the drink, rather than the drink to the insanity. I had, indeed, nearly abandoned all hope of a permanent cure, when I found one in the *death* of my wife. This I can and do endure as becomes a man—it was the horrible never-ending oscillation between hope and despair which I could *not* longer have endured without total loss of reason. In the death of what was my life, then, I receive a new, but—Oh God! how melancholy an existence.

TO GEORGE EVELETH

[New York, Feb. 29, 1848]

The editor of the *Weekly Universe* speaks kindly, and I find no fault with his representing my habits as "shockingly irregular." He could not have had the "personal acquaintance" with me, of which he writes, but has fallen into a very natural error. The fact is thus:— My *habits* are rigorously abstemious, and I omit nothing of the natural regimen requisite for health—*i.e.*, I rise early, eat moderately, drink nothing but water, and take abundant and regular exercise in the open air. But this is my private life—my studious and literary life— and of course escapes the eye of the world. The desire for society comes upon me only when I have become excited by drink. Then *only* I go—that is, at these times only I *have been* in the practice of going among my friends; who seldom, or in fact never, having seen me unless excited, take it for granted that I am always so. Those who *really* know me, know better. In the meantime I shall turn the general error to account. But enough of this—the causes which maddened me to the drinking point are no more, and I am done with drinking for ever.

TO MRS. SARAH HELEN WHITMAN

[These two love letters to Mrs. Whitman are in Poe's most florid Victorian style. The first was written about a week after they had met for the first time. Poe was in error about the difference in their ages; actually Mrs. Whitman was six years his senior. In the second letter, his statement that he married "for another's happiness" is at variance with what he had committed to paper when he wrote to or about Virginia.]

[October 1, 1848]

And now, in the most simple words at my command, let me paint to you the impression made upon me by your personal presence. As you entered the room, pale, timid, hesitating, and evidently oppressed at heart; as your eyes rested appealingly, for one brief moment, upon mine, I felt, for the first time in my life, and tremblingly acknowledged, the existence of spiritual influences altogether out of the reach of my reason. I saw that you were Helen—*my* Helen—the Helen of a thousand dreams—she whose visionary lips had so often lingered upon my own in the divine trance of passion—she whom the great Giver of all Good preordained to be mine—mine only—if not now, alas! then at least hereafter and *forever* in the Heavens. You spoke falteringly and seemed scarcely conscious of what you said. I heard no words—only the soft voice, more familiar to me than my own, and more melodious than the songs of the angels. Your hand rested in mine, and my whole soul shook with a tremulous ecstasy. And then but for very shame but for fear of grieving or oppressing you— I would have fallen at your feet in as pure—in as real a worship as was ever offered to Idol or to God. And when, afterwards, on those two successive evenings of all—Heavenly delights, you passed to and fro about the room—now sitting by my side, now far away, now standing with your hand resting on the back of my chair, while the preternatural thrill of your touch vibrated even through the senseless wood into my heart —while you moved thus restlessly about the room—as if a deep Sorrow or more profound Joy haunted your bosom—my brain reeled beneath the intoxicating spell of your presence (and it was with no human senses that I either saw or heard you. It was my soul only that distinguished you there). I grew faint with the luxury of your voice and blind with the voluptuous lustre of your eyes.

Let me quote to you a passage from your letter:

"You will, perhaps, attempt to convince me that my person is agreeable to you—that my countenance interests you;—but in this respect I am so variable that I should inevitably disappoint you if you hoped to find in me to-morrow the same aspect which one knew today. And again, although my reverence for your intellect and my admiration of your genius make me feel like a child in your presence, you are not perhaps aware that I am many years older than yourself. I fear you do not know it, and that if you had known it you would not have felt for me as you do."

To all this what shall I say—except that the heavenly candor with which you speak oppresses my heart with so rich a burden of love that my eyes overflow with sweet tears. You are mistaken, Helen, very far mistaken about this matter of age. I am older than you; and if illness and sorrow have made you seem older than you are—is not all this the best of reasons for my loving you the more? Cannot my patient cares—my watchful earnest devotion—cannot the magic which lies in such devotion as I feel for you, win back for you much—oh, very much of the freshness of your youth? But grant that what you urge were even true. Do you not feel in

that inmost heart of hearts that the "soul-love" of which
the world speaks so often and so idly, in this instance
at least, but the veriest the most absolute of realities?
Do you not—I ask of your reason, darling, not less than
of your heart—do you not perceive that it is my diviner
nature—my spiritual being—which burns and pants to
commingle with your own? Has the soul age, Helen?
Can immortality regard Time? Can that which began
never and shall never end, consider a few wretched
years of incarnate life? Ah, I could weep—I could almost be angry with you for the wrong you offer to the
purity—to the sacred reality of my affection. And how
am I to answer what you say of your personal appearance? Have I not seen you, Helen? Have I not heard
the more than melody of your voice? Has not my heart
ceased to throb beneath the magic of your smile? Have
I not held your hand in mine and looked steadily into
your soul through the crystal Heaven of your eyes?
Have I done all these things?—or do I dream?—or am
I mad? Were you indeed all that your fancy, enfeebled
and perverted by illness, tempts you to suppose that
you are, still, life of my life! I could but love you—but
worship you the more; it would be so glorious a happiness to prove to you what I feel! But as it is, what can
I—what am I to say? who ever spoke of you without
emotion—without praise who ever saw you and did not
love? But now a deadly terror oppresses me; for I
clearly see that these objections—so groundless—so
futile when urged to one whose nature must be so well
known to you as mine is—can scarcely be meant earnestly; and I tremble lest they but serve to mask others,
more real, and which you hesitate—perhaps in pity—to
confide to me. Alas! I too distinctly perceive also, that
in no instance have you permitted yourself to say that
you *love me.* You are aware, sweet Helen, that on my

part there are insuperable reasons forbidding me to urge upon you my love. Were I not poor—had not my late errors and reckless excesses justly lowered me in the esteem of the good—were I wealthy, or could I offer you worldly honors—ah then—then—how proud would I be to persevere—to—to plead—to pray—to beseech you for your love—in the deepest humility—at your feet—at your feet, Helen, with floods of passionate tears.

And now let me copy here one other passage from your letter—"I find that I cannot now tell you all that I promised. I can only say to you. . . .": [Here four lines of her letter and two lines of his letter are missing.] . . . may God forever shield you from the agony which these *your* words occasion *me!* You will never, *never* know—you can *never* picture to yourself the hopeless, rayless despair with which I now trace these words. Alas Helen! my soul! what is it that I have been saying to you! to what madness have I been urging you? I who am *nothing* to you—*you* who have a dear mother and sister to be blessed by your life and love. But ah, darling! if I am selfish, yet believe me that I truly, truly love you, and that is the most spiritual of love that I speak, even if I speak it from the depths of the most passionate of hearts. Think—oh, think for me, Helen, and for. . . . [The rest of this page is cut off.] . . . comfort you—soothe you—tranquilize you. My love— my faith should instil into your bosom a preternatural calm. You would rest from care—from all worldly agitation. You would get better and finally well. And if *not*, Helen, if not—if you died—then at least I would clasp your dear hand in death, and willingly—oh, joyfully—joyfully—joyfully—go down with you into the night of the grave.

Write me soon—soon—ah soon—but not much. Be

not weary or agitate yourself for my sake. Say to me
those coveted words which would turn Earth into
Heaven. [The rest is missing.]

TO MRS. SARAH HELEN WHITMAN

October 18, 1848

In pressing my last letter between your dear hands,
there passed into your spirit a sense of the love that
glowed within those pages: you say this, and I feel that
indeed it must have been so:—but, in receiving the
paper upon which your eyes now rest, did no shadow
steal over you from the Sorrow within me? Oh, God!
how I curse the impotence of the pen—the inexorable
distance between us! I am pining to speak to *you*—
Helen—to you in person—to be near you while I speak
—gently to press your hand in mine to look into your
soul through your eyes and thus to *be sure* that my voice
passes into your heart. Only thus could I hope to make
you understand what I feel; and even thus I *should* not
hope to make you do so; for it is only Love which can
comprehend Love—and alas! you do not love me. Bear
with me! have patience with me! for indeed my heart is
broken; and let me struggle as I will, I cannot write you
the calm, cold language of a world which I loathe—of
a world in which I have no interest—of a world which
is not mine. I repeat to you that my heart is broken—
that I have no farther object in life—that I have absolutely no wish but *to die*. These are hackneyed phrases;
but they will not now impress you as such—for you
must and do know the passionate agony with which I
write them. "You do not love me"—in this brief sentence lies all I can conceive of despair. I have no resource—no hope; Pride itself fails me now. You do not

love me; or you could not have imposed upon me the torture of eight days silence—of eight days terrible suspense. You do not love me—or, responding to my prayers you would have said to me—"Edgar I do." Ah, Helen, the emotion which now consumes me teaches me too well the nature of the impulses of love! Of what avail to me in my deadly grief are your enthusiastic words of mere admiration? Alas! Alas!—I have been loved, and a relentless Memory contrasts what you say with the unheeded unvalued words of others. But ah—again, and most especially—you do not love me, or you would have felt too thorough a sympathy with the sensitiveness of my nature, to have so wounded me as you have done with this terrible passage of your letter: "How often I have heard men and women say of you—'He has great intellectual power, but no principle—no moral sense.'" Is it possible that such expressions as these could have been repeated to me—to me—by one whom I loved—ah, whom I love—by one at whose feet I knelt—I still kneel—in deeper worship than ever man offered to God? And you proceed to ask me why such opinions exist. You will feel remorse for the question, Helen, when I say to you that, until the moment when those horrible words first met my eye, I would not have believed it *possible* that any such opinions could have existed at all:—but that they do exist breaks my heart and is separating us forever. I love you too truly ever to have offered you my hand—ever to have sought your love—had I *known* my name to be so stained as your expressions imply. Oh God! what shall I say to you Helen, dear Helen!—let me call you now by that sweet name, if I may never so call you again. It is altogether in vain that I tax my Memory or my Conscience. There is no oath that seems to me so sacred as that sworn by the all-divine love I bear you. By this love, then and

by the God who reigns in Heaven, I swear to you that
my soul is incapable of dishonor—that, with the exception of occasional follies and excesses which I bitterly
lament, but to which I have been driven by intolerable
sorrow, and which are hourly committed by others without attracting any notice whatever—I can call to mind
no act of my life which would bring a blush to my cheek
—or to yours. If I have erred at all in this regard, it has
been on the side of what the world would call a Quix-
otic sense of the honorable—of the chivalrous. The indulgence of this sense has been the true voluptuousness
of my life. It was for this species of luxury that, in my
early youth, I deliberately threw away from me a large
fortune, rather than endure a trivial wrong. It was for
this that at a later period, I did violence to my own
heart, and married, for another's happiness, where I
knew that no possibility of my own existed. Ah, how
profound is my love for you, since it forces me into
these egotisms for which you will inevitably despise me!
Nevertheless, I must now speak to you the truth or
nothing. It was mere indulgence, then, of the sense to
which I refer, that, at one dark epoch of my late life,
for the sake of one who, deceiving and betraying, still
loved me much, I sacrificed what seemed in the eyes of
men my honor, rather than abandon what was honor in
hers and in my own. But, alas! for nearly three years I
have been ill, poor, living out of the world; and thus, as
I now painfully see, have afforded opportunity to my
enemies—and especially to one, the most malignant and
pertinacious of all friends. [Line missing.] . . . to slander me, in private society, without my knowledge, and
thus with impunity. Although much, however, may
(and I now see must) have been said to my discredit,
during my retirement, those few who, knowing me well,
have been steadfastly my friends, permitted nothing to

reach my ears—unless in one instancsing where the malignity of the accuser hurried her beyond her usual caution, and thus the accusation was of such a character that I could appeal to a court of justice for redress. The tools employéd in this instance were Mr. Hiram Fuller, Mr. T. D. English. I replied to the charge fully, in a public newspaper—afterward suing the *Mirror* (in which the scandal appeared) obtaining a verdict and obtaining such an amount as, for the time, completely to break up that journal. And you ask me, *why* men so misjudge me—why I have enemies. If your knowledge of my character and of my career does not afford you an answer to the query, at least it does not become me to suggest the answer. Let it suffice that I have had the audacity to remain poor that I might preserve my independence—that, nevertheless, in letters, to a certain extent and in certain regard I have been successful—that I have been a critic—an unscrupulously honest and in many cases a bitter one—that I have been uniformly attacked where I attacked at all—those who stood highest in power and influence—and that, whether in literature or in society, I have seldom refrained from expressing, either directly or indirectly the pure contempt with which the pretensions of ignorance, arrogance, or hostility inspire me. And you who know all this—*you* ask me *why* I have enemies. Ah, Helen, I have a hundred friends for every individual enemy—but has it never occurred to you that you do not live among my friends? Miss Lynch, Miss Fuller, Miss Blackwell, Mrs. Ellet—neither these nor any within their influence, are my friends. Had you read my criticisms generally, you would see, too, how and why it is that the Channings— the Emerson and Hudson coterie—the Longfellow clique, one and all—the cabal of the *N[orth] American Review*—you would see why all these, whom *you* know

best, know me least and are my enemies. Do you not
remember with how deep a sigh I said to you in Providence—"My heart is heavy, Helen, for I see that your
friends are not my own." But the cruel sentence in your
letter would not—could not so deeply have wounded
me, had my soul first been strengthend by those assur-
ances of your love, which I so wildly—so vainly—and,
I now feel, so presumptuously entreated. That our souls
are one, every line which you have ever written asserts
—but our hearts do not beat in unison. Tell me, darling! to your heart has any angel ever whispered that
the very noblest lines in all human poetry are these—
hackneyed though they be!

> *I know not—I ask not if guilt's in thy heart:—*
> *I but know that I love thee whatever thou art.*

When I first read your letter I could do nothing but
shed tears, while I repeated again and again, those
glorious, those all-comprehensive verses, till I could
scarcely hear my own voice for the passionate throb-
bings of my heart.

Forgive me, best and only beloved Helen, if there be
bitterness in my tone. Towards you there is no room in
my soul for any other sentiment than devotion—it is
Fate only I accuse: it is my own unhappy nature which
wins me as the true *love* of no woman whom by any
possibility I could love.

I heard something, a day or two ago, which, had your
last letter never reached me, might not irreparably have
disturbed the relations between us, but which, as it is,
withers forever all the dear hopes upspringing in my
bosom. A few words will explain to you what I mean.
Not long after the receipt of your Valentine I learned,
for the first time, that you were free—unmarried. I will
not pretend to express to you what is absolutely inex-

pressible—that will—long-enduring thrill of joy which pervaded my whole being on hearing that it was not *impossible* I might one day call you by the sacred title, wife: but there was one alloy to this happiness—I *dreaded* to find you in worldly circumstances superior to my own. Let me speak freely to you now, Helen, for perhaps, I may never thus be permitted to speak to you again. Let me speak openly—fearlessly—trusting to the generosity of your own spirit for a true interpretation of my own. I repeat, then, that I *dreaded* to find you in worldly circumstances superior to mine. So great was my *fear* that you were rich, or at least possessed of some property which might cause you to seem rich in the eyes of one so poor as I had always permitted myself to be— that, on the day I refer to, I had not the courage to ask my informant any questions concerning you. I feel that you will have difficulty in comprehending me; but the horror with which, during my sojourn in the world, I have seen affection made the subject of barter, had, long since—long before my marriage—inspired me with the resolution that, under no circumstances, would I marry where "interest," as the world terms it, could be suspected as, on my part, the object of the marriage. As far as this point concerned yourself, however, I was re- lieved the next day, by an assurance that you were wholly dependent upon your mother. May I—dare I add—can you believe me when I say that this assurance was doubly grateful to me by the additional one that you were in ill health and had suffered more from do- mestic trouble than falls usually to the lot of woman? and even if your faith in my nature is not too greatly tasked by such an assertion, can you forbear thinking me unkind, selfish, or ungenerous? You cannot: but oh! the sweet dreams which absorbed me at once! dear dreams of a devotional care for you that end only with

life—of a tender, cherishing, patient, solicitude which
should bring you back, at length to health and to happiness—a care—a solicitude—which should find its
glorious reward in winning me, after long years, that
which I could *feel* to be *your love!* without well understanding *why.* I had been led to fancy you ambitious;
perhaps the fancy arose from your lines:

> Not a bird that roams the forest
> Shall our lofty eyrie share!

but my very soul glowed with ambition for *your* sake,
although I have always condemned it for my own. It
was then only—then when I thought of you—that I
dwelt exultingly upon what I felt that I could accomplish in Letters and in Literary Influence—in the widest
and noblest field of human ambition.

"I will erect," I said, "a prouder throne than any on
which mere monarch ever sat; and on this throne she—
she shall be my queen." When I saw you, however,—
when I touched your gentle hand—when I heard your
soft voice, and perceived how greatly I had misconceived your womanly nature—these triumphant visions
melted sweetly away in the sunshine of a love ineffable;
and I suffered my imagination to stray with you, and
with the few who love us both, to the banks of some
quiet river, in some lovely valley of our land. Here, not
too far secluded from the world, we exercised the taste
controlled by no conventionalities, but the sworn slave
of a Natural Art, in the building for ourselves a cottage
which no human being could ever pass without an
ejaculation of wonder at its strange, weird, and incomprehensible, yet most simple beauty. Oh, the sweet and
gorgeous, but not often rare flowers in which we half
buried it!—the grandeur of the little-distant magnolias
and tulip-trees which stood guarding it—the luxurious

velvet of its lawn—the lustre of the rivulet that ran by the very door—the tasteful yet quiet comfort of the interior—the music—the books—the unostentatious pictures—and, above all, the love—the *love* that threw an unfading *glory* over the whole! Ah, Helen! my heart is indeed, breaking and I must now put an end to these divine dreams. Alas! all is now a dream; for I have lately heard that of you which (taken in connection with your letter and with that of which your letter does not assure me) puts it forever out of my power to ask you —again to ask you—to become my wife. That *many* persons in your presence, have declared me wanting in honor, appeals irresistibly to an instinct of my nature— an instinct which I feel to be honor, let the dishonorable say what they may, and forbids me, under such circumstances, to insult you with my love:—but that you are quite independent in your worldly position (as I have just heard)—in a word *that you are comparatively rich while I am poor,* opens between us a gulf—a gulf, alas! which the Sorrow and the slander of the world have rendered forever impassible by me.

I have not yet been able to procure all the criticisms, etc., of which you spoke, but will forward them by express, in a day or two. Meantime I enclose the lines by Miss Fuller; and "The Domain of Arnheim," which happens to be at hand, and which, moreover, expresses *much of my soul.* It was about the 10th. of Sep., I think, that your sweet MS. verses reached me in Richmond. I lectured in Lowell on the 10th. of July. Your first letter was received by me at Fordham on the evening of Saturday, Sep. 30. I was in Providence, or its neighborhood, during the Monday you mention. In the morning I revisited the cemetery—at 6 P.M. I left the city in the Stonington train for N.Y. I cannot explain to you— since I cannot myself comprehend—the feeling which

urged me not to see you again before going—not to bid
you a second time *farewell*. I had a sad foreboding at
heart. In the seclusion of the cemetery you sat by my
side—on the very spot where my arm first tremblingly
encircled your waist.

EDGAR

TO MRS. NANCY LOCKE
HEYWOOD RICHMOND ("ANNIE")

[The affair—if it can be called that—with Mrs. Whitman
was not yet over when Poe wrote this fervent letter to the
married woman whose love he was also seeking. It tells of his
attempt at suicide and of his return afterwards to Providence.
The "her" he mentions is, of course, Mrs. Whitman. No
original of this letter is known; the present text is taken from
a copy (now in the possession of the University of Virginia)
made many years later by Mrs. Richmond for the benefit of
J. H. Ingram, who was then engaged in writing a biography of
Poe. Ingram wrote on it: "This must be burnt."]

[Fordham, November 16, 1848]

Ah, Annie Annie! *my* Annie! What cruel thoughts
about your Eddy, must have been torturing your heart
during the last terrible fortnight, in which you have
heard *nothing* from me—not even one little word to say
that I still lived & loved you. But Annie, I know that
you *felt* too deeply the nature of my love for you, to
doubt *that*, even for one moment, & this thought has
comforted me in my bitter sorrow— I could bear that
you should imagine *every other evil except that one*—
that my soul had been untrue to yours. Why am I not
with you now *darling* that I might sit by your side, press
your dear hand in mine, & look deep down into the clear
Heaven of your eyes—so that the words which I now

can only *write*, might sing into your heart, and make you comprehend what it is that I would say— And yet Annie, *all* that I wish to say—all that my soul pines to express at this instant, is included in the one word, *love*— To be with you now—so that I might whisper in your ear the divine emotions which agitate me—I would willingly—oh *joyfully* abandon this world with all my hopes of another:—but you *believe* this, Annie— you do believe it, & will always believe it— So long as I think that you know I love you, as no man ever loved woman—so long as I think you comprehend in some measure, the fervor with which I adore you, *so* long, no worldly trouble can ever render me absolutely wretched. But oh, *my darling, my* Annie, my own sweet *sister* Annie, my *pure* beautiful angel—*wife* of my soul—to be mine hereafter & *forever in the Heavens,* how shall I explain to you the *bitter, bitter* anguish which has tortured me since I left you? You saw, you *felt* the agony of grief with which I bade you farewell—you remember my expressions of gloom—of a dreadful horrible foreboding of Ill—Indeed—*indeed* it seemed to me that death approached me even then, & that I was involved in the shadow which went before him— As I clasped you to my heart, I said to myself—"it is for the last time, until we meet in Heaven"— I remember nothing distinctly, from that moment until I found myself in Providence. I went to bed & wept through a long, long hideous night of despair— When the day broke, I arose & endeavored to quiet my mind by a rapid walk in the cold, keen air—but all *would* not do—the demon tormented me still. Finally I procured two ounces of laud-[a]num & without returning, to my Hotel, took the cars back to Boston. When I arrived, I wrote you a letter, in which I opened my whole heart to you—to *you*—my Annie, whom I so madly, so distractedly love— I told you how my struggles were more than I could bear—how my soul revolted from saying the words which were to be said—and that not even for your dear sake, could I bring myself to say them. I then reminded you of that holy promise, which was the last I exacted from you in parting—the promise that, under all circumstances, you would come to me on my bed of death— I implored you to come *then*—mentioning the place where I should be found in Boston. Having written this letter, I swallowed about half the laud[a]num, & hurried to the Post-office—intending not to take the rest until I saw you—for, I did not doubt for one moment, that *my own Annie* would keep her sacred promise. But I had not calculated on the strength of the laudanum, for, before I reached the Post office my reason was entirely gone, & the letter was never put in. Let me pass over, my darling *sister*, the awful horrors which succeeded. A friend was at hand, who aided & (if it can be called easing) eased me, but it is only within the last three days, that I have been able to remember what occurred in that dreary interval. It appears that, after the laudanum was rejected from the stomach, I became calm, & to a casual observer, sane—so that I was suffered to go back to Providence— Here I saw *her,* & spoke for *your* sake, the words which you urged me to speak— Ah Annie Annie! *my* Annie!—*is* your heart *so* strong?—is there *no* hope?—is there *none?*— I feel that I *must* die if I persist, & yet, how can I now retract with honor?— Ah *beloved,* think—think for *me* & for yourself—do I not *love* you Annie? do you not *love me?* Is not this *all?* Beyond this blissful thought, what other consideration *can* there be in this dreary world! It is not *much* that I ask, *sweet sister Annie*—my mother & myself would take a small cottage at Westford—oh *so* small—so *very* humble— I should be far away from the tumult of the world—from the ambition which I loathe— I would labor day & night, and with industry, I could accomplish *so* much—Annie! it would be a Paradise beyond my wildest hopes—I could see some of your beloved family *every* day, & you, often oh very often—I would hear from you continually—regularly & *our* dear mother would be with us & love us both—ah *darling*—do not these pictures touch your inmost heart? Think—oh *think* for me—before the words—the vows are spoken, which put yet another terrible *bar,* between us—before the time goes by, beyond which there must be *no* thinking— I call upon you in the name of God—in the name of the holy love I bear you, to be *sincere* with me— *Can* you, *my* Annie, *bear* to think I am another's? *It would give me supreme—infinite bliss,* to hear you say that you could *not* bear it— I am at home now with my dear muddie who is endeavoring to comfort me—but the sole words which soothe me, are those in which she speaks of *"my Annie"*— She tells me that she has written you, begging you to come on to Fordham— Ah beloved Annie, IS IT NOT POSSIBLE? I am so *ill*—so terribly, hopelessly ILL in body and mind, that I feel I CANNOT live, unless I can feel your sweet, gentle, loving hand pressed upon my forehead— Oh my *pure, virtuous, generous, beautiful, beautiful sister* Annie! is it not POSSIBLE for you to come—if only for one little week? until I subdue this fearful agitation, which if continued, will either destroy my life or, drive me hopelessly mad— Farewell—*here* & hereafter—

forever your own

EDDY—

FROM A LETTER
TO F. W. THOMAS

[Frederick W. Thomas was one of the few men with whom Poe was on intimate terms. They had met in 1840 and corresponded frequently thereafter. Thomas was a lawyer who had written a novel entitled *Clinton Bradshaw*. This letter to him is noteworthy because of what Poe has to say about authorship as a career.]

Fordham, near New York,
Feb. 14, 1849

MY DEAR FRIEND THOMAS,—Your letter dated November 27, has reached me at a little village of the Empire State after having taken at its leisure, a very considerable tour among the P. Offices—occasioned I presume by your endorsement "to forward" wherever I might be—and the fact is where I might *not* have been for the last three months, is the legitimate question. At all events now that I have your well-known MS before me, it is most cordially welcomed. Indeed it seems an age since I heard from you and a decade of ages since I shook you by the hand—although I hear *of* you now and then. Right glad am I to find you once more in a true position—in the field of Letters. Depend upon it after all, Thomas, Literature is the most noble of professions. In fact, it is about the only one fit for a man. For my own part there is no seducing me from the path. I shall be a *littérateur* at least, all my life; nor would I abandon the hopes which still lead me on for all the gold in California. Talking of gold and of the temptations at present held out to "poor-devil authors" did it ever strike you that all that is really valuable to a man of letters—to a poet in especial—is absolutely unpurchasable? Love, fame, the dominion of intellect, the consciousness of power, the thrilling sense of beauty, the free air of Heaven, exercise of body & mind, with the physical and moral health which result—these and such as these are really all that a poet cares for:—then answer me this—*why* should he go to California?

TO MRS. MARIA CLEMM

[These last five letters were all written to Poe's mother-in-law, the woman he had come to look upon as a mother. They mark the stages of his last dreadful journey toward dissolution and death. The first three refer to his experiences in Philadelphia, where he had been out of his mind; the last two to his anticipated marriage to Mrs. Shelton. The Rose he mentions is his sister Rosalie; the Mackenzies are the people who had given her a home. He still says that he "must be somewhere where I can see Annie" (Mrs. Richmond). These are among the last letters Poe ever wrote. He died only a few weeks after writing the last one.]

July 7, [1849]

My *dear, dear* MOTHER,

I have been *so* ill—have had the cholera, or spasms quite as bad, and can now hardly hold the pen.

The very instant you get this, *come* to me. The joy of seeing you will almost compensate for our sorrows. We can but die together. It is no use to reason with *me* now; I must die. I have no desire to live since I have done "Eureka." I could accomplish nothing more. For your sake it would be sweet to live, but we must die together. You have been all in all to me, darling, ever beloved mother, and dearest, truest friend.

I was never *really* insane, except on occasions where my heart was touched.

I have been taken to prison once since I came here for getting drunk; but *then* I was not. It was about Virginia.

TO MRS. MARIA CLEMM

Richmond, Saturday Night. [July 14, 1849]

OH, MY DARLING MOTHER, it is now more than three weeks since I saw you, and in all that time your poor Eddy has scarcely drawn a breath except of intense agony. Perhaps you are sick or gone from Fordham in despair, or dead. If you are but alive, and if I but *see you again*, all the rest is nothing. I love you better than ten thousand lives—so much so that it is cruel in you to let me leave you; nothing but sorrow *ever* comes of it.

Oh, Mother, I am *so* ill while I write—but I resolved that come what would, I would not sleep again without easing your dear heart as far as I could.

My valise was lost for ten days. At last I found it at the depot in Philadelphia, but (you will scarcely credit it) they had opened it and stolen *both lectures*. Oh, Mother, think of the blow to me this evening, when on examining the valise, these lectures were gone. All my object here is over unless I can recover them or re-write one of them.

I am indebted for more than life itself to B[urr]. Never forget him, Mother, while you live. When all failed me, he stood my friend, got me money, and saw me off in the cars for Richmond.

I got here with two dollars over—of which I inclose you one. Oh God, my Mother, shall we ever again meet? If possible, oh COME! My clothes are *so horrible*, and I am so *ill*. Oh, if you could come to me, *my mother*. Write instantly—oh *do* not fail. God forever bless you.

EDDY

TO MRS. MARIA CLEMM

Richmond, Thursday, July 19, [1849]

MY OWN BELOVED MOTHER—

You will see at once, by the handwriting of this letter, that I am better—much better in health and spirits. Oh, if you only knew how your dear letter comforted me! It acted like magic. Most of my suffering arose from that terrible idea which I could not get rid of—the idea that you were dead. For more than ten days I was totally deranged, although I was not drinking one drop; and during this interval I imagined the most horrible calamities.

All was hallucination, arising from an attack which I had never before experienced—an attack of mania-à-potu. May Heaven grant that it prove a warning to me for the rest of my days. If so, I shall not regret even the horrible unspeakable torments I have endured.

To L[ippard] and to C[hauncey] B[urr] (and in some measure, also, to Mr. S[artain]) I am indebted for more than life. They remained with me (L[ippard] and B[urr]) all day on Friday last, comforted me and aided me in coming to my senses. L[ippard] saw G[odey], who said everything kind of me, and sent me five dollars; and [S. D.] P[atterson] sent another five. B[urr] procured me a ticket as far as Baltimore, and the passage from there to Richmond was seven dollars. I have not drank anything since Friday morning, and then only a little Port wine. If *possible*, dearest Mother, I *will* extricate myself from this difficulty for your *dear, dear sake*. So keep up heart.

All is not lost yet, and "the darkest hour is just before daylight." Keep up heart, my own beloved mother—all may yet go well. I will put forth all my energies. When I get my mind a little more composed, I will try to

write something. Oh, give my *dearest*, fondest love to
Mrs. L. Tell her that *never, while I live*, will I forget
her kindness to my darling mother.

TO MRS. MARIA CLEMM

[August, 1849]

[The beginning is missing]

possible. Everybody says that if I lecture again & put
the tickets at 50 cts. I will clear $100. I *never* was re-
ceived with so much enthusiasm. The papers have done
nothing but praise me before the lecture & since. I enclose one of the notices—the only one in which the
slightest word of disparagement appears. It is written
by Daniel—the man whom I challenged when I was
here last year. I have been invited out a great deal—
but could seldom go, on account of not having a dress
coat. To-night Rose & I are to spend the evening at
Elmira's. Last night I was at Poitiaux's—the night before at Strobia's, where I saw my dear friend Eliza
Lambert (Gen. Lambert's sister). She was ill in her
bed-room, but insisted upon our coming up, & we stayed
until nearly 1 o'clock. In a word, I have received nothing but kindness since I have been here, & could have
been quite happy but for my dreadful anxiety about
you. Since the report of my intended marriage, the
McKenzies have overwhelmed me with attentions. Their
house is so crowded that they *could* not ask me to stay.
—And now, my own precious Muddy, the very moment
I get a definite answer about everything, I will write
again & tell you what to do. Elmira talks about visiting
Fordham—but I do not know whether that would do.
I think, perhaps, it would be best for you to give up
everything there & come on here in the Packet. Write

immediately & give me your advice about it—for you know best. Could we be happier in Richmond or Lowell?—for I suppose we could never be happy at Fordham—and, Muddy, I *must* be somewhere where I can see Annie.—Did Mrs. L. get the *Western Quarterly Review?* Thompson is constantly urging me to write for the *Messenger*, but I am so anxious that I cannot—Mr. Loud, the husband of Mrs. St Leon Loud, the hostess of Philadelphia, called on me the other day and offered me $100 to edit his wife's poems. Of course, I accepted the offer. The whole labor will not occupy me 3 days. I am to have them ready by Christmas.—I have seen Bernard often. Eliza is expected but has not come.— When I repeat my lecture here, I will then go to Petersburg & Norfolk.—A Mr. Taverner lectured here on Shakespeare, a few nights after me, and had 8 persons, including myself & the doorkeeper.—I think, upon the whole, dear Muddy, it will be better for you to say that I am ill, or something of that kind, and break up at Fordham, so that you may come on here. Let me know immediately what you think best. You know we could easily pay off what we owe at Fordham & the place is a beautiful one—but I want to live *near Annie*.—And now, dear Muddy, there is one thing I wish you to pay particular attention to. I told Elmira, when I first came here, that I had one of the pencil-sketches of her, that I took a long while ago in Richmond; and I told her that I would write to you about it. So when you write, just copy the following words in your letter:

I have looked again for the pencil-sketch of Mrs. S. but cannot find it anywhere. I took down all the books and shook them one by one, and unless Eliza White has it, I do not know what has become of it. She was looking at it the last time I saw it. The one you spoilt with

Indian Ink ought to be somewhere about the house. I will do my best to [find] it.

I got a sneaking letter to-day from Chivers.—Do not tell me anything about Annie—I cannot bear to hear it now—unless you can tell me that Mr. R[ichmond] is dead.—I have got the wedding ring.—and shall have no difficulty, I think, in getting a dress-coat.

[The rest is missing]

TO MRS. MARIA CLEMM

Richmond, Va., Tuesday—Sep. [1849]

MY OWN DARLING MUDDY,—On arriving here last night from Norfolk I received both your letters, including Mrs. Lewis's. I cannot tell you the joy they gave me —to learn at least that you are well & hopeful. May God forever bless you, my *dear, dear* Muddy ——. Elmira [Shelton] has just got home from the country. I spent last evening with her. I think she loves me more devotedly than any one I ever knew & I cannot help loving her in return. Nothing is as yet definitely settled —and it will not do to hurry matters. I lectured at Norfolk on Monday & cleared enough to settle my bill here at the Madison House with $2, over. I had a highly fashionable audience, but Norfolk is a small place & there were 2 exhibitions the same night. Next Monday I lecture again here & expect to have a large audience. On Tuesday I start for Phil^a. to attend to Mrs. Loud's poems—& *possibly* on Thursday I may start for N. York. If I do I will go straight over to Mrs. Lewis's & send for you. It will be better for me not to go to Fordham.—don't you think so? Write immediately in reply & direct to Phil^a. For fear I should not get the letter sign no name & address it to *E. S. T. Grey, Esqre.* *If possible* I will get married before I start—but there is no telling. Give my dearest love to Mrs. L. My poor, poor Muddy I am still unable to send you even one dollar—but keep up heart—I hope that our troubles are nearly over. I saw John Beatty in Norfolk.

God bless & protect you, my own darling Muddy. I showed your letter to Elmira and she says "it is such a darling precious letter that she loves you for it already."

Your own   EDDY

Don't forget to write immediately to Phil^a. so that your letter will be there when I arrive.

The papers here are praising me to death—and I have been received every where with enthusiasm. Be sure & preserve all the printed scraps I have sent you & keep up my file of the *Lit. World.*

TALES
Of Fantasy

"FANTASY," E. M. Forster has said, "implies the supernatural, but need not express it." Oddly enough, Poe never wrote a ghost story; nowhere in his writings is there a ghost in the sense that we ordinarily think of one. His characters who return from the grave are not spectral visions but the resuscitated dead who rise from the tomb to confront the living with their substantial—though corrupted—flesh. Nevertheless Poe did create characters that had no real existence. The other self, the conscience-symbol of William Wilson, is perhaps the most significant of them.

There were two Poes. One was the hardworking editor, the intellectual critic, the respectable citizen who was interested in art and letters; the other was a disreputable fellow, who frequented low dives and who often wound up literally in the gutter. The outcome of the lifelong struggle between the two warring selves is forecast in "William Wilson," particularly in its prophetic last sentence. The story is autobiographical, not only in its material—the school is the one Poe attended at Stoke Newington—but also in its inner meaning. Of all his stories it tells us most about its author and gives us the greatest insight into the secret workings of his mind. Stevenson dealt with a similar theme in "Markheim," but his story does not have the force of Poe's, for Poe was writing not merely a tale but a symbolic confessional.

"A Tale of the Ragged Mountains" is one of the very few stories to which Poe gave an American setting; its background is the mountains near Charlottesville, where the young Poe often went for long walks when he attended the University of Virginia. It is a contrived story, but it deals with the idea of predestined and inescapable doom that fascinated its author.

"Eleonora" was published a year before Virginia Poe broke a blood vessel and entered upon the slow decline that led to her death, so her husband can hardly have known how closely his story was to be paralleled in real life. The tale is prophetic also in its foretelling of a successor to the dead wife, the "ethereal Ermengarde," for whom one can substitute Mrs. Whitman, Mrs. Richmond, Mrs. Shelton, or any of the other women whose attentions Poe sought after Virginia's death. The first two paragraphs which deal with madness are especially noteworthy.

Hawthorne's story, "The Birthmark," which was published a year after Poe's "The Oval Portrait" appeared, closely resembles it. Hawthorne was surely not a plagiarist, but both he and Poe may have received their inspiration from a common source.

"The Man of the Crowd" is one of Poe's least appreciated stories. It is almost never commented on in any critical review of his work, yet it is one of his most unusual stories, curiously modern in its psychology, and far more original than some of his better-known tales.

WILLIAM WILSON

(*Burton's Gentleman's Magazine,* October, 1839.)

What say of it? what say of CONSCIENCE grim,
That spectre in my path?
                    —CHAMBERLAYNE'S PHARRONIDA

LET me call myself, for the present, William Wilson. The fair page now lying before me need not be sullied with my real appellation. This has been already too much an object for the scorn—for the horror—for the detestation of my race. To the uttermost regions of the globe have not the indignant winds bruited its unparalleled infamy? Oh, outcast of all outcasts most abandoned!—to the earth art thou not forever dead? to its honors, to its flowers, to its golden aspirations?— and a cloud, dense, dismal, and limitless, does it not hang eternally between thy hopes and heaven?

I would not, if I could, here or to-day, embody a record of my later years of unspeakable misery, and unpardonable crime. This epoch—these later years—took unto themselves a sudden elevation in turpitude, whose origin alone it is my present purpose to assign. Men usually grow base by degrees. From me, in an instant, all virtue dropped bodily as a mantle. From comparatively trivial wickedness I passed, with the stride of a giant, into more than the enormities of an Elah-Gabalus. What chance—what one event brought this evil thing to pass, bear with me while I relate. Death approaches; and the shadow which foreruns him has thrown a softening influence over my spirit. I long, in passing through the dim valley, for the sympathy—I had nearly said for the pity—of my fellow men. I would fain have them believe that I have been, in some measure, the slave of circumstances beyond human control. I would wish them to seek out for me, in the details I am about to give, some little oasis of *fatality* amid a wilderness of error. I would have them allow—what they cannot refrain from allowing—that, although temptation may have erewhile existed as great, man was never *thus*, at least, tempted before—certainly, never *thus* fell. And is it therefore that he has never thus suffered? Have I not indeed been living in a dream? And am I not now dying a victim to the horror and the mystery of the wildest of all sublunary visions?

I am the descendant of a race whose imaginative and easily excitable temperament has at all times rendered them remarkable; and, in my earliest infancy, I gave evidence of having fully inherited the family character. As I advanced in years it was more strongly developed; becoming, for many reasons, a cause of serious disquietude to my friends, and of positive injury to myself. I grew self-willed, addicted to the wildest caprices, and a prey to the most ungovernable passions. Weak-minded, and beset with constitutional infirmities akin to my own, my parents could do but little to check the evil propensities which distinguished me. Some feeble and ill-directed efforts resulted in complete failure on their part, and, of course, in total triumph on mine. Thenceforward my voice was a household law; and at an age when few children have abandoned their leading-strings, I was left to the guidance of my own will, and became, in all but name, the master of my own actions.

My earliest recollections of a school-life, are connected with a large, rambling, Elizabethan house, in a misty-looking village of England, where were a vast number of gigantic and gnarled trees, and where all the houses were excessively ancient. In truth, it was a dream-like and spirit-soothing place, that venerable old town. At this moment, in fancy, I feel the refreshing

chilliness of its deeply-shadowed avenues, inhale the
fragrance of its thousand shrubberies, and thrill anew
with undefinable delight, at the deep hollow note of the
church-bell, breaking, each hour, with sullen and sudden roar, upon the stillness of the dusky atmosphere in
which the fretted Gothic steeple lay imbedded and
asleep.

It gives me, perhaps, as much of pleasure as I can
now in any manner experience, to dwell upon minute
recollections of the school and its concerns. Steeped
in misery as I am—misery, alas! only too real—I shall
be pardoned for seeking relief, however slight and temporary, in the weakness of a few rambling details.
These, moreover, utterly trivial, and even ridiculous in
themselves, assume, to my fancy, adventitious importance, as connected with a period and a locality when
and where I recognise the first ambiguous monitions of
the destiny which afterwards so fully overshadowed me.
Let me then remember.

The house, I have said, was old and irregular. The
grounds were extensive, and a high and solid brick wall,
topped with a bed of mortar and broken glass, encompassed the whole. This prison-like rampart formed the
limit of our domain; beyond it we saw but thrice a week
—once every Saturday afternoon, when, attended by
two ushers, we were permitted to take brief walks in a
body through some of the neighbouring fields—and
twice during Sunday, when we were paraded in the
same formal manner to the morning and evening service
in the one church of the village. Of this church the principal of our school was pastor. With how deep a spirit
of wonder and perplexity was I wont to regard him from
our remote pew in the gallery, as, with step solemn and
slow, he ascended the pulpit! This reverend man, with
countenance so demurely benign, with robes so glossy

and so clerically flowing, with wig so minutely pow-
dered, so rigid and so vast,—could this be he who, of
late, with sour visage, and in snuffy habiliments, admin-
istered, ferule in hand, the Draconian laws of the
academy? Oh, gigantic paradox, too utterly monstrous
for solution!

At an angle of the ponderous wall frowned a more
ponderous gate. It was riveted and studded with iron
bolts, and surmounted with jagged iron spikes. What
impressions of deep awe did it inspire! It was never
opened save for the three periodical egressions and in-
gressions already mentioned; then, in every creak of
its mighty hinges, we found a plenitude of mystery—
a world of matter for solemn remark, or for more solemn meditation.

The extensive enclosure was irregular in form, having
many capacious recesses. Of these, three or four of the
largest constituted the play-ground. It was level, and
covered with fine hard gravel. I well remember it had
no trees, nor benches, nor anything similar within it.
Of course it was in the rear of the house. In front lay a
small parterre, planted with box and other shrubs; but
through this sacred division we passed only upon rare
occasions indeed—such as a first advent to school or
final departure thence, or perhaps, when a parent or
friend having called for us, we joyfully took our way
home for the Christmas or Midsummer holy-days.

But the house!—how quaint an old building was
this!—to me how veritably a palace of enchantment!
There was really no end to its windings—to its incomprehensible subdivisions. It was difficult, at any given
time, to say with certainty upon which of its two stories
one happened to be. From each room to every other
there were sure to be found three or four steps either in
ascent or descent. Then the lateral branches were in-

numerable—inconceivable—and so returning in upon themselves, that our most exact ideas in regard to the whole mansion were not very far different from those with which we pondered upon infinity. During the five years of my residence here, I was never able to ascertain with precision, in what remote locality lay the little sleeping apartment assigned to myself and some eighteen or twenty other scholars.

The school-room was the largest in the house—I could not help thinking, in the world. It was very long, narrow, and dismally low, with pointed Gothic windows and a ceiling of oak. In a remote and terror-inspiring angle was a square enclosure of eight or ten feet, comprising the *sanctum*, "during hours," of our principal, the Reverend Dr. Bransby. It was a solid structure, with massy door, sooner than open which in the absence of the "Dominie," we would all have willingly perished by the *peine forte et dure*. In other angles were two other similar boxes, far less reverenced, indeed, but still greatly matters of awe. One of these was the pulpit of the "classical" usher, one of the "English and mathematical." Interspersed about the room, crossing and recrossing in endless irregularity, were innumerable benches and desks, black, ancient, and time-worn, piled desperately with much-bethumbed books, and so beseamed with initial letters, names at full length, grotesque figures, and other multiplied efforts of the knife, as to have entirely lost what little of original form might have been their portion in days long departed. A huge bucket with water stood at one extremity of the room, and a clock of stupendous dimensions at the other.

Encompassed by the massy walls of this venerable academy, I passed, yet not in tedium or disgust, the years of the third lustrum of my life. The teeming brain of childhood requires no external world of incident to occupy or amuse it; and the apparently dismal monotony of a school was replete with more intense excitement than my riper youth has derived from luxury, or my full manhood from crime. Yet I must believe that my first mental development had in it much of the uncommon—even much of the *outré*. Upon mankind at large the events of very early existence rarely leave in mature age any definite impression. All is gray shadow—a weak and irregular remembrance—an indistinct regathering of feeble pleasures and phantasmagoric pains. With me this is not so. In childhood I must have felt with the energy of a man what I now find stamped upon memory in lines as vivid, as deep, and as durable as the *exergues* of the Carthaginian medals.

Yet in fact—in the fact of the world's view—how little was there to remember! The morning's awakening, the nightly summons to bed; the connings, the recitations; the periodical half-holidays, and perambulations; the play-ground, with its broils, its pastimes, its intrigues;—these, by a mental sorcery long forgotten, were made to involve a wilderness of sensation, a world of rich incident, an universe of varied emotion, of excitement the most passionate and spirit-stirring. *"Oh, le bon temps, que ce siècle de fer!"*

In truth, the ardor, the enthusiasm, and the imperiousness of my disposition, soon rendered me a marked character among my schoolmates, and by slow, but natural gradations, gave me an ascendancy over all not greatly older than myself;—over all with a single exception. This exception was found in the person of a scholar, who, although no relation, bore the same Christian and surname as myself;—a circumstance, in fact, little remarkable; for, notwithstanding a noble descent, mine was one of those everyday appellations which seem, by prescriptive right, to have been, time out of mind, the common property of the mob. In this narrative I have therefore designated myself as William Wilson,—a fictitious title not very dissimilar to the real. My namesake alone, of those who in school phraseology constituted "our set," presumed to compete with me in the studies of the class—in the sports and broils of the play-ground—to refuse implicit belief in my assertions, and submission to my will—indeed, to interfere with my arbitrary dictation in any respect whatsoever. If there is on earth a supreme and unqualified despotism, it is the despotism of a master mind in boyhood over the less energetic spirits of its companions.

Wilson's rebellion was to me a source of the greatest embarrassment;—the more so as, in spite of the bravado with which in public I made a point of treating him and his pretensions, I secretly felt that I feared him, and could not help thinking the equality which he maintained so easily with myself, a proof of his true superiority; since not to be overcome cost me a perpetual struggle. Yet this superiority—even this equality—was in truth acknowledged by no one but myself; our associates, by some unaccountable blindness, seemed not even to suspect it. Indeed, his competition, his resistance, and especially his impertinent and dogged interference with my purposes, were not more pointed than private. He appeared to be destitute alike of the ambition which urged, and of the passionate energy of mind which enabled me to excel. In his rivalry he might have been supposed actuated solely by a whimsical desire to thwart, astonish, or mortify myself; although there were times when I could not help observing, with a feeling made up of wonder, abasement, and pique, that he mingled with his injuries, his insults, or his contradictions, a certain most inappropriate, and assuredly most unwelcome *affectionateness* of manner. I could only conceive this singular behaviour to arise from a consummate self-conceit assuming the vulgar airs of patronage and protection.

Perhaps it was this latter trait in Wilson's conduct, conjoined with our identity of name, and the mere accident of our having entered the school upon the same day, which set afloat the notion that we were brothers, among the senior classes in the academy. These do not usually inquire with much strictness into the affairs of their juniors. I have before said, or should have said, that Wilson was not, in the most remote degree, connected with my family. But assuredly if we *had* been brothers we must have been twins; for, after leaving Dr. Bransby's, I casually learned that my namesake was born on the nineteenth of January, 1809[1]—and this is a somewhat remarkable coincidence; for the day is precisely that of my own nativity.

It may seem strange that in spite of the continual anxiety occasioned me by the rivalry of Wilson, and his intolerable spirit of contradiction, I could not bring myself to hate him altogether. We had, to be sure, nearly every day a quarrel in which, yielding me publicly the palm of victory, he, in some manner, contrived to make me feel that it was he who had deserved it; yet a sense of pride on my part, and a veritable dignity on his own, kept us always upon what are called "speaking terms," while there were many points of strong congeniality in our tempers, operating to awake in me a sentiment which our position alone, perhaps, prevented from ripening into friendship. It is difficult, indeed, to define, or even to describe, my real feelings towards him. They formed a motley and heterogeneous admixture;—some

---

[1] Poe changed this date twice in reprintings made during his life-time. The year 1809 is best fitting—his own birth date—for this autobiographical story.—ED.

petulant animosity, which was not yet hatred, some esteem, more respect, much fear, with a world of uneasy curiosity. To the moralist it will be unnecessary to say, in addition, that Wilson and myself were the most inseparable of companions.

It was no doubt the anomalous state of affairs existing between us, which turned all my attacks upon him, (and they were many, either open or covert) into the channel of banter or practical joke (giving pain while assuming the aspect of mere fun) rather than into a more serious and determined hostility. But my endeavours on this head were by no means uniformly successful, even when my plans were the most wittily concocted; for my namesake had much about him, in character, of that unassuming and quiet austerity which, while enjoying the poignancy of its own jokes, has no heel of Achilles in itself, and absolutely refuses to be laughed at. I could find, indeed, but one vulnerable point, and that, lying in a personal peculiarity, arising, perhaps, from constitutional disease, would have been spared by any antagonist less at his wit's end than myself;—my rival had a weakness in the faucial or guttural organs, which precluded him from raising his voice at any time *above a very low whisper*. Of this defect I did not fail to take what poor advantage lay in my power.

Wilson's retaliations in kind were many; and there was one form of his practical wit that disturbed me beyond measure. How his sagacity first discovered at all that so petty a thing would vex me, is a question I never could solve; but, having discovered, he habitually practised the annoyance. I had always felt aversion to my uncourtly patronymic, and its very common, if not plebeian prænomen. The words were venom in my ears; and when, upon the day of my arrival, a second William Wilson came also to the academy, I felt angry

with him for bearing the name, and doubly disgusted
with the name because a stranger bore it, who would be
the cause of its twofold repetition, who would be constantly in my presence, and whose concerns, in the
ordinary routine of the school business, must inevitably,
on account of the detestable coincidence, be often confounded with my own.

The feeling of vexation thus engendered grew
stronger with every circumstance tending to show resemblance, moral or physical, between my rival and
myself. I had not then discovered the remarkable fact
that we were of the same age; but I saw that we were
of the same height, and I perceived that we were even
singularly alike in general contour of person and outline
of feature. I was galled, too, by the rumour touching a
relationship, which had grown current in the upper
forms. In a word, nothing could more seriously disturb
me, (although I scrupulously concealed such disturbance,) than any allusion to a similarity of mind, person,
or condition existing between us. But, in truth, I had
no reason to believe that (with the exception of the matter of relationship, and in the case of Wilson himself,)
this similarity had ever been made a subject of comment, or even observed at all by our schoolfellows. That
he observed it in all its bearings, and as fixedly as I, was
apparent; but that he could discover in such circumstances so fruitful a field of annoyance, can only be
attributed, as I said before, to his more than ordinary
penetration.

His cue, which was to perfect an imitation of myself,
lay both in words and in actions; and most admirably
did he play his part. My dress it was an easy matter to
copy; my gait and general manner were, without difficulty, appropriated; in spite of his constitutional defect,
even my voice did not escape him. My louder tones

were, of course, unattempted, but then the key, it was
identical; *and his singular whisper, it grew the very
echo of my own.*

How greatly this most exquisite portraiture harassed
me, (for it could not justly be termed a caricature,) I
will not now venture to describe. I had but one consolation—in the fact that the imitation, apparently, was
noticed by myself alone, and that I had to endure only
the knowing and strangely sarcastic smiles of my namesake himself. Satisfied with having produced in my
bosom the intended effect, he seemed to chuckle in
secret over the sting he had inflicted, and was charac-
teristically disregardful of the public applause which the
success of his witty endeavours might have so easily
elicited. That the school, indeed, did not feel his design,
perceive its accomplishment, and participate in his
sneer, was, for many anxious months, a riddle I could
not resolve. Perhaps the *gradation* of his copy rendered
it not so readily perceptible; or, more possibly, I owed
my security to the masterly air of the copyist, who, dis-
daining the letter, (which in a painting is all the obtuse
can see,) gave but the full spirit of his original for my
individual contemplation and chagrin.

I have already more than once spoken of the disgust-
ing air of patronage which he assumed toward me, and
of his frequent officious interference with my will. This
interference often took the ungracious character of advice; advice not openly given, but hinted or insinuated.
I received it with a repugnance which gained strength
as I grew in years. Yet, at this distant day, let me do him
the simple justice to acknowledge that I can recall no
occasion when the suggestions of my rival were on the
side of those errors or follies so usual to his immature
age and seeming inexperience; that his moral sense, at
least, if not his general talents and worldly wisdom, was

far keener than my own; and that I might, to-day, have
been a better, and thus a happier man, had I less frequently rejected the counsels embodied in those meaning whispers which I then but too cordially hated and
too bitterly despised.

As it was, I at length grew restive in the extreme
under his distasteful supervision, and daily resented
more and more openly what I considered his intolerable
arrogance. I have said that, in the first years of our connexion as schoolmates, my feelings in regard to him
might have been easily ripened into friendship: but, in
the latter months of my residence at the academy, although the intrusion of his ordinary manner had, beyond doubt, in some measure, abated, my sentiments,
in nearly similar proportion, partook very much of positive hatred. Upon one occasion he saw this, I think,
and afterwards avoided, or made a show of avoiding me.

It was about the same period, if I remember aright,
that, in an altercation of violence with him, in which
he was more than usually thrown off his guard, and
spoke and acted with an openness of demeanour rather
foreign to his nature, I discovered, or fancied I discovered, in his accent, his air, and general appearance,
a something which first startled, and then deeply interested me, by bringing to mind dim visions of my earliest
infancy—wild, confused and thronging memories of a
time when memory herself was yet unborn. I cannot
better describe the sensation which oppressed me than
by saying that I could with difficulty shake off the belief of my having been acquainted with the being who
stood before me, at some epoch very long ago—some
point of the past even infinitely remote. The delusion,
however, faded rapidly as it came; and I mention it at
all but to define the day of the last conversation I there
held with my singular namesake.

The huge old house, with its countless subdivisions, had several large chambers communicating with each other, where slept the greater number of the students. There were, however, (as must necessarily happen in a building so awkwardly planned,) many little nooks or recesses, the odds and ends of the structure; and these the economic ingenuity of Dr. Bransby had also fitted up as dormitories; although, being the merest closets, they were capable of accommodating but a single individual. One of these small apartments was occupied by Wilson.

One night, about the close of my fifth year at the school, and immediately after the altercation just mentioned, finding every one wrapped in sleep, I arose from bed, and, lamp in hand, stole through a wilderness of narrow passages from my own bedroom to that of my rival. I had long been plotting one of those ill-natured pieces of practical wit at his expense in which I had hitherto been so uniformly unsuccessful. It was my intention, now, to put my scheme in operation, and I resolved to make him feel the whole extent of the malice with which I was imbued. Having reached his closet, I noiselessly entered, leaving the lamp, with a shade over it, on the outside. I advanced a step, and listened to the sound of his tranquil breathing. Assured of his being asleep, I returned, took the light, and with it again approached the bed. Close curtains were around it, which, in the prosecution of my plan, I slowly and quietly withdrew, when the bright rays fell vividly upon the sleeper, and my eyes, at the same moment, upon his countenance. I looked;—and a numbness, an iciness of feeling instantly pervaded my frame. My breast heaved, my knees tottered, my whole spirit became possessed with an objectless yet intolerable horror. Gasping for breath, I lowered the lamp in still nearer proximity to the face. Were these—*these* the lineaments of William Wilson? I saw, indeed, that they were his, but I shook as if with a fit of the ague in fancying they were not. What *was* there about them to confound me in this manner? I gazed;—while my brain reeled with a multitude of incoherent thoughts. Not thus he appeared—assuredly not *thus*—in the vivacity of his waking hours. The same name! the same contour of person! the same day of arrival at the academy! And then his dogged and meaningless imitation of my gait, my voice, my habits, and my manner! Was it, in truth, within the bounds of human possibility, that *what I now saw* was the result, merely, of the habitual practice of this sarcastic imitation? Awestricken, and with a creeping shudder, I extinguished the lamp, passed silently from the chamber, and left, at once, the halls of that old academy, never to enter them again.

After a lapse of some months, spent at home in mere idleness, I found myself a student at Eton. The brief interval had been sufficient to enfeeble my remembrance of the events at Dr. Bransby's, or at least to effect a material change in the nature of the feelings with which I remembered them. The truth—the tragedy—of the drama was no more. I could now find room to doubt the evidence of my senses; and seldom called up the subject at all but with wonder at the extent of human credulity, and a smile at the vivid force of the imagination which I hereditarily possessed. Neither was this species of scepticism likely to be diminished by the character of the life I led at Eton. The vortex of thoughtless folly into which I there so immediately and so recklessly plunged, washed away all but the froth of my past hours, engulfed at once every solid or serious impression, and left to memory only the veriest levities of a former existence.

I do not wish, however, to trace the course of my

miserable profligacy here—a profligacy which set at
defiance the laws, while it eluded the vigilance of the
institution. Three years of folly, passed without profit,
had but given me rooted habits of vice, and added, in a
somewhat unusual degree, to my bodily stature, when,
after a week of soulless dissipation, I invited a small
party of the most dissolute students to a secret carousal
in my chambers. We met at a late hour of the night;
for our debaucheries were to be faithfully protracted
until morning. The wine flowed freely, and there were
not wanting other and perhaps more dangerous seduc-
tions; so that the grey dawn had already faintly appeared in the east, while our delirious extravagance
was at its height. Madly flushed with cards and intoxication, I was in the act of insisting upon a toast of more
than wonted profanity, when my attention was suddenly
diverted by the violent, although partial unclosing of
the door of the apartment, and by the eager voice of a
servant from without. He said that some person, apparently in great haste, demanded to speak with me in
the hall.

Wildly excited with wine, the unexpected interruption
rather delighted than surprised me. I staggered forward
at once, and a few steps brought me to the vestibule of
the building. In this low and small room there hung no
lamp; and now no light at all was admitted, save that
of the exceedingly feeble dawn which made its way
through the semi-circular window. As I put my foot
over the threshold, I became aware of the figure of a
youth about my own height, and habited in a white
kerseymere morning frock, cut in the novel fashion of
the one I myself wore at the moment. This the faint
light enabled me to perceive; but the features of his face
I could not distinguish. Upon my entering he strode
hurriedly up to me, and, seizing me by the arm with a

gesture of petulant impatience, whispered the words "William Wilson!" in my ear.

I grew perfectly sober in an instant.

There was that in the manner of the stranger, and in the tremulous shake of his uplifted finger, as he held it between my eyes and the light, which filled me with unqualified amazement; but it was not this which had so violently moved me. It was the pregnancy of solemn admonition in the singular, low, hissing utterance; and, above all, it was the character, the tone, *the key,* of those few, simple, and familiar, yet *whispered* syllables, which came with a thousand thronging memories of by-gone days, and struck upon my soul with the shock of a galvanic battery. Ere I could recover the use of my senses he was gone.

Although this event failed not of a vivid effect upon my disordered imagination, yet was it evanescent as vivid. For some weeks, indeed, I busied myself in earnest inquiry, or was wrapped in a cloud of morbid speculation. I did not pretend to disguise from my perception the identity of the singular individual who thus perseveringly interfered with my affairs, and harassed me with his insinuated counsel. But who and what was this Wilson?—and whence came he?—and what were his purposes? Upon neither of these points could I be satisfied; merely ascertaining, in regard to him, that a sudden accident in his family had caused his removal from Dr. Bransby's academy on the afternoon of the day in which I myself had eloped. But in a brief period I ceased to think upon the subject; my attention being all absorbed in a contemplated departure for Oxford. Thither I soon went; the uncalculating vanity of my parents furnishing me with an outfit and annual establishment, which would enable me to indulge at will in the luxury already so dear to my heart,—to vie in pro-

fuseness of expenditure with the haughtiest heirs of the
wealthiest earldoms in Great Britain.

Excited by such appliances to vice, my constitutional
temperament broke forth with redoubled ardor, and I
spurned even the common restraints of decency in the
mad infatuation of my revels. But it were absurd to
pause in the detail of my extravagance. Let it suffice,
that among spendthrifts I out-Heroded Herod, and that,
giving name to a multitude of novel follies, I added no
brief appendix to the long catalogue of vices then usual
in the most dissolute university of Europe.

It could hardly be credited, however, that I had,
even here, so utterly fallen from the gentlemanly estate,
as to seek acquaintance with the vilest arts of the
gambler by profession, and, having become an adept
in his despicable science, to practise it habitually as a
means of increasing my already enormous income at the
expense of the weak-minded among my fellow-colle-
gians. Such, nevertheless, was the fact. And the very
enormity of this offence against all manly and honour-
able sentiment proved, beyond doubt, the main if not
the sole reason of the impunity with which it was committed. Who, indeed, among my most abandoned associates, would not rather have disputed the clearest evidence of his senses, than have suspected of such courses,
the gay, the frank, the generous William Wilson—the
noblest and most liberal commoner at Oxford—him
whose follies (said his parasites) were but the follies of
youth and unbridled fancy—whose errors but inimitable
whim—whose darkest vice but a careless and dashing
extravagance?

I had been now two years successfully busied in this
way, when there came to the university a young *parvenu* nobleman, Glendinning—rich, said report, as
Herodes Atticus—his riches, too, as easily acquired. I

soon found him of weak intellect, and, of course, marked him as a fitting subject for my skill. I frequently engaged him in play, and contrived, with the gambler's usual art, to let him win considerable sums, the more effectually to entangle him in my snares. At length, my schemes being ripe, I met him (with the full intention that this meeting should be final and decisive) at the chambers of a fellow-commoner, (Mr. Preston,) equally intimate with both, but who, to do him justice, entertained not even a remote suspicion of my design. To give to this a better colouring, I had contrived to have assembled a party of some eight or ten, and was solicitously careful that the introduction of cards should appear accidental, and originate in the proposal of my contemplated dupe himself. To be brief upon a vile topic, none of the low finesse was omitted, so customary upon similar occasions that it is a just matter for wonder how any are still found so besotted as to fall its victim.

We had protracted our sitting far into the night, and I had at length effected the manœuvre of getting Glendinning as my sole antagonist. The game, too, was my favorite *écarté*. The rest of the company, interested in the extent of our play, had abandoned their own cards, and were standing around us as spectators. The *parvenu*, who had been induced by my artifices in the early part of the evening, to drink deeply, now shuffled, dealt, or played, with a wild nervousness of manner for which his intoxication, I thought, might partially, but could not altogether account. In a very short period he had become my debtor to a large amount, when, having taken a long draught of port, he did precisely what I had been coolly anticipating—he proposed to double our already extravagant stakes. With a well-feigned show of reluctance, and not until after my repeated refusal had seduced him into some angry words which gave a colour of *pique* to my compliance, did I finally comply. The result, of course, did but prove how entirely the prey was in my toils; in less than an hour he had quadrupled his debt. For some time his countenance had been losing the florid tinge lent it by the wine; but now, to my astonishment, I perceived that it had grown to a pallor truly fearful. I say to my astonishment. Glendinning had been represented to my eager inquiries as immeasurably wealthy; and the sums which he had as yet lost, although in themselves vast, could not, I supposed, very seriously annoy, much less so violently affect him. That he was overcome by the wine just swallowed, was the idea which most readily presented itself; and, rather with a view to the preservation of my own character in the eyes of my associates, than from any less interested motive, I was about to insist, peremptorily, upon a discontinuance of the play, when some expressions at my elbow from among the company, and an ejaculation evincing utter despair on the part of Glendinning, gave me to understand that I had effected his total ruin under circumstances which, rendering him an object for the pity of all, should have protected him from the ill offices even of a fiend.

What now might have been my conduct it is difficult to say. The pitiable condition of my dupe had thrown an air of embarrassed gloom over all; and, for some moments, a profound silence was maintained, during which I could not help feeling my cheeks tingle with the many burning glances of scorn or reproach cast upon me by the less abandoned of the party. I will even own that an intolerable weight of anxiety was for a brief instant lifted from my bosom by the sudden and extraordinary interruption which ensued. The wide, heavy folding doors of the apartment were all at once thrown open, to their full extent, with a vigorous and rushing impetuosity that extinguished, as if by magic, every candle in the room. Their light, in dying, enabled us just to perceive that a stranger had entered, about my own height, and closely muffled in a cloak. The darkness, however, was now total; and we could only *feel* that he was standing in our midst. Before any one of us could recover from the extreme astonishment into which this rudeness had thrown all, we heard the voice of the intruder.

"Gentlemen," he said, in a low, distinct, and never-to-be-forgotten *whisper* which thrilled to the very marrow of my bones, "Gentlemen, I make no apology for this behaviour, because in thus behaving, I am but fulfilling a duty. You are, beyond doubt, uninformed of the true character of the person who has to-night won at *écarté* a large sum of money from Lord Glendinning. I will therefore put you upon an expeditious and decisive plan of obtaining this very necessary information. Please to examine, at your leisure, the inner linings of the cuff of his left sleeve, and the several little packages which may be found in the somewhat capacious pockets of his embroidered morning wrapper."

While he spoke, so profound was the stillness that one might have heard a pin drop upon the floor. In ceasing, he departed at once, and as abruptly as he had entered. Can I—shall I describe my sensations?—must I say that I felt all the horrors of the damned? Most assuredly I had little time given for reflection. Many hands roughly seized me upon the spot, and lights were immediately reprocured. A search ensued. In the lining of my sleeve were found all the court cards essential in *écarté*, and, in the pockets of my wrapper, a number of packs, fac-similes of those used at our sittings, with the single exception that mine were of the species called, technically, *arrondées;* the honours being slightly convex at the ends, the lower cards slightly convex at the sides. In this disposition, the dupe who cuts, as customary, at the length of the pack, will invariably find that he cuts his antagonist an honour; while the gambler, cutting at the breadth, will, as certainly, cut nothing for his victim which may count in the records of the game.

Any burst of indignation upon this discovery would have affected me less than the silent contempt, or the sarcastic composure, with which it was received.

"Mr. Wilson," said our host, stooping to remove from beneath his feet an exceedingly luxurious cloak of rare furs, "Mr. Wilson, this is your property." (The weather was cold; and, upon quitting my own room, I had thrown a cloak over my dressing wrapper, putting it off upon reaching the scene of play.) "I presume it is super-erogatory to seek here (eyeing the folds of the garment with a bitter smile) for any farther evidence of your skill. Indeed, we have had enough. You will see the necessity, I hope, of quitting Oxford—at all events, of quitting instantly my chambers."

Abased, humbled to the dust as I then was, it is probable that I should have resented this galling language by immediate personal violence, had not my whole attention been at the moment arrested by a fact of the most startling character. The cloak which I had worn was of a rare description of fur; how rare, how extravagantly costly, I shall not venture to say. Its fashion, too, was of my own fantastic invention; for I was fastidious to an absurd degree of coxcombry, in matters of this frivolous nature. When, therefore, Mr. Preston reached me that which he had picked up upon the floor, and near the folding doors of the apartment, it was with an astonishment nearly bordering upon terror, that I perceived my own already hanging on my arm, (where I had no doubt unwittingly placed it,) and that the one presented me was but its exact counterpart in every, in even the minutest possible particular. The singular being who had so disastrously exposed me, had been muffled, I remembered, in a cloak; and none had been worn at all by any of the members of our party with the exception of myself. Retaining some presence of mind, I took the one offered me by Preston; placed it, unnoticed, over my own; left the apartment with a resolute scowl of defiance; and, next morning ere dawn of day, commenced a hurried journey from Oxford to the continent, in a perfect agony of horror and of shame.

I fled in vain. My evil destiny pursued me as if in exultation, and proved, indeed, that the exercise of its mysterious dominion had as yet only begun. Scarcely had I set foot in Paris ere I had fresh evidence of the detestable interest taken by this Wilson in my concerns. Years flew, while I experienced no relief. Villain!—at Rome, with how untimely, yet with how spectral an officiousness, stepped he in between me and my ambition! At Vienna, too—at Berlin—and at Moscow! Where, in truth, had I *not* bitter cause to curse him within my heart? From this inscrutable tyranny did I at length flee, panic-stricken, as from a pestilence; and to the very ends of the earth *I fled in vain.*

And again, and again, in secret communion with my own spirit, would I demand the questions "Who is he? —whence came he?—and what are his objects?" But no answer was there found. And then I scrutinized, with a minute scrutiny, the forms, and the methods, and the leading traits of his impertinent supervision. But even here there was very little upon which to base a conjecture. It was noticeable, indeed, that, in no one of the multiplied instances in which he had of late crossed my path, had he so crossed it except to frustrate those schemes, or to disturb those actions, which, if fully car-

ried out, might have resulted in bitter mischief. Poor
justification this, in truth, for an authority so imperiously
assumed! Poor indemnity for natural rights of self-
agency so pertinaciously, so insultingly denied!

I had also been forced to notice that my tormentor,
for a very long period of time, (while scrupulously and
with miraculous dexterity maintaining his whim of an
identity of apparel with myself,) had so contrived it, in
the execution of his varied interference with my will,
that I saw not, at any moment, the features of his face.
Be Wilson what he might, *this*, at least, was but the
veriest of affectation, or of folly. Could he, for an instant, have supposed that, in my admonisher at Eton—
in the destroyer of my honour at Oxford,—in him who
thwarted my ambition at Rome, my revenge at Paris,
my passionate love at Naples, or what he falsely termed
my avarice in Egypt,—that in this, my arch-enemy and
evil genius, I could fail to recognise the William Wilson
of my school-boy days,—the namesake, the companion,
the rival,—the hated and dreaded rival at Dr. Bransby's?
Impossible!—But let me hasten to the last eventful
scene of the drama.

Thus far I had succumbed supinely to this imperious
domination. The sentiment of deep awe with which I
habitually regarded the elevated character, the majestic
wisdom, the apparent omnipresence and omnipotence
of Wilson, added to a feeling of even terror, with which
certain other traits in his nature and assumptions inspired me, had operated, hitherto, to impress me with
an idea of my own utter weakness and helplessness, and
to suggest an implicit, although bitterly reluctant submission to his arbitrary will. But, of late days, I had
given myself up entirely to wine; and its maddening
influence upon my hereditary temper rendered me more
and more impatient of control. I began to murmur,—to

hesitate,—to resist. And was it only fancy which induced me to believe that, with the increase of my own firmness, that of my tormentor underwent a proportional diminution? Be this as it may, I now began to feel the inspiration of a burning hope, and at length nurtured in my secret thoughts a stern and desperate resolution that I would submit no longer to be enslaved.

It was at Rome, during the Carnival of 18—, that I attended a masquerade in the palazzo of the Neapolitan Duke Di Broglio. I had indulged more freely than usual in the excesses of the wine-table; and now the suffocating atmosphere of the crowded rooms irritated me beyond endurance. The difficulty, too, of forcing my way through the mazes of the company contributed not a little to the ruffling of my temper; for I was anxiously seeking, (let me not say with what unworthy motive) the young, the gay, the beautiful wife of the aged and doting Di Broglio. With a too unscrupulous confidence she had previously communicated to me the secret of the costume in which she would be habited, and now, having caught a glimpse of her person, I was hurrying to make my way into her presence.—At this moment I felt a light hand placed upon my shoulder, and that ever-remembered, low, damnable *whisper* within my ear.

In an absolute phrenzy of wrath, I turned at once upon him who had thus interrupted me, and seized him violently by the collar. He was attired, as I had expected, in a costume altogether similar to my own; wearing a Spanish cloak of blue velvet, begirt about the waist with a crimson belt sustaining a rapier. A mask of black silk entirely covered his face.

"Scoundrel!" I said, in a voice husky with rage, while every syllable I uttered seemed as new fuel to my fury, "scoundrel! imposter! accursed villain! you shall not—

you *shall not* dog me unto death! Follow me, or I stab you where you stand!"—and I broke my way from the ball-room into a small ante-chamber adjoining—dragging him unresistingly with me as I went.

Upon entering, I thrust him furiously from me. He staggered against the wall, while I closed the door with an oath, and commanded him to draw. He hesitated but for an instant; then, with a slight sigh, drew in silence, and put himself upon his defence.

The contest was brief indeed. I was frantic with every species of wild excitement, and felt within my single arm the energy and power of a multitude. In a few seconds I forced him by sheer strength against the wainscoting, and thus, getting him at mercy, plunged my sword, with brute ferocity, repeatedly through and through his bosom.

At that instant some person tried the latch of the door. I hastened to prevent an intrusion, and then immediately returned to my dying antagonist. But what human language can adequately portray *that* astonishment, *that* horror which possessed me at the spectacle then presented to view? The brief moment in which I averted my eyes had been sufficient to produce, apparently, a material change in the arrangements at the upper or farther end of the room. A large mirror,—so at first it seemed to me in my confusion—now stood where none had been perceptible before; and, as I stepped up to it in extremity of terror, mine own image, but with features all pale and dabbled in blood, advanced to meet me with a feeble and tottering gait.

Thus it appeared, I say, but was not. It was my antagonist—it was Wilson, who then stood before me in the agonies of his dissolution. His mask and cloak lay, where he had thrown them, upon the floor. Not a thread in all his raiment—not a line in all the marked and singular lineaments of his face which was not, even in the most absolute identity, *mine own!*

It was Wilson; but he spoke no longer in a whisper, and I could have fancied that I myself was speaking while he said:

"You have conquered, and I yield. Yet, henceforward art thou also dead—dead to the World, to Heaven and to Hope! In me didst thou exist—and, in my death, see by this image, which is thine own, how utterly thou hast murdered thyself."

A TALE OF
THE RAGGED MOUNTAINS
(*Godey's Lady's Book*, April, 1844.)

DURING the fall of the year 1827, while residing near Charlottesville, Virginia, I casually made the acquaintance of Mr. Augustus Bedloe. This young gentleman was remarkable in every respect, and excited in me a profound interest and curiosity. I found it impossible to comprehend him either in his moral or his physical relations. Of his family I could obtain no satisfactory account. Whence he came, I never ascertained. Even about his age—although I call him a young gentleman—there was something which perplexed me in no little degree. He certainly *seemed* young—and he made a point of speaking about his youth—yet there were moments when I should have had little trouble in imagining him a hundred years of age. But in no regard was he more peculiar than in his personal appearance. He was singularly tall and thin. He stooped much. His limbs were exceedingly long and emaciated. His forehead was broad and low. His complexion was absolutely bloodless. His mouth was large and flexible, and his teeth were more wildly uneven, although sound, than I had ever before seen teeth in a human head. The expression of his smile, however, was by no means unpleasing, as might be supposed; but it had no variation whatever. It was one of profound melancholy—of a phaseless and unceasing gloom. His eyes were abnormally large, and round like those of a cat. The pupils, too, upon any accession or diminution of light, underwent contraction or dilation, just such as is observed in the feline tribe. In moments of excitement the orbs grew bright to a degree almost inconceivable; seeming to emit luminous rays, not of a reflected, but of an intrinsic lustre, as does a candle or the sun; yet their ordinary condition was so totally vapid, filmy and dull, as to convey the idea of the eyes of a long-interred corpse.

These peculiarities of person appeared to cause him much annoyance, and he was continually alluding to them in a sort of half explanatory, half apologetic strain, which, when I first heard it, impressed me very painfully. I soon, however, grew accustomed to it, and my uneasiness wore off. It seemed to be his design rather to insinuate than directly to assert that, physically, he had not always been what he was—that a long series of neuralgic attacks had reduced him from a condition of more than usual personal beauty, to that which I saw. For many years past he had been attended by a physician, named Templeton—an old gentleman, perhaps seventy years of age—whom he had first encountered at Saratoga, and from whose attention, while there, he either received, or fancied that he received, great benefit. The result was that Bedloe, who was wealthy, had made an arrangement with Doctor Templeton, by which the latter, in consideration of a liberal annual allowance, had consented to devote his time and medical experience exclusively to the care of the invalid.

Doctor Templeton had been a traveller in his younger days, and, at Paris, had become a convert, in great measure, to the doctrines of Mesmer. It was altogether by means of magnetic remedies that he had succeeded in alleviating the acute pains of his patient; and this success had very naturally inspired the latter with a certain degree of confidence in the opinions from which the remedies had been educed. The Doctor, however, like all enthusiasts, had struggled hard to make a thorough convert of his pupil, and finally so far gained his point as to induce the sufferer to submit to numerous experiments.—By a frequent repetition of these, a result had arisen, which of late days has become so common as to attract little or no attention, but which, at the period of which I write, had very rarely been known in America. I mean to say, that between Doctor Templeton and Bedloe there had grown up, little by little, a very distinct and strongly marked *rapport*, or magnetic relation. I am not prepared to assert, however, that this *rapport* extended beyond the limits of the simple sleep-producing power; but this power itself had attained great intensity. At the first attempt to induce the magnetic somnolency, the mesmerist entirely failed. In the fifth or sixth he succeeded very partially, and after long-continued effort. Only at the twelfth was the triumph complete. After this the will of the patient succumbed rapidly to that of the physician, so that, when I first became acquainted with the two, sleep was brought about almost instantaneously, by the mere volition of the operator, even when the invalid was unaware of his presence. It is only now, in the year 1845, when similar miracles are witnessed daily by thousands, that I dare

venture to record this apparent impossibility as a matter
of serious fact.

The temperament of Bedloe was, in the highest degree, sensitive, excitable, enthusiastic. His imagination
was singularly vigorous and creative; and no doubt it derived additional force from the habitual use of morphine, which he swallowed in great quantity, and without which he would have found it impossible to exist.
It was his practice to take a very large dose of it immediately after breakfast, each morning—or rather immediately after a cup of strong coffee, for he ate nothing
in the forenoon—and then set forth alone, or attended
only by a dog, upon a long ramble among the chain of
wild and dreary hills that lie westward and southward
of Charlottesville, and are there dignified by the title
of the Ragged Mountains.

Upon a dim, warm, misty day, towards the close of
November, and during the strange *interregnum* of the
seasons which in America is termed the Indian Summer
Mr. Bedloe departed, as usual, for the hills. The day
passed, and still he did not return.

About eight o'clock at night, having become seriously
alarmed at his protracted absence, we were about setting out in search of him, when he unexpectedly made
his appearance, in health no worse than usual, and in
rather more than ordinary spirits. The account which he
gave of his expedition, and of the events which had
detained him, was a singular one indeed.

"You will remember," said he, "that it was about nine
in the morning when I left Charlottesville. I bent my
steps immediately to the mountains, and, about ten, entered a gorge which was entirely new to me. I followed
the windings of this pass with much interest.—The
scenery which presented itself on all sides, although

scarcely entitled to be called grand, had about it an indescribable, and to me, a delicious aspect of dreary
desolation. The solitude seemed absolutely virgin. I
could not help believing that the green sods and the
gray rocks upon which I trod, had been trodden never
before by the foot of a human being. So entirely secluded, and in fact inaccessible, except through a series
of accidents, is the entrance of the ravine, that it is by
no means impossible that I was indeed the first adventurer—the very first and sole adventurer who had ever
penetrated its recesses.

"The thick and peculiar mist, or smoke, which distinguishes the Indian Summer, and which now hung
heavily over all objects, served, no doubt, to deepen
the ague impressions which these objects created. So
dense was this pleasant fog, that I could at no time see
more than a dozen yards of the path before me. This
path was excessively sinuous, and as the sun could not
be seen, I soon lost all idea of the direction in which I
journeyed. In the meantime the morphine had its customary effect—that of enduing all the external world
with an intensity of interest. In the quivering of a leaf
—in the hue of a blade of grass—in the shape of a
trefoil—in the humming of a bee—in the gleaming of
a dew-drop—in the breathing of the wind—in the faint
odors that came from the forest—there came a whole
universe of suggestion—a gay and motley train of rhap-
sodical and immethodical thought.

"Busied in this, I walked on for several hours, during
which the mist deepened around me to so great an extent, that at length I was reduced to an absolute groping
of the way. And now an indescribable uneasiness possessed me—a species of nervous hesitation and tremor.
—I feared to tread, lest I should be precipitated into
some abyss. I remembered, too, strange stories told

about these Ragged Hills, and of the uncouth and fierce races of men who tenanted their groves and caverns. A thousand vague fancies oppressed and disconcerted me —fancies the more distressing because vague. Very suddenly my attention was arrested by the loud beating of a drum.

"My amazement was, of course, extreme. A drum in these hills was a thing unknown. I could not have been more surprised at the sound of the trump of the Archangel. But a new and still more astounding source of interest and perplexity arose. There came a wild rattling or jingling sound, as if of a bunch of large keys—and upon the instant a dusky-visaged and half-naked man rushed past me with a shriek. He came so close to my person that I felt his hot breath upon my face. He bore in one hand an instrument composed of an assemblage of steel rings, and shook them vigorously as he ran. Scarcely had he disappeared in the mist, before, panting after him, with open mouth and glaring eyes, there darted a huge beast. I could not be mistaken in its character. It was a hyena.

"The sight of this monster rather relieved than heightened my terrors—for I now made sure that I dreamed, and endeavored to arouse myself to waking consciousness. I stepped boldly and briskly forward. I rubbed my eyes. I called aloud. I pinched my limbs. A small spring of water presented itself to my view, and here, stooping, I bathed my hands and my head and neck. This seemed to dissipate the equivocal sensations which had hitherto annoyed me. I arose, as I thought, a new man, and proceeded steadily and complacently on my unknown way.

"At length, quite overcome by exertion, and by a certain oppressive closeness of the atmosphere, I seated myself beneath a tree. Presently there came a feeble gleam of sunshine, and the shadow of the leaves of the tree fell faintly but definitely upon the grass. At this shadow I gazed wonderingly for many minutes. Its character stupified me with astonishment. I looked upward. The tree was a palm.

"I now arose hurriedly, and in a state of fearful agitation—for the fancy that I dreamed would serve me no longer. I saw—I felt that I had perfect command of my senses—and these senses now brought to my soul a world of novel and singular sensation. The heat became all at once intolerable. A strange odor loaded the breeze. —A low continuous murmur, like that arising from a full, but gently-flowing river, came to my ears, intermingled with the peculiar hum of multitudinous human voices.

"While I listened in an extremity of astonishment which I need not attempt to describe, a strong and brief gust of wind bore off the incumbent fog as if by the wand of an enchanter.

"I found myself at the foot of a high mountain, and looking down into a vast plain, through which wound a majestic river. On the margin of this river stood an Eastern-looking city, such as we read of in the Arabian Tales, but of a character even more singular than any there described. From my position, which was far above the level of the town, I could perceive its every nook and corner, as if delineated on a map. The streets seemed innumerable, and crossed each other irregularly in all directions, but were rather long winding alleys than streets, and absolutely swarmed with inhabitants. The houses were wildly picturesque. On every hand was a wilderness of balconies, of verandahs, of minarets, of shrines, and fantastically carved oriels. Bazaars abounded; and in these were displayed rich wares in infinite variety and profusion—silks, muslins, the most dazzling cutlery, the most magnificent jewels and gems.

Besides these things, were seen, on all sides, banners and palanquins, litters with stately dames close veiled, elephants gorgeously caparisoned, idols grotesquely hewn, drums, banners and gongs, spears, silver and gilded maces. And amid the crowd, and the clamor, and the general intricacy and confusion—amid the million of black and yellow men, turbaned and robed, and of flowing beard, there roamed a countless multitude of holy filleted bulls, while vast legions of the filthy but sacred ape clambered, chattering and shrieking, about the cornices of the mosques, or clung to the minarets and oriels. From the swarming streets to the banks of the river, there descended innumerable flights of steps leading to bathing places, while the river itself seemed to force a passage with difficulty through the vast fleets of deeply-burthened ships that far and wide encumbered its surface. Beyond the limits of the city arose, in frequent majestic groups, the palm and the cocoa, with other gigantic and weird trees of vast age; and here and there might be seen a field of rice, the thatched hut of a peasant, a tank, a stray temple, a gypsy camp, or a solitary graceful maiden taking her way, with a pitcher upon her head, to the banks of the magnificent river.

"You will say now, of course, that I dreamed; but not so. What I saw—what I heard—what I felt—what I thought—had about it nothing of the unmistakeable idiosyncrasy of the dream. All was rigorously self-consistent. At first, doubting that I was really awake, I entered into a series of tests, which soon convinced me that I really was. Now, when one dreams, and, in the dream, suspects that he dreams, the suspicion *never fails to confirm itself,* and the sleeper is almost immediately aroused.—Thus Novalis errs not in saying that 'we are near waking when we dream that we dream.' Had the vision occurred to me as I describe it, without my suspecting it as a dream, then a dream it might absolutely have been, but, occurring as it did, and suspected and tested as it was, I am forced to class it among other phenomena."

"In this I am not sure that you are wrong," observed Dr. Templeton, "but proceed. You arose and descended into the city."

"I arose," continued Bedloe, regarding the Doctor with an air of profound astonishment, "I arose, as you say, and descended into the city. On my way, I fell in with an immense populace, crowding, through every avenue, all in the same direction, and exhibiting in every action the wildest excitement. Very suddenly, and by some inconceivable impulse, I became intensely imbued with personal interest in what was going on. I seemed to feel that I had an important part to play, without exactly understanding what it was. Against the crowd which environed me, however, I experienced a deep sentiment of animosity. I shrank from amid them, and, swiftly, by a circuitous path, reached and entered the city. Here all was the wildest tumult and contention. A small party of men, clad in garments half-Indian, half-European, and officered by gentlemen in a uniform partly British, were engaged, at great odds, with the swarming rabble of the alleys. I joined the weaker party, arming myself with the weapons of a fallen officer, and fighting I knew not whom with the nervous ferocity of despair. We were soon overpowered by numbers, and driven to seek refuge in a species of kiosk. Here we barricaded ourselves, and, for the present, were secure. From a loop-hole near the summit of the kiosk, I perceived a vast crowd, in furious agitation, surrounding and assaulting a gay palace that overhung the river. Presently, from an upper window of this palace, there descended an effeminate-looking person, by means of a

string made of the turbans of his attendants. A boat was
at hand, in which he escaped to the opposite bank of
the river.

"And now a new object took possession of my soul.
I spoke a few hurried but energetic words to my companions, and, having succeeded in gaining over a few
of them to my purpose, made a frantic sally from the
kiosk. We rushed amid the crowd that surrounded it.
They retreated, at first, before us. They rallied, fought
madly, and retreated again. In the mean time we were
borne far from the kiosk, and became bewildered and
entangled among the narrow streets of tall overhanging
houses, into the recesses of which the sun had never
been able to shine. The rabble pressed impetuously
upon us, harassing us with their spears, and overwhelming us with flights of arrows. These latter were very
remarkable, and resembled in some respects the writhing
creese of the Malay. They were made to imitate the
body of a creeping serpent, and were long and black,
with a poisoned barb. One of them struck me upon the
right temple. I reeled and fell. An instantaneous and
dreadful sickness seized me. I struggled—I gasped—I
died."

"You will hardly persist *now,*" said I, smiling, "that
the whole of your adventure was not a dream. You are
not prepared to maintain that you are dead?"

When I said these words, I of course expected some
lively sally from Bedloe in reply; but, to my astonishment, he hesitated, trembled, became fearfully pallid,
and remained silent. I looked towards Templeton. He
sat erect and rigid in his chair—his teeth chattered, and
his eyes were starting from their sockets. "Proceed!" he
at length said hoarsely to Bedloe.

"For many minutes," continued the latter, "my sole
sentiment—my sole feeling—was that of darkness and

nonentity, with the consciousness of death. At length, there seemed to pass a violent and sudden shock through my soul, as if of electricity. With it came the sense of elasticity and of light. This latter I felt—not saw. In an instant I seemed to rise from the ground. But I had no bodily, no visible, audible, or palpable presence. The crowd had departed. The tumult had ceased. The city was in comparative repose. Beneath me lay my corpse, with the arrow in my temple, the whole head greatly swollen and disfigured. But all these things I felt—not saw. I took interest in nothing. Even the corpse seemed a matter in which I had no concern. Volition I had none, but appeared to be impelled into motion, and flitted buoyantly out of the city, retracing the circuitous path by which I had entered it. When I had attained that point of the ravine in the mountains, at which I had encountered the hyena, I again experienced a shock as of a galvanic battery; the sense of weight, of volition, of substance, returned. I became my original self, and bent my steps eagerly homewards—but the past had not lost the vividness of the real—and not now, even for an instant, can I compel my understanding to regard it as a dream."

"Nor was it," said Templeton, with an air of deep solemnity, "yet it would be difficult to say how otherwise it should be termed. Let us suppose only, that the soul of the man of to-day is upon the verge of some stupendous psychal discoveries. Let us content ourselves with this supposition. For the rest I have some explanation to make. Here is a water-colour drawing, which I should have shown you before, but which an unaccountable sentiment of horror has hitherto prevented me from showing."

We looked at the picture which he presented. I saw nothing in it of an extraordinary character; but its

effect upon Bedloe was prodigious. He nearly fainted as
he gazed. And yet it was but a miniature portrait—a
miraculously accurate one, to be sure—of his own very
remarkable features. At least this was my thought as I
regarded it.

"You will perceive," said Templeton, "the date of this
picture—it is here, scarcely visible, in this corner—
1780. In this year was the portrait taken. It is the like-
ness of a dead friend—a Mr. Oldeb—to whom I became
much attached at Calcutta, during the administration of
Warren Hastings. I was then only twenty years old.—
When I first saw you, Mr. Bedloe, at Saratoga, it was the
miraculous similarity which existed between yourself
and the painting, which induced me to accost you, to
seek your friendship, and to bring about those arrangements which resulted in my becoming your constant
companion. In accomplishing this point, I was urged
partly, and perhaps principally, by a regretful memory
of the deceased, but also, in part, by an uneasy, and not
altogether horrorless curiosity respecting yourself.

"In your detail of the vision which presented itself to
you amid the hills, you have described, with the minutest accuracy, the Indian city of Benares, upon the Holy
River. The riots, the combats, the massacre, were the
actual events of the insurrection of Cheyte Sing, which
took place in 1780, when Hastings was put in imminent
peril of his life. The man escaping by the string of turbans, was Cheyte Sing himself. The party in the kiosk
were sepoys and British officers, headed by Hastings. Of
this party I was one, and did all I could to prevent the
rash and fatal sally of the officer who fell, in the crowded
alleys, by the poisoned arrow of a Bengalee. That officer
was my dearest friend. It was Oldeb. You will perceive
by these manuscripts," (here the speaker produced a
note-book in which several pages appeared to have been

freshly written) "that at the very period in which you fancied these things amid the hills, I was engaged in detailing them upon paper here at home."

In about a week after this conversation, the following paragraphs appeared in a Charlottesville paper.

"We have the painful duty of announcing the death of Mr. AUGUSTUS BEDLO, a gentleman whose amiable manners and many virtues have long endeared him to the citizens of Charlottesville.

"Mr. B., for some years past, has been subject to neuralgia, which has often threatened to terminate fatally; but this can be regarded only as the mediate cause of his decease. The proximate cause was one of especial singularity. In an excursion to the Ragged Mountains, a few days since, a slight cold and fever were contracted, attended with great determination of blood to the head. To relieve this, Dr. Templeton resorted to topical bleeding. Leeches were applied to the temples. In a fearfully brief period the patient died, when it appeared that, in the jar containing the leeches, had been introduced, by accident, one of the venomous vermicular sangsues which are now and then found in the neighboring ponds. This creature fastened itself upon a small artery in the right temple. Its close resemblance to the medicinal leech caused the mistake to be overlooked until too late.

"N.B. The poisonous sangsue of Charlottesville may always be distinguished from the medicinal leech by its blackness, and especially by its writhing or vermicular motions, which very nearly resemble those of a snake."

I was speaking with the editor of the paper in question, upon the topic of this remarkable accident, when it occurred to me to ask how it happened that the name of the deceased had been given as Bedlo.

"I presume," said I, "you have authority for this

spelling, but I have always supposed the name to be written with an *e* at the end."

"Authority?—no," he replied. "It is a mere typographical error. The name is Bedlo with an *e*, all the world over, and I never knew it to be spelt otherwise in my life."

"Then," said I mutteringly, as I turned upon my heel, "then indeed has it come to pass that one truth is stranger than any fiction—for Bedlo, without the *e*, what is it but Oldeb conversed? And this man tells me it is a typographical error."

ELEONORA
(The Gift, 1842.)

Sub conservatione formæ specificæ salva anima.
—RAYMOND LULLY

I AM come of a race noted for vigor of fancy and ardor of passion. Men have called me mad; but the question is not yet settled, whether madness is or is not the loftiest intelligence—whether much that is glorious —whether all that is profound—does not spring from disease of thought—from *moods* of mind exalted at the expense of the general intellect. They who dream by day are cognizant of many things which escape those who dream only by night. In their grey visions they obtain glimpses of eternity, and thrill, in awaking, to find that they have been upon the verge of the great secret. In snatches, they learn something of the wisdom which is of good, and more of the mere knowledge which is of evil. They penetrate, however rudderless or compassless, into the vast ocean of the "light ineffable" and again, like the adventurers of the Nubian geographer, *"agressi sunt mare tenebrarum, quid in eo esset exploraturi."*

We will say, then, that I am mad. I grant, at least, that there are two distinct conditions of my mental existence—the condition of a lucid reason, not to be disputed, and belonging to the memory of events forming the first epoch of my life—and a condition of shadow and doubt, appertaining to the present, and to the recollection of what constitutes the second great era of my being. Therefore, what I shall tell of the earlier period, believe; and to what I may relate of the later time, give only such credit as may seem due; or doubt it altogether; or, if doubt it ye cannot, then play unto its riddle the Oedipus.

She whom I loved in youth, and of whom I now pen calmly and distinctly these remembrances, was the sole daughter of the only sister of my mother long departed. Eleonora was the name of my cousin. We had always dwelled together, beneath a tropical sun, in the Valley of the Many-Colored Grass. No unguided footstep ever came upon that vale; for it lay far away up among a range of giant hills that hung beetling around about it, shutting out the sunlight from its sweetest recesses. No path was trodden in its vicinity; and, to reach our happy home, there was need of putting back, with force, the foliage of many thousands of forest trees, and of crushing to death the glories of many millions of fragrant flowers. Thus it was that we lived all alone, knowing nothing of the world without the valley,—I, and my cousin, and her mother.

From the dim regions beyond the mountains at the upper end of our encircled domain, there crept out a narrow and deep river, brighter than all save the eyes of Eleonora; and, winding stealthily about in mazy courses, it passed away, at length, through a shadowy gorge, among hills still dimmer than those whence it had issued. We called it the "River of Silence"; for there seemed to be a hushing influence in its flow. No murmur arose from its bed, and so gently it wandered along, that the pearly pebbles upon which we loved to gaze, far down within its bosom, stirred not at all, but lay in a motionless content, each in its own old station, shining on gloriously forever.

The margin of the river, and of the many dazzling rivulets that glided, through devious ways, into its channel, as well as the spaces that extended from the margins away down into the depths of the streams until they reached the bed of pebbles at the bottom,—these spots, not less than the whole surface of the valley, from the river to the mountains that girdled it in, were carpeted all by a soft green grass, thick, short, perfectly even, and vanilla-perfumed, but so besprinkled throughout with the yellow buttercup, the white daisy, the purple violet, and the ruby-red asphodel, that its exceeding beauty spoke to our hearts, in loud tones, of the love and of the glory of God.

And, here and there, in groves about this grass, like wildernesses of dreams, sprang up fantastic trees, whose tall slender stems stood not upright, but slanted gracefully towards the light that peered at noon-day into the centre of the valley. Their bark was speckled with the vivid alternate splendor of ebony and silver, and was smoother than all save the cheeks of Eleonora; so that but for the brilliant green of the huge leaves that spread from their summits in long tremulous lines, dallying with the Zephyrs, one might have fancied them giant serpents of Syria doing homage to their Sovereign the Sun.

Hand in hand about this valley, for fifteen years,

roamed I with Eleonora before Love entered within
our hearts. It was one evening at the close of the third
lustrum of her life, and of the fourth of my own, that
we sat, locked in each other's embrace, beneath the
serpent-like trees, and looked down within the waters
of the River of Silence at our images therein. We spoke
no words during the rest of that sweet day; and our
words even upon the morrow were tremulous and few.
We had drawn the god Eros from that wave, and now
we felt that he had enkindled within us the fiery souls
of our forefathers. The passions which had for centuries
distinguished our race, came thronging with the fancies
for which they had been equally noted, and together
breathed a delirious bliss over the Valley of the Many-
Colored Grass. A change fell upon all things. Strange
brilliant flowers, star-shaped, burst out upon the trees
where no flowers had been known before. The tints of
the green carpet deepened; and when, one by one, the
white daisies shrank away, there sprang up, in place of
them, ten by ten of the ruby-red asphodel. And life
arose in our paths; for the tall flamingo, hitherto unseen,
with all gay glowing birds, flaunted his scarlet plumage
before us. The golden and silver fish haunted the river,
out of the bosom of which issued, little by little, a murmur that swelled, at length, into a lulling melody more
divine than that of the harp of Æolus—sweeter than all
save the voice of Eleonora. And now, too, a voluminous
cloud, which we had long watched in the regions of
Hesper, floated out thence, all gorgeous in crimson and
gold, and settling in peace above us, sank, day by day,
lower and lower, until its edges rested upon the tops of
the mountains, turning all their dimness into magnificence, and shutting us up, as if forever, within a magic
prison-house of grandeur and of glory.

The loveliness of Eleonora was that of the Seraphim;

but she was a maiden artless and innocent as the brief
life she had led among the flowers. No guile disguised
the fervor of love which animated her heart, and she
examined with me its inmost recesses as we walked together in the Valley of the Many-Colored Grass, and
discoursed of the mighty changes which had lately
taken place therein.

At length, having spoken one day, in tears, of the
last sad change which must befall Humanity, she
thenceforward dwelt only upon this one sorrowful
theme, interweaving it into all our converse, as, in the
songs of the bard of Schiraz, the same images are found
occurring, again and again, in every impressive variation of phrase.

She had seen that the finger of Death was upon her
bosom—that, like the ephemeron, she had been made
perfect in loveliness only to die; but the terrors of the
grave, to her, lay solely in a consideration which she
revealed to me, one evening at twilight, by the banks
of the River of Silence. She grieved to think that, having entombed her in the Valley of the Many-Colored
Grass, I would quit forever its happy recesses, trans-
ferring the love which now was so passionately her own
to some maiden of the outer and every-day world. And,
then and there, I threw myself hurriedly at the feet of
Eleonora, and offered up a vow, to herself and to
Heaven, that I would never bind myself in marriage to
any daughter of Earth—that I would in no manner
prove recreant to her dear memory, or to the memory
of the devout affection with which she had blessed me.
And I called the Mighty Ruler of the Universe to witness the pious solemnity of my vow. And the curse
which I invoked of *Him* and of her, a saint in Helusion,
should I prove traitorous to that promise, involved a
penalty the exceeding great horror of which will not

permit me to make record of it here. And the bright eyes of Eleonora grew brighter at my words; and she sighed as if a deadly burthen had been taken from her breast; and she trembled and very bitterly wept; but she made acceptance of the vow, (for what was she but a child?) and it made easy to her the bed of her death. And she said to me, not many days afterwards, tranquilly dying, that, because of what I had done for the comfort of her spirit, she would watch over me in that spirit when departed, and, if so it were permitted her, return to me visibly in the watches of the night; but, if this thing were, indeed, beyond the power of the souls in Paradise, that she would, at least, give me frequent indications of her presence; sighing upon me in the evening winds, or filling the air which I breathed with perfume from the censers of the angels. And, with these words upon her lips, she yielded up her innocent life, putting an end to the first epoch of my own.

Thus far I have faithfully said. But as I pass the barrier in Time's path formed by the death of my beloved, and proceed with the second era of my existence, I feel that a shadow gathers over my brain, and I mistrust the perfect sanity of the record. But let me on.— Years dragged themselves along heavily, and still I dwelled within the Valley of the Many-Colored Grass; —but a second change had come upon all things. The star-shaped flowers shrank into the stems of the trees, and appeared no more. The tints of the green carpet faded; and, one by one, the ruby-red asphodels withered away; and there sprang up, in place of them, ten by ten, dark eye-like violets that writhed uneasily and were ever encumbered with dew. And Life departed from our paths; for the tall flamingo flaunted no longer his scarlet plumage before us, but flew sadly

from the vale into the hills, with all the gay glowing
birds that had arrived in his company. And the golden
and silver fish swam down through the gorge at the
lower end of our domain and bedecked the sweet river
never again. And the lulling melody that had been
softer than the wind-harp of Æolus and more divine
than all save the voice of Eleonora, it died little by little
away, in murmurs growing lower and lower, until the
stream returned, at length, utterly, into the solemnity
of its original silence. And then, lastly the voluminous
cloud uprose, and, abandoning the tops of the mountains to the dimness of old, fell back into the regions of
Hesper, and took away all its manifold golden and
gorgeous glories from the Valley of the Many-Colored
Grass.

Yet the promises of Eleonora were not forgotten; for
I heard the sounds of the swinging of the censers of
the angels; the streams of a holy perfume floated ever
and ever about the valley; and at lone hours, when my
heart beat heavily, the winds that bathed my brow came
unto me laden with soft sighs; and indistinct murmurs
filled often the night air; and once—oh, but once only!
I was awakened from a slumber like the slumber of
death by the pressing of spiritual lips upon my own.

But the void within my heart refused, even thus, to
be filled. I longed for the love which had before filled
it to overflowing. At length the valley *pained* me
through its memories of Eleonora, and I left it forever
for the vanities and the turbulent triumphs of the
world.

✸   ✸   ✸

I found myself within a strange city, where all things
might have served to blot from recollection the sweet
dreams I had dreamed so long in the Valley of the

Many-Colored Grass. The pomps and pageantries of a
stately court, and the mad clangor of arms, and the
radiant loveliness of woman, bewildered and intoxicated
my brain. But as yet my soul had proved true to its
vows, and the indications of the presence of Eleonora
were still given me in the silent hours of the night. Suddenly, these manifestations they ceased; and the world
grew dark before mine eyes; and I stood aghast at the
burning thoughts which possessed—at the terrible
temptations which beset me; for there came from some
far, far distant and unknown land, into the gay court of
the king I served, a maiden to whose beauty my whole
recreant heart yielded at once—at whose footstool I
bowed down without a struggle, in the most ardent, in
the most abject worship of love. What indeed was my
passion for the young girl of the valley in comparison
with the fervor, and the delirium, and the spirit-lifting
ecstasy of adoration with which I poured out my whole
soul in tears at the feet of the ethereal Ermengarde?—
Oh bright was the seraph Ermengarde! and in that
knowledge I had room for none other. Oh divine was
the angel Ermengarde! and as I looked down into the
depths of her memorial eyes I thought only of them—
and *of her*.

I wedded;—nor dreaded the curse I had invoked;
and its bitterness was not visited upon me. And once—
but once again in the silence of the night, there came
through my lattice the soft sighs which had forsaken
me; and they modelled themselves into familiar and
sweet voice, saying:

"Sleep in peace!—for the Spirit of Love reigneth and
ruleth, and, in taking to thy passionate heart her who is
Ermengarde, thou art absolved, for reasons which shall
be made known to thee in Heaven, of thy vows unto
Eleonora "

THE OVAL PORTRAIT

(*Graham's Magazine*, April, 1842)

THE château into which my valet had ventured to make forcible entrance, rather than permit me, in my desperately wounded condition, to pass a night in the open air, was one of those piles of commingled gloom and grandeur which have so long frowned among the Apennines, not less in fact than in the fancy of Mrs. Radcliffe. To all appearance it had been temporarily and very lately abandoned. We established ourselves in one of the smallest and least sumptuously furnished apartments. It lay in a remote turret of the building. Its decorations were rich, yet tattered and antique. Its walls were hung with tapestry and bedecked with manifold and multiform armorial trophies, together with an unusually great number of very spirited modern paintings in frames of rich golden arabesque. In these paintings, which depended from the walls not only in their main surfaces, but in very many nooks which the bizarre architecture of the château rendered necessary —in these paintings my incipient delirium, perhaps, had caused me to take deep interest; so that I bade Pedro to close the heavy shutters of the room—since it was already night—to light the tongues of a tall candelabrum which stood by the head of my bed—and to throw open far and wide the fringed curtains of black velvet which enveloped the bed itself. I wished all this done that I might resign myself, if not to sleep, at least alternately to the contemplation of these pictures, and the perusal of a small volume which had been found upon the pillow, and which purported to criticise and describe them.

Long—long I read—and devoutly, devotedly I gazed. Rapidly and gloriously the hours flew by, and the deep midnight came. The position of the candelabrum displeased me, and outreaching my hand with difficulty, rather than disturb my slumbering valet, I placed it so as to throw its rays more fully upon the book.

But the action produced an effect altogether unanticipated. The rays of the numerous candles (for there were many) now fell within a niche of the room which had hitherto been thrown into deep shade by one of the bed-posts. I thus saw in vivid light a picture all unnoticed before. It was the portrait of a young girl just ripening into womanhood. I glanced at the painting hurriedly, and then closed my eyes. Why I did this was not at first apparent even to my own perception. But while my lids remained thus shut, I ran over in mind my reason for so shutting them. It was an impulsive movement to gain time for thought—to make sure that my vision had not deceived me—to calm and subdue my fancy for a more sober and more certain gaze. In a very few moments I again looked fixedly at the painting.

That I now saw aright I could not and would not doubt; for the first flashing of the candles upon that canvas had seemed to dissipate the dreamy stupor which was stealing over my senses, and to startle me at once into waking life.

The portrait, I have already said, was that of a young girl. It was a mere head and shoulders, done in what is technically termed a *vignette* manner; much in the style of the favorite heads of Sully. The arms, the bosom and even the ends of the radiant hair, melted imperceptibly into the vague yet deep shadow which formed the back-ground of the whole. The frame was oval, richly gilded and filagreed in *Moresque*. As a thing of art nothing could be more admirable than the painting itself. But it could have been neither the execution of the work, nor the immortal beauty of the countenance, which had so suddenly and so vehemently moved me. Least of all, could it have been that my fancy, shaken from its half slumber, had mistaken the head for that of a living person. I saw at once that the peculiarities of the design, of the *vignetting*, and of the frame, must have instantly dispelled such idea—must have prevented even its momentary entertainment. Thinking earnestly upon these points, I remained, for an hour perhaps, half sitting, half reclining, with my vision riveted upon the portrait. At length, satisfied with the true secret of its effect, I fell back within the bed. I had found the spell of the picture in an absolute *life-likeliness* of expression, which at first startling, finally confounded, subdued and appalled me. With deep and reverent awe I replaced the candelabrum in its former position. The cause of my deep agitation being thus shut from view, I sought eagerly the volume which discussed the paintings and their histories. Turning to the number which designated the oval portrait, I there read the vague and quaint words which follow:

"She was a maiden of rarest beauty, and not more lovely than full of glee. And evil was the hour when she saw, and loved, and wedded the painter. He, passionate, studious, austere, and having already a bride in his Art; she a maiden of rarest beauty, and not more lovely than full of glee: all light and smiles, and frolicksome as the young fawn: loving and cherishing all things: hating only the Art which was her rival: dreading only the pallet and brushes and other untoward instruments which deprived her of the countenance of her lover. It was thus a terrible thing for this lady to hear the painter speak of his desire to portray even his young bride. But she was humble and obedient, and sat meekly for many weeks in the dark high turret-chamber where the light dripped upon the pale canvas only from overhead. But he, the painter, took glory in his work, which went on from hour to hour and from day to day. And he was a passionate, and wild and moody man, who became lost in reveries; so that he *would* not see that the light which fell so ghastlily in that lone turret withered the health and the spirits of his bride, who pined visibly to all but him. Yet she smiled on and still on, uncomplainingly, because she saw that the painter, (who had high renown,) took a fervid and burning pleasure in his task, and wrought day and night to depict her who so loved him, yet who grew daily more dispirited and weak. And in sooth some who beheld the portrait spoke of its resemblance in low words, as of a mighty marvel, and a proof not less of the power of the painter than of his deep love for her whom he depicted so surpassingly well. But at length, as the labor drew nearer to its conclusion, there were admitted none into the turret; for the painter had grown wild with the ardor of his work, and turned his eyes from the canvas rarely, even to regard the countenance of his wife. And he *would* not see that the tints which he spread upon the canvas were drawn from the cheeks of her who sate beside him. And when many weeks had passed, and but little remained to do, save one brush upon the mouth and one tint upon the eye, the spirit of the lady again flickered up as the flame within the socket of the lamp. And then the brush was given, and then the tint was placed; and, for one moment, the painter stood entranced before the work which he had wrought; but in the next, while he yet gazed, he grew tremulous and very pallid, and aghast, and crying with a loud voice, 'This is indeed *Life* itself!' turned suddenly to regard his beloved:—*She was dead!*"

THE MAN OF THE CROWD

(The first printing appeared simultaneously in Burton's *The Gentle-man's Magazine* and in *The Casket*, the contents of which were the same because they were about to be combined into Graham's *Lady's and Gentleman's Magazine*)

Ce grand malheur, de ne pouvoir être seul.—LA BRUYÈRE.

IT was well said of a certain German book that *"es lässt sich nicht lesen"*—it does not permit itself to be read. There are some secrets which do not permit themselves to be told. Men die nightly in their beds, wringing the hands of ghostly confessors, and looking them piteously in the eyes—die with despair of heart and convulsion of throat, on account of the hideousness of mysteries which will not *suffer themselves* to be revealed. Now and then, alas, the conscience of man takes up a burthen so heavy in horror that it can be thrown down only into the grave. And thus the essence of all crime is undivulged.

Not long ago, about the closing in of an evening in autumn, I sat at the large bow window of the D—— Coffee-House in London. For some months I had been ill in health, but was now convalescent, and, with returning strength, found myself in one of those happy moods which are so precisely the converse of *ennui*—moods of the keenest appetency, when the film from the mental vision departs—the ἀχλὺς ἣ πρὶν ἐπῆεν—and the intellect, electrified, surpasses as greatly its everyday condition, as does the vivid yet candid reason of Leibnitz, the mad and flimsy rhetoric of Gorgias. Merely to breathe was enjoyment; and I derived positive pleasure even from many of the legitimate sources of pain. I felt a calm but inquisitive interest in every thing. With a cigar in my mouth and a newspaper in my lap, I had been amusing myself for the greater part of the afternoon, now in poring over advertisements, now in observing the promiscuous company in the room, and now in peering through the smoky panes into the street.

This latter is one of the principal thoroughfares of the city, and had been very much crowded during the whole day. But, as the darkness came on, the throng momently increased; and, by the time the lamps were well lighted, two dense and continuous tides of population were rushing past the door. At this particular period of the evening I had never before been in a similar situation, and the tumultuous sea of human heads filled me, therefore, with a delicious novelty of emotion. I gave up, at length, all care of things within the hotel, and became absorbed in contemplation of the scene without.

At first my observations took an abstract and generalizing turn. I looked at the passengers in masses, and thought of them in their aggregate relations. Soon, however, I descended to details, and regarded with minute interest the innumerable varieties of figure, dress, air, gait, visage, and expression of countenance.

By far the greater number of those who went by had a satisfied business-like demeanor, and seemed to be thinking only of making their way through the press. Their brows were knit, and their eyes rolled quickly; when pushed against by fellow-wayfarers they evinced no symptom of impatience, but adjusted their clothes and hurried on. Others, still a numerous class, were restless in their movements, had flushed faces, and talked and gesticulated to themselves, as if feeling in solitude on account of the very denseness of the company around. When impeded in their progress, these people suddenly ceased muttering, but redoubled their gesticulations, and awaited, with an absent and overdone smile upon the lips, the course of the persons impeding them. If jostled, they bowed profusely to the jostlers, and appeared overwhelmed with confusion.— There was nothing very distinctive about these two large classes beyond what I have noted. Their habiliments belonged to that order which is pointedly termed the decent. They were undoubtedly noblemen, merchants, attorneys, tradesmen, stock-jobbers—the Eupatrids and the common-places of society—men of leisure and men actively engaged in affairs of their own —conducting business upon their own responsibility. They did not greatly excite my attention.

The tribe of clerks was an obvious one; and here I discerned two remarkable divisions. There were the junior clerks of flash houses—young gentlemen with tight coats, bright boots, well-oiled hair, and supercilious lips. Setting aside a certain dapperness of carriage, which may be termed *deskism* for want of a better word, the manner of these persons seemed to me an exact facsimile of what had been the perfection of *bon ton* about twelve or eighteen months before. They wore the cast-off graces of the gentry;—and this, I believe, involves the best definition of the class.

The division of the upper clerks of staunch firms, or of the "steady old fellows," it was not possible to mistake. These were known by their coats and pantaloons of black or brown, made to sit comfortably, with white cravats and waistcoats, broad solid-looking shoes, and thick hose or gaiters.—They had all slightly bald heads, from which the right ears, long used to pen-holding, had an odd habit of standing off on end. I observed that they always removed or settled their hats with both hands, and wore watches, with short gold chains of a substantial and ancient pattern. Theirs was the affectation of respectability;—if indeed there be an affectation so honorable.

There were many individuals of dashing appearance, whom I easily understood as belonging to the race of swell pick-pockets, with which all great cities are in· fested. I watched these gentry with much inquisitive- ness, and found it difficult to imagine how they should ever be mistaken for gentlemen by gentlemen them- selves. Their voluminousness of wristband, with an air of excessive frankness, should betray them at once.

The gamblers, of whom I descried not a few, were still more easily recognisable. They, wore every variety of dress, from that of the desperate thimble-rig bully, with velvet waistcoat, fancy neckerchief, gilt chains, and filagreed buttons, to that of the scrupulously inor- nate clergyman than which nothing could be less liable to suspicion. Still all were distinguished by a certain sodden swarthiness of complexion, a filmy dimness of eye, and pallor and compression of lip. There were two other traits, moreover, by which I could always detect them;—a guarded lowness of tone in conversation, and a more than ordinary extension of the thumb in a direc- tion at right angles with the fingers.—Very often, in company with these sharpers, I observed an order of men somewhat different in habits, but still birds of a kindred feather. They may be defined as the gentlemen who live by their wits. They seem to prey upon the pub- lic in two battalions—that of the dandies and that of the military men. Of the first grade the leading features are long locks and smiles; of the second frogged coats and frowns.

Descending in the scale of what is termed gentility, I found darker and deeper themes for speculation. I saw Jew pedlars, with hawk eyes flashing from coun- tenances whose every other feature wore only an ex- pression of abject humility; sturdy professional street beggars scowling upon mendicants of a better stamp, whom despair alone had driven forth into the night for charity; feeble and ghastly invalids, upon whom death had placed a sure hand, and who sidled and tottered through the mob, looking every one beseechingly in the face, as if in search of some chance consolation, some lost hope; modest young girls returning from long and late labor to a cheerless home, and shrinking more tearfully than indignantly from the glances of ruffians, whose direct contact, even, could not be avoided; women of the town of all kinds and of all ages—the unequivocal beauty in the prime of her womanhood, putting one in mind of the statue in Lucian, with the surface of Parian marble, and the interior filled with filth—the loathsome and utterly lost leper in rags—the wrinkled, bejewelled and paint-begrimed beldame, making a last effort at youth—the mere child of immature form, yet, from long association, an adept in the dreadful coquetries of her trade, and burning with a rabid ambition to be ranked the equal of her elders in vice; drunkards innumerable and indescribable—some in shreds and patches, reeling, inarticulate, with bruised visage and lack-lustre eyes—some in whole although filthy garments, with a slightly unsteady swagger, thick sensual lips, and hearty-looking rubicund faces—others clothed in materials which had once been good, and which even now were scrupulously well brushed—men who walked with a more than naturally firm and springy step, but whose countenances were fearfully pale, whose eyes hideously wild and red, and who clutched with quivering fingers, as they strode through the crowd, at every object which came within their reach; beside these, pie-men, porters, coal-heavers, sweeps; organ-grinders, monkey-exhibiters and ballad mongers, those who vended with those who sang; ragged artisans and exhausted laborers of every description, and all full of a noisy and inordinate vivacity which jarred discordantly upon the ear, and gave an aching sensation to the eye.

As the night deepened, so deepened to me the interest of the scene; for not only did the general character of the crowd materially alter (its gentler features retiring in the gradual withdrawal of the more orderly portion of the people, and its harsher ones coming out into bolder relief, as the late hour brought forth every species of infamy from its den,) but the rays of the gas-lamps, feeble at first in their struggle with the dying day, had now at length gained ascendancy, and threw over every thing a fitful and garish lustre. All was dark yet splendid—as that ebony to which has been likened the style of Tertullian.

The wild effects of the light enchained me to an examination of individual faces; and although the rapidity with which the world of light flitted before the window, prevented me from casting more than a glance upon each visage, still it seemed that, in my then peculiar mental state, I could frequently read, even in that brief interval of a glance, the history of long years.

With my brow to the glass, I was thus occupied in scrutinizing the mob, when suddenly there came into view a countenance (that of a decrepit old man, some sixty-five or seventy years of age,)—a countenance which at once arrested and absorbed my whole attention, on account of the absolute idiosyncrasy of its expression. Any thing even remotely resembling that expression I had never seen before. I well remember that my first thought, upon beholding it, was that Retszch, had he viewed it, would have greatly preferred it to his own pictural incarnations of the fiend. As I endeavored, during the brief minute of my original survey, to form some analysis of the meaning conveyed, there arose confusedly and paradoxically within my mind, the ideas of vast mental power, of caution, of penuriousness, of avarice, of coolness, of malice, of blood-thirstiness, of triumph, of merriment, of excessive terror, of intense—of extreme despair. I felt singularly aroused, startled, fascinated. "How wild a history," I said to myself, "is written within that bosom!" Then came a craving desire to keep the man in view—to know more of him. Hurriedly putting on an overcoat, and seizing my hat and cane, I made my way into the street, and pushed through the crowd in the direction which I had seen him take; for he had already disappeared. With some little difficulty I at length came within sight of him, approached, and followed him closely, yet cautiously, so as not to attract his attention.

I had now a good opportunity of examining his person. He was short in stature, very thin, and apparently very feeble. His clothes, generally, were filthy and ragged; but as he came, now and then, within the strong glare of a lamp, I perceived that his linen, although dirty, was of beautiful texture; and my vision deceived me, or, through a rent in a closely-buttoned and evidently second-handed *roquelaire* which enveloped him, I caught a glimpse both of a diamond and of a dagger. These observations heightened my curiosity, and I resolved to follow the stranger whithersoever he should go.

It was now fully night-fall, and a thick humid fog hung over the city, soon ending in a settled and heavy rain. This change of weather had an odd effect upon the crowd, the whole of which was at once put into new commotion, and overshadowed by a world of umbrellas. The waver, the jostle, and the hum increased in a tenfold degree. For my own part I did not much regard the rain—the lurking of an old fever in my

system rendering the moisture somewhat too dangerously pleasant. Tying a handkerchief about my mouth,
I kept on. For half an hour the old man held his way
with difficulty along the great thoroughfare; and I here
walked close at his elbow through fear of losing sight
of him. Never once turning his head to look back, he
did not observe me. By and by he passed into a cross
street, which, although densely filled with people, was
not quite so much thronged as the main one he had
quitted. Here a change in his demeanor became evident.
He walked more slowly and with less object than before—more hesitatingly. He crossed and re-crossed the
way repeatedly without apparent aim; and the press
was still so thick, that, at every such movement, I was
obliged to follow him closely. The street was a narrow
and long one, and his course lay within it for nearly
an hour, during which the passengers had gradually
diminished to about that number which is ordinarily
seen at noon in Broadway near the Park—so vast a
difference is there between a London populace and
that of the most frequented American city. A second
turn brought us into a square, brilliantly lighted, and
overflowing with life. The old manner of the stranger
re-appeared. His chin fell upon his breast, while his eyes
rolled wildly from under his knit brows, in every direction, upon those who hemmed him in. He urged his way
steadily and perseveringly. I was surprised, however,
to find, upon his having made the circuit of the square,
that he turned and retraced his steps. Still more was I
astonished to see him repeat the same walk several times
—once nearly detecting me as he came round with a
sudden movement.

   In this exercise he spent another hour, at the end of
which we met with far less interruption from passengers
than at first. The rain fell fast; the air grew cool; and

the people were retiring to their homes. With a gesture
of impatience, the wanderer passed into a by-street
comparatively deserted. Down this, some quarter of a
mile long, he rushed with an activity I could not have
dreamed of seeing in one so aged, and which put me to
much trouble in pursuit. A few minutes brought us to
a large and busy bazaar, with the localities of which
the stranger appeared well acquainted, and where his
original demeanor again became apparent, as he forced
his way to and fro, without aim, among the host of
buyers and sellers.

During the hour and a half, or thereabouts, which
we passed in this place, it required much caution on
my part to keep him within reach without attracting
his observation. Luckily I wore a pair of caoutchouc
over-shoes, and could move about in perfect silence.
At no moment did he see that I watched him. He
entered shop after shop, priced nothing, spoke no word,
and looked at all objects with a wild and vacant stare.
I was now utterly amazed at his behavior, and firmly
resolved that we should not part until I had satisfied
myself in some measure respecting him.

A loud-toned clock struck eleven, and the company
were fast deserting the bazaar. A shop-keeper, in putting up a shutter, jostled the old man, and at the instant
I saw a strong shudder come over his frame. He hurried
into the street, looked anxiously around him for an instant, and then ran with incredible swiftness through
many crooked and people-less lanes, until we emerged
once more upon the great thoroughfare whence we had
started—the street of the D—— Hotel. It no longer
wore, however, the same aspect. It was still brilliant
with gas; but the rain fell fiercely, and there were few
persons to be seen. The stranger grew pale. He walked
moodily some paces up the once populous avenue, then,

with a heavy sigh, turned in the direction of the river, and, plunging through a great variety of devious ways, came out, at length, in view of one of the principal theatres. It was about being closed, and the audience were thronging from the doors. I saw the old man gasp as if for breath while he threw himself amid the crowd; but I thought that the intense agony of his countenance had, in some measure, abated. His head again fell upon his breast; he appeared as I had seen him at first. I observed that he now took the course in which had gone the greater number of the audience —but, upon the whole, I was at a loss to comprehend the waywardness of his actions.

As he proceeded, the company grew more scattered, and his old uneasiness and vacillation were resumed. For some time he followed closely a party of some ten or twelve roisterers; but from this number one by one dropped off, until three only remained together, in a narrow and gloomy lane little frequented. The stranger paused, and, for a moment, seemed lost in thought; then, with every mark of agitation, pursued rapidly a route which brought us to the verge of the city, amid regions very different from those we had hitherto traversed. It was the most noisome quarter of London, where everything wore the worst impress of the most deplorable poverty, and of the most desperate crime. By the dim light of an accidental lamp, tall, antique, worm-eaten, wooden tenements were seen tottering to their fall, in directions so many and capricious that scarce the semblance of a passage was discernible between them. The paving-stones lay at random, displaced from their beds by the rankly growing grass. Horrible filth festered in the dammed-up gutters. The whole atmosphere teemed with desolation. Yet, as we proceeded, the sounds of human life revived by sure de-

grees, and at length large bands of the most abandoned
of a London populace were seen reeling to and fro.
The spirits of the old man again flickered up, as a lamp
which is near its death-hour. Once more he strode onward with elastic tread. Suddenly a corner was turned,
a blaze of light burst upon our sight, and we stood
before one of the huge suburban temples of Intemperance—one of the palaces of the fiend, Gin.

It was now nearly day-break; but a number of
wretched inebriates still pressed in and out of the flaunting entrance. With a half shriek of joy the old man
forced a passage within, resumed at once his original
bearing, and stalked backward and forward, without
apparent object, among the throng. He had not been
thus long occupied, however, before a rush to the doors
gave token that the host was closing them for the night.
It was something even more intense than despair that I
then observed upon the countenance of the singular
being whom I had watched so pertinaciously. Yet he
did not hesitate in his career, but, with a mad energy,
retraced his steps at once, to the heart of the mighty
London. Long and swiftly he fled, while I followed him
in the wildest amazement, resolute not to abandon a
scrutiny in which I now felt an interest all-absorbing.
The sun arose while we proceeded, and, when we had
once again reached that most thronged mart of the populous town, the street of the D—— Hotel, it presented
an appearance of human bustle and activity scarcely
inferior to what I had seen on the evening before. And
here, long, amid the momently increasing confusion,
did I persist in my pursuit of the stranger. But, as
usual, he walked to and fro, and during the day did
not pass from out the turmoil of that street. And, as the
shades of the second evening came on, I grew wearied
unto death, and, stopping fully in front of the wanderer,

gazed at him steadfastly in the face. He noticed me not, but resumed his solemn walk, while I, ceasing to follow, remained absorbed in contemplation. "This old man," I said at length, "is the type and the genius of deep crime. He refuses to be alone. *He is the man of the crowd.* It will be in vain to follow; for I shall learn no more of him, nor of his deeds. The worst heart of the world is a grosser book than the *Hortulus Animæ,*[1] and perhaps it is but one of the great mercies of God that *es lässt sich nicht lesen.*"

---

[1] The Hortulus Animæ cum Oratiunculis Aliquibus Superadditis [of Grüninger].

Of Terror

Just as most of Poe's stories are fantasies, so are they tales of terror, but those printed in this section have terror as their major theme. Any man who writes of terror must himself be peculiarly susceptible to fear. Poe was a frightened creature, afraid of a hostile world, but most of all, afraid of the dreadful images that lurked in his own mind. Out of his own fears and his own nightmares came the stuff from which he made his stories. He apparently had a strange dread of deep places; the grave, a pit, and the dark, mysterious abysses of the ocean appear symbolically in all four of these stories.

"Ms Found in a Bottle" is one of the earliest of his tales. It is a Flying Dutchman story in which the phantom ship is sucked down into a giant whirlpool, and so is connected in theme with "A Descent into the Maelström," which also deals with being drawn down into great watery depths.

For sheer writing and the creation of intolerable suspense "The Pit and the Pendulum" is one of Poe's best stories. It is the very essence of nightmare, for it is only in the untrammeled horror of his dreams that the average man meets a situation wherein he is utterly helpless and from which there is no apparent escape. Poe had probably read Juan Antonio Llorente's *Critical History of the Spanish Inquisition* and may have derived the setting of his story from it, but the development of the basic narrative idea came from his own mind, which

119

was so fertile in conjuring up terror that it needed no outside assistance.

No documentary evidence exists to prove it, but there is a good chance that "The Premature Burial" was based on an actual experience encountered in Poe's youth; he indicates as much in the third from the last paragraph. Certainly it is the sort of experience he might very well have had.

MS FOUND IN A BOTTLE

(*The Baltimore Saturday Visiter*, October 19, 1833.)

> Qui n'a plus qu'un moment à vivre
> N'a plus rien à dissimuler.
> —QUINAULT—ATYS

OF MY country and of my family I have little to say. Ill usage and length of years have driven me from the one, and estranged me from the other. Hereditary wealth afforded me an education of no common order, and a contemplative turn of mind enabled me to methodize the stores which early study very diligently garnered up.—Beyond all things, the study of the German moralists gave me great delight; not from any ill-advised admiration of their eloquent madness, but from the ease with which my habits of rigid thought enabled me to detect their falsities. I have often been reproached with the aridity of my genius; a deficiency of imagination has been imputed to me as a crime; and the Pyrrhonism of my opinions has at all times rendered me notorious. Indeed, a strong relish for physical philosophy has, I fear, tinctured my mind with a very common error of this age—I mean the habit of referring occurrences, even the least susceptible of such reference, to the principles of that science. Upon the whole, no person could be less liable than myself to be led away from the severe precincts of truth by the *ignes fatui* of superstition. I have thought proper to premise thus much, lest the incredible tale I have to tell should be considered rather the raving of a crude imagination, than the positive experience of a mind to which the reveries of fancy have been a dead letter and a nullity.

After many years spent in foreign travel, I sailed in the year 18—, from the port of Batavia, in the rich and populous island of Java, on a voyage to the Archipelago of the Sunda islands. I went as passenger—having no other inducement than a kind of nervous restlessness which haunted me as a fiend.

Our vessel was a beautiful ship of about four hundred tons, copper-fastened, and built at Bombay of Malabar teak. She was freighted with cotton-wool and oil, from the Lachadive islands. We had also on board coir, jaggeree, ghee, cocoa-nuts, and a few cases of opium. The stowage was clumsily done, and the vessel consequently crank.

We got under way with a mere breath of wind, and for many days stood along the eastern coast of Java, without any other incident to beguile the monotony of our course than the occasional meeting with some of the small grabs of the Archipelago to which we were bound.

One evening, leaning over the taffrail, I observed a very singular, isolated cloud, to the N. W. It was remarkable, as well for its color, as from its being the first we had seen since our departure from Batavia. I watched it attentively until sunset, when it spread all at once to the eastward and westward, girting in the horizon with a narrow strip of vapor, and looking like a long line of low beach. My notice was soon afterwards attracted by the dusky-red appearance of the moon, and

the peculiar character of the sea. The latter was undergoing a rapid change, and the water seemed more than
usually transparent. Although I could distinctly see the
bottom, yet, heaving the lead, I found the ship in fifteen
fathoms. The air now became intolerably hot, and was
loaded with spiral exhalations similar to those arising
from heated iron. As night came on, every breath of
wind died away, and a more entire calm it is impossible
to conceive. The flame of a candle burned upon the
poop without the least perceptible motion, and a long
hair, held between the finger and thumb, hung without
the possibility of detecting a vibration. However, as the
captain said he could perceive no indication of danger,
and as we were drifting in bodily to shore, he ordered
the sails to be furled, and the anchor let go. No watch
was set, and the crew, consisting principally of Malays,
stretched themselves deliberately upon deck. I went below—not without a full presentiment of evil. Indeed,
every appearance warranted me in apprehending a
Simoon. I told the captain my fears; but he paid no attention to what I said, and left me without deigning to
give a reply. My uneasiness, however, prevented me
from sleeping, and about midnight I went upon deck.—
As I placed my foot upon the upper step of the com-
panion-ladder, I was startled by a loud, humming noise,
like that occasioned by the rapid revolution of a mill-
wheel, and before I could ascertain its meaning, I found
the ship quivering to its centre. In the next instant, a
wilderness of foam hurled us upon our beam-ends, and,
rushing over us fore and aft, swept the entire decks
from stem to stern.

The extreme fury of the blast proved, in a great measure, the salvation of the ship. Although completely
water-logged, yet, as her masts had gone by the board,
she rose, after a minute, heavily from the sea, and,

staggering awhile beneath the immense pressure of the tempest, finally righted.

By what miracle I escaped destruction, it is impossible to say. Stunned by the shock of the water, I found myself, upon recovery, jammed in between the stern-post and rudder. With great difficulty I gained my feet, and looking dizzily around, was, at first, struck with the idea of our being among breakers; so terrific, beyond the wildest imagination, was the whirlpool of mountainous and foaming ocean within which we were engulfed. After a while, I heard the voice of an old Swede, who had shipped with us at the moment of our leaving port. I hallooed to him with all my strength, and presently he came reeling aft. We soon discovered that we were the sole survivors of the accident. All on deck, with the exception of ourselves, had been swept overboard;—the captain and mates must have perished as they slept, for the cabins were deluged with water. Without assistance, we could expect to do little for the security of the ship, and our exertions were at first paralyzed by the momentary expectation of going down. Our cable had, of course, parted like pack-thread, at the first breath of the hurricane, or we should have been instantaneously overwhelmed. We scudded with frightful velocity before the sea, and the water made clear breaches over us. The frame-work of our stern was shattered excessively, and, in almost every respect, we had received considerable injury; but to our extreme joy we found the pumps unchoked, and that we had made no great shifting of our ballast. The main fury of the blast had already blown over, and we apprehended little danger from the violence of the wind; but we looked forward to its total cessation with dismay; well believing, that, in our shattered condition, we should inevitably perish in the tremendous swell which would ensue. But this very just apprehension seemed by no means likely to be soon verified. For five entire days and nights—during which our only subsistence was a small quantity of jaggeree, procured with great difficulty from the forecastle—the hulk flew at a rate defying computation, before rapidly succeeding flaws of wind, which, without equalling the first violence of the Simoon, were still more terrific than any tempest I had before encountered. Our course for the first four days was, with trifling variations, S. E. and by S.; and we must have run down the coast of New Holland.—On the fifth day the cold became extreme, although the wind had hauled round a point more to the northward.—The sun arose with a sickly yellow lustre, and clambered a very few degrees above the horizon— emitting no decisive light.—There were no clouds apparent, yet the wind was upon the increase, and blew with a fitful and unsteady fury. About noon, as nearly as we could guess, our attention was again arrested by the appearance of the sun. It gave out no light, properly so called, but a dull and sullen glow without reflection, as if all its rays were polarized. Just before sinking within the turgid sea, its central fires suddenly went out, as if hurriedly extinguished by some unaccountable power. It was a dim, silver-like rim, alone, as it rushed down the unfathomable ocean.

We waited in vain for the arrival of the sixth day— that day to me has not arrived—to the Swede, never did arrive. Thenceforward we were enshrouded in pitchy darkness, so that we could not have seen an object at twenty paces from the ship. Eternal night continued to envelop us, all unrelieved by the phosphoric sea-brilliancy to which we had been accustomed in the tropics. We observed too, that, although the tempest continued to rage with unabated violence, there was no longer to be discovered the usual appearance of surf, or foam, which had hitherto attended us. All around were horror, and thick gloom, and a black sweltering desert of ebony.—Superstitious terror crept by degrees into the spirit of the old Swede, and my own soul was wrapped up in silent wonder. We neglected all care of the ship, as worse than useless, and securing ourselves, as well as possible, to the stump of the mizen-mast, looked out bitterly into the world of ocean. We had no means of calculating time, nor could we form any guess of our situation. We were, however, well aware of having made farther to the southward than any previous navigators, and felt great amazement at not meeting with the usual impediments of ice. In the meantime every moment threatened to be our last—every mountainous billow hurried to overwhelm us. The swell surpassed anything I had imagined possible, and that we were not instantly buried is a miracle. My companion spoke of the lightness of our cargo, and reminded me of the excellent qualities of our ship; but I could not help feeling the utter hopelessness of hope itself, and prepared myself gloomily for that death which I thought nothing could defer beyond an hour, as, with every knot of way the ship made, the swelling of the black stupendous seas became more dismally appalling. At times we gasped for breath at an elevation beyond the albatross—at times became dizzy with the velocity of our descent into some watery hell, where the air grew stagnant, and no sound disturbed the slumbers of the kraken.

We were at the bottom of one of these abysses, when a quick scream from my companion broke fearfully upon the night. "See! see!" cried he, shrieking in my ears, "Almighty God! see! see!" As he spoke, I became aware of a dull, sullen glare of red light which streamed down the sides of the vast chasm where we lay, and threw a fitful brilliancy upon our deck. Casting my eyes upwards, I beheld a spectacle which froze the current of my blood. At a terrific height directly above us, and upon the very verge of the precipitous descent, hovered a gigantic ship of, perhaps, four thousand tons. Although upreared upon the summit of a wave more than a hundred times her own altitude, her apparent size still exceeded that of any ship of the line or East Indiaman in existence. Her huge hull was of a deep dingy black, unrelieved by any of the customary carvings of a ship. A single row of brass cannon protruded from her open ports, and dashed from their polished surfaces the fires of innumerable battle-lanterns, which swung to and fro about her rigging. But what mainly inspired us with horror and astonishment, was that she bore up under a press of sail in the very teeth of that supernatural sea, and of that ungovernable hurricane. When we first discovered her, her bows were alone to be seen, as she rose slowly from the dim and horrible gulf beyond her. For a moment of intense terror she paused upon the giddy pinnacle, as if in contemplation of her own sublimity, then trembled and tottered, and—came down.

At this instant, I know not what sudden self-possession came over my spirit. Staggering as far aft as I could, I awaited fearlessly the ruin that was to overwhelm. Our own vessel was at length ceasing from her struggles, and sinking with her head to the sea. The shock of the descending mass struck her, consequently, in that portion of her frame which was already under water, and the inevitable result was to hurl me, with irresistible violence, upon the rigging of the stranger.

As I fell, the ship hove in stays, and went about; and to the confusion ensuing I attributed my escape from the notice of the crew. With little difficulty I made my way unperceived to the main hatchway, which was partially open, and soon found an opportunity of secret ing myself in the hold. Why I did so I can hardly tell. An indefinite sense of awe, which at first sight of the navigators of the ship had taken hold of my mind, was perhaps the principle of my concealment. I was unwilling to trust myself with a race of people who had offered, to the cursory glance I had taken, so many points of vague novelty, doubt, and apprehension. I therefore thought proper to contrive a hiding-place in the hold. This I did by removing a small portion of the shifting-boards, in such a manner as to afford me a convenient retreat between the huge timbers of the ship.

I had scarcely completed my work, when a footstep in the hold forced me to make use of it. A man passed by my place of concealment with a feeble and unsteady gait. I could not see his face, but had an opportunity of observing his general appearance. There was about it an evidence of great age and infirmity. His knees tottered beneath a load of years, and his entire frame quivered under the burthen. He muttered to himself, in a low broken tone, some words of a language which I could not understand, and groped in a corner among a pile of singular-looking instruments, and decayed charts of navigation. His manner was a wild mixture of the peevishness of second childhood, and the solemn dignity of a God. He at length went on deck, and I saw him no more.

    *   *   *   *   *

A feeling, for which I have no name, has taken possession of my soul—a sensation which will admit of no analysis, to which the lessons of by-gone times are inadequate, and for which I fear futurity itself will offer me no key. To a mind constituted like my own, the latter consideration is an evil. I shall never—I know that I shall never—be satisfied with regard to the nature of my conceptions. Yet it is not wonderful that these conceptions are indefinite, since they have their origin in sources so utterly novel. A new sense—a new entity is added to my soul.

* * * * *

It is long since I first trod the deck of this terrible ship, and the rays of my destiny are, I think, gathering to a focus. Incomprehensible men! Wrapped up in meditations of a kind which I cannot divine, they pass me by unnoticed. Concealment is utter folly on my part, for the people *will not* see. It was but just now that I passed directly before the eyes of the mate—it was no long while ago that I ventured into the captain's own private cabin, and took thence the materials with which I write, and have written. I shall from time to time continue this journal. It is true that I may not find an opportunity of transmitting it to the world, but I will not fail to make the endeavour. At the last moment I will enclose the MS. in a bottle, and cast it within the sea.

* * * * *

An incident has occurred which has given me new room for meditation. Are such things the operation of ungoverned Chance? I had ventured upon deck and thrown myself down, without attracting any notice, among a pile of ratlin-stuff and old sails, in the bottom of the yawl. While musing upon the singularity of my fate, I unwittingly daubed with a tar-brush the edges of a neatly-folded studding-sail which lay near me on a barrel. The studding-sail is now bent upon the ship, and the thoughtless touches of the brush are spread out into the word DISCOVERY. * * *

I have made many observations lately upon the structure of the vessel. Although well armed, she is not, I think, a ship of war. Her rigging, build, and general equipment, all negative a supposition of this kind. What she *is not*, I can easily perceive—what she *is* I fear it is impossible to say. I know not how it is, but in scrutinizing her strange model and singular cast of spars, her huge size and overgrown suits of canvass, her severely simple bow and antiquated stern, there will occasionally flash across my mind a sensation of familiar things, and there is always mixed up with such indistinct shadows of recollection, an unaccountable memory of old foreign chronicles and ages long ago. * * *

I have been looking at the timbers of the ship. She is built of a material to which I am a stranger. There is a peculiar character about the wood which strikes me as rendering it unfit for the purpose to which it has been applied. I mean its extreme *porousness*, considered independently of the worm-eaten condition which is a consequence of navigation in these seas, and apart from the rottenness attendant upon age. It will appear perhaps an observation somewhat over-curious, but this wood would have every characteristic of Spanish oak, if Spanish oak were distended by any unnatural means.

In reading the above sentence a curious apothegm of an old weather-beaten Dutch navigator comes full upon my recollection. "It is as sure," he was wont to say, when any doubt was entertained of his veracity, "as sure as there is a sea where the ship itself will grow in bulk like the living body of the seaman." * * *

About an hour ago, I made bold to thrust myself among a group of the crew. They paid me no manner of attention, and, although I stood in the very midst of them all, seemed utterly unconscious of my presence. Like the one I had at first seen in the hold, they all bore about them the marks of a hoary old age. Their knees trembled with infirmity; their shoulders were bent

double with decrepitude; their shrivelled skins rattled in
the wind; their voices were low, tremulous and broken;
their eyes glistened with the rheum of years; and their
gray hairs streamed terribly in the tempest. Around
them, on every part of the deck, lay scattered mathematical instruments of the most quaint and obsolete
construction. ° ° °

I mentioned some time ago the bending of a studding-
sail. From that period the ship, being thrown dead off
the wind, has continued her terrific course due south,
with every rag of canvass packed upon her, from her
trucks to her lower studding-sail booms, and rolling
every moment her top-gallant yard-arms into the most
appalling hell of water which it can enter into the mind
of man to imagine. I have just left the deck, where I
find it impossible to maintain a footing, although the
crew seem to experience little inconvenience. It appears
to me a miracle of miracles that our enormous bulk is
not swallowed up at once and forever. We are surely
doomed to hover continually upon the brink of Eternity,
without taking a final plunge into the abyss. From bil-
lows a thousand times more stupendous than any I have
ever seen, we glide away with the facility of the arrowy
sea-gull; and the colossal waters rear their heads above
us like demons of the deep, but like demons confined to
simple threats and forbidden to destroy. I am led to attribute these frequent escapes to the only natural cause
which can account for such effect.—I must suppose the
ship to be within the influence of some strong current,
or impetuous under-tow. ° ° °

I have seen the captain face to face, and in his own
cabin—but, as I expected, he paid me no attention. Although in his appearance there is, to a casual observer,
nothing which might bespeak him more or less than man
—still a feeling of irrepressible reverence and awe

mingled with the sensation of wonder with which I regarded him. In stature he is nearly my own height; that
is, about five feet eight inches. He is of a well-knit and
compact frame of body, neither robust nor remarkably
otherwise. But it is the singularity of the expression
which reigns upon the face—it is the intense, the wonderful, the thrilling evidence of old age, so utter, so
extreme, which excites within my spirit a sense—a sentiment ineffable. His forehead, although little wrinkled,
seems to bear upon it the stamp of a myriad of years.—
His gray hairs are records of the past, and his grayer
eyes are Sybils of the future. The cabin floor was thickly
strewn with strange, iron-clasped folios, and mouldering
instruments of science, and obsolete long-forgotten
charts. His head was bowed down upon his hands, and
he pored, with a fiery unquiet eye, over a paper which I
took to be a commission, and which, at all events, bore
the signature of a monarch. He muttered to himself, as
did the first seaman whom I saw in the hold, some low
peevish syllables of a foreign tongue, and although the
speaker was close at my elbow, his voice seemed to
reach my ears from the distance of a mile. * * *

The ship and all in it are imbued with the spirit of
Eld. The crew glide to and fro like the ghosts of buried
centuries; their eyes have an eager and uneasy meaning;
and when their fingers fall athwart my path in the wild
glare of the battle-lanterns, I feel as I have never felt
before, although I have been all my life a dealer in an-
tiquities, and have imbibed the shadows of fallen columns at Balbec, and Tadmor, and Persepolis, until my
very soul has become a ruin. * * *

When I look around me I feel ashamed of my former
apprehensions. If I trembled at the blast which has
hitherto attended us, shall I not stand aghast at a warring of wind and ocean, to convey any idea of which the

words tornado and Simoon are trivial and ineffective?
All in the immediate vicinity of the ship is the blackness
of eternal night, and a chaos of foamless water; but,
about a league on either side of us, may be seen, indistinctly and at intervals, stupendous ramparts of ice,
towering away into the desolate sky, and looking like the
walls of the universe. * * *

As I imagined, the ship proves to be in a current; if
that appellation can properly be given to a tide which,
howling and shrieking by the white ice, thunders on to
the southward with a velocity like the headlong dashing
of a cataract. * * *

To conceive the horror of my sensations is, I presume,
utterly impossible; yet a curiosity to penetrate the mysteries of these awful regions, predominates even over my
despair, and will reconcile me to the most hideous aspect
of death. It is evident that we are hurrying onwards to
some exciting knowledge—some never-to-be-imparted
secret, whose attainment is destruction. Perhaps this
current leads us to the southern pole itself. It must be
confessed that a supposition apparently so wild has
every probability in its favor. * * *

The crew pace the deck with unquiet and tremulous
step; but there is upon their countenances an expression
more of the eagerness of hope than of the apathy of
despair.

In the meantime the wind is still in our poop, and, as
we carry a crowd of canvass, the ship is at times lifted
bodily from out the sea—Oh, horror upon horror! the
ice opens suddenly to the right, and to the left, and we
are whirling dizzily, in immense concentric circles,
round and round the borders of a gigantic amphitheatre,
the summit of whose walls is lost in the darkness and the
distance. But little time will be left me to ponder upon
my destiny—the circles rapidly grow small—we are

plunging madly within the grasp of the whirlpool—and amid a roaring, and bellowing, and thundering of ocean and of tempest, the ship is quivering, oh God! and—— going down.

Note.—*The "MS Found in a Bottle," was originally published in 1831 [1833], and it was not until many years afterwards that I became acquainted with the maps of Mercator, in which the ocean is represented as rushing, by four mouths, into the (northern) Polar Gulf, to be absorbed into the bowels of the earth; the Pole itself being represented by a black rock, towering to a prodigious height.* [E.A.P.]

A DESCENT
INTO THE MAELSTRÖM
(*Graham's Magazine*, May, 1841.)

The ways of God in Nature, as in Providence, are not as *our* ways; nor are the models that we frame any way commensurate to the vastness, profundity, and unsearchableness of His works, *which have a depth in them greater than the well of Democritus.*

—Joseph Glanville

WE HAD now reached the summit of the loftiest crag. For some minutes the old man seemed too much exhausted to speak.

"Not long ago," said he at length, "and I could have guided you on this route as well as the youngest of my sons; but, about three years past, there happened to me an event such as never happened before to mortal man —or at least such as no man ever survived to tell of— and the six hours of deadly terror which I then endured have broken me up body and soul. You suppose me a *very* old man—but I am not. It took less than a single day to change these hairs from a jetty black to white, to weaken my limbs, and to unstring my nerves, so that I tremble at the least exertion, and am frightened at a shadow. Do you know I can scarcely look over this little cliff without getting giddy?"

The "little cliff," upon whose edge he had so carelessly thrown himself down to rest that the weightier portion of his body hung over it, while he was only kept from falling by the tenure of his elbow on its extreme and slippery edge—this "little cliff" arose, a sheer unobstructed precipice of black shining rock, some fifteen or sixteen hundred feet from the world of crags beneath us. Nothing would have tempted me to within half a dozen yards of its brink. In truth so deeply was I excited by the perilous position of my companion, that I fell at full length upon the ground, clung to the shrubs around me, and dared not even glance upward at the sky—while I struggled in vain to divest myself of the idea that the very foundations of the mountain were in danger from the fury of the winds. It was long before I could reason myself into sufficient courage to sit up and look out into the distance.

"You must get over these fancies," said the guide, "for I have brought you here that you might have the best possible view of the scene of that event I mentioned—and to tell you the whole story with the spot just under your eye."

"We are now," he continued, in that particularizing manner which distinguished him—"we are now close upon the Norwegian coast—in the sixty-eighth degree of latitude—in the great province of Nordland—and in the dreary district of Lofoden. The mountain upon whose top we sit is Helseggen, the Cloudy. Now raise yourself up a little higher—hold on to the grass if you feel giddy—so—and look out, beyond the belt of vapor beneath us, into the sea."

I looked dizzily, and beheld a wide expanse of ocean, whose waters wore so inky a hue as to bring at once to my mind the Nubian geographer's account of the *Mare Tenebrarum*. A panorama more deplorably desolate no human imagination can conceive. To the right and left, as far as the eye could reach, there lay outstretched, like ramparts of the world, lines of horridly black and beetling cliff, whose character of gloom was but the more forcibly illustrated by the surf which reared high up against it its white and ghastly crest, howling and shrieking for ever. Just opposite the promontory upon whose apex we were placed, and at a distance of some five or six miles out at sea, there was visible a small, bleak-looking island; or, more properly, its position was discernible through the wilderness of surge in which it was enveloped. About two miles nearer the land, arose another of smaller size, hideously craggy and barren, and encompassed at various intervals by a cluster of dark rocks.

The appearance of the ocean, in the space between the more distant island and the shore, had something very unusual about it. Although, at the time, so strong a gale was blowing landward that a brig in the remote offing lay to under a double-reefed trysail, and constantly plunged her whole hull out of sight, still there was here nothing like a regular swell, but only a short, quick, angry cross dashing of water in every direction—as well in the teeth of the wind as otherwise. Of foam there was little except in the immediate vicinity of the rocks.

"The island in the distance," resumed the old man, "is called by the Norwegians Vurrgh. The one midway is Moskoe. That a mile to the northward is Ambaaren. Yonder are Iflesen, Hoeyholm, Kieldholm, Suarven, and Buckholm. Farther off—between Moskoe and Vurrgh—

are Otterholm, Flimen, Sandflesen, and Skarholm. These are the true names of the places—but why it has been thought necessary to name them at all, is more than either you or I can understand. Do you hear any thing? Do you see any change in the water?"

We had now been about ten minutes upon the top of Helseggen, to which we had ascended from the interior of Lofoden, so that we had caught no glimpse of the sea until it had burst upon us from the summit. As the old man spoke, I became aware of a loud and gradually increasing sound, like the moaning of a vast herd of buffaloes upon an American prairie; and at the same moment I perceived that what seamen term the *chopping* character of the ocean beneath us, was rapidly changing into a current which set to the eastward. Even while I gazed, this current acquired a monstrous velocity. Each moment added to its speed—to its headlong impetuosity. In five minutes the whole sea, as far as Vurrgh, was lashed into ungovernable fury; but it was between Moskoe and the coast that the main uproar held its sway. Here the vast bed of the waters, seamed and scarred into a thousand conflicting channels, burst suddenly into phrensied convulsion—heaving, boiling, hissing—gyrating in gigantic and innumerable vortices, and all whirling and plunging on to the eastward with a rapidity which water never elsewhere assumes except in precipitous descents.

In a few minutes more, there came over the scene another radical alteration. The general surface grew somewhat more smooth, and the whirlpools, one by one, disappeared, while prodigious streaks of foam became apparent where none had been seen before. These streaks, at length, spreading out to a great distance, and entering into combination, took unto themselves the gyratory motion of the subsided vortices, and seemed to form the germ of another more vast. Suddenly—very suddenly—this assumed a distinct and definite existence, in a circle of more than half a mile in diameter. The edge of the whirl was represented by a broad belt of gleaming spray; but no particle of this slipped into the mouth of the terrific funnel, whose interior, as far as the eye could fathom it, was a smooth, shining, and jet-black wall of water, inclined to the horizon at an angle of some forty-five degrees, speeding dizzily round and round with a swaying and sweltering motion, and sending forth to the winds an appalling voice, half shriek, half roar, such as not even the mighty cataract of Niagara ever lifts up in its agony to Heaven.

The mountain trembled to its very base, and the rock rocked. I threw myself upon my face, and clung to the scant herbage in an excess of nervous agitation.

"This," said I at length, to the old man—"this *can* be nothing else than the great whirlpool of the Maelström."

"So it is sometimes termed," said he. "We Norwegians call it the Moskoe-ström, from the island of Moskoe in the midway."

The ordinary accounts of this vortex had by no means prepared me for what I saw. That of Jonas Ramus, which is perhaps the most circumstantial of any, cannot impart the faintest conception either of the magnificence, or of the horror of the scene—or of the wild bewildering sense of *the novel* which confounds the beholder. I am not sure from what point of view the writer in question surveyed it, nor at what time; but it could neither have been from the summit of Helseggen, nor during a storm. There are some passages of his description, nevertheless, which may be quoted for their details, although their effect is exceedingly feeble in conveying an impression of the spectacle.

"Between Lofoden and Moskoe," he says, "the depth of the water is between thirty-six and forty fathoms; but on the other side, toward Ver (Vurrgh) this depth decreases so as not to afford a convenient passage for a vessel, without the risk of splitting on the rocks, which happens even in the calmest weather. When it is flood, the stream runs up the country between Lofoden and Moskoe with a boisterous rapidity; but the roar of its impetuous ebb to the sea is scarce equalled by the loudest and most dreadful cataracts; the noise being heard several leagues off, and the vortices or pits are of such an extent and depth, that if a ship comes within its attraction, it is inevitably absorbed and carried down to the bottom, and there beat to pieces against the rocks; and when the water relaxes, the fragments thereof are thrown up again. But these intervals of tranquillity are only at the turn of the ebb and flood, and in calm weather, and last but a quarter of an hour, its violence gradually returning. When the stream is most boisterous, and its fury heightened by a storm, it is dangerous to come within a Norway mile of it. Boats, yachts, and ships have been carried away by not guarding against it before they were within its reach. It likewise happens frequently, that whales come too near the stream, and are overpowered by its violence; and then it is impossible to describe their howlings and bellowings in their fruitless struggles to disengage themselves. A bear once, attempting to swim from Lofoden to Moskoe, was caught by the stream and borne down, while he roared terribly, so as to be heard on shore. Large stocks of firs and pine trees, after being absorbed by the current, rise again broken and torn to such a degree as if bristles grew upon them. This plainly shows the bottom to consist of craggy rocks, among which they are whirled to and fro. This stream is regulated by the flux and reflux of the sea—it being constantly high and low water every six hours. In the year 1645, early in the morning of Sexagesima Sunday, it raged with such noise and impetuosity that the very stones of the houses on the coast fell to the ground."

In regard to the depth of the water, I could not see how this could have been ascertained at all in the immediate vicinity of the vortex. The "forty fathoms" must have reference only to portions of the channel close upon the shore either of Moskoe or Lofoden. The depth in the centre of the Moskoe-ström must be immeasurably greater; and no better proof of this fact is necessary than can be obtained from even the sidelong glance into the abyss of the whirl which may be had from the highest crag of Helseggen. Looking down from this pinnacle upon the howling Phlegethon below, I could not help smiling at the simplicity with which the honest Jonas Ramus records, as a matter difficult of belief, the anecdotes of the whales and the bears; for it appeared to me, in fact, a self-evident thing, that the largest ships of the line in existence, coming within the influence of that deadly attraction, could resist it as little as a feather the hurricane, and must disappear bodily and at once.

The attempts to account for the phenomenon—some of which, I remember, seemed to me sufficiently plausible in perusal—now wore a very different and unsatisfactory aspect. The idea generally received is that this, as well as three smaller vortices among the Feroe islands, "have no other cause than the collision of waves rising and falling, at flux and reflux, against a ridge of rocks and shelves, which confines the water so that it precipitates itself like a cataract; and thus the higher the flood rises, the deeper must the fall be, and the natural result of all is a whirlpool or vortex, the prodigious suction of which is sufficiently known by lesser experiments."—These are the words of the *Encyclopædia Britannica*. Kircher and others imagine that in the centre of the channel of the Maelström is an abyss penetrating the globe, and issuing in some very remote part —the Gulf of Bothnia being somewhat decidedly named in one instance. This opinion, idle in itself, was the one to which, as I gazed, my imagination most readily assented; and, mentioning it to the guide, I was rather surprised to hear him say that, although it was the view almost universally entertained of the subject by the Norwegians, it nevertheless was not his own. As to the former notion he confessed his inability to comprehend it; and here I agreed with him—for, however conclusive on paper, it becomes altogether unintelligible, and even absurd, amid the thunder of the abyss.

"You have had a good look at the whirl now," said the old man, "and if you will creep round this crag, so as to get in its lee, and deaden the roar of the water, I will tell you a story that will convince you I ought to know something of the Moskoe-ström."

I placed myself as desired, and he proceeded.

"Myself and my two brothers once owned a schooner-rigged smack of about seventy tons burthen, with which we were in the habit of fishing among the islands beyond Moskoe, nearly to Vurrgh. In all violent eddies at sea there is good fishing, at proper opportunities, if one has only the courage to attempt it; but among the whole of the Lofoden coastmen, we three were the only ones who made a regular business of going out to the islands, as I tell you. The usual grounds are a great way lower down to the southward. There fish can be got at all hours, without much risk, and therefore these places are preferred. The choice spots over here among the rocks, however, not only yield the finest variety, but in far greater abundance; so that we often got in a single day, what the more timid of the craft could not scrape together in a week. In fact, we made it a matter of desperate speculation—the risk of life standing instead of labor, and courage answering for capital.

"We kept the smack in a cove about five miles higher up the coast than this; and it was our practice, in fine weather, to take advantage of the fifteen minutes' slack to push across the main channel of the Moskoe-ström, far above the pool, and then drop down upon anchorage somewhere near Otterholm, or Sandflesen, where the eddies are not so violent as elsewhere. Here we used to remain until nearly time for slack-water again, when we weighed and made for home. We never set out upon this expedition without a steady side wind for going and coming—one that we felt sure would not fail us before our return—and we seldom made a miscalculation upon this point. Twice, during six years, we were forced to stay all night at anchor on account of a dead calm, which is a rare thing indeed just about here; and once we had to remain on the grounds nearly a week, starving to death, owing to a gale which blew up shortly after our arrival, and made the channel too boisterous to be thought of. Upon this occasion we should have been driven out to sea in spite of everything, (for the whirlpools threw us round and round so violently, that, at length, we fouled our anchor and dragged it) if it had not been that we drifted into one of the innumerable cross currents—here to-day and gone to-morrow—which drove us under the lee of Flimen, where, by good luck, we brought up.

"I could not tell you the twentieth part of the difficulties we encountered 'on the ground'—it is a bad spot to be in, even in good weather—but we made shift always to run the gauntlet of the Moskoe-ström itself without accident; although at times my heart has been in my mouth when we happened to be a minute or so behind or before the slack. The wind sometimes was not as strong as we thought it at starting, and then we made rather less way than we could wish, while the current rendered the smack unmanageable. My eldest brother had a son eighteen years old, and I had two stout boys of my own. These would have been of great assistance at such times, in using the sweeps, as well as afterward in fishing—but, somehow, although we ran the risk ourselves, we had not the heart to let the young ones get into the danger—for, after all said and done, it *was* a horrible danger, and that is the truth.

"It is now within a few days of three years since what I am going to tell you occurred. It was on the tenth of July, 18—, a day which the people of this part of the world will never forget—for it was one in which blew the most terrible hurricane that ever came out of the heavens. And yet all the morning, and indeed until late in the afternoon, there was a gentle and steady breeze from the south-west, while the sun shone brightly, so that the oldest seaman among us could not have foreseen what was to follow.

"The three of us—my two brothers and myself—had crossed over to the islands about two o'clock P. M., and soon nearly loaded the smack with fine fish, which, we all remarked, were more plenty that day than we had ever known them. It was just seven, *by my watch,* when we weighed and started for home, so as to make the worst of the Ström at slack water, which we knew would be at eight.

"We set out with a fresh wind on our starboard quarter, and for some time spanked along at a great rate, never dreaming of danger, for indeed we saw not the slightest reason to apprehend it. All at once we were taken aback by a breeze from over Helseggen.

This was most unusual—something that had never happened to us before—and I began to feel a little uneasy, without exactly knowing why. We put the boat on the wind, but could make no headway at all for the eddies, and I was upon the point of proposing to return to the anchorage, when, looking astern, we saw the whole horizon covered with a singular copper-colored cloud that rose with the most amazing velocity.

"In the meantime the breeze that had headed us off fell away, and we were dead becalmed, drifting about in every direction. This state of things, however, did not last long enough to give us time to think about it. In less than a minute the storm was upon us—in less than two the sky was entirely overcast—and what with this and the driving spray, it became suddenly so dark that we could not see each other in the smack.

"Such a hurricane as then blew it is folly to attempt describing. The oldest seaman in Norway never experienced any thing like it. We had let our sails go by the run before it cleverly took us; but, at the first puff, both our masts went by the board as if they had been sawed off—the mainmast taking with it my youngest brother, who had lashed himself to it for safety.

"Our boat was the lightest feather of a thing that ever sat upon water. It had a complete flush deck, with only a small hatch near the bow, and this hatch it had always been our custom to batten down when about to cross the Ström, by way of precaution against the chopping seas. But for this circumstance we should have foundered at once—for we lay entirely buried for some moments. How my elder brother escaped destruction I cannot say, for I never had an opportunity of ascertaining. For my part, as soon as I had let the foresail run, I threw myself flat on deck, with my feet against the narrow gunwale of the bow, and with my hands grasping a ring-bolt near the foot of the foremast. It was mere instinct that prompted me to do this—which was undoubtedly the very best thing I could have done— for I was too much flurried to think.

"For some moments we were completely deluged, as I say, and all this time I held my breath, and clung to the bolt. When I could stand it no longer I raised my-self upon my knees, still keeping hold with my hands, and thus got my head clear. Presently our little boat gave herself a shake, just as a dog does in coming out of the water, and thus rid herself, in some measure, of the seas. I was now trying to get the better of the stupor that had come over me, and to collect my senses so as to see what was to be done, when I felt somebody grasp my arm. It was my elder brother, and my heart leaped for joy, for I had made sure that he was overboard— but the next moment all this joy was turned into horror —for he put his mouth close to my ear, and screamed out the word '*Moskoe-ström!*'

"No one ever will know what my feelings were at that moment. I shook from head to foot as if I had had the most violent fit of the ague. I knew what he meant by that one word well enough—I knew what he wished to make me understand. With the wind that now drove us on, we were bound for the whirl of the Ström, and nothing could save us!

"You perceive that in crossing the Ström *channel,* we always went a long way up above the whirl, even in the calmest weather, and then had to wait and watch carefully for the slack—but now we were driving right upon the pool itself, and in such a hurricane as this! 'To be sure,' I thought, 'we shall get there just about the slack—there is some little hope in that'—but in the next moment I cursed myself for being so great a fool as to dream of hope at all. I knew very well that we were doomed, had we been ten times a ninety-gun ship.

"By this time the first fury of the tempest had spent itself, or perhaps we did not feel it so much, as we scudded before it, but at all events the seas, which at first had been kept down by the wind, and lay flat and frothing, now got up into absolute mountains. A singular change, too, had come over the heavens. Around in every direction it was still as black as pitch, but nearly overhead there burst out, all at once, a circular rift of clear sky—as clear as I ever saw—and of a deep bright blue—and through it there blazed forth the full moon with a lustre that I never before knew her to wear. She lit up every thing about us with the greatest distinctness —but, oh God, what a scene it was to light up!

"I now made one or two attempts to speak to my brother—but in some manner which I could not understand, the din had so increased that I could not make him hear a single word, although I screamed at the top of my voice in his ear. Presently he shook his head, looking as pale as death, and held up one of his fingers, as if to say 'listen!'

"At first I could not make out what he meant—but soon a hideous thought flashed upon me. I dragged my watch from its fob. It was not going. I glanced at its face by the moonlight, and then burst into tears as I flung it far away into the ocean. *It had run down at seven o'clock! We were behind the time of the slack, and the whirl of the Ström was in full fury!*

"When a boat is well built, properly trimmed, and not deep laden, the waves in a strong gale, when she is going large, seem always to slip from beneath her— which appears very strange to a landsman—and this is what is called *riding*, in sea phrase.

"Well, so far we had ridden the swells very cleverly; but presently a gigantic sea happened to take us right under the counter, and bore us with it as it rose—up —up—as if into the sky. I would not have believed that any wave could rise so high. And then down we came with a sweep, a slide, and a plunge, that made me feel sick and dizzy, as if I was falling from some lofty mountain-top in a dream. But while we were up I had thrown a quick glance around—and that one glance was all sufficient. I saw our exact position in an instant. The Moskoe-ström whirlpool was about a quarter of a mile dead ahead—but no more like the every-day Moskoe-ström, than the whirl as you now see it, is like a mill-race. If I had not known where we were, and what we had to expect, I should not have recognised the place at all. As it was, I involuntarily closed my eyes in horror. The lids clenched themselves together as if in a spasm.

"It could not have been more than two minutes afterwards until we suddenly felt the waves subside, and were enveloped in foam. The boat made a sharp half turn to larboard, and then shot off in its new direction like a thunderbolt. At the same moment the roaring noise of the water was completely drowned in a kind of shrill shriek—such a sound as you might imagine given out by the water-pipes of many thousand steam-vessels, letting off their steam all together. We were now in the belt of surf that always surrounds the whirl; and I thought, of course, that another moment would plunge us into the abyss—down which we could only see indistinctly on account of the amazing velocity with which we were borne along. The boat did not seem to sink into the water at all, but to skim like an air-bubble upon the surface of the surge. Her starboard side was next the whirl, and on the larboard arose the world of ocean we had left. It stood like a huge writhing wall between us and the horizon.

"It may appear strange, but now, when we were in the very jaws of the gulf, I felt more composed than when we were only approaching it. Having made up my mind to hope no more, I got rid of a great deal of that terror which unmanned me at first. I suppose it was despair that strung my nerves.

"It may look like boasting—but what I tell you is truth—I began to reflect how magnificent a thing it was to die in such a manner, and how foolish it was in me to think of so paltry a consideration as my own individual life, in view of so wonderful a manifestation of God's power. I do believe that I blushed with shame when this idea crossed my mind. After a little while I became possessed with the keenest curiosity about the whirl itself. I positively felt a *wish* to explore its depths, even at the sacrifice I was going to make; and my principal grief was that I should never be able to tell my old companions on shore about the mysteries I should see. These, no doubt, were singular fancies to occupy a man's mind in such extremity—and I have often thought since, that the revolutions of the boat around the pool might have rendered me a little light-headed.

"There was another circumstance which tended to restore my self-possession; and this was the cessation of the wind, which could not reach us in our present situation—for, as you saw yourself, the belt of surf is considerably lower than the general bed of the ocean, and this latter now towered above us, a high, black, mountainous ridge. If you have never been at sea in a heavy gale, you can form no idea of the confusion of mind occasioned by the wind and spray together. They blind, deafen and strangle you, and take away all power of action or reflection. But we were now, in a great measure, rid of these annoyances—just as death-condemned felons in prison are allowed petty indulgences, forbidden them while their doom is yet uncertain.

"How often we made the circuit of the belt it is impossible to say. We careered round and round for perhaps an hour, flying rather than floating, getting gradually more and more into the middle of the surge, and then nearer and nearer to its horrible inner edge. All this time I had never let go of the ring-bolt. My brother was at the stern, holding on to a large empty water-cask which had been securely lashed under the coop of the counter, and was the only thing on deck that had not been swept overboard when the gale first took us. As we approached the brink of the pit he let go his hold upon this, and made for the ring, from which, in the agony of his terror, he endeavored to force my hands, as it was not large enough to afford us both a secure grasp. I never felt deeper grief than when I saw him attempt this act—although I knew he was a madman when he did it—a raving maniac through sheer fright. I did not care, however, to contest the point with him. I thought it could make no difference whether either of us held on at all; so I let him have the bolt, and went astern to the cask. This there was no great difficulty in doing; for the smack flew round steadily enough, and upon an even keel—only swaying to and fro, with the immense sweeps and swelters of the whirl. Scarcely had I secured myself in my new position, when we gave a wild lurch to starboard, and rushed headlong into the abyss. I muttered a hurried prayer to God, and thought all was over.

"As I felt the sickening sweep of the descent, I had instinctively tightened my hold upon the barrel, and closed my eyes. For some seconds I dared not open them—while I expected instant destruction, and wondered that I was not already in my death-struggles with the water. But moment after moment elapsed. I still lived. The sense of falling had ceased; and the motion of the vessel seemed much as it had been before while in the belt of foam, with the exception that she now lay more along. I took courage and looked once again upon the scene.

"Never shall I forget the sensations of awe, horror, and admiration with which I gazed about me. The boat appeared to be hanging, as if by magic, midway down, upon the interior surface of a funnel vast in circumference, prodigious in depth, and whose perfectly smooth sides might have been mistaken for ebony, but for the bewildering rapidity with which they spun around, and for the gleaming and ghastly radiance they shot forth, as the rays of the full moon, from that circular rift amid the clouds which I have already described, streamed in a flood of golden glory along the black walls, and far away down into the inmost recesses of the abyss.

"At first I was too much confused to observe anything accurately. The general burst of terrific grandeur was all that I beheld. When I recovered myself a little, however, my gaze fell instinctively downward. In this direction I was able to obtain an unobstructed view, from the manner in which the smack hung on the inclined surface of the pool. She was quite upon an even keel—that is to say, her deck lay in a plane parallel with that of the water—but this latter sloped at an angle of more than forty-five degrees, so that we seemed to be lying upon our beam-ends. I could not help observing, nevertheless, that I had scarcely more difficulty in maintaining my hold and footing in this situation, than if we had been upon a dead level; and this, I suppose, was owing to the speed at which we revolved.

"The rays of the moon seemed to search the very bottom of the profound gulf; but still I could make out nothing distinctly, on account of a thick mist in which, everything there was enveloped, and over which there hung a magnificent rainbow, like that narrow and tottering bridge which Mussulmen say is the only pathway between Time and Eternity. This mist, or spray, was no doubt occasioned by the clashing of the great walls of the funnel, as they all met together at the bottom—but the yell that went up to the Heavens from out of that mist, I dare not attempt to describe.

"Our first slide into the abyss itself, from the belt of foam above, had carried us to a great distance down the slope; but our farther descent was by no means proportionate. Round and round we swept—not with any uniform movement—but in dizzying swings and jerks, that sent us sometimes only a few hundred feet—sometimes nearly the complete circuit of the whirl. Our progress downward, at each revolution, was slow, but very perceptible.

"Looking about me upon the wide waste of liquid ebony on which we were thus borne, I perceived that our boat was not the only object in the embrace of the whirl. Both above and below us were visible fragments of vessels, large masses of building timber and trunks of trees, with many smaller articles, such as pieces of house furniture, broken boxes, barrels and staves. I have already described the unnatural curiosity which had taken the place of my original terrors. It appeared to grow upon me as I drew nearer and nearer to my dreadful doom. I now began to watch, with a strange interest, the numerous things that floated in our company. I *must* have been delirious—for I even sought *amusement* in speculating upon the relative velocities of their several descents toward the foam below. 'This fir tree,' I found myself at one time saying, 'will certainly be the next thing that takes the awful plunge and disappears,'—and then I was disappointed to find that the wreck of a Dutch merchant ship overtook it and went down before. At length, after making several guesses of this nature, and being deceived in all—this fact—the fact of my invariable miscalculation, set me upon a train of reflection that made my limbs again tremble, and my heart beat heavily once more.

"It was not a new terror that thus affected me, but the dawn of a more exciting *hope*. This hope arose partly from memory, and partly from present observation. I called to mind the great variety of buoyant matter that strewed the coast of Lofoden, having been absorbed and then thrown forth by the Moskoe-ström. By far the greater number of the articles were shattered in the most extraordinary way—so chafed and roughened as to have the appearance of being stuck full of splinters—but then I distinctly recollected that there were *some* of them which were not disfigured at all. Now I could not account for this difference except by supposing that the roughened fragments were the only ones which had been *completely absorbed*—that the others had entered the whirl at so late a period of the tide, or, from some reason, had descended so slowly after entering, that they did not reach the bottom before the turn of the flood came, or of the ebb, as the case might be. I conceived it possible, in either instance, that they might thus be whirled up again to the level of the ocean, without undergoing the fate of those which had been drawn in more early or absorbed more rapidly. I made, also, three important observations. The first was, that as a general rule, the larger the bodies were, the more rapid their descent;—the second, that, between two masses of equal extent, the one spherical, and the other *of any other shape*, the superiority in speed of descent was with the sphere;—the third, that, between two masses of equal size, the one cylindrical, and the other of any other shape, the cylinder was absorbed the more slowly.

Since my escape, I have had several conversations on this subject with an old school-master of the district; and it was from him that I learned the use of the words 'cylinder' and 'sphere.' He explained to me—although I have forgotten the explanation—how what I observed was, in fact, the natural consequence of the forms of the floating fragments—and showed me how it happened that a cylinder, swimming in a vortex, offered more resistance to its suction, and was drawn in with greater difficulty than an equally bulky body, of any form whatever.[1]

"There was one startling circumstance which went a great way in enforcing these observations, and rendering me anxious to turn them to account, and this was that, at every revolution, we passed something like a barrel, or else the broken yard or the mast of a vessel, while many of these things, which had been on our level when I first opened my eyes upon the wonders of the whirlpool, were now high up above us, and seemed to have moved but little from their original station.

"I no longer hesitated what to do. I resolved to lash myself securely to the water cask upon which I now held, to cut it loose from the counter, and to throw myself with it into the water. I attracted my brother's attention by signs, pointed to the floating barrels that came near us, and did everything in my power to make him understand what I was about to do. I thought at length that he comprehended my design—but, whether this was the case or not, he shook his head despairingly, and refused to move from his station by the ring-bolt. It was impossible to force him; the emergency ad-

---

[1] See Archimedes, "De Incidentibus in Fluido."—lib. 2.

mitted no delay; and so, with a bitter struggle, I resigned him to his fate, fastened myself to the cask by means of the lashings which secured it to the counter, and precipitated myself with it into the sea, without another moment's hesitation.

"The result was precisely what I had hoped it might be. As it is myself who now tell you this tale—as you see that I *did* escape—and as you are already in possession of the mode in which this escape was effected, and must therefore anticipate all that I have farther to say—I will bring my story quickly to conclusion. It might have been an hour, or thereabout, after my quitting the smack, when, having descended to a vast distance beneath me, it made three or four wild gyrations in rapid succession, and, bearing my loved brother with it, plunged headlong, at once and forever, into the chaos of foam below. The barrel to which I was attached sunk very little farther than half the distance between the bottom of the gulf and the spot at which I leaped overboard, before a great change took place in the character of the whirlpool. The slope of the sides of the vast funnel became momently less and less steep. The gyrations of the whirl grew, gradually, less and less violent. By degrees, the froth and the rainbow disappeared, and the bottom of the gulf seemed slowly to uprise. The sky was clear, the winds had gone down, and the full moon was setting radiantly in the west, when I found myself on the surface of the ocean, in full view of the shores of Lofoden, and above the spot where the pool of the Moskoe-ström *had been*. It was the hour of the slack—but the sea still heaved in mountainous waves from the effects of the hurricane. I was borne violently into the channel of the Ström, and in a few minutes, was hurried down the coast into the 'grounds' of the fishermen. A boat picked me up—exhausted from fatigue—and (now that the danger was removed) speechless from the memory of its horror. Those who drew me on board were my old mates and daily companions—but they knew me no more than they would have known a traveller from the spirit-land. My hair, which had been raven-black the day before, was as white as you see it now. They say too that the whole expression of my countenance had changed. I told them my story—they did not believe it. I now tell it to *you*— and I can scarcely expect you to put more faith in it than did the merry fishermen of Lofoden.

THE PIT
AND THE PENDULUM
(*The Gift*, 1843.)

Impia tortorum longos hic turba furores
Sanguinis innocui, non satiata, aluit.
Sospite nunc patriâ, fracto nunc funeris antro,
Mors ubi dira fuit vita salusque patent.
> —QUATRAIN COMPOSED FOR THE GATES
> OF A MARKET TO BE ERECTED UPON
> THE SITE OF THE JACOBIN CLUB
> HOUSE AT PARIS.

I WAS sick—sick unto death with that long agony; and when they at length unbound me, and I was permitted to sit, I felt that my senses were leaving me. The sentence—the dread sentence of death—was the last of distinct accentuation which reached my ears. After that, the sound of the inquisitorial voices seemed merged in one dreamy indeterminate hum. It conveyed to my soul the idea of *revolution*—perhaps from its association in fancy with the burr of a mill-wheel. This only for a brief period; for presently I heard no more. Yet, for a while, I saw; but with how terrible an exaggeration! I saw the lips of the black-robed judges. They appeared to me white—whiter than the sheet upon which I trace these words—and thin even to grotesqueness; thin with the intensity of their expression of firmness—of immoveable resolution—of stern contempt of human torture. I saw that the decrees of what to me was Fate, were still issuing from those lips. I saw them writhe with a deadly locution. I saw them fashion the syllables of my name; and I shuddered because no sound succeeded. I saw, too, for a few moments of delirious horror, the soft and nearly imperceptible waving of the sable draperies which enwrapped the walls of the apartment. And then my vision fell upon the seven tall candles upon the table. At first they wore the aspect of charity, and seemed white slender angels who would save me; but then, all at once, there came a most deadly nausea over my spirit, and I felt every fibre in my frame thrill as if I had touched the wire of a galvanic battery, while the angel forms became meaningless spectres, with heads of flame, and I saw that from them there would be no help. And then there stole into my fancy, like a rich musical note, the thought of what sweet rest there must be in the grave. The thought came gently and stealthily, and it seemed long before it attained full appreciation; but just as my spirit came at length properly to feel and entertain it, the figures of the judges vanished, as if magically, from before me; the tall candles sank into nothingness; their flames went out utterly; the blackness of darkness supervened; all sensations appeared swallowed up in a mad rushing descent as of the soul into Hades. Then silence, and stillness, and night were the universe.

I had swooned; but still will not say that all of consciousness was lost. What of it there remained I will not attempt to define, or even to describe; yet all was not lost. In the deepest slumber—no! In delirium—no! In a swoon—no! In death—no! even in the grave all *is not* lost. Else there is no immortality for man. Arousing from the most profound of slumbers, we break the gossamer web of *some* dream. Yet in a second afterward, (so frail may that web have been) we remember not that we have dreamed. In the return to life from the swoon there are two stages; first, that of the sense of mental or spiritual; secondly, that of the sense of physical, existence. It seems probable that if, upon reaching the second stage, we could recall the impressions of the first, we should find these impressions eloquent in memories of the gulf beyond. And that gulf is—what? How at least shall we distinguish its shadows from those of the tomb? But if the impressions of what I have termed the first stage, are not, at will, recalled, yet, after long interval, do they not come unbidden, while we marvel whence they come? He who has never swooned, is not he who finds strange palaces and wildly familiar faces in coals that glow; is not he who beholds floating in mid-air the sad visions that the many may not view; is not he who ponders over the perfume of some novel flower—is not he whose brain grows bewildered with the meaning of some musical cadence which has never before arrested his attention.

Amid frequent and thoughtful endeavors to remember; amid earnest struggles to regather some token of the state of seeming nothingness into which my soul had lapsed, there have been moments when I have dreamed of success; there have been brief, very brief periods when I have conjured up remembrances which the lucid reason of a later epoch assures me could have had reference only to that condition of seeming unconsciousness. These shadows of memory tell, indistinctly, of tall figures that lifted and bore me in silence down—down —still down—till a hideous dizziness oppressed me at the mere idea of the interminableness of the descent. They tell also of a vague horror at my heart, on account of that heart's unnatural stillness. Then comes a sense of sudden motionlessness throughout all things; as if those who bore me (a ghastly train!) had outrun, in their descent, the limits of the limitless, and paused from the wearisomeness of their toil. After this I call to mind flatness and dampness; and then all is *madness*—the madness of a memory which busies itself among forbidden things.

Very suddenly there came back to my soul motion and sound—the tumultuous motion of the heart, and, in my ears, the sound of its beating. Then a pause in which all is blank. Then again sound, and motion, and touch—a tingling sensation pervading my frame. Then the mere consciousness of existence, without thought— a condition which lasted long. Then, very suddenly, *thought,* and shuddering terror, and earnest endeavor to comprehend my true state. Then a strong desire to lapse into insensibility. Then a rushing revival of soul and a successful effort to move. And now a full memory of the trial, of the judges, of the sable draperies, of the sentence, of the sickness, of the swoon. Then entire forgetfulness of all that followed; of all that a later day and much earnestness of endeavor have enabled me vaguely to recall.

So far, I had not opened my eyes. I felt that I lay upon my back, unbound. I reached out my hand, and it fell heavily upon something damp and hard. There I suffered it to remain for many minutes, while I strove to imagine where and *what* I could be. I longed, yet dared not to employ my vision. I dreaded the first glance at objects around me. It was not that I feared to look upon things horrible, but that I grew aghast lest there should be *nothing* to see. At length, with a wild desperation at heart, I quickly unclosed my eyes. My worst thoughts, then, were confirmed. The blackness of eternal night encompassed me. I struggled for breath. The intensity of the darkness seemed to oppress and stifle me. The atmosphere was intolerably close. I still lay quietly, and made effort to exercise my reason. I brought to mind the inquisitorial proceedings, and attempted from that point to deduce my real condition. The sentence had passed; and it appeared to me that a very long interval of time had since elapsed. Yet not for a moment did I suppose myself actually dead. Such a supposition, notwithstanding what we read in fiction, is altogether inconsistent with real existence;—but where and in what state was I? The condemned to death, I knew, perished usually at the *autos-da-fé*, and one of these had been held on the very night of the day of my trial. Had I been remanded to my dungeon, to await the next sacrifice, which would not take place for many months? This I at once saw could not be. Victims had been in immediate demand. Moreover, my dungeon, as well as all the condemned cells at Toledo, had stone floors, and light was not altogether excluded.

A fearful idea now suddenly drove the blood in torrents upon my heart, and for a brief period, I once more relapsed into insensibility. Upon recovering, I at once started to my feet, trembling convulsively in every fibre. I thrust my arms wildly above and around me in all directions. I felt nothing; yet dreaded to move a step, lest I should be impeded by the walls of a *tomb*. Perspiration burst from every pore, and stood in cold big beads upon my forehead. The agony of suspense grew at length intolerable, and I cautiously moved forward, with my arms extended, and my eyes straining from their sockets, in the hope of catching some faint ray of light. I proceeded for many paces; but still all was blackness and vacancy. I breathed more freely. It seemed evident that mine was not, at least, the most hideous of fates.

And now, as I still continued to step cautiously onward, there came thronging upon my recollection a thousand vague rumors of the horrors of Toledo. Of the dungeons there had been strange things narrated— fables I had always deemed them—but yet strange, and too ghastly to repeat, save in a whisper. Was I left to perish of starvation in this subterranean world of darkness; or what fate, perhaps even more fearful, awaited me? That the result would be death, and a death of more than customary bitterness, I knew too well the character of my judges to doubt. The mode and the hour were all that occupied or distracted me.

My outstretched hands at length encountered some solid obstruction. It was a wall, seemingly of stone masonry—very smooth, slimy, and cold. I followed it up; stepping with all the careful distrust with which certain antique narratives had inspired me. This process, however, afforded me no means of ascertaining the dimensions of my dungeon; as I might make its circuit, and return to the point whence I set out, without being aware of the fact; so perfectly uniform seemed the wall. I therefore sought the knife which had been in my pocket, when led into the inquisitorial chamber; but it was gone; my clothes had been exchanged for a wrapper of coarse serge. I had thought of forcing the blade in some minute crevice of the masonry, so as to identify my point of departure. The difficulty, nevertheless, was but trivial; although, in the disorder of my fancy, it seemed at first insuperable. I tore a part of the hem from the robe and placed the fragment at full length, and at right angles to the wall. In groping my way around the prison, I could not fail to encounter this rag upon completing the circuit. So, at least I thought: but I had not counted upon the extent of the dungeon, or upon my own weakness. The ground was moist and slippery. I staggered onward for some time, when I stumbled and fell. My excessive fatigue induced me to remain prostrate; and sleep soon overtook me as I lay.

Upon awaking, and stretching forth an arm, I found beside me a loaf and a pitcher with water. I was too much exhausted to reflect upon this circumstance, but ate and drank with avidity. Shortly afterward, I resumed my tour around the prison, and with much toil, came at last upon the fragment of the serge. Up to the period when I fell I had counted fifty-two paces, and upon resuming my walk, I had counted forty-eight more;—when I arrived at the rag. There were in all, then, a hundred paces; and, admitting two paces to the yard, I presumed the dungeon to be fifty yards in circuit. I had met, however, with many angles in the wall, and thus I could form no guess at the shape of the vault; for vault I could not help supposing it to be.

I had little object—certainly no hope—in these researches; but a vague curiosity prompted me to continue them. Quitting the wall, I resolved to cross the area of the enclosure. At first I proceeded with extreme caution, for the floor, although seemingly of solid material, was treacherous with slime. At length, however, I took courage, and did not hesitate to step firmly; endeavoring to cross in as direct a line as possible. I had advanced some ten or twelve paces in this manner, when the remnant of the torn hem of my robe became entangled between my legs. I stepped on it, and fell violently on my face.

In the confusion attending my fall, I did not immediately apprehend a somewhat startling circumstance,
which yet, in a few seconds afterward, and while I still
lay prostrate, arrested my attention. It was this—my
chin rested upon the floor of the prison, but my lips and
the upper portion of my head, although seemingly at a
less elevation than the chin, touched nothing. At the
same time my forehead seemed bathed in a clammy
vapor, and the peculiar smell of decayed fungus arose to
my nostrils. I put forward my arm, and shuddered to
find that I had fallen at the very brink of a circular pit,
whose extent, of course, I had no means of ascertaining
at the moment. Groping about the masonry just below
the margin, I succeeded in dislodging a small fragment,
and let it fall into the abyss. For many seconds I hearkened to its reverberations as it dashed against the sides
of the chasm in its descent; at length there was a sullen
plunge into water, succeeded by loud echoes. At the
same moment there came a sound resembling the quick
opening, and as rapid closing of a door overhead, while
a faint gleam of light flashed suddenly through the
gloom, and as suddenly faded away.

I saw clearly the doom which had been prepared for
me, and congratulated myself upon the timely accident
by which I had escaped. Another step before my fall,
and the world had seen me no more. And the death just
avoided, was of that very character which I had regarded as fabulous and frivolous in the tales respecting
the Inquisition. To the victims of its tyranny, there was
the choice of death with its direst physical agonies, or
death with its most hideous moral horrors. I had been
reserved for the latter. By long suffering my nerves had
been unstrung, until I trembled at the sound of my own
voice, and had become in every respect a fitting subject
for the species of torture which awaited me.

Shaking in every limb, I groped my way back to the wall; resolving there to perish rather than risk the terrors of the wells, of which my imagination now pictured many in various positions about the dungeon. In other conditions of mind I might have had courage to end my misery at once by a plunge into one of these abysses; but now I was the veriest of cowards. Neither could I forget what I had read of these pits—that the *sudden* extinction of life formed no part of their most horrible plan.

Agitation of spirit kept me awake for many long hours; but at length I again slumbered. Upon arousing, I found by my side, as before, a loaf and a pitcher of water. A burning thirst consumed me, and I emptied the vessel at a draught. It must have been drugged; for scarcely had I drunk, before I became irresistibly drowsy. A deep sleep fell upon me—a sleep like that of death. How long it lasted of course, I know not; but when, once again, I unclosed my eyes, the objects around me were visible. By a wild sulphurous lustre, the origin of which I could not at first determine, I was enabled to see the extent and aspect of the prison.

In its size I had been greatly mistaken. The whole circuit of its walls did not exceed twenty-five yards. For some minutes this fact occasioned me a world of vain trouble; vain indeed! for what could be of less importance under the terrible circumstances which environed me, than the mere dimensions of my dungeon? But my soul took a wild interest in trifles, and I busied myself in endeavors to account for the error I had committed in my measurement. The truth at length flashed upon me. In my first attempt at exploration I had counted fifty-two paces, up to the period when I fell; I must then have been within a pace or two of the fragment of serge; in fact, I had nearly performed the circuit of the vault. I then slept, and upon awaking, I must have returned upon my steps—thus supposing the circuit nearly double what it actually was. My confusion of mind prevented me from observing that I began my tour with the wall to the left, and ended it with the wall to the right.

I had been deceived, too, in respect to the shape of the enclosure. In feeling my way I had found many angles and thus deduced an idea of great irregularity; so potent is the effect of total darkness upon one arousing from lethargy or sleep! The angles were simply those of a few slight depressions, or niches, at odd intervals. The general shape of the prison was square. What I had taken for masonry seemed now to be iron, or some other metal, in huge plates, whose sutures or joints occasioned the depression. The entire surface of this metallic enclosure was rudely daubed in all the hideous and repulsive devices to which the charnel superstition of the monks has given rise. The figures of fiends in aspects of menace, with skeleton forms, and other more really fearful images, overspread and disfigured the walls. I observed that the outlines of these monstrosities were sufficiently distinct, but that the colors seemed faded and blurred, as if from the effects of a damp atmosphere. I now noticed the floor, too, which was of stone. In the centre yawned the circular pit from whose jaws I had escaped; but it was the only· one in the dungeon.

All this I saw indistinctly and by much effort: for my personal condition had been greatly changed during slumber. I now lay upon my back, and at full length, on a species of low framework of wood. To this I was securely bound by a long strap resembling a surcingle. It passed in many convolutions about my limbs and body, leaving at liberty only my head, and my left arm to such extent that I could, by dint of much exertion, supply myself with food from an earthen dish which lay by my side on the floor. I saw, to my horror, that the pitcher had been removed. I say to my horror; for I was consumed with intolerable thirst. This thirst it appeared to be the design of my persecutors to stimulate: for the food in the dish was meat pungently seasoned.

Looking upward, I surveyed the ceiling of my prison. It was some thirty or forty feet overhead, and constructed much as the side walls. In one of its panels a very singular figure riveted my whole attention. It was the painted figure of Time as he is commonly represented, save that, in lieu of a scythe, he held what, at a casual glance, I supposed to be the pictured image of a huge pendulum such as we see on antique clocks. There was something, however, in the appearance of this machine which caused me to regard it more attentively. While I gazed directly upward at it (for its position was immediately over my own) I fancied that I saw it in motion. In an instant afterward the fancy was confirmed. Its sweep was brief, and of course slow. I watched it for some minutes, somewhat in fear, but more in wonder. Wearied at length with observing its dull movement, I turned my eyes upon the other objects in the cell.

A slight noise attracted my notice, and, looking to the floor, I saw several enormous rats traversing it. They had issued from the well, which lay just within view to my right. Even then, while I gazed, they came up in troops, hurriedly, with ravenous eyes, allured by the scent of the meat. From this it required much effort and attention to scare them away.

It might have been half an hour, perhaps even an hour, (for I could take but imperfect note of time) before I again cast my eyes upward. What I then saw confounded and amazed me. The sweep of the pendulum had increased in extent by nearly a yard. As a natural consequence, its velocity was also much greater. But what mainly disturbed me was the idea that it had perceptibly *descended*. I now observed—with what horror it is needless to say—that its nether extremity was formed of a crescent of glittering steel, about a foot in length from horn to horn; the horns upward, and the under edge evidently as keen as that of a razor. Like a razor also, it seemed massy and heavy, tapering from the edge into a solid and broad structure above. It was appended to a weighty rod of brass, and the whole *hissed* as it swung through the air.

I could no longer doubt the doom prepared for me by monkish ingenuity in torture. My cognizance of the pit had become known to the inquisitorial agents—*the pit* whose horrors had been destined for so bold a recusant as myself—*the pit*, typical of hell, and regarded by rumor as the Ultima Thule of all their punishments. The plunge into this pit I had avoided by the merest of accidents, and I knew that surprise, or entrapment into torment, formed an important portion of all the grotesquerie of these dungeon deaths. Having failed to fall, it was no part of the demon plan to hurl me into the abyss; and thus (there being no alternative) a different and a milder destruction awaited me. Milder! I half smiled in my agony as I thought of such application of such a term.

What boots it to tell of the long, long hours of horror more than mortal, during which I counted the rushing vibrations of the steel! Inch by inch—line by line—with a descent only appreciable at intervals that seemed ages—down and still down it came! Days passed—it might have been that many days passed—ere it swept so closely over me as to fan me with its acrid breath.

The odor of the sharp steel forced itself into my nostrils. I prayed—I wearied heaven with my prayer for its more speedy descent. I grew frantically mad, and struggled to force myself upward against the sweep of the fearful scimitar. And then I fell suddenly calm, and lay smiling at the glittering death, as a child at some rare bauble.

There was another interval of utter insensibility; it was brief; for, upon again lapsing into life there had been no perceptible descent in the pendulum. But it might have been long; for I knew there were demons who took note of my swoon, and who could have arrested the vibration at pleasure. Upon my recovery, too, I felt very—oh, inexpressibly sick and weak, as if through long inanition. Even amid the agonies of that period, the human nature craved food. With painful effort I outstretched my left arm as far as my bonds permitted, and took possession of the small remnant which had been spared me by the rats. As I put a portion of it within my lips, there rushed to my mind a half formed thought of joy—of hope. Yet what business had *I* with hope? It was, as I say, a half formed thought —man has many such which are never completed. I felt that it was of joy—of hope; but I felt also that it had perished in its formation. In vain I struggled to perfect—to regain it. Long suffering had nearly annihilated all my ordinary powers of mind. I was an imbecile —an idiot.

The vibration of the pendulum was at right angles to my length. I saw that the crescent was designed to cross the region of the heart. It would fray the serge of my robe—it would return and repeat its operations —again—and again. Notwithstanding its terrifically wide sweep (some thirty feet or more) and the hiss-ing vigor of its descent, sufficient to sunder these very walls of iron, still the fraying of my robe would be all that, for several minutes, it would accomplish. And at this thought I paused. I dared not go farther than this reflection. I dwelt upon it with a pertinacity of attention —as if, in so dwelling, I could arrest *here* the descent of the steel. I forced myself to ponder upon the sound of the crescent as it should pass across the garment— upon the peculiar thrilling sensation which the friction of cloth produces on the nerves. I pondered upon all this frivolity until my teeth were on edge.

Down—steadily down it crept. I took a frenzied pleasure in contrasting its downward with its lateral velocity. To the right—to the left—far and wide—with the shriek of a damned spirit; to my heart with the stealthy pace of the tiger! I alternately laughed and howled as the one or the other idea grew predominant.

Down—certainly, relentlessly down! It vibrated within three inches of my bosom! I struggled violently, furiously, to free my left arm. This was free only from the elbow to the hand. I could reach the latter, from the platter beside me, to my mouth, with great effort, but no farther. Could I have broken the fastenings above the elbow, I would have seized and attempted to arrest the pendulum. I might as well have attempted to arrest an avalanche!

Down—still unceasingly—still inevitably down! I gasped and struggled at each vibration. I shrunk convulsively at its every sweep. My eyes followed its outward or upward whirls with the eagerness of the most unmeaning despair; they closed themselves spasmodically at the descent, although death would have been a relief, oh! how unspeakable! Still I quivered in every nerve to think how slight a sinking of the machinery would precipitate that keen, glistening axe upon my bosom. It was *hope* prompted the nerve to quiver—

the frame to shrink. It was *hope*—the hope that triumphs on the rack—that whispers to the death-condemned even in the dungeons of the Inquisition.

I saw that some ten or twelve vibrations would bring the steel in actual contact with my robe, and with this observation there suddenly came over my spirit all the keen, collected calmness of despair. For the first time during many hours—or perhaps days—I *thought*. It now occurred to me that the bandage, or surcingle, which enveloped me, was *unique*. I was tied by no separate cord. The first stroke of the razor-like crescent athwart any portion of the band, would so detach it that it might be unwound from my person by means of my left hand. But how fearful, in that case, the proximity of the steel! The result of the slightest struggle how deadly! Was it likely, moreover, that the minions of the torturer had not foreseen and provided for this possibility! Was it probable that the bandage crossed my bosom in the track of the pendulum? Dreading to find my faint, and, as it seemed, my last hope frustrated, I so far elevated my head as to obtain a distinct view of my breast. The surcingle enveloped my limbs and body close in all directions—*save in the path of the destroying crescent*.

Scarcely had I dropped my head back into its original position, when there flashed upon my mind what I cannot better describe than as the unformed half of that idea of deliverance to which I have previously alluded, and of which a moiety only floated indeterminately through my brain when I raised food to my burning lips. The whole thought was now present—feeble, scarcely sane, scarcely definite,—but still entire. I proceeded at once, with the nervous energy of despair, to attempt its execution.

For many hours the immediate vicinity of the low

framework upon which I lay, had been literally swarming with rats. They were wild, bold, ravenous; their red eyes glaring upon me as if they waited but for motionlessness on my part to make me their prey. "To what food," I thought, "have they been accustomed in the well?"

They had devoured, in spite of all my efforts to prevent them, all but a small remnant of the contents of the dish. I had fallen into an habitual see-saw, or wave of the hand about the platter: and, at length, the unconscious uniformity of the movement deprived it of effect. In their voracity the vermin frequently fastened their sharp fangs in my fingers. With the particles of the oily and spicy viand which now remained, I thoroughly rubbed the bandage wherever I could reach it; then, raising my hand from the floor, I lay breathlessly still.

At first the ravenous animals were startled and terrified at the change—at the cessation of movement. They shrank alarmedly back; many sought the well. But this was only for a moment. I had not counted in vain upon their voracity. Observing that I remained without motion, one or two of the boldest leaped upon the frame-work, and smelt at the surcingle. This seemed the signal for a general rush. Forth from the well they hurried in fresh troops. They clung to the wood—they overran it, and leaped in hundreds upon my person. The measured movement of the pendulum disturbed them not at all. Avoiding its strokes they busied themselves with the anointed bandage. They pressed—they swarmed upon me in ever accumulating heaps. They writhed upon my throat; their cold lips sought my own; I was half stifled by their thronging pressure; disgust, for which the world has no name, swelled my bosom, and chilled, with a heavy clamminess, my heart. Yet one minute, and I felt that the struggle would be over.

Plainly I perceived the loosening of the bandage. I knew that in more than one place it must be already severed. With a more than human resolution I lay *still*.

Nor had I erred in my calculations—nor had I endured in vain. I at length felt that I was *free*. The surcingle hung in ribands from my body. But the stroke of the pendulum already pressed upon my bosom. It had divided the serge of the robe. It had cut through the linen beneath. Twice again it swung, and a sharp sense of pain shot through every nerve. But the moment of escape had arrived. At a wave of my hand my deliverers hurried tumultuously away. With a steady movement—cautious, sidelong, shrinking, and slow—I slid from the embrace of the bandage and beyond the reach of the scimitar. For the moment, at least, *I was free.*

Free!—and in the grasp of the Inquisition! I had scarcely stepped from my wooden bed of horror upon the stone floor of the prison, when the motion of the hellish machine ceased and I beheld it drawn up, by some invisible force, through the ceiling. This was a lesson which I took desperately to heart. My every motion was undoubtedly watched. Free!—I had but escaped death in one form of agony, to be delivered unto worse than death in some other. With that thought I rolled my eyes nervously around on the barriers of iron that hemmed me in. Something unusual—some change which, at first, I could not appreciate distinctly —it was obvious, had taken place in the apartment. For many minutes of a dreamy and trembling abstraction, I busied myself in vain, unconnected conjecture. During this period, I became aware, for the first time, of the origin of the sulphurous light which illumined the cell. It proceeded from a fissure, about half an inch in width, extending entirely around the prison at the base of the walls, which thus appeared, and were, completely separated from the floor. I endeavored, but of course in vain, to look through the aperture.

As I arose from the attempt, the mystery of the alteration in the chamber broke at once upon my understanding. I have observed that, although the outlines of the figures upon the walls were sufficiently distinct, yet the colours seemed blurred and indefinite. These had now assumed, and were momentarily assuming, a startling and most intense brilliancy, that gave to the spectral and fiendish portraitures an aspect that might have thrilled even firmer nerves than my own. Demon eyes, of a wild and ghastly vivacity, glared upon me in a thousand directions, where none had been visible before, and gleamed with the lurid lustre of a fire that I could not force my imagination to regard as unreal.

Unreal!—Even while I breathed there came to my nostrils the breath of the vapour of heated iron! A suffocating odour pervaded the prison! A deeper glow settled each moment in the eyes that glared at my agonies! A richer tint of crimson diffused itself over the pictured horrors of blood. I panted! I gasped for breath! There could be no doubt of the design of my tormentors —oh! most unrelenting! oh! most demoniac of men! I shrank from the glowing metal to the centre of the cell. Amid the thought of the fiery destruction that impended, the idea of the coolness of the well came over my soul like balm. I rushed to its deadly brink. I threw my straining vision below. The glare from the enkindled roof illumined its inmost recesses. Yet, for a wild moment, did my spirit refuse to comprehend the meaning of what I saw. At length it forced—it wrestled its way into my soul—it burned itself in upon by shuddering reason.—Oh! for a voice to speak!—oh! horror!—oh!

any horror but this! With a shriek, I rushed from the margin, and buried my face in my hands—weeping bitterly.

The heat rapidly increased, and once again I looked up, shuddering as with a fit of the ague. There had been a second change in the cell—and now the change was obviously in the *form*. As before, it was in vain that I, at first, endeavoured to appreciate or understand what was taking place. But not long was I left in doubt. The Inquisitorial vengeance had been hurried by my two-fold escape, and there was to be no more dallying with the King of Terrors. The room had been square. I saw that two of its iron angles were now acute—two, consequently, obtuse. The fearful difference quickly increased with a low rumbling or moaning sound. In an instant the apartment had shifted its form into that of a lozenge. But the alteration stopped not here—I neither hoped nor desired it to stop. I could have clasped the red walls to my bosom as a garment of eternal peace. "Death," I said, "any death but that of the pit!" Fool! might I have not known that *into the pit* it was the object of the burning iron to urge me? Could I resist its glow? or, if even that, could I withstand its pressure? And now, flatter and flatter grew the lozenge, with a rapidity that left me no time for contemplation. Its centre, and of course, its greatest width, came just over the yawning gulf. I shrank back—but the closing walls pressed me resistlessly onward. At length for my seared and writhing body there was no longer an inch of foothold on the firm floor of the prison. I struggled no more, but the agony of my soul found vent in one loud, long, and final scream of despair. I felt that I tottered upon the brink—I averted my eyes—

There was a discordant hum of human voices! There was a loud blast as of many trumpets! There was a

harsh grating as of a thousand thunders! The fiery walls
rushed back! An out-stretched arm caught my own as
I fell, fainting, into the abyss. It was that of General
Lasalle. The French army had entered Toledo. The
Inquisition was in the hands of its enemies.

THE PREMATURE BURIAL

(The Dollar Newspaper, July 31, 1844.)

THERE are certain themes of which the interest is
all-absorbing, but which are too entirely horrible for
the purposes of legitimate fiction. These the mere
romanticist must eschew, if he do not wish to offend, or
to disgust. They are with propriety handled, only when
the severity and majesty of Truth sanctify and sustain
them. We thrill, for example, with the most intense of
"pleasurable pain," over the accounts of the Passage of
the Beresina, of the Earthquake at Lisbon, of the Plague
at London, of the Massacre of St. Bartholomew, or of
the stifling of the hundred and twenty-three prisoners in
the Black Hole at Calcutta. But, in these accounts, it
is the fact—it is the reality—it is the history which excites. As inventions, we should regard them with simple
abhorrence.

I have mentioned some few of the more prominent
and august calamities on record; but, in these, it is the
extent, not less than the character of the calamity, which
so vividly impresses the fancy. I need not remind the
reader that, from the long and weird catalogue of human miseries, I might have selected many individual
instances more replete with essential suffering than any
of these vast generalities of disaster. The true wretchedness, indeed—the ultimate woe—is particular, not

diffuse. That the ghastly extremes of agony are endured by man the unit, and never by man the mass—for this let us thank a merciful God!

To be buried while alive, is, beyond question, the most terrific of these extremes which has ever fallen to the lot of mere mortality. That it was frequently, very frequently, so fallen, will scarcely be denied by those who think. The boundaries which divide Life from Death, are at best shadowy and vague. Who shall say where the one ends, and where the other begins? We know that there are diseases in which occur total cessations of all the apparent functions of vitality, and yet in which these cessations are merely suspensions, properly so called. They are only temporary pauses in the incomprehensible mechanism. A certain period elapses, and some unseen mysterious principle again sets in motion the magic pinions and the wizard wheels. The silver cord was not for ever loosed, nor the golden bowl irreparably broken. But where, meantime, was the soul?

Apart, however, from the inevitable conclusion, *à priori,* that such causes must produce such effects—that the well known occurrence of such cases of suspended animation must naturally give rise, now and then, to premature interments—apart from this consideration, we have the direct testimony of medical and ordinary experience, to prove that a vast number of such interments have actually taken place. I might refer at once, if necessary, to a hundred well authenticated instances. One of very remarkable character, and of which the circumstances may be fresh in the memory of some of my readers, occurred, not very long ago, in the neighboring city of Baltimore, where it occasioned a painful, intense, and widely extended excitement. The wife of one of the most respectable citizens—a lawyer of eminence and a member of Congress—was seized with a sudden and unaccountable illness, which completely baffled the skill of her physicians. After much suffering she died, or was supposed to die. No one suspected, indeed, or had reason to suspect, that she was not actually dead. She presented all the ordinary appearances of death. The face assumed the usual pinched and sunken outline. The lips were of the usual marble pallor. The eyes were lustreless. There was no warmth. Pulsation had ceased. For three days the body was preserved unburied, during which it had acquired a stony rigidity. The funeral, in short, was hastened, on account of the rapid advance of what was supposed to be decomposition.

The lady was deposited in her family vault, which, for three subsequent years, was undisturbed. At the expiration of this term, it was opened for the reception of a sarcophagus;—but, alas! how fearful a shock awaited the husband, who, personally, threw open the door. As its portals swung outwardly back, some white-apparelled object fell rattling within his arms. It was the skeleton of his wife in her yet unmouldered shroud.

A careful investigation rendered it evident that she had revived within two days after her intombment—that her struggles within the coffin had caused it to fall from a ledge, or shelf, to the floor, where it was so broken as to permit her escape. A lamp which had been accidentally left, full of oil, within the tomb, was found empty; it might have been exhausted, however, by evaporation. On the uppermost of the steps which led down into the dread chamber, was a large fragment of the coffin, with which it seemed that she had endeavored to arrest attention, by striking the iron door. While thus occupied, she probably swooned, or possibly died, through sheer terror; and, in falling, her shroud became entangled in some iron-work which projected interiorly. Thus she remained, and thus she rotted, erect.

In the year 1810, a case of living inhumation happened in France, attended with circumstances which go far to warrant the assertion that truth is, indeed, stranger than fiction. The heroine of the story was a Mademoiselle Victorine Lafourcade, a young girl of illustrious family, of wealth, and of great personal beauty. Among her numerous suitors was Julien Bossuet, a poor *littérateur*, or journalist, of Paris. His talents and general amiability had recommended him to the notice of the heiress, by whom he seems to have been truly beloved; but her pride of birth decided her, finally, to reject him, and to wed a Monsieur Rénelle, a banker, and a diplomatist of some eminence. After marriage, however, this gentleman neglected, and, perhaps, even more positively ill-treated her. Having passed with him some wretched years, she died,—at least her condition so closely resembled death as to deceive every one who saw her. She was buried—not in a vault—but in an ordinary grave in the village of her nativity. Filled with despair, and still inflamed by the memory of a profound attachment, the lover journeys from the capital to the remote province in which the village lies, with the romantic purpose of disinterring the corpse, and possessing himself of its luxuriant tresses. He reaches the grave. At midnight he unearths the coffin, opens it, and is in the act of detaching the hair, when he is arrested by the unclosing of the beloved eyes. In fact, the lady had been buried alive. Vitality had not altogether departed; and she was aroused, by the caresses of her lover, from the lethargy which had been mistaken for death. He bore her frantically to his lodgings in the village. He employed certain powerful restoratives suggested by no little medical learning. In fine, she revived. She recognized her preserver. She remained with him until, by slow degrees, she fully recovered her original health. Her woman's heart was not adamant, and this last lesson of love sufficed to soften it. She bestowed it upon Bossuet. She returned no more to her husband, but concealing from him her resurrection, fled with her lover to America. Twenty years afterwards, the two returned to France, in the persuasion that time had so greatly altered the lady's appearance that her friends would be unable to recognize her. They were mistaken, however; for, at the first meeting, Monsieur Rénelle did actually recognize and make claim to his wife. This claim she resisted; and a judicial tribunal sustained her in her resistance; deciding that the peculiar circumstances, with the long lapse of years, had extinguished, not only equitably but legally, the authority of the husband.

The *Chirurgical Journal* of Leipsic—a periodical, of high authority and merit, which some American bookseller would do well to translate and republish—records, in a late number, a very distressing event of the character in question.

An officer of artillery, a man of gigantic stature and of robust health, being thrown from an unmanageable horse, received a very severe contusion upon the head, which rendered him insensible at once; the skull was slightly fractured; but no immediate danger was apprehended. Trepanning was accomplished successfully. He was bled, and many other of the ordinary means of relief were adopted. Gradually, however, he fell into a more and more hopeless state of stupor; and, finally, it was thought that he died.

The weather was warm; and he was buried, with indecent haste, in one of the public cemeteries. His funeral took place on Thursday. On the Sunday following, the grounds of the cemetery were, as usual, much thronged with visiters; and, about noon, an intense excitement was created by the declaration of a peasant that, while sitting upon the grave of the officer, he had distinctly felt a commotion of the earth, as if occasioned by some one struggling beneath. At first little attention was paid to the man's asseveration; but his evident terror, and the dogged obstinacy with which he persisted in his story, had, at length, their natural effect upon the crowd. Spades were hurriedly procured, and the grave, which was shamefully shallow, was, in a few minutes, so far thrown open that the head of its occupant appeared. He was then, seemingly, dead; but he sat nearly erect within his coffin, the lid of which, in his furious struggles, he had partially uplifted.

He was forthwith conveyed to the nearest hospital, and there pronounced to be still living, although in an asphytic condition. After some hours he revived, recognized individuals of his acquaintance, and, in broken sentences, spoke of his agonies in the grave.

From what he related, it was clear that he must have been conscious of life for more than an hour, while inhumed, before lapsing into insensibility. The grave was carelessly and loosely filled with an exceedingly porous soil; and thus some air was necessarily admitted. He heard the footsteps of the crowd overhead, and endeavored to make himself heard in turn. It was the tumult within the grounds of the cemetery, he said, which appeared to awaken him from a deep sleep—but no sooner was he awake than he became fully aware of the awful horrors of his position.

This patient, it is recorded, was doing well, and seemed to be in a fair way of ultimate recovery, but fell a victim to the quackeries of medical experiment. The galvanic battery was applied; and he suddenly expired in one of those ecstatic paroxysms which, occasionally, it superinduces.

The mention of the galvanic battery, nevertheless, recalls to my memory a well known and very extraordinary case in point, where its action proved the means of restoring to animation a young attorney of London who had been interred for two days. This occurred in 1831, and created, at the time, a very profound sensation wherever it was made the subject of converse.

The patient, Mr. Edward Stapleton, had died, apparently, of typhus fever, accompanied with some anomalous symptoms which had excited the curiosity of his medical attendants. Upon his seeming decease, his friends were requested to sanction a *post mortem* examination, but declined to permit it. As often happens when such refusals are made, the practitioners resolved to disinter the body and dissect it at leisure, in private. Arrangements were easily effected with some of the numerous corps of body-snatchers with which London abounds; and, upon the third night after the funeral, the supposed corpse was unearthed from a grave eight feet deep, and deposited in the operating chamber of one of the private hospitals.

An incision of some extent had been actually made in the abdomen, when the fresh and undecayed appearance of the subject suggested an application of the battery. One experiment succeeded another, and the customary effects supervened, with nothing to characterize them in any respect, except, upon one or two occasions, a more than ordinary degree of life-likeness in the convulsive action.

It grew late. The day was about to dawn; and it was thought expedient, at length, to proceed at once to the dissection. A student, however, was especially desirous of testing a theory of his own, and insisted upon applying the battery to one of the pectoral muscles. A rough gash was made, and a wire hastily brought in contact; when the patient, with a hurried but quite unconvulsive movement, arose from the table, stepped into the middle of the floor, gazed about him uneasily for a few seconds, and then—spoke. What he said was unintelligible; but words were uttered; the syllabification was distinct. Having spoken, he fell heavily to the floor.

For some moments all were paralyzed with awe—but the urgency of the case soon restored them their presence of mind. It was seen that Mr. Stapleton was alive, although in a swoon. Upon exhibition of ether he revived and was rapidly restored to health, and to the society of his friends—from whom, however, all knowledge of his resuscitation was withheld, until a relapse was no longer to be apprehended. Their wonder—their rapturous astonishment—may be conceived.

The most thrilling peculiarity of this incident, nevertheless, is involved in what Mr. S. himself asserts. He declares that at no period was he altogether insensible —that, dully and confusedly, he was aware of every thing which happened to him, from the moment in which he was pronounced *dead* by his physicians, to that in which he fell swooning to the floor of the Hospital. "I am alive" were the uncomprehended words which, upon recognizing the locality of the dissecting-room, he had endeavored, in his extremity, to utter.

It were an easy matter to multiply such histories as these—but I forbear—for, indeed, we have no need of such to establish the fact that premature interments occur. When we reflect how very rarely, from the nature of the case, we have it in our power to detect them, we must admit that they may *frequently* occur without our cognizance. Scarcely, in truth, is a grave-yard ever encroached upon, for any purpose, to any great extent, that skeletons are not found in postures which suggest the most fearful of suspicions.

Fearful indeed the suspicion—but more fearful the doom! It may be asserted, without hesitation, that *no* event is so terribly well adapted to inspire the supreme-ness of bodily and of mental distress, as is burial before death. The unendurable oppression of the lungs—the stifling fumes from the damp earth—the clinging of the death garments—the rigid embrace of the narrow house —the blackness of the absolute Night—the silence like a sea that overwhelms—the unseen but palpable pres-ence of the Conqueror Worm—these things, with thoughts of the air and grass above, with memory of dear friends who would fly to save us if but informed of our fate, and with consciousness that of this fate they can *never* be informed—that our hopeless portion is that of the really dead—these considerations, I say, carry into the heart, which still palpitates, a degree of ap-palling and intolerable horror from which the most dar-ing imagination must recoil. We know of nothing so agonizing upon Earth—we can dream of nothing half so hideous in the realms of the nethermost Hell. And thus all narratives upon this topic have an interest profound; an interest, nevertheless, which, through the sacred awe of the topic itself, very properly and very peculiarly depends upon our conviction of the *truth* of the matter narrated. What I have now to tell, is of my own actual knowledge—of my own positive and personal experi-ence.

For several years I had been subject to attacks of the singular disorder which physicians have agreed to term catalepsy, in default of a more definitive title. Although both the immediate and the predisposing causes, and even the actual diagnosis, of this disease, are still mysteries, its obvious and apparent character is sufficiently well understood. Its variations seem to be chiefly of degree. Sometimes the patient lies, for a day only, or even for a shorter period, in a species of exaggerated lethargy. He is senseless and externally motionless; but the pulsation of the heart is still faintly perceptible; some traces of warmth remain; a slight color lingers within the centre of the cheek; and, upon application of a mirror to the lips, we can detect a torpid, unequal, and vacillating action of the lungs. Then again the duration of the trance is for weeks— even for months; while the closest scrutiny, and the most rigorous medical tests, fail to establish any material distinction between the state of the sufferer and what we conceive of absolute death. Very usually, he is saved from premature interment solely by the knowledge of his friends that he has been previously subject to catalepsy, by the consequent suspicion excited, and, above all, by the non-appearance of decay. The advances of the malady are, luckily, gradual. The first manifestations, although marked, are unequivocal. The fits grow successively more and more distinctive, and endure each for a longer term than the preceding. In this lies the principal security from inhumation. The unfortunate whose *first* attack should be of the extreme character which is occasionally seen, would almost inevitably be consigned alive to the tomb.

My own case differed in no important particular from those mentioned in medical books. Sometimes, without any apparent cause, I sank, little by little, into a condition of hemi-syncope, or half swoon; and, in this condition, without pain, without ability to stir, or, strictly speaking, to think, but with a dull lethargic consciousness of life and of the presence of those who surrounded my bed, I remained, until the crisis of the disease restored me, suddenly, to perfect sensation. At other times I was quickly and impetuously smitten. I grew sick, and numb, and chilly, and dizzy, and so fell prostrate at once. Then, for weeks, all was void, and black, and silent, and Nothing became the universe. Total annihilation could be no more. From these latter attacks I awoke, however, with a gradation slow in proportion to the suddenness of the seizure. Just as the day dawns to the friendless and houseless beggar who roams the streets throughout the long desolate winter night—just so tardily—just so wearily—just so cheerily came back the light of the Soul to me.

Apart from the tendency to trance, however, my general health appeared to be good; nor could I perceive that it was at all affected by the one prevalent malady— unless, indeed, an idiosyncrasy in my ordinary *sleep* may be looked upon as superinduced. Upon awaking from slumber, I could never gain, at once, thorough possession of my senses, and always remained, for many minutes, in much bewilderment and perplexity;—the mental faculties in general, but the memory in especial, being in a condition of absolute abeyance.

In all that I endured there was no physical suffering, but of moral distress an infinitude. My fancy grew charnel. I talked "of worms, of tombs and epitaphs." I was lost in reveries of death, and the idea of premature burial held continual possession of my brain. The ghastly Danger to which I was subjected, haunted me day and night. In the former, the torture of meditation was excessive—in the latter, supreme. When the grim Darkness overspread the Earth, then, with very horror of thought, I shook—shook as the quivering plumes upon the hearse. When Nature could endure wakefulness no longer, it was with a struggle that I consented to sleep

—for I shuddered to reflect that, upon awaking, I might find myself the tenant of a grave. And when, finally, I sank into slumber, it was only to rush at once into a world of phantasms, above which, with vast, sable, overshadowing wings, hovered, predominant, the one sepulchral Idea.

From the innumerable images of gloom which thus oppressed me in dreams, I select for record but a solitary vision. Methought I was immersed in a cataleptic trance of more than usual duration and profundity. Suddenly there came an icy hand upon my forehead, and an impatient, gibbering voice whispered the word "Arise!" within my ear.

I sat erect. The darkness was total. I could not see the figure of him who had aroused me. I could call to mind neither the period at which I had fallen into the trance, nor the locality in which I then lay. While I remained motionless, and busied in endeavors to collect my thoughts, the cold hand grasped me fiercely by the wrist, shaking it petulantly, while the gibbering voice said again:

"Arise! did I not bid thee arise?"

"And who," I demanded, "art thou?"

"I have no name in the regions which I inhabit," replied the voice mournfully; "I was mortal, but am fiend. I was merciless, but am pitiful. Thou dost feel that I shudder.—My teeth chatter as I speak, yet it is not with the chilliness of the night—of the night without end. But this hideousness is insufferable. How canst *thou* tranquilly sleep? I cannot rest for the cry of these great agonies. These sights are more than I can bear. Get thee up! Come with me into the outer Night, and let me unfold to thee the graves. Is not this a spectacle of woe?—Behold!"

I looked; and the unseen figure, which still grasped

me by the wrist, had caused to be thrown open the graves of all mankind; and from each issued the faint phosphoric radiance of decay; so that I could see into the innermost recesses, and there view the shrouded bodies in their sad and solemn slumbers with the worm. But, alas! the real sleepers were fewer, by many millions, than those who slumbered not at all; and there was a feeble struggling; and there was a general sad unrest; and from out the depths of the countless pits there came a melancholy rustling from the garments of the buried. And, of those who seemed tranquilly to repose, I saw that a vast number had changed, in a greater or less degree, the rigid and uneasy position in which they had originally been entombed. And the voice again said to me, as I gazed:

"Is it not—oh, is it *not* a pitiful sight?"—but, before I could find words to reply, the figure had ceased to grasp my wrist, the phosphoric lights expired, and the graves were closed with a sudden violence, while from out them arose a tumult of despairing cries, saying again —"Is it not—oh, God! is it *not* a very pitiful sight?"

Phantasies such as these, presenting themselves at night, extended their terrific influence far into my waking hours.—My nerves became thoroughly unstrung, and I fell a prey to perpetual horror. I hesitated to ride, or to walk, or to indulge in any exercise that would carry me from home. In fact, I no longer dared trust myself out of the immediate presence of those who were aware of my proneness to catalepsy, lest, falling into one of my usual fits, I should be buried before my real condition could be ascertained. I doubted the care, the fidelity of my dearest friends. I dreaded that, in some trance of more than customary duration, they might be prevailed upon to regard me as irrecoverable. I even went so far as to fear that, as I occasioned much trouble, they might

be glad to consider any very protracted attack as sufficient excuse for getting rid of me altogether. It was in
vain they endeavored to reassure me by the most solemn
promises. I exacted the most sacred oaths, that under no
circumstances they would bury me until decomposition
had so materially advanced as to render farther preservation impossible. And, even then, my mortal terrors
would listen to no reason—would accept no consolation.
I entered into a series of elaborate precautions. Among
other things, I had the family vault so remodelled as to
admit of being readily opened from within. The slightest
pressure upon a long lever that extended far into the
tomb would cause the iron portals to fly back. There
were arrangements also for the free admission of air
and light, and convenient receptacles for food and
water, within immediate reach of the coffin intended for
my reception. This coffin was warmly and softly padded,
and was provided with a lid, fashioned upon the principle of the vault-door, with the addition of springs so
contrived that the feeblest movement of the body would
be sufficient to set it at liberty. Besides all this, there
was suspended from the roof of the tomb, a large bell,
the rope of which, it was designed, should extend
through a hole in the coffin, and so be fastened to one
of the hands of the corpse. But, alas! what avails the
vigilance against the Destiny of man? Not even these
well contrived securities sufficed to save from the uttermost agonies of living inhumation, a wretch to these
agonies foredoomed!

There arrived an epoch—as often before there had
arrived—in which I found myself emerging from total
unconsciousness into the first feeble and indefinite sense
of existence.—Slowly—with a tortoise gradation—approached the faint gray dawn of the psychal day. A
torpid uneasiness. An apathetic endurance of dull pain.

No care—no hope—no effort. Then, after long interval, a ringing in the ears; then, after a lapse still longer, a pricking or tingling sensation in the extremities; then a seemingly eternal period of pleasurable quiescence, during which the awakening feelings are struggling into thought; then a brief re-sinking into non-entity; then a sudden recovery. At length the slight quivering of an eyelid, and immediately thereupon, an electric shock of a terror, deadly and indefinite, which sends the blood in torrents from the temples to the heart. And now the first positive effort to think. And now the first endeavor to remember. And now a partial and evanescent success. And now the memory has so far regained its dominion that, in some measure, I am cognizant of my state. I feel that I am not awaking from ordinary sleep. I recollect that I have been subject to catalepsy. And now, at last, as if by the rush of an ocean, my shuddering spirit is overwhelmed by the one grim Danger—by the one spectral and ever-prevalent Idea.

For some minutes after this fancy possessed me, I remained without motion. And why? I could not summon courage to move. I dared not make the effort which was to satisfy me of my fate—and yet there was something at my heart which whispered me *it was sure.* Despair—such as no other species of wretchedness ever calls into being—despair alone urged me, after long irresolution, to uplift the heavy lids of my eyes. I uplifted them. It was dark—all dark. I knew that the fit was over. I knew that the crisis of my disorder had long passed. I knew that I had now fully recovered the use of my visual faculties—and yet it was dark—all dark— the intense and utter raylessness of the Night that endureth for evermore.

I endeavored to shriek; and my lips and my parched tongue moved convulsively together in the attempt—

but no voice issued from the cavernous lungs, which, oppressed as if by the weight of some incumbent mountain, gasped and palpitated, with the heart, at every elaborate and struggling inspiration.

The movement of the jaws, in this effort to cry aloud, showed me that they were bound up, as is usual with the dead. I felt, too, that I lay upon some hard substance; and by something similar my sides were, also, closely compressed. So far, I had not ventured to stir any of my limbs—but now I violently threw up my arms, which had been lying at length, with the wrists crossed. They struck a solid wooden substance, which extended above my person at an elevation of not more than six inches from my face. I could no longer doubt that I reposed within a coffin at last.

And now, amid all my infinite miseries, came sweetly the cherub Hope—for I thought of my precautions. I writhed, and made spasmodic exertions to force open the lid: it would not move. I felt my wrists for the bell-rope: it was not to be found. And now the Comforter fled forever, and a still sterner Despair reigned triumphant; for I could not help perceiving the absence of the paddings which I had so carefully prepared—and then, too, there came suddenly to my nostrils the strong peculiar odor of moist earth. The conclusion was irresistible. I was *not* within the vault. I had fallen into a trance while absent from home—while among strangers —when, or how, I could not remember—and it was they who had buried me as a dog—nailed up in some common coffin—and thrust, deep, deep, and forever, into some ordinary and nameless *grave*.

As this awful conviction forced itself, thus, into the innermost chambers of my soul, I once again struggled to cry aloud. And in this second endeavor I succeeded. A long, wild, and continuous shriek, or yell, of agony, resounded through the realms of the subterrene Night.

"Hillo! hillo, there!" said a gruff voice in reply.

"What the devil's the matter now?" said a second.

"Get out o' that!" said a third.

"What do you mean by yowling in that ere kind of style, like a cattymount?" said a fourth; and hereupon I was seized and shaken without ceremony, for several minutes, by a junto of very rough-looking individuals. They did not arouse me from my slumber—for I was wide awake when I screamed—but they restored me to the full possession of my memory.

This adventure occurred near Richmond, in Virginia. Accompanied by a friend, I had proceeded, upon a gunning expedition, some miles down the banks of James River. Night approached, and we were overtaken by a storm. The cabin of a small sloop lying at anchor in the stream, and laden with garden mould, afforded us the only available shelter. We made the best of it, and passed the night on board. I slept in one of the only two berths in the vessel—and the berths of a sloop of sixty or seventy tons, need scarcely be described. That which I occupied had no bedding of any kind. Its extreme width was eighteen inches. The distance of its bottom from the deck overhead, was precisely the same. I found it a matter of exceeding difficulty to squeeze myself in. Nevertheless, I slept soundly; and the whole of my vision—for it was no dream, and no nightmare—arose naturally from the circumstances of my position—from my ordinary bias of thought—and from the difficulty, to which I have alluded, of collecting my senses, and especially of regaining my memory, for a long time after awaking from slumber. The men who shook me were the crew of the sloop, and some laborers engaged to unload it. From the load itself came the earthy smell. The bandage about the jaws was a silk handkerchief in which I had bound up my head, in default of my customary night-cap.

The tortures endured, however, were indubitably quite equal, for the time, to those of actual sepulture. They were fearfully—they were inconceivably hideous; but out of Evil proceeded Good; for their very excess wrought in my spirit an inevitable revulsion. My soul acquired tone—acquired temper. I went abroad. I took vigorous exercise. I breathed the free air of Heaven. I thought upon other subjects than Death. I discarded my medical books. Buchan I burned. I read no *Night Thoughts*—no fustian about church-yards—no bugaboo tales—*such as this*. In short, I became a new man, and lived a man's life. From that memorable night, I dismissed forever my charnel apprehensions, and with them vanished the cataleptic disorder, of which, perhaps, they had been less the consequence than the cause.

There are moments when, even to the sober eye of Reason, the world of our sad Humanity may assume the semblance of a Hell—but the imagination of man is no Carathis, to explore with impunity its every cavern. Alas! the grim legion of sepulchral terrors cannot be regarded as altogether fanciful—but, like the Demons in whose company Afrasiab made his voyage down the Oxus, they must sleep, or they will devour us—they must be suffered to slumber, or we perish.

Of Death

All but three of the stories printed in this volume deal with death or the threat of death. It was Poe's favorite subject, the idea he was most obsessed with, so that nearly all his work consists of variations on this single theme. No American writer has dwelt so constantly on the subject, delved into it so deeply, and made death's doings his own to the extent that Poe did. His terror is the fear of death, his fantasy stems from the unknown that lies beyond the grave, his only mode of revenge is that of killing, and his interest in ratiocination springs from the universal desire to find out who murdered whom.

"The Assignation" is one of his early stories and is probably derived from Hoffman's "Doge and Dogaressa." It is not one of Poe's best, but it shows him in his most romantic vein.

"Berenice" and "Morella" are preliminary studies for "Ligeia," which Poe repeatedly called his best story. "Berenice" ends in a climax so grotesque that it becomes ludicrous; "Morella" is a step farther toward the eventual masterpiece. All three stories deal with the death of a beautiful woman—the subject which Poe called "the most poetical topic in the world." In the case of "Ligeia," however, the theme is not merely death but the triumphant return from the grave, an idea which is hesitatingly projected in the earlier and simpler story, "Morella." "Ligeia" is a masterpiece of suspense and development. For this masterpiece Poe was paid

191

ten dollars by the editors of the magazine that first printed it.

"The Fall of the House of Usher" is probably Poe's best-known tale and is surely one of the great short stories of the world. Atmosphere plays an important part in it, and so does symbolism. It is a composite of material used in "Ligeia," "The Premature Burial," and "The Assignation," but it goes beyond all those tales in its integration of characters and background.

"The Facts in the Case of M. Valdemar" is a blending of two of Poe's chief interests—mesmerism and the corruption of the flesh. The story created a sensation in England, where it was printed as a pamphlet under the title "*In Articulo Mortis.*" Many British readers accepted its obvious fiction as fact.

"The Masque of the Red Death" probably had its origin in the cholera plague which struck Baltimore in the late summer of 1831. It is one of Poe's most grotesque fantasies, a symbolic Dance of Death, which rises to a climax that has strange and terrible implications. The writing is done in Poe's most baroque manner, but here the lush style seems peculiarly fitting.

THE ASSIGNATION

(First published under the title, "The Visionary" in Godey's *Lady's Book*, for January, 1834)

> Stay for me there! I will not fail
> To meet thee in that hollow vale.
>   (Exequy on the death of his wife,
>   *Henry King, Bishop of Chichester.*)

ILL-FATED and mysterious man!—bewildered in the brilliancy of thine own imagination, and fallen in the

flames of thine own youth! Again in fancy I behold
thee! Once more thy form hath risen before me!—not
—oh not as thou art—in the cold valley and shadow—
but as thou *shouldst be*—squandering away a life of
magnificent meditation in that city of dim visions, thine
own Venice—which is a star-beloved Elysium of the
sea, and the wide windows of whose Palladian palaces
look down with a deep and bitter meaning upon the
secrets of her silent waters. Yes! I repeat it—as thou
shouldst be. There are surely other worlds than this—
other thoughts than the thoughts of the multitude—
other speculations than the speculations of the sophist.
Who then shall call thy conduct into question? who
blame thee for thy visionary hours, or denounce those
occupations as a wasting away of life, which were but
the overflowings of thine everlasting energies?

It was at Venice, beneath the covered archway there
called the *Ponte di Sospiri*, that I met for the third
or fourth time the person of whom I speak. It is with
a confused recollection that I bring to mind the circumstances of that meeting. Yet I remember—ah! how
should I forget?—the deep midnight, the Bridge of
Sighs, the beauty of woman, and the Genius of Romance that stalked up and down the narrow canal.

It was a night of unusual gloom. The great clock of
the Piazza had sounded the fifth hour of the Italian
evening. The square of the Campanile lay silent and
deserted, and the lights in the old Ducal Palace were
dying fast away. I was returning home from the Pia-
zetta, by way of the Grand Canal. But as my gondola
arrived opposite the mouth of the canal San Marco, a
female voice from its recesses broke suddenly upon the
night, in one wild, hysterical, and long continued shriek.
Startled at the sound, I sprang upon my feet: while the
gondolier, letting slip his single oar, lost it in the pitchy

darkness beyond a chance of recovery, and we were consequently left to the guidance of the current which here sets from the greater into the smaller channel. Like some huge and sable-feathered condor, we were slowly drifting down towards the Bridge of Sighs, when a thousand flambeaux flashing from the windows, and down the staircases of the Ducal Palace, turned all at once that deep gloom into a livid and preternatural day.

A child, slipping from the arms of its own mother, had fallen from an upper window of the lofty structure into the deep and dim canal. The quiet waters had closed placidly over their victim; and, although my own gondola was the only one in sight, many a stout swimmer, already in the stream, was seeking in vain upon the surface, the treasure which was to be found, alas! only within the abyss. Upon the broad black marble flagstones at the entrance of the palace, and a few steps above the water, stood a figure which none who then saw can have ever since forgotten. It was the Marchesa Aphrodite—the adoration of all Venice—the gayest of the gay—the most lovely where all were beautiful—but still the young wife of the old and intriguing Mentoni, and the mother of that fair child, her first and only one, who now deep beneath the murky water, was thinking in bitterness of heart upon her sweet caresses, and exhausting its little life in struggles to call upon her name.

She stood alone. Her small, bare, and silvery feet gleamed in the black mirror of marble beneath her. Her hair, not as yet more than half loosened for the night from its ball-room array, clustered, amid a shower of diamonds, round and round her classical head, in curls like those of the young hyacinth. A snowy-white and gauze-like drapery seemed to be nearly the sole covering to her delicate form; but the mid-summer and

midnight air was hot, sullen, and still, and no motion
in the statue-like form itself, stirred even the folds of
that raiment of very vapor which hung around it as the
heavy marble hangs around the Niobe. Yet—strange to
say!—her large lustrous eyes were not turned downwards upon that grave wherein her brightest hope lay
buried—but riveted in a widely different direction! The
prison of the Old Republic is, I think, the stateliest
building in all Venice—but how could that lady gaze so
fixedly upon it, when beneath her lay stifling her only
child? Yon dark, gloomy niche, too, yawns right opposite her chamber window—what, then, *could* there be
in its shadows—in its architecture—in its ivy-wreathed
and solemn cornices—that the Marchesa di Mentoni had
not wondered at a thousand times before? Nonsense!
Who does not remember that, at such a time as this, the
eye, like a shattered mirror, multiplies the images of its
sorrow, and sees in innumerable far off places, the woe
which is close at hand?

Many steps above the Marchesa, and within the arch
of the water-gate, stood, in full dress, the Satyr-like
figure of Mentoni himself. He was occasionally occupied
in thrumming a guitar, and seemed *ennuyé* to the very
death, as at intervals he gave directions for the recovery
of his child. Stupefied and aghast, I had myself no
power to move from the upright position I had assumed
upon first hearing the shriek, and must have presented
to the eyes of the agitated group a spectral and ominous
appearance, as with pale countenance and rigid limbs,
I floated down among them in that funereal gondola.

All efforts proved in vain. Many of the most energetic
in the search were relaxing their exertions, and yielding
to a gloomy sorrow. There seemed but little hope for
the child; (how much less than for the mother!) but
now, from the interior of that dark niche which has been

already mentioned as forming a part of the Old Republican prison, and as fronting the lattice of the Marchesa,
a figure muffled in a cloak, stepped out within reach of
the light, and, pausing a moment upon the verge of the
giddy descent, plunged headlong into the canal. As, in
an instant afterwards, he stood with the still living and
breathing child within his grasp, upon the marble flagstones by the side of the Marchesa, his cloak, heavy with
the drenching water, became unfastened, and, falling in
folds about his feet, discovered to the wonder-stricken
spectators the graceful person of a very young man,
with the sound of whose name the greater part of
Europe was then ringing.

No word spoke the deliverer. But the Marchesa! She
will now receive her child—she will press it to her
heart—she will cling to its little form, and smother it
with her caresses. Alas! *another's* arms have taken it
from the stranger—*another's* arms have taken it away,
and borne it afar off, unnoticed, into the palace! And
the Marchesa! Her lip—her beautiful lip trembles: tears
are gathering in her eyes—those eyes which, like
Pliny's acanthus, are "soft and almost liquid." Yes!
tears are gathering in those eyes—and see! the entire
woman thrills throughout the soul, and the statue has
started into life! The pallor of the marble countenance,
the swelling of the marble bosom, the very purity of the
marble feet, we behold suddenly flushed over with a tide
of ungovernable crimson; and a slight shudder quivers
about her delicate frame, as a gentle air at Napoli about
the rich silver lilies in the grass.

Why *should* that lady blush! To this demand there is
no answer—except that, having left, in the eager haste
and terror of a mother's heart, the privacy of her own
boudoir, she has neglected to enthrall her tiny feet in
their slippers, and utterly forgotten to throw over her

Venetian shoulders that drapery which is their due. What other possible reason could there have been for her so blushing?—for the glance of those wild appealing eyes? for the unusual tumult of that throbbing bosom? —for the convulsive pressure of that trembling hand? —that hand which fell, as Mentoni turned into the palace, accidentally, upon the hand of the stranger. What reason could there have been for the low—the singularly low tone of those unmeaning words which the lady uttered hurriedly in bidding him adieu? "Thou hast conquered—" she said, or the murmurs of the water deceived me—"thou hast conquered—one hour after sunrise—we shall meet—so let it be!"

*   *   *

The tumult had subsided, the lights had died away within the palace, and the stranger, whom I now recognised, stood alone upon the flags. He shook with inconceivable agitation, and his eye glanced around in search of a gondola. I could not do less than offer him the service of my own; and he accepted the civility. Having obtained an oar at the water-gate, we proceeded together to his residence, while he rapidly recovered his self-possession, and spoke of our former slight acquaintance in terms of great apparent cordiality.

There are some subjects upon which I take pleasure in being minute. The person of the stranger—let me call him by this title, who to all the world was still a stranger—the person of the stranger is one of these subjects. In height he might have been below rather than above the medium size: although there were moments of intense passion when his frame actually *expanded* and belied the assertion. The light, almost slender symmetry of his figure, promised more of that ready activity which he evinced at the Bridge of Sighs, than of that Herculean strength which he has been known to wield without an effort, upon occasions of more dangerous emergency. With the mouth and chin of a deity —singular, wild, full, liquid eyes, whose shadows varied from pure hazel to intense and brilliant jet— and a profusion of curling, black hair, from which a forehead of unusual breadth gleamed forth at intervals all light and ivory—his were features than which I have seen none more classically regular, except, perhaps, the marble ones of the Emperor Commodus. Yet his countenance was, nevertheless, one of those which all men have seen at some period of their lives, and have never afterwards seen again. It had no peculiar—it had no settled predominant expression to be fastened upon the memory; a countenance seen and instantly forgotten— but forgotten with a vague and never-ceasing desire of recalling it to mind. Not that the spirit of each rapid passion failed, at any time, to throw its own distinct image upon the mirror of that face—but that the mirror, mirror-like, retained no vestige of the passion, when the passion had departed.

Upon leaving him on the night of our adventure, he solicited me, in what I thought an urgent manner, to call upon him *very* early the next morning. Shortly after sunrise, I found myself accordingly at his Palazzo, one of those huge structures of gloomy, yet fantastic pomp, which tower above the waters of the Grand Canal in the vicinity of the Rialto. I was shown up a broad winding staircase of mosaics, into an apartment whose unparalleled splendor burst through the opening door with an actual glare, making me blind and dizzy with luxuriousness.

I knew my acquaintance to be wealthy. Report had spoken of his possessions in terms which I had even ventured to call terms of ridiculous exaggeration. But as I gazed about me, I could not bring myself to believe that the wealth of any subject in Europe could have supplied the princely magnificence which burned and blazed around.

Although, as I say, the sun had arisen, yet the room was still brilliantly lighted up. I judge from this circumstance, as well as from an air of exhaustion in the countenance of my friend, that he had not retired to bed during the whole of the preceding night. In the architecture and embellishments of the chamber, the evident design had been to dazzle and astound. Little attention had been paid to the *decora* of what is technically called *keeping*, or to the proprieties of nationality. The eye wandered from object to object, and rested upon none—neither the *grotesques* of the Greek painters, nor the sculptures of the best Italian days, nor the huge carvings of untutored Egypt. Rich draperies in every part of the room trembled to the vibration of low, melancholy music, whose origin was not to be discovered. The senses were oppressed by mingled and conflicting perfumes, reeking up from strange convolute censers, together with multitudinous flaring and flickering tongues of emerald and violet fire. The rays of the newly risen sun poured in upon the whole, through windows formed each of a single pane of crimson-tinted glass. Glancing to and fro, in a thousand reflections, from curtains which rolled from their cornices like cataracts of molten silver, the beams of natural glory mingled at length fitfully with the artificial light, and lay weltering in subdued masses upon a carpet of rich, liquid-looking cloth of Chili gold.

"Ha! ha! ha!—ha! ha! ha!"—laughed the proprietor, motioning me to a seat as I entered the room, and throwing himself back at full length upon an ottoman. "I see," said he, perceiving that I could not immediately reconcile myself to the *bienséance* of so singular a welcome—"I see you are astonished at my apartment—at my statues—my pictures—my originality of conception in architecture and upholstery—absolutely drunk, eh? with my magnificence? But pardon me, my dear sir, (here his tone of voice dropped to the very spirit of cordiality,) pardon me for my uncharitable laughter. You appeared so *utterly* astonished. Besides, some things are so completely ludicrous that a man *must* laugh or die. To die laughing must be the most glorious of all glorious deaths! Sir Thomas More—a very fine man was Sir Thomas More—Sir Thomas More died laughing, you remember. Also in the *Absurdities* of Ravisius Textor, there is a long list of characters who came to the same magnificent end. Do you know, however," continued he musingly, "that at Sparta (which is now Palæochori), at Sparta, I say, to the west of the citadel, among a chaos of scarcely visible ruins, is a kind of *socle*, upon which are still legible the letters ΛΑΣΜ. They are undoubtedly part of ΓΕΛΑΣΜΑ. Now at Sparta were a thousand temples and shrines to a thousand different divinities. How exceedingly strange that the altar of Laughter should have survived all the others! But in the present instance," he resumed, with a singular alteration of voice and manner, "I have no right to be merry at your expense. You might well have been amazed. Europe cannot produce anything so fine as this, my little regal cabinet. My other apartments are by no means of the same order; mere *ultras* of fashionable insipidity. This is better than fashion—is it not? Yet this has but to be seen to become the rage—that is, with those who could afford it at the cost of their entire patrimony. I have guarded, however, against any such profanation. With one exception you are the only human being besides myself and my *valet*, who has been

admitted within the mysteries of these imperial precincts, since they have been bedizened as you see!"

I bowed in acknowledgment; for the overpowering
sense of splendor and perfume, and music, together with
the unexpected eccentricity of his address and manner,
prevented me from expressing, in words, my appreciation of what I might have construed into a compliment.

"Here," he resumed, arising and leaning on my arm
as he sauntered around the apartment, "here are paintings from the Greeks to Cimabue, and from Cimabue
to the present hour. Many are chosen, as you see, with
little deference to the opinions of Virtù. They are all,
however, fitting tapestry for a chamber such as this.
Here too, are some *chefs d'œuvre* of the unknown great
—and here unfinished designs by men, celebrated in
their day, whose very names the perspicacity of the
academies has left to silence and to me. What think
you," said he, turning abruptly as he spoke—"what
think you of this Madonna della Pietà?"

"It is Guido's own!" I said with all the enthusiasm
of my nature, for I had been poring intently over its
surpassing loveliness. "It is Guido's own!—how *could*
you have obtained it?—she is undoubtedly in painting
what the Venus is in sculpture."

"Ha!" said he thoughtfully, "the Venus—the beautiful
Venus?—the Venus of the Medici?—she of the diminutive head and the gilded hair? Part of the left arm
(here his voice dropped so as to be heard with difficulty), and all the right are restorations, and in the
coquetry of that right arm lies, I think, the quintessence
of all affectation. Give *me* the Canova! The Apollo, too!
—is a copy—there can be no doubt of it—blind fool
that I am, who cannot behold the boasted inspiration of
the Apollo! I cannot help—pity me!—I cannot help
preferring the Antinous. Was it not Socrates who said

that the statuary found his statue in the block of marble?
Then Michæl Angelo was by no means original in his
couplet—

> *Non ha l'ottimo artista alcun concetto*
> *Che un marmo solo in se non circonscriva.*"

It has been, or should be remarked, that, in the manner of the true gentleman, we are always aware of a
difference from the bearing of the vulgar, without being
at once precisely able to determine in what such difference consists. Allowing the remark to have applied in
its full force to the outward demeanor of my acquaintance, I felt it, on that eventful morning, still more fully
applicable to his moral temperament and character.
Nor can I better define that peculiarity of spirit which
seemed to place him so essentially apart from all other
human beings, than by calling it a *habit* of intense and
continual thought, pervading even his most trivial actions—intruding upon his moments of dalliance—and
interweaving itself with his very flashes of merriment—
like adders which writhe from out the eyes of the grinning masks in the cornices around the temples of Persepolis.

I could not help, however, repeatedly observing,
through the mingled tone of levity and solemnity with
which he rapidly descanted upon matters of little importance, a certain air of trepidation—a degree of nervous *unction* in action and in speech—an unquiet excitability of manner which appeared to me at all times
unaccountable, and upon some occasions even filled me
with alarm. Frequently, too, pausing in the middle of a
sentence whose commencement he had apparently forgotten, he seemed to be listening in the deepest attention, as if either in momentary expectation of a visiter,

or to sounds which must have had existence in his imagination alone.

It was during one of these reveries or pauses of apparent abstraction, that, in turning over a page of the poet and scholar Politian's beautiful tragedy "The Orfeo," (the first native Italian tragedy,) which lay near me upon an ottoman, I discovered a passage underlined in pencil. It was a passage towards the end of the third act—a passage of the most heart-stirring excitement—a passage which, although tainted with impurity, no man shall read without a thrill of novel emotion—no woman without a sigh. The whole page was blotted with fresh tears, and, upon the opposite interleaf, were the following English lines, written in a hand so very different from the peculiar characters of my acquaintance, that I had some difficulty in recognising it as his own.

> Thou wast that all to me, love,
>   For which my soul did pine—
> A green isle in the sea, love,
>   A fountain and a shrine,
> All wreathed with fairy fruits and flowers;
>   And all the flowers were mine.
>
> Ah, dream too bright to last;
>   Ah, starry Hope that didst arise
> But to be overcast!
>   A voice from out the Future cries
> "Onward!"—but o'er the Past
>   (Dim gulf!) my spirit hovering lies,
> Mute, motionless, aghast!
>
> For alas! alas! with me
>   The light of life is o'er.

"No more—no more—no more,"
(Such language holds the solemn sea
  To the sands upon the shore,)
Shall bloom the thunder-blasted tree,
  Or the stricken eagle soar!

Now all my hours are trances;
  And all my nightly dreams
Are where the dark eye glances,
  And where thy footstep gleams,
In what ethereal dances,
  By what eternal streams.

Alas! for that accursed time
  They bore thee o'er the billow,
From Love to titled age and crime,
  And an unholy pillow—
From me, and from our misty clime,
  Where weeps the silver willow! [1]

That these lines were written in English—a language
with which I had not believed their author acquainted
—afforded me little matter for surprise. I was too well
aware of the extent of his acquirements, and of the
singular pleasure he took in concealing them from
observation, to be astonished at any similar discovery;
but the place of date, I must confess, occasioned me
no little amazement. It had been originally written
London, and afterwards carefully overscored—not,
however, so effectually as to conceal the word from a
scrutinizing eye. I say this occasioned me no little

---

[1] This poem was, of course, written by Poe and was included
(without the final stanza) in his collected poetry under the title "To
One in Paradise." [Ed.]

amazement; for I well remember that, in a former conversation with my friend, I particularly inquired if he had at any time met in London the Marchesa di Mentoni, (who for some years previous to her marriage had resided in that city,) when his answer, if I mistake not, gave me to understand that he had never visited the metropolis of Great Britain. I might as well here mention, that I have more than once heard, (without of course giving credit to a report involving so many improbabilities,) that the person of whom I speak was not only by birth, but in education, an *Englishman.*

*   *   *

"There is one painting," said he, without being aware of my notice of the tragedy—"there is still one painting which you have not seen." And throwing aside a drapery, he discovered a full length portrait of the Marchesa Aphrodite.

Human art could have done no more in the delineation of her superhuman beauty. The same ethereal figure which stood before me the preceding night upon the steps of the Ducal Palace, stood before me once again. But in the expression of the countenance, which was beaming all over with smiles, there still lurked (incomprehensible anomaly!) that fitful stain of melancholy which will ever be found inseparable from the perfection of the beautiful. Her right arm lay folded over her bosom. With her left she pointed downward to a curiously fashioned vase. One small, fairy foot, alone visible, barely touched the earth—and, scarcely discernible in the brilliant atmosphere which seemed to encircle and enshrine her loveliness, floated a pair of the most delicately imagined wings. My glance fell from the painting to the figure of my friend, and the vigorous words of Chapman's *Bussy D' Ambois* quivered instinctively upon my lips:

> *He is up*
> *There like a Roman statue! He will stand*
> *Till Death hath made him marble!*

"Come!" he said at length, turning towards a table of richly enamelled and massive silver, upon which were a few goblets fantastically stained, together with two large Etruscan vases, fashioned in the same extraordinary model as that in the foreground of the portrait, and filled with what I supposed to be Johannisberger. "Come!" he said abruptly, "let us drink! It is early—but let us drink. It is *indeed* early," he continued, musingly, as a cherub with a heavy golden hammer, made the apartment ring with the first hour after sunrise—"it is *indeed* early, but what matters it? let us drink! Let us pour out an offering to yon solemn sun which these gaudy lamps and censers are so eager to subdue!" And, having made me pledge him in a bumper, he swallowed in rapid succession several goblets of the wine.

"To dream," he continued, resuming the tone of his desultory conversation, as he held up to the rich light of a censer one of the magnificent vases—"to dream has been the business of my life. I have therefore framed for myself, as you see, a bower of dreams. In the heart of Venice could I have erected a better? You behold around you, it is true, a medley of architectural embellishments. The chastity of Ionia is offended by antediluvian devices, and the sphynxes of Egypt are outstretched upon carpets of gold. Yet the effect is incongruous to the timid alone. Proprieties of place, and especially of time, are the bugbears which terrify mankind from the contemplation of the magnificent. Once I was myself a decorist: but that sublimation of folly has palled upon my soul. All this is now the fitter for my purpose. Like these arabesque censers, my spirit is writhing in fire, and the delirium of this scene is fashioning me for the wilder visions of that land of real dreams whither I am now rapidly departing." He here paused abruptly, bent his head to his bosom, and seemed to listen to a sound which I could not bear. At length, erecting his frame, he looked upwards and ejaculated the lines of the Bishop of Chichester:—

> Stay for me there! I will not fail
> To meet thee in that hollow vale.

In the next instant, confessing the power of the wine, he threw himself at full length upon an ottoman.

A quick step was now heard upon the staircase, and a loud knock at the door rapidly succeeded. I was hastening to anticipate a second disturbance, when a page of Mentoni's household burst into the room, and faltered out, in a voice choking with emotion, the incoherent words, "My mistress!—my mistress!—poisoned! —poisoned! Oh beautiful—oh beautiful Aphrodite!"

Bewildered, I flew to the ottoman, and endeavored to arouse the sleeper to a sense of the startling intelligence. But his limbs were rigid—his lips were livid—his lately beaming eyes were riveted in *death*. I staggered back towards the table—my hand fell upon a cracked and blackened goblet—and a consciousness of the entire and terrible truth flashed suddenly over my soul.

BERENICE

(*The Southern Literary Messenger*, March, 1835.)

*Dicebant mihi sodales, si sepulchrum amicæ visitarem,
curas meas aliquantulum fore levatas.* —EBN ZAIAT

MISERY is manifold. The wretchedness of earth
is multiform. Overreaching the wide horizon as
the rainbow, its hues are as various as the hues of that
arch,—as distinct too, yet as intimately blended. Overreaching the wide horizon as the rainbow! How is it that
from beauty I have derived a type of unloveliness?—
from the covenant of peace a simile of sorrow? But as, in
ethics, evil is a consequence of good, so, in fact, out of
joy is sorrow born. Either the memory of past bliss is the
anguish of to-day, or the agonies which *are* have their
origin in the ecstasies which *might have been.*

My baptismal name is Egæus; that of my family I will
not mention. Yet there are no towers in the land more
time-honored than my gloomy, gray, hereditary halls.
Our line has been called a race of visionaries; and in
many striking particulars—in the character of the family
mansion—in the frescos of the chief saloon—in the
tapestries of the dormitories—in the chiselling of some
buttresses in the armory—but more especially in the gallery of antique paintings—in the fashion of the library
chamber—and, lastly, in the very peculiar nature of the
library's contents, there is more than sufficient evidence
to warrant the belief.

The recollections of my earliest years are connected
with that chamber, and with its volumes—of which
latter I will say no more. Here died my mother. Herein
was I born. But it is mere idleness to say that I had not
lived before—that the soul has no previous existence.

You deny it?—let us not argue the matter. Convinced myself, I seek not to convince. There is, however, a remembrance of aërial forms—of spiritual and meaning eyes—of sounds, musical yet sad—a remembrance which will not be excluded; a memory like a shadow, vague, variable, indefinite, unsteady; and like a shadow, too, in the impossibility of my getting rid of it while the sunlight of my reason shall exist.

In that chamber was I born. Thus awaking from the long night of what seemed, but was not, nonentity, at once into the very regions of fairy-land—into a palace of imagination—into the wild dominions of monastic thought and erudition—it is not singular that I gazed around me with a startled and ardent eye—that I loitered away my boyhood in books, and dissipated my youth in reverie; but it *is* singular that as years rolled away, and the noon of manhood found me still in the mansion of my fathers—it *is* wonderful what stagnation there fell upon the springs of my life—wonderful how total an inversion took place in the character of my commonest thought. The realities of the world affected me as visions, and as visions only, while the wild ideas of the land of dreams became, in turn,—not the material of my every-day existence—but in very deed that existence utterly and solely in itself.

o   o   o

Berenice and I were cousins, and we grew up together in my paternal halls. Yet differently we grew—I ill of health, and buried in gloom—she agile, graceful, and overflowing with energy; hers the ramble on the hill-side—mine the studies of the cloister—I living within my own heart, and addicted body and soul to the most intense and painful meditation—she roaming carelessly through life with no thought of the shadows in her path, or the silent flight of the raven-winged hours. Berenice!—I call upon her name—Berenice!—and from the gray ruins of memory a thousand tumultuous recollections are startled at the sound! Ah! vividly is her image before me now, as in the early days of her light-heartedness and joy! Oh! gorgeous yet fantastic beauty! Oh! sylph amid the shrubberies of Arnheim!—O! Naiad among its fountains!—and then—then all is mystery and terror, and a tale which should not be told. Disease—a fatal disease—fell like the simoom upon her frame, and, even while I gazed upon her, the spirit of change swept over her, pervading her mind, her habits, and her character, and, in a manner the most subtle and terrible, disturbing even the identity of her person! Alas! the destroyer came and went, and the victim—where was she? I knew her not—or knew her no longer as Berenice.

Among the numerous train of maladies superinduced by that fatal and primary one which effected a revolution of so horrible a kind in the moral and physical being of my cousin, may be mentioned as the most distressing and obstinate in its nature, a species of epilepsy not unfrequently terminating in *trance* itself—trance very nearly resembling positive dissolution, and from which her manner of recovery was, in most instances, startlingly abrupt. In the mean time my own disease—for I have been told that I should call it by no other appellation—my own disease, then, grew rapidly upon me, and assumed finally a monomaniac character of a novel and extraordinary form—hourly and momently gaining vigor —and at length obtaining over me the most incomprehensible ascendancy. This monomania, if I must so term it, consisted in a morbid irritability of those properties of the mind in metaphysical science termed the *attentive*. It is more than probable that I am not understood; but I fear, indeed, that it is in no manner possible to convey to the mind of the merely general reader, an adequate idea of that nervous *intensity of interest* with which, in my case, the powers of meditation (not to speak technically) busied and buried themselves, in the contemplation of even the most ordinary objects of the universe.

To muse for long unwearied hours with my attention riveted to some frivolous device on the margin, or in the typography of a book; to become absorbed for the better part of a summer's day, in a quaint shadow falling aslant upon the tapestry, or upon the door; to lose myself for an entire night in watching the steady flame of a lamp, or the embers of a fire; to dream away whole days over the perfume of a flower; to repeat monotonously some common word, until the sound, by dint of frequent repetition, ceased to convey any idea whatever to the mind; to lose all sense of motion or physical existence, by means of absolute bodily quiescence long and obstinately persevered in;—such were a few of the most common and least pernicious vagaries induced by a condition of the mental faculties, not, indeed, altogether unparalleled, but certainly bidding defiance to anything like analysis or explanation.

Yet let me not be misapprehended.—The undue, earnest, and morbid attention thus excited by objects in their own nature frivolous, must not be confounded in character with that ruminating propensity common to all mankind, and more especially indulged in by persons of ardent imagination. It was not even, as might be at first supposed, an extreme condition, or exaggeration of such propensity, but primarily and essentially distinct and different. In the one instance, the dreamer, or enthusiast, being interested by an object usually *not* frivolous, imperceptibly loses sight of this object in a wilderness of deductions and suggestions issuing therefrom, until, at the conclusion of a day dream *often replete with luxury,* he finds the *incitamentum* or first cause of his musings entirely vanished and forgotten. In my case the primary object was *invariably frivolous,* although assuming, through the medium of my distempered vision, a refracted and unreal importance. Few deductions, if any, were made; and those few pertinaciously returning in upon the original object as a centre. The meditations were *never* pleasurable; and, at the termination of the reverie, the first cause, so far from being out of sight, had attained that supernaturally exaggerated interest which was the prevailing feature of the disease. In a word, the powers of mind more particularly exercised were, with me, as I have said before, the *attentive,* and are, with the daydreamer, the *speculative.*

My books, at this epoch, if they did not actually serve to irritate the disorder, partook, it will be perceived, largely, in their imaginative and inconsequential nature, of the characteristic qualities of the disorder itself. I well remember, among others, the treatise of the noble Italian Cœlius Secundus Curio *"de Amplitudine Beati Regni Dei;"* St. Augustine's great work, *The City of God;* and Tertullian *"de Carne Christi,"* in which the paradoxical sentence *"Mortuus est Dei filius; credibile est quia ineptum est: et sepultus resurrexit; certum est quia impossibile est"* occupied my undivided time, for many weeks of laborious and fruitless investigation.

Thus it will appear that, shaken from its balance only by trivial things, my reason bore resemblance to that ocean-crag spoken of by Ptolemy Hephestion, which steadily resisting the attacks of human violence, and the fiercer fury of the waters and the winds, trembled only to the touch of the flower called Asphodel. And although, to a careless thinker, it might appear a matter beyond doubt, that the alteration produced by her unhappy malady, in the *moral* condition of Berenice, would afford me many objects for the exercise of that intense and abnormal meditation whose nature I have been at some trouble in explaining, yet such was not in any degree the case. In the lucid intervals of my infirmity, her calamity, indeed, gave me pain, and, taking deeply to heart that total wreck of her fair and gentle life, I did not fail to ponder frequently and bitterly upon the wonder-working means by which so strange a revolution had been so suddenly brought to pass. But these reflections partook not of the idiosyncrasy of my disease, and were such as would have occurred, under similar circumstances, to the ordinary mass of mankind. True to its own character, my disorder revelled in the less important but more startling changes wrought in the *physical* frame of Berenice—in the singular and most appalling distortion of her personal identity.

During the brightest days of her unparalleled beauty, most surely I had never loved her. In the strange anomaly of my existence, feelings with me, *had never been* of the heart, and my passions *always were* of the mind. Through the gray of the early morning—among the trellissed shadows of the forest at noonday—and in the silence of my library at night, she had flitted by my eyes, and I had seen her—not as the living and breathing Berenice, but as the Berenice of a dream—not as a being of the earth, earthy, but as the abstraction of such a being—not as a thing to admire, but to analyze—not as an object of love, but as the theme of the most abstruse although desultory speculation. And *now*—now I shuddered in her presence, and grew pale at her approach; yet bitterly lamenting her fallen and desolate condition, I called to mind that she had loved me long, and, in an evil moment, I spoke to her of marriage.

And at length the period of our nuptials was approaching, when, upon an afternoon in the winter of the year,—one of those unseasonably warm, calm, and misty days which are the nurse of the beautiful Halcyon,[1]—I sat, (and sat, as I thought, alone,) in the inner apartment of the library. But uplifting my eyes I saw that Berenice stood before me.

Was it my own excited imagination—or the misty influence of the atmosphere—or the uncertain twilight of the chamber—or the gray draperies which fell around her figure—that caused in it so vacillating and indistinct an outline? I could not tell. She spoke no word, and I— not for worlds could I have uttered a syllable. An icy chill ran through my frame; a sense of insufferable anxiety oppressed me; a consuming curiosity pervaded my soul; and sinking back upon the chair, I remained for some time breathless and motionless, with my eyes riveted upon her person. Alas! its emaciation was excessive, and not one vestige of the former being, lurked in any single line of the contour. My burning glances at length fell upon the face.

The forehead was high, and very pale, and singularly placid; and the once jetty hair fell partially over it, and overshadowed the hollow temples with innumerable ringlets now of a vivid yellow, and jarring discordantly, in their fantastic character, with the reigning melancholy of the countenance. The eyes were lifeless, and lustreless, and seemingly pupil-less, and I shrank involuntarily from their glassy stare to the contemplation of the thin and shrunken lips. They parted; and in a smile of peculiar meaning, *the teeth* of the changed Berenice disclosed themselves slowly to my view.

[1] For as Jove, during the winter season, gives twice seven days of warmth, men have called this clement and temperate time the nurse of the beautiful Halcyon—Simonides.

Would to God that I had never beheld them, or that, having done so, I had died!

* * * * *

The shutting of a door disturbed me, and, looking up, I found that my cousin had departed from the chamber. But from the disordered chamber of my brain, had not, alas! departed, and would not be driven away, the white and ghastly *spectrum* of the teeth. Not a speck on their surface—not a shade on their enamel—not an indenture in their edges—but what that period of her smile had sufficed to brand in upon my memory. I saw them *now* even more unequivocally than I beheld them *then*. The teeth!—the teeth!—they were here, and there, and every where, and visibly and palpably before me; long, narrow, and excessively white, with the pale lips writhing about them, as in the very moment of their first terrible development. Then came the full fury of my *monomania*, and I struggled in vain against its strange and irresistible influence. In the multiplied objects of the external world I had no thoughts but for the teeth. For these I longed with a phrenzied desire. All other matters and all different interests became absorbed in their single contemplation. They—they alone were present to the mental eye, and they, in their sole individuality, became the essence of my mental life. I held them in every light. I turned them in every attitude. I surveyed their characteristics. I dwelt upon their peculiarities. I pondered upon their conformation. I mused upon the alteration in their nature. I shuddered as I assigned to them in imagination a sensitive and sentient power, and even when unassisted by the lips, a capability of moral expression. Of Mad'selle Sallé it has been well said, *"que tous ses pas étaient des sentiments,"* and of Berenice I more seriously believed *que toutes ses dents étaient*

des idées, Des idées!—ah here was the idiotic thought
that destroyed me! *Des idées!*—ah *therefore* it was that
I coveted them so madly! I felt that their possession
could alone ever restore me to peace, in giving me back
to reason.

And the evening closed in upon me thus—and then
the darkness came, and tarried, and went—and the day
again dawned—and the mists of a second night were
now gathering around—and still I sat motionless in that
solitary room; and still I sat buried in meditation, and
still the *phantasma* of the teeth maintained its terrible
ascendancy as, with the most vivid and hideous distinctness, it floated about amid the changing lights and shadows of the chamber. At length there broke in upon my
dreams a cry as of horror and dismay; and thereunto,
after a pause, succeeded the sound of troubled voices,
intermingled with many low moanings of sorrow, or of
pain. I arose from my seat and, throwing open one of the
doors of the library, saw standing out in the ante-
chamber a servant maiden, all in tears, who told me
that Berenice was—no more. She had been seized with
epilepsy in the early morning, and now, at the closing in
of the night, the grave was ready for its tenant, and all
the preparations for the burial were completed.

*   *   *   *   *

I found myself sitting in the library, and again sitting
there alone. It seemed that I had newly awakened from
a confused and exciting dream. I knew that it was now
midnight, and I was well aware that since the setting of
the sun Berenice had been interred. But of that dreary
period which intervened I had no positive—at least no
definite comprehension. Yet its memory was replete with
horror—horror more horrible from being vague, and terror more terrible from ambiguity. It was a fearful page

in the record of my existence, written all over with dim, and hideous, and unintelligible recollections. I strived to decypher them, but in vain; while ever and anon, like the spirit of a departed sound, the shrill and piercing shriek of a female voice seemed to be ringing in my ears. I had done a deed—what was it? I asked myself the question aloud, and the whispering echoes of the chamber answered me, *"what was it?"*

On the table beside me burned a lamp, and near it lay a little box. It was of no remarkable character, and I had seen it frequently before, for it was the property of the family physician; but how came it *there*, upon my table, and why did I shudder in regarding it? These things were in no manner to be accounted for, and my eyes at length dropped to the open pages of a book, and to a sentence underscored therein. The words were the singular but simple ones of the poet Ebn Zaiat, *"Dicebant mihi sodales si sepulchrum amicae visitarem, curas meas aliquantulum fore levatas."* Why then, as I perused them, did the hairs of my head erect themselves on end, and the blood of my body become congealed within my veins?

There came a light tap at the library door, and pale as the tenant of a tomb, a menial entered upon tiptoe. His looks were wild with terror, and he spoke to me in a voice tremulous, husky, and very low. What said he?—some broken sentences I heard. He told of a wild cry disturbing the silence of the night—of the gathering together of the household—of a search in the direction of the sound;—and then his tones grew thrillingly distinct as he whispered me of a violated grave —of a disfigured body enshrouded, yet still breathing, still palpitating, still *alive!*

He pointed to my garments;—they were muddy and clotted with gore. I spoke not, and he took me gently by the hand;—it was indented with the impress of human nails. He directed my attention to some object against the wall;—I looked at it for some minutes;— it was a spade. With a shriek I bounded to the table, and grasped the box that lay upon it. But I could not force it open; and in my tremor it slipped from my hands, and fell heavily, and burst into pieces; and from it, with a rattling sound, there rolled out some instruments of dental surgery, intermingled with thirty-two small, white and ivory-looking substances that were scattered to and fro about the floor.

MORELLA

(*Southern Literary Messenger*, April, 1835.)

Αὐτὸ καθ᾽ αὑτὸ μεθ αὑτοῦ, μονοειδὲς ἀεὶ ὄν.
Itself, by itself solely, ONE everlastingly, and single.
PLATO. *Sympos.* [211, XXIX.]

WITH a feeling of deep yet most singular affection I regarded my friend Morella. Thrown by accident into her society many years ago, my soul, from our first meeting, burned with fires it had never before known; but the fires were not of Eros, and bitter and tormenting to my spirit was the gradual conviction that I could in no manner define their unusual meaning, or regulate their vague intensity. Yet we met; and fate bound us together at the altar; and I never spoke of passion, nor thought of love. She, however, shunned society, and, attaching herself to me alone, rendered me happy. It is a happiness to wonder;—it is a happiness to dream.

Morella's erudition was profound. As I hope to live, her talents were of no common order—her powers of mind were gigantic. I felt this, and, in many matters, became her pupil. I soon, however, found that, perhaps on account of her Presburg education, she placed before me a number of those mystical writings which are usually considered the mere dross of the early German literature. These, for what reason I could not imagine, were her favorite and constant study—and that, in process of time they became my own, should be attributed to the simple but effectual influence of habit and example.

In all this, if I err not, my reason had little to do. My convictions, or I forget myself, were in no manner acted upon by the ideal, nor was any tincture of the mysticism which I read, to be discovered, unless I am greatly mistaken, either in my deeds or in my thoughts. Persuaded of this, I abandoned myself implicitly to the guidance of my wife, and entered with an unflinching heart into the intricacies of her studies. And then—then, when, poring over forbidden pages, I felt a forbidden spirit enkindling within me—would Morella place her cold hand upon my own, and rake up from the ashes of a dead philosophy some low, singular words, whose strange meaning burned themselves in upon my memory. And then, hour after hour, would I linger by her side, and dwell upon the music of her voice—until, at length, its melody was tainted with terror,—and there fell a shadow upon my soul—and I grew pale, and shuddered inwardly at those too unearthly tones. And thus, joy suddenly faded into horror, and the most beautiful became the most hideous, as Hinnon became Ge-Henna.

It is unnecessary to state the exact character of those disquisitions which, growing out of the volumes I have mentioned, formed, for so long a time, almost the sole conversation of Morella and myself. By the learned in what might be termed theological morality they will be readily conceived, and by the unlearned they would, at all events, be little understood. The wild Pantheism of Fichte; the modified Παλιγγενεσία of the Pythagoreans; and, above all, the doctrines of *Identity* as urged by Schelling, were generally the points of discussion presenting the most of beauty to the imaginative Morella. That identity which is termed personal, Mr. Locke, I think, truly defines to consist in the saneness of a rational being. And since by person we understand an intelligent essence having reason, and since there is a consciousness which always accompanies thinking, it is this which makes us all to be that which we call *ourselves*—thereby distinguishing us from other beings that think, and giving us our personal identity. But the *principium individuationis*—the notion of that identity *which at death is or is not lost forever*, was to me—at all times, a consideration of intense interest; not more from the perplexing and exciting nature of its consequences, than from the marked and agitated manner in which Morella mentioned them.

But, indeed, the time had now arrived when the mystery of my wife's manner oppressed me as a spell. I could no longer bear the touch of her wan fingers, nor the low tone of her musical language, nor the lustre of her melancholy eyes. And she knew all this, but did not upbraid; she seemed conscious of my weakness or my folly, and, smiling, called it Fate. She seemed, also, conscious of a cause, to me unknown, for the gradual alienation of my regard; but she gave me no hint or token of its nature. Yet was she woman, and pined away daily. In time, the crimson spot settled steadily upon the cheek, and the blue veins upon the pale forehead became prominent; and, one instant, my nature melted into pity, but, in the next, I met the glance of her meaning eyes, and then my soul sickened and became giddy with the giddiness of one who gazes downward into some dreary and unfathomable abyss.

Shall I then say that I longed with an earnest and consuming desire for the moment of Morella's decease? I did; but the fragile spirit clung to its tenement of clay for many days—for many weeks and irksome months—until my tortured nerves obtained the mastery over my mind, and I grew furious through delay, and, with the heart of a fiend, cursed the days, and the hours, and the bitter moments, which seemed to lengthen and lengthen as her gentle life declined—like shadows in the dying of the day.

But one autumnal evening, when the winds lay still in heaven, Morella called me to her bed-side. There was a dim mist over all the earth, and a warm glow upon the waters, and, amid the rich October leaves of the forest, a rainbow from the firmament had surely fallen.

"It is a day of days," she said, as I approached; "a day of all days either to live or die. It is a fair day for the sons of earth and life—ah, more fair for the daughters of heaven and death!"

I kissed her forehead, and she continued:

"I am dying, yet shall I live."

"Morella!"

"The days have never been when thou couldst love me—but her whom in life thou didst abhor, in death thou shalt adore."

"Morella!"

"I repeat that I am dying. But within me is a pledge of that affection—ah, how little!—which thou didst feel for me, Morella. And when my spirit departs shall the child live—thy child and mine, Morella's. But thy days shall be days of sorrow—that sorrow which is the most lasting of impressions, as the cypress is the most enduring of trees. For the hours of thy happiness are

over; and joy is not gathered twice in a life, as the roses
of Pæstum twice in a year. Thou shalt no longer, then,
play the Teian with time, but, being ignorant of the
myrtle and the vine, thou shalt bear about with thee
thy shroud on the earth, as do the Moslemin at Mecca."

"Morella!" I cried, "Morella! how knowest thou this?"
—but she turned away her face upon the pillow, and,
a slight tremor coming over her limbs, she thus died,
and I heard her voice no more.

Yet, as she had foretold, her child—to which in dying
she had given birth, and which breathed not until the
mother breathed no more—her child, a daughter, lived.
And she grew strangely in stature and intellect, and was
the perfect resemblance of her who had departed, and
I loved her with a love more fervent than I had believed
it possible to feel for any denizen of earth.

But, ere long, the heaven of this pure affection became darkened, and gloom, and horror, and grief, swept
over it in clouds. I said the child grew strangely in
stature and intelligence. Strange indeed was her rapid
increase in bodily size—but terrible, oh! terrible were
the tumultuous thoughts which crowded upon me while
watching the development of her mental being. Could it
be otherwise, when I daily discovered in the conceptions of the child the adult powers and faculties of the
woman?—when the lessons of experience fell from the
lips of infancy? and when the wisdom or the passions of
maturity I found hourly gleaming from its full and
speculative eye? When, I say, all this became evident
to my appalled senses—when I could no longer hide it
from my soul, nor throw it off from those perceptions
which trembled to receive it—is it to be wondered at
that suspicions, of a nature fearful and exciting, crept in
upon my spirit, or that my thoughts fell back aghast
upon the wild tales and thrilling theories of the en-

tombed Morella? I snatched from the scrutiny of the
world a being whom destiny compelled me to adore,
and in the rigorous seclusion of my home, watched with
an agonizing anxiety over all which concerned the beloved.

And, as years rolled away, and I gazed, day after
day, upon her holy, and mild, and eloquent face, and
pored over her maturing form, day after day did I discover new points of resemblance in the child to her
mother, the melancholy and the dead. And, hourly, grew
darker these shadows of similitude, and more full, and
more definite, and more perplexing, and more hideously
terrible in their aspect. For that her smile was like her
mother's I could bear; but then I shuddered at its too
perfect *identity*—that her eyes were like Morella's I
could endure; but then they too often looked down into
the depths of my soul with Morella's own intense and
bewildering meaning. And in the contour of the high
forehead, and in the ringlets of the silken hair, and in
the wan fingers which buried themselves therein, and in
the sad musical tones of her speech, and above all—oh,
above all—in the phrases and expressions of the dead
on the lips of the loved and the living, I found food for
consuming thought and horror—for a worm that *would*
not die.

Thus passed away two lustra of her life, and, as yet,
my daughter remained nameless upon the earth. "My
child" and "my love" were the designations usually
prompted by a father's affection, and the rigid seclusion
of her days precluded all other intercourse. Morella's
name died with her at her death. Of the mother I had
never spoken to the daughter;—it was impossible to
speak. Indeed, during the brief period of her existence
the latter had received no impressions from the outward
world save such as might have been afforded by the

narrow limits of her privacy. But at length the ceremony
of baptism presented to my mind, in its unnerved and
agitated condition, a present deliverance from the
terrors of my destiny. And at the baptismal font I hesitated for a name. And many titles of the wise and
beautiful, of old and modern times, of my own and foreign lands, came thronging to my lips, with many, many
fair titles of the gentle, and the happy, and the good.
What prompted me, then, to disturb the memory of the
buried dead? What demon urged me to breathe that
sound, which, in its very recollection was wont to make
ebb the purple blood in torrents from the temples to the
heart? What fiend spoke from the recesses of my soul,
when, amid those dim aisles, and in the silence of the
night, I whispered within the ears of the holy man the
syllables—Morella? What more than fiend convulsed
the features of my child, and overspread them with hues
of death, as starting at that scarcely audible sound, she
turned her glassy eyes from the earth to heaven, and,
falling prostrate on the black slabs of our ancestral
vault, responded—"I am here!"

Distinct, coldly, calmly distinct, fell those few simple
sounds within my ear, and thence, like molten lead,
rolled hissingly into my brain. Years—years may pass
away, but the memory of that epoch—never! Nor was
I indeed ignorant of the flowers and the vine—but the
hemlock and the cypress overshadowed me night and
day. And I kept no reckoning of time or place, and the
stars of my fate faded from heaven, and therefore the
earth grew dark, and its figures passed by me, like
flitting shadows, and among them all I beheld only—
Morella. The winds of the firmament breathed but one
sound within my ears, and the ripples upon the sea
murmured evermore—Morella. But she died; and with
my own hands I bore her to the tomb; and I laughed

with a long and bitter laugh as I found no traces of the
first, in the charnel where I laid the second—Morella.

LIGEIA

(The Baltimore *American Museum*, September, 1838.)

AND the will therein lieth, which dieth not. Who knoweth
the mysteries of the will, with its vigor? For God is but a
great will pervading all things by nature of its intentness.
Man doth not yield himself to the angels, nor unto death
utterly, save only through the weakness of his feeble will.
                                        —JOSEPH GLANVILLE

I CANNOT, for my soul, remember how, when, or
even precisely where, I first became acquainted with
the lady Ligeia. Long years have since elapsed, and my
memory is feeble through much suffering. Or, perhaps,
I cannot *now* bring these points to mind, because, in
truth, the character of my beloved, her rare learning, her
singular yet placid cast of beauty, and the thrilling and
enthralling eloquence of her low musical language, made
their way into my heart by paces so steadily and stealthily progressive that they have been unnoticed and unknown. Yet I believe that I met her first and most
frequently in some large, old, decaying city near the
Rhine. Of her family—I have surely heard her speak.
That it is of a remotely ancient date cannot be doubted.
Ligeia! Ligeia! Buried in studies of a nature more than
all else adapted to deaden impressions of the outward
world, it is by that sweet word alone—by Ligeia—that
I bring before mine eyes in fancy the image of her who
is no more. And now, while I write, a recollection flashes
upon me that I have *never known* the paternal name of
her who was my friend and my betrothed, and who be-

came the partner of my studies, and finally the wife of my bosom. Was it a playful charge on the part of my Ligeia? or was it a test of my strength of affection, that I should institute no inquiries upon this point? or was it rather a caprice of my own—a wildly romantic offering on the shrine of the most passionate devotion? I but indistinctly recall the fact itself—what wonder that I have utterly forgotten the circumstances which originated or attended it? And, indeed, if ever that spirit which is entitled *Romance*—if ever she, the wan and the misty-winged *Ashtophet* of idolatrous Egypt, presided, as they tell, over marriages ill-omened, then most surely she presided over mine.

There is one dear topic, however, on which my memory fails me not. It is the *person* of Ligeia. In stature she was tall, somewhat slender, and, in her latter days, even emaciated. I would in vain attempt to portray the majesty, the quiet ease, of her demeanor, or the incomprehensible lightness and elasticity of her footfall. She came and departed as a shadow. I was never made aware of her entrance into my closed study save by the dear music of her low sweet voice, as she placed her marble hand upon my shoulder. In beauty of face no maiden ever equalled her. It was the radiance of an opium-dream—an airy and spirit-lifting vision more wildly divine than the phantasies which hovered about the slumbering souls of the daughters of Delos. Yet her features were not of that regular mould which we have been falsely taught to worship in the classical labors of the heathen. "There is no exquisite beauty," says Bacon, Lord Verulam, speaking truly of all the forms and *genera* of beauty, "without some *strangeness* in the proportion." Yet, although I saw that the features of Ligeia were not of a classic regularity—although I perceived that her loveliness was indeed "exquisite," and felt that there was much of "strangeness" pervading it, yet I have tried in vain to detect the irregularity and to trace home my own perception of "the strange." I examined the contour of the lofty and pale forehead—it was faultless —how cold indeed that word when applied to a majesty so divine!—the skin rivalling the purest ivory, the commanding extent and repose, the gentle prominence of the regions above the temples; and then the raven-black, the glossy, the luxuriant and naturally-curling tresses, setting forth the full force of the Homeric epithet, "hyacinthine!" I looked at the delicate outlines of the nose—and nowhere but in the graceful medallions of the Hebrews had I beheld a similar perfection. There were the same luxurious smoothness of surface, the same scarcely perceptible tendency to the aquiline, the same harmoniously curved nostrils speaking the free spirit. I regarded the sweet mouth. Here was indeed the triumph of all things heavenly—the magnificent turn of the short upper lip—the soft, voluptuous slumber of the under—the dimples which sported, and the color which spoke—the teeth glancing back, with a brilliancy almost startling, every ray of the holy light which fell upon them in her serene and placid, yet most exultingly radiant of all smiles. I scrutinized the formation of the chin—and here, too, I found the gentleness of breadth, the softness and the majesty, the fullness and the spirituality, of the Greek—the contour which the god Apollo revealed but in a dream, to Cleomenes, the son of the Athenian. And then I peered into the large eyes of Ligeia.

For eyes we have no models in the remotely antique. It might have been, too, that in these eyes of my beloved lay the secret to which Lord Verulam alludes. They were, I must believe, far larger than the ordinary eyes of our own race. They were even fuller than the fullest

of the gazelle eyes of the tribe of the valley of Nourja-
had. Yet it was only at intervals—in moments of intense
excitement—that this peculiarity became more than
slightly noticeable in Ligeia. And at such moments was
her beauty—in my heated fancy thus it appeared perhaps—the beauty of beings either above or apart from
the earth—the beauty of the fabulous Houri of the
Turk. The hue of the orbs was the most brilliant of
black, and, far over them, hung jetty lashes of great
length. The brows, slightly irregular in outline, had the
same tint. The "strangeness," however, which I found
in the eyes, was of a nature distinct from the formation,
or the color, or the brilliancy of the features, and must,
after all, be referred to the *expression*. Ah, word of no
meaning! behind whose vast latitude of mere sound we
intrench our ignorance of so much of the spiritual. The
expression of the eyes of Ligeia! How for long hours
have I pondered upon it! How have I, through the
whole of a midsummer night, struggled to fathom it!
What was it—that something more profound than the
well of Democritus—which lay far within the pupils of
my beloved? What *was* it? I was possessed with a passion to discover. Those eyes! those large, those shining,
those divine orbs! they became to me twin stars of Leda,
and I to them devoutest of astrologers.

There is no point, among the many incomprehensible
anomalies of the science of mind, more thrillingly exciting than the fact—never, I believe, noticed in the
schools—that, in our endeavors to recall to memory
something long forgotten, we often find ourselves *upon
the very verge* of remembrance, without being able, in
the end, to remember. And thus how frequently, in my
intense scrutiny of Ligeia's eyes, have I felt approaching the full knowledge of their expression—felt it approaching—yet not quite be mine—and so at length

entirely depart! And (strange, oh strangest mystery of all!) I found, in the commonest objects of the universe, a circle of analogies to that expression. I mean to say that, subsequently to the period when Ligeia's beauty passed into my spirit, there dwelling as in a shrine, I derived, from many existences in the material world, a sentiment such as I felt always aroused within me by her large and luminous orbs. Yet not the more could I define that sentiment, or analyze, or even steadily view it. I recognized it, let me repeat, sometimes in the survey of a rapidly-growing vine—in the contemplation of a moth, a butterfly, a chrysalis, a stream of running water. I have felt it in the ocean; in the falling of a meteor. I have felt it in the glances of unusually aged people. And there are one or two stars in heaven—(one especially, a star of the sixth magnitude, double and changeable, to be found near the large star in Lyra) in a telescopic scrutiny of which I have been made aware of the feeling. I have been filled with it by certain sounds from stringed instruments, and not unfrequently by passages from books. Among innumerable other instances, I well remember something in a volume of Joseph Glanvill, which (perhaps merely from its quaintness—who shall say?) never failed to inspire me with the sentiment;—"And the will therein lieth, which dieth not. Who knoweth the mysteries of the will, with its vigor? For God is but a great will pervading all things by nature of its intentness. Man doth not yield him to the angels, nor unto death utterly, save only through the weakness of his feeble will."

Length of years, and subsequent reflection, have enabled me to trace, indeed, some remote connection between this passage in the English moralist and a portion of the character of Ligeia. An *intensity* in thought, action, or speech, was possibly, in her, a result, or at least an index, of that gigantic volition which, during our long intercourse, failed to give other and more immediate evidence of its existence. Of all the women whom I have ever known, she, the outwardly calm, the ever-placid Ligeia, was the most violently a prey to the tumultuous vultures of stern passion. And of such passion I could form no estimate, save by the miraculous expansion of those eyes which at once so delighted and appalled me—by the almost magical melody, modulation, distinctness and placidity of her very low voice—and by the fierce energy (rendered doubly effective by contrast with her manner of utterance) of the wild words which she habitually uttered.

I have spoken of the learning of Ligeia: it was immense—such as I have never known in woman. In the classical tongues was she deeply proficient, and as far as my own acquaintance extended in regard to the modern dialects of Europe, I have never known her at fault. Indeed upon any theme of the most admired, because simply the most abstruse of the boasted erudition of the academy, have I *ever* found Ligeia at fault? How singularly—how thrillingly, this one point in the nature of my wife has forced itself, at this late period only, upon my attention! I said her knowledge was such as I have never known in woman—but where breathes the man who has traversed, and successfully, *all* the wide areas of moral, physical, and mathematical science? I saw not then what I now clearly perceive, that the acquisitions of Ligeia were gigantic, were astounding; yet I was sufficiently aware of her infinite supremacy to resign myself, with a child-like confidence, to her guidance through the chaotic world of metaphysical investigation at which I was most busily occupied during the earlier years of our marriage. With how vast a triumph—with how vivid a delight—with how much of all that is ethereal in hope—did I *feel*, as she bent over me in studies but little sought—but less known—that delicious vista by slow degrees expanding before me, down whose long, gorgeous, and all untrodden path, I might at length pass onward to the goal of a wisdom too divinely precious not to be forbidden!

How poignant, then, must have been the grief with which, after some years, I beheld my well-grounded expectations take wings to themselves and fly away! Without Ligeia I was but as a child groping benighted. Her presence, her readings alone, rendered vividly luminous the many mysteries of the transcendentalism in which we were immersed. Wanting the radiant lustre of her eyes, letters, lambent and golden, grew duller than Saturnian lead. And now those eyes shone less and less frequently upon the pages over which I pored. Ligeia grew ill. The wild eyes blazed with a too—too glorious effulgence; the pale fingers became of the transparent waxen hue of the grave, and the blue veins upon the lofty forehead swelled and sank impetuously with the tides of the most gentle emotion. I saw that she must die —and I struggled desperately in spirit with the grim Azrael. And the struggles of the passionate wife were, to my astonishment, even more energetic than my own. There had been much in her stern nature to impress me with the belief that, to her, death would have come without its terrors;—but not so. Words are impotent to convey any just idea of the fierceness of resistance with which she wrestled with the Shadow. I groaned in anguish at the pitiable spectacle. I would have soothed— I would have reasoned; but, in the intensity of her wild desire for life,—for life—*but* for life—solace and reason were alike the uttermost of folly. Yet not until the last instance, amid the most convulsive writhings of her fierce spirit, was shaken the external placidity of her de-

meanor. Her voice grew more gentle—grew more low
—yet I would not wish to dwell upon the wild meaning
of the quietly uttered words. My brain reeled as I hearkened entranced, to a melody more than mortal—to assumptions and aspirations which mortality had never
before known.

That she loved me I should not have doubted; and I
might have been easily aware that, in a bosom such as
hers, love would have reigned no ordinary passion. But
in death only, was I fully impressed with the strength of
her affection. For long hours, detaining my hand, would
she pour out before me the overflowing of a heart whose
more than passionate devotion amounted to idolatry.
How had I deserved to be so blessed by such confessions?—how had I deserved to be so cursed with the removal of my beloved in the hour of her making them?
But upon this subject I cannot bear to dilate. Let me say
only, that in Ligeia's more than womanly abandonment
to a love, alas! all unmerited, all unworthily bestowed,
I at length recognized the principle of her longing with
so wildly earnest a desire for the life which was now
fleeing so rapidly away. It is this wild longing—it is
this eager vehemence of desire for life—*but* for life—
that I have no power to portray—no utterance capable
of expressing.

At high noon of the night in which she departed,
beckoning me, peremptorily, to her side, she bade me
repeat certain verses composed by herself not many
days before. I obeyed her.—They were these:

> *Lo! 'tis a gala night*
> *Within the lonesome latter years!*
> *An angel throng, bewinged, bedight*
> *In veils, and drowned in tears,*
> *Sit in a theatre, to see*
> *A play of hopes and fears,*

While the orchestra breathes fitfully
 The music of the spheres.

Mimes, in the form of God on high,
 Mutter and mumble low,
And hither and thither fly—
 Mere puppets they, who come and go
At bidding of vast formless things
 That shift the scenery to and fro,
Flapping from out their Condor wings
 Invisible Wo!

That motley drama!—oh, be sure
 It shall not be forgot!
With its Phantom chased forever more,
 By a crowd that seize it not,
Through a circle that ever returneth in
 To the self-same spot,
And much of Madness and more of Sin
 And Horror the soul of the plot.

But see, amid the mimic rout,
 A crawling shape intrude!
A blood-red thing that writhes from out
 The scenic solitude!
It writhes!—it writhes!—with mortal pangs
 The mimes become its food,
And the seraphs sob at vermin fangs
 In human gore imbued.

Out—out are the lights—out all!
 And over each quivering form,
The curtain, a funeral pall,
 Comes down with the rush of a storm,
And the angels, all pallid and wan,
 Uprising, unveiling, affirm
That the play is the tragedy, "Man,"
 And its hero the Conqueror Worm.

"O God!" half shrieked Ligeia, leaping to her feet and extending her arms aloft with a spasmodic movement, as I made an end of these lines—"O God! O Divine Father!—shall these things be undeviatingly so?—shall this Conqueror be not once conquered? Are we not part and parcel in Thee? Who—who knoweth the mysteries of the will with its vigor? Man doth not yield him to the angels, *nor unto death utterly*, save only through the weakness of his feeble will."

And now, as if exhausted with emotion, she suffered her white arms to fall, and returned solemnly to her bed of death. And as she breathed her last sighs, there came mingled with them a low murmur from her lips. I bent to them my ear and distinguished, again, the concluding words of the passage in Glanvill—*"Man doth not yield him to the angels, nor unto death utterly, save only through the weakness of his feeble will."*

She died;—and I, crushed into the very dust with sorrow, could no longer endure the lonely desolation of my dwelling in the dim and decaying city by the Rhine. I had no lack of what the world calls wealth. Ligeia had brought me far more, very far more than ordinarily falls to the lot of mortals. After a few months, therefore, of weary and aimless wandering, I purchased, and put in some repair, an abbey, which I shall not name, in one of the wildest and least frequented portions of fair England. The gloomy and dreary grandeur of the building, the almost savage aspect of the domain, the many melancholy and time-honored memories connected with both, had much in unison with the feelings of utter abandonment which had driven me into that remote and unsocial region of the country. Yet although the external abbey, with its verdant decay hanging about it, suffered but little alteration, I gave way, with a child-like perversity, and perchance with a faint hope of al-

leviating my sorrows, to a display of more than regal
magnificence within.—For such follies, even in childhood, I had imbibed a taste and now they came back to
me as if in the dotage of grief. Alas, I feel how much
even of incipient madness might have been discovered
in the gorgeous and fantastic draperies, in the solemn
carvings of Egypt, in the wild cornices and furniture,
in the Bedlam patterns of the carpets of tufted gold! I
had become a bounden slave in the trammels of opium,
and my labors and my orders had taken a coloring from
my dreams. But these absurdities I must not pause to
detail. Let me speak only of that one chamber, ever
accursed, whither in a moment of mental alienation, I
led from the altar as my bride—as the successor of the
unforgotten Ligeia—the fair-haired and blue-eyed Lady
Rowena Trevanion, of Tremaine.

There is no individual portion of the architecture and
decoration of that bridal chamber which is not now
visibly before me. Where were the souls of the haughty
family of the bride, when, through thirst of gold, they
permitted to pass the threshold of an apartment so bedecked, a maiden and a daughter so beloved? I have
said that I minutely remember the details of the chamber—yet I am sadly forgetful on topics of deep moment—and here there was no system, no keeping, in the
fantastic display, to take hold upon the memory. The
room lay in a high turret of the castellated abbey, was
pentagonal in shape, and of capacious size. Occupying
the whole southern face of the pentagon was the sole
window—an immense sheet of unbroken glass from
Venice—a single pane, and tinted of a leaden hue, so
that the rays of either the sun or moon, passing through
it, fell with a ghastly lustre on the objects within. Over
the upper portion of this huge window, extended the
trellice-work of an aged vine, which clambered up the

massy walls of the turret. The ceiling, of gloomy-looking
oak, was excessively lofty, vaulted, and elaborately
fretted with the wildest and most grotesque specimens
of a semi-Gothic, semi-Druidical device. From out of the
most central recess of this melancholy vaulting, depended, by a single chain of gold with long links, a huge
censer of the same metal, Saracenic in pattern, and
with many perforations so contrived that there writhed
in and out of them, as if endued with a serpent vitality,
a continual succession of parti-colored fires.

Some few ottomans and golden candelabra, of Eastern figure, were in various stations about—and there
was the couch, too—the bridal couch—of an Indian
model, and low, and sculptured of solid ebony, with a
pall-like canopy above. In each of the angles of the
chamber stood on end a gigantic sarcophagus of black
granite, from the tombs of the kings over against Luxor,
with their aged lids full of immemorial sculpture. But in
the draping of the apartment lay, alas! the chief
phantasy of all. The lofty walls, gigantic in height—
even unproportionably so—were hung from summit to
foot, in vast folds, with a heavy and massive-looking
tapestry—tapestry of a material which was found alike
as a carpet on the floor, as a covering for the ottomans
and the ebony bed, as a canopy for the bed, and as the
gorgeous volutes of the curtains which partially shaded
the window. The material was the richest cloth of gold.
It was spotted all over, at irregular intervals, with arabesque figures, about a foot in diameter, and wrought
upon the cloth in patterns of the most jetty black. But
these figures partook of the true character of the arabesque only when regarded from a single point of view.
By a contrivance now common, and indeed traceable
to a very remote period of antiquity, they were made
changeable in aspect. To one entering the room, they

bore the appearance of simple monstrosities; but upon a farther advance, this appearance gradually departed; and step by step, as the visitor moved his station in the chamber, he saw himself surrounded by an endless succession of the ghastly forms which belong to the superstition of the Norman, or arise in the guilty slumbers of the monk. The phantasmagoric effect was vastly heightened by the artificial introduction of a strong continual current of wind behind the draperies—giving a hideous and uneasy animation to the whole.

In halls such as these—in a bridal chamber such as this—I passed, with the Lady of Tremaine, the unhallowed hours of the first month of our marriage—passed them with but little disquietude. That my wife dreaded the fierce moodiness of my temper—that she shunned me and loved me but little—I could not help perceiving; but it gave me rather pleasure than otherwise. I loathed her with a hatred belonging more to demon than to man. My memory flew back, (oh, with what intensity of regret!) to Ligeia, the beloved, the august, the beautiful, the entombed. I revelled in recollections of her purity, of her wisdom, of her lofty, her ethereal nature, of her passionate, her idolatrous love. Now, then, did my spirit fully and freely burn with more than all the fires of her own. In the excitement of my opium dreams (for I was habitually fettered in the shackles of the drug) I would call aloud upon her name, during the silence of the night, or among the sheltered recesses of the glens by day, as if, through the wild eagerness, the solemn passion, the consuming ardor of my longing for the departed, I could restore her to the pathway she had abandoned—ah, *could* it be forever?—upon the earth.

About the commencement of the second month of the marriage, the Lady Rowena was attacked with sudden illness, from which her recovery was slow. The fever which consumed her rendered her nights uneasy; and in her perturbed state of half-slumber, she spoke of sounds, and of motions, in and about the chamber of the turret, which I concluded had no origin save in the distemper of her fancy, or perhaps in the phantasmagoric influences of the chamber itself. She became at length convalescent—finally well. Yet but a brief period elapsed, ere a second more violent disorder again threw her upon a bed of suffering; and from this attack her frame, at all times feeble, never altogether recovered. Her illnesses were, after this epoch, of alarming character, and of more alarming recurrence, defying alike the knowledge and the great exertions of her physicians. With the increase of the chronic disease which had thus, apparently, taken too sure hold upon her constitution to be eradicated by human means, I could not fail to observe a similar increase in the nervous irritation of her temperament, and in her excitability by trivial causes of fear. She spoke again, and now more frequently and pertinaciously, of the sounds—of the slight sounds—and of the unusual motions among the tapestries, to which she had formerly alluded.

One night, near the closing in of September, she pressed this distressing subject with more than usual emphasis upon my attention. She had just awakened from an unquiet slumber, and I had been watching, with feelings half of anxiety, half of vague terror, the workings of her emaciated countenance. I sat by the side of her ebony bed, upon one of the ottomans of India. She partly arose, and spoke, in an earnest low whisper, of sounds which she *then* heard, but which I could not hear—of motions which she *then* saw, but which I could not perceive. The wind was rushing hurriedly behind the tapestries, and I wished to show her (what, let me confess it, I could not *all* believe) that those almost inarticulate breathings, and those very gentle variations of the figures upon the wall, were but the natural effects of that customary rushing of the wind. But a deadly pallor, overspreading her face, had proved to me that my exertions to reassure her would be fruitless. She appeared to be fainting, and no attendants were within call. I remembered where was deposited a decanter of light wine which had been ordered by her physicians, and hastened across the chamber to procure it. But, as I stepped beneath the light of the censer, two circumstances of a startling nature attracted my attention. I had felt that some palpable although invisible object had passed lightly by my person; and I saw that there lay upon the golden carpet, in the very middle of the rich lustre thrown from the censer, a shadow—a faint, indefinite shadow of angelic aspect—such as might be fancied for the shadow of a shade. But I was wild with the excitement of an immoderate dose of opium, and heeded these things but little, nor spoke of them to Rowena. Having found the wine, I recrossed the chamber, and poured out a goblet-ful, which I held to the lips of the fainting lady. She had now partially recovered, however, and took the vessel herself, while I sank upon an ottoman near me, with my eyes fastened upon her person. It was then that I became distinctly aware of a gentle foot-fall upon the carpet, and near the couch; and in a second thereafter, as Rowena was in the act of raising the wine to her lips, I saw, or may have dreamed that I saw, fall within the goblet, as if from some invisible spring in the atmosphere of the room, three or four large drops of a brilliant and ruby colored fluid. If this I saw—not so Rowena. She swallowed the wine unhesitatingly, and I forbore to speak to her of a circumstance which must, after all, I considered, have been but the suggestion of a vivid imagination, rendered morbidly active by the terror of the lady, by the opium, and by the hour.

Yet I cannot conceal it from my own perception that, immediately subsequent to the fall of the ruby-drops, a rapid change for the worse took place in the disorder of my wife; so that, on the third subsequent night, the hands of her menials prepared her for the tomb, and on the fourth, I sat alone, with her shrouded body, in that fantastic chamber which had received her as my bride. —Wild visions, opium-engendered, flitted, shadow-like, before me. I gazed with unquiet eye upon the sarcophagi in the angels of the room, upon the varying figures of the drapery, and upon the writhing of the parti-colored fires in the censer overhead. My eyes then fell, as I called to mind the circumstances of a former night, to the spot beneath the glare of the censer where I had seen the faint traces of the shadow. It was there, however, no longer; and breathing with greater freedom, I turned my glances to the pallid and rigid figure upon the bed. Then rushed upon me a thousand memories of Ligeia—and then came back upon my heart, with the turbulent violence of a flood, the whole of that unutterable wo with which I had regarded *her* thus enshrouded. The night waned; and still, with a bosom full of bitter thoughts of the one only and supremely beloved, I remained gazing upon the body of Rowena.

It might have been midnight, or perhaps earlier, or later, for I had taken no note of time, when a sob, low, gentle, but very distinct, startled me from my revery.— I *felt* that it came from the bed of ebony—the bed of death. I listened in an agony of superstitious terror—but there was no repetition of the sound. I strained my vision to detect any motion in the corpse—but there was not the slightest perceptible. Yet I could not have been deceived. I *had* heard the noise, however faint, and my

soul was awakened within me. I resolutely and perseveringly kept my attention riveted upon the body. Many
minutes elapsed before any circumstance occurred tending to throw light upon the mystery. At length it became
evident that a slight, a very feeble, and barely noticeable
tinge of color had flushed up within the cheeks, and
along the sunken small veins of the eyelids. Through a
species of unutterable horror and awe, for which the
language of mortality has no sufficiently energetic expression, I felt my heart cease to beat, my limbs grow
rigid where I sat. Yet a sense of duty finally operated to
restore my self-possession. I could no longer doubt that
we had been precipitate in our preparations—that
Rowena still lived. It was necessary that some immediate exertion be made; yet the turret was altogether
apart from the portion of the abbey tenanted by the
servants—there were none within call—I had no means
of summoning them to my aid without leaving the room
for many minutes—and this I could not venture to do. I
therefore struggled alone in my endeavors to call back
the spirit still hovering. In a short period it was certain,
that a relapse had taken place; the color disappeared
from both eyelid and cheek, leaving a wanness even
more than that of marble; the lips became doubly
shrivelled and pinched up in the ghastly expression of
death; a repulsive clamminess and coldness overspread
rapidly the surface of the body; and all the usual
rigorous stiffness immediately supervened. I fell back
with a shudder upon the couch from which I had been
so startlingly aroused, and again gave myself up to passionate waking visions of Ligeia.

An hour thus elapsed when (could it be possible?)
I was a second time aware of some vague sound issuing
from the region of the bed. I listened—in extremity of
horror. The sound came again—it was a sigh. Rushing

to the corpse, I saw—distinctly saw—a tremor upon the lips. In a minute afterward they relaxed, disclosing a bright line of the pearly teeth. Amazement now struggled in my bosom with the profound awe which had hitherto reigned there alone. I felt that my vision grew dim, that my reason wandered; and it was only by a violent effort that I at length succeeded in nerving myself to the task which duty thus once more had pointed out. There was now a partial glow upon the forehead and upon the cheek and throat; a perceptible warmth pervaded the whole frame; there was even a slight pulsation at the heart. The lady *lived;* and with redoubled ardor I betook myself to the task of restoration. I chafed and bathed the temples and the hands, and used every exertion which experience, and no little medical reading, could suggest. But in vain. Suddenly, the color fled, the pulsation ceased, the lips resumed the expression of the dead, and, in an instant afterward, the whole body took upon itself the icy chilliness, the livid hue, the intense rigidity, the sunken outline, and all the loathsome peculiarities of that which has been, for many days, a tenant of the tomb.

And again I sunk into visions of Ligeia—and again, (what marvel that I shudder while I write?) *again* there reached my ears a low sob from the region of the ebony bed. But why shall I minutely detail the unspeakable horrors of that night? Why shall I pause to relate how, time after time, until near the period of the gray dawn, this hideous drama of revification was repeated; how each terrific relapse was only into a sterner and apparently more irredeemable death; how each agony wore the aspect of a struggle with some invisible foe; and how each struggle was succeeded by I know not what of wild change in the personal appearance of the corpse? Let me hurry to a conclusion.

The greater part of the fearful night had worn away, and she who had been dead, once again stirred—and now more vigorously than hitherto, although arousing from a dissolution more appalling in its utter hopelessness than any. I had long ceased to struggle or to move, and remained sitting rigidly upon the ottoman, a helpless prey to a whirl of violent emotions, of which extreme awe was perhaps the least terrible, the least consuming. The corpse, I repeat, stirred, and now more vigorously than before. The hues of life flushed up with unwonted energy into the countenance—the limbs relaxed—and, save that the eyelids were yet pressed heavily together, and that the bandages and draperies of the grave still imparted their charnel character to the figure, I might have dreamed that Rowena had indeed shaken off, utterly, the fetters of Death. But if this idea was not, even then, altogether adopted, I could at least doubt no longer, when, arising from the bed, tottering, with feeble steps, with closed eyes, and with the manner of one bewildered in a dream, the thing that was enshrouded advanced boldly and palpably into the middle of the apartment.

I trembled not—I stirred not—for a crowd of unutterable fancies connected with the air, the stature, the demeanor of the figure, rushing hurriedly through my brain, had paralyzed—had chilled me into stone. I stirred not—but gazed upon the apparition. There was a mad disorder in my thoughts—a tumult unappeasable. Could it, indeed, be the *living* Rowena who confronted me? Could it indeed be Rowena *at all*—the fair-haired, the blue-eyed Lady Rowena Trevanion of Tremaine? Why, *why* should I doubt it? The bandage lay heavily about the mouth—but then might it not be the mouth of the breathing Lady of Tremaine? And the cheeks—there were the roses as in her noon of life—yes, these might indeed be the fair cheeks of the living Lady of Tremaine. And the chin, with its dimples, as in health, might it not be hers?—but *had she then grown taller since her malady?* What inexpressible madness seized me with that thought? One bound, and I had reached her feet! Shrinking from my touch, she let fall from her head, unloosened, the ghastly cerements which had confined it, and there streamed forth, into the rushing atmosphere of the chamber, huge masses of long and dishevelled hair; *it was blacker than the raven wings of the midnight!* And now slowly opened *the eyes* of the figure which stood before me. "Here then, at least," I shrieked aloud, "'can I never—can I never be mistaken —these are the full, and the black, and the wild eyes— of my lost love—of the lady—of the LADY LIGEIA."

THE FALL OF THE HOUSE OF USHER

(*Burton's Gentleman's Magazine*, September, 1839.)

> *Son cœur est un luth suspendu;*
> *Sitôt qu'on le touche il résonne.*
> —DE BÉRANGER

DURING the whole of a dull, dark, and soundless day in the autumn of the year, when the clouds hung oppressively low in the heavens, I had been passing alone, on horseback, through a singularly dreary tract of country; and at length found myself, as the shades of the evening drew on, within view of the melancholy House of Usher. I know not how it was—but, with the first glimpse of the building, a sense of insufferable gloom pervaded my spirit. I say insufferable;

for the feeling was unrelieved by any of that half-pleasurable, because poetic, sentiment, with which the mind usually receives even the sternest natural images of the desolate or terrible. I looked upon the scene before me—upon the mere house, and the simple landscape features of the domain—upon the bleak walls—upon the vacant eye-like windows—upon a few rank sedges—and upon a few white trunks of decayed trees—with an utter depression of soul which I can compare to no earthly sensation more properly than to the after-dream of the reveller upon opium—the bitter lapse into everyday life—the hideous dropping off of the veil. There was an iciness, a sinking, a sickening of the heart—an unredeemed dreariness of thought which no goading of the imagination could torture into aught of the sublime. What was it—I paused to think—what was it that so unnerved me in the contemplation of the House of Usher? It was a mystery all insoluble; nor could I grapple with the shadowy fancies that crowded upon me as I pondered. I was forced to fall back upon the unsatisfactory conclusion, that while, beyond doubt, there *are* combinations of very simple natural objects which have the power of thus affecting us, still the analysis of this power lies among considerations beyond our depth. It was possible, I reflected, that a mere different arrangement of the particulars of the scene, of the details of the picture, would be sufficient to modify, or perhaps to annihilate its capacity for sorrowful impression; and, acting upon this idea, I reined my horse to the precipitous brink of a black and lurid tarn that lay in unruffled lustre by the dwelling, and gazed down—but with a shudder even more thrilling than before—upon the remodelled and inverted images of the gray sedge, and the ghastly tree-stems, and the vacant and eye-like windows.

Nevertheless, in this mansion of gloom I now proposed to myself a sojourn of some weeks. Its proprietor, Roderick Usher, had been one of my boon companions in boyhood; but many years had elapsed since our last meeting. A letter, however, had lately reached me in a distant part of the country—a letter from him—which, in its wildly importunate nature, had admitted of no other than a personal reply. The MS. gave evidence of nervous agitation. The writer spoke of acute bodily illness—of a mental disorder which oppressed him— and of an earnest desire to see me, as his best, and indeed his only personal friend, with a view of attempting, by the cheerfulness of my society, some alleviation of his malady. It was the manner in which all this, and much more, was said—it was the apparent *heart* that went with his request—which allowed me no room for hesitation; and I accordingly obeyed forthwith what I still considered a very singular summons.

Although, as boys, we had been even intimate associates, yet I really knew little of my friend. His reserve had been always excessive and habitual. I was aware, however, that his very ancient family had been noted, time out of mind, for a peculiar sensibility of temperament, displaying itself, through long ages, in many works of exalted art, and manifested, of late, in repeated deeds of munificent yet unobtrusive charity, as well as in a passionate devotion to the intricacies, perhaps even more than to the orthodox and easily recognisable beauties, of musical science. I had learned, too, the very remarkable fact, that the stem of the Usher race, all time-honoured as it was, had put forth, at no period, any enduring branch; in other words, that the entire family lay in the direct line of descent, and had always, with very trifling and very temporary variation, so lain. It was this deficiency, I considered, while running over in thought the perfect keeping of the character of the premises with the accredited character of the people, and while speculating upon the possible influence which the one, in the long lapse of centuries, might have exercised upon the other—it was this deficiency, perhaps, of collateral issue, and the consequent un-deviating transmission, from sire to son, of the patri-mony with the name, which had, at length, so identified the two as to merge the original title of the estate in the quaint and equivocal appellation of the "House of Usher"—an appellation which seemed to include, in the minds of the peasantry who used it, both the family and the family mansion.

I have said that the sole effect of my somewhat child-ish experiment—that of looking down within the tarn —had been to deepen the first singular impression. There can be no doubt that the consciousness of the rapid increase of my superstition—for why should I not so term it?—served mainly to accelerate the increase itself. Such, I have long known, is the paradoxical law of all sentiments having terror as a basis. And it might have been for this reason only, that, when I again up-lifted my eyes to the house itself, from its image in the pool, there grew in my mind a strange fancy—a fancy so ridiculous, indeed, that I but mention it to show the vivid force of the sensations which oppressed me. I had so worked upon my imagination as really to believe that about the whole mansion and domain there hung an atmosphere peculiar to themselves and their immedi-ate vicinity—an atmosphere which had no affinity with the air of heaven, but which had reeked up from the decayed trees, and the gray wall, and the silent tarn —a pestilent and mystic vapour, dull, sluggish, faintly discernible, and leaden-hued.

Shaking off from my spirit what *must* have been a

dream, I scanned more narrowly the real aspect of the building. Its principal feature seemed to be that of an excessive antiquity. The discoloration of ages had been great. Minute fungi overspread the whole exterior, hanging in a fine tangled web-work from the eaves. Yet all this was apart from any extraordinary dilapidation. No portion of the masonry had fallen; and there appeared to be a wild inconsistency between its still perfect adaptation of parts, and the crumbling condition of the individual stones. In this there was much that reminded me of the specious totality of old wood-work which has rotted for long years in some neglected vault, with no disturbance from the breath of the external air. Beyond this indication of extensive decay, however, the fabric gave little token of instability. Perhaps the eye of a scrutinising observer might have discovered a barely perceptible fissure, which, extending from the roof of the building in front, made its way down the wall in a zigzag direction, until it became lost in the sullen waters of the tarn.

Noticing these things, I rode over a short causeway to the house. A servant in waiting took my horse, and I entered the Gothic archway of the hall. A valet, of stealthy step, thence conducted me, in silence, through many dark and intricate passages in my progress to the *studio* of his master. Much that I encountered on the way contributed, I know not how, to heighten the vague sentiments of which I have already spoken. While the objects around me—while the carvings of the ceilings, the sombre tapestries of the walls, the ebon blackness of the floors, and the phantasmagoric armorial trophies which rattled as I strode, were but matters to which, or to such as which, I had been accustomed from my infancy—while I hesitated not to acknowledge how familiar was all this—I still wondered to find how unfamiliar were the fancies which ordinary images were stirring up. On one of the staircases, I met the physician of the family. His countenance, I thought, wore a mingled expression of low cunning and perplexity. He accosted me with trepidation and passed on. The valet now threw open a door and ushered me into the presence of his master.

The room in which I found myself was very large and lofty. The windows were long, narrow, and pointed, and at so vast a distance from the black oaken floor as to be altogether inaccessible from within. Feeble gleams of encrimsoned light made their way through the trellised panes, and served to render sufficiently distinct the more prominent objects around; the eye, however, struggled in vain to reach the remoter angles of the chamber, or the recesses of the vaulted and fretted ceiling. Dark draperies hung upon the walls. The general furniture was profuse, comfortless, antique, and tattered. Many books and musical instruments lay scattered about, but failed to give any vitality to the scene. I felt that I breathed an atmosphere of sorrow. An air of stern, deep, and irredeemable gloom hung over and pervaded all.

Upon my entrance, Usher arose from a sofa on which he had been lying at full length, and greeted me with a vivacious warmth which had much in it, I at first thought, of an overdone cordiality—of the constrained effort of the *ennuyé* man of the world. A glance, however, at his countenance, convinced me of his perfect sincerity. We sat down; and for some moments, while he spoke not, I gazed upon him with a feeling half of pity, half of awe. Surely, man had never before so terribly altered, in so brief a period, as had Roderick Usher! It was with difficulty that I could bring myself to admit the identity of the wan being before me with the companion of my early boyhood. Yet the character of his face had been at all times remarkable. A cadaverousness of complexion; an eye large, liquid, and luminous beyond comparison; lips somewhat thin and very pallid, but of a surpassingly beautiful curve; a nose of delicate Hebrew model, but with a breadth of nostril unusual in similar formations; a finely moulded chin, speaking, in its want of prominence, of a want of moral energy; hair of a more than web-like softness and tenuity; these features, with an inordinate expansion above the regions of the temple, made up altogether a countenance not easily to be forgotten. And now in the mere exaggeration of the prevailing character of these features, and of the expression they were wont to convey, lay so much of change that I doubted to whom I spoke. The now ghastly pallor of the skin, and the now miraculous lustre of the eye, above all things startled and even awed me. The silken hair, too, had been suffered to grow all unheeded, and as, in its wild gossamer texture, it floated rather than fell about the face, I could not, even with effort, connect its Arabesque expression with any idea of simple humanity.

In the manner of my friend I was at once struck with an incoherence—an inconsistency; and I soon found this to arise from a series of feeble and futile struggles to overcome an habitual trepidancy—an excessive nervous agitation. For something of this nature I had indeed been prepared, no less by his letter, than by reminiscences of certain boyish traits, and by conclusions deduced from his peculiar physical conformation and temperament. His action was alternately vivacious and sullen. His voice varied rapidly from a tremulous indecision (when the animal spirits seemed utterly in abeyance) to that species of energetic concision—that abrupt, weighty, unhurried, and hollow-sounding enunciation—that leaden, self-balanced and perfectly modulated guttural utterance, which may be observed in the lost drunkard, or the irreclaimable eater of opium, during the periods of his most intense excitement.

It was thus that he spoke of the object of my visit, of his earnest desire to see me, and of the solace he expected me to afford him. He entered, at some length, into what he conceived to be the nature of his malady. It was, he said, a constitutional and a family evil, and one for which he despaired to find a remedy—a mere nervous affection, he immediately added, which would undoubtedly soon pass off. It displayed itself in a host of unnatural sensations. Some of these, as he detailed them, interested and bewildered me; although, perhaps, the terms, and the general manner of the narration had their weight. He suffered much from a morbid acuteness of the senses; the most insipid food was alone endurable; he could wear only garments of certain texture; the odours of all flowers were oppressive; his eyes were tortured by even a faint light; and there were but peculiar sounds, and these from stringed instruments, which did not inspire him with horror.

To an anomalous species of terror I found him a bounden slave. "I shall perish," said he, "I *must* perish in this deplorable folly. Thus, thus, and not otherwise, shall I be lost. I dread the events of the future, not in themselves, but in their results. I shudder at the thought of any, even the most trivial, incident, which may operate upon this intolerable agitation of soul. I have, indeed, no abhorrence of danger, except in its absolute effect—in terror. In this unnerved—in this pitiable condition—I feel that the period will sooner or later arrive when I must abandon life and reason together, in some struggle with the grim phantasm, FEAR."

I learned, moreover, at intervals, and through broken

and equivocal hints, another singular feature of his mental condition. He was enchained by certain superstitious impressions in regard to the dwelling which he tenanted, and whence, for many years, he had never ventured forth—in regard to an influence whose superstitious force was conveyed in terms too shadowy here to be re-stated—an influence which some peculiarities in the mere form and substance of his family mansion, had, by dint of long sufferance, he said, obtained over his spirit—an effect which the *physique* of the gray walls and turrets, and of the dim tarn into which they all looked down, had, at length, brought about upon the *morale* of his existence.

He admitted, however, although with hesitation, that much of the peculiar gloom which thus afflicted him could be traced to a more natural and far more palpable origin—to the severe and long-continued illness—indeed to the evidently approaching dissolution—of a tenderly beloved sister—his sole companion for long years—his last and only relative on earth. "Her decease," he said, with a bitterness which I can never forget, "would leave him (him the hopeless and the frail) the last of the ancient race of the Ushers." While he spoke, the lady Madeline (for so was she called) passed slowly through a remote portion of the apartment, and, without having noticed my presence, disappeared. I regarded her with an utter astonishment not unmingled with dread—and yet I found it impossible to account for such feelings. A sensation of stupor oppressed me, as my eyes followed her retreating steps. When a door, at length, closed upon her, my glance sought instinctively and eagerly the countenance of the brother—but he had buried his face in his hands, and I could only perceive that a far more than ordinary wanness had overspread the emaciated fingers through which trickled many passionate tears.

The disease of the lady Madeline had long baffled the skill of her physicians. A settled apathy, a gradual wasting away of the person, and frequent although transient affections of a partially cataleptical character, were the unusual diagnosis. Hitherto she had steadily borne up against the pressure of her malady, and had not betaken herself finally to bed; but, on the closing in of the evening of my arrival at the house, she succumbed (as her brother told me at night with inexpressible agitation) to the prostrating power of the destroyer; and I learned that the glimpse I had obtained of her person would thus probably be the last I should obtain—that the lady, at least while living, would be seen by me no more.

For several days ensuing, her name was unmentioned by either Usher or myself: and during this period I was busied in earnest endeavours to alleviate the melancholy of my friend. We painted and read together; or I listened, as if in a dream, to the wild improvisations of his speaking guitar. And thus, as a closer and still closer intimacy admitted me more unreservedly into the recesses of his spirit, the more bitterly did I perceive the futility of all attempt at cheering a mind from which darkness, as if an inherent positive quality, poured forth upon all objects of the moral and physical universe, in one unceasing radiation of gloom.

I shall ever bear about me a memory of the many solemn hours I thus spent alone with the master of the House of Usher. Yet I should fail in any attempt to convey an idea of the exact character of the studies, or of the occupations, in which he involved me, or led me the way. An excited and highly distempered ideality threw a sulphureous lustre over all. His long improvised dirges will ring forever in my ears. Among other things, I hold painfully in mind a certain singular perversion and amplification of the wild air of the last waltz of Von Weber. From the paintings over which his elaborate fancy brooded, and which grew, touch by touch, into vaguenesses at which I shuddered the more thrillingly, because I shuddered knowing not why;—from these paintings (vivid as their images now are before me) I would in vain endeavour to educe more than a small portion which should lie within the compass of merely written words. By the utter simplicity, by the nakedness of his designs, he arrested and overawed attention. If ever mortal painted an idea, that mortal was Roderick Usher. For me at least—in the circumstances then surrounding me—there arose out of the pure abstractions which the hypochondriac contrived to throw upon his canvas, an intensity of intolerable awe, no shadow of which felt I ever yet in the contemplation of the certainly glowing yet too concrete reveries of Fuseli.

One of the phantasmagoric conceptions of my friend, partaking not so rigidly of the spirit of abstraction, may be shadowed forth, although feebly, in words. A small picture presented the interior of an immensely long and rectangular vault or tunnel, with low walls, smooth, white, and without interruption or device. Certain accessory points of the design served well to convey the idea that this excavation lay at an exceeding depth below the surface of the earth. No outlet was observed in any portion of its vast extent, and no torch, or other artificial source of light was discernible; yet a flood of intense rays rolled throughout, and bathed the whole in a ghastly and inappropriate splendour.

I have just spoken of that morbid condition of the

auditory nerve which rendered all music intolerable to the sufferer, with the exception of certain effects of stringed instruments. It was, perhaps, the narrow limits to which he thus confined himself upon the guitar, which gave birth, in great measure, to the fantastic character of his performances. But the fervid *facility* of his *impromptus* could not be so accounted for. They must have been, and were, in the notes, as well as in the words of his wild fantasias (for he not unfrequently accompanied himself with rhymed verbal improvisations), the result of that intense mental collectedness and concentration to which I have previously alluded as observable only in particular moments of the highest artificial excitement. The words of one of these rhapsodies I have easily remembered. I was, perhaps, the more forcibly impressed with it, as he gave it, because, in the under or mystic current of its meaning, I fancied that I perceived, and for the first time, a full consciousness on the part of Usher, of the tottering of his lofty reason upon her throne. The verses, which were entitled "The Haunted Palace," ran very nearly, if not accurately, thus:

> *In the greenest of our valleys,*
> *By good angels tenanted,*
> *Once a fair and stately palace—*
> *Radiant palace—reared its head.*
> *In the monarch Thought's dominion—*
> *It stood there!*
> *Never seraph spread a pinion*
> *Over fabric half so fair.*
>
> *Banners yellow, glorious, golden,*
> *On its roof did float and flow;*
> *(This—all this—was in the olden*
> *Time long ago)*

And every gentle air that dallied,
    In that sweet day,
Along the ramparts plumed and pallid,
    A winged odour went away.

Wanderers in that happy valley
    Through two luminous windows saw
Spirits moving musically
    To a lute's well-tunèd law,
Round about a throne, where sitting
    (Porphyrogene!)
In state his glory well befitting,
    The ruler of the realm was seen.

And all with pearl and ruby glowing
    Was the fair palace door,
Through which came flowing, flowing, flowing
    And sparkling evermore,
A troop of Echoes whose sweet duty
    Was but to sing,
In voices of surpassing beauty,
    The wit and wisdom of their king.

But evil things, in robes of sorrow,
    Assailed the monarch's high estate;
(Ah, let us mourn, for never morrow
    Shall dawn upon him, desolate!)
And, round about his home, the glory
    That blushed and bloomed
Is but a dim-remembered story
    Of the old time entombed.

And travellers now within that valley,
    Through the red-litten windows, see
Vast forms that move fantastically
    To a discordant melody;

While, like a rapid ghastly river,
Through the pale door,
A hideous throng rush out forever,
And laugh—but smile no more.

I well remember that suggestions arising from this ballad, led us into a train of thought wherein there became manifest an opinion of Usher's which I mention not so much on account of its novelty, (for other men[1] have thought thus,) as on account of the pertinacity with which he maintained it. This opinion, in its general form, was that of the sentience of all vegetable things. But, in his disordered fancy, the idea had assumed a more daring character, and trespassed, under certain conditions, upon the kingdom of inorganization. I lack words to express the full extent, or the earnest *abandon* of his persuasion. The belief, however, was connected (as I have previously hinted) with the gray stones of the home of his forefathers. The conditions of the sentience had been here, he imagined, fulfilled in the method of collocation of these stones—in the order of their arrangement, as well as in that of the many *fungi* which overspread them, and of the decayed trees which stood around—above all, in the long undisturbed endurance of this arrangement, and in its reduplication in the still waters of the tarn. Its evidence —the evidence of the sentience—was to be seen, he said, (and I here started as he spoke,) in the gradual yet certain condensation of an atmosphere of their own about the waters and the walls. The result was discoverable, he added, in that silent, yet importunate and terrible influence which for centuries had moulded

[1] Watson, Dr. Percival, Spallanzani, and especially the Bishop of Landaff.—*See* Chemical Essays, *vol. v.* [E.A.P.]

the destinies of his family, and which made *him* what
I now saw him—what he was. Such opinions need no
comment, and I will make none.

Our books—the books which, for years, had formed
no small portion of the mental existence of the invalid
—were, as might be supposed, in strict keeping with
this character of phantasm. We pored together over
such works as the *Ververt et Chartreuse* of Gresset;
the *Belphegor* of Machiavelli; the *Heaven and Hell*
of Swedenborg; the *Subterranean Voyage of Nicholas
Klimm* by Holberg; the *Chiromancy* of Robert Flud,
of Jean D'Indaginé, and of De la Chambre; the *Journey into the Blue Distance of Tieck;* and the *City of
the Sun* of Campanella. One favourite volume was a
small octavo edition of the *Directorium Inquisitorum*,
by the Dominican Eymeric de Gironne; and there were
passages in Pomponius Mela, about the old African
Satyrs and Ægipans, over which Usher would sit
dreaming for hours. His chief delight, however, was
found in the perusal of an exceedingly rare and curious
book in quarto Gothic—the manual of a forgotten
church—the *Vigiliæ Mortuorum secundum Chorum Ec-
clesiæ Maguntinæ.*

I could not help thinking of the wild ritual of this
work, and of its probable influence upon the hypochondriac, when, one evening, having informed me abruptly
that the lady Madeline was no more, he stated his intention of preserving her corpse for a fortnight, (previously to its final interment,) in one of the numerous
vaults within the main walls of the building. The
worldly reason, however, assigned for this singular
proceeding, was one which I did not feel at liberty to
dispute. The brother had been led to his resolution
(so he told me) by consideration of the unusual character of the malady of the deceased, of certain obtru-

sive and eager inquiries on the part of her medical men, and of the remote and exposed situation of the burial-ground of the family. I will not deny that when I called to mind the sinister countenance of the person whom I met upon the staircase, on the day of my arrival at the house, I had no desire to oppose what I regarded as at best but a harmless, and by no means an unnatural, precaution.

At the request of Usher, I personally aided him in the arrangements for the temporary entombment. The body having been encoffined, we two alone bore it to its rest. The vault in which we placed it (and which had been so long unopened that our torches, half smothered in its oppressive atmosphere, gave us little opportunity for investigation) was small, damp, and entirely without means of admission for light; lying, at great depth, immediately beneath that portion of the building in which was my own sleeping apartment. It had been used, apparently, in remote feudal times, for the worst purposes of a donjon-keep, and, in later days, as a place of deposit for powder, or some other highly combustible substance, as a portion of its floor, and the whole interior of a long archway through which we reached it, were carefully sheathed with copper. The door, of massive iron, had been, also, similarly protected. Its immense weight caused an unusually sharp grating sound, as it moved upon its hinges.

Having deposited our mournful burden upon tressels within this region of horror, we partially turned aside the yet unscrewed lid of the coffin, and looked upon the face of the tenant. A striking similitude between the brother and sister now first arrested my attention; and Usher, divining, perhaps, my thoughts, murmured out some few words from which I learned that the deceased and himself had been twins, and that sympathies of a scarcely intelligible nature had always existed between them. Our glances, however, rested not long upon the dead—for we could not regard her unawed. The disease which had thus entombed the lady in the maturity of youth, had left, as usual in all maladies of a strictly cataleptical character, the mockery of a faint blush upon the bosom and the face, and that suspiciously lingering smile upon the lip which is so terrible in death. We replaced and screwed down the lid, and, having secured the door of iron, made our way, with toil, into the scarcely less gloomy apartments of the upper portion of the house.

And now, some days of bitter grief having elapsed, an observable change came over the features of the mental disorder of my friend. His ordinary manner had vanished. His ordinary occupations were neglected or forgotten. He roamed from chamber to chamber with hurried, unequal, and objectless step. The pallor of his countenance had assumed, if possible, a more ghastly hue—but the luminousness of his eye had utterly gone out. The once occasional huskiness of his tone was heard no more; and a tremulous quaver, as if of extreme terror, habitually characterized his utterance. There were times, indeed, when I thought his unceasingly agitated mind was labouring with some oppressive secret, to divulge which he struggled for the necessary courage. At times, again, I was obliged to resolve all into the mere inexplicable vagaries of madness, for I beheld him gazing upon vacancy for long hours, in an attitude of the profoundest attention, as if listening to some imaginary sound. It was no wonder that his condition terrified—that it infected me. I felt creeping upon me, by slow yet certain degrees, the wild influences of his own fantastic yet impressive superstitions.

It was, especially, upon retiring to bed late in the night of the seventh or eighth day after the placing of the lady Madeline within the donjon, that I experienced the full power of such feelings. Sleep came not near my couch—while the hours waned and waned away. I struggled to reason off the nervousness which had dominion over me. I endeavoured to believe that much, if not all of what I felt, was due to the bewildering influence of the gloomy furniture of the room —of the dark and tattered draperies, which, tortured into motion by the breath of a rising tempest, swayed fitfully to and fro upon the walls, and rustled uneasily about the decorations of the bed. But my efforts were fruitless. An irrepressible tremour gradually pervaded my frame; and, at length, there sat upon my very heart an incubus of utterly causeless alarm. Shaking this off with a gasp and a struggle, I uplifted myself upon the pillows, and, peering earnestly within the intense darkness of the chamber, hearkened—I know not why, except that an instinctive spirit prompted me—to certain low and indefinite sounds which came, through the pauses of the storm, at long intervals, I knew not whence. Overpowered by an intense sentiment of horror, unaccountable yet unendurable, I threw on my clothes with haste (for I felt that I should sleep no more during the night), and endeavoured to arouse myself from the pitiable condition into which I had fallen, by pacing rapidly to and fro through the apartment.

I had taken but few turns in this manner, when a light step on an adjoining staircase arrested my attention. I presently recognised it as that of Usher. In an instant afterward he rapped, with a gentle touch, at my door, and entered, bearing a lamp. His countenance was, as usual, cadaverously wan—but, moreover, there was a species of mad hilarity in his eyes— an evidently restrained *hysteria* in his whole demeanour. His air appalled me—but anything was preferable to the solitude which I had so long endured, and I even welcomed his presence as a relief.

"And you have not seen it?" he said abruptly, after having stared about him for some moments in silence— "you have not then seen it?—but, stay! you shall." Thus speaking, and having carefully shaded his lamp, he hurried to one of the casements, and threw it freely open to the storm.

The impetuous fury of the entering gust nearly lifted us from our feet. It was, indeed, a tempestuous yet sternly beautiful night, and one wildly singular in its terror and its beauty. A whirlwind had apparently collected its force in our vicinity; for there were frequent and violent alterations in the direction of the wind; and the exceeding density of the clouds (which hung so low as to press upon the turrets of the house) did not prevent our perceiving the life-like velocity with which they flew careering from all points against each other, without passing away into the distance. I say that even their exceeding density did not prevent our perceiving this—yet we had no glimpse of the moon or stars—nor was there any flashing forth of the lightning. But the under surfaces of the huge masses of agitated vapour, as well as all terrestrial objects immediately around us, were glowing in the unnatural light of a faintly luminous and distinctly visible gaseous exhalation which hung about and enshrouded the mansion.

"You must not—you shall not behold this!" said I,

shudderingly, to Usher, as I led him, with a gentle violence, from the window to a seat. "These appearances, which bewilder you, are merely electrical phenomena not uncommon—or it may be that they have their ghastly origin in the rank miasma of the tarn. Let us close this casement; the air is chilling and dangerous to your frame. Here is one of your favourite romances. I will read, and you shall listen; and so we will pass away this terrible night together."

The antique volume which I had taken up was the *Mad Trist* of Sir Launcelot Canning; but I had called it a favourite of Usher's more in sad jest than in earnest; for, in truth, there is little in its uncouth and unimaginative prolixity which could have had interest for the lofty and spiritual ideality of my friend. It was, however, the only book immediately at hand; and I indulged a vague hope that the excitement which now agitated the hypochondriac, might find relief (for the history of mental disorder is full of similar anomalies) even in the extremeness of the folly which I should read. Could I have judged, indeed, by the wild overstrained air of vivacity with which he hearkened, or apparently hearkened, to the words of the tale, I might well have congratulated myself upon the success of my design.

I had arrived at that well-known portion of the story where Ethelred, the hero of the Trist, having sought in vain for peaceable admission into the dwelling of the hermit, proceeds to make good an entrance by force. Here, it will be remembered, the words of the narrative run thus:

"And Ethelred, who was by nature of a doughty heart, and who was now mighty withal, on account of the powerfulness of the wine which he had drunken, waited no longer to hold parley with the hermit, who, in sooth, was of an obstinate and maliceful turn, but, feeling the rain upon his shoulders, and fearing the rising of the tempest, uplifted his mace outright, and, with blows, made quickly room in the plankings of the door for his gauntleted hand; and now pulling therewith sturdily, he so cracked, and ripped, and tore all asunder, that the noise of the dry and hollow-sounding wood alarumed and reverberated throughout the forest."

At the termination of this sentence I started, and for a moment, paused; for it appeared to me (although I at once concluded that my excited fancy had deceived me)—it appeared to me that, from some very remote portion of the mansion, there came, indistinctly, to my ears, what might have been, in its exact similarity of character, the echo (but a stifled and dull one certainly) of the very cracking and ripping sound which Sir Launcelot had so particularly described. It was, beyond doubt, the coincidence alone which had arrested my attention; for, amid the rattling of the sashes of the casements, and the ordinary commingled noises of the still increasing storm, the sound, in itself, had nothing, surely, which would have interested or disturbed me. I continued the story:

"But the good champion Ethelred, now entering within the door, was sore enraged and amazed to perceive no signal of the maliceful hermit; but, in the stead thereof, a dragon of a scaly and prodigious demeanour, and of a fiery tongue, which sate in guard before a palace of gold, with a floor of silver; and upon the wall there hung a shield of shining brass with this legend enwritten—

Who entereth herein, a conqueror hath bin;
Who slayeth the dragon, the shield he shall win.

And Ethelred uplifted his mace, and struck upon the
head of the dragon, which fell before him, and gave
up his pesty breath, with a shriek so horrid and harsh,
and withal so piercing, that Ethelred had fain to close
his ears with his hands against the dreadful noise of it,
the like whereof was never before heard."

Here again I paused abruptly, and now with a feeling of wild amazement—for there could be no doubt
whatever that, in this instance, I did actually hear
(although from what direction it proceeded I found it
impossible to say) a low and apparently distant, but
harsh, protracted, and most unusual screaming or grating sound—the exact counterpart of what my fancy
had already conjured up for the dragon's unnatural
shriek as described by the romancer.

Oppressed, as I certainly was, upon the occurrence
of the second and most extraordinary coincidence, by a
thousand conflicting sensations, in which wonder and
extreme terror were predominant, I still retained sufficient presence of mind to avoid exciting, by any observation, the sensitive nervousness of my companion.
I was by no means certain that he had noticed the
sounds in question; although, assuredly, a strange alteration had, during the last few minutes, taken place
in his demeanour. From a position fronting my own,
he had gradually brought round his chair, so as to sit
with his face to the door of the chamber; and thus I
could but partially perceive his features, although I
saw that his lips trembled as if he were murmuring
inaudibly. His head had dropped upon his breast—
yet I knew that he was not asleep, from the wide and
rigid opening of the eye as I caught a glance of it in
profile. The motion of his body, too, was at variance
with this idea—for he rocked from side to side with a
gentle yet constant and uniform sway. Having rapidly

taken notice of all this, I resumed the narrative of Sir Launcelot, which thus proceeded:

"And now, the champion, having escaped from the terrible fury of the dragon, bethinking himself of the brazen shield, and of the breaking up of the enchantment which was upon it, removed the carcass from out of the way before him, and approached valorously over the silver pavement of the castle to where the shield was upon the wall; which in sooth tarried not for his full coming, but fell down at his feet upon the silver floor, with a mighty great and terrible ringing sound."

No sooner had these syllables passed my lips, than—as if a shield of brass had indeed, at the moment, fallen heavily upon a floor of silver—I became aware of a distinct, hollow, metallic, and clangorous, yet apparently muffled reverberation. Completely unnerved, I leaped to my feet; but the measured rocking movement of Usher was undisturbed. I rushed to the chair in which he sat. His eyes were bent fixedly before him, and throughout his whole countenance there reigned a stony rigidity. But, as I placed my hand upon his shoulder, there came a strong shudder over his whole person; a sickly smile quivered about his lips; and I saw that he spoke in a low, hurried, and gibbering murmur, as if unconscious of my presence. Bending closely over him, I at length drank in the hideous import of his words.

"Not hear it?—yes, I hear it, and *have* heard it. Long —long—long—many minutes, many hours, many days, have I heard it—yet I dared not—oh, pity me, miserable wretch that I am!—I dared not—I *dared* not speak! *We have put her living in the tomb!* Said I not that my senses were acute? I *now* tell you that I heard her first feeble movements in the hollow coffin. I heard them— many, many days ago—yet I dared not—*I dared not speak!* And now—to-night—Ethelred—ha! ha! the breaking of the hermit's door, and the death-cry of the dragon, and the clangour of the shield!—say, rather, the rending of her coffin, and the grating of the iron hinges of her prison, and her struggles within the coppered archway of the vault! Oh whither shall I fly? Will she not be here anon? Is she not hurrying to upbraid me for my haste? Have I not heard her footstep on the stair? Do I not distinguish that heavy and horrible beating of her heart? MADMAN!" here he sprang furiously to his feet, and shrieked out his syllables, as if in the effort he were giving up his soul—"MADMAN! I TELL YOU THAT SHE NOW STANDS WITHOUT THE DOOR!"

As if in the superhuman energy of his utterance there had been found the potency of a spell—the huge antique panels to which the speaker pointed, threw slowly back, upon the instant, their ponderous and ebony jaws. It was the work of the rushing gust—but then without those doors there DID stand the lofty and enshrouded figure of the lady Madeline of Usher. There was blood upon her white robes, and the evidence of some bitter struggle upon every portion of her emaciated frame. For a moment she remained trembling and reeling to and fro upon the threshold, then, with a low moaning cry, fell heavily inward upon the person of her brother, and in her violent and now final death-agonies, bore him to the floor a corpse, and a victim to the terrors he had anticipated.

From that chamber, and from that mansion, I fled aghast. The storm was still abroad in all its wrath as I found myself crossing the old causeway. Suddenly there shot along the path a wild light, and I turned to see whence a gleam so unusual could have issued; for the vast house and its shadows were alone behind me. The radiance was that of the full, setting, and blood-red moon which now shone vividly through that once barely-discernible fissure of which I have before spoken as extending from the roof of the building, in a zigzag direction, the base. While I gazed, this fissure rapidly widened—there came a fierce breath of the whirlwind —the entire orb of the satellite burst at once upon my sight—my brain reeled as I saw the mighty walls rushing asunder—there was a long tumultuous shouting sound like the voice of a thousand waters—and the deep and dank tarn at my feet closed sullenly and silently over the fragments of the "House of Usher."

THE FACTS IN THE CASE
OF M. VALDEMAR

(*The American Review*, December, 1845.)

OF COURSE I shall not pretend to consider it any matter for wonder, that the extraordinary case of M. Valdemar has excited discussion. It would have been a miracle had it not—especially under the circumstances. Through the desire of all parties concerned, to keep the affair from the public, at least for the present, or until we had farther opportunities for investigation—through our endeavors to effect this—a garbled or exaggerated account made its way into society, and became the source of many unpleasant misrepresentations, and, very naturally, of a great deal of disbelief.

It is now rendered necessary that I give the *facts*— as far as I comprehend them myself. They are, succinctly, these:

My attention, for the last three years, had been repeatedly drawn to the subject of Mesmerism; and, about nine months ago, it occurred to me, quite suddenly, that in the series of experiments made hitherto, there had been a very remarkable and most unaccountable omission:—no person had as yet been mesmerized *in articulo mortis*. It remained to be seen, first, whether, in such condition, there existed in the patient any susceptibility to the magnetic influence; secondly, whether, if any existed, it was impaired or increased by the condition; thirdly, to what extent, or for how long a period, the encroachments of Death might be arrested by the process. There were other points to be ascertained, but these most excited my curiosity—the last in especial, from the immensely important character of its consequences.

In looking around me for some subject by whose means I might test these particulars, I was brought to think of my friend, M. Ernest Valdemar, the well-known compiler of the "Bibliotheca Forensica," and author (under the *nom de plume* of Issachar Marx) of the Polish versions of "Wallenstein" and "Gargantua." M. Valdemar, who has resided principally at Harlaem, N. Y., since the year 1839, is (or was) particularly noticeable for the extreme spareness of his person— his lower limbs much resembling those of John Randolph; and, also, for the whiteness of his whiskers, in violent contrast to the blackness of his hair—the latter, in consequence, being very generally mistaken for a wig. His temperament was markedly nervous, and rendered him a good subject for mesmeric experiment. On two or three occasions I had put him to sleep with little difficulty, but was disappointed in other results which his peculiar constitution had naturally led me to anticipate. His will was at no period positively, or thoroughly, under my control, and in regard to *clairvoyance*, I could accomplish with him nothing to be relied upon.

I always attributed my failure at these points to the disordered state of his health. For some months previous to my becoming acquainted with him, his physicians had declared him in a confirmed phthisis. It was his custom, indeed, to speak calmly of his approaching dissolution, as of a matter neither to be avoided nor regretted.

When the ideas to which I have alluded first occurred to me, it was of course very natural that I should think of M. Valdemar. I knew the steady philosophy of the man too well to apprehend any scruples from *him;* and he had no relatives in America who would be likely to interfere. I spoke to him frankly upon the subject; and, to my surprise, his interest seemed vividly excited. I say to my surprise; for, although he had always yielded his person freely to my experiments, he had never before given me any tokens of sympathy with what I did. His disease was of that character which would admit of exact calculation in respect to the epoch of its termination in death; and it was finally arranged between us that he would send for me about twenty-four hours before the period announced by his physicians as that of his decease.

It is now rather more than seven months since I received, from M. Valdemar himself, the subjoined note:

My dear P——,
    You may as well come *now.* D—— and F—— are agreed that I cannot hold out beyond tomorrow midnight; and I think they have hit the time very nearly.

VALDEMAR

I received this note within half an hour after it was written, and in fifteen minutes more I was in the dying man's chamber. I had not seen him for ten days, and was appalled by the fearful alteration which the brief interval had wrought in him. His face wore a leaden hue; the eyes were utterly lustreless; and the emaciation was so extreme that the skin had been broken through by the cheek-bones. His expectoration was excessive. The pulse was barely perceptible. He retained, nevertheless, in a very remarkable manner, both his mental power and a certain degree of physical strength. He spoke with distinctness—took some palliative medicines without aid—and, when I entered the room, was occupied in penciling memoranda in a pocket-book. He was propped up in the bed by pillows. Doctors D—— and F—— were in attendance.

After pressing Valdemar's hand, I took these gentlemen aside, and obtained from them a minute account of the patient's condition. The left lung had been for eighteen months in a semi-osseous or cartilaginous state, and was, of course, entirely useless for all purposes of vitality. The right, in its upper portion, was also partially, if not thoroughly, ossified, while the lower region was merely a mass of purulent tubercles, running one into another. Several extensive perforations existed; and, at one point, permanent adhesion to the ribs had taken place. These appearances in the right lobe were of comparatively recent date. The ossification had proceeded with very unusual rapidity; no sign of it had been discovered a month before, and the adhesion had only been observed during the three previous days. Independently of the phthisis, the patient was suspected of aneurism of the aorta; but on this point the osseous symptoms rendered an exact diagnosis impossible. It was the opinion of both physicians that M. Valdemar would die about midnight on the morrow (Sunday). It was then seven o'clock on Saturday evening.

On quitting the invalid's bed-side to hold conversation with myself, Doctors D—— and F—— had bidden him a final farewell. It had not been their intention to return; but, at my request, they agreed to look in upon the patient about ten the next night.

When they had gone, I spoke freely with M. Valdemar on the subject of his approaching dissolution, as well as, more particularly, of the experiment proposed. He still professed himself quite willing and even anxious to have it made, and urged me to commence it at once. A male and a female nurse were in attendance; but I did not feel myself altogether at liberty to engage in a task of this character with no more reliable witnesses than these people, in case of sudden accident, might prove. I therefore postponed operations until about eight the next night, when the arrival of a medical student with whom I had some acquaintance, (Mr. Theodore L——l,) relieved me from farther embarrassment. It had been my design, originally, to wait for the physicians; but I was induced to proceed, first, by the urgent entreaties of M. Valdemar, and secondly, by my conviction that I had not a moment to lose, as he was evidently sinking fast.

Mr. L——l was so kind as to accede to my desire that he would take notes of all that occurred; and it is from his memoranda that what I now have to relate is, for the most part, either condensed or copied *verbatim*.

It wanted about five minutes of eight when, taking the patient's hand, I begged him to state, as distinctly as he could, to Mr. L——l, whether he (M. Valdemar) was entirely willing that I should make the experiment of mesmerizing him in his then condition.

He replied feebly, yet quite audibly, "Yes, I wish to be mesmerized"—adding immediately afterwards, "I fear you have deferred it too long."

While he spoke thus, I commenced the passes which I had already found most effectual in subduing him. He was evidently influenced with the first lateral stroke of my hand across his forehead; but although I exerted all my powers, no farther perceptible effect was induced until some minutes after ten o'clock, when Doctors D—— and F—— called, according to appointment. I explained to them, in a few words, what I designed, and as they opposed no objection, saying that the patient was already in the death agony, I proceeded without hesitation—exchanging, however, the lateral passes for downward ones, and directing my gaze entirely into the right eye of the sufferer.

By this time his pulse was imperceptible and his breathing was stertorous, and at intervals of half a minute.

This condition was nearly unaltered for a quarter of an hour. At the expiration of this period, however, a natural although a very deep sigh escaped the bosom of the dying man, and the stertorous breathing ceased— that is to say, its stertorousness was no longer apparent; the intervals were undiminished. The patient's extremities were of an icy coldness.

At five minutes before eleven I perceived unequivocal signs of the mesmeric influence. The glassy roll of the eye was changed for that expression of uneasy *inward* examination which is never seen except in cases of sleep-waking, and which it is quite impossible to mistake. With a few rapid lateral passes I made the lids quiver, as in incipient sleep, and with a few more I closed them altogether. I was not satisfied, however, with this, but continued the manipulations vigorously, and with the fullest exertion of the will, until I had completely stiffened the limbs of the slumberer, after placing them in a seemingly easy position. The legs were at full length; the arms were nearly so, and reposed on the bed at a moderate distance from the loins. The head was very slightly elevated.

When I had accomplished this, it was fully midnight, and I requested the gentlemen present to examine M. Valdemar's condition. After a few experiments, they admitted him to be in an unusually perfect state of mesmeric trance. The curiosity of both the physicians was greatly excited. Dr. D—— resolved at once to remain with the patient all night, while Dr. F—— took leave with a promise to return at daybreak. Mr. L——l and the nurses remained.

We left M. Valdemar entirely undisturbed until about three o'clock in the morning, when I approached him and found him in precisely the same condition as when Dr. F—— went away—that is to say, he lay in the same position; the pulse was imperceptible; the breathing was gentle (scarcely noticeable, unless through the application of a mirror to the lips); the eyes were closed naturally; and the limbs were as rigid and as cold as marble. Still, the general appearance was certainly not that of death.

As I approached M. Valdemar I made a kind of half effort to influence his right arm into pursuit of my own, as I passed the latter gently to and fro above his person. In such experiments with this patient I had never perfectly succeeded before, and assuredly I had little thought of succeeding now; but to my astonishment, his arm very readily, although feebly, followed every direction I assigned it with mine. I determined to hazard a few words of conversation.

"M. Valdemar," I said, "are you asleep?" He made no answer, but I perceived a tremor about the lips, and was thus induced to repeat the question, again and again. At its third repetition, his whole frame was agitated by a very slight shivering; the eyelids unclosed themselves so far as to display a white line of the ball; the lips moved sluggishly, and from between them, in a barely audible whisper, issued the words:

"Yes;—asleep now. Do not wake me!—let me die so!"

I here felt the limbs and found them as rigid as ever. The right arm, as before, obeyed the direction of my hand. I questioned the sleep-waker again:

"Do you still feel pain in the breast, M. Valdemar?"

The answer now was immediate, but even less audible than before:

"No pain—I am dying."

I did not think it advisable to disturb him farther just then, and nothing more was said or done until the arrival of Dr. F——, who came a little before sunrise, and expressed unbounded astonishment at finding the patient still alive. After feeling the pulse and applying a mirror to the lips, he requested me to speak to the sleep-waker again. I did so, saying:

"M. Valdemar, do you still sleep?"

As before, some minutes elapsed ere a reply was made; and during the interval the dying man seemed to be collecting his energies to speak. At my fourth repetition of the question, he said very faintly, almost inaudibly:

"Yes; still asleep—dying."

It was now the opinion, or rather the wish, of the physicians, that M. Valdemar should be suffered to remain undisturbed in his present apparently tranquil condition, until death should supervene—and this, it was generally agreed, must now take place within a few minutes. I concluded, however, to speak to him once more, and merely repeated my previous question.

While I spoke, there came a marked change over the countenance of the sleep-waker. The eyes rolled

themselves slowly open, the pupils disappearing up-
wardly; the skin generally assumed a cadaverous hue,
resembling not so much parchment as white paper;
and the circular hectic spots which, hitherto, had been
strongly defined in the centre of each cheek, *went out*
at once. I use this expression, because the suddenness
of their departure put me in mind of nothing so much
as the extinguishment of a candle by a puff of the breath.
The upper lip, at the same time, writhed itself away
from the teeth, which it had previously covered completely; while the lower jaw fell with an audible jerk,
leaving the mouth widely extended, and disclosing in
full view the swollen and blackened tongue. I presume
that no member of the party then present had been
unaccustomed to death-bed horrors; but so hideous
beyond conception was the appearance of M. Valdemar
at this moment, that there was a general shrinking
back from the region of the bed.

I now feel that I have reached a point of this narrative at which every reader will be startled into positive
disbelief. It is my business, however, simply to proceed.

There was no longer the faintest sign of vitality in
M. Valdemar; and concluding him to be dead, we were
consigning him to the charge of the nurses, when a
strong vibratory motion was observable in the tongue.
This continued for perhaps a minute. At the expiration
of this period, there issued from the distended and
motionless jaws a voice—such as it would be madness
in me to attempt describing. There are, indeed, two
or three epithets which might be considered as applicable to it in part; I might say, for example, that the
sound was harsh, and broken and hollow; but the
hideous whole is indescribable, for the simple reason
that no similar sounds have ever jarred upon the ear
of humanity. There were two particulars, nevertheless

which I thought then, and still think, might fairly be stated as characteristic of the intonation—as well adapted to convey some idea of its unearthly peculiarity. In the first place, the voice seemed to reach our ears— at least mine—from a vast distance, or from some deep cavern within the earth. In the second place, it impressed me (I fear, indeed, that it will be impossible to make myself comprehended) as gelatinous or glutinous matters impress the sense of touch.

I have spoken both of "sound" and of "voice." I mean to say that the sound was one of distinct—of even wonderfully, thrillingly distinct—syllabification. M. Valdemar *spoke*—obviously in reply to the question I had propounded to him a few minutes before. I had asked him, it will be remembered, if he still slept. He now said:

"Yes;—no;—I *have been* sleeping—and now—now —*I am dead.*"

No person present even affected to deny, or attempted to repress, the unutterable, shuddering horror which these few words, thus uttered, were so well calculated to convey. Mr. L——l (the student) swooned. The nurses immediately left the chamber, and could not be induced to return. My own impressions I would not pretend to render intelligible to the reader. For nearly an hour, we busied ourselves, silently—without the utterance of a word—in endeavors to revive Mr. L——l. When he came to himself, we addressed ourselves again to an investigation of M. Valdemar's condition.

It remained in all respects as I have last described it, with the exception that the mirror no longer afforded evidence of respiration. An attempt to draw blood from the arm failed. I should mention, too, that this limb was no farther subject to my will. I endeavored in vain to make it follow the direction of my hand.

The only real indication, indeed, of the mesmeric influence, was now found in the vibratory movement of the tongue, whenever I addressed M. Valdemar a question. He seemed to be making an effort to reply, but had no longer sufficient volition. To queries put to him by any other person than myself he seemed utterly insensible—although I endeavored to place each member of the company in mesmeric *rapport* with him. I believe that I have now related all that is necessary to an understanding of the sleep-waker's state at this epoch. Other nurses were procured; and at ten o'clock I left the house in company with the two physicians and Mr. L——l.

In the afternoon we all called again to see the patient. His condition remained precisely the same. We had now some discussion as to the propriety and feasibility of awakening him; but we had little difficulty in agreeing that no good purpose would be served by so doing. It was evident that, so far, death (or what is usually termed death) had been arrested by the mesmeric process. It seemed clear to us all that to awaken M. Valdemar would be merely to insure his instant, or at least his speedy dissolution.

From this period until the close of last week—*an interval of nearly seven months*—we continued to make daily calls at M. Valdemar's house, accompanied, now and then, by medical and other friends. All this time the sleeper-waker remained *exactly* as I have last described him. The nurses' attentions were continual.

It was on Friday last that we finally resolved to make the experiment of awakening, or attempting to awaken him; and it is the (perhaps) unfortunate result of this latter experiment which has given rise to so much discussion in private circles—to so much of what I cannot help thinking unwarranted popular feeling.

For the purpose of relieving M. Valdemar from the mesmeric trance, I made use of the customary passes. These, for a time, were unsuccessful. The first indication of revival was afforded by a partial descent of the iris. It was observed, as especially remarkable, that this lowering of the pupil was accompanied by the profuse out-flowing of a yellowish ichor (from beneath the lids) of a pungent and highly offensive odor.

It was now suggested that I should attempt to influence the patient's arm, as heretofore. I made the attempt and failed. Dr. F—— then intimated a desire to have me put a question. I did so, as follows:

"M. Valdemar, can you explain to us what are your feelings or wishes now?"

There was an instant return of the hectic circles on the cheeks; the tongue quivered, or rather rolled violently in the mouth (although the jaws and lips remained rigid as before;) and at length the same hideous voice which I have already described, broke forth:

"For God's sake!—quick!—quick!—put me to sleep —or, quick!—waken me!—quick!—*I say to you that I am dead!*"

I was thoroughly unnerved, and for an instant remained undecided what to do. At first I made an endeavor to re-compose the patient; but, failing in this through total abeyance of the will, I retraced my steps and as earnestly struggled to awaken him. In this attempt I soon saw that I should be successful—or at least I soon fancied that my success would be complete —and I am sure that all in the room were prepared to see the patient awaken.

For what really occurred, however, it is quite impossible that any human being could have been prepared.

As I rapidly made the mesmeric passes, amid ejaculations of "dead! dead!" absolutely *bursting* from the tongue and not from the lips of the sufferer, his whole frame at once—within the space of a single minute, or even less, shrunk—crumbled—absolutely *rotted* away beneath my hands. Upon the bed, before that whole company, there lay a nearly liquid mass of loathsome—of detestable putridity.

THE MASQUE
OF THE RED DEATH

(*Graham's Magazine*, May, 1842.)

THE "Red Death" had long devastated the country. No pestilence had ever been so fatal, or so hideous. Blood was its Avatar and its seal—the redness and the horror of blood. There were sharp pains, and sudden dizziness, and then profuse bleeding at the pores, with dissolution. The scarlet stains upon the body and especially upon the face of the victim, were the pest ban which shut him out from the aid and from the sympathy of his fellow-men. And the whole seizure, progress and termination of the disease, were the incidents of half an hour.

But the Prince Prospero was happy and dauntless and sagacious. When his dominions were half depopulated, he summoned to his presence a thousand hale and light-hearted friends from among the knights and dames of his court, and with these retired to the deep seclusion of one of his castellated abbeys. This was an extensive and magnificent structure, the creation of the prince's own eccentric yet august taste. A strong and lofty wall girdled it in. This wall had gates of iron. The courtiers, having entered, brought furnaces and massy hammers and welded the bolts. They resolved to leave means neither of ingress or egress to the sudden impulses of despair or of frenzy from within. The abbey was amply provisioned. With such precautions the courtiers might bid defiance to contagion. The external world could take care of itself. In the meantime it was folly to grieve, or to think. The prince had provided all the appliances of pleasure. There were buffoons, there were improvisatori, there were ballet-dancers, there were musicians, there was Beauty, there was wine. All these and security were within. Without was the "Red Death."

It was toward the close of the fifth or sixth month of his seclusion, and while the pestilence raged most furiously abroad, that the Prince Prospero entertained his thousand friends at a masked ball of the most un-usual magnificence.

It was a voluptuous scene, that masquerade. But first let me tell of the rooms in which it was held. There were seven—an imperial suite. In many palaces, how-ever, such suites form a long and straight vista, while the folding doors slide back nearly to the walls on either hand, so that the view of the whole extent is scarcely impeded. Here the case was very different; as might have been expected from the duke's love of the *bizarre*. The apartments were so irregularly disposed that the vision embraced but little more than one at a time. There was a sharp turn at every twenty or thirty yards, and at each turn a novel effect. To the right and left, in the middle of each wall, a tall and narrow Gothic window looked out upon a closed corridor which pur-sued the windings of the suite. These windows were of stained glass whose color varied in accordance with the prevailing hue of the decorations of the chamber into which it opened. That at the eastern extremity was hung, for example, in blue—and vividly blue were its windows. The second chamber was purple in its ornaments and tapestries, and here the panes were purple. The third was green throughout, and so were the casements. The fourth was furnished and lighted with orange —the fifth with white—the sixth with violet. The seventh apartment was closely shrouded in black velvet tapestries that hung all over the ceiling and down the walls, falling in heavy folds upon a carpet of the same material and hue. But in this chamber only, the color of the windows failed to correspond with the decorations. The panes here were scarlet—a deep blood color. Now in no one of the seven apartments was there any lamp or candelabrum, amid the profusion of golden ornaments that lay scattered to and fro or depended from the roof. There was no light of any kind emanating from lamp or candle within the suite of chambers. But in the corridors that followed the suite, there stood, opposite to each window, a heavy tripod, bearing a brazier of fire that projected its rays through the tinted glass and so glaringly illumined the room. And thus were produced a multitude of gaudy and fantastic appearances. But in the western or black chamber the effect of the fire-light that streamed upon the dark hangings through the blood-tinted panes, was ghastly in the extreme, and produced so wild a look upon the countenances of those who entered, that there were few of the company bold enough to set foot within its precincts at all.

It was in this apartment, also, that there stood against the western wall, a gigantic clock of ebony. Its pendulum swung to and fro with a dull, heavy, monotonous clang; and when the minute-hand made the circuit of the face, and the hour was to be stricken, there came from the brazen lungs of the clock a sound which was clear and loud and deep and exceedingly musical, but of so peculiar a note and emphasis that, at each lapse of an hour, the musicians of the orchestra were constrained to pause, momentarily, in their performance, to hearken to the sound; and thus the waltzers perforce ceased their evolutions; and there was a brief disconcert of the whole gay company; and, while the chimes of the clock yet rang, it was observed that the giddiest grew pale, and the more aged and sedate passed their hands over their brows as if in confused reverie or meditation. But when the echoes had fully ceased, a light laughter at once pervaded the assembly; the musicians looked at each other and smiled as if at their own nervousness and folly, and made whispering vows, each to the other, that the next chiming of the clock should produce in them no similar emotion; and then, after the lapse of sixty minutes, (which embrace three thousand and six hundred seconds of the Time that flies,) there came yet another chiming of the clock, and then were the same disconcert and tremulousness and meditation as before.

But, in spite of these things, it was a gay and magnificent revel. The tastes of the duke were peculiar. He had a fine eye for colors and effects. He disregarded the *decora* of mere fashion. His plans were bold and fiery, and his conceptions glowed with barbaric lustre. There are some who would have thought him mad. His followers felt that he was not. It was necessary to hear and see and touch him to be *sure* that he was not.

He had directed, in great part, the moveable embellishments of the seven chambers, upon occasion of this great *fête;* and it was his own guiding taste which had given character to the masqueraders. Be sure they were grotesque. There were much glare and glitter and piquancy and phantasm—much of what has been since seen in *Hernani*. There were arabesque figures with unsuited limbs and appointments. There were delirious fancies such as the madman fashions. There was much of the beautiful, much of the wanton, much of the *bizarre*, something of the terrible, and not a little of that which might have excited disgust. To and fro in the seven chambers there stalked, in fact, a multitude of dreams. And these—the dreams—writhed in and about, taking hue from the rooms, and causing the wild music of the orchestra to seem as the echo of their steps. And, anon, there strikes the ebony clock which stands in the hall of the velvet. And then, for a moment, all is still, and all is silent save the voice of the clock. The dreams are stiff-frozen as they stand. But the echoes of the chime die away— they have endured but an instant—and a light, half-subdued laughter floats after them as they depart. And now again the music swells, and the dreams live, and writhe to and fro more merrily than ever, taking hue from the many-tinted windows through which stream the rays from the tripods. But to the chamber which lies most westwardly of the seven, there are now none of the maskers who venture; for the night is waning away; and there flows a ruddier light through the blood-colored panes; and the blackness of the sable drapery appals; and to him whose foot falls upon the sable carpet, there comes from the near clock of ebony a muffled peal more solemnly emphatic than any which reaches *their* ears who indulge in the more remote gaieties of the other apartments.

But these other apartments were densely crowded, and in them beat feverishly the heart of life. And the revel went whirlingly on, until at length there commenced the sounding of midnight upon the clock. And then the music ceased, as I have told; and the evolutions of the waltzers were quieted; and there was an uneasy cessation of all things as before. But now there were twelve strokes to be sounded by the bell of the clock; and thus it happened, perhaps, that more of thought crept, with more of time, into the meditations of the thoughtful among those who revelled. And thus, too, it happened, perhaps, that before the last echoes of the last chime had utterly sunk into silence, there were many individuals in the crowd who had found leisure to become aware of the presence of a masked figure which had arrested the attention of no single individual before. And the rumor of this new presence having spread itself whisperingly around, there arose at length from the whole company a buzz, or murmur, expressive of disapprobation and surprise—then, finally, of terror, of horror, and of disgust.

In an assembly of phantasms such as I have painted, it may well be supposed that no ordinary appearance could have excited such sensation. In truth the masquerade license of the night was nearly unlimited; but the figure in question had out-Heroded Herod, and gone beyond the bounds of even the prince's indefinite decorum. There are chords in the hearts of the most reckless which cannot be touched without emotion. Even with the utterly lost, to whom life and death are equally jests, there are matters of which no jest can be made. The whole company, indeed, seemed now deeply to feel that in the costume and bearing of the stranger neither wit nor propriety existed. The figure was tall and gaunt, and shrouded from head to foot in the habiliments of the grave. The mask which concealed the visage was made so nearly to resemble the countenance of a stiffened corpse that the closest scrutiny must have had difficulty in detecting the cheat. And yet all this might have been endured, if not approved, by the mad revellers around. But the mummer had gone so far to assume the type of the Red Death. His vesture was dabbled in *blood*—and his broad brow, with all the features of the face, was besprinkled with the scarlet horror.

When the eyes of Prince Prospero fell upon this spectral image (which with a slow and solemn movement, as if more fully to sustain its *rôle*, stalked to and fro among the waltzers) he was seen to be convulsed, in the first moment with a strong shudder either of terror or distaste; but, in the next, his brow reddened with rage.

"Who dares?" he demanded hoarsely of the courtiers who stood near him—"who dares insult us with this blasphemous mockery? Seize him and unmask him —that we may know whom we have to hang at sunrise, from the battlements!"

It was in the eastern or blue chamber in which stood the Prince Prospero as he uttered these words. They rang throughout the seven rooms loudly and clearly— for the prince was a bold and robust man, and the music had become hushed at the waving of his hand.

It was in the blue room where stood the prince, with a group of pale courtiers by his side. At first, as he spoke, there was a slight rushing movement of this group in the direction of the intruder, who at the moment was also near at hand, and now, with deliberate and stately step, made closer approach to the speaker. But from a certain nameless awe with which the mad assumptions of the mummer had inspired the whole party, there were found none who put forth hand to seize him; so that, unimpeded, he passed within a yard of the prince's person; and, while the vast assembly, as if with one impulse, shrank from the centres of the rooms to the walls, he made his way uninterruptedly, but with the same solemn and measured step which had distinguished him from the first, through the blue chamber to the purple—through the purple to the green—through the green to the orange—through this again to the white—and even thence to the violet, ere a decided movement had been made to arrest him. It was then, however, that the Prince Prospero, maddening with rage and the shame of his own momentary cowardice, rushed hurriedly through the six chambers, while none followed him on account of a deadly terror that had seized upon all. He bore aloft a drawn dagger, and had approached, in rapid impetuosity, to within three or four feet of the retreating figure, when the latter, having attained the extremity of the velvet apartment, turned suddenly and confronted his pursuer. There was a sharp cry—and the dagger dropped gleaming upon the sable carpet, upon which, instantly afterwards, fell prostrate in death the Prince Prospero. Then, summoning the wild courage of despair, a throng of the revellers at once threw themselves into the black apartment, and, seizing the mummer, whose tall figure stood erect and motion-less within the shadow of the ebony clock, gasped in unutterable horror at finding the grave-cerements and corpse-like mask which they handled with so violent a rudeness, untenanted by any tangible form.

And now was acknowledged the presence of the Red Death. He had come like a thief in the night. And one by one dropped the revellers in the blood-bedewed halls of their revel, and died each in the despairing posture of his fall. And the life of the ebony clock went out with that of the last of the gay. And the flames of the tripods expired. And Darkness and Decay and the Red Death held illimitable dominion over all.

Of Revenge and Murder

EDITOR'S PREFACE

Poe was a man with a grievance; he knew that he possessed a fine intellect and extraordinary ability, but he never received the rewards to which he must have felt entitled. He saw other less able and less gifted writers highly praised and paid substantially for their obviously inferior work. He also saw John Allan's illegitimate children awarded legacies, while he, the adopted son, got nothing. He did not take these slights easily; he burned with sullen anger and probably indulged in daydreams of revenge. There was a sadistic streak in him too, a malicious and wanton desire to hurt others for the perverse satisfaction it gave him. His attempts at humor show this; some of his lesser-known tales like "The Spectacles" and "The Man that Was Used Up" are not only in bad taste but are offensively cruel.

The four tales in this section are all murder stories; the first two are concerned with killings committed without any ascertainable reason; the second two are tales of murder committed for revenge.

"The Tell-Tale Heart" and "The Black Cat" have a lot in common with each other and with a third, less important story, aptly entitled "The Imp of the Perverse." All three tales deal with a murderer who has committed a successful crime and is apparently about to escape the consequences. Then through sheer perverseness, the killer betrays himself and confesses his guilt. Like "William Wilson," they are tales of conscience. The respectable Mr. Poe was troubled by his other, darker self, and the conflict is mirrored in these stories.

"The Tell-Tale Heart" is one of Poe's most compact and brilliantly executed tales. It has none of the Gothic trappings that date some of his work, so that it reads like a modern, tautly written psychological story.

"The Black Cat," its companion piece, is one of the most celebrated of Poe's short pieces of fiction. Although it is artistically inferior to "The Tell-Tale Heart," the image of the sinister cat makes an ineradicable impression upon the mind of the reader. It is noteworthy that both these stories have to do with an eye, the symbol of watchfulness, of censure, and the reminder of guilt.

The associative links that connect the Poe stories are numerous. The idea of disposing of a body by walling it up in a vault that occurs in "The Black Cat" reoccurs in "The Cask of Amontillado"—and with an additional twist of horror, for in the latter story the victim is entombed alive. "The Cask of Amontillado" has revenge as its sole motive. It is interesting to note that the family arms of the avenger are described as a foot crushing a serpent whose fangs are imbedded in its heel, together with the motto: *"Nemo me impune lacessit."*

Even more sadistic and vengeful is "Hop-Frog," the tale of a crippled court jester who strikes back at his tormentors in a peculiarly horrible way. This seldom-read tale is one of the most unconsciously self-revealing documents its author left to the world. The dwarf and his beloved come from "some barbarous region that no person ever heard of"; the king and his seven fat ministers force the dwarf to drink, although they know that "wine excited the poor cripple almost to madness"; when the dwarf hesitates, the king throws the contents of the goblet in the girl's face; then the dwarf conceives his dreadful revenge and carries it out with implacable determination. This story was written in February 1849, just eight months before its author's death. It was written after Poe's wife had died of poverty and starvation, after a lifetime of rejection and failure, and immediately after the humiliating experience Poe had gone through with Mrs. Whitman and her family and friends. Unable to take physical revenge upon those who had made him suffer, he struck back at them in his daydreams and—symbolically—in his writing.

THE TELL-TALE HEART
(*The Pioneer*, January, 1843.)

TRUE!—nervous—very, very dreadfully nervous I had been and am; but why *will* you say that I am mad? The disease had sharpened my senses—not destroyed—not dulled them. Above all was the sense of hearing acute. I heard all things in the heaven and in the earth. I heard many things in hell. How, then, am I mad? Hearken! and observe how healthily—how calmly I can tell you the whole story.

It is impossible to say how first the idea entered my brain; but once conceived, it haunted me day and night. Object there was none. Passion there was none. I loved the old man. He had never wronged me. He had never given me insult. For his gold I had no desire. I think it was his eye! yes, it was this! He had the eye of a vulture—a pale blue eye, with a film over it. Whenever it fell upon me, my blood ran cold; and so by degrees—very gradually—I made up my mind to take the life of the old man, and thus rid myself of the eye forever.

Now this is the point. You fancy me mad. Madmen know nothing. But you should have seen *me*. You should have seen how wisely I proceeded—with what caution

—with what foresight—with what dissimulation I went to work! I was never kinder to the old man than during the whole week before I killed him. And every night, about midnight, I turned the latch of his door and opened it—oh so gently! And then, when I had made an opening sufficient for my head, I put in a dark lantern, all closed, closed, so that no light shone out, and then I thrust in my head. Oh, you would have laughed to see how cunningly I thrust it in! I moved it slowly—very, very slowly, so that I might not disturb the old man's sleep. It took me an hour to place my whole head within the opening so far that I could see him as he lay upon his bed. Ha!—would a madman have been so wise as this? And then, when my head was well in the room, I undid the lantern cautiously—oh, so cautiously— cautiously (for the hinges creaked)—I undid it just so much that a single thin ray fell upon the vulture eye. And this I did for seven long nights—every night just at midnight—but I found the eye always closed; and so it was impossible to do the work; for it was not the old man who vexed me, but his Evil Eye. And every morning, when the day broke, I went boldly into the chamber, and spoke courageously to him, calling him by name in a hearty tone, and inquiring how he had passed the night. So you see he would have been a very profound old man, indeed, to suspect that every night, just at twelve, I looked in upon him while he slept.

Upon the eighth night I was more than usually cautious in opening the door. A watch's minute hand moves more quickly than did mine. Never before that night, had I *felt* the extent of my own powers—of my sagacity. I could scarcely contain my feelings of triumph. To think that there I was, opening the door, little by little, and he not even to dream of my secret deeds or thoughts. I fairly chuckled at the idea; and perhaps he heard me; for he moved on the bed suddenly, as if startled. Now you may think that I drew back—but no. His room was as black as pitch with the thick darkness, (for the shutters were close fastened, through fear of robbers,) and so I knew that he could not see the opening of the door, and I kept pushing it on steadily, steadily.

I had my head in, and was about to open the lantern, when my thumb slipped upon the tin fastening, and the old man sprang up in bed, crying out—"Who's there?"

I kept quite still and said nothing. For a whole hour I did not move a muscle, and in the meantime I did not hear him lie down. He was still sitting up in the bed listening;—just as I have done, night after night, hearkening to the death watches in the wall.

Presently I heard a slight groan, and I knew it was the groan of mortal terror. It was not a groan of pain or of grief—oh, no!—it was the low stifled sound that arises from the bottom of the soul when over-charged with awe. I knew the sound well. Many a night, just at midnight, when all the world slept, it has welled up from my own bosom, deepening, with its dreadful echo. the terrors that distracted me. I say I knew it well. I knew what the old man felt, and pitied him, although I chuckled at heart. I knew that he had been lying awake ever since the first slight noise, when he had turned in the bed. His fears had been ever since growing upon him. He had been trying to fancy them causeless, but could not. He had been saying to himself—"It is nothing but the wind in the chimney—it is only a mouse crossing the floor," or "it is merely a cricket which has made a single chirp." Yes, he had been trying to comfort himself with these suppositions: but he had found all in vain. *All in vain;* because Death, in approaching him had stalked with his black shadow before him, and enveloped the victim. And it was the mournful influence of the unperceived shadow that caused him to feel— although he neither saw nor heard—to *feel* the presence of my head within the room.

When I had waited a long time, very patiently, without hearing him lie down, I resolved to open a little —a very, very little crevice in the lantern. So I opened it—you cannot imagine how stealthily, stealthily— until, at length a simple dim ray, like the thread of the spider, shot from out the crevice and fell full upon the vulture eye.

It was open—wide, wide open—and I grew furious as I gazed upon it. I saw it with perfect distinctness— all a dull blue, with a hideous veil over it that chilled the very marrow in my bones; but I could see nothing else of the old man's face or person: for I had directed the ray as if by instinct, precisely upon the damned spot.

And have I not told you that what you mistake for madness is but over acuteness of the senses?—now, I say, there came to my ears a low, dull, quick sound, such as a watch makes when enveloped in cotton. I knew *that* sound well, too. It was the beating of the old man's heart. It increased my fury, as the beating of a drum stimulates the soldier into courage.

But even yet I refrained and kept still. I scarcely breathed. I held the lantern motionless. I tried how steadily I could maintain the ray upon the eye. Mean- time the hellish tattoo of the heart increased. It grew quicker and quicker, and louder and louder every in- stant. The old man's terror *must* have been extreme! It grew louder, I say, louder every moment!—do you mark me well? I have told you that I am nervous: so I am. And now at the dead hour of the night, amid the dreadful silence of that old house, so strange a noise as this excited me to uncontrollable terror. Yet, for some minutes longer I refrained and stood still. But the beating grew louder, louder! I thought the heart must burst. And now a new anxiety seized me—the sound would be heard by a neighbour! The old man's hour had come! With a loud yell, I threw open the lantern and leaped into the room. He shrieked once—once only. In an instant I dragged him to the floor, and pulled the heavy bed over him. I then smiled gaily, to find the deed so far done. But, for many minutes, the heart beat on with a muffled sound. This, however, did not vex me; it would not be heard through the wall. At length it ceased. The old man was dead. I removed the bed and examined the corpse. Yes, he was stone, stone dead. I placed my hand upon the heart and held it there many minutes. There was no pulsation. He was stone dead. His eye would trouble me no more.

If still you think me mad, you will think so no longer when I describe the wise precautions I took for the concealment of the body. The night waned, and I worked hastily, but in silence. First of all I dismembered the corpse. I cut off the head and the arms and the legs.

I then took up three planks from the flooring of the chamber, and deposited all between the scantlings. I then replaced the boards so cleverly, so cunningly, that no human eye—not even *his*—could have detected any thing wrong. There was nothing to wash out—no stain of any kind—no blood-spot whatever. I had been too wary for that. A tub had caught all—ha! ha!

When I had made an end of these labors, it was four o'clock—still dark as midnight. As the bell sounded the hour, there came a knocking at the street door. I went down to open it with a light heart,—for what had I *now* to fear? There entered three men, who introduced themselves, with perfect suavity, as officers of the police.

A shriek had been heard by a neighbour during the night; suspicion of foul play had been aroused; information had been lodged at the police office, and they (the officers) had been deputed to search the premises.

I smiled,—for *what* had I to fear? I bade the gentlemen welcome. The shriek, I said, was my own in a dream. The old man, I mentioned, was absent in the country. I took my visitors all over the house. I bade them search—search *well*. I led them, at length, to *his* chamber. I showed them his treasures, secure, undisturbed. In the enthusiasm of my confidence, I brought chairs into the room, and desired them *here* to rest from their fatigues, while I myself, in the wild audacity of my perfect triumph, placed my own seat upon the very spot beneath which reposed the corpse of the victim.

The officers were satisfied. My *manner* had convinced them. I was singularly at ease. They sat, and while I answered cheerily, they chatted of familiar things. But, ere long, I felt myself getting pale and wished them gone. My head ached, and I fancied a ringing in my ears: but still they sat and still chatted. The ringing became more distinct:—it continued and became more distinct: I talked more freely to get rid of the feeling: but it continued and gained definiteness—until, at length, I found that the noise was *not* within my ears.

No doubt I now grew *very* pale;—but I talked more fluently, and with a heightened voice. Yet the sound increased—and what could I do? It was *a low, dull, quick sound—much such a sound as a watch makes when enveloped in cotton*. I gasped for breath—and yet the officers heard it not. I talked more quickly—more vehemently; but the noise steadily increased. I arose and argued about trifles, in a high key and with violent gesticulations; but the noise steadily increased. Why *would* they not be gone? I paced the floor to and fro

with heavy strides, as if excited to fury by the observations of the men—but the noise steadily increased. Oh
God! what *could* I do? I foamed—I raved—I swore! I
swung the chair upon which I had been sitting, and
grated it upon the boards, but the noise arose over all
and continually increased. It grew louder—louder—
louder! And still the men chatted pleasantly, and smiled.
Was it possible they heard not? Almighty God!—no, no!
They heard!—they suspected!—they *knew!*—they were
making a mockery of my horror!—this I thought, and
this I think. But anything was better than this agony!
Anything was more tolerable than this derision! I could
bear those hypocritical smiles no longer! I felt that I
must scream or die! and now—again!—hark! louder!
louder! louder! *louder!*

"Villains!" I shrieked, "dissemble no more! I admit
the deed!—tear up the planks! here, here!—it is the
beating of his hideous heart!"

THE BLACK CAT

(The Philadelphia *United States Saturday Post*, August 19, 1843.)

FOR the most wild, yet most homely narrative
which I am about to pen, I neither expect nor solicit
belief. Mad indeed would I be to expect it, in a case
where my very senses reject their own evidence. Yet,
mad am I not—and very surely do I not dream. But to-
morrow I die, and to-day I would unburthen my soul.
My immediate purpose is to place before the world,
plainly, succinctly, and without comment, a series of
mere household events. In their consequences, these
events have terrified—have tortured—have destroyed
me. Yet I will not attempt to expound them. To me,

they have presented little but Horror—to many they will seem less terrible than *baroques*. Hereafter, perhaps, some intellect may be found which will reduce my phantasm to the common-place—some intellect more calm, more logical, and far less excitable than my own, which will perceive, in the circumstances I detail with awe, nothing more than an ordinary succession of very natural causes and effects.

From my infancy I was noted for the docility and humanity of my disposition. My tenderness of heart was even so conspicuous as to make me the jest of my companions. I was especially fond of animals, and was indulged by my parents with a great variety of pets. With these I spent most of my time, and never was so happy as when feeding and caressing them. This peculiarity of character grew with my growth, and, in my manhood, I derived from it one of my principal sources of pleasure. To those who have cherished an affection for a faithful and sagacious dog, I need hardly be at the trouble of explaining the nature or the intensity of the gratification thus derivable. There is something in the unselfish and self-sacrificing love of a brute, which goes directly to the heart of him who has had frequent occasion to test the paltry friendship and gossamer fidelity of mere *Man*.

I married early, and was happy to find in my wife a disposition not uncongenial with my own. Observing my partiality for domestic pets, she lost no opportunity of procuring those of the most agreeable kind. We had birds, gold fish, a fine dog, rabbits, a small monkey, and *a cat*.

This latter was a remarkably large and beautiful animal, entirely black, and sagacious to an astonishing degree. In speaking of his intelligence, my wife, who at heart was not a little tinctured with superstition, made frequent allusion to the ancient popular notion, which regarded all black cats as witches in disguise. Not that she was ever *serious* upon this point—and I mention the matter at all for no better reason than that it happens, just now, to be remembered.

Pluto—this was the cat's name—was my favorite pet and playmate. I alone fed him, and he attended me wherever I went about the house. It was even with difficulty that I could prevent him from following me through the streets.

Our friendship lasted, in this manner, for several years, during which my general temperament and character—through the instrumentality of the Fiend Intemperance—had (I blush to confess it) experienced a radical alteration for the worse. I grew, day by day, more moody, more irritable, more regardless of the feelings of others. I suffered myself to use intemperate language to my wife. At length, I even offered her personal violence. My pets, of course, were made to feel the change in my disposition. I not only neglected, but ill-used them. For Pluto, however, I still retained sufficient regard to restrain me from maltreating him, as I made no scruple of maltreating the rabbits, the monkey, or even the dog, when by accident, or through affection, they came in my way. But my disease grew upon me—for what disease is like Alcohol!—and at length even Pluto, who was now becoming old, and consequently somewhat peevish—even Pluto began to experience the effects of my ill temper.

One night, returning home, much intoxicated, from one of my haunts about town, I fancied that the cat avoided my presence. I seized him; when, in his fright at my violence, he inflicted a slight wound upon my hand with his teeth. The fury of a demon instantly possessed me. I knew myself no longer. My original soul seemed, at once, to take its flight from my body; and a more than fiendish malevolence, gin-nurtured, thrilled every fibre of my frame. I took from my waist-coat-pocket a pen-knife, opened it, grasped the poor beast by the throat, and deliberately cut one of its eyes from the socket! I blush, I burn, I shudder, while I pen the damnable atrocity.

When reason returned with the morning—when I had slept off the fumes of the night's debauch—I experienced a sentiment half of horror, half of remorse, for the crime of which I had been guilty; but it was, at best, a feeble and equivocal feeling, and the soul remained untouched. I again plunged into excess, and soon drowned in wine all memory of the deed.

In the meantime the cat slowly recovered. The socket of the lost eye presented, it is true, a frightful appearance, but he no longer appeared to suffer any pain. He went about the house as usual, but, as might be expected, fled in extreme terror at my approach. I had so much of my old heart left, as to be at first grieved by this evident dislike on the part of a creature which had once so loved me. But this feeling soon gave place to irritation. And then came, as if to my final and irrevocable overthrow, the spirit of PERVERSENESS. Of this spirit philosophy takes no account. Yet I am not more sure that my soul lives, than I am that perverseness is one of the primitive impulses of the human heart —one of the indivisible primary faculties, or sentiments, which give direction to the character of Man. Who has not, a hundred times, found himself committing a vile or a silly action, for no other reason than because he knows he should *not?* Have we not a perpetual inclination, in the teeth of our best judgment, to violate that which is *Law,* merely because we understand it to be such? This spirit of perverseness, I say, came to my final overthrow. It was this unfathomable longing of the soul *to vex itself*—to offer violence to its own nature—to do wrong for the wrong's sake only—that urged me to continue and finally to consummate the injury I had inflicted upon the unoffending brute. One morning, in cool blood, I slipped a noose about its neck and hung it to the limb of a tree;—hung it with the tears streaming from my eyes, and with the bitterest remorse at my heart;—hung it *because* I knew that it had loved me, and *because* I felt it had given me no reason of offence;—hung it *because* I knew that in so doing I was committing a sin—a deadly sin that would so jeopardize my immortal soul as to place it—if such a thing were possible—even beyond the reach of the infinite mercy of the Most Merciful and Most Terrible God.

On the night of the day on which this cruel deed was done, I was aroused from sleep by the cry of fire. The curtains of my bed were in flames. The whole house was blazing. It was with great difficulty that my wife, a servant, and myself, made our escape from the conflagration. The destruction was complete. My entire worldly wealth was swallowed up, and I resigned myself thenceforward to despair.

I am above the weakness of seeking to establish a sequence of cause and effect, between the disaster and the atrocity. But I am detailing a chain of facts—and wish not to leave even a possible link imperfect. On the day succeeding the fire, I visited the ruins. The walls, with one exception, had fallen in. This exception was found in a compartment wall, not very thick, which stood about the middle of the house, and against which had rested the head of my bed. The plastering had here, in great measure, resisted the action of the fire—

a fact which I attributed to its having been recently spread. About this wall a dense crowd were collected, and many persons seemed to be examining a particular portion of it with very minute and eager attention. The words "strange!" "singular!" and other similar expressions, excited my curiosity. I approached and saw, as if graven in *bas relief* upon the white surface, the figure of a gigantic *cat*. The impression was given with an accuracy truly marvellous. There was a rope about the animal's neck.

When I first beheld this apparition—for I could scarcely regard it as less—my wonder and my terror were extreme. But at length reflection came to my aid. The cat, I remembered, had been hung in a garden adjacent to the house. Upon the alarm of fire, this garden had been immediately filled by the crowd—by some one of whom the animal must have been cut from the tree and thrown, through an open window, into my chamber. This had probably been done with the view of arousing me from sleep. The falling of other walls had compressed the victim of my cruelty into the substance of the freshly-spread plaster; the lime of which, with the flames, and the *ammonia* from the carcass, had then accomplished the portraiture as I saw it.

Although I thus readily accounted to my reason, if not altogether to my conscience, for the startling fact just detailed, it did not the less fail to make a deep impression upon my fancy. For months I could not rid myself of the phantasm of the cat; and, during this period, there came back into my spirit a half-sentiment that seemed, but was not, remorse. I went so far as to regret the loss of the animal, and to look about me, among the vile haunts which I now habitually frequented, for another pet of the same species, and of somewhat similar appearance, with which to supply its place.

One night as I sat, half stupified, in a den of more than infamy, my attention was suddenly drawn to some black object, reposing upon the head of one of the immense hogsheads of Gin, or of Rum, which constituted the chief furniture of the apartment. I had been looking steadily at the top of this hogshead for some minutes, and what now caused me surprise was the fact that I had not sooner perceived the object thereupon. I approached it, and touched it with my hand. It was a black cat—a very large one—fully as large as Pluto, and closely resembling him in every respect but one. Pluto had not a white hair upon any portion of his body; but this cat had a large, although indefinite splotch of white, covering nearly the whole region of the breast.

Upon my touching him, he immediately arose, purred loudly, rubbed against my hand, and appeared delighted with my notice. This, then, was the very creature of which I was in search. I at once offered to purchase it of the landlord; but this person made no claim to it—knew nothing of it—had never seen it before.

I continued my caresses, and, when I prepared to go home, the animal evinced a disposition to accompany me. I permitted it to do so; occasionally stooping and patting it as I proceeded. When it reached the house it domesticated itself at once, and became immediately a great favorite with my wife.

For my own part, I soon found a dislike to it arising within me. This was just the reverse of what I had anticipated; but I know not how or why it was—its evident fondness for myself rather disgusted and annoyed. By slow degrees, these feelings of disgust and

annoyance rose into the bitterness of hatred. I avoided
the creature; a certain sense of shame, and the remembrance of my former deed of cruelty, preventing me
from physically abusing it. I did not, for some weeks,
strike, or otherwise violently ill use it; but gradually—
very gradually—I came to look upon it with unutterable loathing, and to flee silently from its odious presence, as from the breath of a pestilence.

What added, no doubt, to my hatred of the beast,
was the discovery, on the morning after I brought it
home, that, like Pluto, it also had been deprived of one
of its eyes. This circumstance, however, only endeared
it to my wife, who, as I have already said, possessed,
in a high degree, that humanity of feeling which had
once been my distinguishing trait, and the source of
many of my simplest and purest pleasures.

With my aversion to this cat, however, its partiality
for myself seemed to increase. It followed my footsteps with a pertinacity which it would be difficult to
make the reader comprehend. Whenever I sat, it would
crouch beneath my chair, or spring upon my knees,
covering me with its loathsome caresses. If I arose to
walk it would get between my feet and thus nearly
throw me down, or, fastening its long and sharp claws
in my dress, clamber, in this manner, to my breast. At
such times, although I longed to destroy it with a blow,
I was yet withheld from so doing, partly by a memory
of my former crime, but chiefly—let me confess it at
once—by absolute *dread* of the beast.

This dread was not exactly a dread of physical evil
—and yet I should be at a loss how otherwise to define
it. I am almost ashamed to own—yes, even in this
felon's cell, I am almost ashamed to own—that the
terror and horror with which the animal inspired me,
had been heightened by one of the merest chimæras

it would be possible to conceive. My wife had called
my attention, more than once, to the character of the
mark of white hair, of which I have spoken, and which
constituted the sole visible difference between the
strange beast and the one I had destroyed. The reader
will remember that this mark, although large, had been
originally very indefinite; but, by slow degrees—degrees nearly imperceptible, and which for a long time
my Reason struggled to reject as fanciful—it had, at
length, assumed a rigorous distinctness of outline. It
was now the representation of an object that I shudder
to name—and for this, above all, I loathed, and
dreaded, and would have rid myself of the monster
had I dared—it was now, I say, the image of a hideous
—of a ghastly thing—of the GALLOWS!—oh, mournful
and terrible engine of Horror and of Crime—of Agony
and of Death!

And now was I indeed wretched beyond the wretchedness of mere Humanity. And *a brute beast*—whose
fellow I had contemptuously destroyed—*a brute beast*
to work out for *me*—for me a man, fashioned in the
image of the High God—so much of insufferable wo!
Alas! neither by day nor by night knew I the blessing
of Rest any more! During the former the creature left
me no moment alone; and, in the latter, I started, hourly,
from dreams of unutterable fear, to find the hot breath
of *the thing* upon my face, and its vast weight—an
incarnate Night-Mare that I had no power to shake off
—incumbent eternally upon my *heart!*

Beneath the pressure of torments such as these, the
feeble remnant of the good within me succumbed. Evil
thoughts became my sole intimates—the darkest and
most evil of thoughts. The moodiness of my usual
temper increased to hatred of all things and of all mankind; while, from the sudden, frequent, and ungovern-

able outbursts of a fury to which I now blindly abandoned myself, my uncomplaining wife, alas! was the most usual and the most patient of sufferers.

One day she accompanied me, upon some household errand, into the cellar of the old building which our poverty compelled us to inhabit. The cat followed me down the steep stairs, and, nearly throwing me headlong, exasperated me to madness. Uplifting an axe, and forgetting, in my wrath, the childish dread which had hitherto stayed my hand, I aimed a blow at the animal which, of course, would have proved instantly fatal had it descended as I wished. But this blow was arrested by the hand of my wife. Goaded, by the interference, into a rage more than demoniacal, I withdrew my arm from her grasp and buried the axe in her brain. She fell dead upon the spot, without a groan.

This hideous murder accomplished, I set myself forthwith, and with entire deliberation, to the task of concealing the body. I knew that I could not remove it from the house, either by day or by night, without the risk of being observed by the neighbors. Many projects entered my mind. At one period I thought of cutting the corpse into minute fragments, and destroying them by fire. At another, I resolved to dig a grave for it in the floor of the cellar. Again, I deliberated about casting it in the well in the yard—about packing it in a box, as if merchandize, with the usual arrangements, and so getting a porter to take it from the house. Finally I hit upon what I considered a far better expedient than either of these. I determined to wall it up in the cellar —as the monks of the middle ages are recorded to have walled up their victims.

For a purpose such as this the cellar was well adapted. Its walls were loosely constructed, and had lately been plastered throughout with a rough plaster, which the dampness of the atmosphere had prevented from hardening. Moreover, in one of the walls was a projection, caused by a false chimney, or fireplace, that had been filled up, and made to resemble the rest of the cellar. I made no doubt that I could readily displace the bricks at this point, insert the corpse, and wall the whole up as before, so that no eye could detect anything suspicious.

And in this calculation I was not deceived. By means of a crow-bar I easily dislodged the bricks, and, having carefully deposited the body against the inner wall, I propped it in that position, while, with little trouble, I re-laid the whole structure as it originally stood. Having procured mortar, sand, and hair, with every possible precaution, I prepared a plaster which could not be distinguished from the old, and with this I very carefully went over the new brick-work. When I had finished, I felt satisfied that all was right. The wall did not present the slightest appearance of having been disturbed. The rubbish on the floor was picked up with the minutest care. I looked around triumphantly, and said to myself—"Here at least, then, my labor has not been in vain."

My next step was to look for the beast which had been the cause of so much wretchedness; for I had, at length, firmly resolved to put it to death. Had I been able to meet with it, at the moment, there could liave been no doubt of its fate; but it appeared that the crafty animal had been alarmed at the violence of my previous anger, and forebore to present itself in my present mood. It is impossible to describe, or to imagine, the deep, the blissful sense of relief which the absence of the detested creature occasioned in my bosom. It did not make its appearance during the night—and thus for one night at least, since its introduction into the house, I soundly and tranquilly slept; aye, *slept* even with the burden of murder upon my soul!

The second and the third day passed, and still my tormentor came not. Once again I breathed as a free-·man. The monster, in terror, had fled the premises forever! I should behold it no more! My happiness was supreme! The guilt of my dark deed disturbed me but little. Some few inquiries had been made, but these had been readily answered. Even a search had been instituted—but of course nothing was to be discovered. I looked upon my future felicity as secured.

Upon the fourth day of the assassination, a party of the police came, very unexpectedly, into the house, and proceeded again to make rigorous investigation of the premises. Secure, however, in the inscrutability of my place of concealment, I felt no embarrassment what-ever. The officers bade me accompany them in their search. They left no nook or corner unexplored. At length, for the third or fourth time, they descended into the cellar. I quivered not a muscle. My heart beat calmly as that of one who slumbers in innocence. I walked the cellar from end to end. I folded my arms upon my bosom, and roamed easily to and fro. The police were thoroughly satisfied and prepared to de-part. The glee at my heart was too strong to be re-strained. I burned to say if but one word, by way of triumph, and to render doubly sure their assurance of my guiltlessness.

"Gentlemen," I said at last, as the party ascended the steps, "I delight to have allayed your suspicions. I wish you all health, and a little more courtesy. By the bye, gentlemen, this—this is a very well constructed house." [In the rabid desire to say something easily, I scarcely knew what I uttered at all.]—"I may say an *excellently* well constructed house. These walls—are you going, gentlemen?—these walls are solidly put together;" and here, through the mere phrenzy of bravado, I rapped heavily, with a cane which I held in my hand, upon that very portion of the brick-work behind which stood the corpse of the wife of my bosom.

But may God shield and deliver me from the fangs of the Arch-Fiend! No sooner had the reverberation of my blows sunk into silence, than I was answered by a voice from within the tomb!—by a cry, at first muffled and broken, like the sobbing of a child, and then quickly swelling into one long, loud, and continuous scream, utterly anomalous and inhuman—a howl—a wailing shriek, half of horror and half of triumph, such as might have arisen only out of hell, conjointly from the throats of the damned in their agony and of the demons that exult in the damnation.

Of my own thoughts it is folly to speak. Swooning, I staggered to the opposite wall. For one instant the party upon the stairs remained motionless, through extremity of terror and of awe. In the next, a dozen stout arms were toiling at the wall. It fell bodily. The corpse, already greatly decayed and clotted with gore, stood erect before the eyes of the spectators. Upon its head, with red extended mouth and solitary eye of fire, sat the hideous beast whose craft had seduced me into murder, and whose informing voice had consigned me to the hangman. I had walled the monster up within the tomb!

THE CASK OF AMONTILLADO

(*Godey's Lady's Book*, November, 1846.)

THE thousand injuries of Fortunato I had borne as I best could, but when he ventured upon insult I vowed revenge. You, who so well know the nature of my soul, will not suppose, however, that I gave utterance to a threat. *At length* I would be avenged; this was a point definitely settled—but the very definitiveness with which it was resolved precluded the idea of risk. I must not only punish but punish with impunity. A wrong is unredressed when retribution overtakes its redresser. It is equally unredressed when the avenger fails to make himself felt as such to him who has done the wrong.

It must be understood that neither by word nor deed had I given Fortunato cause to doubt my good will. I continued, as was my wont, to smile in his face, and he did not perceive that my smile *now* was at the thought of his immolation.

He had a weak point—this Fortunato—although in other regards he was a man to be respected and even feared. He prided himself on his connoisseurship in wine. Few Italians have the true virtuoso spirit. For the most part their enthusiasm is adopted to suit the time and opportunity, to practise imposture upon the British and Austrian *millionaires*. In painting and gemmary, Fortunato, like his countrymen, was a quack, but in the matter of old wines he was sincere. In this respect I did not differ from him materially;—I was skilful in the Italian vintages myself, and bought largely whenever I could.

It was about dusk, one evening during the supreme madness of the carnival season, that I encountered my friend. He accosted me with excessive warmth, for he had been drinking much. The man wore motley. He had on a tight-fitting parti-striped dress, and his head was surmounted by the conical cap and bells. I was so pleased to see him that I thought I should never have done wringing his hand.

I said to him—"My dear Fortunato, you are luckily met. How remarkably well you are looking to-day. But I have received a pipe of what passes for Amontillado, and I have my doubts."

"How?" said he. "Amontillado? A pipe? Impossible! And in the middle of the carnival!"

"I have my doubts," I replied; "and I was silly enough to pay the full Amontillado price without consulting you in the matter. You were not to be found, and I was fearful of losing a bargain."

"Amontillado!"

"I have my doubts."

"Amontillado!"

"And I must satisfy them."

"Amontillado!"

"As you are engaged, I am on my way to Luchresi. If any one has a critical turn it is he. He will tell me——"

"Luchresi cannot tell Amontillado from Sherry."

"And yet some fools will have it that his taste is a match for your own."

"Come, let us go."

"Whither?"

"To your vaults."

"My friend, no; I will not impose upon your good nature. I perceive you have an engagement. Luchresi——"

"I have no engagement;—come."

"My friend, no. It is not the engagement, but the severe cold with which I perceive you are afflicted.

The vaults are insufferably damp. They are encrusted with nitre."

"Let us go, nevertheless. The cold is merely nothing. Amontillado! You have been imposed upon. And as for Luchresi, he cannot distinguish Sherry from Amontillado."

Thus speaking, Fortunato possessed himself of my arm; and putting on a mask of black silk and drawing a *roquelaire* closely about my person, I suffered him to hurry me to my palazzo.

There were no attendants at home; they had absconded to make merry in honour of the time. I had told them that I should not return until the morning, and had given them explicit orders not to stir from the house. These orders were sufficient, I well knew, to insure their immediate disappearance, one and all, as soon as my back was turned.

I took from their sconces two flambeaux, and giving one to Fortunato, bowed him through several suites of rooms to the archway that led into the vaults. I passed down a long and winding staircase, requesting him to be cautious as he followed. We came at length to the foot of the descent, and stood together upon the damp ground of the catacombs of the Montresors.

The gait of my friend was unsteady, and the bells upon his cap jingled as he strode.

"The pipe," he said.

"It is farther on," said I; "but observe the white web-work which gleams from these cavern walls."

He turned towards me, and looked into my eyes with two filmy orbs that distilled the rheum of intoxication.

"Nitre?" he asked, at length.

"Nitre," I replied. "How long have you had that cough?"

"Ugh! ugh! ugh!—ugh! ugh! ugh!—ugh! ugh! ugh!—ugh! ugh! ugh!—ugh! ugh! ugh!"

My poor friend found it impossible to reply for many minutes.

"It is nothing," he said, at last.

"Come," I said, with decision, "we will go back; your health is precious. You are rich, respected, admired, beloved; you are happy, as once I was. You are a man to be missed. For me it is no matter. We will go back; you will be ill, and I cannot be responsible. Besides, there is Luchresi——"

"Enough," he said; "the cough is a mere nothing; it will not kill me. I shall not die of a cough."

"True—true," I replied; "and, indeed, I had no intention of alarming you unnecessarily—but you should use all proper caution. A draught of this Medoc will defend us from the damps."

Here I knocked off the neck of a bottle which I drew from a long row of its fellows that lay upon the mould.

"Drink," I said, presenting him the wine.

He raised it to his lips with a leer. He paused and nodded to me familiarly, while his bells jingled.

"I drink," he said, "to the buried that repose around us."

"And I to your long life."

He again took my arm, and we proceeded.

"These vaults," he said, "are extensive."

"The Montresors," I replied, "were a great and numerous family."

"I forget your arms."

"A huge human foot d'or, in a field azure; the foot crushes a serpent rampant whose fangs are imbedded in the heel."

"And the motto?"

"*Nemo me impune lacessit.*"

"Good!" he said.

The wine sparkled in his eyes and the bells jingled. My own fancy grew warm with the Medoc. We had passed through long walls of piled skeletons, with casks and puncheons intermingling, into the inmost recesses of the catacombs. I paused again, and this time I made bold to seize Fortunato by an arm above the elbow.

"The nitre!" I said; "see, it increases. It hangs like moss upon the vaults. We are below the river's bed. The drops of moisture trickle among the bones. Come, we will go back ere it is too late. Your cough——"

"It is nothing," he said; "let us go on. But first, another draught of the Medoc."

I broke and reached him a flagon of De Grâve. He emptied it at a breath. His eyes flashed with a fierce light. He laughed and threw the bottle upwards with a gesticulation I did not understand.

I looked at him in surprise. He repeated the movement—a grotesque one.

"You do not comprehend?" he said.

"Not I," I replied.

"Then you are not of the brotherhood."

"How?"

"You are not of the masons."

"Yes, yes," I said; "yes, yes."

"You? Impossible! A mason?"

"A mason," I replied.

"A sign," he said, "a sign."

"It is this," I answered, producing from beneath the folds of my *roquelaire* a trowel.

"You jest," he exclaimed, recoiling a few paces. "But let us proceed to the Amontillado."

"Be it so," I said, replacing the tool beneath the cloak and again offering him my arm. He leaned upon it heavily. We continued our route in search of the

Amontillado. We passed through a range of low arches, descended, passed on, and descending again, arrived at a deep crypt, in which the foulness of the air caused our flambeaux rather to glow than flame.

At the most remote end of the crypt there appeared another less spacious. Its walls had been lined with human remains, piled to the vault overhead, in the fashion of the great catacombs of Paris. Three sides of this interior crypt were still ornamented in this manner. From the fourth side the bones had been thrown down, and lay promiscuously upon the earth, forming at one point a mound of some size. Within the wall thus exposed by the displacing of the bones, we perceived a still interior crypt or recess, in depth about four feet, in width three, in height six or seven. It seemed to have been constructed for no especial use within itself, but formed merely the interval between two of the colossal supports of the roof of the catacombs, and was backed by one of their circumscribing walls of solid granite.

It was in vain that Fortunato, uplifting his dull torch, endeavoured to pry into the depth of the recess. Its termination the feeble light did not enable us to see.

"Proceed," I said; "herein is the Amontillado. As for Luchresi——"

"He is an ignoramus," interrupted my friend, as he stepped unsteadily forward, while I followed immediately at his heels. In an instant he had reached the extremity of the niche, and finding his progress arrested by the rock, stood stupidly bewildered. A moment more and I had fettered him to the granite. In its surface were two iron staples, distant from each other about two feet, horizontally. From one of these depended a short chain, from the other a padlock. Throwing the links about his waist, it was but the work of a few seconds to secure it. He was too much astounded to resist

Withdrawing the key I stepped back from the recess.

"Pass your hand," I said, "over the wall; you cannot help feeling the nitre. Indeed, it is *very* damp. Once more let me *implore* you to return. No? Then I must positively leave you. But I must first render you all the little attentions in my power."

"The Amontillado!" ejaculated my friend, not yet recovered from his astonishment.

"True," I replied; "the Amontillado."

As I said these words I busied myself among the pile of bones of which I have before spoken. Throwing them aside, I soon uncovered a quantity of building stone and mortar. With these materials and with the aid of my trowel, I began vigorously to wall up the entrance of the niche.

I had scarcely laid the first tier of the masonry when I discovered that the intoxication of Fortunato had in a great measure worn off. The earliest indication I had of this was a low moaning cry from the depth of the recess. It was *not* the cry of a drunken man. There was then a long and obstinate silence. I laid the second tier, and the third, and the fourth; and then I heard the furious vibrations of the chain. The noise lasted for several minutes, during which, that I might hearken to it with the more satisfaction, I ceased my labours and sat down upon the bones. When at last the clanking subsided, I resumed the trowel, and finished without interruption the fifth, the sixth, and the seventh tier. The wall was now nearly upon a level with my breast. I again paused, and holding the flambeaux over the mason-work, threw a few feeble rays upon the figure within.

A succession of loud and shrill screams, bursting suddenly from the throat of the chained form, seemed to thrust me violently back. For a brief moment I hesitated,

I trembled. Unsheathing my rapier, I began to grope with it about the recess; but the thought of an instant reassured me. I placed my hand upon the solid fabric of the catacombs, and felt satisfied. I reapproached the wall; I replied to the yells of him who clamoured. I re-echoed, I aided, I surpassed them in volume and in strength. I did this, and the clamourer grew still.

It was now midnight, and my task was drawing to a close. I had completed the eighth, the ninth and the tenth tier. I had finished a portion of the last and the eleventh; there remained but a single stone to be fitted and plastered in. I struggled with its weight; I placed it partially in its destined position. But now there came from out the niche a low laugh that erected the hairs upon my head. It was succeeded by a sad voice, which I had difficulty in recognizing as that of the noble Fortunato. The voice said—

"Ha! ha! ha!—he! he! he!—a very good joke, indeed—an excellent jest. We will have many a rich laugh about it at the palazzo—he! he! he!—over our wine—he! he! he!"

"The Amontillado!" I said.

"He! he! he!—he! he! he!—yes, the Amontillado. But is it not getting late? Will not they be awaiting us at the palazzo, the Lady Fortunato and the rest? Let us be gone."

"Yes," I said, "let us be gone."

"*For the love of God, Montresor!*"

"Yes," I said, "for the love of God!"

But to these words I hearkened in vain for a reply. I grew impatient. I called aloud—

"Fortunato!"

No answer. I called again—

"Fortunato!"

No answer still. I thrust a torch through the remain-

ing aperture and let it fall within. There came forth in
return only a jingling of the bells. My heart grew sick;
it was the dampness of the catacombs that made it so.
I hastened to make an end of my labour. I forced the
last stone into its position; I plastered it up. Against
the new masonry I re-erected the old rampart of bones.
For the half of a century no mortal has disturbed them.
In pace requiescat!

HOP-FROG

(*The Flag of Our Union*, 1849.)

I NEVER knew any one so keenly alive to a joke as
the king was. He seemed to live only for joking. To
tell a good story of the joke kind, and to tell it well, was
the surest road to his favor. Thus it happened that his
seven ministers were all noted for their accomplish-
ments as jokers. They all took after the king, too, in
being large, corpulent, oily men, as well as inimitable
jokers. Whether people grow fat by joking, or whether
there is something in fat itself which predisposes to a
joke, I have never been quite able to determine; but
certain it is that a lean joker is a *rara avis in terris*.

About the refinements, or, as he called them, the
"ghosts" of wit, the king troubled himself very little.
He had an especial admiration for *breadth* in a jest,
and would often put up with *length*, for the sake of it.
Over-niceties wearied him. He would have preferred
Rabelais's *Gargantua*, to the *Zadig* of Voltaire: and,
upon the whole, practical jokes suited his taste far better than verbal ones.

At the date of my narrative, professing jesters had
not altogether gone out of fashion at court. Several of

the great continental "powers" still retained their "fools," who wore motley, with caps and bells, and who were expected to be always ready with sharp witticisms, at a moment's notice, in consideration of the crumbs that fell from the royal table.

Our king, as a matter of course, retained his "fool." The fact is, he *required* something in the way of folly —if only to counterbalance the heavy wisdom of the seven wise men who were his ministers—not to mention himself.

His fool, or professional jester, was not *only* a fool, however. His value was trebled in the eyes of the king, by the fact of his being also a dwarf and a cripple. Dwarfs were as common at court, in those days, as fools; and many monarchs would have found it difficult to get through their days (days are rather longer at court than elsewhere) without both a jester to laugh *with*, and a dwarf to laugh *at*. But, as I have already observed, your jesters, in ninety-nine cases out of a hundred, are fat, round and unwieldy—so that it was no small source of self-gratulation with our king that, in Hop-Frog (this was the fool's name,) he possessed a triplicate treasure in one person.

I believe the name "Hop-Frog" was *not* that given to the dwarf by his sponsors at baptism, but it was conferred upon him, by general consent of the seven ministers, on account of his inability to walk as other men do. In fact, Hop-Frog could only get along by a sort of interjectional gait—something between a leap and a wriggle —a movement that afforded illimitable amusement, and of course consolation, to the king, for (notwithstanding the protuberance of his stomach and a constitutional swelling of the head) the king, by his whole court, was accounted a capital figure.

But although Hop-Frog, through the distortion of his

legs, could move only with great pain and difficulty along a road or floor, the prodigious muscular power which nature seemed to have bestowed upon his arms, by way of compensation for deficiency in the lower limbs, enabled him to perform many feats of wonderful dexterity, where trees or ropes were in question, or anything else to climb. At such exercises he certainly much more resembled a squirrel, or a small monkey, than a frog.

I am not able to say, with precision, from what country Hop-Frog originally came. It was from some barbarous region, however, that no person ever heard of —a vast distance from the court of our king. Hop-Frog, and a young girl very little less dwarfish than himself (although of exquisite proportions, and a marvellous dancer,) had been forcibly carried off from their respective homes in adjoining provinces, and sent as presents to the king, by one of his ever-victorious generals.

Under these circumstances, it is not to be wondered at that a close intimacy arose between the two little captives. Indeed, they soon became sworn friends. Hop-Frog, who, although he made a great deal of sport, was by no means popular, had it not in his power to render Trippetta many services; but *she*, on account of her grace and exquisite beauty (although a dwarf,) was universally admired and petted: so she possessed much influence; and never failed to use it, whenever she could, for the benefit of Hop-Frog.

On some grand state occasion—I forget what—the king determined to have a masquerade; and whenever a masquerade, or anything of that kind, occurred at our court, then the talents both of Hop-Frog and Trippetta were sure to be called in play. Hop-Frog, in especial, was so inventive in the way of getting up pageants, suggesting novel characters, and arranging costume, for masked balls, that nothing could be done, it seems, without his assistance.

The night appointed for the *fête* had arrived. A gorgeous hall had been fitted up, under Trippetta's eye, with every kind of device which could possibly give *éclat* to a masquerade. The whole court was in a fever of expectation. As for costumes and characters, it might well be supposed that everybody had come to a decision on such points. Many had made up their minds (as to what *rôles* they should assume) a week, or even a month, in advance; and, in fact, there was not a particle of indecision anywhere—except in the case of the king and his seven ministers. Why *they* hesitated I never could tell, unless they did it by way of a joke. More probably, they found it difficult, on account of being so fat, to make up their minds. At all events, time flew; and, as a last resource, they sent for Trippetta and Hop-Frog.

When the two little friends obeyed the summons of the king, they found him sitting at his wine with the seven members of his cabinet council; but the monarch appeared to be in a very ill humor. He knew that Hop-Frog was not fond of wine; for it excited the poor cripple almost to madness; and madness is no comfortable feeling. But the king loved his practical jokes, and took pleasure in forcing Hop-Frog to drink and (as the king called it) "to be merry."

"Come here, Hop-Frog," said he, as the jester and his friend entered the room: "swallow this bumper to the health of your absent friends (here Hop-Frog sighed,) and then let us have the benefit of your invention. We want characters—*characters,* man—something novel—out of the way. We are wearied with this everlasting sameness. Come, drink! the wine will brighten your wits."

Hop-Frog endeavored, as usual, to get up a jest in reply to these advances from the king; but the effort was too much. It happened to be the poor dwarf's birthday, and the command to drink to his "absent friends" forced the tears to his eyes. Many large, bitter drops fell into the goblet as he took it, humbly, from the hand of the tyrant.

"Ah! ha! ha! ha!" roared the latter, as the dwarf reluctantly drained the beaker. "See what a glass of good wine can do! Why, your eyes are shining already!"

Poor fellow! his large eyes *gleamed*, rather than shone; for the effect of wine on his excitable brain was not more powerful than instantaneous. He placed the goblet nervously on the table, and looked round upon the company with a half-insane stare. They all seemed highly amused at the success of the king's "*joke*."

"And now to business," said the prime minister, a *very* fat man.

"Yes," said the king; "come, Hop-Frog, lend us your assistance. Characters, my fine fellow; we stand in need of characters—all of us—ha! ha! ha!" and as this was seriously meant for a joke, his laugh was chorused by the seven.

Hop-Frog also laughed, although feebly and somewhat vacantly.

"Come, come," said the king, impatiently, "have you nothing to suggest?"

"I am endeavoring to think of something *novel*," replied the dwarf, abstractedly, for he was quite bewildered by the wine.

"Endeavoring!" cried the tyrant, fiercely; "what do you mean by *that?* Ah, I perceive. You are sulky, and want more wine. Here, drink this!" and he poured out another goblet full and offered it to the cripple, who merely gazed at it, gasping for breath.

"Drink, I say!" shouted the monster, "or by the fiends—"

The dwarf hesitated. The king grew purple with rage. The courtiers smirked. Trippetta, pale as a corpse, advanced to the monarch's seat, and, falling on her knees before him, implored him to spare her friend.

The tyrant regarded her, for some moments, in evident wonder at her audacity. He seemed quite at a loss what to do or say—how most becomingly to express his indignation. At last, without uttering a syllable, he pushed her violently from him, and threw the contents of the brimming goblet in her face.

The poor girl got up as best she could, and, not daring even to sigh, resumed her position at the foot of the table.

There was a dead silence for about half a minute, during which the falling of a leaf, or of a feather might have been heard. It was interrupted by a low, but harsh and protracted *grating* sound which seemed to come at once from every corner of the room.

"What—what—*what* are you making that noise for?" demanded the king, turning furiously to the dwarf.

The latter seemed to have recovered, in great measure, from his intoxication, and looking fixedly but quietly into the tyrant's face, merely ejaculated:

"I—I? How could it have been me?"

"The sound appeared to come from without," observed one of the courtiers. "I fancy it was the parrot at the window, whetting his bill upon his cage-wires."

"True," replied the monarch, as if much relieved by the suggestion; "but, on the honor of a knight, I could have sworn that it was the gritting of this vagabond's teeth."

Hereupon the dwarf laughed (the king was too confirmed a joker to object to any one's laughing), and displayed a set of large, powerful, and very repulsive teeth. Moreover, he avowed his perfect willingness to swallow as much wine as desired. The monarch was pacified; and having drained another bumper with no very perceptible ill effect, Hop-Frog entered at once, and with spirit, into the plans for the masquerade.

"I cannot tell what was the association of idea," observed he, very tranquilly, and as if he had never tasted wine in his life, "but *just after* your majesty had struck the girl and thrown the wine in her face—*just after* your majesty had done this, and while the parrot was making that odd noise outside the window, there came into my mind a capital diversion—one of my own country frolics—often enacted among us, at our masquerades: but here it will be new altogether. Unfortunately, however, it requires a company of eight persons, and—"

"Here we *are!*" cried the king, laughing at his acute discovery of the coincidence; "eight to a fraction—I and my seven ministers. Come! what is the diversion?"

"We call it," replied the cripple, "the Eight Chained Ourang-Outangs, and it really is excellent sport if well enacted."

"*We* will enact it," remarked the king, drawing himself up, and lowering his eyelids.

"The beauty of the game," continued Hop-Frog, "lies in the fright it occasions among the women."

"Capital!" roared in chorus the monarch and his ministry.

"*I* will equip you as ourang-outangs," proceeded the dwarf; "leave all that to me. The resemblance shall be so striking, that the company of masqueraders will take you for real beasts—and, of course, they will be as much terrified as astonished."

"O, this is exquisite!" exclaimed the king. "Hop-Frog! I will make a man of you."

"The chains are for the purpose of increasing the confusion by their jangling. You are supposed to have escaped, *en masse*, from your keepers. Your majesty cannot conceive the *effect* produced, at a masquerade, by eight chained ourang-outangs, imagined to be real ones by most of the company; and rushing in with savage cries, among the crowd of delicately and gorgeously habited men and women. The *contrast* is inimitable."

"It *must* be," said the king: and the council arose hurriedly (as it was growing late), to put in execution the scheme of Hop-Frog.

His mode of equipping the party as ourang-outangs was very simple, but effective enough for his purposes. The animals in question had, at the epoch of my story, very rarely been seen in any part of the civilized world; and as the imitations made by the dwarf were sufficiently beast-like and more than sufficiently hideous, their truthfulness to nature was thus thought to be secured.

The king and his ministers were first encased in tight-fitting stockinet shirts and drawers. They were then saturated with tar. At this stage of the process, some one of the party suggested feathers; but the suggestion was at once overruled by the dwarf, who soon convinced the eight, by ocular demonstration, that the hair of such a brute as the ourang-outang was much more efficiently represented by *flax*. A thick coating of the latter was accordingly plastered upon the coating of tar. A long chain was now procured. First, it was passed about the waist of the king, *and tied;* then about another of the party, and also tied; then about all successively, in the same manner. When this chaining arrangement was complete, and the party stood as far apart from each other as possible, they formed a circle; and to make all things appear natural, Hop-Frog passed the residue of the chain, in two diameters, at right angles, across the circle, after the fashion adopted, at the present day, by those who capture Chimpanzees, or other large apes, in Borneo.

The grand saloon in which the masquerade was to take place, was a circular room, very lofty, and receiving the light of the sun only through a single window at top. At night (the season for which the apartment was especially designed,) it was illuminated principally by a large chandelier, depending by a chain from the centre of the sky-light, and lowered, or elevated, by means of a counter-balance as usual; but (in order not to look unsightly) this latter passed outside the cupola and over the roof.

The arrangements of the room had been left to Trippetta's superintendence; but, in some particulars, it seems, she had been guided by the calmer judgment of her friend the dwarf. At his suggestion it was that, on this occasion, the chandelier was removed. Its waxen drippings (which, in weather so warm, it was quite impossible to prevent,) would have been seriously detrimental to the rich dresses of the guests, who, on account of the crowded state of the saloon, could not *all* be expected to keep from out its centre—that is to say, from under the chandelier. Additional sconces were set in various parts of the hall, out of the way; and a flambeau, emitting sweet odor, was placed in the right hand of each of the Caryatides that stood against the wall— some fifty or sixty altogether.

The eight ourang-outangs, taking Hop-Frog's advice, waited patiently until midnight (when the room was thoroughly filled with masqueraders) before making their appearance. No sooner had the clock ceased striking, however, than they rushed, or rather rolled in, all together—for the impediment of their chains caused most of the party to fall, and all to stumble as they entered.

The excitement among the masqueraders was prodigious, and filled the heart of the king with glee. As had been anticipated, there were not a few of the guests who supposed the ferocious-looking creatures to be beasts of *some* kind in reality, if not precisely ourang-outangs. Many of the women swooned with affright; and had not the king taken the precaution to exclude all weapons from the saloon, his party might soon have expiated their frolic in their blood. As it was, a general rush was made for the doors; but the king had ordered them to be locked immediately upon his entrance; and, at the dwarf's suggestion, the keys had been deposited with *him*.

While the tumult was at its height, and each masquerader attentive only to his own safety—(for, in fact, there was much *real* danger from the pressure of the excited crowd,)—the chain by which the chandelier ordinarily hung, and which had been drawn up on its removal, might have been seen very gradually to descend, until its hooked extremity came within three feet of the floor.

Soon after this, the king and his seven friends, having reeled about the hall in all directions, found themselves, at length, in its centre, and, of course, in immediate contact with the chain. While they were thus situated, the dwarf, who had followed closely at their heels, inciting them to keep up the commotion, took hold of their own chain at the intersection of the two portions which crossed the circle diametrically and at right angles. Here, with the rapidity of thought, he

inserted the hook from which the chandelier had been
wont to depend; and, in an instant, by some unseen
agency, the chandelier-chain was drawn so far upward
as to take the hook out of reach, and, as an inevitable
consequence, to drag the ourang-outangs together in
close connection, and face to face.

The masqueraders, by this time, had recovered, in
some measure, from their alarm; and, beginning to regard the whole matter as a well-contrived pleasantry,
set up a loud shout of laughter at the predicament of
the apes.

"Leave them to *me!*" now screamed Hop-Frog, his
shrill voice making itself easily heard through all the
din. "Leave them to *me*. I fancy *I* know them. If I can
only get a good look at them, *I* can soon tell who they
are."

Here, scrambling over the heads of the crowd, he
managed to get to the wall; when, seizing a flambeau
from one of the Caryatides, he returned, as he went,
to the centre of the room—leaped, with the agility of
a monkey, upon the king's head—and thence clambered
a few feet up the chain—holding down the torch to
examine the group of ourang-outangs, and still screaming, "*I* shall soon find out who they are!"

And now, while the whole assembly (the apes included) were convulsed with laughter, the jester suddenly uttered a shrill whistle; when the chain flew
violently up for about thirty feet—dragging with it the
dismayed and struggling ourang-outangs, and leaving
them suspended in mid-air between the sky-light and
the floor. Hop-Frog, clinging to the chain as it rose,
still maintained his relative position in respect to the
eight maskers, and still (as if nothing were the matter)
continued to thrust his torch down towards them, as
though endeavoring to discover who they were.

So thoroughly astonished were the whole company at this ascent, that a dead silence, of about a minute's duration, ensued. It was broken by just such a low, harsh, *grating* sound, as had before attracted the attention of the king and his councillors, when the former threw the wine in the face of Trippetta. But, on the present occasion, there could be no question as to *whence* the sound issued. It came from the fang-like teeth of the dwarf, who ground them and gnashed them as he foamed at the mouth, and glared, with an expression of maniacal rage, into the upturned countenances of the king and his seven companions.

"Ah, ha!" said at length the infuriated jester. "Ah, ha! I begin to see who these people *are*, now!" Here, pretending to scrutinize the king more closely, he held the flambeau to the flaxen coat which enveloped him, and which instantly burst into a sheet of vivid flame. In less than half a minute the whole eight ourang-outangs were blazing fiercely, amid the shrieks of the multitude who gazed at them from below, horror-stricken, and without the power to render them the slightest assistance.

At length the flames, suddenly increasing in virulence, forced the jester to climb higher up the chain, to be out of their reach; and, as he made this movement, the crowd again sank, for a brief instant, into silence. The dwarf seized his opportunity, and once more spoke:

"I now see *distinctly*," he said, "what manner of people these maskers are. They are a great king and his seven privy-councillors—a king who does not scruple to strike a defenceless girl, and his seven councillors who abet him in the outrage. As for myself, I am simply Hop-Frog, the jester—and *this is my last jest*."

Owing to the high combustibility of both the flax and the tar to which it adhered, the dwarf had scarcely made an end of his brief speech before the work of vengeance was complete. The eight corpses swung in their chains, a fetid, blackened, hideous, and indistinguishable mass. The cripple hurled his torch at them, clambered leisurely to the ceiling, and disappeared through the sky-light.

It is supposed that Trippetta, stationed on the roof of the saloon, had been the accomplice of her friend in his fiery revenge, and that, together, they effected their escape to their own country: for neither was seen again.

Of Mystery and Ratiocination

"Poe," wrote Joseph Wood Krutch in his study of him, "invented the detective story in order that he might not go mad."

The invention of this new genre, however, did not prevent its originator from finally giving way to the insanity that had threatened him all his life. But a man who fears the irrational will make a fetish of logic and take comfort in the apparent immutability of the laws of reason. In 1841 Poe was still fighting to preserve his sanity, and it was then that he published his pioneer detective story, "The Murders in the Rue Morgue." Five years before that time, however, he had written his analytical essay "Maelzel's Chess-Player" (q.v.), which shows that his interest in the deductive method was of early origin.

Poe was a man of superior intellect, but he found it difficult to establish his superiority, so he was constantly attempting to demonstrate it. As a boy he tried to surpass his companions in sports; as a man he tried to impress his contemporaries with a show of erudition. When he created the character of his detective, C. Auguste Dupin, he projected an idealization of himself as he would like to have been—a cool, infallible thinking machine that brought the power of reason to bear on all of life's problems and triumphantly solved them. He put in Dupin everything that he approved of in himself and endowed him with everything that he himself lacked. Thus we find that Dupin was of good family, not

wealthy but with some independent means (Poe would
have asked for no more), an excellent judge of character, and a sharp, shrewd man of the world who chose to
remain isolated from it in order to pursue his own
esoteric studies.

There are only three Dupin stories. The first one,
"The Murders in the Rùe Morgue," describes the detective and gives several preliminary indications of his remarkable deductive powers. "The Mystery of Marie
Rogêt" is less successful, but it was an attempt to solve
an actual murder case. Poe described the origins of the
story in a letter written to Dr. J. E. Snodgrass in June
1842:

The story is based upon that of the real murder of Mary
Cecilia Rogers, which created so vast an excitement some
months ago in New York. I have handled the design in a very
singular and entirely *novel* manner. A young grisette, one
Marie Rogêt, has been murdered under precisely similar circumstances with *Mary Rogers.* Thus under pretence of showing how Dupin (the hero of the Rue Morgue) unravelled the
mystery of Marie's assassination, I, in fact, enter into a very
rigorous examination of the *real* tragedy in New York. *No
point* is omitted. I examine, each by each, the opinions and
arguments of our press on the subject, and show (I think
satisfactorily) that this subject has never yet been *approached.*
The press has been entirely on a wrong scent. In fact, I really
believe, not only that I have demonstrated the falsity of the
idea that the girl was the victim of a gang, but have indicated
the assassin. My main object, however . . . is the analysis of
the *principles of investigation* in cases of like character. Dupin
reasons the matter throughout.

In "The Purloined Letter," the third and last Dupin
story, the detective does a bit of really brilliant reasoning when he is called upon to find an important letter
which a clever man is known to have hidden. "The Purloined Letter" is one of the very few Poe stories that
does not deal with death or violence.

Just as Poe, long before the writing of the three Dupin stories, had displayed his interest in deductive reasoning in "Maelzel's Chess-Player," so did he fore-shadow "The Gold-Bug" in a series of articles on Cryptography in 1841. The scene of "The Gold-Bug" is Sullivan's Island in Charleston Harbor, where Poe had spent some time during his army career. The goldbug is a composite of two real insects which are commonly found on that island, the gold beetle, *Callichroma*, and the click beetle, *Alaus Oculatus*, which bears a sort of death's head marking on its back.

"The Gold-Bug" is one of the most popular stories Poe ever wrote. Even in his day it had a wide reading and was often reprinted. Shortly after publication it was dramatized by Silas S. Steele and produced in Philadelphia, evidently without success, for no copy of the play—or even of the playbill—is known.

THE MURDERS IN THE RUE MORGUE

(*Graham's Magazine*, April, 1841.)

What song the Syrens sang, or what name Achilles assumed when he hid himself among women, although puzzling questions are not beyond *all* conjecture.

—SIR THOMAS BROWNE, *Urn-Burial*

THE mental features discoursed of as the analytical, are, in themselves, but little susceptible of analysis. We appreciate them only in their effects. We know of them, among other things, that they are always to their possessor, when inordinately possessed, a source of the liveliest enjoyment. As the strong man exults in his physical ability, delighting in such exercises as call his muscles into action, so glories the analyst in that moral activity which *disentangles*. He derives pleasure from even the most trivial occupations bringing his talents into play. He is fond of enigmas, of conundrums, of hieroglyphics; exhibiting in his solutions of each a degree of *acumen* which appears to the ordinary apprehension preternatural. His results, brought about by the very soul and essence of method, have, in truth, the whole air of intuition. The faculty of re-solution is possibly much invigorated by mathematical study, and especially by that highest branch of it which, unjustly, and merely on account of its retrograde operations, has been called, as if *par excellence*, analysis. Yet to calculate is not in itself to analyze. A chess-player, for example, does the one without effort at the other. It follows that the game of chess, in its effects upon mental character, is greatly misunderstood. I am not now writing a treatise, but simply prefacing a somewhat peculiar narrative by observations very much at random; I will, therefore, take occasion to assert that the higher powers of the reflective intellect are more decidedly and more usefully tasked by the unostentatious game of draughts than by all the elaborate frivolity of chess. In this latter, where the pieces have different and *bizarre* motions, with various and variable values, what is only complex is mistaken (a not unusual error) for what is profound. The *attention* is here called powerfully into play. If it flag for an instant, an oversight is committed, resulting in injury or defeat. The possible moves being not only manifold but involute, the chances of such oversights are multiplied; and in nine cases out of ten it is the more concentrative rather than the more acute player who conquers. In draughts, on the contrary,

where the moves are *unique* and have but little variation, the probabilities of inadvertence are diminished,
and the mere attention being left comparatively unem-
ployed, what advantages are obtained by either party
are obtained by superior *acumen*. To be less abstract
—Let us suppose a game of draughts where the pieces
are reduced to four kings, and where, of course, no
oversight is to be expected. It is obvious that here the
victory can be decided (the players being at all equal)
only by some *recherché* movement, the result of some
strong exertion of the intellect. Deprived of ordinary resources, the analyst throws himself into the spirit of his
opponent, identifies himself therewith, and not unfrequently sees thus, at a glance, the sole methods (sometimes indeed absurdly simple ones) by which he may
seduce into error or hurry into miscalculation.

Whist has long been noted for its influence upon what
is termed the calculating power; and men of the highest order of intellect have been known to take an
apparently unaccountable delight in it, while eschewing
chess as frivolous. Beyond doubt there is nothing of a
similar nature so greatly tasking the faculty of analysis.
The best chess-player in Christendom *may* be little more
than the best player of chess; but proficiency in whist
implies capacity for success in all these more important
undertakings where mind struggles with mind. When
I say proficiency, I mean that perfection in the game
which includes a comprehension of *all* the sources
whence legitimate advantage may be derived. These
are not only manifold but multiform, and lie frequently
among recesses of thought altogether inaccessible to the
ordinary understanding. To observe attentively is to
remember distinctly; and, so far, the concentrative
chess-player will do very well at whist; while the rules
of Hoyle (themselves based upon the mere mechanism

of the game) are sufficiently and generally comprehensible. Thus to have a retentive memory, and to proceed by "the book," are points commonly regarded as the sum total of good playing. But it is in matters beyond the limits of mere rule that the skill of the analyst is evinced. He makes, in silence, a host of observations and inferences. So, perhaps, do his companions; and the difference in the extent of the information obtained, lies not so much in the validity of the inference as in the quality of the observation. The necessary knowledge is that of *what* to observe. Our player confines himself not at all; nor, because the game is the object, does he reject deductions from things external to the game. He examines the countenance of his partner, comparing it carefully with that of each of his opponents. He considers the mode of assorting the cards in each hand; often counting trump by trump, and honor by honor, through the glances bestowed by their holders upon each. He notes every variation of face as the play progresses, gathering a fund of thought from the differences in the expression of certainty, of surprise, of triumph, or chagrin. From the manner of gathering up a trick he judges whether the person taking it can make another in the suit. He recognizes what is played through feint, by the air with which it is thrown upon the table. A casual or inadvertent word; the accidental dropping or turning of a card, with the accompanying anxiety or carelessness in regard to its concealment; the counting of the tricks, with the order of their arrangement; embarrassment, hesitation, eagerness or trepidation—all afford, to his apparently intuitive perception, indications of the true state of affairs. The first two or three rounds having been played, he is in full possession of the contents of each hand, and thenceforward puts down his cards with as absolute a pre cision of purpose as if the rest of the party had turned outward the faces of their own.

The analytical power should not be confounded with simple ingenuity; for while the analyst is necessarily ingenious, the ingenious man is often remarkably incapable of analysis. The constructive or combining power, by which ingenuity is usually manifested, and to which the phrenologists (I believe erroneously) have assigned a separate organ, supposing it a primitive faculty, has been so frequently seen in those whose intellect bordered otherwise upon idiocy, as to have attracted general observation among writers on morals. Between ingenuity and the analytic ability there exists a difference far greater, indeed, than that between the fancy and the imagination, but of a character very strictly analogous. It will be found, in fact, that the ingenious are always fanciful, and the *truly* imaginative never otherwise than analytic.

The narrative which follows will appear to the reader somewhat in the light of a commentary upon the propositions just advanced.

Residing in Paris during the spring and part of the summer of 18—, I there became acquainted with a Monsieur C. Auguste Dupin. This young gentleman was of an excellent—indeed of an illustrious family, but, by a variety of untoward events, had been reduced to such poverty that the energy of his character succumbed beneath it, and he ceased to bestir himself in the world, or to care for the retrieval of his fortunes. By courtesy of his creditors, there still remained in his possession a small remnant of his patrimony; and, upon the income arising from this, he managed, by means of a rigorous economy, to procure the necessaries of life, without troubling himself about its superfluities. Books, indeed, were his sole luxuries, and in Paris these are easily obtained.

Our first meeting was at an obscure library in the Rue Montmartre, where the accident of our both being in search of the same very rare and very remarkable volume brought us into closer communion. We saw each other again and again. I was deeply interested in the little family history which he detailed to me with all that candor which a Frenchman indulges whenever mere self is the theme. I was astonished, too, at the vast extent of his reading; and, above all, I felt my soul enkindled within me by the wild fervor, and the vivid freshness of his imagination. Seeking in Paris the objects I then sought, I felt that the society of such a man would be to me a treasure beyond price; and this feeling I frankly confided to him. It was at length arranged that we should live together during my stay in the city; and as my worldly circumstances were somewhat less embarrassed than his own, I was permitted to be at the expense of renting, and furnishing in a style which suited the rather fantastic gloom of our common temper, a time-eaten and grotesque mansion, long deserted through superstitions into which we did not inquire, and tottering to its fall in a retired and desolate portion of the Faubourg St. Germain.

Had the routine of our life at this place been known to the world, we should have been regarded as madmen —although, perhaps, as madmen of a harmless nature. Our seclusion was perfect. We admitted no visitors. Indeed the locality of our retirement had been carefully kept a secret from my own former associates; and it had been many years since Dupin had ceased to know or be known in Paris. We existed within ourselves alone.

It was a freak of fancy in my friend (for what else

shall I call it?) to be enamored of the Night for her own
sake; and into this *bizarrerie,* as into all his others, I
quietly fell; giving myself up to his wild whims with
a perfect *abandon.* The sable divinity would not herself dwell with us always; but we could counterfeit
her presence. At the first dawn of the morning we
closed all the massy shutters of our old building; lighted
a couple of tapers which, strongly perfumed, threw out
only the ghastliest and feeblest of rays. By the aid of
these we then busied our souls in dreams—reading,
writing, or conversing, until warned by the clock of the
advent of the true Darkness. Then we sallied forth into
the streets, arm and arm, continuing the topics of the
day, or roaming far and wide until a late hour, seeking,
amid the wild lights and shadows of the populous city,
that infinity of mental excitement which quiet observation can afford.

At such times I could not help remarking and admiring (although from his rich ideality I had been prepared
to expect it) a peculiar analytic ability in Dupin. He
seemed, too, to take an eager delight in its exercise—
if not exactly in its display—and did not hesitate to
confess the pleasure thus derived. He boasted to me,
with a low chuckling laugh, that most men, in respect
to himself, wore windows in their bosoms, and was
wont to follow up such assertions by direct and very
startling proofs of his intimate knowledge of my own.
His manner at these moments was frigid and abstract;
his eyes were vacant in expression; while his voice,
usually a rich tenor, rose into a treble which would
have sounded petulantly but for the deliberateness and
entire distinctness of the enunciation. Observing him
in these moods, I often dwelt meditatively upon the
old philosophy of the Bi-Part Soul, and amused myself

with the fancy of a double Dupin—the creative and the resolvent.

Let it not be supposed, from what I have just said, that I am detailing any mystery, or penning any romance. What I have described in the Frenchman, was merely the result of an excited, or perhaps of a diseased intelligence. But of the character of his remarks at the periods in question an example will best convey the idea.

We were strolling one night down a long dirty street, in the vicinity of the Palais Royal. Being both, apparently, occupied with thought, neither of us had spoken a syllable for fifteen minutes at least. All at once Dupin broke forth with these words:—

"He is a very little fellow, that's true, and would do better for the *Théâtre des Variétés*."

"There can be no doubt of that," I replied unwittingly, and not at first observing (so much had I been absorbed in reflection) the extraordinary manner in which the speaker had chimed in with my meditations. In an instant afterward I recollected myself, and my astonishment was profound.

"Dupin," said I, gravely, "this is beyond my comprehension. I do not hesitate to say that I am amazed, and can scarcely credit my senses. How was it possible you should know I was thinking of ———?" Here I paused, to ascertain beyond a doubt whether he really knew of whom I thought.

——— "of Chantilly," said he, "why do you pause? You were remarking to yourself that his diminutive figure unfitted him for tragedy."

This was precisely what had formed the subject of my reflections. Chantilly was a *quondam* cobbler of the Rue St. Denis, who, becoming stage-mad, had attempted the *rôle* of Xerxes, in Crébillon's tragedy so called, and been notoriously Pasquinaded for his pains.

"Tell me, for Heaven's sake," I exclaimed, "the method—if method there is—by which you have been enabled to fathom my soul in this matter." In fact I was even more startled than I would have been willing to express.

"It was the fruiterer," replied my friend, "who brought you to the conclusion that the mender of soles was not of sufficient height for Xerxes *et id genus omne.*"

"The fruiterer!—you astonish me—I know no fruiterer whomsoever."

"The man who ran up against you as we entered the street—it may have been fifteen minutes ago."

I now remembered that, in fact, a fruiterer, carrying upon his head a large basket of apples, had nearly thrown me down, by accident, as we passed from the Rue C——— into the thoroughfare where we stood; but what this had to do with Chantilly I could not possibly understand.

There was not a particle of *charlatanerie* about Dupin. "I will explain," he said, "and that you may comprehend all clearly, we will first retrace the course of your meditations, from the moment in which I spoke to you until that of the *recontre* with the fruiterer in question. The larger links of the chain run thus—Chantilly, Orion, Dr. Nichols, Epicurus, Stereotomy, the street stones, the fruiterer."

There are few persons who have not, at some period of their lives, amused themselves in retracing the steps by which particular conclusions of their own minds have been attained. The occupation is often full of interest; and he who attempts it for the first time is astonished by the apparently illimitable distance and incoherence between the starting-point and the goal. What, then, must have been my amazement when I heard the Frenchman speak what he had just spoken, and when I could not help acknowledging that he had spoken the truth. He continued:

"We had been talking of horses, if I remember aright, just before leaving the Rue C———. This was the last subject we discussed. As we crossed into this street, a fruiterer, with a large basket upon his head, brushing quickly past us, thrust you upon a pile of paving-stones collected at a spot where the causeway is undergoing repair. You stepped upon one of the loose fragments, slipped, slightly strained your ankle, appeared vexed or sulky, muttered a few words, turned to look at the pile, and then proceeded in silence. I was not particularly attentive to what you did; but observation has become with me, of late, a species of necessity.

"You kept your eyes upon the ground—glancing, with a petulant expression, at the holes and ruts in the pavement, (so that I saw you were still thinking of the stones,) until we reached the little alley called Lamartine, which has been paved, by way of experiment, with the overlapping and riveted blocks. Here your countenance brightened up, and, perceiving your lips move, I could not doubt that you murmured the word 'stereotomy,' a term very affectedly applied to this species of pavement. I knew that you could not say to yourself 'stereotomy' without being brought to think of atomies, and thus of the theories of Epicurus; and since, when we discussed this subject not very long ago, I mentioned to you how singularly, yet with how little notice, the vague guesses of that noble Greek had met with confirmation in the late nebular cosmogony, I felt that you could not avoid casting your eyes upward to the great *nebula* in Orion, and I certainly expected that you

would do so. You did look up; and I was now assured
that I had correctly followed your steps. But in that
bitter *tirade* upon Chantilly, which appeared in yesterday's '*Musée*,' the satirist, making some disgraceful allu-
sions to the cobbler's change of name upon assuming the
buskin, quoted a Latin line about which we have often
conversed. I mean the line

Perdidit antiquum litera prima sonum.

I had told you that this was in reference to Orion, formerly written Urion; and, from certain pungencies connected with this explanation, I was aware that you could
not have forgotten it. It was clear, therefore, that you
would not fail to combine the two ideas of Orion and
Chantilly. That you did combine them I saw by the
character of the smile which passed over your lips. You
thought of the poor cobbler's immolation. So far, you
had been stooping in your gait; but now I saw you draw
yourself up to your full height. I was then sure that you
reflected upon the diminutive figure of Chantilly. At
this point I interrupted your meditations to remark that
as, in fact, he *was* a very little fellow—that Chantilly—
he would do better at the *Théâtre des Variétés*."

Not long after this, we were looking over an evening
edition of the *Gazette des Tribunaux*, when the following paragraphs arrested our attention.

"Extraordinary Murders.—This morning, about
three o'clock, the inhabitants of the Quartier St. Roch
were aroused from sleep by a succession of terrific
shrieks, issuing, apparently, from the fourth story of a
house in the Rue Morgue, known to be in the sole oc-
cupancy of one Madame L'Espanaye, and her daughter, Mademoiselle Camille L'Espanaye. After some delay, occasioned by a fruitless attempt to procure admission in the usual manner, the gateway was broken

in with a crowbar, and eight or ten of the neighbors entered, accompanied by two *gendarmes*. By this time the cries had ceased; but, as the party rushed up the first flight of stairs, two or more rough voices, in angry contention, were distinguished, and seemed to proceed from the upper part of the house. As the second landing was reached, these sounds, also, had ceased, and everything remained perfectly quiet. The party spread themselves, and hurried from room to room. Upon arriving at a large back chamber in the fourth story, (the door of which, being found locked, with the key inside, was forced open,) a spectacle presented itself which struck every one present not less with horror than with astonishment.

"The apartment was in the wildest disorder—the furniture broken and thrown about in all directions. There was only one bedstead; and from this the bed had been removed, and thrown into the middle of the floor. On a chair lay a razor, besmeared with blood. On the hearth were two or three long and thick tresses of grey human hair, also dabbled in blood, and seeming to have been pulled out by the roots. Upon the floor were found four Napoleons, an ear-ring of topaz, three large silver spoons, three smaller of *métal d'Alger*, and two bags, containing nearly four thousand francs in gold. The drawers of a *bureau*, which stood in one corner, were open, and had been, apparently, rifled, although many articles still remained in them. A small iron safe was discovered under the *bed* (not under the bedstead). It was open, with the key still in the door. It had no contents beyond a few old letters, and other papers of little consequence.

"Of Madame L'Espanaye no traces were here seen; but an unusual quantity of soot being observed in the fire-place, a search was made in the chimney, and (horrible to relate!) the corpse of the daughter, head downward, was dragged therefrom; it having been thus forced up the narrow aperture for a considerable distance. The body was quite warm. Upon examining it, many excoriations were perceived, no doubt occasioned by the violence with which it had been thrust up and disengaged. Upon the face were many severe scratches, and, upon the throat, dark bruises, and deep indentations of finger nails, as if the deceased had been throttled to death.

"After a thorough investigation of every portion of the house, without farther discovery, the party made its way into a small paved yard in the rear of the building, where lay the corpse of the old lady, with her throat so entirely cut that, upon an attempt to raise her, the head fell off. The body, as well as the head, was fearfully mutilated—the former so much so as scarcely to retain any semblance of humanity.

"To this horrible mystery there is not as yet, we believe, the slightest clew."

The next day's paper had these additional particulars.

"*The Tragedy in the Rue Morgue*. Many individuals have been examined in relation to this most extraordinary and frightful affair." [The word '*affaire*' has not yet, in France, the levity of import which it conveys with us,] "but nothing whatever has transpired to throw light upon it. We give below all the material testimony elicited.

"*Pauline Dubourg*, laundress, deposes that she has known both the deceased for three years, having washed for them during that period. The old lady and her daughter seemed on good terms—very affectionate towards each other. They were excellent pay. Could not speak in regard to their mode or means of living. Believed that Madame L. told fortunes for a living. Was reputed to have money put by. Never met any persons in the house when she called for the clothes or took them home. Was sure that they had no servant in employ. There appeared to be no furniture in any part of the building except in the fourth story.

"*Pierre Moreau*, tobacconist, deposes that he has been in the habit of selling small quantities of tobacco and snuff to Madame L'Espanaye for nearly four years. Was born in the neighborhood, and has always resided there. The deceased and her daughter had occupied the house in which the corpses were found, for more than six years. It was formerly occupied by a jeweller, who under-let the upper rooms to various persons. The house was the property of Madame L. She became dissatisfied with the abuse of the premises by her tenant, and moved into them herself, refusing to let any portion. The old lady was childish. Witness had seen the daughter some five or six times during the six years. The two lived an exceedingly retired life—were reputed to have money. Had heard it said among the neighbors that Madame L. told fortunes—did not believe it. Had never seen any person enter the door except the old lady and her daughter, a porter once or twice, and a physician some eight or ten times.

"Many other persons, neighbors, gave evidence to the same effect. No one was spoken of as frequenting the house. It was not known whether there were any living connexions of Madam L. and her daughter. The shutters of the front windows were seldom opened. Those in the rear were always closed, with the exception of the large back room, fourth story. The house was a good house—not very old.

"*Isidore Musèt, gendarme,* deposes that he was called to the house about three o'clock in the morning. and found some twenty or thirty persons at the gateway, endeavoring to gain admittance. Forced it open, at length, with a bayonet—not with a crowbar. Had but little difficulty in getting it open, on account of its being a double or folding gate, and bolted neither at bottom nor top. The shrieks were continued until the gate was forced—and then suddenly ceased. They seemed to be screams of some person (or persons) in great agony—were loud and drawn out, not short and quick. Witness led the way up stairs. Upon reaching the first landing, heard two voices in loud and angry contention—the one a gruff voice, the other much shriller—a very strange voice. Could distinguish some words of the former, which was that of a Frenchman. Was positive that it was not a woman's voice. Could distinguish the words 'sacré' and 'diable.' The shrill voice was that of a foreigner. Could not be sure whether it was the voice of a man or of a woman. Could not make out what was said, but believed the language to be Spanish. The state of the room and of the bodies was described by this witness as we described them yesterday.

"Henri Duval, a neighbor, and by trade a silversmith, deposes that he was one of the party who first entered the house. Corroborates the testimony of Musèt in general. As soon as they forced an entrance, they reclosed the door, to keep out the crowd, which collected very fast, notwithstanding the lateness of the hour. The shrill voice, the witness thinks, was that of an Italian. Was certain it was not French. Could not be sure that it was a man's voice. It might have been a woman's. Was not acquainted with the Italian language. Could not distinguish the words, but was convinced by the intonation that the speaker was an Italian. Knew Madame L. and her daughter. Had conversed with both frequently. Was sure that the shrill voice was not that of either of the deceased.

"—— *Odenheimer, restaurateur.* This witness volunteered his testimony. Not speaking French, was examined through an interpreter. Is a native of Amsterdam. Was passing the house at the time of the shrieks. They lasted for several minutes—probably ten. They were long and loud—very awful and distressing. Was one of those who entered the building. Corroborated the previous evidence in every respect but one. Was sure that the shrill voice was that of a man—of a Frenchman. Could not distinguish the words uttered. They were loud and quick—unequal—spoken apparently in fear as well as in anger. The voice was harsh—not so much shrill as harsh. Could not call it a shrill voice. The gruff voice said repeatedly 'sacré,' 'diable' and once 'mon Dieu.'

"*Jules Mignaud,* banker, of the firm of Mignaud et Fils, Rue Deloraine. Is the elder Mignaud. Madame L'Espanaye had some property. Had opened an account with his banking house in the spring of the year —— (eight years previously). Made frequent deposits in small sums. Had checked for nothing until the third day before her death, when she took out in person the sum of 4000 francs. This sum was paid in gold, and a clerk sent home with the money.

"*Adolphe Le Bon,* clerk to Mignaud et Fils, deposes that on the day in question, about noon, he accompanied Madame L'Espanaye to her residence with the 4000 francs, put up in two bags. Upon the door being opened, Mademoiselle L. appeared and took from his hands one of the bags, while the old lady relieved him of the other. He then bowed and departed. Did not see any person in the street at the time. It is a bye-street—very lonely.

"*William Bird,* tailor, deposes that he was one of the party who entered the house. Is an Englishman. Has

lived in Paris two years. Was one of the first to ascend
the stairs. Heard the voices in contention. The gruff
voice was that of a Frenchman. Could make out several
words, but cannot now remember all. Heard distinctly
'sacré' and 'mon Dieu.' There was a sound at the moment as if of several persons struggling—a scraping and
scuffling sound. The shrill voice was very loud—louder
than the gruff one. Is sure that it was not the voice of
an Englishman. Appeared to be that of a German.
Might have been a woman's voice. Does not understand
German.

"Four of the above-named witnesses, being recalled,
deposed that the door of the chamber in which was
found the body of Mademoiselle L. was locked on the
inside when the party reached it. Every thing was perfectly silent—no groans or noises of any kind. Upon
forcing the door no person was seen. The windows,
both of the back and front room, were down and firmly
fastened from within. A door between the two rooms
was closed, but not locked. The door leading from the
front room into the passage was locked, with the key
on the inside. A small room in the front of the house, on
the fourth story, at the head of the passage, was open,
the door being ajar. This room was crowded with old
beds, boxes, and so forth. These were carefully removed
and searched. There was not an inch of any portion of
the house which was not carefully searched. Sweeps
were sent up and down the chimneys. The house was
a four story one, with garrets (mansardes). A trap-door
on the roof was nailed down very securely—did not appear to have been opened for years. The time elapsing
between the hearing of the voices in contention and the
breaking open of the room door, was variously stated
by the witnesses. Some made it as short as three minutes

—some as long as five. The door was opened with difficulty.

"*Alfonzo Garcio,* undertaker, deposes that he resides in the Rue Morgue. Is a native of Spain. Was one of the party who entered the house. Did not proceed up stairs. Is nervous, and was apprehensive of the consequences of agitation. Heard the voices in contention. The gruff voice was that of a Frenchman. Could not distinguish what was said. The shrill voice was that of an Englishman—is sure of this. Does not understand the English language, but judges by the intonation.

"*Alberto Montani,* confectioner, deposes that he was among the first to ascend the stairs. Heard the voices in question. The gruff voice was that of a Frenchman. Distinguished several words. The speaker appeared to be expostulating. Could not make out the words of the shrill voice. Spoke quick and unevenly. Thinks it the voice of a Russian. Corroborates the general testimony. Is an Italian. Never conversed with a native of Russia.

"Several witnesses, recalled, here testified that the chimneys of all the rooms on the fourth story were too narrow to admit the passage of a human being. By 'sweeps' were meant cylindrical sweeping-brushes, such as are employed by those who clean chimneys. These brushes were passed up and down every flue in the house. There is no back pasage by which any one could have descended while the party proceeded up stairs. The body of Mademoiselle L'Espanaye was so firmly wedged in the chimney that it could not be got down until four or five of the party united their strength.

"*Paul Dumas,* physician, deposes that he was called to view the bodies about day-break. They were both then lying on the sacking of the bedstead in the chamber where Mademoiselle L. was found. The corpse of the

young lady was much bruised and excoriated. The fact
that it had been thrust up the chimney would sufficiently
account for these appearances. The throat was greatly
chafed. There were several deep scratches just below
the chin, together with a series of livid spots which
were evidently the impression of fingers. The face was
fearfully discolored, and the eye-balls protruded. The
tongue had been partially bitten through. A large bruise
was discovered upon the pit of the stomach, produced,
apparently, by the pressure of a knee. In the opinion
of M. Dumas, Mademoiselle L'Espanaye had been
throttled to death by some person or persons unknown.
The corpse of the mother was horribly mutilated. All the
bones of the right leg and arm were more or less shattered. The left *tibia* much splintered, as well as all the
ribs of the left side. Whole body dreadfully bruised
and discolored. It was not possible to say how the injuries had been inflicted. A heavy club of wood, or a
broad bar of iron—a chair—any large, heavy, and obtuse weapon would have produced such results, if
wielded by the hands of a very powerful man. No
woman could have inflicted the blows with any weapon.
The head of the deceased, when seen by witness, was
entirely separated from the body, and was also greatly
shattered. The throat had evidently been cut with some
very sharp instrument—probably with a razor.

"*Alexandre Etienne,* surgeon, was called with M.
Dumas to view the bodies. Corroborated the testimony,
and the opinions of M. Dumas.

"Nothing farther of importance was elicited, although
several other persons were examined. A murder so mysterious, and so perplexing in all its particulars, was never
before committed in Paris—if indeed a murder has been
committed at all. The police are entirely at fault—an

unusual occurrence in affairs of this nature. There is
1ot, however, the shadow of a clew apparent."

The evening edition of the paper stated that the greatest excitement still continued in the Quartier St. Roch—
that the premises in question had been carefully re-
searched, and fresh examinations of witnesses instituted,
but all to no purpose. A postscript, however mentioned
that Adolphe Le Bon had been arrested and imprisoned
—although nothing appeared to criminate him, beyond
the facts already detailed.

Dupin seemed singularly interested in the progress of
this affair—at least so I judged from his manner, for he
made no comments. It was only after the announcement
that Le Bon had been imprisoned, that he asked me my
opinion respecting the murders.

I could merely agree with all Paris in considering
them an insoluble mystery. I saw no means by which it
would be possible to trace the murderer.

"We must not judge of the means," said Dupin, "by
this shell of an examination. The Parisian police, so
much extolled for *acumen,* are cunning, but no more.
There is no method in their proceedings, beyond the
method of the moment. They make a vast parade of
measures; but, not infrequently, these are so ill adapted
to the objects proposed, as to put us in mind of Monsieur Jourdain's calling for his *robe-de-chambre—pour
mieux entendre la musique.* The results attained by them
are not unfrequently surprising, but, for the most part,
are brought about by simple diligence and activity.
When these qualities are unavailing, their schemes fail.
Vidocq, for example, was a good guesser, and a persevering man. But, without educated thought, he erred
continually by the very intensity of his investigations.
He impaired his vision by holding the object too close.

He might see, perhaps, one or two points with unusual clearness, but in so doing he, necessarily, lost sight of the matter as a whole. Thus there is such a thing as being too profound. Truth is not always in a well. In fact, as regards the more important knowledge, I do believe that she is invariably superficial. The depth lies in the valleys where we seek her, and not upon the mountain-tops where she is found. The modes and sources of this kind of error are well typified in the contemplation of the heavenly bodies. To look at a star by glances—to view it in a side-long way, by turning toward it the exterior portions of the *retina* (more susceptible of feeble impressions of light than the interior), is to behold the star distinctly—is to have the best appreciation of its lustre —a lustre which grows dim just in proportion as we turn our vision *fully* upon it. A greater number of rays actually fall upon the eye in the latter case, but, in the former, there is the more refined capacity for comprehension. By undue profundity we perplex and enfeeble thought; and it is possible to make even Venus herself vanish from the firmament by a scrutiny too sustained, too concentrated, or too direct.

"As for these murders, let us enter into some examinations for ourselves, before we make up an opinion respecting them. An inquiry will afford us amusement," [I thought this an odd term, so applied, but said nothing] "and, besides, Le Bon once rendered me a service for which I am not ungrateful. We will go and see the premises with our own eyes. I know G——, the Prefect of Police, and shall have no difficulty in obtaining the necessary permission."

The permission was obtained, and we proceeded at once to the Rue Morgue. This is one of those miserable thoroughfares which intervene between the Rue Richelieu and the Rue St. Roch. It was late in the afternoon when we reached it; as this quarter is at a great distance from that in which we resided. The house was readily found; for there were still many persons gazing up at the closed shutters, with an objectless curiosity, from the opposite site of the way. It was an ordinary Parisian house, with a gateway, on one side of which was a glazed watch-box, with a sliding panel in the window, indicating a *loge de concierge*. Before going in we walked up the street, turned down an alley, and then, again turning, passed in the rear of the building—Dupin, meanwhile, examining the whole neighborhood, as well as the house, with a minuteness of attention for which I could see no possible object.

Retracing our steps, we came again to the front of the dwelling, rang, and, having shown our credentials, were admitted by the agents in charge. We went up stairs— into the chamber where the body of Mademoiselle L'Espanaye had been found, and where both the deceased still lay. The disorders of the room had, as usual, been suffered to exist. I saw nothing beyond what had been stated in the *Gazette des Tribunaux*. Dupin, scrutinized every thing—not excepting the bodies of the victims. We then went into the other rooms, and into the yard; a *gendarme* accompanying us throughout. The examination occupied us until dark, when we took our departure. On our way home my companion stopped in for a moment at the office of one of the daily papers.

I have said that the whims of my friend were manifold, and that *Je les menageais:*—for this phrase there is no English equivalent. It was his humor, now, to decline all conversation on the subject of the murder, until about noon the next day. He then asked me, suddenly, if I had observed any thing *peculiar* at the scene of the atrocity.

There was something in his manner of emphasizing

the word "peculiar," which caused me to shudder, without knowing why.

"No, nothing *peculiar*," I said; "nothing more, at least, than we both saw stated in the paper."

"The *Gazette*," he replied, "has not entered, I fear, into the unusual horror of the thing. But dismiss the idle opinions of this print. It appears to me that this mystery is considered insoluble, for the very reason which should cause it to be regarded as easy of solution —I mean for the *outré* character of its features. The police are confounded by the seeming absence of motive —not for the murder itself—but for the atrocity of the murder. They are puzzled, too, by the seeming impossibility of reconciling the voices heard in contention, with the facts that no one was discovered up stairs but the assassinated Mademoiselle L'Espanaye, and that there were no means of egress without the notice of the party ascending. The wild disorder of the room; the corpse thrust, with the head downward, up the chimney; the frightful mutilation of the body of the old lady; these considerations, with those just mentioned, and others which I need not mention, have sufficed to paralyze the powers, by putting completely at fault the boasted *acumen*, of the government agents. They have fallen into the gross but common error of confounding the unusual with the abstruse. But it is by these deviations from the plane of the ordinary, that reason feels its way, if at all, in its search for the true. In investigations such as we are now pursuing, it should not be so much asked 'what has occurred,' as 'what has occurred that has never occurred before.' In fact, the facility with which I shall arrive, or have arrived, at the solution of this mystery, is in the direct ratio of its apparent insolubility in the eyes of the police."

I stared at the speaker in mute astonishment.

"I am now awaiting," continued he, looking toward the door of our apartment—"I am now awaiting a person who, although perhaps not the perpetrator of these butcheries, must have been in some measure implicated in their perpetration. Of the worst portion of the crimes committed, it is probable that he is innocent. I hope that I am right in this supposition; for upon it I build my expectation of reading the entire riddle. I look for the man here—in this room—every moment. It is true that he may not arrive; but the probability is that he will. Should he come, it will be necessary to detain him. Here are pistols; and we both know how to use them when occasion demands their use."

I took the pistols, scarcely knowing what I did, or believing what I heard, while Dupin went on, very much as if in a soliloquy. I have already spoken of his abstract manner at such times. His discourse was addressed to myself; but his voice, although by no means loud, had that intonation which is commonly employed in speaking to some one at a great distance. His eyes, vacant in expression, regarded only the wall.

"That the voices heard in contention," he said, "by the party upon the stairs, were not the voices of the women themselves, was fully proved by the evidence. This relieves us of all doubt upon the question whether the old lady could have first destroyed the daughter, and afterward have committed suicide. I speak of this point chiefly for the sake of method; for the strength of Madame L'Espanaye would have been utterly unequal to the task of thrusting her daughter's corpse up the chimney as it was found; and the nature of the wounds upon her own person entirely preclude the idea of self-destruction. Murder, then, has been committed by some third party; and the voices of this third party were those heard in contention. Let me now advert—not to the whole testimony respecting these voices—but to what was *peculiar* in that testimony. Did you observe anything peculiar about it?"

I remarked that, while all the witnesses agreed in supposing the gruff voice to be that of a Frenchman, there was much disagreement in regard to the shrill, or, as one individual termed it, the harsh voice.

"That was the evidence itself," said Dupin, "but it was not the peculiarity of the evidence. You have observed nothing distinctive. Yet there *was* something to be observed. The witnesses, as you remark, agreed about the gruff voice; they were here unanimous. But in regard to the shrill voice, the peculiarity is—not that they disagreed—but that, while an Italian, an Englishman, a Spaniard, a Hollander, and a Frenchman attempted to describe it, each one spoke of it as that *of a foreigner.* Each is sure that it was not the voice of one of his own countrymen. Each likens it—not to the voice of an individual of any nation with whose language he is conversant—but the converse. The Frenchman supposes it the voice of a Spaniard, and 'might have distinguished some words *had he been acquainted with the Spanish.*' The Dutchman maintains it to have been that of a Frenchman; but we find it stated that '*not understanding French this witness was examined through an interpreter.*' The Englishman thinks it the voice of a German, and '*does not understand German.*' The Spaniard 'is sure' that it was that of an Englishman, but 'judges by the intonation' altogether, '*as he has no knowledge of the English.*' The Italian believes it the voice of a Russian, but '*has never conversed with a native of Russia.*' A second Frenchman differs, moreover, with the first, and is positive that the voice was that of an Italian; but, *not being cognizant of that tongue,* is, like the Spaniard, 'convinced by the intonation.' Now, how strangely unusual must that voice have really been, about which such testimony as this *could* have been elicited!—in whose *tones,* even, denizens of the five great divisions of Europe could recognise nothing familiar! You will say that it might have been the voice of an Asiatic—of an African. Neither Asiatics nor Africans abound in Paris; but, without denying the inference, I will now merely call your attention to three points. The voice is termed by one witness 'harsh rather than shrill.' It is represented by two others to have been 'quick and *unequal.*' No words—no sounds resembling words— were by any witness mentioned as distinguishable.

"I know not," continued Dupin, "what impression I may have made, so far, upon your own understanding; but I do not hesitate to say that legitimate deductions even from this portion of the testimony—the portion respecting the gruff and shrill voices—are in themselves sufficient to engender a suspicion which should give direction to all farther progress in the investigation of the mystery. I said 'legitimate deductions;' but my meaning is not thus fully expressed. I designed to imply that the deductions are the *sole* proper ones, and that the suspicion arises *inevitably* from them as the single result. What the suspicion is, however, I will not say just yet. I merely wish you to bear in mind that, with myself, it was sufficiently forcible to give a definite form —a certain tendency—to my inquiries in the chamber.

"Let us now transport ourselves, in fancy, to this chamber. What shall we first seek here? The means of egress employed by the murderers. It is not too much to say that neither of us believe in præternatural events. Madame and Mademoiselle L'Espanaye were not destroyed by spirits. The doers of the deed were material, and escaped materially. Then how? Fortunately, there is but one mode of reasoning upon the point, and that mode *must* lead us to a definite decision.—Let us examine, each by each, the possible means of egress. It is clear that the assassins were in the room where Mademoiselle L'Espanaye was found, or at least in the room adjoining, when the party ascended the stairs. It is then only from these two apartments that we have to seek issues. The police have laid bare the floors, the ceilings, and the masonry of the walls, in every direction. No *secret* issues could have escaped their vigilance. But, not trusting to *their* eyes, I examined with my own. There were, then, *no* secret issues. Both doors leading from the rooms into the passage were securely locked, with the keys inside. Let us turn to the chimneys. These, although of ordinary width for some eight or ten feet above the hearths, will not admit, throughout their extent, the body of a large cat. The impossibility of egress, by means already stated, being thus absolute, we are reduced to the windows. Through those of the front room no one could have escaped without notice from the crowd in the street. The murderers *must* have passed, then, through those of the back room. Now, brought to this conclusion in so unequivocal a manner as we are, it is not our part, as reasoners, to reject it on account of apparent impossibilities. It is only left for us to prove that these apparent 'impossibilities' are, in reality, not such.

"There are two windows in the chamber. One of them is unobstructed by furniture, and is wholly visible. The lower portion of the other is hidden from view by the head of the unwieldy bedstead which is thrust close up against it. The former was found securely fastened from within. It resisted the utmost force of those who endeavored to raise it. A large gimlet-hole had been pierced in its frame to the left, and a very stout nail was found fitted therein, nearly to the head. Upon examining the other window, a similar nail was seen similarly fitted in it; and a vigorous attempt to raise this sash, failed also. The police were now entirely satisfied that egress had not been in these directions. And, *therefore*, it was thought a matter of supererogation to withdraw the nails and open the windows.

"My own examination was somewhat more particular, and was so for the reason I have just given—because here it was, I knew, that all apparent impossibilities *must* be proved to be not such in reality.

"I proceeded to think thus—*à posteriori*. The murderers *did* escape from one of these windows. This being so, they could not have re-fastened the sashes from the inside, as they were found fastened;—the consideration which put a stop, through its obviousness, to the scrutiny of the police in this quarter. Yet the sashes *were* fastened. They *must*, then, have the power of fastening themselves. There was no escape from this conclusion. I stepped to the unobstructed casement, withdrew the nail with some difficulty, and attempted to raise the sash. It resisted all my efforts, as I had anticipated. A concealed spring must, I now knew, exist; and this corroboration of my idea convinced me that my premises, at least, were correct, however mysterious still appeared the circumstances attending the nails. A careful search soon brought to light the hidden spring. I pressed it, and, satisfied with the discovery, forebore to upraise the sash.

"I now replaced the nail and regarded it attentively. A person passing out through this window might have reclosed it, and the spring would have caught—but the nail could not have been replaced. The conclusion was plain, and again narrowed in the field of my investigations. The assassins *must* have escaped through the other window. Supposing, then, the springs upon each sash to be the same, as was probable, there *must* be found a difference between the nails, or at least between the modes of their fixture. Getting upon the sacking of the bedstead, I looked over the head-board minutely at the second casement. Passing my hand down behind the board, I readily discovered and pressed the spring, which was, as I had supposed, identical in character with its neighbor. I now looked at the nail. It was as stout as the other, and apparently fitted in the same manner—driven in nearly up to th'e head.

"You will say that I was puzzled; but, if you think so, you must have misunderstood the nature of the inductions. To use a sporting phrase, I had not been once 'at fault.' The scent had never for an instant been lost. There was no flaw in any link of the chain. I had traced the secret to its ultimate result,—and that result was *the nail*. It had, I say, in every respect, the appearance of its fellow in the other window; but this fact was an absolute nullity (conclusive as it might seem to be) when compared with the consideration that here, at this point, terminated the clew. 'There *must* be something wrong,' I said, 'about the nail.' I touched it; and the head, with about a quarter of an inch of the shank, came off in my fingers. The rest of the shank was in the gimlet-hole, where it had been broken off. The fracture was an old one (for its edges were incrusted with rust), and had apparently been accomplished by the blow of a hammer, which had partially imbedded, in the top of the bottom sash, the head portion of the nail. I now carefully replaced this head portion in the indentation whence I had taken it, and the resemblance to a perfect nail was complete—the fissure was invisible. Pressing the spring, I gently raised the sash for a few inches; the head went up with it, remaining firm in its bed. I closed the window, and the semblance of the whole nail was again perfect.

"The riddle, so far, was now unriddled. The assassin had escaped through the window which looked upon the bed. Dropping of its own accord upon his exit (or perhaps purposely closed), it had become fastened by the spring; and it was the retention of this spring which had been mistaken by the police for that of the nail,— farther inquiry being thus considered unnecessary.

"The next question is that of the mode of descent. Upon this point I had been satisfied in my walk with you around the building. About five feet and a half from the casement in question there runs a lightning-rod. From this rod it would have been impossible for any one to reach the window itself, to say nothing of entering it. I observed, however, that the shutters of the fourth story were of the peculiar kind called by Parisian carpenters *ferrades*—a kind rarely employed at the present day, but frequently seen upon very old mansions at Lyons and Bordeaux. They are in the form of an ordinary door, (a single, not a folding door) except that the upper half is latticed or worked in open trellis—thus affording an excellent hold for the hands. In the present instance these shutters are fully three feet and a half broad. When we saw them from the rear of the house, they were both about half open—that is to say, they stood off at right angles from the wall. It is probable that the police, as well as myself, examined the back of the tenement; but, if so, in looking at these *ferrades* in the line of their breadth (as they must have done), they did not perceive this great breadth itself, or, at all events, failed to take it into due consideration. In fact, having once satisfied themselves that no egress could have been made in this quarter, they would naturally bestow here a very cursory examination. It was clear to me, however, that the shutter belonging to the window at the head of the bed, would, if swung fully back to the wall, reach to within two feet of the lightning-rod. It was also evident that, by exertion of a very unusual degree of activity and courage, an entrance into the window, from the rod, might have been thus effected. —By reaching to the distance of two feet and a half (we now suppose the shutter open to its whole extent) a robber might have taken a firm grasp upon the trellis-work. Letting go, then, his hold upon the rod, placing his feet securely against the wall, and springing boldly from it, he might have swung the shutter so as to close it, and, if we imagine the window open at the time, might even have swung himself into the room.

"I wish you to bear especially in mind that I have spoken of a *very* unusual degree of activity as requisite to success in so hazardous and so difficult a feat. It is my design to show you, first, that the thing might possibly have been accomplished:—but, secondly and *chiefly,* I wish to impress upon your understanding the *very extraordinary*—the almost præternatural character of that agility which could have accomplished it.

"You will say, no doubt, using the language of the law, that 'to make out my case' I should rather under-value, than insist upon a full estimation of the activity required in this matter. This may be the practice in law, but it is not the usage of reason. My ultimate object is only the truth. My immediate purpose is to lead you to place in juxta-position that *very unusual* activity of which I have just spoken, with that *very peculiar* shrill (or harsh) and *unequal* voice, about whose nationality no two persons could be found to agree, and in whose utterance no syllabification could be detected."

At these words a vague and half-formed conception of

the meaning of Dupin flitted over my mind. I seemed
to be upon the verge of comprehension, without power
to comprehend—as men, at times, find themselves upon
the brink of remembrance, without being able, in the
end, to remember. My friend went on with his discourse.

"You will see," he said, "that I have shifted the question from the mode of egress to that of ingress. It was
my design to suggest that both were effected in the
same manner, at the same point. Let us now revert to
the interior of the room. Let us survey the appearances
here. The drawers of the bureau, it is said, had been
rifled, although many articles of apparel still remained
within them. The conclusion here is absurd. It is a mere
guess—a very silly one—and no more. How are we to
know that the articles found in the drawers were not all
these drawers had originally contained? Madame L'Espanaye and her daughter lived an exceedingly retired
life—saw no company—seldom went out—had little use
for numerous changes of habiliment. Those found were
at least of as good quality as any likely to be possessed
by these ladies. If a thief had taken any, why did he not
take the best—why did he not take all? In a word, why
did he abandon four thousand francs in gold to en-
cumber himself with a bundle of linen? The gold *was*
abandoned. Nearly the whole sum mentioned by Monsieur Mignaud, the banker, was discovered, in bags,
upon the floor. I wish you, therefore, to discard from
your thoughts the blundering idea of *motive,* engendered in the brains of the police by that portion of the
evidence which speaks of money delivered at the door of
the house. Coincidences ten times as remarkable as this
(the delivery of the money, and murder committed
within three days upon the party receiving it), happen
to all of us every hour of our lives, without attracting
even momentary notice. Coincidences, in general, are

great stumbling-blocks in the way of that class of thinkers who have been educated to know nothing of the
theory of probabilities—that theory to which the most
glorious objects of human research are indebted for the
most glorious of illustration. In the present instance, had
the gold been gone, the fact of its delivery three days
before would have formed something more than a coincidence. It would have been corroborative of this idea
of motive. But, under the real circumstances of the case,
if we are to suppose gold the motive of this outrage, we
must also imagine the perpetrator so vacillating an idiot
as to have abandoned his gold and his motive together.

"Keeping now steadily in mind the points to which I
have drawn your attention—that peculiar voice, that unusual agility, and that startling absence of motive in a
murder so singularly atrocious as this—let us glance at
the butchery itself. Here is a woman strangled to death
by manual strength, and thrust up a chimney, head
downward. Ordinary assassins employ no such modes of
murder as this. Least of all, do they thus dispose of the
murdered. In the manner of thrusting the corpse up the
chimney, you will admit that there was something *excessively outré*—something altogether irreconcilable
with our common notions of human action, even when
we suppose the actors the most depraved of men. Think,
too, how great must have been that strength which
could have thrust the body *up* such an aperture so
forcibly that the united vigor of several persons was
found barely sufficient to drag it *down!*

"Turn, now, to other indications of the employment
of a vigor most marvellous. On the hearth were thick
tresses—very thick tresses—of grey human hair. These
had been torn out by the roots. You are aware of the
great force necessary in tearing thus from the head even
twenty or thirty hairs together. You saw the locks in

question as well as myself. Their roots (a hideous
sight!) were clotted with fragments of the flesh of the
scalp—sure token of the prodigious power which had
been exerted in uprooting perhaps half a million of hairs
at a time. The throat of the old lady was not merely cut,
but the head absolutely severed from the body: the
instrument was a mere razor. I wish you also to look at
the *brutal* ferocity of these deeds. Of the bruises upon
the body of Madame L'Espanaye I do not speak. Monsieur Dumas, and his worthy coadjutor Monsieur Etienne, have pronounced that they were inflicted by some
obtuse instrument; and so far these gentlemen are very
correct. The obtuse instrument was clearly the stone
pavement in the yard, upon which the victim had fallen
from the window which looked in upon the bed. This
idea, however simple it may now seem, escaped the
police for the same reason that the breadth of the shutters escaped them—because, by the affair of the nails,
their perceptions had been hermetically sealed against
the possibility of the windows having ever been opened
at all.

"If now, in addition to all these things, you have
properly reflected upon the odd disorder of the chamber,
we have gone so far as to combine the ideas of an agility
astounding, a strength superhuman, a ferocity brutal, a
butchery without motive, a *grotesquerie* in horror absolutely alien from humanity, and a voice foreign in tone
to the ears of men of many nations, and devoid of all
distinct or intelligible syllabification. What result, then,
has ensued? What impression have I made upon your
fancy?"

I felt a creeping of the flesh as Dupin asked me the
question. "A madman," I said, "has done this deed—
some raving maniac, escaped from a neighboring *Maison
de Santé.*"

"In some respects," he replied, "your idea is not irrelevant. But the voices of madmen, even in their wildest paroxysms, are never found to tally with that peculiar voice heard upon the stairs. Madmen are of some nation, and their language, however incoherent in its words, has always the coherence of syllabification. Besides, the hair of a madman is not such as I now hold in my hand. I disentangled this little tuft from the rigidly clutched fingers of Madame L'Espanaye. Tell me what you can make of it."

"Dupin!" I said, completely unnerved; "this hair is most unusual—this is no *human* hair."

"I have not asserted that it is," said he; "but, before we decide this point, I wish you to glance at the little sketch I have here traced upon this paper. It is a *facsimile* drawing of what has been described in one portion of the testimony as 'dark bruises, and deep indentations of finger nails,' upon the throat of Mademoiselle L'Espanaye, and in another, (by Messrs. Dumas and Etienne, as a 'series of livid spots, evidently the impression of fingers.'

"You will perceive," continued my friend, spreading out the paper upon the table before us, "that this drawing gives the idea of a firm and fixed hold. There is no *slipping* apparent. Each finger has retained—possibly until the death of the victim—the fearful grasp by which it originally imbedded itself. Attempt, now, to place all your fingers, at the same time, in the respective impressions as you see them."

I made the attempt in vain.

"We are possibly not giving this matter a fair trial," he said. "The paper is spread out upon a plane surface; but the human throat is cylindrical. Here is a billet of wood, the circumference of which is about that of the throat. Wrap the drawing around it, and try the experiment again."

I did so; but the difficulty was even more obvious than before.

"This,' I said, "is the mark of no human hand."

"Read now," replied Dupin, "this passage from Cuvier."

It was a minute anatomical and generally descriptive account of the large fulvous Ourang-Outang of the East Indian Islands. The gigantic stature, the prodigious strength and activity, the wild ferocity, and the imitative propensities of these mammalia are sufficiently well known to all. I understood the full horrors of the murder at once.

"The description of the digits," said I, as I made an end of reading, "is in exact accordance with this drawing. I see that no animal but an Ourang-Outang, of the species here mentioned, could have impressed the indentations as you have traced them. This tuft of tawny hair, too, is identical in character with that of the beast of Cuvier. But I cannot possibly comprehend the particulars of this frightful mystery. Besides, there were *two* voices heard in contention, and one of them was unquestionably the voice of a Frenchman."

"True; and you will remember an expression attributed almost unanimously, by the evidence, to this voice,—the expression, 'mon Dieu!' This, under the circumstances, has been justly characterized by one of the witnesses (Montani, the confectioner,) as an expression of remonstrance or expostulation. Upon these two words, therefore, I have mainly built my hopes of a full solution of the riddle. A Frenchman was cognizant of the murder. It is possible—indeed it is far more than probable—that he was innocent of all participation in the bloody transactions which took place. The Ourang-Outang may have escaped from him. He may have traced it to the chamber; but, under the agitating circumstances which ensued, he could never have recaptured it. It is still at large. I will not pursue these guesses—for I have no right to call them more—since the shades of reflection upon which they are based are scarcely of sufficient depth to be appreciable by my own intellect, and since I could not pretend to make them intelligible to the understanding of another. We will call them guesses then, and speak of them as such. If the Frenchman in question is indeed, as I suppose, innocent of this atrocity, this advertisement, which I left last night, upon our return home, at the office of *Le Monde*, (a paper devoted to the shipping interest, and much sought by sailors,) will bring him to our residence."

He handed me a paper, and I read thus:

CAUGHT—*In the Bois de Boulogne, early in the morning of the —— inst;* (the morning of the murder,) *a very large Ourang-Outang of the Bornese species. The owner, (who is ascertained to be a sailor, belonging to a Maltese vessel,) may have the animal again, upon identifying it satisfactorily, and paying a few charges arising from its capture and keeping. Call at No. ——, Rue ——, Faubourg St. Germain—au troisième.*

"How was it possible," I asked, "that you should know the man to be a sailor, and belonging to a Maltese vessel?"

"I do *not* know it," said Dupin. "I am not *sure* of it. Here, however, is a small piece of ribbon, which from its form, and from its greasy appearance, has evidently been used in tying the hair in one of those long *queues* of which sailors are so fond. Moreover, this knot is one which few besides sailors can tie, and is peculiar to the

Maltese. I picked the ribbon up at the foot of the light-ning-rod. It could not have belonged to either of the deceased. Now if, after all, I am wrong in my induction from this ribbon, that the Frenchman was a sailor be-longing to a Maltese vessel, still I can have done no harm in saying what I did in the advertisement. If I am in error, he will merely suppose that I have been misled by some circumstance into which he will not take the trouble to inquire. But if I am right, a great point is gained. Cognizant although innocent of the murder, the Frenchman will naturally hesitate about replying to the advertisement—about demanding the Ourang-Outang. He will reason thus:—'I am innocent; I am poor; my Ourang-Outang is of great value—to one in my circum-stances a fortune of itself—why should I lose it through idle apprehensions of danger? Here it is, within my grasp. It was found in the Bois de Boulogne—at a vast distance from the scene of that butchery. How can it ever be suspected that a brute beast should have done the deed? The police are at fault—they have failed to procure the slightest clew. Should they even trace the animal, it would be impossible to prove me cognizant of the murder, or to implicate me in guilt on account of that cognizance. Above all, *I am known*. The advertiser designates me as the possessor of the beast. I am not sure to what limit his knowledge may extend. Should I avoid claiming a property of so great value, which it is known that I possess, I will render the animal, at least, liable to suspicion. It is not my policy to attract atten-tion either to myself or to the beast. I will answer the advertisement, get the Ourang-Outang, and keep it close until this matter has blown over.'"

At this moment we heard a step upon the stairs.

"Be ready," said Dupin, "with your pistols, but neither use them nor show them until at a signal from myself."

The front door of the house had been left open, and the visitor had entered, without ringing, and advanced several steps upon the staircase. Now, however, he seemed to hesitate. Presently we heard him descending. Dupin was moving quickly to the door, when we again heard him coming up. He did not turn back a second time, but stepped up with decision and rapped at the door of our chamber.

"Come in," said Dupin, in a cheerful and hearty tone.

A man entered. He was a sailor, evidently,—a tall, stout, and muscular-looking person, with a certain dare-devil expression of countenance, not altogether unprepossessing. His face, greatly sunburnt, was more than half hidden by whisker and *mustachio*. He had with him a huge oaken cudgel, but appeared to be otherwise unarmed. He bowed awkwardly, and bade us "good evening," in French accents, which, although somewhat Neufchatelish, were still sufficiently indicative of a Parisian origin.

"Sit down, my friend," said Dupin. "I suppose you have called about the Ourang-Outang. Upon my word, I almost envy you the possession of him; a remarkably fine, and no doubt a very valuable animal. How old do you suppose him to be?"

The sailor drew a long breath, with the air of a man relieved of some intolerable burden, and then replied, in an assured tone:

"I have no way of telling—but he can't be more than four or five years old. Have you got him here?"

"Oh no; we had no conveniences for keeping him here. He is at a livery stable in the Rue Dubourg, just by. You can get him in the morning. Of course you are prepared to identify the property?"

"To be sure I am, sir."

"I shall be sorry to part with him," said Dupin.

"I don't mean that you should be at all this trouble for nothing, sir," said the man. "Couldn't expect it. Am very willing to pay a reward for the finding of the animal—that is to say, any thing in reason."

"Well," replied my friend, "that is all very fair, to be sure. Let me think!—what should I have? Oh! I will tell you. My reward shall be this. You shall give me all the information in your power about these murders in the Rue Morgue."

Dupin said the last words in a very low tone, and very quietly. Just as quietly, too, he walked toward the door, locked it, and put the key in his pocket. He then drew a pistol from his bosom and placed it, without the least flurry, upon the table.

The sailor's face flushed up as if he were struggling with suffocation. He started to his feet and grasped his cudgel; but the next moment he fell back into his seat, trembling violently, and with the countenance of death itself. He spoke not a word. I pitied him from the bottom of my heart.

"My friend," said Dupin, in a kind tone, "you are alarming yourself unnecessarily—you are indeed. We mean you no harm whatever. I pledge you the honor of a gentleman, and of a Frenchman, that we intend you no injury. I perfectly well know that you are innocent of the atrocities in the Rue Morgue. It will not do, however, to deny that you are in some measure implicated in them. From what I have already said, you must know that I have had means of information about this matter— means of which you could never have dreamed. Now the thing stands thus. You have done nothing which you could have avoided—nothing, certainly, which renders you culpable. You were not even guilty of robbery, when you might have robbed with impunity. You have nothing to conceal. You have no reason for concealment. On the other hand, you are bound by every principle of honor to confess all you know. An innocent man is now imprisoned, charged with that crime of which you can point out the perpetrator."

The sailor had recovered his presence of mind, in a great measure, while Dupin uttered these words; but his original boldness of bearing was all gone.

"So help me God," said he, after a brief pause, "I *will* tell you all I know about this affair;—but I do not expect you to believe one half I say—I would be a fool indeed if I did. Still, I *am* innocent, and I will make a clean breast if I die for it."

What he stated was, in substance, this. He had lately made a voyage to the Indian Archipelago. A party, of which he formed one, landed at Borneo, and passed into the interior on an excursion of pleasure. Himself and a companion had captured the Ourang-Outang. This companion dying, the animal fell into his own exclusive possession. After great trouble, occasioned by the intractable ferocity of his captive during the home voyage, he at length succeeded in lodging it safely at his own residence in Paris, where, not to attract toward himself the unpleasant curiosity of his neighbors, he kept it carefully secluded, until such time as it should recover from a wound in the foot, received from a splinter on board ship. His ultimate design was to sell it.

Returning home from some sailors' frolic on the night, or rather in the morning of the murder, he found the beast occupying his own bed-room, into which it had broken from a closet adjoining, where it had been, as was thought, securely confined. Razor in hand, and fully lathered, it was sitting before a looking-glass, attempting the operation of shaving, in which it had no doubt previously watched its master through the key-hole of the closet. Terrified at the sight of so dangerous a weapon in the possession of an animal so ferocious, and so well able to use it, the man, for some moments, was at a loss what to do. He had been accustomed, however, to quiet the creature, even in its fiercest moods, by the use of a whip, and to this he now resorted. Upon sight of it, the Ourang-Outang sprang at once through the door of the chamber, down the stairs, and thence, through a window, unfortunately open, into the street.

The Frenchman followed in despair; the ape, razor still in hand, occasionally stopping to look back and gesticulate at its pursuer, until the latter had nearly come up with it. It then again made off. In this manner the chase continued for a long time. The streets were profoundly quiet, as it was nearly three o'clock in the morning. In passing down an alley in the rear of the Rue Morgue, the fugitive's attention was arrested by a light gleaming from the open window of Madame L'Espanaye's chamber, in the fourth story of her house. Rushing to the building, it perceived the lightning-rod, clambered up with inconceivable agility, grasped the shutter, which was thrown fully back against the wall, and, by its means, swung itself directly upon the headboard of the bed. The whole feat did not occupy a minute. The shutter was kicked open again by the Ourang-Outang as it entered the room.

The sailor, in the meantime, was both rejoiced and perplexed. He had strong hopes of now recapturing the brute, as it could scarcely escape from the trap into which it had ventured, except by the rod, where it might be intercepted as it came down. On the other hand, there was much cause for anxiety as to what it might do in the house. This latter reflection urged the man still to follow the fugitive. A lightning-rod is ascended without difficulty, especially by a sailor; but, when he had arrived as high as the window, which lay far to his left, his career was stopped; the most that he could accomplish was to reach over so as to obtain a glimpse of the interior of the room. At this glimpse he nearly fell from his hold through excess of horror. Now it was that those hideous shrieks arose upon the night, which had startled from slumber the inmates of the Rue Morgue. Madame L'Espanaye and her daughter, habited in their night clothes, had apparently been arranging some papers in the iron chest already mentioned, which had been wheeled into the middle of the room. It was open, and its contents lay beside it on the floor. The victims must have been sitting with their backs toward the window; and, from the time elapsing between the ingress of the beast and the screams, it seems probable that it was not immediately perceived. The flapping-to of the shutter would naturally have been attributed to the wind.

As the sailor looked in, the gigantic animal had seized Madame L'Espanaye by the hair, (which was loose, as she had been combing it,) and was flourishing the razor about her face, in imitation of the motions of a barber. The daughter lay prostrate and motionless; she had swooned. The screams and struggles of the old lady (during which the hair was torn from her head) had the effect of changing the probably pacific purposes of the Ourang-Outang into those of wrath. With one determined sweep of its muscular arm it nearly severed her head from her body. The sight of blood inflamed its anger into phrenzy. Gnashing its teeth, and flashing fire from its eyes, it flew upon the body of the girl, and imbedded its fearful talons in her throat, retaining its grasp until she expired. Its wandering and wild glances fell at this moment upon the head of the bed, over which the face of its master, rigid with horror, was just discernible. The fury of the beast, who no doubt bore still in mind the dreaded whip, was instantly converted into fear. Conscious of having deserved punishment, it seemed desirous of concealing its bloody deeds, and skipped about the chamber in an agony of nervous agitation; throwing down and breaking the furniture as it moved, and dragging the bed from the bedstead. In conclusion, it seized first the corpse of the daughter, and thrust it up the chimney, as it was found; then that of the old lady, which it immediately hurled through the window head-long.

As the ape approached the casement with its muti-lated burden, the sailor shrank aghast to the rod, and, rather gliding than clambering down it, hurried at once home—dreading the consequences of the butchery, and gladly abandoning, in his terror, all solicitude about the fate of the Ourang-Outang. The words heard by the party upon the staircase were the Frenchman's exclama-tions of horror and affright, commingled with the fiend-ish jabberings of the brute.

I have scarcely anything to add. The Ourang-Outang must have escaped from the chamber, by the rod, just before the breaking of the door. It must have closed the window as it passed through it. It was subsequently caught by the owner himself, who obtained for it a very large sum at the *Jardin des Plantes*. Le Bon was in-stantly released, upon our narration of the circumstances (with some comments from Dupin) at the *bureau* of the Prefect of Police. This functionary, however well dis-posed to my friend, could not altogether conceal his chagrin at the turn which affairs had taken, and was fain to indulge in a sarcasm or two, about the propriety of every person minding his own business.

"Let them talk," said Dupin, who had not thought it necessary to reply. "Let him discourse; it will ease his conscience. I am satisfied with having defeated him in his own castle. Nevertheless, that he failed in the solution of this mystery, is by no means that matter for wonder which he supposes it; for, in truth, our friend the Prefect is somewhat too cunning to be profound. In his wisdom is no *stamen*. It is all head and no body, like the pictures of the Goddess Laverna,—or, at best, all head and shoulders, like a codfish. But he is a good creature after all. I like him especially for one master stroke of cant, by which he has attained his reputation for ingenuity. I mean the way he has '*de nier ce qui est, et d'expliquer ce qui n'est pas.*'" [1]

THE MYSTERY OF
MARIE ROGÊT [2]

A SEQUEL TO "THE MURDERS IN THE RUE MORGUE."
(*Snowden's Ladies' Companion*, November, December, 1842;
February 1843.)

Es giebt eine Reihe idealischer Begebenheiten, die der Wirklichkeit parallel läuft. Selten fallen sie zusammen. Menschen und Zufälle modificiren gewönlich die idealische Begebenheit, so dass sie unvollkommen erscheint, und ihre Folgen gleichfalls unvollkommen sind. So bei der Reformation: statt des Protestantismus kam das Lutherthum hervor.

[1] Rousseau, Nouvelle Héloïse.
[2] On the original publication of "Marie Rogêt," the footnotes now appended were considered unnecessary; but the lapse of several years since the tragedy upon which the tale is based, renders it expedient to give them, and also to say a few words in explanation of the general design. A young girl, Mary Cecilia Rogers, was murdered in the vicinity of New York; and, although her death occasioned an intense and long-enduring excitement, the mystery attending it had remained unsolved at the period when the present paper was written and published (November, 1842). Herein, under pretence of relating the fate of a Parisian grisette, the author has followed, in minute

There are ideal series of events which run parallel with the real ones. They rarely coincide. Men and circumstances generally modify the ideal train of events, so that it seems imperfect, and its consequences are equally imperfect. Thus with the Reformation; instead of Protestantism came Lutheranism.—NOVALIS.[1] *Moralische Ansichten.*

THERE are few persons, even among the calmest thinkers, who have not occasionally been startled into a vague yet thrilling half-credence in the supernatural, by *coincidences* of so seemingly marvellous a character that, as *mere* coincidences, the intellect has been unable to receive them. Such sentiments—for the half-credences of which I speak have never the full force of *thought*—are seldom thoroughly stifled unless by reference to the doctrine of chance, or, as it is technically termed, the Calculus of Probabilities. Now this Calculus is, in its essence, purely mathematical; and thus we have the anomaly of the most rigidly exact in science applied to the shadow and spirituality of the most intangible in speculation.

The extraordinary details which I am now called upon to make public, will be found to form, as regards sequence of time, the primary branch of a series of scarcely intelligible *coincidences,* whose secondary or detail, the essential, while merely paralleling the inessential facts of the real murder of Mary Rogers. Thus all argument founded upon the fiction is applicable to the truth; and the investigation of the truth was the object.

The "*Mystery of Marie Rogêt*" was composed at a distance from the scene of the atrocity, and with no other means of investigation than the newspapers afforded. Thus much escaped the writer of which he could have availed himself had he been on the spot, and visited the localities. It may not be improper to record, nevertheless, that the confessions of two persons, (one of them the Madame Deluc of the narrative) made, at different periods, long subsequent to the publication, confirmed, in full, not only the general conclusion, but absolutely all the chief hypothetical details by which that conclusion was attained. [E.A.P.]

[1] The nom de plume of Von Hardenberg.

concluding branch will be recognized by all readers in the late murder of MARY CECILIA ROGERS, at New York.

When, in an article entitled "The Murders in the Rue Morgue," I endeavored, about a year ago, to depict some very remarkable features in the mental character of my friend, the Chevalier C. Auguste Dupin, it did not occur to me that I should ever resume the subject. This depicting of character constituted my design; and this design was fulfilled in the train of circumstances brought to instance Dupin's idiosyncrasy. I might have adduced other examples, but I should have proven no more. Late events, however, in their surprising development, have startled me into some farther details, which will carry with them the air of extorted confession. Hearing what I have lately heard, it would be indeed strange should I remain silent in regard to what I both heard and saw so long ago.

Upon the winding up of the tragedy involved in the deaths of Madame L'Espanaye and her daughter, the Chevalier dismissed the affair at once from his attention, and relapsed into his old habits of moody reverie. Prone, at all times, to abstraction, I readily fell in with his humor; and, continuing to occupy our chambers in the Faubourg Saint Germain, we gave the Future to the winds, and slumbered tranquilly in the Present, weaving the dull world around us into dreams.

But these dreams were not altogether uninterrupted. It may readily be supposed that the part played by my friend, in the drama at the Rue Morgue, had not failed of its impression upon the fancies of the Parisian police. With its emissaries, the name of Dupin had grown into a household word. The simple character of those inductions by which he had disentangled the mystery never having been explained even to the Prefect, or to any other individual than myself, of course it is not surprising that the affair was regarded as little less than miraculous, or that the Chevalier's analytical abilities acquired for him the credit of intuition. His frankness would have led him to disabuse every inquirer of such prejudice; but his indolent humor forbade all farther agitation of a topic whose interest to himself had long ceased. It thus happened that he found himself the cynosure of the policial eyes; and the cases were not few in which attempt was made to engage his services at the Prefecture. One of the most remarkable instances was that of the murder of a young girl named Marie Rogêt.

This event occurred about two years after the atrocity in the Rue Morgue. Marie, whose Christian and family name will at once arrest attention from their resemblance to those of the unfortunate "cigar-girl," was the only daughter of the widow Estelle Rogêt. The father had died during the child's infancy, and from the period of his death, until within eighteen months before the assassination which forms the subject of our narrative, the mother and daughter had dwelt together in the Rue Pavée Saint André;[1] Madame there keeping a *pension*, assisted by Marie. Affairs went on thus until the latter had attained her twenty-second year, when her great beauty attracted the notice of a perfumer, who occupied one of the shops in the basement of the Palais Royal, and whose custom lay chiefly among the desperate adventurers infesting that neighborhood. Monsieur Le Blanc[2] was not unaware of the advantages to be derived from the attendance of the fair Marie in his perfumery; and his liberal proposals were accepted eagerly by the girl, although with somewhat more of hestitation by Madame.

[1] *Nassau Street.*
[2] *Anderson.*

The anticipations of the shopkeeper were realized, and his rooms soon became notorious through the charms of the sprightly *grisette*. She had been in his employ about a year, when her admirers were thrown into confusion by her sudden disappearance from the shop. Monsieur Le Blanc was unable to account for her absence, and Madame Rogêt was distracted with anxiety and terror. The public papers immediately took up the theme, and the police were upon the point of making serious investigations, when, one fine morning, after the lapse of a week, Marie, in good health, but with a somewhat saddened air, made her re-appearance at her usual counter in the perfumery. All inquiry, except that of a private character, was of course immediately hushed. Monsieur Le Blanc professed total ignorance, as before. Marie, with Madame, replied to all questions, that the last week had been spent at the house of a relation in the country. Thus the affair died away, and was generally forgotten; for the girl, ostensibly to relieve herself from the impertinence of curiosity, soon bade a final adieu to the perfumer, and sought the shelter of her mother's residence in the Rue Pavée Saint André.

It was about three years after this return home, that her friends were alarmed by her sudden disappearance for the second time. Three days elapsed, and nothing was heard of her. On the fourth her corpse was found floating in the Seine,[1] near the shore which is opposite the Quartier of the Rue Saint André, and at a point not very far distant from the secluded neighborhood of the Barrière du Roule.[2]

The atrocity of this murder, (for it was at once evident that murder had been committed,) the youth and

[1] The Hudson.
[2] Weehawken.

beauty of the victim, and, above all, her previous notoriety, conspired to produce intense excitement in the
minds of the sensitive Parisians. I can call to mind no
similar occurrence producing so general and so intense
an effect. For several weeks, in the discussion of this
one absorbing theme, even the momentous political
topics of the day were forgotten. The Prefect made unusual exertions; and the powers of the whole Parisian
police were, of course, tasked to the utmost extent.

Upon the first discovery of the corpse, it was not
supposed that the murderer would be able to elude, for
more than a very brief period, the inquisition which
was immediately set on foot. It was not until the expiration of a week that it was deemed necessary to
offer a reward; and even then this reward was limited
to a thousand francs. In the mean time the investigation proceeded with vigor, if not always with judgment,
and numerous individuals were examined to no purpose; while, owing to the continual absence of all clue
to the mystery, the popular excitement greatly increased. At the end of the tenth day it was thought
advisable to double the sum originally proposed; and,
at length, the second week having elapsed without
leading to any discoveries, and the prejudice which
always exists in Paris against the Police having given
vent to itself in several serious *émeutes,* the Prefect took
it upon himself to offer the sum of twenty thousand
francs "for the conviction of the assassin," or, if more
than one should prove to have been implicated, "for
the conviction of any one of the assassins." In the
proclamation setting forth this reward, a full pardon
was promised to any accomplice who should come forward in evidence against his fellow; and to the whole
was appended, wherever it appeared, the private plac-
ard of a committee of citizens, offering ten thousand

francs, in addition to the amount proposed by the Prefecture. The entire reward thus stood at no less than thirty thousand francs, which will be regarded as an extraordinary sum when we consider the humble condition of the girl, and the great frequency, in large cities, of such atrocities as the one described.

No one doubted now that the mystery of this murder would be immediately brought to light. But although, in one or two instances, arrests were made which promised elucidation, yet nothing was elicited which could implicate the parties suspected; and they were discharged forthwith. Strange as it may appear, the third week from the discovery of the body had passed, without any light being thrown upon the subject, before even a rumor of the events which had so agitated the public mind, reached the ears of Dupin and myself. Engaged in researches which had absorbed our whole attention, it had been nearly a month since either of us had gone abroad, or received a visiter, or more than glanced at the leading political articles in one of the daily papers. The first intelligence of the murder was brought us by G——, in person. He called upon us early in the afternoon of the thirteenth of July, 18—, and remained with us until late in the night. He had been piqued by the failure of all his endeavors to ferret out the assassins. His reputation—so he said with a peculiarly Parisian air—was at stake. Even his honor was concerned. The eyes of the public were upon him; and there was really no sacrifice which he would not be willing to make for the development of the mystery. He concluded a somewhat droll speech with a compliment upon what he was pleased to term the *tact* of Dupin, and made him a direct, and certainly a liberal proposition, the precise nature of which I do not feel myself at liberty to disclose, but which has no bearing upon the proper subject of my narrative.

The compliment my friend rebutted as best he could, but the proposition he accepted at once, although its advantages were altogether provisional. This point being settled, the Prefect broke forth at once into explanations of his own views, interspersing them with long comments upon the evidence; of which latter we were not yet in possession. He discoursed much, and beyond doubt, learnedly; while I hazarded an occasional suggestion as the night wore drowsily away. Dupin, sitting steadily in his accustomed arm-chair, was the embodiment of respectful attention. He wore spectacles during the whole interview; and an occasional glance beneath their green glasses, sufficed to convince me that he slept not the less soundly, because silently, throughout the seven or eight leaden-footed hours which immediately preceded the departure of the Prefect.

In the morning, I procured, the Prefecture, a full report of all the evidence elicited, and, at the various newspaper offices, a copy of every paper in which, from first to last, had been published any decisive information in regard to this sad affair. Freed from all that was positively disproved, this mass of information stood thus:

Marie Rogêt left the residence of her mother, in the Rue Pavée St. André, about nine o'clock in the morning of Sunday, June the twenty-second, 18—. In going out, she gave notice to a Monsieur Jacques St. Eustache,[1] and to him only, of her intention to spend the day with an aunt who resided in the Rue des Drômes. The Rue des Drômes is a short and narrow but populous thoroughfare, not far from the banks of the river, and, at a distance of some two miles, in the most direct course possible, from the *pension* of Madame Rogêt. St. Eustache

[1] *Payne.*

was the accepted suitor of Marie, and lodged, as well as took his meals, at the *pension*. He was to have gone for his betrothed at dusk, and to have escorted her home. In the afternoon, however, it came on to rain heavily; and, supposing that she would remain all night at her aunt's, (as she had done under similar circumstances before,) he did not think it necessary to keep his promise. As night drew on, Madame Rogêt (who was an infirm old lady, seventy years of age,) was heard to express a fear "that she should never see Marie again;" but this observation attracted little attention at the time.

On Monday, it was ascertained that the girl had not been to the Rue des Drômes; and when the day elapsed without tidings of her, a tardy search was instituted at several points in the city, and its environs. It was not, however, until the fourth day from the period of her disappearance that any thing satisfactory was ascertained respecting her. On this day, (Wednesday, the twenty-fifth day of June,) a Monsieur Beauvais,[1] who, with a friend, had been making inquiries for Marie near the Barriére du Roule, on the shore of the Seine which is opposite the Rue Pavée St. André, was informed that a corpse had just been towed ashore by some fishermen, who had found it floating in the river. Upon seeing the body, Beauvais, after some hesitation, identified it as that of the perfumery-girl. His friend recognized it more promptly.

The face was suffused with dark blood, some of which issued from the mouth. No foam was seen, as in the case of the merely drowned. There was no discoloration in the cellular tissue. About the throat were bruises and impressions of fingers. The arms were bent over on the chest and were rigid. The right hand was clenched; the left partially open. On the left wrist were two circular

[1] *Crommelin.*

excoriations, apparently the effect of ropes, or of a rope in more than one volution. A part of the right wrist, also, was much chafed, as well as the back throughout its extent, but more especially at the shoulder-blades. In bringing the body to the shore the fishermen had attached to it a rope; but none of the excoriations had been effected by this. The flesh of the neck was much swollen. There were no cuts apparent, or bruises which appeared the effect of blows. A piece of lace was found tied so tightly around the neck as to be hidden from sight; it was completely buried in the flesh, and was fastened by a knot which lay just under the left ear. This alone would have sufficed to produce death. The medical testimony spoke confidently of the virtuous character of the deceased. She had been subjected, it said, to brutal violence. The corpse was in such condition when found, that there could have been no difficulty in its recognition by friends.

The dress was much torn and otherwise disordered. In the outer garment, a slip, about a foot wide, had been torn upward from the bottom hem to the waist, but not torn off. It was wound three times around the waist, and secured by a sort of hitch in the back. The dress immediately beneath the frock was of fine muslin; and from this a slip eighteen inches wide had been torn entirely out—torn very evenly and with great care. It was found around her neck, fitting loosely, and secured with a hard knot. Over this muslin slip and the slip of lace, the strings of a bonnet were attached; the bonnet being appended. The knot by which the strings of the bonnet were fastened, was not a lady's, but a slip or sailor's knot.

After the recognition of the corpse, it was not, as usual, taken to the Morgue, (this formality being superfluous,) but hastily interred not far. from the spot at which it was brought ashore. Through the exertions of Beauvais, the matter was industriously hushed up, as far as possible; and several days had elapsed before any public emotion resulted. A weekly paper,[1] however, at length took up the theme; the corpse was disinterred, and a re-examination instituted; but nothing was elicited beyond what has been already noted. The clothes, however, were now submitted to the mother and friends of the deceased, and fully identified as those worn by the girl upon leaving home.

Meantime, the excitement increased hourly. Several individuals were arrested and discharged. St. Eustache fell especially under suspicion; and he failed, at first, to give an intelligible account of his whereabouts during the Sunday on which Marie left home. Subsequently, however, he submitted to Monsieur G——, affidavits, accounting satisfactorily for every hour of the day in question. As time passed and no discovery ensued, a thousand contradictory rumors were circulated, and journalists busied themselves in *suggestions*. Among these, the one which attracted the most notice, was the idea that Marie Rogêt still lived—that the corpse found in the Seine was that of some other unfortunate. It will be proper that I submit to the reader some passages which embody the suggestion alluded to. These passages are *literal* translations from *L'Etoile*,[2] a paper conducted, in general, with much ability.

Mademoiselle Rogêt left her mother's house on Sunday morning, June the twenty-second, 18—, with the ostensible purpose of going to see her aunt or some other connexion, in the Rue des Drômes. From that hour, nobody is proved to have seen her.

[1] *The N. Y. Mercury.*
[2] *The N. Y. Brother Jonathan, edited by H. Hastings Weld, Esq.*

There is no trace or tidings of her at all. . . .
There has no person, whatever, come forward, so
far, who saw her at all, on that day, after she left
her mother's door. . . . Now, though we have no
evidence that Marie Rogêt was in the land of the
living after nine o'clock on Sunday, June the
twenty-second, we have proof that, up to that hour,
she was alive. On Wednesday noon, at twelve, a
female body was discovered afloat on the shore of
the Barrière du Roule. This was, even if we presume that Marie Rogêt was thrown into the river
within three hours after she left her mother's
house, only three days from the time she left her
home—three days to an hour. But it is folly to
suppose that the murder, if murder was committed on her body, could have been consummated soon enough to have enabled her murderers
to throw the body into the river before midnight.
Those who are guilty of such horrid crimes, choose
darkness rather than light. . . . Thus we see that
if the body found in the river *was* that of Marie
Rogêt, it could only have been in the water two and
a half days, or three at the outside. All experience
has shown that drowned bodies, or bodies thrown
into the water immediately after death by violence,
require from six to ten days for sufficient decomposition to take place to bring them to the top of
the water. Even when a cannon is fired over a
corpse, and it rises before at least five or six days'
immersion, it sinks again, if let alone. Now, we
ask, what was there in this case to cause a departure from the ordinary course of nature? . . . If
the body had been kept in its mangled state on
shore until Tuesday night, some trace would be
found on shore of the murderers. It is a doubtful

point, also, whether the body would be so soon afloat, even were it thrown in after having been dead two days. And, furthermore, it is exceedingly improbable that any villains who had committed such a murder as is here supposed, would have thrown the body in without weight to sink it, when such a precaution could have so easily been taken.

The editor here proceeds to argue that the body must have been in the water "not three days merely, but, at least, five times three days," because it was so far decomposed that Beauvais had great difficulty in recognizing it. This latter point, however, was fully disproved. I continue the translation:

What, then, are the facts on which M. Beauvais says that he has no doubt the body was that of Marie Rogêt? He ripped up the gown sleeve, and says he found marks which satisfied him of the identity. The public generally supposed those marks to have consisted of some description of scars. He rubbed the arm and found *hair* upon it—something as indefinite, we think, as can readily be imagined —as little conclusive as finding an arm in the sleeve. M. Beauvais did not return that night, but sent word to Madame Rogêt, at seven o'clock, on Wednesday evening, that an investigation was still in progress respecting her daughter. If we allow that Madame Rogêt, from her age and grief, could not go over, (which is allowing a great deal,) there certainly must have been some one who would have thought it worth while to go over and attend the investigation, if they thought the body was that of Marie. Nobody went over. There was nothing said or heard about the matter in the Rue Pavée

St. André, that reached even the occupants of the same building. M. St. Eustache, the lover and intended husband of Marie, who boarded in her mother's house, deposes that he did not hear of the discovery of the body of his intended until the next morning, when M. Beauvais came into his chamber and told him of it. For an item of news like this, it strikes us it was very coolly received.

In this way the journal endeavored to create the impression of an apathy on the part of the relatives of Marie, inconsistent with the supposition that these relatives believed the corpse to be hers. Its insinuations amount to this:—that Marie, with the connivance of her friends, had absented herself from the city for reasons involving a charge against her chastity; and that these friends, upon the discovery of a corpse in the Seine, somewhat resembling that of the girl, had availed themselves of the opportunity to impress the public with the belief of her death. But *L'Etoile* was again over hasty. It was distinctly proved that no apathy, such as was imagined, existed; that the old lady was exceedingly feeble, and so agitated as to be unable to attend to any duty; that St. Eustache, so far from receiving the news coolly, was distracted with grief, and bore himself so frantically, that M. Beauvais prevailed upon a friend and relative to take charge of him, and prevent his attending the examination at disinterment. Moreover, although it was stated by *L'Etoile*, that the corpse was re-interred at the public expense—that an advantageous offer of private sepulture was absolutely declined by the family—and that no member of the family attended the ceremonial:—although, I say, all this was asserted by *L'Etoile* in furtherance of the impression it designed to convey—yet *all* this was satisfactorily disproved. In a subsequent number of the paper, an attempt was made to throw suspicion upon Beauvais himself. The editor says:

> Now, then, a change comes over the matter. We are told that, on one occasion, while a Madame B—— was at Madame Rogêt's house, M. Beauvais, who was going out, told her that a *gendarme* was expected there, and that she, Madame B., must not say anything to the *gendarme* until he returned, but let the matter be for him. . . . In the present posture of affairs, M. Beauvais appears to have the whole matter locked up in his head. A single step cannot be taken without M. Beauvais; for, go which way you will, you run against him. . . . For some reason, he determined that nobody shall have any thing to do with the proceedings but himself, and he has elbowed the male relatives out of the way, according to their representations, in a very singular manner. He seems to have been very much averse to permitting the relatives to see the body.

By the following fact, some color was given to the suspicion thus thrown upon Beauvais. A visiter at his office, a few days prior to the girl's disappearance, and during the absence of its occupant, had observed *a rose* in the key-hole of the door, and the name *"Marie"* inscribed upon a slate which hung near at hand.

The general impression, so far as we were enabled to glean it from the newspapers, seemed to be, that Marie had been the victim of *a gang* of desperadoes—that by these she had been borne across the river, maltreated and murdered. *Le Commerciel,*[1] however, a print of

---

[1] N. Y. Journal of Commerce.

extensive influence, was earnest in combating this popular idea. I quote a passage or two from its columns:

> We are persuaded that pursuit has hitherto been on a false scent, so far as it has been directed to the Barrière du Roule. It is impossible that a person so well known to thousands as this young woman was, should have passed three blocks without some one having seen her; and any one who saw her would have remembered it, for she interested all who knew her. It was when the streets were full of people, when she went out. . . . It is impossible that she could have gone to the Barrière du Roule, or to the Rue des Drômes, without being recognized by a dozen persons; yet no one has come forward who saw her outside of her mother's door, and there is no evidence, except the testimony concerning her *expressed intentions,* that she did go out at all. Her gown was torn, bound round her, and tied; and by that the body was carried as a bundle. If the murder had been committed at the Barrière du Roule, there would have been no necessity for any such arrangement. The fact that the body was found floating near the Barrière, is no proof as to where it was thrown into the water. . . . A piece of one of the unfortunate girl's petticoats, two feet long and one foot wide, was torn out and tied under her chin around the back of her head, probably to prevent screams. This was done by fellows who had no pocket-handkerchiefs.

A day or two before the Prefect called upon us, however, some important information reached the police, which seemed to overthrow, at least, the chief portion of *Le Commerciel's* argument. Two small boys, sons of a Madame Deluc, while roaming among the woods near the Barrière du Roule, chanced to penetrate a close thicket, within which were three or four large stones, forming a kind of seat, with a back and footstool. On the upper stone lay a white petticoat; on the second a silk scarf. A parasol, gloves, and a pocket-handkerchief were also here found. The handkerchief bore the name "Marie Rogêt." Fragments of dress were discovered on the brambles around. The earth was trampled, the bushes were broken, and there was every evidence of a struggle. Between the thicket and the river, the fences were found taken down, and the ground bore evidence of some heavy burthen having been dragged along it.

A weekly paper, *Le Soleil*,[1] had the following comments upon this discovery—comments which merely echoed the sentiment of the whole Parisian press:

The things had all evidently been there at least three or four weeks; they were all mildewed down hard with the action of the rain, and stuck together from mildew. The grass had grown around and over some of them. The silk on the parasol was strong, but the threads of it were run together within. The upper part, where it had been doubled and folded, was all mildewed and rotten, and tore on its being opened. . . . The pieces of her frock torn out by the bushes were about three inches wide and six inches long. One part was the hem of the frock, and it had been mended; the other piece was part of the skirt, not the hem. They looked like strips torn off, and were on the thorn bush, about a foot from the ground. . . . There can be no doubt, therefore, that the spot of this appalling outrage has been discovered.

[1] *Phil.* Saturday Evening Post, edited by C. J. Peterson, Esq.

Consequent upon this discovery, new evidence appeared. Madame Deluc testified that she keeps a roadside inn not far from the bank of the river, opposite the Barrière du Roule. The neighborhood is secluded—particularly so. It is the usual Sunday resort of blackguards from the city, who cross the river in boats. About three o'clock, in the afternoon of the Sunday in question, a young girl arrived at the inn, accompanied by a young man of dark complexion. The two remained here for some time. On their departure, they took the road to some thick woods in the vicinity. Madame Deluc's attention was called to the dress worn by the girl, on account of its resemblance to one worn by a deceased relative. A scarf was particularly noticed. Soon after the departure of the couple, a gang of miscreants made their appearance, behaved boisterously, ate and drank without making payment, followed in the route of the young man and girl, returned to the inn about dusk, and recrossed the river as if in great haste.

It was soon after dark, upon this same evening, that Madame Deluc, as well as her eldest son, heard the screams of a female in the vicinity of the inn. The screams were violent but brief. Madame D. recognized not only the scarf which was found in the thicket, but the dress which was discovered upon the corpse. An omnibus-driver, Valence,[1] now also testified that he saw Marie Rogêt cross a ferry on the Seine, on the Sunday in question, in company with a young man of dark complexion. He, Valence, knew Marie, and could not be mistaken in her identity. The articles found in the thicket were fully identified by the relatives of Marie.

The items of evidence and information thus collected by myself, from the newspapers, at the suggestion of Dupin, embraced only one more point—but this was a

[1] Adam.

point of seemingly vast consequence. It appears that, immediately after the discovery of the clothes as above described, the lifeless, or nearly lifeless body of St. Eustache, Marie's betrothed, was found in the vicinity of what all now supposed the scene of the outrage. A phial labelled "laudanum," and emptied, was found near him. His breath gave evidence of the poison. He died without speaking. Upon his person was found a letter, briefly stating his love for Marie, with his design of self-destruction.

"I need scarcely tell you," said Dupin, as he finished the perusal of my notes, "that this is a far more intricate case than that of the Rue Morgue; from which it differs in one important respect. This is an *ordinary,* although an atrocious instance of crime. There is nothing peculiarly *outré* about it. You will observe that, for this reason, the mystery has been considered easy, when, for this reason, it should have been considered difficult, of solution. Thus, at first, it was thought unnecessary to offer a reward. The myrmidons of G—— were able at once to comprehend how and why such an atrocity *might have been* committed. They could picture to their imaginations a mode—many modes—and a motive—many motives; and because it was not impossible that either of these numerous modes and motives *could* have been the actual one, they have taken it for granted that one of them *must.* But the ease with which these variable fancies were entertained, and the very plausibility which each assumed, should have been understood as indicative rather of the difficulties than of the facilities which must attend elucidation. I have before observed that it is by prominences above the plane of the ordinary, that reason feels her way, if at all, in her search for the true, and that the proper question in cases such as this, is not so much 'what has occurred? as 'what has occurred

that has never occurred before?' In the investigations at
the house of Madame L'Espanaye, the agents of G——
were discouraged and confounded by that very *unusualness* which, to a properly regulated intellect, would have
afforded the surest omen of success; while this same intellect might have been plunged in despair at the ordinary character of all that met the eye in the case of the
perfumery-girl, and yet told of nothing but easy triumph
to the functionaries of the Prefecture.

"In the case of Madame L'Espanaye and her daughter,
there was, even at the beginning of our investigation,
no doubt that murder had been committed. The idea
of suicide was excluded at once. Here, too, we are freed,
at the commencement, from all supposition of self-
murder. The body found at the Barrière du Roule, was
found under such circumstances as to leave us no room
for embarrassment upon this important point. But it
has been suggested that the corpse discovered, is not
that of the Marie Rogêt for the conviction of whose
assassin, or assassins, the reward is offered, and respecting whom, solely, our agreement has been arranged with
the Prefect. We both know this gentleman well. It will
not do to trust him too far. If, dating our inquiries from
the body found, and thence tracing a murderer, we yet
discover this body to be that of some other individual
than Marie; or, if starting from the living Marie, we
find her, yet find her unassassinated—in either case we
lose our labor; since it is Monsieur G—— with whom
we have to deal. For our own purpose, therefore, if not
for the purpose of justice, it is indispensable that our
first step should be the determination of the identity
of the corpse with the Marie Rogêt who is missing.

"With the public the arguments of *L'Etoile* have had
weight; and that the journal itself is convinced of their
importance would appear from the manner in which it

commences one of its essays upon the subject—'Several of the morning papers of the day,' it says, 'speak of the *conclusive* article in Monday's *Etoile*.' To me, this article appears conclusive of little beyond the zeal of its inditer. We should bear in mind that, in general, it is the object of our newspapers rather to create a sensation—to make a point—than to further the cause of truth. The latter end is only pursued when it seems coincident with the former. The print which merely falls in with ordinary opinion (however well founded this opinion may be) earns for itself no credit with the mob. The mass of the people regard as profound only him who suggests *pungent contradictions* of the general idea. In ratiocination, not less than in literature, it is the *epigram* which is the most immediately and the most universally appreciated. In both, it is of the lowest order of merit.

"What I mean to say is, that it is the mingled epigram and melodrame of the idea, that Marie Rogêt still lives, rather than any true plausibility in this idea, which have suggested it to *L'Etoile,* and secured it a favorable reception with the public. Let us examine the heads of this journal's argument; endeavoring to avoid the incoherence with which it is originally set forth.

"The first aim of the writer is to show, from the brevity of the interval between Marie's disappearance and the finding of the floating corpse, that this corpse cannot be that of Marie. The reduction of this interval to its smallest possible dimension, becomes thus, at once, an object with the reasoner. In the rash pursuit of this object, he rushes into mere assumption at the outset. 'It is folly to suppose,' he says, 'that the murder, if murder was committed on her body, could have been consummated soon enough to have enabled her murderers to throw the body into the river before midnight.' We demand at once, and very naturally, *why?* Why is it folly to suppose that the murder was committed *within five minutes* after the girl's quitting her mother's house? Why is it folly to suppose that the murder was committed at any given period of the day? There have been assassinations at all hours. But, had the murder taken place at any moment between nine o'clock in the morning of Sunday, and a quarter before midnight, there would still have been time enough 'to throw the body into the river before midnight.' This assumption, then, amounts precisely to this—that the murder was not committed on Sunday at all—and, if we allow *L'Etoile* to assume this, we may permit it any liberties whatever. The paragraph beginning 'It is folly to suppose that the murder, etc.,' however it appears as printed in *L'Etoile,* may be imagined to have existed actually *thus* in the brain of its inditer—'It is folly to suppose that the murder, if murder was committed on the body, could have been committed soon enough to have enabled her murderers to throw the body into the river before midnight; it is folly, we say, to suppose all this, and to suppose at the same time, (as we are resolved to suppose,) that the body was *not* thrown in until *after* midnight'—a sentence sufficiently inconsequential in itself, but not so utterly preposterous as the one printed.

"Were it my purpose," continued Dupin, "merely to *make out a case* against this passage of *L'Etoile's* argument, I might safely leave it where it is. It is not, however, with *L'Etoile* that we have to do, but with the truth. The sentence in question has but one meaning, as it stands; and this meaning I have fairly stated: but it is material that we go behind the mere words, for an idea which these words have obviously intended, and failed to convey. It was the design of the journalist to say that, at whatever period of the day or night of Sunday this murder was committed, it was improbable that the assassins would have ventured to bear the corpse to the river before midnight. And herein lies, really, the assumption of which I complain. It is assumed that the murder was committed at such a position, and under such circumstances, that *the bearing it* to the river became necessary. Now, the assassination might have taken place upon the river's brink, or on the river itself; and, thus, the throwing the corpse in the water might have been resorted to, at any period of the day or night, as the most obvious and most immediate mode of disposal. You will understand that I suggest nothing here as probable, or as coincident with my own opinion. My design, so far, has no reference to the *facts* of the case. I wish merely to caution you against the whole tone of *L'Etoile's suggestion*, by calling your attention to its *ex parte* character at the outset.

"Having prescribed thus a limit to suit its own preconceived notions; having assumed that, if this were the body of Marie, it could have been in the water but a very brief time; the journal goes on to say:

All experience has shown that drowned bodies, or bodies thrown into the water immediately after death by violence, require from six to ten days for sufficient decomposition to take place to bring them to the top of the water. Even when a cannon is fired over a corpse, and it rises before at least five or six days' immersion, it sinks again if let alone.

"These assertions have been tacitly received by every paper in Paris, with the exception of *Le Moniteur*.[1] This latter print endeavors to combat that portion of the paragraph which has reference to 'drowned bodies'

---

[1] *The* N. Y. Commercial Advertiser, *edited by Col. Stone.*

only, by citing some five or six instances in which the bodies of individuals known to be drowned were found floating after the lapse of less time than is insisted upon by *L'Etoile*. But there is something excessively unphilosophical in the attempt on the part of *Le Moniteur*, to rebut the general assertion of *L'Etoile*, by a citation of particular instances militating against that assertion. Had it been possible to adduce fifty instead of five examples of bodies found floating at the end of two or three days, these fifty examples could still have been properly regarded only as exceptions to *L'Etoile's* rule, until such time as the rule itself should be confuted. Admitting the rule, (and this *Le Moniteur* does not deny, insisting merely upon its exceptions,) the argument of *L'Etoile* is suffered to remain in full force; for this argument does not pretend to involve more than a question of the *probability* of the body having risen to the surface in less than three days; and this probability will be in favor of *L'Etoile's* position until the instances so childishly adduced shall be sufficient in number to establish an antagonistical rule.

"You will see at once that all argument upon this head should be urged, if at all, against the rule itself; and for this end we must examine the *rationale* of the rule. Now the human body, in general, is neither much lighter nor much heavier than the water of the Seine; that is to say, the specific gravity of the human body, in its natural condition, is about equal to the bulk of fresh water which it displaces. The bodies of fat and fleshy persons, with small bones, and of women generally, are lighter than those of the lean and large-boned, and of men; and the specific gravity of the water of a river is somewhat influenced by the presence of the tide from sea. But, leaving this tide out of question, it may be said that *very* few human bodies will sink at all, even in fresh water, *of their own accord.* Almost any one, falling into a river, will be enabled to float, if he suffer the specific gravity of the water fairly to be adduced in comparison with his own—that is to say, if he suffer his whole person to be immersed, with as little exception as possible. The proper position for one who cannot swim, is the upright position of the walker on land, with the head thrown fully back, and immersed; the mouth and nostrils alone remaining above the surface. Thus circumstanced, we shall find that we float without difficulty and without exertion. It is evident, however, that the gravities of the body, and of the bulk of water displaced, are very nicely balanced, and that a trifle will cause either to preponderate. An arm, for instance, uplifted from the water, and thus deprived of its support, is an additional weight sufficient to immerse the whole head, while the accidental aid of the smallest piece of timber will enable us to elevate the head so as to look about. Now, in the struggles of one unused to swimming, the arms are invariably thrown upward, while an attempt is made to keep the head in its usual perpendicular position. The result is the immersion of the mouth and nostrils, and the inception, during efforts to breathe while beneath the surface, of water into the lungs. Much is also received into the stomach, and the whole body becomes heavier by the difference between the weight of the air originally distending these cavities, and that of the fluid which now fills them. This difference is sufficient to cause the body to sink, as a general rule; but is insufficient in the cases of individuals with small bones and an abnormal quantity of flaccid or fatty matter. Such individuals float even after drowning.

"The corpse, being supposed at the bottom of the river, will there remain until, by some means, its specific gravity again becomes less than that of the bulk of

water which it displaces. This effect is brought about
by decomposition, or otherwise. The result of decomposition is the generation of gas, distending the cellular
tissues and all the cavities, and giving the *puffed* appearance which is so horrible. When this distension has
so far progressed that the bulk of the corpse is materially increased without a corresponding increase of
mass or weight, its specific gravity becomes less than
that of the water displaced, and it forthwith makes its
appearance at the surface. But decomposition is modified by innumerable circumstances—is hastened or re-
tarded by innumerable agencies; for example, by the
heat or cold of the season, by the mineral impregnation
or purity of the water, by its depth or shallowness, by
its currency or stagnation, by the temperament of the
body, by its infection or freedom from disease before
death. Thus it is evident that we can assign no period,
with any thing like accuracy, at which the corpse shall
rise through decomposition. Under certain conditions
this result would be brought about within an hour;
under others, it might not take place at all. There are
chemical infusions by which the animal frame can be
preserved *forever* from corruption; the Bi-chloride of
Mercury is one. But, apart from decomposition, there
may be, and very usually is, a generation of gas within
the stomach, from the acetous fermentation of vegetable
matter (or within other cavities from other causes)
sufficient to induce a distension which will bring the
body to the surface. The effect produced by the firing
of a cannon is that of simple vibration. This may either
loosen the corpse from the soft mud or ooze in which it
is imbedded, thus permitting it to rise when other agencies have already prepared it for so doing; or it may
overcome the tenacity of some putrescent portions of

the cellular tissue; allowing the cavities to distend under the influence of the gas.

"Having thus before us the whole philosophy of this subject, we can easily test by it the assertions of *L'Etoile.* 'All experience shows,' says this paper, 'that drowned bodies, or bodies thrown into the water immediately after death by violence, require from six to ten days for sufficient decomposition to take place to bring them to the top of the water. Even when a cannon is fired over a corpse, and it rises before at least five or six days' immersion, it sinks again if let alone.'

"The whole of this paragraph must now appear a tissue of inconsequence and incoherence. All experience does *not* show that 'drowned bodies' *require* from six to ten days for sufficient decomposition to take place to bring them to the surface. Both science and experience show that the period of their rising is, and necessarily must be, indeterminate. If, moreover, a body has risen to the surface through firing of cannon, it will *not* 'sink again if let alone,' until decomposition has so far progressed as to permit the escape of the generated gas. But I wish to call your attention to the distinction which is made between 'drowned bodies,' and 'bodies thrown into the water immediately after death by violence.' Although the writer admits the distinction, he yet includes them all in the same category. I have shown how it is that the body of a drowning man becomes specifically heavier than its bulk of water, and that he would not sink at all, except for the struggles by which he elevates his arms above the surface, and his gasps for breath while beneath the surface—gasps which supply by water the place of the original air in the lungs. But these struggles and these gasps would not occur in the body 'thrown into the water immediately after death by violence.' Thus, in the latter instance, *the body, as a general rule, would not sink at all*—a fact of which *L'Etoile* is evidently ignorant. When decomposition had proceeded to a very great extent—when the flesh had in a great measure left the bones—then, indeed, but not *till* then, should we lose sight of the corpse.

"And now what are we to make of the argument, that the body found could not be that of Marie Rogêt, because, three days only having elapsed, this body was found floating? If drowned, being a woman, she might never have sunk; or having sunk, might have re-appeared in twenty-four hours, or less. But no one supposes her to have been drowned; and, dying before being thrown into the river, she might have been found floating at any period afterwards whatever.

"'But,' says *L'Etoile*, 'if the body had been kept in its mangled state on shore until Tuesday night, some trace would be found on shore of the murderers.' Here it is at first difficult to perceive the intention of the reasoner. He means to anticipate what he imagines would be an objection to his theory—viz.: that the body was kept on shore two days, suffering rapid decomposition—*more* rapid than if immersed in water. He supposes that, had this been the case, it *might* have appeared at the surface on the Wednesday, and thinks that *only* under such circumstances it could so have appeared. He is accordingly in haste to show that it *was not* kept on shore; for, if so, 'some trace would be found on shore of the murderers.' I presume you smile at the *sequitur*. You cannot be made to see how the mere *duration* of the corpse on the shore could operate to *multiply traces* of the assassins. Nor can I.

"'And furthermore it is exceedingly improbable,' continues our journal, 'that any villains who had committed such a murder as is here supposed, would have thrown the body in without weight to sink it, when such a precaution could have so easily been taken.' Observe, here, the laughable confusion of thought! No one—not even *L'Etoile*—disputes the murder committed *on the body found*. The marks of violence are too obvious. It is our reasoner's object merely to show that this body is not Marie's. He wishes to prove that *Marie* is not assassinated—not that the corpse was not. Yet his observation proves only the latter point. Here is a corpse without weight attached. Murderers, casting it in, would not have failed to attach a weight. Therefore it was not thrown in by murderers. This is all which is proved, if any thing is. The question of identity is not even approached, and *L'Etoile* has been at great pains merely to gainsay now what it has admitted only a moment before. 'We are perfectly convinced,' it says, 'that the body found was that of a murdered female.'

"Nor is this the sole instance, even in this division of his subject, where our reasoner unwittingly reasons against himself. His evident object, I have already said, is to reduce, as much as possible, the interval between Marie's disappearance and the finding of the corpse. Yet we find him *urging* the point that no person saw the girl from the moment of her leaving her mother's house. 'We have no evidence,' he says, 'that Marie Rogêt was in the land of the living after nine o'clock on Sunday, June the twenty-second.' As his argument is obviously an *ex parte* one, he should, at least, have left this matter out of sight; for had any one been known to see Marie, say on Monday, or on Tuesday, the interval in question would have been much reduced, and, by his own ratiocination, the probability much diminished of the corpse being that of the *grisette*. It is, nevertheless, amusing to observe that *L'Etoile* insists upon its point in the full belief of its furthering its general argument.

"Reperuse now that portion of this argument which has reference to the identification of the corpse by Beauvais. In regard to the *hair* upon the arm, *L'Etoile* has been obviously disingenuous. M. Beauvais, not being an idiot, could never have urged, in identification of the corpse, simply *hair upon its arm.* No arm is *without* hair. The *generality* of the expression of *L'Etoile* is a mere perversion of the witness' phraseology. He must have spoken of some *peculiarity* in this hair. It must have been a peculiarity of color, of quantity, of length, or of situation.

"'Her foot,' says the journal, 'was small—so are thousands of feet. Her garter is no proof whatever— nor is her shoe—for shoes and garters are sold in packages. The same may be said of the flowers in her hat. One thing upon which M. Beauvais strongly insists is, that the clasp on the garter found, had been set back to take it in. This amounts to nothing; for most women find it proper to take a pair of garters home and fit them to the size of the limbs they are to encircle, rather than to try them in the store where they purchase.' Here it is difficult to suppose the reasoner in earnest. Had M. Beauvais, in his search for the body of Marie, discovered a corpse corresponding in general size and appearance to the missing girl, he would have been warranted (without reference to the question of habiliment at all) in forming an opinion that his search had been successful. If, in addition to the point of general size and contour, he had found upon the arm a peculiar hairy appearance which he had observed upon the living Marie, his opinion might have been justly strengthened; and the increase of positiveness might well have been in the ratio of the peculiarity, or unusualness, of the hairy mark. If, the feet of Marie being small, those of the corpse were also small, the increase of probability that the body was that of Marie would not be an increase in a ratio merely arithmetical, but in one highly geometrical, or accumulative. Add to all this shoes such as she had been known to wear upon the day of her disappearance, and, although these shoes may be 'sold in packages,' you so far augment the probability as to verge upon the certain. What of itself, would be no evidence of identity, becomes through its corroborative position, proof most sure. Give us, then, flowers in the hat corresponding to those worn by the missing girl, and we seek for nothing farther. If only *one* flower, we seek for nothing farther—what then if two or three, or more? Each successive one is multiple evidence—proof not *added* to proof, but *multiplied* by hundreds or thousands. Let us now discover, upon the deceased, garters such as the living used, and it is almost folly to proceed. But these garters are found to be tightened, by the setting back of a clasp, in just such a manner as her own had been tightened by Marie, shortly previous to her leaving home. It is now madness or hypocrisy to doubt. What *L'Etoile* says in respect to this abbreviation of the garter's being an usual occurrence, shows nothing beyond its own pertinacity in error. The elastic nature of the clasp-garter is self-demonstration of the *unusualness* of the abbreviation. What is made to adjust itself must of necessity require foreign adjustment but rarely. It must have been by an accident, in its strictest sense, that these garters of Marie needed the tightening described. They alone would have amply established her identity. But it is not that the corpse was found to have the garters of the missing girl, or found to have her shoes, or her bonnet, or the flowers of her bonnet, or her feet, or a peculiar mark upon the arm, or her general size and appearance—it is that the corpse had each, and *all collectively*. Could it be proved that the editor of

L'Etoile really entertained a doubt, under the circumstances, there would be no need, in his case, of a commission *de lunatico inquirendo*. He has thought it sagacious to echo the small talk of the lawyers, who, for the most part, content themselves with echoing the rectangular precepts of the courts. I would here observe that very much of what is rejected as evidence by a court, is the best of evidence to the intellect. For the court, guiding itself by the general principles of evidence—the recognized and *booked* principles—is averse from swerving at particular instances. And this steadfast adherence to principle, with rigorous disregard of the conflicting exception, is a sure mode of attaining the *maximum* of attainable truth, in any long sequence of time. The practise, *in mass,* is therefore philosophical; but it is not the less certain that it engenders vast individual error.[1]

"In respect to the insinuations levelled at Beauvais, you will be willing to dismiss them in a breath. You have already fathomed the true character of this good gentleman. He is a *busy-body,* with much of romance and little of wit. Any one so constituted will readily so conduct himself, upon occasion of *real* excitement, as to render himself liable to suspicion on the part of the over-acute, or the ill-disposed. M. Beauvais (as it appears from your notes) had some personal interviews with the editor of *L'Etoile,* and offended him by venturing an opinion that the corpse, notwithstanding the

[1] "A theory based on the qualities of an object, will prevent its being unfolded according to its objects; and he who arranges topics in reference to their causes, will cease to value them according to their results. Thus the jurisprudence of every nation will show that, when law becomes a science and a system, it ceases to be justice. The errors into which a blind devotion to principles of classification has led the common law, will be seen by observing how often the legislature has been obliged to come forward to restore the equity its scheme had lost."—Landor.

theory of the editor, was, in sober fact, that of Marie. 'He persists,' says the paper, 'in asserting the corpse to be that of Marie, but cannot give a circumstance, in addition to those which we have commented upon, to make others believe.' Now, without re-adverting to the fact that stronger evidence 'to make others believe,' could *never* have been adduced, it may be remarked that a man may very well be understood to believe, in a case of this kind, without the ability to advance a single reason for the belief of a second party. Nothing is more vague than impressions of individual identity. Each man recognizes his neighbor, yet there are few instances in which any one is prepared *to give a reason* for his recognition. The editor of *L'Etoile* had no right to be offended at M. Beauvais' unreasoning belief.

"The suspicious circumstances which invest him, will be found to tally much better with my hypothesis of *romantic busy-bodyism*, than with the reasoner's suggestion of guilt. Once adopting the more charitable interpretation, we shall find no difficulty in comprehending the rose in the key-hole; the 'Marie' upon the slate; the 'elbowing the male relatives out of the way;' the 'aversion to permitting them to see the body;' the caution given to Madame B——, that she must hold no conversation with the *gendarme* until his return (Beauvais'); and, lastly, his apparent determination 'that nobody should have anything to do with the proceedings except himself.' It seems to me unquestionable that Beauvais was a suitor of Marie's; that she coquetted with him; and that he was ambitious of being thought to enjoy her fullest intimacy and confidence. I shall say nothing more upon this point; and, as the evidence fully rebuts the assertion of *L'Etoile*, touching the matter of *apathy* on the part of the mother and other relatives— an apathy inconsistent with the supposition of their believing the corpse to be that of the perfumery-girl—we shall now proceed as if the question of *identity* were settled to our perfect satisfaction."

"And what," I here demanded, "do you think of the opinions of *Le Commerciel?*"

"That, in spirit, they are far more worthy of attention than any which have been promulgated upon the subject. The deductions from the premises are philosophical and acute; but the premises, in two instances, at least, are founded in imperfect observation. *Le Commerciel* wishes to intimate that Marie was seized by some gang of low ruffians not far from her mother's door. 'It is impossible,' it urges, 'that a person so well known to thousands as this young woman was, should have passed three blocks without some one having seen her.' This is the idea of a man long resident in Paris—a public man—and one whose walks to and fro in the city, have been mostly limited to the vicinity of the public offices. He is aware that *he* seldom passes so far as a dozen blocks from his own *bureau,* without being recognized and accosted. And, knowing the extent of his personal acquaintance with others, and of others with him, he compares his notoriety with that of the perfumery-girl, finds no great difference between them, and reaches at once the conclusion that she, in her walks, would be equally liable to recognition with himself in his. This could only be the case were her walks of the same unvarying, methodical character, and within the same *species* of limited region as are his own. He passes to and fro, at regular intervals, within a confined periphery, abounding in individuals who are led to observation of his person through interest in the kindred nature of his occupation with their own. But the walks of Marie may, in general, be supposed discursive. In this particular instance, it will be understood as most probable, that she proceeded upon a route of more than average diversity from her accustomed ones. The parallel which we imagine to have existed in the mind of *Le Commerciel* would only be sustained in the event of the two individuals traversing the whole city. In this case, granting the personal acquaintances to be equal, the chances would be also equal that an equal number of personal encounters would be made. For my own part, I should hold it not only as possible, but as very far more than probable, that Marie might have proceeded, at any given period, by any one of the many routes between her own residence and that of her aunt, without meeting a single individual whom she knew, or by whom she was known. In viewing this question in its full and proper light, we must hold steadily in mind the great disproportion between the personal acquaintances of even the most noted individual in Paris, and the entire population of Paris itself.

"But whatever force there may still appear to be in the suggestion of *Le Commerciel*, will be much diminished when we take into consideration *the hour* at which the girl went abroad. 'It was when the streets were full of people,' says *Le Commerciel*, 'that she went out.' But not so. It was nine o'clock in the morning. Now at nine o'clock of every morning in the week, *with the exception of Sunday*, the streets of the city are, it is true, thronged with people. At nine on Sunday, the populace are chiefly within doors *preparing for church*. No observing person can have failed to notice the peculiarly deserted air of the town, from about eight until ten on the morning of every Sabbath. Between ten and eleven the streets are thronged, but not at so early a period as that designated.

"There is another point at which there seems a deficiency of *observation* on the part of *Le Commerciel*.

'A piece,' it says, 'of one of the unfortunate girl's petticoats, two feet long, and one foot wide, was torn out
and tied under her chin, and around the back of her
head, probably to prevent screams. This was done by
fellows who had no pocket-handkerchiefs.' Whether
this idea is, or is not well founded, we will endeavor to
see hereafter; but by 'fellows who have no pocket-
handkerchiefs,' the editor intends the lowest class of
ruffians. These, however, are the very description of
people who will always be found to have handkerchiefs
even when destitute of shirts. You must have had occasion to observe how absolutely indispensable, of late
years, to the thorough blackguard, has become the
pocket-handkerchief."

"And what are we to think," I asked, "of the article
in *Le Soleil?*"

"That it is a pity its inditer was not born a parrot—
in which case he would have been the most illustrious
parrot of his race. He has merely repeated the individual
items of the already published opinion; collecting them,
with a laudable industry, from this paper and from
that. 'The things had all *evidently* been there,' he says,
'at least, three or four weeks, and there can be *no doubt*
that the spot of this appalling outrage has been discovered.' The facts here re-stated by *Le Soleil,* are very
far indeed from removing my own doubts upon this subject, and we will examine them more particularly hereafter in connexion with another division of the theme.

"At present we must occupy ourselves with other investigations. You cannot fail to have remarked the extreme laxity of the examination of the corpse. To be
sure, the question of identity was readily determined, or
should have been; but there were other points to be
ascertained. Had the body been in any respect *de-
spoiled?* Had the deceased any articles of jewelry about

her person upon leaving home? if so, had she any when
found? These are important questions utterly untouched
by the evidence; and there are others of equal moment,
which have met with no attention. We must endeavor to
satisfy ourselves by personal inquiry. The case of St.
Eustache must be re-examined. I have no suspicion of
this person; but let us proceed methodically. We will
ascertain beyond a doubt the validity of the *affidavits*
in regard to his whereabouts on the Sunday. Affidavits
of this character are readily made matter of mystification. Should there be nothing wrong here, however, we
will dismiss St. Eustache from our investigations. His
suicide, however corroborative of suspicion, were there
found to be deceit in the affidavits, is, without such deceit, in no respect an unaccountable circumstance, or
one which need cause us to deflect from the line of ordinary analysis.

"In that which I now propose, we will discard the
interior points of this tragedy, and concentrate our attention upon its outskirts. Not the least usual error, in
investigations such as this, is the limiting of inquiry to
the immediate, with total disregard of the collateral
or circumstantial events. It is the mal-practice of the
courts to confine evidence and discussion to the bounds
of apparent relevancy. Yet experience has shown, and
a true philosophy will always show, that a vast, perhaps the larger portion of truth, arises from the seemingly irrelevant. It is through the spirit of this principle, if not precisely through its letter, that modern
science has resolved to *calculate upon the unforeseen.*
But perhaps you do not comprehend me. The history
of human knowledge has so uninterruptedly shown that
to collateral, or incidental, or accidental events we are
indebted for the most numerous and most valuable discoveries, that it has at length become necessary, in any

prospective view of improvement, to make not only large, but the largest allowances for inventions that shall arise by chance, and quite out of the range of ordinary expectation. It is no longer philosophical to base, upon what has been, a vision of what is to be. *Accident* is admitted as a portion of the substructure. We make chance a matter of absolute calculation. We subject the unlooked for and unimagined, to the mathematical *formulæ* of the schools.

"I repeat that it is no more than fact, that the *larger* portion of all truth has sprung from the collateral; and it is but in accordance with the spirit of the principle involved in this fact, that I would divert inquiry, in the present case, from the trodden and hitherto unfruitful ground of the event itself, to the contemporary circumstances which surround it. While you ascertain the validity of the affidavits, I will examine the newspapers more generally than you have as yet done. So far, we have only reconnoitred the field of investigation; but it will be strange indeed if a comprehensive survey, such as I propose, of the public prints, will not afford us some minute points which shall establish a *direction* for inquiry."

In pursuance of Dupin's suggestion, I made scrupulous examination of the affair of the affidavits. The result was a firm conviction of their validity, and of the consequent innocence of St. Eustache. In the mean time my friend occupied himself, with what seemed to me a minuteness altogether objectless, in a scrutiny of the various newspaper files. At the end of a week he placed before me the following extracts:

About three years and a half ago, a disturbance very similar to the present, was caused by the disappearance of this same Marie Rogêt, from the *parfumerie* of Monsieur Le Blanc, in the Palais Royal. At the end of a week, however, she re-appeared at her customary *comptoir* as well as ever, with the exception of a slight paleness not altogether usual. It was given out by Monsieur Le Blanc and her mother, that she had merely been on a visit to some friend in the country; and the affair was speedily hushed up. We presume that the present absence is a freak of the same nature, and that, at the expiration of a week, or perhaps of a month, we shall have her among us again.—*Evening Paper—Monday, June 23.*[1]

An evening journal of yesterday, refers to a former mysterious disappearance of Mademoiselle Rogêt. It is well known that, during the week of her absence from Le Blanc's *parfumerie,* she was in the company of a young naval officer, much noted for his debaucheries. A quarrel, it is supposed, providentially led to her return home. We have the name of the Lothario in question, who is, at present, stationed in Paris, but, for obvious reasons, forbear to make it public.—*Le Mercure—Tuesday Morning, June 24.*[2]

An outrage of the most atrocious character was perpetrated near this city the day before yesterday. A gentleman, with his wife and daughter, engaged, about dusk, the services of six young men, who were idly rowing a boat to and fro near the banks of the Seine, to convey him across the river. Upon reaching the opposite shore, the three passengers stepped out, and had proceeded so far as to be beyond the view of the boat, when the daughter discovered that she had left in it her parasol. She returned for it, was seized by the gang, carried out into the stream, gagged, brutally treated, and finally taken to the shore at a point not far from that at which she had originally entered the boat with her parents. The villains have escaped for the time, but the police are upon their trail, and some of them will soon be taken.—*Morning Paper—June 25.*[1]

We have received one or two communications, the object of which is to fasten the crime of the late atrocity upon Mennais;[2] but as this gentleman has been fully exonerated by a legal inquiry, and as the arguments of our several correspondents appear to be more zealous than profound, we do not think it advisable to make them public.—*Morning Paper—June 28.*[3]

We have received several forcibly written communications, apparently from various sources, and which go far to render it a matter of certainty that the unfortunate Marie Rogêt has become a victim of one of the numerous bands of blackguards which infest the vicinity of the city upon Sunday. Our own opinion is decidedly in favor of this supposition. We shall endeavor to make room for some of these arguments hereafter.—*Evening Paper.—Tuesday, June 31.*[4]

On Monday, one of the bargemen connected with the revenue service, saw an empty boat floating down the Seine. Sails were lying in the bottom of the boat. The bargeman towed it under the barge office. The next morning it was taken from

[1] N. Y. Courier and Inquirer.

[2] *Mennais was one of the parties originally suspected and arrested, but discharged through total lack of evidence.*

[3] N. Y. Courier and Inquirer.

[4] N. Y. Evening Post.

thence, without the knowledge of any of the officers. The rudder is now at the barge office.—*La
Diligence—Thursday, June 26.*[1]

Upon reading these various extracts, they not only
seemed to me irrelevant, but I could perceive no mode
in which any one of them could be brought to bear
upon the matter in hand. I waited for some explanation
from Dupin.

"It is not my present design," he said, "to *dwell* upon
the first and second of these extracts. I have copied
them chiefly to show you the extreme remissness of the
police, who, as far as I can understand from the Prefect,
have not troubled themselves, in any respect, with an
examination of the naval officer alluded to. Yet it is
mere folly to say that between the first and second disappearance of Marie, there is no *supposable* connection.
Let us admit the first elopement to have resulted in a
quarrel between the lovers, and the return home of the
betrayed. We are now prepared to view a second *elopement* (if we *know* that an elopement has again taken
place) as indicating a renewal of the betrayer's advances, rather than as the result of new proposals by a
second individual—we are prepared to regard it as a
'making up' of the old *amour,* rather than as the commencement of a new one. The chances are ten to one,
that he who had once eloped with Marie, would again
propose an elopement, rather than that she to whom
proposals of elopement had been made by one individual, should have them made to her by another. And
here let me call your attention to the fact, that the time
elapsing between the first ascertained, and the second
supposed elopement, is a few months more than the
general period of the cruises of our men-of-war. Had the

[1] *N. Y. Standard.*

lover been interrupted in his first villany by the necessity
of departure to sea, and had he seized the first moment
of his return to renew the base designs not yet altogether accomplished—or not yet altogether accomplished *by him?* Of all these things we know nothing.

"You will say, however, that, in the second instance,
there was *no* elopement as imagined. Certainly not—
but are we prepared to say that there was not the frustrated design? Beyond St. Eustache, and perhaps Beauvais, we find no recognized, no open, no honorable
suitors of Marie. Of none other is there any thing said.
Who, then, is the secret lover, of whom the relatives
(*at least most of them*) know nothing, but whom Marie
meets upon the morning of Sunday, and who is so deeply
in her confidence, that she hesitates not to remain with
him until the shades of the evening descend, amid the
solitary groves of the Barrière du Roule? Who is that
secret lover, I ask, of whom, at least, *most* of the relatives know nothing? And what means the singular
prophecy of Madame Rogêt on the morning of Marie's
departure?—'I fear that I shall never see Marie again.'

"But if we cannot imagine Madame Rogêt privy to
the design of elopement, may we not at least suppose
this design entertained by the girl? Upon quitting home,
she gave it to be understood that she was about to visit
her aunt in the Rue des Drômes, and St. Eustache was
requested to call for her at dark. Now, at first glance,
this fact strongly militates against my suggestion;—but
let us reflect. That she *did* meet some companion, and
proceed with him across the river, reaching the Barrière
du Roule at so late an hour as three o'clock in the afternoon, is known. But in consenting so to accompany this
individual, (*for whatever purpose—to her mother known
or unknown,*) she must have thought of her expressed intention when leaving home, and of the surprise and

suspicion aroused in the bosom of her affianced suitor,
St. Eustache, when, calling for her, at the hour appointed, in the Rue des Drômes, he should find that she
had not been there, and when, moreover, upon returning
to the *pension* with this alarming intelligence, he should
become aware of her continued absence from home.
She must have thought of these things, I say. She must
have foreseen the chagrin of St. Eustache, the suspicion
of all. She could not have thought of returning to brave
this suspicion; but the suspicion becomes a point of
trivial importance to her, if we suppose her *not* intending
to return.

"We may imagine her thinking thus—'I am to meet a
certain person for the purpose of elopement, or for certain other purposes known only to myself. It is necessary
that there be no chance of interruption—there must be
sufficient time given us to elude pursuit—I will give it
to be understood that I shall visit and spend the day
with my aunt at the Rue des Drômes—I will tell St.
Eustache not to call for me until dark—in this way, my
absence from home for the longest possible period, without causing suspicion or anxiety, will be accounted for,
and I shall gain more time than in any other manner.
If I bid St. Eustache call for me at dark, he will be sure
not to call before; but, if I wholly neglect to bid him call,
my time for escape will be diminished, since it will be
expected that I return the earlier, and my absence will
the sooner excite anxiety. Now, if it were my design to
return *at all*—if I had in contemplation merely a stroll
with the individual in question—it would not be my
policy to bid St. Eustache call; for, calling, he will be
sure to ascertain that I have played him false—a fact
of which I might keep him for ever in ignorance, by
leaving home without notifying him of my intention, by
returning before dark, and by then stating that I had

been to visit my aunt in the Rue des Drômes. But, as it is my design *never* to return—or not for some weeks—or not until certain concealments are effected—the gaining of time is the only point about which I need give myself any concern.'

"You have observed, in your notes, that the most general opinion in relation to this sad affair is, and was from the first, that the girl had been the victim of *a gang* of blackguards. Now, the popular opinion, under certain conditions, is not to be disregarded. When arising of itself—when manifesting itself in a strictly spontaneous manner—we should look upon it as analogous with that *intuition* which is the idiosyncrasy of the individual man of genius. In ninety-nine cases from the hundred I would abide by its decision. But it is important that we find no palpable traces of *suggestion*. The opinion must be rigorously *the public's own;* and the distinction is often exceedingly difficult to perceive and to maintain. In the present instance, it appears to me that this 'public opinion,' in respect to *a gang*, has been superinduced by the collateral event which is detailed in the third of my extracts. All Paris is excited by the discovered corpse of Marie, a girl young, beautiful and notorious. This corpse is found, bearing marks of violence, and floating in the river. But it is now made known that, at the very period, or about the very period, in which it is supposed that the girl was assassinated, an outrage similar in nature to that endured by the deceased, although less in extent, was perpetrated, by a gang of young ruffians, upon the person of a second young female. Is it wonderful that the one known atrocity should influence the popular judgment in regard to the other unknown? This judgment awaited direction, and the known outrage seemed so opportunely to afford it! Marie, too, was found in the river; and upon this very river was this known outrage committed. The connexion of the two events had about it so much of the palpable, that the true wonder would have been a *failure* of the populace to appreciate and to seize it. But, in fact, the one atrocity, known to be so committed, is, if any thing, evidence that the other, committed at a time nearly coincident, was *not* so committed. It would have been a miracle indeed, if, while a gang of ruffians were perpetrating, at a given locality, a most unheard-of wrong, there should have been another similar gang, in a similar locality, in the same city, under the same circumstances, with the same means and appliances, engaged in a wrong of precisely the same aspect, at precisely the same period of time! Yet in what, if not in this marvellous train of coincidence, does the accidentally *suggested* opinion of the populace call upon us to believe?

"Before proceeding farther, let us consider the supposed scene of the assassination, in the thicket at the Barrière du Roule. This thicket, although dense, was in the close vicinity of a public road. Within were three or four large stones, forming a kind of seat with a back and footstool. On the upper stone was discovered a white petticoat; on the second, a silk scarf. A parasol, gloves, and a pocket-handkerchief, were also here found. The handkerchief bore the name, 'Marie Rogêt.' Fragments of dress were seen on the branches around. The earth was trampled, the bushes were broken, and there was every evidence of a violent struggle.

"Notwithstanding the acclamation with which the discovery of this thicket was received by the press, and the unanimity with which it was supposed to indicate the precise scene of the outrage, it must be admitted that there was some very good reason for doubt. That it *was* the scene, I may or I may not believe—but there was excellent reason for doubt. Had the *true* scene been, as *Le Commerciel* suggested, in the neighborhood of the Rue Pavée St. André, the perpetrators of the crime, supposing them still resident in Paris, would naturally have been stricken with terror at the public attention thus acutely directed into the proper channel; and, in certain classes of minds, there would have arisen, at once, a sense of the necessity of some exertion to re-divert this attention. And thus, the thicket of the Bar-rière du Roule having been already suspected, the idea of placing the articles where they were found, might have been naturally entertained. There is no real evidence, although *Le Soleil* so supposes, that the articles discovered had been more than a very few days in the thicket; while there is much circumstantial proof that they could not have remained there, without attracting attention, during the twenty days elapsing between the fatal Sunday and the afternoon upon which they were found by the boys. 'They were all *mildewed* down hard,' says *Le Soleil*, adopting the opinions of its pred-ecessors, 'with the action of the rain, and stuck to-gether from *mildew*. The grass had grown around and over some of them. The silk of the parasol was strong, but the threads of it were run together within. The upper part, where it had been doubled and folded, was all *mildewed* and rotten, and tore on being opened.' In respect to the grass having 'grown around and over some of them,' it is obvious that the fact could only have been ascertained from the words, and thus from the recollections, of two small boys; for these boys re-moved the articles and took them home before they had been seen by a third party. But grass will grow, especi-ally in warm and damp weather, (such as was that of the period of the murder,) as much as two or three inches in a single day. A parasol lying upon a newly

turfed ground, might, in a week, be entirely concealed
from sight by the upspringing grass. And touching that
mildew upon which the editor of *Le Soleil* so pertinaciously insists, that he employs the word no less than
three times in the brief paragraph just quoted, is he
really unaware of the nature of this *mildew?* Is he to
be told that it is one of the many classes of *fungus,* of
which the most ordinary feature is its upspringing and
decadence within twenty-four hours?

"Thus we see, at a glance, that what has been most
triumphantly adduced in support of the idea that the
articles had been 'for at least three or four weeks'
in the thicket, is most absurdly null as regards any
evidence of that fact. On the other hand, it is exceedingly difficult to believe that these articles could have
remained in the thicket specified, for a longer period
than a single week—for a longer period than from one
Sunday to the next. Those who know any thing of the
vicinity of Paris, know the extreme difficulty of finding
seclusion, unless at a great distance from its suburbs.
Such a thing as an unexplored, or even an unfrequently
visited recess, amid its woods or groves, is not for a
moment to be imagined. Let any one who, being at
heart a lover of nature, is yet chained by duty to the
dust and heat of this great metropolis—let any such
one attempt, even during the week-days, to slake his
thirst for solitude amid the scenes of natural loveliness
which immediately surround us. At every second step,
he will find the growing charm dispelled by the voice
and personal intrusion of some ruffian or party of
carousing blackguards. He will seek privacy amid the
densest foliage, all in vain. Here are the very nooks
where the unwashed most abound—here are the
temples most desecrate. With sickness of the heart the
wanderer will flee back to the polluted Paris as to a less

odious because less incongruous sink of pollution. But if the vicinity of the city is so beset during the working days of the week, how much more so on the Sabbath! It is now especially that, released from the chains of labor, or deprived of the customary opportunities of crime, the town blackguard seeks the precincts of the town, not through love of the rural, which in his heart he despises, but by way of escape from the restraints and conventionalities of society. He desires less the fresh air and the green trees, than the utter *license* of the country. Here, at the road-side inn, or beneath the foliage of the woods, he indulges, unchecked by any eye except those of his boon companions, in all the mad excess of a counterfeit hilarity—the joint offspring of liberty and of rum. I say nothing more than what must be obvious to every dispassionate observer, when I repeat that the circumstance of the articles in question having remained undiscovered, for a longer period than from one Sunday to another, in *any* thicket in the immediate neighborhood of Paris, is to be looked upon as little less than miraculous.

"But there are not wanting other grounds for the suspicion that the articles were placed in the thicket with the view of diverting attention from the real scene of the outrage. And, first, let me direct your notice to the *date* of the discovery of the articles. Collate this with the date of the fifth extract made by myself from the newspapers. You will find that the discovery followed, almost immediately, the urgent communications sent to the evening paper. These communications, although various, and apparently from various sources, tended all to the same point—viz., the directing of attention to *a gang* as the perpetrators of the outrage, and to the neighborhood of the Barrière du Roule as its scene. Now here, of course, the suspicion is not that,

in consequence of these communications, or of the public attention by them directed, the articles were found
by the boys; but the suspicion might and may well
have been, that the articles were not *before* found by
the boys, for the reason that the articles had not before
been in the thicket; having been deposited there only
at so late a period as at the date, or shortly prior to the
date of the communications, by the guilty authors of
these communications themselves.

"This thicket was a singular—an exceedingly singular one. It was unusually dense. Within its naturally
walled enclosure were three extraordinary stones, *forming a seat with a back and footstool.* And this thicket,
so full of a natural art, was in the immediate vicinity,
within a few rods, of the dwelling of Madame Deluc,
whose boys were in the habit of closely examining the
shrubberies about them in search of the bark of the
sassafras. Would it be a rash wager—a wager of one
thousand to one—that *a day* never passed over the
heads of these boys without finding at least one of them
ensconced in the umbrageous hall, and enthroned upon
its natural throne? Those who would hesitate at such a
wager, have either never been boys themselves, or have
forgotten the boyish nature. I repeat—it is exceedingly
hard to comprehend how the articles could have remained in this thicket undiscovered, for a longer period
than one or two days; and that thus there is good
ground for suspicion, in spite of the dogmatic ignorance
of *Le Soleil,* that they were, at a comparatively late
date, deposited where found.

"But there are still other and stronger reasons for believing them so deposited, than any which I have as
yet urged. And, now, let me beg your notice to the
highly artificial arrangement of the articles. On the
upper stone lay a white petticoat; on the *second* a silk

scarf; scattered around, were a parasol, gloves, and a pocket-handkerchief bearing the name, 'Marie Rogêt.' Here is just such an arrangement as would *naturally* be made by a not-over-acute person wishing to dispose the articles *naturally*. But it is by no means a *really* natural arrangement. I should rather have looked to see the things *all* lying on the ground and trampled under foot. In the narrow limits of that bower, it would have been scarcely possible that the petticoat and scarf should have retained a position upon the stones, when subjected to the brushing to and fro of many struggling persons. 'There was evidence,' it is said, 'of a struggle; and the earth was trampled, the bushes were broken,' —but the petticoat and the scarf are found deposited as if upon shelves. 'The pieces of the frock torn out by the bushes were about three inches wide and six inches long. One part was the hem of the frock and it had been mended. They *looked like strips torn off.*' Here, inadvertently, *Le Soleil* has employed an exceedingly suspicious phrase. The pieces, as described, do indeed 'look like strips torn off;' but purposely and by hand. It is one of the rarest of accidents that a piece is 'torn off,' from any garment such as is now in question, by the agency *of a thorn*. From the very nature of such fabrics, a thorn or nail becoming entangled in them, tears them rectangularly—divides them into two longitudinal rents, at right angles with each other, and meeting at an apex where the thorn enters—but it is scarcely possible to conceive the piece 'torn off.' I never so knew it, nor did you. To tear a piece *off* from such fabric, two distinct forces, in different directions, will be, in almost every case, required. If there be two edges to the fabric—if, for example, it be a pocket-handkerchief, and it is desired to tear from it a slip, then, and then only, will the one force serve the purpose. But in the

present case the question is of a dress, presenting but
one edge. To tear a piece from the interior, where no
edge is presented, could only be effected by a miracle
through the agency of thorns, and no *one* thorn could
accomplish it. But, even where an edge is presented,
two thorns will be necessary, operating, the one in two
distinct directions, and the other in one. And this in the
supposition that the edge is unhemmed. If hemmed,
the matter is nearly out of the question. We thus see
the numerous and great obstacles in the way of pieces
being 'torn off' through the simple agency of 'thorns;'
yet we are required to believe not only that one piece
but that many have been so torn. 'And one part,' too,
'was the hem of the frock!' Another piece was *'part of
the skirt, not the hem,'*—that is to say, was torn completely out, through the agency of thorns, from the un-
edged interior of the dress! These, I say, are things
which one may well be pardoned for disbelieving; yet,
taken collectedly, they form, perhaps, less of reasonable
ground for suspicion, than the one startling circumstance of the articles having been left in this thicket at
all, by any *murderers* who had enough precaution to
think of removing the corpse. You will not have apprehended me rightly, however, if you suppose it my
design to *deny* this thicket as the scene of the outrage.
There might have been a wrong *here,* or, more possibly,
an accident at Madame Deluc's. But, in fact, this is a
point of minor importance. We are not engaged in an
attempt to discover the scene, but to produce the perpetrators of the murder. What I have adduced, notwithstanding the minuteness with which I have adduced it, has been with the view, first, to show the
folly of the positive and headlong assertions of *Le Soleil,*
but secondly and chiefly, to bring you, by the most
natural route, to a further contemplation of the doubt

whether this assassination has, or has not been, the work of *a gang*.

"We will resume this question by mere allusion to the revolting details of the surgeon examined at the inquest. It is only necessary to say that his published *inferences,* in regard to the number of the ruffians, have been properly ridiculed as unjust and totally baseless, by all the reputable anatomists of Paris. Not that the matter *might not* have been as inferred, but that there was no ground for the inference:—was there not much for another?

"Let us reflect now upon 'the traces of a struggle;' and let me ask what these traces have been supposed to demonstrate. A gang. But do they not rather demonstrate the absence of a gang? What *struggle* could have taken place—what struggle so violent and so enduring as to have left its 'traces' in all directions—between a weak and defenceless girl and the *gang* of ruffians imagined? The silent grasp of a few rough arms and all would have been over. The victim must have been absolutely passive at their will. You will here bear in mind that the arguments urged against the thicket as the scene, are applicable, in chief part, only against it as the scene of an outrage committed by *more than a single individual.* If we imagine but *one* violator, we can conceive, and thus only conceive, the struggle of so violent and so obstinate a nature as to have left the 'traces' apparent.

"And again. I have already mentioned the suspicion to be excited by the fact that the articles in question were suffered to remain *at all* in the thicket where discovered. It seems almost impossible that these evidences of guilt should have been accidentally left where found. There was sufficient presence of mind (it is supposed) to remove the corpse; and yet a more positive evidence than the corpse itself (whose features might have been quickly obliterated by decay,) is allowed to lie conspicuously in the scene of the outrage—I allude to the handkerchief with the *name* of the deceased. If this was accident, it was not the accident *of a gang*. We can imagine it only the accident of an individual. Let us see. An individual has committed the murder. He is alone with the ghost of the departed. He is appalled by what lies motionless before him. The fury of his passion is over, and there is abundant room in his heart for the natural awe of the deed. His is none of that confidence which the presence of numbers inevitably inspires. He is *alone* with the dead. He trembles and is bewildered. Yet there is a necessity for disposing of the corpse. He bears it to the river, but leaves behind him the other evidences of guilt; for it is difficult, if not impossible to carry all the burthen at once, and it will be easy to return for what is left. But in his toilsome journey to the water his fears redouble within him. The sounds of life encompass his path. A dozen times he hears or fancies the step of an observer. Even the very lights from the city bewilder him. Yet, in time, and by long and frequent pauses of deep agony, he reaches the river's brink, and disposes of his ghastly charge—perhaps through the medium of a boat. But *now* what treasure does the world hold—what threat of vengeance could it hold out—which would have power to urge the return of that lonely murderer over that toilsome and perilous path, to the thicket and its blood-chilling recollections? He returns *not*, let the consequences be what they may. He *could* not return if he would. His sole thought is immediate escape. He turns his back *forever* upon those dreadful shrubberies, and flees as from the wrath to come.

"But how with a gang? Their number would have

inspired them with confidence; if, indeed, confidence
is ever wanting in the breast of the arrant blackguard;
and of arrant blackguards alone are the supposed *gangs*
ever constituted. Their number, I say, would have prevented the bewildering and unreasoning terror which
I have imagined to paralyze the single man. Could we
suppose an oversight in one, or two, or three, this oversight would have been remedied by a fourth. They
would have left nothing behind them; for their number
would have enabled them to carry *all* at once. There
would have been no need of *return*.

"Consider now the circumstances that, in the outer
garment of the corpse when found, 'a slip, about a foot
wide, had been torn upward from the bottom hem to
the waist, wound three times round the waist, and secured by a sort of hitch in the back.' This was done with
the obvious design of affording *a handle* by which to
carry the body. But would any *number* of men have
dreamed of resorting to such an expedient? To three
or four, the limbs of the corpse would have afforded
not only a sufficient, but the best possible hold. The
device is that of a single individual; and this brings us
to the fact that 'between the thicket and the river, the
rails of the fences were found taken down, and the
ground bore evident traces of some heavy burden having been dragged along it!' But would a *number* of men
have put themselves to the superfluous trouble of taking down a fence, for the purpose of dragging through
it a corpse which they might have *lifted over* any fence
in an instant? Would a *number* of men have so *dragged*
a corpse at all as to have left evident *traces* of the dragging?

"And here we must refer to an observation of *Le
Commerciel;* an observation upon which I have already,
in some measure, commented. 'A piece,' says this jour-

nal, 'of one of the unfortunate girl's petticoats was torn out and tied under her chin, and around the back of her head, probably to prevent screams. This was done by fellows who had no pocket-handkerchiefs.'

"I have before suggested that a genuine blackguard is never *without* a pocket-handkerchief. But it is not to this fact that I now especially advert. That it was not through want of a handkerchief for the purpose imagined by *Le Commerciel*, that this bandage was employed, is rendered apparent by the handkerchief left in the thicket; and the object was not 'to prevent screams' appears, also, from the bandage having been employed in preference to what would so much better have answered the purpose. But the language of the evidence speaks of the strip in question as 'found around the neck, fitting loosely, and secured with a hard knot.' These words are sufficiently vague, but differ materially from those of *Le Commerciel*. The slip was eighteen inches wide, and therefore, although of muslin, would form a strong band when folded or rumpled longitudinally. And thus rumpled it was discovered. My inference is this. The solitary murderer, having borne the corpse, for some distance, (whether from the thicket or elsewhere) by means of the bandage *hitched* around its middle, found the weight, in this mode of procedure, too much for his strength. He resolved to drag the burthen—the evidence goes to show that it *was* dragged. With this object in view, it became necessary to attach something like a rope to one of the extremities. It could be best attached about the neck, where the head would prevent its slipping off. And, now, the murderer bethought him, unquestionably, of the bandage about the loins. He would have used this, but for its volution about the corpse, the *hitch* which embarrassed it, and the reflection that it had not been

'torn off' from the garment. It was easier to tear a new
slip from the petticoat. He tore it, made it fast about
the neck, and so *dragged* his victim to the brink of the
river. That this 'bandage,' only attainable with trouble
and delay, and but imperfectly answering its purpose
—that this bandage was employed *at all*, demonstrates
that the necessity for its employment sprang from circumstances arising at a period when the handkerchief
was no longer attainable—that is to say, arising, as we
have imagined, after quitting the thicket, (if the thicket
it was), and on the road between the thicket and the
river.

"But the evidence, you will say, of Madame Deluc (!)
points especially to the presence of *a gang*, in the
vicinity of the thicket, at or about the epoch of the murder. This I grant. I doubt if there were not a *dozen* gangs,
such as described by Madame Deluc, in and about the
vicinity of the Barrière du Roule at *or about* the period
of this tragedy. But the gang which has drawn upon
itself the pointed animadverison, although the somewhat
tardy and very suspicious evidence of Madame Deluc, is
the *only* gang which is represented by that honest and
scrupulous old lady as having eaten her cakes and swallowed her brandy, without putting themselves to the
trouble of making her payment. *Et hinc illæ iræ?*

"But what *is* the precise evidence of Madame Deluc?
'A gang of miscreants made their appearance, behaved
boisterously, ate and drank without making payment,
followed in the route of the young man and girl, returned
to the inn *about dusk,* and recrossed the river as if in
great haste.'

"Now this 'great haste' very possibly seemed *greater*
haste in the eyes of Madame Deluc, since she dwelt
lingeringly and lamentingly upon her violated cakes and
ale—cakes and ale for which she might still have enter-

tained a faint hope of compensation. Why, otherwise, since it was *about dusk*, should she make a point of the *haste?* It is no cause for wonder, surely, that even a gang of blackguards should make *haste* to get home, when a wide river is to be crossed in small boats, when storm impends, and when night *approaches*.

"I say *approaches;* for the night had *not yet arrived*. It was only *about dusk* that the indecent haste of these 'miscreants' offended the sober eyes of Madame Deluc. But we are told that it was upon this very evening that Madame Deluc, as well as her eldest son, 'heard the screams of a female in the vicinity of the inn.' And in what words does Madame Deluc designate the period of the evening at which these screams were heard? 'It was *soon after dark*,' she says. But 'soon *after* dark,' is, at least, *dark;* and '*about dusk*' is as certainly daylight. Thus it is abundantly clear that the gang quitted the Barrière du Roule *prior* to the screams overheard (?) by Madame Deluc. And although, in all the many reports of the evidence, the relative expressions in question are distinctly and invariably employed just as I have employed them in this conversation with yourself, no notice whatever of the gross discrepancy has, as yet, been taken by any of the public journals, or by any of the Myrmidons of police.

"I shall add but one to the arguments against *a gang;* but this *one* has, to my own understanding at least, a weight altogether irresistible. Under the circumstances of large reward offered, and full pardon to any King's evidence, it is not to be imagined, for a moment, that some member of *a gang* of low ruffians, or of any body of men, would not long ago have betrayed his accomplices. Each one of a gang so placed, is not so much greedy of reward, or anxious for escape, as *fearful of betrayal*. He betrays eagerly and early that *he may not himself be betrayed.* That the secret has not been divulged, is the very best of proof that it is, in fact, a secret. The horrors of this dark deed are known only to *one,* or two, living human beings, and to God.

"Let us sum up now the meagre yet certain fruits of our long analysis. We have attained the idea either of a fatal accident under the roof of Madame Deluc, or of a murder perpetrated, in the thicket at the Barrière du Roule, by a lover, or at least by an intimate and secret associate of the deceased. This associate is of swarthy complexion. This complexion, the 'hitch' in the bandage, and the 'sailor's knot,' with which the bonnet-ribbon is tied, point to a seaman. His companionship with the deceased, a gay, but not an abject young girl, designates him as above the grade of the common sailor. Here the well written and urgent communications to the journals are much in the way of corroboration. The circumstance of the first elopement, as mentioned by *Le Mercure,* tends to blend the idea of this seaman with that of the 'naval officer' who is first known to have led the unfortunate into crime.

"And here, most fitly, comes the consideration of the continued absence of him of the dark complexion. Let me pause to observe that the complexion of this man is dark and swarthy; it was no common swarthiness which constituted the *sole* point of remembrance, both as regards Valence and Madame Deluc. But why is this man absent? Was he murdered by the gang? If so, why are there only *traces* of the assassinated *girl?* The scene of the two outrages will naturally be supposed identical. And where is his corpse? The assassins would most probably have disposed of both in the same way. But it may be said that this man lives, and is deterred from making himself known, through dread of being charged with the murder. This consideration might be supposed to operate upon him now—at this late period—since it has been given in evidence that he was seen with Marie —but it would have had no force at the period of the deed. The first impulse of an innocent man would have been to announce the outrage, and to aid in identifying the ruffians. This, *policy* would have suggested. He had been seen with the girl. He had crossed the river with her in an open ferry-boat. The denouncing of the assassins would have appeared, even to an idiot, the surest and sole means of relieving himself from suspicion. We cannot suppose him, on the night of the fatal Sunday, both innocent himself and incognizant of an outrage committed. Yet only under such circumstances is it possible to imagine that he would have failed, if alive, in the denouncement of the assassins.

"And what means are ours, of attaining the truth? We shall find these means multiplying and gathering distinctness as we proceed. Let us sift to the bottom this affair of the first elopement. Let us know the full history of 'the officer,' with his present circumstances, and his whereabouts at the precise period of the murder. Let us carefully compare with each other the various communications sent to the evening paper, in which the object was to inculpate *a gang*. This done, let us compare these communications, both as regards style and MS., with those sent to the morning paper, at a previous period, and insisting so vehemently upon the guilt of Mennais. And, all this done, let us again compare these various communications with the known MSS. of the officer. Let us endeavor to ascertain, by repeated questionings of Madame Deluc and her boys, as well as of the omnibus-driver, Valence, something more of the personal appearance and bearing of the 'man of dark complexion.' Queries, skilfully directed, will not fail to elicit, from some of these parties, information on this particular point (or upon others)—information which the parties themselves may not even be aware of possessing. And let us now trace *the boat* picked up by the barge-man on the morning of Monday the twenty-third of June, and which was removed from the barge-office, without cognizance of the officer in attendance, and *without the rudder*, at some period prior to the discovery of the corpse. With a proper caution and perseverance we shall infallibly trace this boat; for not only can the bargeman who picked it up identify it, but the *rudder is at hand*. The rudder *of a sail-boat* would not have been abandoned, without inquiry, by one altogether at ease in heart. And here let me pause to insinuate a question. There was no *advertisement* of the picking up of this boat. It was silently taken to the barge-office, and as silently removed. But its owner or employer—how *happened* he, at so early a period as Tuesday morning, to be informed, without the agency of advertisement, of the locality of the boat taken up on Monday, unless we imagine some connexion with the *navy*—some personal permanent connexion leading to cognizance of its minute interests—its petty local news?

"In speaking of the lonely assassin dragging his burden to the shore, I have already suggested the probability of his availing himself *of a boat*. Now we are to understand that Marie Rogêt *was* precipitated from a boat. This would naturally have been the case. The corpse could not have been trusted to the shallow waters of the shore. The peculiar marks on the back and shoulders of the victim tell of the bottom ribs of a boat. That the body was found without weight is also corroborative of the idea. If thrown from the shore a weight would have been attached. We can only account for its absence by supposing the murderer to have neglected the precaution of supplying himself with it before pushing off. In the act of consigning the corpse to the water, he would unquestionably have noticed his oversight; but then no remedy would have been at hand. Any risk would have been preferred to a return to that accursed shore. Having rid himself of his ghastly charge, the murderer would have hastened to the city. There, at some obscure wharf, he would have leaped on land. But the boat—would he have secured it? He would have been in too great haste for such things as securing a boat. Moreover, in fastening it to the wharf, he would have felt as if securing evidence against himself. His natural thought would have been to cast from him, as far as possible, all that had held connection with his crime. He would not only have fled from the wharf, but he would not have permitted *the boat* to remain. Assuredly he would have cast it adrift. Let us pursue our fancies.—In the morning, the wretch is stricken with unutterable horror at finding that the boat has been picked up and detained at a locality which he is in the daily habit of frequenting— at a locality, perhaps, which his duty compels him to frequent. The next night, *without daring to ask for the rudder,* he removes it. Now *where* is that rudderless boat? Let it be one of our first purposes to discover. With the first glimpse we obtain of it, the dawn of our success shall begin. This boat shall guide us, with a rapidity which will surprise even ourselves, to him who employed it in the midnight of the fatal Sabbath. Corroboration will rise upon corroboration, and the murderer will be traced."

[For reasons which we shall not specify, but which to many readers will appear obvious, we have taken the liberty of here omitting, from the MSS placed in our hands, such portion as details the *following up* of the apparently slight clew obtained by Dupin. We feel it advisable only to state, in brief, that the result desired was brought to pass; and that the Prefect fulfilled punctually, although with reluctance, the terms of his compact with the Chevalier. Mr. Poe's article concludes with the following words.—*Eds.*[1]]

It will be understood that I speak of coincidences *and no more*. What I have said above upon this topic must suffice. In my own heart there dwells no faith in præter-nature. That Nature and its God are two, no man who thinks, will deny. That the latter, creating the former, can, at will, control or modify it, is also unquestionable. I say "at will;" for the question is of will, and not, as the insanity of logic has assumed, of power. It is not that the Deity *cannot* modify his laws, but that we insult him in imagining a possible necessity for modification. In their origin these laws were fashioned to embrace *all* contingencies which *could* lie in the Future. With God all is *Now*.

I repeat, then, that I speak of these things only as of coincidences. And farther: in what I relate it will be seen that between the fate of the unhappy Mary Cecilia Rogers, so far as that fate is known, and the fate of one Marie Rogêt up to a certain epoch in her history, there has existed a parallel in the contemplation of whose wonderful exactitude the reason becomes embarrassed. I say all this will be seen. But let it not for a moment be supposed that, in proceeding with the sad narrative of Marie from the epoch just mentioned, and in tracing to its *dénouement* the mystery which enshrouded her, it is my covert design to hint at an extension of the parallel, or even to suggest that the measures adopted in Paris for the discovery of the assassin of a grisette, or measures founded in any similar ratiocination, would produce any similar result.

For, in respect to the latter branch of the supposition,

[1] *Of the magazine in which the article was originally published.*

it should be considered that the most trifling variation
in the facts of the two cases might give rise to the most
important miscalculations, by diverting thoroughly the
two courses of events; very much as, in arithmetic, an
error which, in its own individuality, may be inappreciable, produces, at length, by dint of multiplication
at all points of the process, a result enormously at
variance with truth. And, in regard to the former branch,
we must not fail to hold in view that the very Calculus
of Probabilities to which I have referred, forbids all
idea of the extension of the parallel:—forbids it with
a positiveness strong and decided just in proportion as
this parallel has already been long-drawn and exact.
This is one of those anomalous propositions which,
seemingly appealing to thought altogether apart from
the mathematical, is yet one which only the mathematician can fully entertain. Nothing, for example, is more
difficult than to convince the merely general reader that
the fact of sixes having been thrown twice in succession
by a player at dice, is sufficient cause for betting the
largest odds that sixes will not be thrown in the third
attempt. A suggestion to this effect is usually rejected by
the intellect at once. It does not appear that the two
throws which have been completed, and which lie now
absolutely in the Past, can have influence upon the
throw which exists only in the Future. The chance for
throwing sixes seems to be precisely as it was at any
ordinary time—that is to say, subject only to the influence of the various other throws which may be made
by the dice. And this is a reflection which appears so
exceedingly obvious that attempts to controvert it are
received more frequently with a derisive smile than
with anything like respectful attention. The error here
involved—a gross error redolent of mischief—I cannot
pretend to expose within the limits assigned me at

present; and with the philosophical it needs no exposure.
It may be sufficient here to say that it forms one of an
infinite series of mistakes which arise in the path of
Reason through her propensity for seeking truth *in
detail.*

THE PURLOINED LETTER
(The Gift, 1845.)

Nil sapientiæ odiosius acumine nimio.
                                        —SENECA

AT PARIS, just after dark one gusty evening in the
autumn of 18—, I was enjoying the twofold luxury
of meditation and a meerschaum, in company with my
friend C. Auguste Dupin, in his little back library, or
book-closet, *au troisième, No. 33, Rue Dunôt, Faubourg
St. Germain.* For one hour at least we had maintained
a profound silence; while each, to any casual observer,
might have seemed intently and exclusively occupied
with the curling eddies of smoke that oppressed the
atmosphere of the chamber. For myself, however, I
was mentally discussing certain topics which had formed
matter for conversation between us at an earlier period
of the evening; I mean the affair of the Rue Morgue,
and the mystery attending the murder of Marie Rogêt.
I looked upon it, therefore, as something of a coincidence, when the door of our apartment was thrown
open and admitted our old acquaintance, Monsieur
G——, the Prefect of the Parisian police.

We gave him a hearty welcome; for there was nearly
half as much of the entertaining as of the contemptible
about the man, and we had not seen him for several

years. We had been sitting in the dark, and Dupin now arose for the purpose of lighting a lamp, but sat down again, without doing so, upon G.'s saying that he had called to consult us, or rather to ask the opinion of my friend, about some official business which had occasioned a great deal of trouble.

"If it is any point requiring reflection," observed Dupin, as he forbore to enkindle the wick, "we shall examine it to better purpose in the dark."

"That is another of your odd notions," said the Prefect, who had a fashion of calling every thing "odd" that was beyond his comprehension, and thus lived amid an absolute legion of "oddities."

"Very true," said Dupin, as he supplied his visiter with a pipe, and rolled towards him a comfortable chair.

"And what is the difficulty now?" I asked. "Nothing more in the assassination way, I hope?"

"Oh no; nothing of that nature. The fact is, the business is *very* simple indeed, and I make no doubt that we can manage it sufficiently well ourselves; but then I thought Dupin would like to hear the details of it, because it is so excessively *odd*."

"Simple and odd," said Dupin.

"Why, yes; and not exactly that, either. The fact is, we have all been a good deal puzzled because the affair *is* so simple, and yet baffles us altogether."

"Perhaps it is the very simplicity of the thing which puts you at fault," said my friend.

"What nonsense you *do* talk!" replied the Prefect, laughing heartily.

"Perhaps the mystery is a little *too* plain," said Dupin.

"Oh, good heavens! who ever heard of such an idea?"

"A little *too* self-evident."

"Ha! ha! ha!—ha! ha! ha!—ho! ho! ho!"—roared

our visiter, profoundly amused, "oh, Dupin, will be the death of me yet!"

"And what, after all, *is* the matter on hand?" I asked.

"Why, I will tell you," replied the Prefect, as he gave a long, steady, and contemplative puff, and settled himself in his chair. "I will tell you in a few words; but, before I begin, let me caution you that this is an affair demanding the greatest secrecy, and that I should most probably lose the position I now hold, were it known that I confided it to any one."

"Proceed," said I.

"Or not," said Dupin.

"Well, then; I have received personal information, from a very high quarter, that a certain document of the last importance, has been purloined from the royal apartments. The individual who purloined it is known; this beyond a doubt; he was seen to take it. It is known, also, that it still remains in his possession."

"How is this known?" asked Dupin.

"It is clearly inferred," replied the Prefect, "from the nature of the document, and from the non-appearance of certain results which would at once arise from its passing *out* of the robber's possession;—that is to say, from his employing it as he must design in the end to employ it."

"Be a little more explicit," I said.

"Well, I may venture so far as to say that the paper gives its holder a certain power in a certain quarter where such power is immensely valuable." The Prefect was fond of the cant of diplomacy.

"Still I do not quite understand," said Dupin.

"No? Well; the disclosure of the document to a third person, who shall be nameless, would bring in question the honor of a personage of most exalted station; and this fact gives the holder of the document an ascendancy over the illustrious personage whose honor and peace are so jeopardized."

"But this ascendancy," I interposed, "would depend upon the robber's knowledge of the loser's knowledge of the robber. Who would dare—"

"The thief," said G., "is the Minister D——, who dares all things, those unbecoming as well as those becoming a man. The method of the theft was not less ingenious than bold. The document in question—a letter, to be frank—had been received by the personage robbed while alone in the royal *boudoir*. During its perusal she was suddenly interrupted by the entrance of the other exalted personage from whom especially it was her wish to conceal it. After a hurried and vain endeavor to thrust it in a drawer, she was forced to place it, open as it was, upon a table. The address, however, was uppermost, and, the contents thus unexposed, the letter escaped notice. At this juncture enters the Minister D——. His lynx eye immediately perceives the paper, recognises the handwriting of the address, observes the confusion of the personage addressed, and fathoms her secret. After some business transactions, hurried through in his ordinary manner, he produces a letter somewhat similar to the one in question, opens it, pretends to read it, and then places it in close juxtaposition to the other. Again he converses, for some fifteen minutes, upon the public affairs. At length, in taking leave, he takes also from the table the letter to which he had no claim. Its rightful owner saw, but, of course, dared not call attention to the act, in the presence of the third personage who stood at her elbow. The minister decamped; leaving his own letter—one of no importance—upon the table."

"Here, then," said Dupin to me, "you have precisely

what you demand to make the ascendancy complete—
the robber's knowledge of the loser's knowledge of the
robber."

"Yes," replied the Prefect; "and the power thus attained has, for some months past, been wielded, for
political purposes, to a very dangerous extent. The personage robbed is more thoroughly convinced, every day,
of the necessity of reclaiming her letter. But this, of
course, cannot be done openly. In fine, driven to despair,
she has committed the matter to me."

"Than whom," said Dupin, amid a perfect whirlwind of smoke, "no more sagacious agent could, I suppose, be desired, or even imagined."

"You flatter me," replied the Prefect; "but it is possible that some such opinion may have been entertained."

"It is clear," said I, "as you observe, that the letter is
still in possession of the minister; since it is this possession, and not any employment of the letter, which
bestows the power. With the employment the power
departs."

"True," said G.; "and upon this conviction I proceeded. My first care was to make thorough search
of the minister's hotel; and here my chief embarrassment lay in the necessity of searching without his knowledge. Beyond all things, I have been warned of the
danger which would result from giving him reason to
suspect our design."

"But," said I, "you are quite *au fait* in these investigations. The Parisian police have done this thing often
before."

"O yes; and for this reason I did not despair. The
habits of the minister gave me, too, a great advantage.
He is frequently absent from home all night. His servants
are by no means numerous. They sleep at a distance

from their master's apartment, and, being chiefly Neapolitans, are readily made drunk. I have keys, as you know, with which I can open any chamber or cabinet in Paris. For three months a night has not passed, during the greater part of which I have not been engaged, personally, in ransacking the D—— Hôtel. My honor is interested, and, to mention a great secret, the reward is enormous. So I did not abandon the search until I had become fully satisfied that the thief is a more astute man than myself. I fancy that I have investigated every nook and corner of the premises in which it is possible that the paper can be concealed."

"But is it not possible," I suggested, "that although the letter may be in possession of the minister, as it unquestionably is, he may have concealed it elsewhere than upon his own premises?"

"This is barely possible," said Dupin. "The present peculiar condition of affairs at court, and especially of those intrigues in which D—— is known to be involved, would render the instant availability of the document— its susceptibility of being produced at a moment's notice —a point of nearly equal importance with its possession."

"Its susceptibility of being produced?" said I.

"That is to say, of being *destroyed*," said Dupin.

"True," I observed; "the paper is clearly then upon the premises. As for its being upon the person of the minister, we may consider that as out of the question."

"Entirely," said the Prefect. "He has been twice waylaid, as if by footpads, and his person rigorously searched under my own inspection."

"You might have spared yourself this trouble," said Dupin. "D——, I presume, is not altogether a fool, and, if not, must have anticipated these waylayings, as a matter of course."

"Not *altogether* a fool," said G., "but then he's a poet, which I take to be only one remove from a fool."

"True," said Dupin, after a long and thoughtful whiff from his meerschaum, "although I have been guilty of certain doggerel myself."

"Suppose you detail," said I, "the particulars of your search."

"Why the fact is, we took our time, and we searched *every where*. I have had long experience in these affairs. I took the entire building, room by room; devoting the nights of a whole week to each. We examined, first, the furniture of each apartment. We opened every possible drawer; and I presume you know that, to a properly trained police agent, such a thing as a *secret* drawer is impossible. Any man is a dolt who permits a 'secret' drawer to escape him in a search of this kind. The thing is *so* plain. There is a certain amount of bulk—of space —to be accounted for in every cabinet. Then we have accurate rules. The fiftieth part of a line could not escape us. After the cabinets we took the chairs. The cushions we probed with the fine long needles you have seen me employ. From the tables we removed the tops."

"Why so?"

"Sometimes the top of a table, or other similarly arranged piece of furniture, is removed by the person wishing to conceal an article; then the leg is excavated, the article deposited within the cavity, and the top replaced. The bottoms and tops of bed-posts are employed in the same way."

"But could not the cavity be detected by sounding?" I asked.

"By no means, if, when the article is deposited, a sufficient wadding of cotton be placed around it. Besides, in our case, we were obliged to proceed without noise."

"But you could not have removed—you could not have taken to pieces *all* articles of furniture in which it would have been possible to make a deposit in the manner you mention. A letter may be compressed into a thin spiral roll, not differing much in shape or bulk from a large knitting-needle, and in this form it might be inserted into the rung of a chair, for example. You did not take to pieces all the chairs?"

"Certainly not; but we did better—we examined the rungs of every chair in the hotel, and, indeed, the jointings of every description of furniture, by the aid of a most powerful microscope. Had there been any traces of recent disturbance we should not have failed to detect it instantly. A single grain of gimlet-dust, for example, would have been as obvious as an apple. Any disorder in the glueing—any unusual gaping in the joints—would have sufficed to insure detection."

"I presume you looked to the mirrors, between the boards and the plates, and you probed the beds and the bed-clothes, as well as the curtains and carpets."

"That of course; and when we had absolutely completed every particle of the furniture in this way, then we examined the house itself. We divided its entire surface into compartments, which we numbered, so that none might be missed; then we scrutinized each individual square inch throughout the premises, including the two houses immediately adjoining, with the microscope, as before."

"The two houses adjoining!" I exclaimed; "you must have had a great deal of trouble."

"We had; but the reward offered is prodigious."

"You include the *grounds* about the houses?"

"All the grounds are paved with brick. They gave us comparatively little trouble. We examined the moss between the bricks, and found it undisturbed."

"You looked among D——'s papers, of course, and into the books of the library?"

"Certainly; we opened every package and parcel; we not only opened every book, but we turned over every leaf in each volume, not contenting ourselves with a mere shake, according to the fashion of some of our police officers. We also measured the thickness of every book-*cover*, with the most accurate admeasurement, and applied to each the most jealous scrutiny of the microscope. Had any of the bindings been recently meddled with, it would have been utterly impossible that the fact should have escaped observation. Some five or six volumes, just from the hands of the binder, we carefully probed, longitudinally, with the needles."

"You explored the floors beneath the carpets?"

"Beyond doubt. We removed every carpet, and examined the boards with the microscope."

"And the paper on the walls?"

"Yes."

"You looked into the cellars?"

"We did."

"Then," I said, "you have been making a miscalculation, and the letter is *not* upon the premises, as you suppose."

"I fear you are right there," said the Prefect. "And now, Dupin, what would you advise me to do?"

"To make a thorough re-search of the premises."

"That is absolutely needless," replied G——. "I am not more sure that I breathe than I am that the letter is not at the Hôtel."

"I have no better advice to give you," said Dupin. "You have, of course, an accurate description of the letter?"

"Oh yes!"—And here the Prefect, producing a memorandum-book, proceeded to read aloud a minute account of the internal, and especially of the external appearance of the missing document. Soon after finishing the perusal of this description, he took his departure, more entirely depressed in spirits than I had ever known the good gentleman before.

In about a month afterwards he paid us another visit, and found us occupied very nearly as before. He took a pipe and a chair and entered into some ordinary conversation. At length I said,—

"Well, but G——, what of the purloined letter? I presume you have at last made up your mind that there is no such thing as overreaching the Minister?"

"Confound him, say I—yes; I made the re-examination, however, as Dupin suggested—but it was all labor lost, as I knew it would be."

"How much was the reward offered, did you say?" asked Dupin.

"Why, a very great deal—a *very* liberal reward—I don't like to say how much, precisely; but one thing I *will* say, that I wouldn't mind giving my individual check for fifty thousand francs to any one who could obtain me that letter. The fact is, it is becoming of more and more importance every day; and the reward has been lately doubled. If it were trebled, however, I could do no more than I have done."

"Why, yes," said Dupin, drawlingly, between the whiffs of his meerschaum, "I really—think, G——, you have not exerted yourself—to the utmost in this matter. You might—do a little more, I think, eh?"

"How?—in what way?"

"Why—puff, puff—you might—puff, puff—employ counsel in the matter, eh?—puff, puff, puff. Do you remember the story they tell of Abernethy?"

"No; hang Abernethy!"

"To be sure! hang him and welcome. But, once upon

a time, a certain rich miser conceived the design of spunging upon this Abernethy for a medical opinion. Getting up, for this purpose, an ordinary conversation in a private company, he insinuated his case to the physician, as that of an imaginary individual.

" 'We will suppose,' said the miser, 'that his symptoms are such and such; now, doctor, what would *you* have directed him to take?'

" 'Take!' said Abernethy, 'why, take *advice*, to be sure.' "

"But," said the Prefect, a little discomposed, "I am *perfectly* willing to take advice, and to pay for it. I would *really* give fifty thousand francs to any one who would aid me in the matter."

"In that case," replied Dupin, opening a drawer, and producing a check-book, "you may as well fill me up a check for the amount mentioned. When you have signed it, I will hand you the letter."

I was astounded. The Prefect appeared absolutely thunder-stricken. For some minutes he remained speechless and motionless, looking incredulously at my friend with open mouth, and eyes that seemed starting from their sockets; then, apparently recovering himself in some measure, he seized a pen, and after several pauses and vacant stares, finally filled up and signed a check for fifty thousand francs, and handed it across the table to Dupin. The latter examined it carefully and deposited it in his pocket-book; then, unlocking an *escritoire*, took thence a letter and gave it to the Prefect. This functionary grasped it in a perfect agony of joy, opened it with a trembling hand, cast a rapid glance at its contents, and then, scrambling and struggling to the door, rushed at length unceremoniously from the room and from the house, without having uttered a syllable since Dupin had requested him to fill up the check.

When he had gone, my friend entered into some explanations.

"The Parisian police," he said, "are exceedingly able in their way. They are persevering, ingenious, cunning, and thoroughly versed in the knowledge which their duties seem chiefly to demand. Thus, when G—— detailed to us his mode of searching the premises at the Hôtel D——, I felt entire confidence in his having made a satisfactory investigation—so far as his labors extended."

"So far as his labors extended?" said I.

"Yes," said Dupin. "The measures adopted were not only the best of their kind, but carried out to absolute perfection. Had the letter been deposited within the range of their search, these fellows would, beyond a question, have found it."

I merely laughed—but he seemed quite serious in all that he said.

"The measures, then," he continued, "were good in their kind, and well executed; their defect lay in their being inapplicable to the case, and to the man. A certain set of highly ingenious resources are, with the Prefect, a sort of Procrustean bed, to which he forcibly adapts his designs. But he perpetually errs by being too deep or too shallow, for the matter in hand; and many a schoolboy is a better reasoner than he. I knew one about eight years of age, whose success at guessing in the game of 'even and odd' attracted universal admiration. This game is simple, and is played with marbles. One player holds in his hand a number of these toys, and demands of another whether that number is even or odd. If the guess is right, the guesser wins one; if wrong, he loses one. The boy to whom I allude won all the marbles of the school. Of course he had some principle of guessing; and this lay in mere observation and admeasurement of the astuteness of his opponents. For example, an arrant simpleton is his opponent, and, holding up his closed hand, asks, 'are they even or odd?' Our school-boy replies, 'odd,' and loses; but upon the second trial he wins, for he then says to himself, 'the simpleton had them even upon the first trial, and his amount of cunning is just sufficient to make him have them odd upon the second; I will therefore guess odd;'—he guesses odd, and wins. Now, with a simpleton a degree above the first, he would have reasoned thus: 'This fellow finds that in the first instance I guessed odd, and, in the second, he will propose to himself upon the first impulse, a simple variation from even to odd, as did the first simpleton; but then a second thought will suggest that this is too simple a variation, and finally he will decide upon putting it even as before. I will therefore guess even;'—he guesses even, and wins. Now this mode of reasoning in the schoolboy, whom his fellows termed 'lucky,'—what, in its last analysis, is it?"

"It is merely," I said, "an identification of the rea-soner's intellect with that of his opponent."

"It is," said Dupin; "and, upon inquiring of the boy by what means he effected the *thorough* identification in which his success consisted, I received answer as follows: 'When I wish to find out how wise, or how stupid, or how good, or how wicked is any one, or what are his thoughts at the moment, I fashion the expression of my face, as accurately as possible, in accordance with the expression of his, and then wait to see what thoughts or sentiments arise in my mind or heart, as if to match or correspond with the expression.' This response of the schoolboy lies at the bottom of all the spurious profundity which has been attributed to Rochefoucauld, to La Bougive, to Machiavelli, and to Campanella."

"And the identification," I said, "of the reasoner's

intellect with that of his opponent, depends, if I understand you aright, upon the accuracy with which the
opponent's intellect is admeasured."

"For its practical value it depends upon this," replied
Dupin; "and the Prefect and his cohort fail so frequently,
first, by default of this identification, and, secondly,
by ill-admeasurement, or rather through non-admeasure-
ment, of the intellect with which they are engaged. They
consider only their *own* ideas of ingenuity; and, in
searching for anything hidden, advert only to the modes
in which *they* would have hidden it. They are right in
this much—that their own ingenuity is a faithful representative of that of the *mass;* but when the cunning of
the individual felon is diverse in character from their
own, the felon foils them, of course. This always happens when it is above their own, and very usually when
it is below. They have no variation of principle in their
investigations; at best, when urged by some unusual
emergency—by some extraordinary reward—they extend or exaggerate their old modes of *practice,* without
touching their principles. What, for example, in this
case of D——, has been done to vary the principle of
action? What is all this boring, and probing, and sounding, and scrutinizing with the microscope, and dividing
the surface of the building into registered square inches
—what is it all but an exaggeration *of the application*
of the one principle or set of principles of search, which
are based upon the one set of notions regarding human
ingenuity, to which the Prefect, in the long routine of
his duty, has been accustomed? Do you not see he has
taken it for granted that *all* men proceed to conceal a
letter,—not exactly in a gimlet-hole bored in a chair-
leg—but, at least, in *some* out-of-the-way hole or corner
suggested by the same tenor of thought which would
urge a man to secrete a letter in a gimlet-hole bored

in a chair-leg? And do you not see also, that such *recherchés* nooks for concealment are adapted only for ordinary occasions, and would be adopted only by ordinary intellects; for, in all cases of concealment, a disposal of the article concealed—a disposal of it in this *recherché* manner,—is, in the very first instance, presumable and presumed; and thus its discovery depends, not at all upon the acumen, but altogether upon the mere care, patience, and determination of the seekers; and where the case is of importance—or, what amounts to the same thing in the policial eyes, when the reward is of magnitude,—the qualities in question have *never* been known to fail. You will now understand what I meant in suggesting that, had the purloined letter been hidden any where within the limits of the Prefect's examination—in other words, had the principle of its concealment been comprehended within the principles of the Prefect—its discovery would have been a matter altogether beyond question. This functionary, however, has been thoroughly mystified; and the remote source of his defeat lies in the supposition that the Minister is a fool, because he has acquired renown as a poet. All fools are poets; this the Prefect *feels;* and he is merely guility of a *non distributio medii* in thence inferring that all poets are fools."

"But is this really the poet?" I asked. "There are two brothers, I know; and both have attained reputation in letters. The Minister I believe has written learnedly on the Differential Calculus. He is a mathematician, and no poet."

"You are mistaken; I know him well; he is both. As poet *and* mathematician, he would reason well; as mere mathematician, he could not have reasoned at all, and thus would have been at the mercy of the Prefect."

"You surprise me," I said, "by these opinions, which

have been contradicted by the voice of the world. You do not mean to set at naught the well-digested idea of centuries. The mathematical reason has long been regarded as *the* reason *par excellence*."

"'*Il y a à parier*,'" replied Dupin, quoting from Chamfort, "'*que toute idée publique, toute convention reçue, est une sottise, car elle a convenu au plus grand nombre.*' The mathematicians, I grant you, have done their best to promulgate the popular error to which you allude, and which is none the less an error for its promulgation as truth. With an art worthy a better cause, for example, they have insinuated the term 'analysis' into application to algebra. The French are the originators of this particular deception; but if a term is of any importance— if words derive any value from applicability—then 'analysis' conveys 'algebra' about as much as, in Latin, '*ambitus*' implies 'ambition,' '*religio*' 'religion,' or '*homines honesti*,' a set of *honorable* men."

"You have a quarrel on hand, I see," said I, "with some of the algebraists of Paris; but proceed."

"I dispute the availability, and thus the value, of that reason which is cultivated in any especial form other than the abstractly logical. I dispute, in particular, the reason educed by mathematical study. The mathematics are the science of form and quantity; mathematical reasoning is merely logic applied to observation upon form and quantity. The great error lies in supposing that even the truths of what is called *pure* algebra, are abstract of general truth. And this error is so egregious that I am confounded at the universality with which it has been received. Mathematical axioms are *not* axioms of general truth. What is true of *relation*— of form and quantity—is often grossly false in regard to morals, for example. In this latter science it is very usually *un*true that the aggregated parts are equal to the whole. In chemistry also the axiom fails. In the consideration of motive it fails; for two motives, each of a given value, have not, necessarily, a value when united, equal to the sum of their values apart. There are numerous other mathematical truths which are only truths within the limits of *relation*. But the mathematician argues, from his *finite truths*, through habit, as if they were of an absolutely general applicability—as the world indeed imagines them to be. Bryant, in his very learned 'Mythology,' mentions an analogous source of error, when he says that 'although the Pagan fables are not believed, yet we forget ourselves continually, and make inferences from them as existing realities.' With the algebraists, however, who are Pagans themselves, the 'Pagan fables' *are* believed, and the inferences are made, not so much through lapse of memory, as through an unaccountable addling of the brains. In short, I never yet encountered the mere mathematician who could be trusted out of equal roots, or one who did not clandestinely hold it as a point of his faith that x^2+px was absolutely and unconditionally equal to q. Say to one of these gentlemen, by way of experiment, if you please, that you believe occasions may occur where x^2+px is *not* altogether equal to q, and, having made him understand what you mean, get out of his reach as speedily as convenient, for, beyond doubt, he will endeavor to knock you down.

"I mean to say," continued Dupin, while I merely laughed at his last observations, "that if the Minister had been no more than a mathematician, the Prefect would have been under no necessity of giving me this check. I knew him, however, as both mathematician and poet, and my measures were adapted to his capacity, with reference to the circumstances by which he was surrounded. I knew him as a courtier, too, and

as a bold *intriguant.* Such a man, I considered, could
not fail to be aware of the ordinary policial modes of
action. He could not have failed to anticipate—and
events have proved that he did not fail to anticipate—
the waylayings to which he was subjected. He must
have foreseen, I reflected, the secret investigations of
his premises. His frequent absences from home at night,
which were hailed by the Prefect as certain aids to his
success, I regarded only as *ruses,* to afford opportunity
for thorough search to the police, and thus the sooner
to impress them with the conviction to which G——,
in fact, did finally arrive—the conviction that the letter
was not upon the premises. I felt, also, that the whole
train of thought, which I was at some pains in detailing
to you just now, concerning the invariable principle of
policial action in searches for articles concealed—I felt
that this whole train of thought would necessarily pass
through the mind of the Minister. It would imperatively
lead him to despise all the ordinary *nooks* of concealment. *He* could not, I reflected, be so weak as not to
see that the most intricate and remote recess of his
hotel would be as open as his commonest closets to the
eyes, to the probes, to the gimlets, and to the micro-
scopes of the Prefect. I saw, in fine, that he would be
driven, as a matter of course, to *simplicity,* if not deliberately induced to it as a matter of choice. You will
remember, perhaps, how desperately the Prefect
laughed when I suggested, upon our first interview,
that it was just possible this mystery troubled him so
much on account of its being so *very* self-evident."

"Yes," said I, "I remember his merriment well. I
really thought he would have fallen into convulsions."

"The material world," continued Dupin, "abounds
with very strict analogies to the immaterial; and thus
some color of truth has been given to the rhetorical

dogma, that metaphor, or simile, may be made to strengthen an argument, as well as to embellish a description. The principle of the *vis inertiæ*, for example, seems to be identical in physics and metaphysics. It is not more true in the former, that a large body is with more difficulty set in motion than a smaller one, and that its subsequent *momentum* is commensurate with this difficulty, than it is, in the latter, that intellects of the vaster capacity, while more forcible, more constant, and more eventful in their movements than those of inferior grade, are yet the less readily moved, and more embarrassed and full of hesitation in the first few steps of their progress. Again: have you ever noticed which of the street signs, over the shop doors, are the most attractive of attention?"

"I have never given the matter a thought," I said.

"There is a game of puzzles," he resumed, "which is played upon a map. One party playing requires another to find a given word—the name of town, river, state or empire—any word, in short, upon the motley and perplexed surface of the chart. A novice in the game generally seeks to embarrass his opponents by giving them the most minutely lettered names; but the adept selects such words as stretch, in large characters, from one end of the chart to the other. These, like the over-largely lettered signs and placards of the street, escape observation by dint of being excessively obvious; and here the physical oversight is precisely analogous with the moral inapprehension by which the intellect suffers to pass unnoticed those considerations which are too obtrusively and too palpably self-evident. But this is a point, it appears, somewhat above or beneath the understanding of the Prefect. He never once thought it probable, or possible, that the Minister had deposited the letter immediately beneath the nose of the whole world, by way of best preventing any portion of that world from perceiving it.

"But the more I reflected upon the daring, dashing, and discriminating ingenuity of D——; upon the fact that the document must always have been *at hand,* if he intended to use it to good purpose; and upon the decisive evidence, obtained by the Prefect, that it was not hidden within the limits of that dignitary's ordinary search—the more satisfied I became that, to conceal this letter, the Minister had resorted to the comprehensive and sagacious expedient of not attempting to conceal it at all.

"Full of these ideas, I prepared myself with a pair of green spectacles, and called one fine morning, quite by accident, at the Ministerial hotel. I found D—— at home, yawning, lounging, and dawdling, as usual, and pretending to be in the last extremity of *ennui.* He is, perhaps, the most really energetic human being now alive—but that is only when nobody sees him.

"To be even with him, I complained of my weak eyes, and lamented the necessity of the spectacles, under cover of which I cautiously and thoroughly surveyed the apartment, while seemingly intent only upon the conversation of my host.

"I paid special attention to a large writing-table near which he sat, and upon which lay confusedly, some miscellaneous letters and other papers, with one or two musical instruments and a few books. Here, however, after a long and very deliberate scrutiny, I saw nothing to excite particular suspicion.

"At length my eyes, in going the circuit of the room, fell upon a trumpery fillagree card-rack of pasteboard, that hung dangling by a dirty blue ribbon, from a little brass knob just beneath the middle of the mantel-piece. In this rack, which had three or four compartments, were five or six visiting cards and a solitary letter. This last was much soiled and crumpled. It was torn nearly in two, across the middle—as if a design, in the first instance, to tear it entirely up as worthless, had been altered, or stayed, in the second. It had a large black seal, bearing the D—— cipher *very* conspicuously, and was addressed, in a diminutive female hand, to D——, the minister, himself. It was thrust carelessly, and even, as it seemed, contemptuously, into one of the upper divisions of the rack.

"No sooner had I glanced at this letter, than I concluded it to be that of which I was in search. To be sure, it was, to all appearance, radically different from the one of which the Prefect had read us so minute a description. Here the seal was large and black, with the D—— cipher; there it was small and red, with the ducal arms of the S—— family. Here, the address, to the Minister, was diminutive and feminine; there the superscription, to a certain royal personage, was markedly bold and decided; the size alone formed a point of correspondence. But, then, the *radicalness* of these differences, which was excessive; the dirt; the soiled and torn condition of the paper, so inconsistent with the *true* methodical habits of D——, and so suggestive of a design to delude the beholder into an idea of the worthlessness of the document; these things, together with the hyperobtrusive situation of this document, full in the view of every visiter, and thus exactly in accordance with the conclusions to which I had previously arrived; these things, I say, were strongly corroborative of suspicion, in one who came with the intention to suspect.

"I protracted my visit as long as possible, and, while I maintained a most animated discussion with the Minister, on a topic which I knew well had never failed to interest and excite him, I kept my attention really riveted upon the letter. In this examination, I committed to memory its external appearance and arrangement in the rack; and also fell, at length, upon a discovery which set at rest whatever trivial doubt I might have entertained. In scrutinizing the edges of the paper, I observed them to be more *chafed* than seemed necessary. They presented the *broken* appearance which is manifested when a stiff paper, having been once folded and pressed with a folder, is refolded in a reversed direction, in the same creases or edges which had formed the original fold. This discovery was sufficient. It was clear to me that the letter had been turned, as a glove, inside out, re-directed, and re-sealed. I bade the Minister good morning, and took my departure at once, leaving a gold snuff-box upon the table.

"The next morning I called for the snuff-box, when we resumed, quite eagerly, the conversation of the preceding day. While thus engaged, however, a loud report, as if of a pistol, was heard immediately beneath the windows of the hotel, and was succeeded by a series of fearful screams, and the shoutings of a mob. D—— rushed to a casement, threw it open, and looked out. In the meantime, I stepped to the card-rack, took the letter, put it in my pocket, and replaced it by a *fac-simile*, (so far as regards externals,) which I had carefully prepared at my lodgings; imitating the D—— cipher, very readily, by means of a seal formed of bread.

"The disturbance in the street had been occasioned by the frantic behavior of a man with a musket. He had fired it among a crowd of women and children. It proved, however, to have been without ball, and the fellow was suffered to go his way as a lunatic or a drunkard. When he had gone, D—— came from the window, whither I had followed him immediately upon

securing the object in view. Soon afterwards I bade
him farewell. The pretended lunatic was a man in my
own pay."

"But what purpose had you," I asked, "in replacing
the letter by a *fac-simile?* Would it not have been
better, at the first visit, to have seized it openly, and
departed?"

"D——," replied Dupin, "is a desperate man, and a
man of nerve. His hotel, too, is not without attendants
devoted to his interests. Had I made the wild attempt
you suggest, I might never have left the Ministerial
presence alive. The good people of Paris might have
heard of me no more. But I had an object apart from
these considerations. You know my political preposses-
sions. In this matter, I act as a partisan of the lady
concerned. For eighteen months the Minister has had
her in his power. She has now him in hers; since, being
unaware that the letter is not in his possession, he will
proceed with his exactions as if it was. Thus will he inevitably commit himself, at once, to his political destruction. His downfall, too, will not be more precipitate than
awkward. It is all very well to talk about the *facilis des-
census Averni;* but in all kinds of climbing, as Catalani
said of singing, it is far more easy to get up than to come
down. In the present instance I have no sympathy—
at least no pity—for him who descends. He is that
monstrum horrendum, an unprincipled man of genius.
I confess, however, that I should like very well to know
the precise character of his thoughts, when, being de-
fied by her whom the Prefect terms 'a certain personage,' he is reduced to opening the letter which I left
for him in the card-rack."

"How? did you put any thing particular in it?"

"Why—it did not seem altogether right to leave
the interior blank—that would have been insulting.

D——, at Vienna once, did me an evil turn, which I told him, quite good-humoredly, that I should remember. So, as I knew he would feel some curiosity in regard to the identity of the person who had outwitted him, I thought it a pity not to give him a clue. He is well acquainted with my MS., and I just copied into the middle of the blank sheet the words—

—— *Un dessein si funeste,*
S'il n'est digne d'Atrée, est digne de Thyeste.

They are to be found in Crébillon's *Atrée.*"

THE GOLD-BUG

(The Philadelphia *Dollar Newspaper*, 1843.)

What ho! what ho! this fellow is dancing mad!
He hath been bitten by the Tarantula.
—ALL IN THE WRONG

MANY years ago, I contracted an intimacy with a Mr. William Legrand. He was of an ancient Huguenot family, and had once been wealthy; but a series of misfortunes had reduced him to want. To avoid the mortification consequent upon his disasters, he left New Orleans, the city of his forefathers, and took up his residence at Sullivan's Island, near Charleston, South Carolina.

This island is a very singular one. It consists of little else than the sea sand, and is about three miles long. Its breadth at no point exceeds a quarter of a mile. It is separated from the main land by a scarcely perceptible creek, oozing its way through a wilderness of reeds and slime, a favorite resort of the marsh-hen. The vegetation, as might be supposed, is scant, or at least dwarfish. No trees of any magnitude are to be seen. Near the western extremity, where Fort Moultrie stands, and where are some miserable frame buildings, tenanted, during summer, by the fugitives from Charleston dust and fever, may be found, indeed, the bristly palmetto; but the whole island, with the exception of this western point, and a line of hard, white beach on the seacoast, is covered with a dense undergrowth of the sweet myrtle, so much prized by the horticulturists of England. The shrub here often attains the height of fifteen or twenty feet, and forms an almost impenetrable coppice, burthening the air with its fragrance.

In the inmost recesses of this coppice, not far from the eastern or more remote end of the island, Legrand had built himself a small hut, which he occupied when I first, by mere accident, made his acquaintance. This soon ripened into friendship—for there was much in the recluse to excite interest and esteem. I found him well educated, with unusual powers of mind, but infected with misanthropy, and subject to perverse moods of alternate enthusiasm and melancholy. He had with him many books, but rarely employed them. His chief amusements were gunning and fishing, or sauntering along the beach and through the myrtles, in quest of shells or entomological specimens;—his collection of the latter might have been envied by a Swammerdamm. In these excursions he was usually accompanied by an old negro, called Jupiter, who had been manumitted before the reverses of the family, but who could be induced, neither by threats nor by promises, to abandon what he considered his right of attendance upon the footsteps of his young "Massa Will." It is not improbable that the relatives of Legrand, conceiving him to be somewhat unsettled in intellect, had contrived to instil this obstinacy into Jupiter, with a view to the supervision and guardianship of the wanderer.

The winters in the latitude of Sullivan's Island are seldom very severe, and in the fall of the year it is a rare event indeed when a fire is considered necessary. About the middle of October, 18—, there occurred, however, a day of remarkable chilliness. Just before sunset I scrambled my way through the evergreens to the hut of my friend, whom I had not visited for several weeks—my residence being, at that time, in Charleston, a distance of nine miles from the island, while the facilities of passage and re-passage were very far behind those of the present day. Upon reaching the hut I rapped, as was my custom, and getting no reply, sought for the key where I knew it was secreted, unlocked the door and went in. A fine fire was blazing upon the hearth. It was a novelty, and by no means an ungrateful one. I threw off an overcoat, took an arm-chair by the crackling logs, and awaited patiently the arrival of my hosts.

Soon after dark they arrived, and gave me a most cordial welcome. Jupiter, grinning from ear to ear, bustled about to prepare some marsh-hens for supper. Legrand was in one of his fits—how else shall I term them?—of enthusiasm. He had found an unknown bivalve, forming a new genus, and, more than this, he had hunted down and secured, with Jupiter's assistance, a *scarabæus* which he believed to be totally new, but in respect to which he wished to have my opinion on the morrow.

"And why not to-night?" I asked, rubbing my hands over the blaze, and wishing the whole tribe of *scarabæi* at the devil.

"Ah, if I had only known you were here!" said Legrand, "but it's so long since I saw you; and how could

I foresee that you would pay me a visit this very night of all others? As I was coming home I met Lieutenant G——, from the fort, and, very foolishly, I lent him the bug; so it will be impossible for you to see it until morning. Stay here to-night, and I will send Jup down for it at sunrise. It is the loveliest thing in creation!"

"What?—sunrise?"

"Nonsense! no!—the bug. It is of a brilliant gold color —about the size of a large hickory-nut—with two jet black spots near one extremity of the back, and another, somewhat longer, at the other. The *antennæ* are—"

"Dey ain't *no* tin in him, Massa Will, I keep a tellin on you," here interrupted Jupiter; "de bug is a goole bug, solid, ebery bit of him, inside and all, sep him wing—neber feel half so hebby a bug in my life."

"Well, suppose it is, Jup," replied Legrand, some-what more earnestly, it seemed to me, than the case demanded, "is that any reason for your letting the birds burn? The color"—here he turned to me—"is really almost enough to warrant Jupiter's idea. You never saw a more brilliant metallic lustre than the scales emit—but of this you cannot judge till to-morrow. In the mean time I can give you some idea of the shape." Saying this, he seated himself at a small table, on which were a pen and ink, but no paper. He looked for some in a drawer, but found none.

"Never mind," said he at length, "this will answer;" and he drew from his waistcoat pocket a scrap of what I took to be very dirty foolscap, and made upon it a rough drawing with the pen. While he did this, I re-tained my seat by the fire, for I was still chilly. When the design was complete, he handed it to me without rising. As I received it, a loud growl was heard, suc-ceeded by a scratching at the door. Jupiter opened it, and a large Newfoundland, belonging to Legrand, rushed in, leaped upon my shoulders, and loaded me with caresses; for I had shown him much attention during previous visits. When his gambols were over, I looked at the paper, and, to speak the truth, found myself not a little puzzled at what my friend had depicted.

"Well!" I said, after contemplating it for some minutes, "this *is* a strange *scarabæus*, I must confess: new to me: never saw anything like it before—unless it was a skull, or a death's-head—which it more nearly resembles than anything else that has come under *my* observation."

"A death's-head!" echoed Legrand—"Oh—yes—well, it has something of that appearance upon paper, no doubt. The two upper black spots look like eyes, eh? and the longer one at the bottom like a mouth—and then the shape of the whole is oval."

"Perhaps so," said I; "but, Legrand, I fear you are no artist. I must wait until I see the beetle itself, if I am to form any idea of its personal appearance."

"Well, I don't know," said he, a little nettled, "I draw tolerably—*should* do it at least—have had good masters, and flatter myself that I am not quite a blockhead."

"But, my dear fellow, you are joking then," said I, "this is a very passable *skull*—indeed, I may say that it is a very *excellent* skull, according to the vulgar notions about such specimens of physiology—and your *scarabæus* must be the queerest *scarabæus* in the world if it resembles it. Why, we may get up a very thrilling bit of superstition upon this hint. I presume you will call the bug *scarabæus caput hominis*, or something of that kind—there are many similar titles in the Natural Histories. But where are the *antennæ* you spoke of?"

"The *antennæ!*" said Legrand, who seemed to be

getting unaccountably warm upon the subject; "I am sure you must see the *antennæ*. I made them as distinct as they are in the original insect, and I presume that is sufficient."

"Well, well," I said, "perhaps you have—still I don't see them;" and I handed him the paper without additional remark, not wishing to ruffle his temper; but I was much surprised at the turn affairs had taken; his ill humor puzzled me—and, as for the drawing of the beetle, there were positively *no antennæ* visible, and the whole *did* bear a very close resemblance to the ordinary cuts of a death's-head.

He received the paper very peevishly, and was about to crumple it, apparently to throw it in the fire, when a casual glance at the design seemed suddenly to rivet his attention. In an instant his face grew violently red —in another as excessively pale. For some minutes he continued to scrutinize the drawing minutely where he sat. At length he arose, took a candle from the table, and proceeded to seat himself upon a sea-chest in the farthest corner of the room. Here again he made an anxious examination of the paper, turning it in all directions. He said nothing, however, and his conduct greatly astonished me; yet I thought it prudent not to exacerbate the growing moodiness of his temper by any comment. Presently he took from his coat pocket a wallet, placed the paper carefully in it, and deposited both in a writing-desk, which he locked. He now grew more composed in his demeanor; but his original air of enthusiasm had quite disappeared. Yet he seemed not so much sulky as abstracted. As the evening wore away he became more and more absorbed in reverie, from which no sallies of mine could arouse him. It had been my intention to pass the night at the hut, as I had frequently done before, but, seeing my host in this mood,

I deemed it proper to take leave. He did not press me to remain, but, as I departed, he shook my hand with even more than his usual cordiality.

It was about a month after this (and during the interval I had seen nothing of Legrand) when I received a visit, at Charleston, from his man, Jupiter. I had never seen the good old negro look so dispirited, and I feared that some serious disaster had befallen my friend.

"Well, Jup," said I, "what is the matter now?—how is your master?"

"Why, to speak de troof, massa, him not so berry well as mought be."

"Not well! I am truly sorry to hear it. What does he complain of?"

"Dar! dat 's it!—him neber plain of notin—but him berry sick for all dat."

"*Very* sick, Jupiter!—why didn't you say so at once? Is he confined to bed?"

"No, dat he aint!—he aint find nowhar—dat's just whar de shoe pinch—my mind is got to be berry hebby bout poor Massa Will."

"Jupiter, I should like to understand what it is you are talking about. You say your master is sick. Hasn't he told you what ails him?"

"Why, massa, taint worf while for to git mad bout de matter—Massa Will say noffin at all aint de matter wid him—but den what make him go about looking dis here way, wid he head down and he soldiers up, and as white as a gose? And den he keep a syphon all de time—"

"Keeps a what, Jupiter?"

"Keeps a syphon wid de figgurs on de slate—de queerest figgurs I ebber did see. Ise gittin to be skeered,

I tell you. Hab for to keep mighty tight eye pon him noovers. Todder day he gib me slip fore de sun up and was gone de whole ob de blessed day. I had a big stick ready cut for to gib him d—d good beating when he did come—but Ise sich a fool dat I had n't de heart arter all—he look so berry poorly."

"Eh?—what?—ah yes!—upon the whole I think you had better not be too severe with the poor fellow—don't flog him, Jupiter—he can't very well stand it—but can you form no idea of what has occasioned this illness, or rather this change of conduct? Has anything unpleasant happened since I saw you?"

"No, massa, dey aint bin noffin onpleasant *since* den—'t was *fore* den I 'm feared—'t was de berry day you was dare."

"How? what do you mean?"

"Why, massa, I mean de bug—dare now."

"The what?"

"De bug—I 'm berry sartain dat Massa Will bin bit somewhere bout de head by dat goole-bug."

"And what cause have you, Jupiter, for such a supposition?"

"Claws enuff, massa, and mouff too. I nebber did see sich a d—d bug—he kick and he bite ebery ting what cum near him. Massa Will cotch him fuss, but had for to let him go gin mighty quick, I tell you—den was de time he must ha got de bite. I did n't like de look ob de bug mouff, myself, no how, so I wouldn't take hold ob him wid my finger, but I cotch him wid a piece ob paper dat I found. I rap him up in de paper and stuff piece ob it in he mouff—dat was de way."

"And you think, then, that your master was really bitten by the beetle, and that the bite made him sick?"

"I don't tink noffin about it—I nose it. What make

him dream bout de goole so much, if taint cause he bit by de goole-bug? Ise heerd bout dem goole-bugs fore dis."

"But how do you know he dreams about gold?"

"How I know? why cause he talk about it in he sleep—dat's how I nose."

"Well, Jup, perhaps you are right; but to what fortunate circumstance am I to attribute the honor of a visit from you to-day?"

"What de matter, massa?"

"Did you bring any message from Mr. Legrand?"

"No, massa, I bring dis here pissel;" and here Jupiter handed me a note which ran thus:

MY DEAR ——

Why have I not seen you for so long a time? I hope you have not been so foolish as to take offence at any little *brusquerie* of mine; but no, that is improbable.

Since I saw you I have had great cause for anxiety. I have something to tell you, yet scarcely know how to tell it, or whether I should tell it at all.

I have not been quite well for some days past, and poor old Jup annoys me, almost beyond endurance, by his well-meant attentions. Would you believe it?—he had prepared a huge stick, the other day, with which to chastise me for giving him the slip, and spending the day, *solus,* among the hills on the main land. I verily believe that my ill looks alone saved me a flogging.

I have made no addition to my cabinet since we met.

If you can, in any way, make it convenient, come over with Jupiter. *Do* come. I wish to see you *to-night,* upon business of importance. I assure you that it is of the *highest* importance.

Ever yours,

WILLIAM LEGRAND

There was something in the tone of this note which gave me great uneasiness. Its whole style differed materially from that of Legrand. What could he be dreaming of? What new crotchet possessed his excitable brain? What "business of the highest importance" could *he* possibly have to transact? Jupiter's account of him boded no good. I dreaded lest the continued pressure of misfortune had, at length, fairly unsettled the reason of my friend. Without a moment's hesitation, therefore, I prepared to accompany the negro.

Upon reaching the wharf, I noticed a scythe and three spades, all apparently new, lying in the bottom of the boat in which we were to embark.

"What is the meaning of all this, Jup?" I inquired.

"Him syfe, massa, and spade."

"Very true; but what are they doing here?"

"Him de syfe and de spade what Massa Will sis pon my buying for him in de town, and de debbil's own lot of money I had to gib for em."

"But what, in the name of all that is mysterious, is your 'Massa Will' going to do with scythes and spades?"

"Dat's more dan *I* know, and debbil take me if I don't blieve 't is more dan he know, too. But it's all cum ob de bug."

Finding that no satisfaction was to be obtained of Jupiter, whose whole intellect seemed to be absorbed by "de bug," I now stepped into the boat and made sail. With a fair and strong breeze we soon ran into the little cove to the northward of Fort Moultrie, and a walk of some two miles brought us to the hut. It was about three in the afternoon when we arrived. Legrand had been awaiting us in eager expectation. He grasped my hand with a nervous *empressement* which alarmed me and strengthened the suspicions already entertained. His countenance was pale even to ghastliness, and his deep-set eyes glared with unnatural lustre. After some inquiries respecting his health, I asked him, not knowing what better to say, if he had yet obtained the *scarabæus* from Lieutenant G——.

"Oh, yes," he replied, coloring violently, "I got it from him the next morning. Nothing should tempt me to part with that *scarabæus*. Do you know that Jupiter is quite right about it?"

"In what way?" I asked, with a sad foreboding at heart.

"In supposing it to be a bug of *real gold*." He said this with an air of profound seriousness, and I felt inexpressibly shocked.

"This bug is to make my fortune," he continued, with a triumphant smile, "to reinstate me in my family possessions. Is it any wonder, then, that I prize it? Since Fortune has thought fit to bestow it upon me, I have only to use it properly and I shall arrive at the gold of which it is the index. Jupiter, bring me that *scarabæus!*"

"What! de bug, massa? I 'd rudder not go fer trubble dat bug—you mus git him for your own self." Hereupon Legrand arose, with a grave and stately air, and brought me the beetle from a glass case in which it was enclosed. It was a beautiful *scarabæus*, and, at that time, unknown to naturalists—of course a great prize in a scientific point of view. There were two round, black spots near one extremity of the back, and a long one near the other. The scales were exceedingly hard and glossy, with all the appearance of burnished gold. The weight of the insect was very remarkable, and, taking all things into consideration, I could hardly blame Jupiter for his opinion respecting it; but what to make of Legrand's agreement with that opinion, I could not, for the life of me, tell.

"I sent for you," said he, in a grandiloquent tone, when I had completed my examination of the beetle, "I sent for you, that I might have your counsel and assistance in furthering the views of Fate and of the bug"—

"My dear Legrand," I cried, interrupting him, "you are certainly unwell, and had better use some little precautions. You shall go to bed, and I will remain with you a few days, until you get over this. You are feverish and"—

"Feel my pulse," said he.

I felt it, and, to say the truth, found not the slightest indication of fever.

"But you may be ill and yet have no fever. Allow me this once to prescribe for you. In the first place, go to bed. In the next"—

"You are mistaken," he interposed, "I am as well as I can expect to be under the excitement which I suffer. If you really wish me well, you will relieve this excitement."

"And how is this to be done?"

"Very easily. Jupiter and myself are going upon an expedition into the hills, upon the main land, and, in this expedition, we shall need the aid of some person in whom we can confide. You are the only one we can trust. Whether we succeed or fail, the excitement which you now perceive in me will be equally allayed."

"I am anxious to oblige you in any way," I replied; "but do you mean to say that this infernal beetle has any connection with your expedition into the hills?"

"It has."

"Then, Legrand, I can become a party to no such absurd proceeding."

"I am sorry—very sorry—for we shall have to try it by ourselves."

"Try it by yourselves! The man is surely mad!—
but stay!—how long do you propose to be absent?"

"Probably all night. We shall start immediately, and
be back, at all events, by sunrise."

"And will you promise me, upon your honor, that
when this freak of yours is over, and the bug business
(good God!) settled to your satisfaction, you will then
return home and follow my advice implicitly, as that
of your physician?"

"Yes; I promise; and now let us be off, for we have
no time to lose."

With a heavy heart I accompanied my friend. We
started about four o'clock—Legrand, Jupiter, the dog,
and myself. Jupiter had with him the scythe and spades
—the whole of which he insisted upon carrying—more
through fear, it seemed to me, of trusting either of the
implements within reach of his master, than from any
excess of industry or complaisance. His demeanor was
dogged in the extreme, and "dat d—d bug" were the
sole words which escaped his lips during the journey.
For my own part, I had charge of a couple of dark
lanterns, while Legrand contented himself with the
scarabæus, which he carried attached to the end of a
bit of whip-cord; twirling it to and fro, with the air of
a conjuror, as he went. When I observed this last, plain
evidence of my friend's aberration of mind, I could
scarcely refrain from tears. I thought it best, however,
to humor his fancy, at least for the present, or until I
could adopt some more energetic measures with a
chance of success. In the mean time I endeavored, but
all in vain, to sound him in regard to the object of the
expedition. Having succeeded in inducing me to accompany him, he seemed unwilling to hold conversation upon any topic of minor importance, and to all my
questions vouchsafed no other reply than "we shall see!"

We crossed the creek at the head of the island by means of a skiff, and, ascending the high grounds on the shore of the main land, proceeded in a northwesterly direction, through a tract of country excessively wild and desolate, where no trace of a human footstep was to be seen. Legrand led the way with decision, pausing only for an instant, here and there, to consult what appeared to be certain landmarks of his own contrivance upon a former occasion.

In this manner we journeyed for about two hours, and the sun was just setting when we entered a region infinitely more dreary than any yet seen. It was a species of table land, near the summit of an almost inaccessible hill, densely wooded from base to pinnacle, and interspersed with huge crags that appeared to lie loosely upon the soil, and in many cases were prevented from precipitating themselves into the valleys below, merely by the support of the trees against which they reclined. Deep ravines, in various directions, gave an air of still sterner solemnity to the scene.

The natural platform to which we had clambered was thickly overgrown with brambles, through which we soon discovered that it would have been impossible to force our way but for the scythe; and Jupiter, by direction of his master, proceeded to clear for us a path to the foot of an enormously tall tulip-tree, which stood, with some eight or ten oaks, upon the level, and far surpassed them all, and all other trees which I had then ever seen, in the beauty of its foliage and form, in the wide spread of its branches, and in the general majesty of its appearance. When we reached this tree, Legrand turned to Jupiter, and asked him if he thought he could climb it. The old man seemed a little staggered by the question, and for some moments made no reply. At length he approached the huge trunk, walked slowly around it, and examined it with minute attention. When he had completed his scrutiny, he merely said,

"Yes, massa, Jup climb any tree he ebber see in he life."

"Then up with you as soon as possible, for it will soon be too dark to see what we are about."

"How far mus go up, massa?" inquired Jupiter.

"Get up the main trunk first, and then I will tell you which way to go—and here—stop! take this beetle with you."

"De bug, Massa Will!—de goole bug!" cried the negro, drawing back in dismay—"what for mus tote de bug way up de tree?—d—n if I do!"

"If you are afraid, Jup, a great big negro like you, to take hold of a harmless little dead beetle, why you can carry it up by this string—but, if you do not take it up with you in some way, I shall be under the necessity of breaking your head with this shovel."

"What de matter now, massa?" said Jup, evidently shamed into compliance; "always want for to raise fuss wid old nigger. Was only funnin any how. *Me* feered de bug! what I keer for de bug?" Here he took cautiously hold of the extreme end of the string, and, maintaining the insect as far from his person as circumstances would permit, prepared to ascend the tree.

In youth, the tulip-tree, or *Liriodendron Tulipiferum*, the most magnificent of American foresters, has a trunk peculiarly smooth, and often rises to a great height without lateral branches; but, in its riper age, the bark becomes gnarled and uneven, while many short limbs make their appearance on the stem. Thus the difficulty of ascension, in the present case, lay more in semblance than in reality. Embracing the huge cylinder, as closely as possible, with his arms and knees, seizing with his hands some projections, and resting his naked toes upon others, Jupiter, after one or two narrow escapes from falling, at length wriggled himself into the first great fork, and seemed to consider the whole business as virtually accomplished. The *risk* of the achievement was, in fact, now over, although the climber was some sixty or seventy feet from the ground.

"Which way mus go now, Massa Will?" he asked.

"Keep up the largest branch—the one on this side," said Legrand. The negro obeyed him promptly, and apparently with but little trouble, ascending higher and higher, until no glimpse of his squat figure could be obtained through the dense foliage which enveloped it. Presently his voice was heard in a sort of halloo.

"How much fudder is got for go?"

"How high up are you?" asked Legrand.

"Ebber so fur," replied the negro; "can see de sky fru de top ob de tree."

"Never mind the sky, but attend to what I say. Look down the trunk and count the limbs below you on this side. How many limbs have you passed?"

"One, two, tree, four, fibe—I done pass fibe big limb, massa, pon dis side."

"Then go one limb higher."

In a few minutes the voice was heard again, announcing that the seventh limb was attained.

"Now, Jup," cried Legrand, evidently much excited, "I want you to work your way out upon that limb as far as you can. If you see anything strange, let me know."

By this time what little doubt I might have entertained of my poor friend's insanity, was put finally at rest. I had no alternative but to conclude him stricken with lunacy, and I became seriously anxious about getting him home. While I was pondering upon what was best to be done, Jupiter's voice was again heard.

"Mos feerd for to ventur pon dis limb berry far—tis dead limb putty much all de way."

"Did you say it was a *dead* limb, Jupiter?" cried Legrand in a quavering voice.

"Yes, massa, him dead as de door-nail—done up for sartain—done departed dis here life."

"What in the name of heaven shall I do?" asked Legrand, seemingly in the greatest distress.

"Do!" said I, glad of an opportunity to interpose a word, "why come home and go to bed. Come now!— that's a fine fellow. It's getting late, and, besides, you remember your promise."

"Jupiter," cried he, without heeding me in the least, "do you hear me?"

"Yes, Massa Will, hear you ebber so plain."

"Try the wood well, then, with your knife, and see if you think it *very* rotten."

"Him rotten, massa, sure nuff," replied the negro in a few moments, "but not so berry rotten as mought be. Mought ventur out lettle way pon de limb by myself, dat's true."

"By yourself!—what do you mean?"

"Why I mean de bug. 'T is *berry* hebby bug. Spose I drop him down fuss, and den de limb won't break wid just de weight ob one nigger."

"You infernal scoundrel!" cried Legrand, apparently much relieved, "what do you mean by telling me such nonsense as that? As sure as you let that beetle fall!—I'll break your neck. Look here, Jupiter! do you hear me?"

"Yes, massa, need n't hollo at poor nigger dat style."

"Well! now listen!—if you will venture out on the limb as far as you think safe, and not let go the beetle, I'll make you a present of a silver dollar as soon as you get down."

"I'm gwine, Massa Will—deed I is," replied the negro very promptly—"mos out to the eend now."

"*Out to the end!*" here fairly screamed Legrand, "do you say you are out to the end of that limb?"

"Soon be to de eend, massa,—o-o-o-o-oh! Lor-gol-a-marcy! what *is* dis here pon de tree?"

"Well!" cried Legrand, highly delighted, "what is it?"

"Why taint noffin but a skull—somebody bin lef him head up de tree, and de crows done gobble ebery bit ob de meat off."

"A skull, you say!—very well!—how is it fastened to the limb?—what holds it on?"

"Sure nuff, massa; mus look. Why dis berry curious sarcumstance, pon my word—dare's a great big nail in de skull, what fastens ob it on to de tree."

"Well now, Jupiter, do exactly as I tell you—do you hear?"

"Yes, massa."

"Pay attention, then!—find the left eye of the skull."

"Hum! hoo! dat's good! why dar aint no eye lef at all."

"Curse your stupidity! do you know your right hand from your left?"

"Yes, I nose dat—nose all bout dat—tis my left hand what I chops de wood wid."

"To be sure! you are left-handed; and your left eye is on the same side as your left hand. Now, I suppose, you can find the left eye of the skull, or the place where the left eye has been. Have you found it?"

Here was a long pause. At length the negro asked,

"Is de left eye of de skull pon de same side as de lef hand of de skull, too?—cause de skull aint got not a bit ob a hand at all—nebber mind! I got de lef eye now—here the lef eye! what mus do wid it?"

"Let the beetle drop through it, as far as the string

will reach—but be careful and not let go your hold of the string."

"All dat done, Massa Will; mighty easy ting for to put de bug fru de hole—look out for him dar below!"

During this colloquy no portion of Jupiter's person could be seen; but the beetle, which he had suffered to descend, was now visible at the end of the string, and glistened, like a globe of burnished gold, in the last rays of the setting sun, some of which still faintly illumined the eminence upon which we stood. The *scarabæus* hung quite clear of any branches, and, if allowed to fall, would have fallen at our feet. Legrand immediately took the scythe, and cleared with it a circular space, three or four yards in diameter, just beneath the insect, and, having accomplished this, ordered Jupiter to let go the string and come down from the tree.

Driving a peg, with great nicety, into the ground, at the precise spot where the beetle fell, my friend now produced from his pocket a tape-measure. Fastening one end of this at that point of the trunk of the tree which was nearest the peg, he unrolled it till it reached the peg, and thence farther unrolled it, in the direction already established by the two points of the tree and the peg, for the distance of fifty feet—Jupiter clearing away the brambles with the scythe. At the spot thus attained a second peg was driven, and about this, as a centre, a rude circle, about four feet in diameter, described. Taking now a spade himself, and giving one to Jupiter and one to me, Legrand begged us to set about digging as quickly as possible.

To speak the truth, I had no especial relish for such amusement at any time, and, at that particular moment, would most willingly have declined it; for the night was coming on, and I felt much fatigued with the exercise already taken; but I saw no mode of escape, and was fearful of disturbing my poor friend's equanimity by a refusal. Could I have depended, indeed, upon Jupiter's aid, I would have had no hesitation in attempting to get the lunatic home by force; but I was too well assured of the old negro's disposition, to hope that he would assist me, under any circumstances, in a personal contest with his master. I made no doubt that the latter had been infected with some of the innumerable Southern superstitions about money buried, and that his phantasy had received confirmation by the finding of the *scarabæus*, or, perhaps, by Jupiter's obstinacy in maintaining it to be "a bug of real gold." A mind disposed to lunacy would readily be led away by such suggestions—especially if chiming in with favorite preconceived ideas—and then I called to mind the poor fellow's speech about the beetle's being "the index of his fortune." Upon the whole, I was sadly vexed and puzzled, but, at length, I concluded to make a virtue of necessity—to dig with a good will, and thus the sooner to convince the visionary, by ocular demonstration, of the fallacy of the opinions he entertained.

The lanterns having been lit, we all fell to work with a zeal worthy a more rational cause; and, as the glare fell upon our persons and implements, I could not help thinking how picturesque a group we composed, and how strange and suspicious our labors must have appeared to any interloper who, by chance, might have stumbled upon our whereabouts.

We dug very steadily for two hours. Little was said; and our chief embarrassment lay in the yelpings of the dog, who took exceeding interest in our proceedings. He, at length, became so obstreperous that we grew fearful of his giving the alarm to some stragglers in the vicinity; —or, rather, this was the apprehension of Legrand;—for myself, I should have rejoiced at any interruption which might have enabled me to get the wanderer home. The noise was, at length, very effectually silenced by Jupiter, who, getting out of the hole with a dogged air of deliberation, tied the brute's mouth up with one of his suspenders, and then returned, with a grave chuckle, to his task.

When the time mentioned had expired, we had reached a depth of five feet, and yet no signs of any treasure became manifest. A general pause ensued, and I began to hope that the farce was at an end. Legrand, however, although evidently much disconcerted, wiped his brow thoughtfully and recommenced. We had excavated the entire circle of four feet diameter, and now we slightly enlarged the limit, and went to the farther depth of two feet. Still nothing appeared. The gold-seeker, whom I sincerely pitied, at length clambered from the pit, with the bitterest disappointment imprinted upon every feature, and proceeded, slowly and reluctantly, to put on his coat, which he had thrown off at the beginning of his labor. In the mean time I made no remark. Jupiter, at a signal from his master, began to gather up his tools. This done, and the dog having been unmuzzled, we turned in profound silence towards home.

We had taken, perhaps, a dozen steps in this direction, when, with a loud oath, Legrand strode up to Jupiter, and seized him by the collar. The astonished negro opened his eyes and mouth to the fullest extent, let fall the spades, and fell upon his knees.

"You scoundrel," said Legrand, hissing out the syllables from between his clenched teeth—"you infernal black villain!—speak, I tell you!—answer me this instant, without prevarication!—which—which is your left eye?"

"Oh, my golly, Massa Will! aint dis here my lef eye

for sartain?" roared the terrified Jupiter, placing his hand upon his *right* organ of vision, and holding it there with a desperate pertinacity, as if in immediate dread of his master's attempt at a gouge.

"I thought so!—I knew it!—hurrah!" vociferated Legrand, letting the negro go, and executing a series of curvets and caracols, much to the astonishment of his valet, who, arising from his knees, looked, mutely, from his master to myself, and then from myself to his master.

"Come! we must go back," said the latter, "the game's not up yet;" and he again led the way to the tulip-tree.

"Jupiter," said he, when we reached its foot, "come here! was the skull nailed to the limb with the face outward, or with the face to the limb?"

"De face was out, massa, so dat de crows could get at de eyes good, widout any trouble."

"Well, then, was it this eye or that through which you let the beetle fall?"—here Legrand touched each of Jupiter's eyes.

"T was dis eye, massa—de lef eye—jis as you tell me," and here it was his right eye that the negro indicated.

"That will do—we must try it again."

Here my friend, about whose madness I now saw, or fancied that I saw, certain indications of method, removed the peg which marked the spot where the beetle fell, to a spot about three inches to the westward of its former position. Taking, now, the tape-measure from the nearest point of the trunk to the peg, as before, and continuing the extension in a straight line to the distance of fifty feet, a spot was indicated, removed, by several yards, from the point at which he had been digging.

Around the new position a circle, somewhat larger than in the former instance, was now described, and we again set to work with the spades. I was dreadfully

weary, but, scarcely understanding what had occasioned
the change in my thoughts, I felt no longer any great
aversion from the labor imposed. I had become most unaccountably interested—nay, even excited. Perhaps
there was something, amid all the extravagant demeanor
of Legrand—some air of forethought, or of deliberation, which impressed me. I dug eagerly, and now and
then caught myself actually looking, with something
that very much resembled expectation, for the fancied
treasure, the vision of which had demented my unfortunate companion. At a period when such vagaries of
thought most fully possessed me, and when we had been
at work perhaps an hour and a half, we were again
interrupted by the violent howlings of the dog. His uneasiness, in the first instance, had been, evidently, but
the result of playfulness or caprice, but he now assumed
a bitter and serious tone. Upon Jupiter's again attempting to muzzle him, he made furious resistance, and, leaping into the hole, tore up the mould frantically with his
claws. In a few seconds he had uncovered a mass of
human bones, forming two complete skeletons, intermingled with several buttons of metal, and what appeared to be the dust of decayed woollen. One or two
strokes of a spade upturned the blade of a large Spanish
knife, and, as we dug farther, three or four loose pieces
of gold and silver coin came to light.

At sight of these the joy of Jupiter could scarcely be
restrained, but the countenance of his master wore an
air of extreme disappointment. He urged us, however,
to continue our exertions, and the words were hardly uttered when I stumbled and fell forward, having caught
the toe of my boot in a large ring of iron that lay half
buried in the loose earth.

We now worked in earnest, and never did I pass ten
minutes of more intense excitement. During this interval

we had fairly unearthed an oblong chest of wood, which, from its perfect preservation, and wonderful hardness, had plainly been subjected to some mineralizing process—perhaps that of the Bi-chloride of Mercury. This box was three feet and a half long, three feet broad, and two and a half feet deep. It was firmly secured by bands of wrought iron, riveted, and forming a kind of trellis-work over the whole. On each side of the chest, near the top, were three rings of iron—six in all—by means of which a firm hold could be obtained by six persons. Our utmost united endeavors served only to disturb the coffer very slightly in its bed. We at once saw the impossibility of removing so great a weight. Luckily, the sole fastenings of the lid consisted of two sliding bolts. These we drew back—trembling and panting with anxiety. In an instant, a treasure of incalculable value lay gleaming before us. As the rays of the lanterns fell within the pit, there flashed upwards, from a confused heap of gold and of jewels, a glow and a glare that absolutely dazzled our eyes.

I shall not pretend to describe the feelings with which I gazed. Amazement was, of course, predominant. Legrand appeared exhausted with excitement, and spoke very few words. Jupiter's countenance wore, for some minutes, as deadly a pallor as it is possible, in the nature of things, for any negro's visage to assume. He seemed stupified—thunderstricken. Presently he fell upon his knees in the pit, and, burying his naked arms up to the elbows in gold, let them there remain, as if enjoying the luxury of a bath. At length, with a deep sigh, he exclaimed, as if in a soliloquy,

"And dis all cum ob de goole-bug! de putty goole-bug! de poor little goole-bug, what I boosed in dat sabage kind ob style! Aint you shamed ob yourself, nigger? —answer me dat!"

It became necessary, at last, that I should arouse both master and valet to the expediency of removing the treasure. It was growing late, and it behooved us to make exertion, that we might get every thing housed before daylight. It was difficult to say what should be done; and much time was spent in deliberation—so confused were the ideas of all. We, finally, lightened the box by removing two thirds of its contents, when we were enabled, with some trouble, to raise it from the hole. The articles taken out were deposited among the brambles, and the dog left to guard them, with strict orders from Jupiter neither, upon any pretence, to stir from the spot, nor to open his mouth until our return. We then hurriedly made for home with the chest; reaching the hut in safety, but after excessive toil, at one o'clock in the morning. Worn out as we were, it was not in human nature to do more just then. We rested until two, and had supper; starting for the hills immediately afterwards, armed with three stout sacks, which, by good luck, were upon the premises. A little before four we arrived at the pit, divided the remainder of the booty, as equally as might be, among us, and, leaving the holes unfilled, again set out for the hut, at which, for the second time, we deposited our golden burthens, just as the first streaks of the dawn gleamed from over the tree-tops in the East.

We were now thoroughly broken down; but the intense excitement of the time denied us repose. After an unquiet slumber of some three or four hours' duration, we arose, as if by preconcert, to make examination of our treasure.

The chest had been full to the brim, and we spent the whole day, and the greater part of the next night, in a scrutiny of its contents. There had been nothing like order or arrangement. Every thing had been heaped in promiscuously. Having assorted all with care, we found ourselves possessed of even vaster wealth than we had at first supposed. In coin there was rather more than four hundred and fifty thousand dollars—estimating the value of the pieces, as accurately as we could, by the tables of the period. There was not a particle of silver. All was gold of antique date and of great variety— French, Spanish, and German money, with a few English guineas, and some counters, of which we had never seen specimens before. There were several very large and heavy coins, so worn that we could make nothing of their inscriptions. There was no American money. The value of the jewels we found more difficulty in estimating. There were diamonds—some of them exceedingly large and fine—a hundred and ten in all, and not one of them small; eighteen rubies of remarkable brilliancy;— three hundred and ten emeralds, all very beautiful; and twenty-one sapphires, with an opal. These stones had all been broken from their settings and thrown loose in the chest. The settings themselves, which we picked out from among the other gold, appeared to have been beaten up with hammers, as if to prevent identification. Besides all this, there was a vast quantity of solid gold ornaments;—nearly two hundred massive finger and ear rings;—rich chains—thirty of these, if I remember;— eighty-three very large and heavy crucifixes;—five gold censers of great value;—a prodigious golden punch-bowl, ornamented with richly chased vine-leaves and Bacchanalian figures; with two sword-handles exquisitely embossed, and many other smaller articles which I cannot recollect. The weight of these valuables exceeded three hundred and fifty pounds avoirdupois; and in this estimate I have not included one hundred and ninety-seven superb gold watches; three of the number being worth each five hundred dollars, if one. Many of them were very old, and as time keepers valueless, the works having suffered, more or less, from corrosion—but all were richly jewelled and in cases of great worth. We estimated the entire contents of the chest, that night, at a million·and a half of dollars; and, upon the subsequent disposal of the trinkets and jewels (a few being retained for our own use), it was found that we had greatly undervalued the treasure.

When, at length, we had concluded our examination, and the intense excitement of the time had, in some measure, subsided, Legrand, who saw that I was dying with impatience for a solution of this most extraordinary riddle, entered into a full detail of all the circumstances connected with it.

"You remember," said he, "the night when I handed you the rough sketch I had made of the *scarabæus*. You recollect also, that I became quite vexed at you for insisting that my drawing resembled a death's-head. When you first made this assertion I thought you were jesting; but afterwards I called to mind the peculiar spots on the back of the insect, and admitted to myself that your remark had some little foundation in fact. Still, the sneer at my graphic powers irritated me—for I am considered a good artist—and, therefore, when you handed me the scrap of parchment, I was about to crumple it up and throw it angrily into the fire."

"The scrap of paper, you mean," said I.

"No; it had much of the appearance of paper, and at first I supposed it to be such, but when I came to draw upon it, I discovered it, at once, to be a piece of very thin parchment. It was quite dirty, you remember. Well, as I was in the very act of crumpling it up, my glance fell upon the sketch at which you had been looking, and you may imagine my astonishment when I perceived, in fact, the figure of a death's-head just where, it seemed to me, I had made the drawing of the beetle. For a moment I was too much amazed to think with accuracy. I knew that my design was very different in detail from this—although there was a certain similarity in general outline. Presently I took a candle, and seating myself at the other end of the room, proceeded to scrutinize the parchment more closely. Upon turning it over, I saw my own sketch upon the reverse, just as I had made it. My first idea, now, was mere surprise at the really remarkable similarity of outline—at the singular coincidence involved in the fact that, unknown to me, there should have been a skull upon the other side of the parchment, immediately beneath my figure of the *scarabæus,* and that this skull, not only in outline, but in size, should so closely resemble my drawing. I say the singularity of this coincidence absolutely stupefied me for a time. This is the usual effect of such coincidences. The mind struggles to establish a connection—a sequence of cause and effect—and, being unable to do so, suffers a species of temporary paralysis. But, when I recovered from this stupor, there dawned upon me gradually a conviction which startled me even far more than the coincidence. I began distinctly, positively, to remember that there had been *no* drawing on the parchment when I made my sketch of the *scarabæus.* I became perfectly certain of this; for I recollected turning up first one side and then the other, in search of the cleanest spot. Had the skull been then there, of course I could not have failed to notice it. Here was indeed a mystery which I felt it impossible to explain; but, even at that early moment, there seemed to glimmer, faintly, within the most remote and secret chambers of my intellect, a glow-worm-like conception of that truth which last night's adventure brought to so magnificent a demonstration. I arose at once, and putting the parchment securely away, dismissed all farther reflection until I should be alone.

"When you had gone, and when Jupiter was fast asleep, I betook myself to a more methodical investigation of the affair. In the first place I considered the manner in which the parchment had come into my possession. The spot where we discovered the *scarabæus* was on the coast of the main land, about a mile eastward of the island, and but a short distance above high water mark. Upon my taking hold of it, it gave me a sharp bite, which caused me to let it drop. Jupiter, with his accustomed caution, before seizing the insect, which had flown towards him, looked about him for a leaf, or something of that nature, by which to take hold of it. It was at this moment that his eyes, and mine also, fell upon the scrap of parchment, which I then supposed to be paper. It was lying half buried in the sand, a corner sticking up. Near the spot where we found it, I observed the remnants of the hull of what appeared to have been a ship's long boat. The wreck seemed to have been there for a very great while; for the resemblance to boat timbers could scarcely be traced.

"Well, Jupiter picked up the parchment, wrapped the beetle in it, and gave it to me. Soon afterwards we turned to go home, and on the way met Lieutenant G——. I showed him the insect, and he begged me to let him take it to the fort. On my consenting, he thrust it forthwith into his waistcoat pocket, without the parchment in which it had been wrapped, and which I had continued to hold in my hand during his inspection. Perhaps he dreaded my changing my mind, and 'hought it best to make sure of the prize at once—you know how enthusiastic he is on all subjects connected with Natural History. At the same time, without being conscious of it, I must have deposited the parchment in my own pocket.

"You remember that when I went to the table, for the purpose of making a sketch of the beetle, I found no paper where it was usually kept. I looked in the drawer, and found none there. I searched my pockets, hoping to find an old letter—and then my hand fell upon the parchment. I thus detail the precise mode in which it came into my possession; for the circumstances impressed me with peculiar force.

"No doubt you will think me fanciful—but I had already established a kind of *connection*. I had put together two links of a great chain. There was a boat lying on a sea-coast, and not far from the boat was a parchment—*not a paper*—with a skull depicted on it. You will, of course, ask 'where is the connection?' I reply that the skull, or death's-head, is the well-known emblem of the pirate. The flag of the death's-head is hoisted in all engagements.

"I have said that the scrap was parchment, and not paper. Parchment is durable—almost imperishable. Matters of little moment are rarely consigned to parchment; since, for the mere ordinary purposes of drawing or writing, it is not nearly so well adapted as paper. This reflection suggested some meaning—some relevancy—in the death's-head. I did not fail to observe, also, the *form* of the parchment. Although one of its corners had been, by some accident, destroyed, it could be seen that the original form was oblong. It was just such a slip, indeed, as might have been chosen for a memorandum—for a record of something to be long remembered and carefully preserved."

"But," I interposed, "you say that the skull was *not* upon the parchment when you made the drawing of the beetle. How then do you trace any connection between the boat and the skull—since this latter, according to your own admission, must have been designed (God only knows how or by whom) at some period subsequent to your sketching the *scarabæus?*"

"Ah, hereupon turns the whole mystery; although the secret, at this point, I had comparatively little difficulty in solving. My steps were sure, and could afford but a single result. I reasoned, for example, thus: When I drew the *scarabæus*, there was no skull apparent on the parchment. When I had completed the drawing, I gave it to you, and observed you narrowly until you returned it. *You*, therefore, did not design the skull, and no one else was present to do it. Then it was not done by human agency. And nevertheless it was done.

"At this stage of my reflections I endeavored to remember, and *did* remember, with entire distinctness, every incident which occurred about the period in question. The weather was chilly (oh rare and happy accident!), and a fire was blazing on the hearth. I was heated with exercise and sat near the table. You, however, had drawn a chair close to the chimney. Just as I placed the parchment in your hand, and as you were in the act of inspecting it, Wolf, the Newfoundland, entered, and leaped upon your shoulders. With your left hand you caressed him and kept him off, while your right, holding the parchment, was permitted to fall listlessly between your knees, and in close proximity to the fire. At one moment I thought the blaze had caught it, and was about to caution you, but, before I could speak, you had withdrawn it, and were engaged in its examination. When I considered all these particulars, I doubted not for a moment that *heat* had been the agent in bringing to light, on the parchment, the skull which I saw designed on it. You are well aware that chemical preparations exist, and have existed time out of mind, by means of which it is possible to write on either paper or vellum,

so that the characters shall become visible only when
subjected to the action of fire. Zaffre, digested in *aqua
regia*, and diluted with four times its weight of water, is
sometimes employed; a green tint results. The regulus of
cobalt, dissolved in spirit of nitre, gives a red. These
colors disappear at longer or shorter intervals after the
material written on cools, but again become apparent
upon the re-application of heat.

"I now scrutinized the death's-head with care. Its
outer edges—the edges of the drawing nearest the edge
of the vellum—were far more *distinct* than the others. It
was clear that the action of the caloric had been imperfect or unequal. I immediately kindled a fire, and subjected every portion of the parchment to a glowing heat.
At first, the only effect was the strengthening of the
faint lines in the skull; but, on persevering in the experiment, there became visible, at the corner of the slip,
diagonally opposite to the spot in which the death's-head
was delineated, the figure of what I at first supposed to
be a goat. A closer scrutiny, however, satisfied me that it
was intended for a kid."

"Ha! ha!" said I, "to be sure I have no right to laugh
at you—a million and a half of money is too serious a
matter for mirth—but you are not about to establish a
third link in your chain—you will not find any especial
connection between your pirates and a goat—pirates,
you know, have nothing to do with goats; they appertain
to the farming interest."

"But I have just said that the figure was *not* that of a
goat."

"Well, a kid then—pretty much the same thing."

"Pretty much, but not altogether," said Legrand.
"You may have heard of one *Captain* Kidd. I at once
looked on the figure of the animal as a kind of punning
or hieroglyphical signature. I say signature; because its

position on the vellum suggested this idea. The death's-
head at the corner diagonally opposite, had, in the same
manner, the air of a stamp, or seal. But I was sorely put
out by the absence of all else—of the body to my imagined instrument—of the text for my context."

"I presume you expected to find a letter between the
stamp and the signature."

"Something of that kind. The fact is, I felt irresistibly
impressed with a presentiment of some vast good fortune impending. I can scarcely say why. Perhaps, after
all, it was rather a desire than an actual belief;—but do
you know that Jupiter's silly words, about the bug being
of solid gold, had a remarkable effect on my fancy? And
then the series of accidents and coincidences—these
were so *very* extraordinary. Do you observe how mere
an accident it was that these events should have occurred on the *sole* day of all the year in which it has
been, or may be, sufficiently cool for fire, and that without the fire, or without the intervention of the dog at the
precise moment in which he appeared, I should never
have become aware of the death's-head, and so never
the possessor of the treasure?"

"But proceed—I am all impatience."

"Well; you have heard, of course, the many stories
current—the thousand vague rumors afloat about money
buried, somewhere on the Atlantic coast, by Kidd and
his associates. These rumors must have had some foundation in fact. And that the rumors have existed so long
and so continuously could have resulted, it appeared to
me, only from the circumstance of the buried treasure
still *remaining* entombed. Had Kidd concealed his plun-
der for a time, and afterwards reclaimed it, the rumors
would scarcely have reached us in their present unvarying form. You will observe that the stories told are all

about money-seekers, not about money-finders. Had the
pirate recovered his money, there the affair would have
dropped. It seemed to me that some accident—say the
loss of a memorandum indicating its locality—had deprived him of the means of recovering it; and that this
accident had become known to his followers, who otherwise might never have heard that treasure had been
concealed at all, and who, busying themselves in vain,
because unguided attempts, to regain it, had given first
birth, and then universal currency, to the reports which
are now so common. Have you ever heard of any important treasure being unearthed along the coast?"

"Never."

"But that Kidd's accumulations were immense, is well
known. I took it for granted, therefore, that the earth
still held them; and you will scarcely be surprised when
I tell you that I felt a hope, nearly amounting to certainty, that the parchment so strangely found, involved a
lost record of the place of deposit."

"But how did you proceed?"

"I held the vellum again to the fire, after increasing
the heat; but nothing appeared. I now thought it possible that the coating of dirt might have something to do
with the failure; so I carefully rinsed the parchment by
pouring warm water over it, and, having done this, I
placed it in a tin pan, with the skull downwards, and
put the pan upon a furnace of lighted charcoal. In a few
minutes, the pan having become thoroughly heated, I
removed the slip, and, to my inexpressible joy, found it
spotted, in several places, with what appeared to be figures arranged in lines. Again I placed it in the pan, and
suffered it to remain another minute. On taking it off,
the whole was just as you see it now."

Here Legrand, having re-heated the parchment, sub-

mitted it to my inspection. The following characters
were rudely traced, in a red tint, between the death's-
head and the goat:

53‡‡†305))6*;4826)4‡.)4‡);806*;48†8¶60))85;]8*
:‡*8†83(88)5*†;46(;88*96*?;8)*‡(;485);5*†2:*‡(;4
956*2(5*—4)8¶8*;4069285);)6†8)4‡‡;1(‡9;48081;8:
8‡1;48†85;4)485†528806*81(‡9;48;(88;4(‡?34;48)4‡
;161;:188;‡?;

"But," said I, returning him the slip, "I am as much in
the dark as ever. Were all the jewels of Golconda awaiting me on my solution of this enigma, I am quite sure
that I should be unable to earn them."

"And yet," said Legrand, "the solution is by no means
so difficult as you might be led to imagine from the first
hasty inspection of the characters. These characters, as
any one might readily guess, form a cipher—that is to
say, they convey a meaning; but then, from what is
known of Kidd, I could not suppose him capable of
constructing any of the more abstruse cryptographs. I
made up my mind, at once, that this was of a simple
species—such, however, as would appear, to the crude
intellect of the sailor, absolutely insoluble without the
key."

"And you really solved it?"

"Readily; I have solved others of an abstruseness ten
thousand times greater. Circumstances, and a certain
bias of mind, have led me to take interest in such riddles, and it may well be doubted whether human ingenuity can construct an enigma of the kind which human ingenuity may not, by proper application, resolve.
In fact, having once established connected and legible
characters, I scarcely gave a thought to the mere difficulty of developing their import.

"In the present case—indeed in all cases of secret writing—the first question regards the *language* of the cipher; for the principles of solution, so far, especially, as the more simple ciphers are concerned, depend on, and are varied by, the genius of the particular idiom. In general, there is no alternative but experiment (directed by probabilities) of every tongue known to him who attempts the solution, until the true one be attained. But, with the cipher now before us, all difficulty is removed by the signature. The pun on the word 'Kidd' is appreciable in no other language than the English. But for this consideration I should have begun my attempts with the Spanish and French, as the tongues in which a secret of this kind would most naturally have been written by a pirate of the Spanish main. As it was, I assumed the cryptograph to be English.

"You observe there are no divisions between the words. Had there been divisions, the task would have been comparatively easy. In such case I should have commenced with a collation and analysis of the shorter words, and, had a word of a single letter occurred, as is most likely, (*a* or I, for example,) I should have considered the solution as assured. But, there being no division, my first step was to ascertain the predominant letters, as well as the least frequent. Counting all, I constructed a table, thus:

Of the character 8 there are 33.
          ;   "   26.
          4   "   19.
    ‡)   "   16.
          ❋   "   13.
          5   "   12.
          6   "   11.
    † 1   "   8.

Of the character 0 there are 6.

$$9\ 2 \qquad ``\qquad 5.$$
$$:\ 3 \qquad ``\qquad 4.$$
$$?\qquad ``\qquad 3.$$
$$\P \qquad ``\qquad 2.$$
$$]\ - \qquad ``$$

"Now, in the English, the letter which most frequently occurs is *e*. Afterwards, the succession runs thus: *a o i d h n r s t u y c f g l m w b k p q x z. E* however predominates so remarkably that an individual sentence of any length is rarely seen, in which it is not the prevailing character.

"Here, then, we have, in the very beginning, the groundwork for something more than a mere guess. The general use which may be made of the table is obvious —but, in this particular cipher, we shall only very partially require its aid. As our predominant character is 8, we will commence by assuming it as the *e* of the natural alphabet. To verify the supposition, let us observe if the 8 be seen often in couples—for *e* is doubled with great frequency in English—in such words, for example, as 'meet,' 'fleet,' 'speed,' 'seen,' 'been,' 'agree,' &c. In the present instance we see it doubled no less than five times, although the cryptograph is brief.

"Let us assume 8, then, as *e*. Now, of all *words* in the language, 'the' is most usual; let us see, therefore, whether there are not repetitions of any three characters, in the same order of collocation, the last of them being 8. If we discover repetitions of such letters, so arranged, they will most probably represent the word 'the.' On inspection, we find no less than seven such arrangements, the characters being ;48. We may, therefore, assume that the semicolon represents *t*, that 4 represents *h*, and

that 8 represents *e*—the last being now well confirmed.
Thus a great step has been taken.

"But, having established a single word, we are enabled to establish a vastly important point; that is to
say, several commencements and terminations of other
words. Let us refer, for example, to the last instance but
one, in which the combination ;48 occurs—not far from
the end of the cipher. We know that the semicolon immediately ensuing is the commencement of a word, and,
of the six characters succeeding this 'the,' we are cognizant of no less than five. Let us set these characters
down, thus, by the letters we know them to represent,
leaving a space for the unknown—

t eeth.

"Here we are enabled, at once, to discard the *'th,'* as
forming no portion of the word commencing with the
first *t;* since, by experiment of the entire alphabet for a
letter adapted to the vacancy we perceive that no word
can be formed of which this *th* can be a part. We are
thus narrowed into

t ee,

and, going through the alphabet, if necessary, as before,
we arrive at the word 'tree,' as the sole possible reading.
We thus gain another letter, *r*, represented by (, with
the words 'the tree' in juxtaposition.

"Looking beyond these words, for a short distance, we
again see the combination ;48, and employ it by way of
termination to what immediately precedes. We have
thus this arrangement:

the tree ;4(‡?34 the,

or, substituting the natural letters, where known, it
reads thus:

the tree thr‡?3h the.

"Now, if, in place of the unknown characters, we
leave blank spaces, or substitute dots, we read thus:

the tree thr...h the,

when the word *'through'* makes itself evident at once. But this discovery gives us three new letters, *o, u* and *g,* represented by ‡ ? and 3.

"Looking now, narrowly, through the cipher for combinations of known characters, we find, not very far from the beginning, this arrangement,

83(88, or egree,

which, plainly, is the conclusion of the word 'degree,' and gives us another letter, *d,* represented by †.

"Four letters beyond the word 'degree,' we perceive the combination

;46(;88*.

"Translating the known characters, and representing the unknown by dots, as before, we read thus:

th.rtee.

an arrangement immediately suggestive of the word 'thirteen,' and again furnishing us with two new characters, *i* and *n,* represented by 6 and *

"Referring, now, to the beginning of the cryptograph, we find the combination,

53‡‡†.

"Translating, as before, we obtain

.good,

which assures us that the first letter is *A,* and that the first two words are 'A good.'

"To avoid confusion, it is now time that we arrange our key, as far as discovered, in a tabular form. It will stand thus:

5	represents	a
†	"	d
8	"	e
3	"	g
4	"	h
6	"	i

* represents n
‡   "   o
("   r
;   "   t

"We have, therefore, no less than ten of the most important letters represented, and it will be unnecessary to proceed with the details of the solution. I have said enough to convince you that ciphers of this nature are readily soluble, and to give you some insight into the *rationale* of their development. But be assured that the specimen before us appertains to the very simplest species of cryptograph. It now only remains to give you the full translation of the characters upon the parchment, as unriddled. Here it is:

"*A good glass in the bishop's hostel in the devil's seat twenty-one degrees and thirteen minutes northeast and by north main branch seventh limb east side shoot from the left eye of the death's-head a bee line from the tree through the shot fifty feet out.*"

"But," said I, "the enigma seems still in as bad a condition as ever. How is it possible to extort a meaning from all this jargon about 'devil's seats,' 'death's-heads,' and 'bishop's hostels?'"

"I confess," replied Legrand, "that the matter still wears a serious aspect, when regarded with a casual glance. My first endeavor was to divide the sentence into the natural division intended by the cryptographist."

"You mean, to punctuate it?"

"Something of that kind."

"But how was it possible to effect this?"

"I reflected that it had been a *point* with the writer to run his words together without division, so as to increase the difficulty of solution. Now, a not over-acute man, in pursuing such an object, would be nearly certain to overdo the matter. When, in the course of his composition, he arrived at a break in his subject which would naturally require a pause, or a point, he would be exceedingly apt to run his characters, at this place, more than usually close together. If you will observe the MS., in the present instance, you will easily detect five such cases of unusual crowding. Acting on this hint, I made the division thus:

"A good glass in the Bishop's hostel in the Devil's seat —twenty-one degrees and thirteen minutes—northeast and by north—main branch seventh limb east side— shoot from the left eye of the death's-head—a bee-line from the tree through the shot fifty feet out."

"Even this division," said I, "leaves me still in the dark."

"It left me also in the dark," replied Legrand, "for a few days; during which I made diligent inquiry, in the neighborhood of Sullivan's Island, for any building which went by the name of the 'Bishop's Hotel;' for, of course, I dropped the obsolete word 'hostel.' Gaining no information on the subject, I was on the point of extending my sphere of search, and proceeding in a more systematic manner, when, one morning, it entered into my head, quite suddenly, that this 'Bishop's Hostel' might have some reference to an old family, of the name of Bessop, which, time out of mind, had held possession of an ancient manor-house, about four miles to the northward of the island. I accordingly went over to the plantation, and reinstituted my inquiries among the older negroes of the place. At length one of the most aged of the women said that she had heard of such a place as *Bessop's Castle,* and thought that she could guide me to it, but that it was not a castle, nor a tavern, but a high rock.

"I offered to pay her well for her trouble, and, after some demur, she consented to accompany me to the spot. We found it without much difficulty, when, dismissing her, I proceeded to examine the place. The 'castle' consisted of an irregular assemblage of cliffs and rocks—one of the latter being quite remarkable for its height as well as for its insulated and artificial appearance. I clambered to its apex, and then felt much at a loss as to what should be next done.

"While I was busied in reflection, my eyes fell upon a narrow ledge in the eastern face of the rock, perhaps a yard below the summit on which I stood. This ledge projected about eighteen inches, and was not more than a foot wide, while a niche in the cliff just above it, gave it a rude resemblance to one of the hollow-backed chairs used by our ancestors. I made no doubt that here was the 'Devil's seat' alluded to in the MS., and now I seemed to grasp the full secret of the riddle.

"The 'good glass,' I knew, could have reference to nothing but a telescope; for the word 'glass' is rarely employed in any other sense by seamen. Now here, I at once saw, was a telescope to be used, and a definite point of view, *admitting no variation,* from which to use it. Nor did I hesitate to believe that the phrases, 'twenty-one degrees and thirteen minutes,' and 'northeast and by north,' were intended as directions for the levelling of the glass. Greatly excited by these discoveries, I hurried home, procured a telescope, and returned to the rock.

"I let myself down to the ledge, and found that it was impossible to retain a seat on it unless in one particular position. This fact confirmed my preconceived idea. I proceeded to use the glass. Of course, the 'twenty-one degrees and thirteen minutes' could allude to nothing but elevation above the visible horizon, since the horizontal direction was clearly indicated by the words, 'northeast and by north.' This latter direction I at once established by means of a pocket-compass; then, pointing the glass as nearly at an angle of twenty-one degrees of elevation as I could do it by guess, I moved it cautiously up or down, until my attention was arrested by a circular rift or opening in the foliage of a large tree that overtopped its fellows in the distance. In the centre of this rift I perceived a white spot, but could not, at first, distinguish what it was. Adjusting the focus of the telescope, I again looked, and now made it out to be a human skull.

"On this discovery I was so sanguine as to consider the enigma solved; for the phrase 'main branch, seventh limb, east side,' could refer only to the position of the skull on the tree, while 'shoot from the left eye of the death's-head' admitted, also, of but one interpretation, in regard to a search for buried treasure. I perceived that the design was to drop a bullet from the left eye of the skull, and that a bee-line, or, in other words, a straight line, drawn from the nearest point of the trunk through 'the shot,' (or the spot where the bullet fell,) and thence extended to a distance of fifty feet, would indicate a definite point—and beneath this point I thought it at least *possible* that a deposit of value lay concealed."

"All this," I said, "is exceedingly clear, and, although ingenious, still simple and explicit. When you left the Bishop's Hotel, what then?"

"Why, having carefully taken the bearings of the tree, I turned homewards. The instant that I left 'the devil's seat,' however, the circular rift vanished; nor could I get a glimpse of it afterwards, turn as I would. What seems to me the chief ingenuity in this whole business, is the fact (for repeated experiment has convinced me it is a

fact) that the circular opening in question is visible from
no other attainable point of view than that afforded by
the narrow ledge on the face of the rock.

"In this expedition to the 'Bishop's Hotel' I had been
attended by Jupiter, who had, no doubt, observed, for
some weeks past, the abstraction of my demeanor, and
took especial care not to leave me alone. But, on the
next day, getting up very early, I contrived to give him
the slip, and went into the hills in search of the tree.
After much toil I found it. When I came home at night
my valet proposed to give me a flogging. With the rest
of the adventure I believe you are as well acquainted as
myself."

"I suppose," said I, "you missed the spot, in the first
attempt at digging, through Jupiter's stupidity in letting
the bug fall through the right instead of through the left
eye of the skull."

"Precisely. This mistake made a difference of about
two inches and a half in the 'shot'—that is to say, in the
position of the peg nearest the tree; and had the treasure
been *beneath* the 'shot,' the error would have been of
little moment; but 'the shot,' together with the nearest
point of the tree, were merely two points for the establishment of a line of direction; of course the error, however trivial in the beginning, increased as we proceeded
with the line, and by the time we had gone fifty feet,
threw us quite off the scent. But for my deep-seated
convictions that treasure was here somewhere actually
buried, we might have had all our labor in vain."

"I presume the fancy of *the skull*, of letting fall a bullet through the skull's eye—was suggested to Kidd by
the piratical flag. No doubt he felt a kind of poetical
consistency in recovering his money through this ominous insignium."

"Perhaps so; still I cannot help thinking that common-sense had quite as much to do with the matter as poetical consistency. To be visible from the Devil's seat, it was necessary that the object, if small, should be white; and there is nothing like your human skull for retaining and even increasing its whiteness under exposure to all vicissitudes of weather."

"But your grandiloquence, and your conduct in swinging the beetle—how excessively odd! I was sure you were mad. And why did you insist on letting fall the bug, instead of a bullet, from the skull?"

"Why, to be frank, I felt somewhat annoyed by your evident suspicions touching my sanity, and so resolved to punish you quietly, in my own way, by a little bit of sober mystification. For this reason I swung the beetle, and for this reason I let it fall from the tree. An observation of yours about its great weight suggested the latter idea."

"Yes, I perceive; and now there is only one point which puzzles me. What are we to make of the skeletons found in the hole?"

"That is a question I am no more able to answer than yourself. There seems, however, only one plausible way of accounting for them—and yet it is dreadful to believe in such atrocity as my suggestion would imply. It is clear that Kidd—if Kidd indeed secreted this treasure, which I doubt not—it is clear that he must have had assistance in the labor. But, the worst of this labor concluded, he may have thought it expedient to remove all participants in his secret. Perhaps a couple of blows with a mattock were sufficient, while his coadjutors were busy in the pit; perhaps it required a dozen—who shall tell?"

ARTICLES

"Maelzel's Chess-Player" is not only a brilliant and interesting bit of deductive reasoning, but is also one of the more significant of the Poe documents. Here is the work that prefigured the Dupin stories, and here the intellectual and analytical part of Poe's versatile mind is seen at its best.

Johann Nepomuk Maelzel, the German showman who exhibited the famous Automaton Chess-Player, was an inventor of musical mechanisms. He devised elaborate musical instruments like the orchestrion and the panharmonicon, which delighted the curiosity-seeking audiences of his day. The metronome has popularly been attributed to him, but its principle was known long before his time, and the device which was named "Maelzel's metronome" was stolen by him from a Dutch inventor. Nevertheless he must have been a remarkable person; he was a friend of Beethoven and collaborated with him in giving several concerts in which his musical gadgets played part of the great symphonic scores. He died in 1838, after which his Chess-Player passed into the possession of a Dr. J. K. Mitchell of Philadelphia. It was unfortunately destroyed in a fire in 1854.

Poe's article on Cryptography is another product of that part of him which worshiped reason and logic. It is evidence, too, of his constant need to demonstrate his own superiority. To the present-day cipher expert his articles will seem elementary, but in Poe's time it was a contribution to a subject which few Americans had tried to investigate.

MAELZEL'S CHESS-PLAYER

(*The Southern Literary Messenger*, April, 1836.)

PERHAPS no exhibition of the kind has ever elicited
so general attention as the Chess-Player of Maelzel.
Wherever seen it has been an object of intense curiosity,
to all persons who think. Yet the question of its *modus
operandi* is still undetermined. Nothing has been written
on this topic which can be considered as decisive—and
accordingly we find everywhere men of mechanical
genius, of great general acuteness, and discriminative
understanding, who make no scruple in pronouncing the
Automaton a *pure machine*, unconnected with human
agency in its movements, and consequently, beyond all
comparison, the most astonishing of the inventions of
mankind. And such it would undoubtedly be, were they
right in their supposition. Assuming this hypothesis, it
would be grossly absurd to compare with the Chess-
Player, any similar thing of either modern or ancient
days. Yet there have been many and wonderful automata. In Brewster's *Letters on Natural Magic*, we
have an account of the most remarkable. Among these
may be mentioned, as having beyond doubt existed,
firstly, the coach invented by M. Camus for the amusement of Louis XIV. when a child. A table, about four
feet square, was introduced into the room appropriated
for the exhibition. Upon this table was placed a carriage
six inches in length, made of wood, and drawn by two
horses of the same material. One window being down, a
lady was seen on the back seat. A coachman held the
reins on the box, and a footman and page were in their
places behind. M. Camus now touched a spring; whereupon the coachman smacked his whip, and the horses
proceeded in a natural manner, along the edge of the

table, drawing after them the carriage. Having gone as far as possible in this direction, a sudden turn was made to the left, and the vehicle was driven at right angles to its former course, and still closely along the edge of the table. In this way the coach proceeded until it arrived opposite the chair of the young prince. It then stopped, the page descended and opened the door, the lady alighted, and presented a petition to her sovereign. She then re-entered. The page put up the steps, closed the door, and resumed his station. The coachman whipped his horses, and the carriage was driven back to its original position.

The magician of M. Maillardet is also worthy of notice. We copy the following account of it from the *Letters* before mentioned of Dr. B., who derived his information principally from the Edinburgh *Encyclopædia*.

"One of the most popular pieces of mechanism which we have seen, is the Magician constructed by M. Maillardet, for the purpose of answering certain given questions. A figure, dressed like a magician, appears seated at the bottom of a wall, holding a wand in one hand, and a book in the other. A number of questions, ready prepared, are inscribed on oval medallions, and the spectator takes any of these he chooses, and to which he wishes an answer, and having placed it in a drawer ready to receive it, the drawer shuts with a spring till the answer is returned. The magician then arises from his seat, bows his head, describes circles with his wand, and consulting the book as if in deep thought, he lifts it towards his face. Having thus appeared to ponder over the proposed question, he raises his wand, and striking with it the wall above his head, two folding doors fly open, and display an appropriate answer to the question. The doors again close, the magician resumes his original position, and the drawer opens to return the medallion. There are twenty of these medallions, all containing different questions, to which the magician returns the most suitable and striking answers. The medallions are thin plates of brass, of an elliptical form, exactly resembling each other. Some of the medallions have a question inscribed on each side, both of which the magician answers in succession. If the drawer is shut without a medallion being put into it, the magician rises, consults his book, shakes his head, and resumes his seat. The folding doors remain shut, and the drawer is returned empty. If two medallions are put into the drawer together, an answer is returned only to the lower one. When the machinery is wound up, the movements continue about an hour, during which time about fifty questions may be answered. The inventor stated that the means by which the different medallions acted upon the machinery, so as to produce the proper answers to the questions which they contained, were extremely simple."

The duck of Vaucanson was still more remarkable. It was of the size of life, and so perfect an imitation of the living animal that all the spectators were deceived. It executed, says Brewster, all the natural movements and gestures, it ate and drank with avidity, performed all the quick motions of the head and throat which are peculiar to the duck, and like it muddled the water which it drank with its bill. It produced also the sound of quacking in the most natural manner. In the anatomical structure the artists exhibited the highest skill. Every bone in the real duck had its representative in the automaton, and its wings were anatomically exact. Every cavity, apophysis, and curvature was imitated, and each bone executed its proper movements. When corn was thrown down before it, the duck stretched out its neck to pick it up, swallowed, and digested it.[1]

But if these machines were ingenious, what shall we think of the calculating machine of Mr. Babbage? What shall we think of an engine of wood and metal which can not only compute astronomical and navigation tables to any given extent, but render the exactitude of its operations mathematically certain through its power of correcting its possible errors? What shall we think of a machine which can not only accomplish all this, but actually print off its elaborate results, when obtained, without the slightest intervention of the intellect of man? It will, perhaps, be said in reply, that a machine such as we have described is altogether above comparison with the Chess-Player of Maelzel. By no means—it is altogether beneath it—that is to say provided we assume (what should never for a moment be assumed) that the Chess-Player is a *pure machine*, and performs its operations without any immediate human agency. Arithmetical or algebraical calculations are, from their very nature, fixed and determinate. Certain *data* being given, certain results necessarily and inevitably follow. These results have dependence upon nothing, and are influenced by nothing but the *data* originally given. And the question to be solved proceeds, or should proceed, to its final determination, by a succession of unerring steps liable to no change, and subject to no modification. This being the case, we can without difficulty conceive the *possibility* of so arranging a piece of mechanism, that upon starting it in accordance with the *data* of the question to be solved, it should continue its movements

[1] *Under the head* Androides *in the* Edinburgh *Encyclopædia may be found a full account of the principal automata of ancient and modern times.* [E.A.P.]

regularly, progressively, and undeviatingly towards the required solution, since these movements, however complex, are never imagined to be otherwise than finite and determinate. But the case is widely different with the Chess-Player. With him there is no determinate progression. No one move in chess necessarily follows upon any one other. From no particular disposition of the men at one period of a game can we predicate their disposition at a different period. Let us place the *first move* in a game of chess, in juxtaposition with the *data* of an algebraical question, and their great difference will be immediately perceived. From the latter—from the *data*—the second step of the question, dependent thereupon, inevitably follows. It is modelled by the *data*. It must be *thus* and not otherwise. But from the first move in the game of chess no especial second move follows of necessity. In the algebraical question, as it proceeds towards solution, the *certainty* of its operations remains altogether unimpaired. The second step having been a consequence of the *data*, the third step is equally a consequence of the second, the fourth of the third, the fifth of the fourth, and so on, *and not possibly otherwise*, to the end. But in proportion to the progress made in a game of chess, is the *uncertainty* of each ensuing move. A few moves having been made, *no* step is certain. Different spectators of the game would advise different moves. All is then dependent upon the variable judgment of the players. Now even granting (what should not be granted) that the movements of the Automaton Chess-Player were in themselves determinate, they would be necessarily interrupted and disarranged by the indeterminate will of his antagonist. There is then no analogy whatever between the operations of the Chess-Player and those of the calculating machine of Mr. Babbage, and if we choose to call the former a *pure machine,* we must be prepared to admit that it is, beyond all comparison, the most wonderful of the inventions of mankind. Its original projector, however, Baron Kempelen, had no scruple in declaring it to be a "very ordinary piece of mechanism—a *bagatelle* whose effects appeared so marvellous only from the boldness of the conception, and the fortunate choice of the methods adopted for promoting the illusion." But it is needless to dwell upon this point. It is quite certain that the operations of the Automaton are regulated by *mind*, and by nothing else. Indeed this matter is susceptible of a mathematical demonstration, *a priori*. The only question then is of the *manner* in which human agency is brought to bear. Before entering upon this subject it would be as well to give a brief history and description of the Chess-Player for the benefit of such of our readers as may never have had an opportunity of witnessing Mr. Maelzel's exhibition.

The Automaton Chess-Player was invented in 1769, by Baron Kempelen, a nobleman of Presburg in Hungary, who afterwards disposed of it, together with the secret of its operations, to its present possessor. Soon after its completion it was exhibited in Presburg, Paris, Vienna, and other continental cities. In 1783 and 1784, it was taken to London by Mr. Maelzel. Of late years it has visited the principal towns in the United States.

Wherever seen, the most intense curiosity was excited by its appearance, and numerous have been the attempts, by men of all classes, to fathom the mystery of its evolutions. The cut above gives a tolerable representation of the figure as seen by the citizens of Richmond a few weeks ago. The right arm, however, should lie more at length upon the box, a chess-board should appear upon it, and the cushion should not be seen while the pipe is held. Some immaterial alterations have been made in the costume of the player since it came into the possession of Maelzel—the plume, for example, was not originally worn.

At the hour appointed for exhibition, a curtain is withdrawn, or folding doors are thrown open, and the machine rolled to within about twelve feet of the nearest of the spectators, between whom and it (the machine) a rope is stretched. A figure is seen habited as a Turk, and seated, with its legs crossed, at a large box apparently of maple which serves it as a table. The exhibiter will, if requested, roll the machine to any portion of the room, suffer it to remain altogether on any designated spot, or even shift its location repeatedly during the progress of a game. The bottom of the box is elevated considerably above the floor by means of the castors or brazen rollers on which it moves, a clear view of the surface immediately beneath the Automaton being thus afforded to the spectators. The chair on which the figure sits is affixed permanently to the box. On the top of this latter is a chess-board, also permanently affixed. The right arm of the Chess-Player is extended at full length before him, at right angles with his body, and lying, in an apparently careless position, by the side of the board. The back of the hand is upwards. The board itself is eighteen inches square. The left arm of the figure is bent at the elbow, and in the left hand is a pipe. A green drapery conceals the back of the Turk, and falls partially over the front of both shoulders. To judge from the external appearance of the box, it is divided into five compartments—three cupboards of equal dimensions, and two drawers occupying that portion of the chest lying beneath the cupboards. The foregoing observations apply to the appearance of the Automaton upon its first introduction into the presence of the spectators.

Maelzel now informs the company that he will disclose to their view the mechanism of the machine. Taking from his pocket a bunch of keys, he unlocks, with one of them, door marked 1 in the cut above, and throws the cupboard fully open to the inspection of all present. Its whole interior is apparently filled with wheels, pinions, levers, and other machinery, crowded very closely together, so that the eye can penetrate but a little distance into the mass. Leaving this door open to its full extent, he goes now round to the back of the box, and raising the drapery of the figure, opens another door situated precisely in the rear of the one first opened. Holding a lighted candle at this door, and shifting the position of the whole machine repeatedly at the same time, a bright light is thrown entirely through the cupboard, which is now clearly seen to be full, completely full, of machinery. The spectators being satisfied of this fact, Maelzel closes the back door, locks it, takes the key from the lock, lets fall the drapery of the figure, and comes round to the front. The door marked 1, it will be remembered, is still open. The exhibiter now proceeds to open the drawer which lies beneath the cupboards at the bottom of the box—for although there are apparently two drawers, there is really only one—the two handles and two keyholes being intended merely for ornament. Having opened this drawer to its full extent, a small cushion, and a set of chess-men, fixed in a framework made to support them perpendicularly, are discovered. Leaving this drawer, as well as cupboard No. 1, open, Maelzel now unlocks door No. 2 and door No. 3, which are discovered to be folding doors, opening into one and the same compartment. To the right of this compartment, however (that is to say the spectators' right), a small division, six inches wide, and filled with machinery, is partitioned off. The main compartment itself (in speaking of that portion of the box visible upon opening doors 2 and 3, we shall always call it the main compartment) is lined with dark cloth and contains no machinery whatever beyond two pieces of steel, quadrant shaped, and situated one in each of the rear top corners of the compartment. A small protuberance about eight inches square, and also covered with dark cloth, lies on the floor of the compartment near the rear corner on the spectators' left hand. Leaving doors No. 2 and No. 3 open as well as the drawer, and door No. 1, the exhibiter now goes round to the back of the main compartment, and unlocking another door there, displays clearly all the interior of the main compartment, by introducing a candle behind it and within it. The whole box being thus apparently disclosed to the scrutiny of the company, Maelzel, still leaving the doors and drawer open, rolls the Automaton entirely round, and exposes the back of the Turk by lifting up the drapery. A door about ten inches square is thrown open in the loins of the figure, and a smaller one also in the left thigh. The interior of the figure, as seen through these apertures, appears to be crowded with machinery. In general, every spectator is now thoroughly satisfied of having beheld and completely scrutinized, at one and the same time, every individual portion of the Automaton, and the idea of any person being concealed in the interior, during so complete an exhibition of that interior, if ever entertained, is immediately dismissed as preposterous in the extreme.

M. Maelzel, having rolled the machine back into its original position, now informs the company that the Automaton will play a game of chess with any one disposed to encounter him. This challenge being accepted, a small table is prepared for the antagonist, and placed close by the rope, but on the spectators' side of it, and so situated as not to prevent the company from obtaining a full view of the Automaton. From a drawer in this table is taken a set of chess-men, and Maelzel arranges them generally, but not always, with his own hands, on the chess-board, which consists merely of the usual number of squares painted upon the table. The antagonist having taken his seat, the exhibiter approaches the drawer of the box, and takes therefrom the cushion, which after removing the pipe from the hand of the Automaton, he places under its left arm as a support. Then taking also from the drawer the Automaton's set of chess-men, he arranges them upon the chess-board before the figure. He now proceeds to close the doors and to lock them—leaving the bunch of keys in door No. 1. He also closes the drawer, and finally winds up the machine by applying a key to an aperture in the left end (the spectators' left) of the box. The game now commences—the Automaton taking the first move. The duration of the contest is usually limited to half an hour, but if it be not finished at the expiration of this period, and the antagonist still contend that he can beat the Automaton, M. Maelzel has seldom any objection to continue it. Not to weary the company, is the ostensible, and no doubt the real object of the limitation. It will of course be understood that when a move is made at his own table by the antagonist, the corresponding move is made at

the box of the Automaton, by Maelzel himself, who then
acts as the representative of the antagonist. On the other
hand, when the Turk moves, the corresponding move is
made at the table of the antagonist, also by M. Maelzel,
who then acts as the representative of the Automaton. In
this manner it is necessary that the exhibiter should
often pass from one table to the other. He also frequently goes in the rear of the figure to remove the
chess-men which it has taken, and which it deposits,
when taken, on the box to the left (to its own left) of the
board. When the Automaton hesitates in relation to its
move, the exhibiter is occasionally seen to place himself
very near its right side, and to lay his hand, now and
then, in a careless manner, upon the box. He has also
a peculiar shuffle with his feet, calculated to induce
suspicion of collusion with the machine in minds which
are more cunning than sagacious. These peculiarities,
are, no doubt, mere mannerisms of M. Maelzel, or, if he
is aware of them at all, he puts them in practice with a
view of exciting in the spectators a false idea of the pure
mechanism in the Automaton.

The Turk plays with his left hand. All the movements
of the arm are at right angles. In this manner, the hand
(which is gloved and bent in a natural way), being
brought directly above the piece to be moved, descends
finally upon it, the fingers receiving it in most cases without difficulty. Occasionally, however, when the piece is
not precisely in its proper situation, the Automaton fails
in his attempt at seizing it. When this occurs, no second
effort is made, but the arm continues its movement in
the direction originally intended, precisely as if the
piece were in the fingers. Having thus designated the
spot whither the move should have been made, the arm
returns to its cushion, and Maelzel performs the evolu-
tion which the Automaton pointed out. At every move-

ment of the figure the machinery is heard in motion. During the progress of the game, the figure now and then rolls its eyes, as if surveying the board, moves its head, and pronounces the word *echec* (check) when necessary.[1] If a false move be made by his antagonist, he raps briskly on the box with the fingers of his right hand, shakes his head roughly, and replacing the pieces falsely moved, in its former situation, assumes the next move himself. Upon beating the game, he waves his head with an air of triumph, looks around complacently upon the spectators, and drawing his left arm farther back than usual, suffers his fingers alone to rest upon the cushion. In general, the Turk is victorious—once or twice he has been beaten. The game being ended, Maelzel will again, if desired, exhibit the mechanism of the box in the same manner as before. The machine is then rolled back, and a curtain hides it from the view of the company.

There have been many attempts at solving the mystery of the Automaton. The most general opinion in relation to it, an opinion too not unfrequently adopted by men who should have known better, was, as we have before said, that no immediate human agency was employed—in other words, that the machine was purely a machine and nothing else. Many, however, maintained that the exhibiter himself regulated the movements of the figure by mechanical means operating through the feet of the box. Others, again, spoke confidently of a magnet. Of the first of these opinions we shall say nothing at present more than we have already said. In relation to the second it is only necessary to repeat what we have before stated, that the machine is rolled about on

---

[1] *The making the Turk pronounce the word echec, is an improvement by M. Maelzel. When in possession of Baron Kempelen, the figure indicated a check by rapping on the box with his right hand.* [E.A.P.]

castors, and will, at the request of a spectator, be moved to and fro to any portion of the room, even during the progress of the game. The supposition of the magnet is also untenable—for if a magnet were the agent, any other magnet in the pocket of a spectator would disarrange the entire mechanism. The exhibiter, however, will suffer the most powerful loadstone to remain even upon the box during the whole of the exhibition.

The first attempt at a written explanation of the secret, at least the first attempt of which we ourselves have any knowledge, was made in a large pamphlet printed at Paris in 1785. The author's hypothesis amounted to this—that a dwarf actuated the machine. This dwarf he supposed to conceal himself during the opening of the box, by thrusting his legs into two hollow cylinders, which were represented to be (but which are not) among the machinery in the cupboard No. 1, while his body was out of the box entirely, and covered by the drapery of the Turk. When the doors were shut, the dwarf was enabled to bring his body within the box, the noise produced by some portion of the machinery allowing him to do so unheard, and also to close the door by which he entered. The interior of the Automaton being then exhibited, and no person discovered, the spectators, says the author of this pamphlet, are satisfied that no one is within any portion of the machine. The whole hypothesis was too obviously absurd to require comment, or refutation, and accordingly we find that it attracted very little attention.

In 1789 a book was published at Dresden by M. I. F. Freyhere in which another endeavour was made to unravel the mystery. Mr. Freyhere's book was a pretty large one, and copiously illustrated by coloured engravings. His supposition was that "a well-taught boy, very thin and tall of his age (sufficiently so, that he could be concealed in a drawer almost immediately under the chess-board,") played the game of chess and effected all the evolutions of the Automaton. This idea, although even more silly than that of the Parisian author, met with a better reception, and was in some measure believed to be the true solution of the wonder, until the inventor put an end to the discussion by suffering a close examination of the top of the box.

These bizarre attempts at explanation were followed by others equally bizarre. Of late years, however, an anonymous writer by a course of reasoning exceedingly unphilosophical, has contrived to blunder upon a plausible solution—although we cannot consider it altogether the true one. His Essay was first published in a Baltimore weekly paper, was illustrated by cuts, and was entitled "An attempt to analyze the Automaton Chess-Player of M. Maelzel." This Essay we suppose to have been the original of the *pamphlet* to which Sir David Brewster alludes in his *Letters on Natural Magic,* and which he has no hesitation in declaring a thorough and satisfactory explanation. The *results* of the analysis are undoubtedly, in the main, just; but we can only account for Brewster's pronouncing the Essay a thorough and satisfactory explanation, by supposing him to have bestowed upon it a very cursory and inattentive perusal. In the compendium of the Essay, made use of in the *Letters on Natural Magic,* it is quite impossible to arrive at any distinct conclusion in regard to the adequacy or inadequacy of the analysis, on account of the gross misarrangement and deficiency of the letters of reference employed. The same fault is to be found in the "Attempt," etc., as we originally saw it. The solution consists in a series of minute explanations, (accompanied by wood-cuts, the whole occupying many pages,) in which the object is to show the *possibility* of *so shifting the partitions* of the box, as to allow a human being, concealed in the interior, to move portions of his body from one part of the box to another, during the exhibition of the mechanism—thus eluding the scrutiny of the spectators. There can be no doubt, as we have before observed, and as we will presently endeavour to show, that the principle, or rather the result of this solution is the true one. Some person *is* concealed in the box during the whole time of exhibiting the interior. We object, however, to the whole verbose description of the *manner* in which the partitions are shifted, to accommodate the movements of the person concealed. We object to it as a mere theory assumed in the first place, and to which circumstances are afterwards made to adapt themselves. It was not, and could not have been, arrived at by any inductive reasoning. In whatever way the shifting is managed, it is, of course, concealed at every step from observation. To show that certain movements might possibly be effected in a certain way, is very far from showing that they are actually so effected. There may be an infinity of other methods by which the same results may be obtained. The probability of the one assumed proving the correct one is then as unity to infinity. But, in reality, this particular point, the shifting of the partitions, is of no consequence whatever. It was altogether unnecessary to devote seven or eight pages for the purpose of proving what no one in his senses would deny, viz.: that the wonderful mechanical genius of Baron Kempelen could invent the necessary means for shutting a door or slipping aside a panel, with a human agent too at his service in actual contact with the panel or the door, and the whole operations carried on, as the author of the Essay himself shows, and as we shall attempt to show more fully hereafter, entirely out of reach of the observation of the spectators.

In attempting ourselves an explanation of the Automaton, we will, in the first place, endeavour to show how its operations are effected, and afterwards describe, as briefly as possible, the nature of the *observations* from which we have deduced our result.

It will be necessary for a proper understanding of the subject, that we repeat here in a few words, the routine adopted by the exhibiter in disclosing the interior of the box—a routine from which he *never* deviates in any material particular. In the first place he opens the door No. 1. Leaving this open, he goes round to the rear of the box, and opens a door precisely at the back of door No. 1. To this back door he holds a lighted candle. He then *closes the back door,* locks it, and coming round to the front, opens the drawer to its full extent. This done, he opens the doors No. 2 and No. 3 (the folding doors), and displays the interior of the main compartment. Leaving open the main compartment, the drawer, and the front door of cupboard No. 1, he now goes to the rear again, and throws open the back door of the main compartment. In shutting up the box no particular order is observed, except that the folding doors are always closed before the drawer.

Now, let us suppose that when the machine is first rolled into the presence of the spectators, a man is already within it. His body is situated behind the dense machinery in cupboard No. 1, (the rear portion of which machinery is so contrived as to slip *en masse,* from the main compartment to the cupboard No. 1, as occasion may require,) and his legs lie at full length in the main compartment. When Maelzel opens the door No. 1, the man within is not in any danger of discovery, for the keenest eye cannot penetrate more than about two

inches into the darkness within. But the case is otherwise when the back door of the cupboard No. 1 is
opened. A bright light then pervades the cupboard, and
the body of the man would be discovered if it were
there. But it is not. The putting the key in the lock of the
back door was a signal on hearing which the person
concealed brought his body forward to an angle as acute
as possible—throwing it altogether, or nearly so, into the
main compartment. This, however, is a painful position,
and cannot be long maintained. Accordingly we find
that Maelzel *closes the back door*. This being done, there
is no reason why the body of the man may not resume its
former situation—for the cupboard is again so dark as
to defy scrutiny. The drawer is now opened, and the
legs of the person within drop down behind it in the
space it formerly occupied.[1] There is, consequently, now
no longer any part of the man in the main compartment
—his body being behind the machinery in cupboard No.
1, and his legs in the space occupied by the drawer. The
exhibiter, therefore, finds himself at liberty to display
the main compartment. This he does—opening both its
back and front doors—and no person is discovered. The
spectators are now satisfied that the whole of the box is
exposed to view—and exposed, too, all portions of it at
one and the same time. But of course this is not the case.
They neither see the space behind the drawer, nor the
interior of cupboard No. 1,—the front door of which
latter the exhibiter virtually shuts in shutting its back

---

[1] *Sir David Brewster supposes that there is always a large space
behind this drawer even when shut—in other words that the drawer
is a "false drawer," and does not extend to the back of the box. But
the idea is altogether untenable. So common-place a trick would be
immediately discovered—especially as the drawer is always opened to
its full extent, and an opportunity thus offered of comparing its
depth with that of the box.* [E.A.P.]

door. Maelzel, having now rolled the machine around, lifted up the drapery of the Turk, opened the doors in his back and thigh, and shown his trunk to be full of machinery, brings the whole back into its original position, and closes the doors. The man within is now at liberty to move about. He gets up into the body of the Turk just so high as to bring his eyes above the level of the chess-board. It is very probable that he seats himself upon the little square block or protuberance which is seen in a corner of the main compartment when the doors are open. In this position he sees the chess-board through the bosom of the Turk which is of gauze. Bringing his right arm across his breast he actuates the little machinery necessary to guide the left arm and the fingers of the figure. This machinery is situated just beneath the left shoulder of the Turk, and is consequently easily reached by the right hand of the man concealed, if we suppose his right arm brought across the breast. The motions of the head and eyes, and of the right arm of the figure, as well as the sound *echec* are produced by other mechanism in the interior, and actuated at will by the man within. The whole of this mechanism—that is to say all the mechanism essential to the machine—is most probably contained within the little cupboard (of about six inches in breadth) partitioned off at the right (the spectators' right) of the main compartment.

In this analysis of the operations of the Automaton, we have purposely avoided any allusion to the manner in which the partitions are shifted, and it will now be readily comprehended that this point is a matter of no importance, since, by mechanism within the ability of any common carpenter, it might be effected in an infinity of different ways, and since we have shown that, however performed, it is performed out of the view of the spectators. Our result is founded upon the following *observations* taken during frequent visits to the exhibition of Maelzel.[1]

1. The moves of the Turk are not made at regular intervals of time, but accommodate themselves to the moves of the antagonist—although this point (of regularity) so important in all kinds of mechanical contrivance, might have been readily brought about by limiting the time allowed for the moves of the antagonist. For example, if this limit were three minutes, the moves of the Automaton might be made at any given intervals longer than three minutes. The fact then of irregularity, when regularity might have been so easily attained, goes to prove that regularity is unimportant to the action of the Automaton—in other words, that the Automaton is not *a pure machine*.

2. When the Automaton is about to move a piece, a distinct motion is observable just beneath the left shoulder, and which motion agitates in a slight degree, the drapery covering the front of the left shoulder. This motion invariably precedes, by about two seconds, the movement of the arm itself—and the arm never, in any instance, moves without this preparatory motion in the shoulder. Now let the antagonist move a piece, and let the corresponding move be made by Maelzel, as usual, upon the board of the Automaton. Then let the antagonist narrowly watch the Automaton, until he detect the preparatory motion in the shoulder. Immediately upon detecting this motion, and before the arm itself begins

---

[1] Some of these observations are intended merely to prove that the machine must be regulated by mind, and it may be thought a work of supererogation to advance farther arguments in support of what has been already fully decided. But our object is to convince, in especial, certain of our friends upon whom a train of suggestive reasoning will have more influence than the most positive a priori demonstration. [E.A.P.]

to move, let him withdraw his piece, as if perceiving an error in his manœuvre. It will then be seen that the movement of the arm, which, in all other cases, immediately succeeds the motion in the shoulder, is withheld— is not made—although Maelzel has not yet performed, on the board of the Automaton, any move corresponding to the withdrawal of the antagonist. In this case, that the Automaton was about to move is evident—and that he did not move, was an effect plainly produced by the withdrawal of the antagonist, and without any intervention of Maelzel.

This fact fully proves, 1—that the intervention of Maelzel, in performing the moves of the antagonist on the board of the Automaton, is not essential to the movements of the Automaton, 2—that its movements are regulated by *mind*—by some person who sees the board of the antagonist, 3—that its movements are not regulated by the mind of Maelzel, whose back was turned toward the antagonist at the withdrawal of his move.

3. The Automaton does not invariably win the game. Were the machine a pure machine this would not be the case—it would always win. The *principle* being discovered by which a machine can be made to *play* a game of chess, an extension of the same principle would enable it to *win* a game—a farther extension would enable it to *win all* games—that is, to beat any possible game of an antagonist. A little consideration will convince any one that the difficulty of making a machine beat all games, is not in the least degree greater, as regards the principle of the operations necessary, than that of making it beat a single game. If then we regard the Chess-Player as a machine, we must suppose, (what is highly improbable,) that its inventor preferred leaving it incomplete to perfecting it—a supposition rendered still more absurd, when we reflect that the leaving it

incomplete would afford an argument against the possibility of its being a pure machine—the very argument we now adduce.

4. When the situation of the game is difficult or complex, we never perceive the Turk either shake his head or roll his eyes. It is only when his next move is obvious, or when the game is so circumstanced that to a man in the Automaton's place there would be no necessity for reflection. Now these peculiar movements of the head and eyes are movements customary with persons engaged in meditation, and the ingenious Baron Kempelen would have adapted these movements (were the machine a pure machine) to occasions proper for their display—that is, to occasions of complexity. But the reverse is seen to be the case, and this reverse applies precisely to our supposition of a man in the interior. When engaged in meditation about the game, he has no time to think of setting in motion the mechanism of the Automaton by which are moved the head and the eyes. When the game, however, is obvious, he has time to look about him, and accordingly, we see the head shake and the eyes roll.

5. When the machine is rolled round to allow the spectators an examination of the back of the Turk, and when his drapery is lifted up and the doors in the trunk and thigh thrown open, the interior of the trunk is seen to be crowded with machinery. In scrutinizing this machinery while the Automaton was in motion, that is to say while the whole machine was moving on the castors, it appeared to us that certain portions of the mechanism changed their shape and position in a degree too great to be accounted for by the simple laws of perspective; and subsequent examinations convince us that these undue alterations were attributable to mirrors in the interior of the trunk. The introduction of mirrors

among the machinery could not have been intended to influence, in any degree, the machinery itself. Their operation, whatever that operation should prove to be, must necessarily have reference to the eye of the spectator. We at once concluded that these mirrors were so placed to multiply to the vision some few pieces of machinery within the trunk so as to give it the appearance of being crowded with mechanism. Now the direct inference from this is that the machine is not a pure machine. For if it were, the inventor, so far from wishing its mechanism to appear complex, and using deception for the purpose of giving it this appearance, would have been especially desirous of convincing those who witnessed his exhibition, of the *simplicity* of the means by which results so wonderful were brought about.

6. The external appearance, and especially, the deportment of the Turk, are, when we consider them as imitations of *life*, but very indifferent imitations. The countenance evinces no ingenuity, and is surpassed, in its resemblance to the human face, by the very commonest of wax-works. The eyes roll unnaturally in the head, without any corresponding motions of the lids or brows. The arm, particularly, performs its operations in an exceedingly stiff, awkward, jerking, and rectangular manner. Now, all this is the result either of inability in Maelzel to do better, or of intentional neglect—accidental neglect being out of the question, when we consider that the whole time of the ingenious proprietor is occupied in the improvement of his machines. Most assuredly we must not refer the unlifelike appearances to inability—for all the rest of Maelzel's automata are evidence of his full ability to copy the motions and peculiarities of life with the most wonderful exactitude. The rope-dancers, for example, are inimitable. When the clown laughs, his lips, his eyes, his eye-brows, and

eye-lids—indeed, all the features of his countenance—
are imbued with their appropriate expressions. In both
him and his companion, every gesture is so entirely easy,
and free from the semblance of artificiality, that, were
it not for the diminutiveness of their size, and the fact
of their being passed from one spectator to another previous to their exhibition on the rope, it would be difficult to convince any assemblage of persons that these
wooden automata were not living creatures. We cannot,
therefore, doubt Mr. Maelzel's ability, and we must
necessarily suppose that he intentionally suffered his
Chess-Player to remain the same artificial and unnatural
figure which Baron Kempelen (no doubt also through
design) originally made it. What this design was it is
not difficult to conceive. Were the Automaton lifelike in
its motions, the spectator would be more apt to attribute
its operations to their true cause (that is, to human
agency within) than he is now, when the awkward and
rectangular manœuvres convey the idea of pure and
unaided mechanism.

7. When, a short time previous to the commencement
of the game, the Automaton is wound up by the exhibiter as usual, an ear in any degree accustomed to the
sounds produced in winding up a system of machinery,
will not fail to discover, instantaneously, that the axis
turned by the key in the box of the Chess-Player, cannot
possibly be connected with either a weight, a spring, or
any system of machinery whatever. The inference here
is the same as in our last observation. The winding up
is inessential to the operations of the Automaton, and
is performed with the design of exciting in the spectators the false idea of mechanism.

8. When the question is demanded explicitly of
Maelzel—"Is the Automaton a pure machine or not?"
his reply is invariably the same—"I will say nothing

about it." Now the notoriety of the Automaton, and the great curiosity it has everywhere excited, are owing more especially to the prevalent opinion that it *is* a pure machine, than to any other circumstance. Of course, then, it is the interest of the proprietor to represent it as a pure machine. And what more obvious, and more effectual method could there be of impressing the spectators with this desired idea, than a positive and explicit declaration to that effect? On the other hand, what more obvious and effectual method could there be of exciting a disbelief in the Automaton's being a pure machine, than by withholding such explicit declaration? For, people will naturally reason thus,—It is Maelzel's interest to represent this thing a pure machine—he refuses to do so, directly, in words, although he does not scruple, and is evidently anxious to do so, indirectly by actions —were it actually what he wishes to represent it by actions, he would gladly avail himself of the more direct testimony of words—the inference is, that a consciousness of its *not* being a pure machine, is the reason of his silence—his actions cannot implicate him in a falsehood —his words may.

9. When, in exhibiting the interior of the box, Maelzel has thrown open the door No. 1, and also the door immediately behind it, he holds a lighted candle at the back door (as mentioned above) and moves the entire machine to and fro with a view of convincing the company that the cupboard No. 1 is entirely filled with machinery. When the machine is thus moved about, it will be apparent to any careful observer that, whereas that portion of the machinery near the front door No. 1 is perfectly steady and unwavering, the portion farther within fluctuates, in a very slight degree, with the movements of the machine. This circumstance first aroused in us the suspicion that the more remote portion of the

machinery was so arranged as to be easily slipped, *en masse*, from its position when occasion should require it. This occasion we have already stated to occur when the man concealed within brings his body into an erect position upon the closing of the back door.

10. Sir David Brewster states the figure of the Turk to be of the size of life—but in fact it is far above the ordinary size. Nothing is more easy than to err in our notions of magnitude. The body of the Automaton is generally insulated, and having no means of immediately comparing it with any human form, we suffer ourselves to consider it as of ordinary dimensions. This mistake may, however, be corrected by observing the Chess-Player when, as is sometimes the case, the exhibiter approaches it. Mr. Maelzel, to be sure, is not very tall, but upon drawing near the machine, his head will be found at least eighteen inches below the head of the Turk, although the latter, it will be remembered, is in a sitting position.

11. The box behind which the Automaton is placed is precisely three feet six inches long, two feet four inches deep, and two feet six inches high. These dimensions are fully sufficient for the accommodation of a man very much above the common size—and the main compartment alone is capable of holding any ordinary man in the position we have mentioned as assumed by the person concealed. As these are facts, which any one who doubts them may prove by actual calculation, we deem it unnecessary to dwell upon them. We will only suggest that, although the top of the box is apparently a board of about three inches in thickness, the spectator may satisfy himself by stooping and looking up at it when the main compartment is open, that it is in reality very thin. The height of the drawer also will be misconceived by those who examine it in a cursory manner. There is

a space of about three inches between the top of the drawer as seen from the exterior, and the bottom of the cupboard—a space which must be included in the height of the drawer. These contrivances to make the room within the box appear less than it actually is, are referrible to a design on the part of the inventor, to impress the company again with a false idea, viz., that no human being can be accommodated within the box.

12. The interior of the main compartment is lined throughout with *cloth*. This cloth we suppose to have a twofold object. A portion of it may form, when tightly stretched, the only partitions which there is any necessity for removing during the changes of the man's position, viz.: the partition between the rear of the main compartment and the rear of cupboard No. 1, and the partition between the main compartment, and the space behind the drawer when open. If we imagine this to be the case, the difficulty of shifting the partitions vanishes at once, if indeed any such difficulty could be supposed under any circumstances to exist. The second object of the cloth is to deaden and render indistinct all sounds occasioned by the movements of the person within.

13. The antagonist (as we have before observed) is not suffered to play at the board of the Automaton, but is seated at some distance from the machine. The reason which, most probably, would be assigned for this circumstance, if the question were demanded, is, that were the antagonist otherwise situated, his person would intervene between the machine and the spectators, and preclude the latter from a distinct view. But this difficulty might be easily obviated, either by elevating the seats of the company, or by turning the end of the box towards them during the game. The true cause of the restriction is, perhaps, very different. Were

the antagonist seated in contact with the box, the secret
would be liable to discovery, by his detecting, with the
aid of a quick ear, the breathings of the man concealed.

14. Although M. Maelzel, in disclosing the interior
of the machine, sometimes slightly deviates from the
routine which we have pointed out, yet *never* in any
instance does he *so* deviate from it as to interfere with
our solution. For example, he has been known to open,
first of all, the drawer—but he never opens the main
compartment without first closing the back door of
cupboard No. 1—he never opens the main compartment
without first pulling out the drawer—he never shuts the
drawer without first shutting the main compartment—
he never opens the back door of cupboard No. 1 while
the main compartment is open—and the game of chess
is never commenced until the whole machine is closed.
Now, if it were observed that *never, in any single instance,* did M. Maelzel differ from the routine we have
pointed out as necessary to our solution, it would be
one of the strongest possible arguments in corroboration of it—but the argument becomes infinitely strengthened if we duly consider the circumstance that he *does*
occasionally deviate from the routine, but never does *so*
deviate as to falsify the solution.

15. There are six candles on the board of the Automaton during exhibition. The question naturally arises
—"Why are so many employed, when a single candle,
or, at farthest, two, would have been amply sufficient
to afford the spectators a clear view of the board, in a
room otherwise so well lit up as the exhibition room
always is—when, moreover, if we suppose the machine
a *pure machine,* there can be no necessity for so much
light, or indeed any light at all, to enable *it* to perform
its operations—and when, especially, only a single
candle is placed upon the table of the antagonist?" The

first and most obvious inference is, that so strong a light is requisite to enable the man within to see through the transparent material (probably fine gauze) of which the breast of the Turk is composed. But when we consider the *arrangement* of the candles, another reason immediately presents itself. There are six lights (as we have said before) in all. Three of these are on each side of the figure. Those most remote from the spectators are the longest—those in the middle are about two inches shorter—and those nearest the company about two inches shorter still—and the candles on one side differ in height from the candles respectively opposite on the other, by a ratio different from two inches— that is to say, the longest candle on one side is about three inches shorter than the longest candle on the other, and so on. Thus it will be seen that no two of the candles are of the same height, and thus also the difficulty of ascertaining the *material* of the breast of the figure (against which the light is especially directed) is greatly augmented by the dazzling effect of the complicated crossings of the rays—crossings which are brought about by placing the centres of radiation all upon different levels.

16. While the Chess-Player was in possession of Baron Kempelen, it was more than once observed, first, that an Italian in the suite of the Baron was never visible during the playing of a game at chess by the Turk, and secondly, that the Italian being taken seriously ill, the exhibition was suspended until his recovery. This Italian professed a *total* ignorance of the game of chess, although all others of the suite played well. Similar observations have been made since the Automaton has been purchased by Maelzel. There is a man, *Schlumberger*, who attends him wherever he goes, but who has no ostensible occupation other than that of assisting

in the packing and unpacking of the Automaton. This man is about the medium size, and has a remarkable stoop in the shoulders. Whether he professes to play chess or not, we are not informed. It is quite certain, however, that he is never to be seen during the exhibition of the Chess-Player, although frequently visible just before and just after the exhibition. Moreover, some years ago Maelzel visited Richmond with his automata, and exhibited them, we believe, in the house now occupied by M. Bossieux as a Dancing Academy. *Schlumberger* was suddenly taken ill, and during his illness there was no exhibition of the Chess-Player. These facts are well known to many of our citizens. The reason assigned for the suspension of the Chess-Player's performances, was *not* the illness of *Schlumberger*. The inferences from all this we leave, without farther comment, to the reader.

17. The Turk plays with his *left* arm. A circumstance so remarkable cannot be accidental. Brewster takes no notice of it whatever, beyond a mere statement, we believe, that such is the fact. The early writers of treatises on the Automaton, seem not to have observed the matter at all, and have no reference to it. The author of the pamphlet alluded to by Brewster mentions it, but acknowledges his inability to account for it. Yet it is obviously from such prominent discrepancies or incongruities as this that deduction are to be made (if made at all) which shall lead us to the truth.

The circumstance of the Automaton's playing with his left hand cannot have connexion with the operations of the machine considered merely as such. Any mechanical arrangement which would cause the figure to move, in any given manner, the left arm—could, if reversed, cause it to move, in the same manner, the right. But these principles cannot be extended to the human organization, wherein there is a marked and radical difference in the construction, and at all events, in the powers, of the right and left arms. Reflecting upon this latter fact, we naturally refer the incongruity noticeable in the Chess-Player to this peculiarity in the human organization. If so, we must imagine some *reversion*—for the Chess-Player plays precisely as a man *would not*. These ideas, once entertained, are sufficient of themselves to suggest the notion of a man in the interior. A few more imperceptible steps lead us, finally, to the result. The Automaton plays with his left arm, because under no other circumstances could the man within play with his right—a *desideratum,* of course. Let us, for example, imagine the Automaton to play with his right arm. To reach the machinery which moves the arm, and which we have before explained to lie just beneath the shoulder, it would be necessary for the man within either to use his right arm in an exceedingly painful and awkward position (viz., brought up close to his body and tightly compressed between his body and the side of the Automaton), or else to use his left arm brought across his breast. In neither case could he act with the requisite ease or precision. On the contrary, the Automaton playing, as it actually does, with the left arm, all difficulties vanish. The right arm of the man within is brought across his breast, and his right fingers act, without any constraint, upon the machinery in the shoulder of the figure.

We do not believe that any reasonable objections can be urged against this solution of the Automaton Chess-Player.

FROM A FEW WORDS
ON SECRET WRITING

(*Graham's Magazine*, July, 1841.)

A S WE can scarcely imagine a time when there did not exist a necessity, or at least a desire, of transmitting information from one individual to another in such manner as to elude general comprehension, so we may well suppose the practice of writing in cipher to be of great antiquity, De la Guilletière, therefore, who, in his *Lacedæmon Ancient and Modern*, maintains that the Spartans were the inventors of Cryptography, is obviously in error. He speaks of the *scytala* as being the origin of the art; but he should only have cited it as one of its earliest instances, so far as our records extend. The *scytalæ* were two wooden cylinders, precisely similar in all respects. The general of an army, in going upon any expedition, received from the *ephori* one of these cylinders, while the other remained in their possession. If either party had occasion to communicate with the other, a narrow strip of parchment was so wrapped around the *scytala* that the edges of the skin fitted accurately each to each. The writing was then inscribed longitudinally, and the epistle unrolled and despatched. If, by mischance, the messenger was intercepted, the letter proved unintelligible to his captors. If he reached his destination safely, however, the party addressed had only to involve the second cylinder in the strip to decipher the inscription. The transmission to our own times of this obvious mode of Cryptography is due, probably, to the *historical* uses of the *scytala* rather than to anything else. Similar means of secret intercommunication must have existed almost contemporaneously with the invention of letters.

It may be as well to remark, in passing, that in none of the treatises on the subject of this paper which have fallen under our cognisance have we observed any suggestion of a method—other than those which apply alike to all ciphers—for the solution of the cipher by *scytala*. We read of instances, indeed, in which the intercepted parchments were deciphered; but we are not informed that this was ever done except accidentally. Yet a solution might be obtained with absolute certainty in this manner. The strip of skin being intercepted, let there be prepared a cone of great length comparatively —say six feet long—and whose circumference at base shall at least equal the length of the strip. Let this latter be rolled upon the cone near the base, edge to edge, as above described; then, still keeping edge to edge, and maintaining the parchment close upon the cone, let it be gradually slipped towards the apex. In this process, some of those words, syllables, or letters, whose connection is intended, will be sure to come together at that point of the cone where its diameter equals that of the *scytala* upon which the cipher was written. And, as in passing up the cone to its apex, all possible diameters are passed over, there is no chance of a failure. The circumference of the *scytala* being thus ascertained, a similar one can be made, and the cipher applied to it.

Few persons can be made to believe that it is not quite an easy thing to invent a method of secret writing which shall baffle investigation. Yet it may be roundly asserted that human ingenuity cannot concoct a cipher which human ingenuity cannot resolve. In the facility with which such writing is deciphered, however, there exist very remarkable differences in different intellects. Often, in the case of two indivduals of acknowledged equality as regards ordinary mental efforts, it will be found that, while one cannot unriddle the commonest cipher, the other will scarcely be puzzled by the most abstruse. It may be observed, generally, that in such investigations the analytic ability is very forcibly called into action; and, for this reason, cryptographical solutions might with great propriety be introduced into academies as the means of giving tone to the most important of the powers of mind.

Were two individuals, totally unpractised in Cryptography, desirous of holding by letter a correspondence which should be unintelligible to all but themselves, it is most probable that they would at once think of a peculiar alphabet, to which each should have a key. At first it would, perhaps, be arranged that *a* should stand for *z, b* for *y, c* for *x, d* for *w,* &c., &c.; that is to say, the order of the letters would be reversed. Upon second thoughts, this arrangement appearing too obvious, a more complex mode would be adopted. The first thirteen letters might be written beneath the last thirteen, thus:

n o p q r s t u v w x y z
a b c d e f g h i j k l m ;

and, so placed, *a* might stand for *n* and *n* for *a, o* for *b* and *b* for *o,* &c., &c. This, again, having an air of regularity which might be fathomed, the key alphabet might be constructed absolutely at random.

Thus,   a might stand for p
          b   "   "   x
          c   "   "   u
          d   "   "   o, &c.

The correspondents, unless convinced of their error by the solution of their cipher, would no doubt be willing

to rest in this latter arrangement as affording full security. But if not, they would be likely to hit upon the
plan of arbitrary marks used in place of the usual characters. For example,

$$
\begin{array}{lllll}
(& \text{might be employed for} & & & \text{a} \\
. & \text{''} & & \text{''} & \text{b} \\
: & \text{''} & & \text{''} & \text{c} \\
; & \text{''} & & \text{''} & \text{d} \\
) & \text{''} & & \text{''} & \text{e, \&c.}
\end{array}
$$

A letter composed of such characters would have an
intricate appearance unquestionably. If, still, however, it did not give full satisfaction, the idea of a perpetually shifting alphabet might be conceived, and thus
effected. Let two circular pieces of pasteboard be prepared, one about half an inch in diameter less than the
other. Let the centre of the smaller be placed upon the
centre of the larger, and secured for a moment from
slipping; while *radii* are drawn from the common centre
to the circumference of the smaller circle, and thus
extended to the circumference of the greater. Let there
be twenty-six of these *radii*, forming on each pasteboard twenty-six spaces. In each of these spaces on the
under circle write one of the letters of the alphabet,
so that the whole alphabet be written—if at random
so much the better. Do the same with the upper circle.
Now run a pin through the common centre, and let the
upper circle revolve, while the under one is held fast.
Now stop the revolution of the upper circle, and, while
both lie still, write the epistle required; using for *a* that
letter in the smaller circle which tallies with *a* in the
larger, for *b* that letter in the smaller circle which tallies
with *b* in the larger, &c., &c. In order that an epistle
thus written may be read by the person for whom it is

intended, it is only necessary that he should have in his possession circles constructed as those just described, and that he should know any two of the characters (one in the under and one in the upper circle) which were in juxtaposition when his correspondent wrote the cipher. Upon this latter point he is informed by looking at the two initial letters of the document which serve as a key. Thus, if he sees *a m* at the beginning, he concludes that, by turning his circles so as to put these characters in conjunction, he will arrive at the alphabet employed.

At a cursory glance, these various modes of constructing a cipher seem to have about them an air of inscrutable secrecy. It appears almost an impossibility to unriddle what has been put together by so complex a method. And to some persons the difficulty might be great; but to others—to those skilled in deciphering—such enigmas are very simple indeed. The reader should bear in mind that the basis of the whole art of solution, as far as regards these matters, is found in the general principles of the formation of language itself, and thus is altogether independent of the particular laws which govern any cipher, or the construction of its key. The difficulty of reading a cryptographical puzzle is by no means always in accordance with the labor or ingenuity with which it has been constructed. The sole use of the key, indeed, is for those *au fait* to the cipher; in its perusal by a third party, no reference is had to it at all. The lock of the secret is picked. In the different methods of Cryptography specified above, it will be observed that there is a gradually increasing complexity. But this complexity is only in shadow. It has no substance whatever. It appertains merely to the formation, and has no bearing upon the solution, of the cipher. The last mode mentioned is not in the least degree more difficult to be deciphered than the first—whatever may be the difficulty of either.

* * *

A very common and somewhat too obvious mode of secret correspondence is the following. A card is interspersed, at irregular intervals, with oblong spaces, about the length of ordinary words of three syllables in a bourgeois type. Another card is made exactly coinciding. One is in possession of each party. When a letter is to be written, the key-card is placed upon the paper and words conveying the true meaning inscribed in the spaces. The card is then removed and the blanks filled up, so as to make out a signification different from the real one. When the person addressed receives the cipher, he has merely to apply to it his own card, when the superfluous words are concealed, and the significant ones alone appear. The chief objection to this cryptograph is the difficulty of so filling the blanks as not to give a forced appearance to the sentences. Differences, also, in the handwriting between the words written in the spaces, and those inscribed upon removal of the card, will always be detected by a close observer.

A pack of cards is sometimes made the vehicle of a cipher, in this manner. The parties determine, in the first place, upon certain arrangements of the pack. For example: it is agreed that, when a writing is to be commenced, a natural sequence of the spots shall be made; with spades at top, hearts next, diamonds next, and clubs last. This order being obtained, the writer proceeds to inscribe upon the top card the first letter of his epistle, upon the next the second, upon the next the third, and so on until the pack is exhausted, when, of course, he will have written fifty-two letters. He now shuffles the pack according to a preconcerted plan. For example: he takes three cards from the bottom and places them at top, then one from top, placing it at bottom, and so on, for a given number of times. This done, he again inscribes fifty-two characters as before, proceeding thus until his epistle is written. The pack being received by the correspondent, he has only to place the cards in the order agreed upon for commencement, to read, letter by letter, the first fifty-two characters as intended. He has then only to shuffle in the manner prearranged for the second perusal, to decipher the series of the next fifty-two letters—and so on to the end. The objection to this cryptograph lies in the nature of the missive. A *pack of cards*, sent from one party to another, would scarcely fail to excite suspicion, and it cannot be doubted that it is far better to secure ciphers from being considered as such, than to waste time in attempts at rendering them scrutiny-proof when intercepted. Experience shows that the most cunningly constructed cryptograph, if suspected, can and will be unriddled.

An unusually secure mode of secret intercommunication might be thus devised. Let the parties each furnish themselves with a copy of the same edition of a book—the rarer the edition the better—as also the rarer the book. In the cryptograph, numbers are used altogether, and these numbers refer to the locality of letters in the volume. For example—a cipher is received commencing, 121-6-8. The party addressed refers to page 121, and looks at the sixth letter from the left of the page in the eighth line from the top. Whatever letter he there finds is the initial letter of the epistle —and so on. This method is very secure; yet it is *pos-*

sible to decipher any cryptograph written by its means
—and it is greatly objectionable otherwise, on account
of the time necessarily required for its solution, even
with the key-volume.

It is not to be supposed that Cryptography, as a
serious thing, as the means of imparting important information, has gone out of use at the present day. It is
still commonly practised in diplomacy; and there are
individuals, even now, holding office in the eye of various foreign governments, whose real business is that
of deciphering. We have already said that a peculiar
mental action is called into play in the solution of cryptographical problems, at least in those of the higher
order. Good cryptographists are rare indeed; and thus
their services, although seldom required, are necessarily
well requited.

*   *   *

In these cursory observations we have by no means
attempted to exhaust the subject of Cryptography. With
such object in view, a folio might be required. We have,
indeed, mentioned only a few of the ordinary modes of
cipher. Even two thousand years ago, Æneas Tacticus
detailed twenty distinct methods; and modern ingenuity
has added much to the science. Our design has been
chiefly suggestive; and perhaps we have already bored
the readers of the Magazine. To those who desire
farther information upon this topic, we may say that
there are extant treatises, by Trithemius, Cap. Porta,
Vigenere, and P. Nicéron. The works of the two latter
may be found, we believe, in the library of the Harvard
University. If, however, there should be sought in these
disquisitions—or in any—*rules for the solution* of
cipher, the seeker will be disappointed. Beyond some

hints in regard to the general structure of language, and some minute exercises in their practical application, he will find nothing upon record which he does not in his own intellect possess.

CRITICISM

While Poe was still alive, James Russell Lowell, who did not bestow praise lightly or carelessly, said of him:

Mr. Poe is at once the most discriminating, philosophical, and fcarless critic upon imaginative works who has written in America. It may be that we should qualify our remark a little, and say that he *might* be, rather than he always *is,* for he seems sometimes to mistake his phial of prussic-acid for his inkstand. If we do not always agree with him in his premises, we are, at least, satisfied that his deductions are logical, and that we are reading the thoughts of a man who thinks for himself, and says what he thinks, and knows well what he is talking about. His analytic power would furnish bravely forth some score of ordinary critics.

And in our own time Edmund Wilson, who, like Lowell, is chary of his praise, has written:

His literary articles and lectures . . . surely constitute the most remarkable body of criticism ever produced in the United States. . . . His prose is as taut as in his stories, but it has cast off the imagery of his fiction to become sharp and precise: our only first-rate classical prose of this period.

Because of his constant need to earn money, much of Poe's critical ability was dissipated on the writing of day-to-day reviews of ephemeral trash. Consequently he left behind only a small body of writing on critical theory. He developed relatively few ideas, the most important of which are his thesis that the short story should attempt to convey only a single impression, and his insistence upon beauty as the chief aim in art. His ingenious essay, "The Philosophy of Composition," which is an *ex post facto* attempt to show how he wrote "The Raven," is fascinating—if the reader does not take it too seriously. For Poe is trying here to apply the same faculties he used in deciphering a cryptogram, or in working out a solution of the Mary Rogers murder case to explain the processes of artistic creation. He makes out a plausible case, but, like his reconstruction of the murder, one wonders whether he has reconstructed the event as it actually took place or constructed *de nouveau* an entirely different affair.

The excerpt which sets forth Poe's critical ideas on the short story comes from a lengthy review he wrote of Hawthorne's *Twice-Told Tales*. Here Poe expounds his often-repeated thesis that in order to be successful a work of art must be short enough to be grasped at a single sitting. He is correct enough so far as the short story is concerned, but he was perhaps making a virtue of what was in his own case almost a necessity. He was a writer for magazines, a writer who did short pieces because he had to, for he never had funds enough to finance himself through the creation of a long work. His only book-length work of fiction, *The Narrative of Arthur Gordon Pym*, was written hastily for money. Consequently, he was rather hostile to the novel (although he admitted to having ghosted a two-volume novel, the title of which has never been identified).

When he attempted to apply this thesis to poetry, saying (in "The Poetic Principle") that "a long poem does not exist," he veered close to nonsense. A short poem may convey a great intensification of experience and through its very brevity make an impact on the reader. But that does not damn the long poem. It is a different thing—just as the novel is different from the short story.

"The Poetic Principle," which was written at the very

end of Poe's life as a lecture and published posthu-
mously, and his "Letter to B———" (probably to Elam
Bliss, his publisher), which was written almost at the
very beginning of his career as a preface to the *Poems*
of 1831, constitute Poe's most important contributions
to the theoretical criticism of poetry. The earlier piece,
written at the age of twenty-two, is the more remarkable; it shows that Poe might have become a first-rate
critic if time and circumstance had worked in his favor
instead of against him. Unfortunately, much of his critical theory was derivative. He owed a great debt to
Coleridge—a debt which he did not acknowledge.

THE PHILOSOPHY
OF COMPOSITION
(*Graham's Magazine*, April, 1846.)

CHARLES DICKENS, in a note now lying before me, alluding to an examination I once made
of the mechanism of *Barnaby Rudge*, says—"By the
way, are you aware that Godwin wrote his *Caleb Williams* backwards? He first involved his hero in a web
of difficulties, forming the second volume, and then, for
the first, cast about him for some mode of accounting
for what had been done."

I cannot think this the *precise* mode of procedure on
the part of Godwin—and indeed what he himself acknowledges, is not altogether in accordance with Mr.
Dickens' idea—but the author of *Caleb Williams* was
too good an artist not to perceive the advantage derivable from at least a somewhat similar process. Nothing is more clear than that every plot, worth the name,
must be elaborated to its *dénouement* before anything

be attempted with the pen. It is only with the *dénoue-ment* constantly in view that we can give a plot its in-dispensable air of consequence, or causation, by mak-ing the incidents, and especially the tone at all points, tend to the development of the intention.

There is a radical error, I think, in the usual mode of constructing a story. Either history affords a thesis—or one is suggested by an incident of the day—or, at best, the author sets himself to work in the combination of striking events to form merely the basis of his narra-tive—designing, generally, to fill in with description, dialogue, or autorial comment, whatever crevices of fact, or action, may, from page to page, render them selves apparent.

I prefer commencing with the consideration of an *effect*. Keeping originality *always* in view—for he is false to himself who ventures to dispense with so ob-vious and so easily attainable a source of interest—I say to myself, in the first place, "Of the innumerable effects, or impressions, of which the heart, the intellect, or (more generally) the soul is susceptible, what one shall I, on the present occasion, select?" Having chosen a novel, first, and secondly a vivid effect, I consider whether it can be best wrought by incident or tone—whether by ordinary incidents and peculiar tone, or the converse, or by peculiarity both of incident and tone—afterward looking about me (or rather within) for such combinations of event, or tone, as shall best aid me in the construction of the effect.

I have often thought how interesting a magazine paper might be written by any author who would—that is to say who could—detail, step by step, the proc-esses by which any one of his compositions attained its ultimate point of completion. Why such a paper has never been given to the world, I am much at a loss to say—but, perhaps, the autorial vanity has had more to do with the omission than any one other cause. Most writers—poets in especial—prefer having it understood that they compose by a species of fine frenzy—an ec-static intuition—and would positively shudder at let-ting the public take a peep behind the scenes, at the elaborate and vacillating crudities of thought—at the true purposes seized only at the last moment—at the innumerable glimpses of idea that arrived not at the maturity of full view—at the fully matured fancies discarded in despair as unmanageable—at the cautious selections and rejections—at the painful erasures and interpolations—in a word, at the wheels and pinions—the tackle for scene-shifting—the step-ladders and demon-traps—the cock's feathers, the red paint and the black patches, which, in ninety-nine cases out of the hundred, constitute the properties of the literary *histrio*.

I am aware, on the other hand, that the case is by no means common, in which an author is at all in con-dition to retrace the steps by which his conclusions have been attained. In general, suggestions, having arisen pell-mell, are pursued and forgotten in a similar man-ner.

For my own part, I have neither sympathy with the repugnance alluded to, nor, at any time the least diffi-culty in recalling to mind the progressive steps of any of my compositions; and, since the interest of an analy-sis, or reconstruction, such as I have considered a *desideratum,* is quite independent of any real or fancied interest in the thing analyzed, it will not be regarded as a breach of decorum on my part to show the *modus operandi* by which some one of my own works was put together. I select "The Raven," as most generally known. It is my design to render it manifest that no one point in its composition is referrible either to accident or intuition—that the work proceeded, step by step, to its completion with the precision and rigid consequence of a mathematical problem.

Let us dismiss, as irrelevant to the poem, *per se*, the circumstance—or say the necessity—which, in the first place, gave rise to the intention of composing *a* poem that should suit at once the popular and the critical taste.

We commence, then, with this intention.

The initial consideration was that of extent. If any literary work is too long to be read at one sitting, we must be content to dispense with the immensely important effect derivable from unity of impression—for, if two sittings be required, the affairs of the world interfere, and every thing like totality is at once destroyed. But since, *ceteris paribus*, no poet can afford to dispense with *any thing* that may advance his design, it but remains to be seen whether there is, in extent, any advantage to counterbalance the loss of unity which attends it. Here I say no, at once. What we term a long poem is, in fact, merely a succession of brief ones— that is to say, of brief poetical effects. It is needless to demonstrate that a poem is such, only inasmuch as it intensely excites, by elevating, the soul; and all intense excitements are, through a psychal necessity, brief. For this reason, at least one half of the *Paradise Lost* is essentially prose—a succession of poetical excitements interspersed, *inevitably*, with corresponding depressions —the whole being deprived, through the extremeness of its length, of the vastly important artistic element, totality, or unity, of effect.

It appears evident, then, that there is a distinct limit, as regards length, to all works of literary art— the limit of a single sitting—and that, although in certain classes of prose composition, such as *Robinson*

Crusoe, (demanding no unity,) this limit may be advantageously overpassed, it can never properly be overpassed in a poem. Within this limit, the extent of a poem may be made to bear mathematical relation to its merit—in other words, to the excitement or elevation —again in other words, to the degree of the true poetical effect which it is capable of inducing; for it is clear that the brevity must be in direct ratio of the intensity of the intended effect:—this, with one proviso—that a certain degree of duration is absolutely requisite for the production of any effect at all.

Holding in view these considerations, as well as that degree of excitement which I deemed not above the popular, while not below the critical, taste, I reached at once what I conceived the proper *length* for my intended poem—a length of about one hundred lines. It is, in fact, a hundred and eight.

My next thought concerned the choice of an impression, or effect, to be conveyed: and here I may as well observe that, throughout the construction, I kept steadily in view the design of rendering the work *universally* appreciable. I should be carried too far out of my immediate topic were I to demonstrate a point upon which I have repeatedly insisted, and which, with the poetical, stands not in the slightest need of demonstration—the point, I mean, that Beauty is the sole legitimate province of the poem. A few words, however, in elucidation of my real meaning, which some of my friends have evinced a disposition to misrepresent. That pleasure which is at once the most intense, the most elevating, and the most pure, is, I believe, found in the contemplation of the beautiful. When, indeed, men speak of Beauty, they mean, precisely, not a quality, as is supposed, but an effect—they refer, in short, just to that intense and pure elevation of *soul—not* of intellect, or of heart—upon which I have commented, and which is experienced in consequence of contemplating "the beautiful." Now I designate Beauty as the province of the poem, merely because it is an obvious rule of Art that effects should be made to spring from direct causes —that objects should be attained through means best adapted for their attainment—no one as yet having been weak enough to deny that the peculiar elevation alluded to is *most readily* attained in the poem. Now the object, Truth, or the satisfaction of the intellect, and the object Passion, or the excitement of the heart, are, although attainable, to a certain extent, in poetry, far more readily attainable in prose. Truth, in fact, demands a precision, and Passion a *homeliness* (the truly passionate will comprehend me) which are absolutely antagonistic to that Beauty which, I maintain, is the excitement, or pleasurable elevation, of the soul. It by no means follows from any thing here said, that Passion, or even Truth, may not be introduced, and even profitably introduced, into a poem—for they may serve in elucidation, or aid the general effect, as do discords in music, by contrast—but the true artist will always contrive, first, to tone them into proper subservience to the predominant aim, and, secondly, to enveil them, as far as possible, in that Beauty which is the atmosphere and the essence of the poem.

Regarding, then, Beauty as my province, my next question referred to the *tone* of its highest manifestation —and all experience has shown that this tone is one of *sadness*. Beauty of whatever kind, in its supreme development, invariably excites the sensitive soul to tears. Melancholy is thus the most legitimate of all the poetical tones.

The length, the province, and the tone, being thus determined, I betook myself to ordinary induction, with the view of obtaining some artistic piquancy which might serve me as a key-note in the construction of the poem—some pivot upon which the whole structure might turn. In carefully thinking over all the usual artistic effects—or more properly *points,* in the theatrical sense—I did not fail to perceive immediately that no one had been so universally employed as that of the *refrain.* The universality of its employment sufficed to assure me of its intrinsic value, and spared me the necessity of submitting it to analysis. I considered it, however, with regard to its susceptibility of improvement, and soon saw it to be in a primitive condition. As commonly used, the *refrain,* or burden, not only is limited to lyric verse, but depends for its impression upon the force of monotone—both in sound and thought. The pleasure is deduced solely from the sense of identity—of repetition. I resolved to diversify, and to heighten, the effect, by adhering, in general, to the monotone of sound, while I continually varied that of thought: that is to say, I determined to produce continuously novel effects, by the variation *of the application* of the *refrain*—the *refrain* itself remaining, for the most part, unvaried.

These points being settled, I next bethought me of the *nature* of my *refrain.* Since its application was to be repeatedly varied, it was clear that the *refrain* itself must be brief, for there would have been an insurmountable difficulty in frequent variations of application in any sentence of length. In proportion to the brevity of the sentence, would, of course, be the facility of the variation. This led me at once to a single word as the best *refrain.*

The question now arose as to the *character* of the word. Having made up my mind to a *refrain,* the division of the poem into stanzas was, of course, a corollary: the *refrain* forming the close of each stanza. That such a close, to have force, must be sonorous and susceptible of protracted emphasis, admitted no doubt: and these considerations inevitably led me to the long *o* as the most sonorous vowel, in connection with *r* as the most producible consonant.

The sound of the *refrain* being thus determined, it became necessary to select a word embodying this sound, and at the same time in the fullest possible keeping with that melancholy which I had predetermined as the tone of the poem. In such a search it would have been absolutely impossible to overlook the word "Nevermore." In fact, it was the very first which presented itself.

The next *desideratum* was a pretext for the continuous use of the one word "Nevermore." In observing the difficulty which I at once found in inventing a sufficiently plausible reason for its continuous repetition, I did not fail to perceive that this difficulty arose solely from the pre-assumption that the word was to be so continuously or monotonously spoken by *a human* being —I did not fail to perceive, in short, that the difficulty lay in the reconciliation of this monotony with the exercise of reason on the part of the creature repeating the word. Here, then, immediately arose the idea of a *non-*reasoning creature capable of speech; and, very naturally, a parrot, in the first instance, suggested itself, but was superseded forthwith by a Raven, as equally capable of speech, and infinitely more in keeping with the intended *tone*.

I had now gone so far as the conception of a Raven —the bird of ill omen—monotonously repeating the one word, "Nevermore," at the conclusion of each stanza, in a poem of melancholy tone, and in length about one hundred lines. Now, never losing sight of the object *supremeness*, or perfection, at all points, I asked myself—"Of all melancholy topics, what, according to the *universal* understanding of mankind, is the *most* melancholy?" Death—was the obvious reply. "And when," I said, "is this most melancholy of topics most poetical?" From what I have already explained at some length, the answer, here also, is obvious— "When it most closely allies itself to *Beauty:* the death, then, of a beautiful woman is, unquestionably, the most poetical topic in the world—and equally is it beyond doubt that the lips best suited for such topic are those of a bereaved lover."

I had now to combine the two ideas, of a lover lamenting his deceased mistress and a Raven continuously repeating the word "Nevermore."—I had to combine these, bearing in mind my design of varying, at every turn, the *application* of the word repeated; but the only intelligible mode of such combination is that of imagining the Raven employing the word in answer to the queries of the lover. And here it was that I saw at once the opportunity afforded for the effect on which I had been depending—that is to say, the effect of the *variation of application.* I saw that I could make the first query propounded by the lover—the first query to which the Raven should reply "Nevermore"—that I could make this first query a commonplace one—the second less so—the third still less, and so on—until at length the lover, startled from his original *nonchalance* by the melancholy character of the word itself—by its frequent repetition—and by a consideration of the ominous reputation of the fowl that uttered it—is at length excited to superstition, and wildly propounds queries of a far different character—queries whose solution he has passionately at heart—propounds them half in superstition and half in that species of despair which delights in self-torture—propounds them not altogether because he believes in the prophetic or demoniac character of the bird (which, reason assures him, is merely repeating a lesson learned by rote) but because he experiences a phrenzied pleasure in so modeling his questions as to receive from the *expected* "Nevermore" the most delicious because the most intolerable of sorrow. Perceiving the opportunity thus afforded me—or, more strictly, thus forced upon me in the progress of the construction—I first established in mind the climax, or concluding query—that query to which "Nevermore" should be in the last place an answer—that in reply to which this word "Nevermore" should involve the utmost conceivable amount of sorrow and despair.

Here then the poem may be said to have its beginning—at the end, where all works of art should begin—for it was here, at this point of my preconsiderations, that I first put pen to paper in the composition of the stanza:

*"Prophet," said I, "thing of evil! prophet still if bird or
    devil!*
*By that heaven that bends above us—by that God we
    both adore,*
*Tell this soul with sorrow laden, if within the distant
    Aidenn,*
*It shall clasp a sainted maiden whom the angels name
    Lenore—*
*Clasp a rare and radiant maiden whom the angels name
    Lenore."*
        Quoth the Raven "Nevermore."

I composed this stanza, at this point, first that, by establishing the climax, I might the better vary and graduate, as regards seriousness and importance, the preceding queries of the lover—and, secondly, that I might definitely settle the rhythm, the metre, and the length and general arrangement of the stanza—as well as graduate the stanzas which were to precede, so that none of them might surpass this in rhythmical effect. Had I been able, in the subsequent composition, to construct more vigorous stanzas, I should, without scruple, have purposely enfeebled them, so as not to interfere with the climacteric effect.

And here I may as well say a few words of the versification. My first object (as usual) was originality. The extent to which this has been neglected, in versification, is one of the most unaccountable things in the world. Admitting that there is little possibility of variety in mere *rhythm*, it is still clear that the possible varieties of metre and stanza are absolutely infinite—and yet, *for centuries, no man, in verse, has ever done, or ever seemed to think of doing, an original thing*. The fact is, that originality (unless in minds of very unusual force) is by no means a matter, as some suppose, of impulse or intuition. In general, to be found, it must be elaborately sought, and although a positive merit of the highest class, demands in its attainment less of invention than negation.

Of course, I pretend to no originality in either the rhythm or metre of the "Raven." The former is trochaic —the latter is octameter acatalectic, alternating with heptameter catalectic repeated in the *refrain* of the fifth verse, and terminating with tetrameter catalectic. Less pedantically—the feet employed throughout (trochees) consist of a long syllable followed by a short: the first line of the stanza consists of eight of these feet—the second of seven and a half (in effect two-thirds)—the third of eight—the fourth of seven and a half—the fifth the same—the sixth three and a half. Now, each of these lines, taken individually, has been employed before, and what originality the "Raven" has, is in their *combination into stanza;* nothing even remotely approaching this combination has ever been attempted. The effect of this originality of combination is aided by other unusual, and some altogether novel effects, arising from an extension of the application of the principles of rhyme and alliteration.

The next point to be considered was the mode of bringing together the lover and the Raven—and the first branch of this consideration was the *locale.* For this the most natural suggestion might seem to be a forest, or the fields—but it has always appeared to me that a close *circumscription of space* is absolutely necessary to the effect of insulated incident:—it has the force of a frame to a picture. It has an indisputable moral power in keeping concentrated the attention, and, of course, must not be confounded with mere unity of place.

I determined, then, to place the lover in his chamber—in a chamber rendered sacred to him by memories of her who had frequented it. The room is represented as richly furnished—this in mere pursuance of the ideas I have already explained on the subject of Beauty, as the sole true poetical thesis.

The *locale* being thus determined, I had now to introduce the bird—and the thought of introducing him through the window, was inevitable. The idea of making the lover suppose, in the first instance, that the flapping of the wings of the bird against the shutter, is a "tapping" at the door, originated in a wish to increase, by prolonging, the reader's curiosity, and in a desire to admit the incidental effect arising from the lover's throwing open the door, finding all dark, and thence adopting the half-fancy that it was the spirit of his mistress that knocked.

I made the night tempestuous, first, to account for the Raven's seeking admission, and secondly, for the effect of contrast with the (physical) serenity within the chámber.

I made the bird alight on the bust of Pallas, also for the effect of contrast between the marble and the plumage—it being understood that the bust was absolutely *suggested* by the bird—the bust of *Pallas* being chosen, first, as most in keeping with the scholarship of the lover, and, secondly, for the sonorousness of the word, Pallas, itself.

About the middle of the poem, also, I have availed myself of the force of contrast, with a view of deepening the ultimate impression. For example, an air of the fantastic—approaching as nearly to the ludicrous as was admissible—is given to the Raven's entrance. He comes in "with many a flirt and flutter."

Not the least obeisance made he—*not a moment stopped*
    or stayed he,
But with mien of lord or lady, *perched above my cham-*
    ber door.

In the two stanzas which follow, the design is more obviously carried out:—

Then this ebony bird beguiling my sad fancy into smil-
    ing
By the grave and stern decorum of the countenance it
    wore,
"Though thy crest be shorn and shaven *thou," I said,*
    "art sure no craven,

Ghastly grim and ancient Raven wandering from the
*   nightly shore—*
Tell me what thy lordly name is on the Night's Plutonian
*   shore?"*
                    Quoth the Raven "Nevermore."

Much I marvelled this ungainly fowl *to hear discourse*
*   so plainly*
Though its answer little meaning—little relevancy bore;
For we cannot help agreeing that no living human being
Ever yet was blessed with seeing bird above his cham-
    ber door—
Bird or beast upon the sculptured bust above his cham-
    ber door,
            With such name as "Nevermore."

The effect of the *dénouement* being thus provided
for, I immediately drop the fantastic for a tone of the
most profound seriousness:—this tone commencing in
the stanza directly following the one last quoted, with
the line,

But the Raven, sitting lonely on that placid bust, spoke
*   only, etc.*

From this epoch the lover no longer jests—no longer
sees any thing even of the fantastic in the Raven's
demeanor. He speaks of him as a "grim, ungainly,
ghastly, gaunt, and ominous bird of yore," and feels
the "fiery eyes" burning into his "bosom's core." This
revolution of thought, or fancy, on the lover's part, is
intended to induce a similar one on the part of the
reader—to bring the mind into a proper frame for the
dénouement—which is now brought about as rapidly
and as *directly* as possible.

With the *dénouement* proper—with the Raven's reply, "Nevermore," to the lover's final demand if he shall meet his mistress in another world—the poem, in its obvious phase, that of a simple narrative, may be said to have its completion. So far, every thing is within the limits of the accountable—of the real. A raven, having learned by rote the single word "Nevermore," and having escaped 'from the custody of its owner, is driven at midnight, through the violence of a storm, to seek admission at a window from which a light still gleams —the chamber-window of a student, occupied half in poring over a volume, half in dreaming of a beloved mistress deceased. The casement being thrown open at the fluttering of the bird's wings, the bird itself perches on the most convenient seat out of the immediate reach of the student, who, amused by the incident and the oddity of the visitor's demeanour, demands of it, in jest and without looking for a reply, its name. The raven addressed, answers with its customary word, "Nevermore"—a word which finds immediate echo in the melancholy heart of the student, who, giving utterance aloud to certain thoughts suggested by the occasion, is again startled by the fowl's repetition of "Nevermore." The student now guesses the state of the case, but is impelled, as I have before explained, by the human thirst for self-torture, and in part by superstition, to propound such queries to the bird as will bring him, the lover, the most of the luxury of sorrow, through the anticipated answer "Nevermore." With the indulgence, to the extreme, of this self-torture, the narration, in what I have termed its first or obvious phase, has a natural termination, and so far there has been no overstepping of the limits of the real.

But in subjects so handled, however skilfully, or with however vivid an array of incident, there is always a certain hardness or nakedness, which repels the artistical eye. Two things are invariably required—first, some amount of complexity, or more properly, adaptation; and, secondly, some amount of suggestiveness—some under-current, however indefinite, of meaning. It is this latter, in especial, which imparts to a work of art so much of that *richness* (to borrow from colloquy a forcible term) which we are too fond of confounding with *the ideal*. It is the *excess* of the suggested meaning— it is the rendering this the upper instead of the under current of the theme—which turns into prose (and that of the very flattest kind) the so called poetry of the so called transcendentalists.

Holding these opinions, I added the two concluding stanzas of the poem—their suggestiveness being thus made to pervade all the narrative which has preceded them. The under-current of meaning is rendered first apparent in the lines—

> *"Take thy beak from out my heart, and take thy form*
> *from off my door!"*
> *Quoth the Raven "Nevermore!"*

It will be observed that the words, "from out my heart," involve the first metaphorical expression in the poem. They, with the answer, "Nevermore," dispose the mind to seek a moral in all that has been previously narrated. The reader begins now to regard the Raven as emblematical—but it is not until the very last line of the very last stanza, that the intention of making him emblematical of *Mournful and Never-ending Remembrance* is permitted distinctly to be seen:

> *And the Raven, never flitting, still is sitting, still is sitting,*

*On the pallid bust of Pallas, just above my chamber
    door;
And his eyes have all the seeming of a demon's that is
    dreaming,
And the lamplight o'er him streaming throws his shadow
    on the floor;
And my soul* from out that shadow *that lies floating on
    the floor*
        Shall be lifted—nevermore

THE SHORT STORY
(From a review of Hawthorne's *Twice-Told Tales*.)

THE tale proper affords the fairest field which can
be afforded by the wide domains of mere prose, for
the exercise of the highest genius. Were I bidden to
say how this genius could be most advantageously employed for the best display of its powers, I should answer, without hesitation, "in the composition of a
rhymed poem not to exceed in length what might be
perused in an hour."

Were I called upon, however, to designate that class
of composition which, next to such a poem as I have
suggested, should best fulfil the demands and serve the
purposes of ambitious genius, should offer it the most
advantageous field of exertion, and afford it the fairest opportunity of display, I should speak at once of the
brief prose tale. History, philosophy, and other matters
of that kind, we leave out of the question, of course.
Of course, I say, and in spite of the gray-beards. These
grave topics, to the end of time, will be best illustrated
by what a discriminating world, turning up its nose at
the drab pamphlets, has agreed to understand as *talent*.

The ordinary novel is objectionable, from its length, for reasons analogous to those which render length objectionable in the poem. As the novel cannot be read at one sitting, it cannot avail itself of the immense benefit of *totality*. Worldly interests, intervening during the pauses of perusal, modify, counteract and annul the impressions intended. But simple cessation in reading would, of itself, be sufficient to destroy the true unity. In the brief tale, however, the author is enabled to carry out his full design without interruption. During the hour of perusal, the soul of the reader is at the writer's control.

A skilful artist has constructed a tale. He has not fashioned his thoughts to accommodate his incidents, but having deliberately conceived a certain *single effect* to be wrought, he then invents such incidents, he then combines such events, and discusses them in such tone as may best serve him in establishing this preconceived effect. If his very first sentence tend not to the outbringing of this effect, then in his very first step has he committed a blunder. In the whole composition there should be no word written of which the tendency, direct or indirect, is not to the one pre-established design. And by such means, with such care and skill, a picture is at length painted which leaves in the mind of him who contemplates it with a kindred art, a sense of the fullest satisfaction. The idea of the tale, its thesis, has been presented unblemished, because undisturbed— an end absolutely demanded, yet, in the novel, altogether unattainable.

We have said that the tale has a point of superiority even over the poem. In fact, while the *rhythm* of this latter is an essential aid in the development of the poet's highest idea—the idea of the Beautiful—the artificialities of this rhythm are an inseparable bar to the development of all points of thought or expression which have their basis in *Truth*. But Truth is often, and in very great degree, the aim of the tale. Some of the finest tales are tales of ratiocination. Thus the field of this species of composition, if not in so elevated a region on the mountain of Mind, is a table-land of far vaster extent than the domain of the mere poem. Its products are never so rich, but infinitely more numerous, and more appreciable by the mass of mankind. The writer of the prose tale, in short, may bring to his theme a vast variety of modes or inflections of thought and expression—(the ratiocinative, for example, the sarcastic, or the humorous) which are not only antagonistical to the nature of the poem, but absolutely forbidden by one of its most peculiar and indispensable adjuncts; we allude, of course, to rhythm. It may be added here, *par parenthèse*, that the author who aims at the purely beautiful in a prose tale is laboring at great disadvantage. For Beauty can be better treated in the poem. Not so with terror, or passion, or horror, or a multitude of such other points. And here it will be seen how full of prejudice are the usual animadversions against those *tales of effect*, many fine examples of which were found in the earlier numbers of *Blackwood*. The impressions produced were wrought in a legitimate sphere of action, and constituted a legitimate although sometimes an exaggerated interest. They were relished by every man of genius: although there were found many men of genius who condemned them without just ground. The true critic will but demand that the design intended be accomplished, to the fullest extent, by the means most advantageously applicable.

FROM
THE POETIC PRINCIPLE
(*The Home Journal*, August 31, 1850.)

IN SPEAKING of the Poetic Principle, I have no design to be either thorough or profound. While discussing, very much at random, the essentiality of what
we call Poetry, my principal purpose will be to cite for
consideration, some few of those minor English or American poems which best suit my own taste, or which, upon
my own fancy, have left the most definite impression.
By "minor poems" I mean, of course, poems of little
length. And here, in the beginning, permit me to say a
few words in regard to a somewhat peculiar principle,
which, whether rightfully or wrongfully, has always
had its influence in my own critical estimate of the
poem. I hold that a long poem does not exist. I maintain that the phrase, "a long poem," is simply a flat
contradiction in terms.

I need scarcely observe that a poem deserves its title
only inasmuch as it excites, by elevating the soul. The
value of the poem is in the ratio of this elevating excitement. But all excitements are, through a psychal
necessity, transient. That degree of excitement which
would entitle a poem to be so called at all, cannot be
sustained throughout a composition of any great length.
After the lapse of half an hour, at the very utmost, it
flags—fails—a revulsion ensues—and then the poem is,
in effect, and in fact, no longer such.

There are, no doubt, many who have found difficulty
in reconciling the critical dictum that the *Paradise Lost*
is to be devoutly admired throughout, with the absolute impossibility of maintaining for it, during perusal,
the amount of enthusiasm which that critical dictum
would demand. This great work, in fact, is to be re-

garded as poetical, only when, losing sight of that vital requisite in all works of Art, Unity, we view it merely as a series of minor poems. If, to preserve its Unity— its totality of effect or impression—we read it (as would be necessary) at a single sitting, the result is but a constant alternation of excitement and depression. After a passage of what we feel to be true poetry, there follows, inevitably, a passage of platitude which no critical pre-judgment can force us to admire; but if, upon completing the work, we read it again; omitting the first book—that is to say, commencing with the second— we shall be surprised at now finding that admirable which we before condemned—that damnable which we had previously so much admired. It follows from all this that the ultimate, aggregate, or absolute effect of even the best epic under the sun, is a nullity:—and this is precisely the fact.

In regard to the Iliad, we have, if not positive proof, at least very good reason, for believing it intended as a series of lyrics; but, granting the epic intention, I can say only that the work is based in an imperfect sense of art. The modern epic is, of the supposititious ancient model, but an inconsiderate and blindfold imitation. But the day of these artistic anomalies is over. If, at any time, any very long poem *were* popular in reality, which I doubt, it is at least clear that no very long poem will ever be popular again.

That the extent of a poetical work is, *ceteris paribus,* the measure of its merit, seems undoubtedly, when we thus state it, a proposition sufficiently absurd—yet we are indebted for it to the Quarterly Reviews. Surely there can be nothing in mere *size,* abstractly considered —there can be nothing in mere *bulk,* so far as a volume is concerned, which has so continuously elicited admiration from these saturnine pamphlets! A mountain, to be sure, by the mere sentiment of physical magnitude which it conveys, *does* impress us with a sense of the sublime—but no man is impressed after *this* fashion by the material grandeur of even *The Columbiad*. Even the Quarterlies have not instructed us to be so impressed by it. *As yet,* they have not *insisted* on our estimating Lamartine by the cubic foot, or Pollok by the pound— but what else are we to *infer* from their continual prating about "sustained effort"? If, by "sustained effort," any little gentleman has accomplished an epic, let us frankly commend him for the effort—if this indeed be a thing commendable—but let us forbear praising the epic on the effort's account. It is to be hoped that common sense, in the time to come, will prefer deciding upon a work of art, rather by the impression it makes, by the effect it produces, than by the time it took to impress the effect or by the amount of "sustained effort" which had been found necessary in effecting the impression. The fact is, that perseverance is one thing, and genius quite another—nor can all the Quarterlies in Christendom confound them. By-and-by, this proposition, with many which I have been just urging, will be received as self-evident. In the meantime, by being generally condemned as falsities, they will not be essentially damaged as truths.

On the other hand, it is clear that a poem may be improperly brief. Undue brevity degenerates into mere epigrammatism. A *very* short poem, while now and then producing a brilliant or vivid, never produces a profound or enduring effect. There must be the steady pressing down of the stamp upon the wax. De Béranger has wrought innumerable things, pungent and spirit-stirring; but, in general, they have been too imponderous to stamp themselves deeply into the public attention; and thus, as so many feathers of fancy, have been blown aloft only to be whistled down the wind.

*   *   *

While the epic mania—while the idea that, to merit in poetry, prolixity is indispensable—has, for some years past, been gradually dying out of the public mind, by mere dint of its own absurdity—we find it succeeded by a heresy too palpably false to be long tolerated, but one which, in the brief period it has already endured, may be said to have accomplished more in the corruption of our Poetical Literature than all its other enemies combined. I allude to the heresy of *The Didactic*. It has been assumed, tacitly and avowedly, directly and indirectly, that the ultimate object of all Poetry is Truth. Every poem, it is said, should inculcate a moral; and by this moral is the poetical merit of the work to be adjudged. We Americans especially have patronised this happy idea; and we Bostonians, very especially, have developed it in full. We have taken it into our heads that to write a poem simply for the poem's sake, and to acknowledge such to have been our design, would be to confess ourselves radically wanting in the true Poetic dignity and force:—but the simple fact is, that, would we but permit ourselves to look into our own souls, we should immediately there discover that under the sun there neither exists nor *can* exist any work more thoroughly dignified—more supremely noble than this very poem—this poem *per se*—this poem which is a poem and nothing more—this poem written solely for the poem's sake.

With as deep a reverence for the True as ever inspired the bosom of man, I would, nevertheless, limit, in some measure, its modes of inculcation. I would limit to en-

force them. I would not enfeeble them by dissipation.
The demands of Truth are severe. She has no sympathy
with the myrtles. All *that* which is so indispensable in
Song, is precisely all *that* with which *she* has nothing
whatever to do. It is but making her a flaunting paradox,
to wreathe her in gems and flowers. In enforcing a truth,
we need severity rather than efflorescence of language.
We must be simple, precise, terse. We must be cool,
calm, unimpassioned. In a word, we must be in that
mood which, as nearly as possible, is the exact converse
of the poetical. *He* must be blind, indeed, who does
not perceive the radical and chasmal differences between the truthful and the poetical modes of inculcation. He must be theory-mad beyond redemption who,
in spite of these differences, shall still persist in attempting to reconcile the obstinate oils and waters of
Poetry and Truth.

Dividing the world of mind into its three most immediately obvious distinctions, we have the Pure Intellect, Taste, and the Moral Sense. I place Taste in the
middle, because it is just this position which, in the
mind, it occupies. It holds intimate relations with
either extreme; but from the Moral Sense is separated
by so faint a difference that Aristotle has not hesitated
to place some of its operations among the virtues themselves. Nevertheless, we find the *offices* of the trio
marked with a sufficient distinction. Just as the Intellect
concerns itself with Truth, so Taste informs us of the
Beautiful while the Moral Sense is regardful of Duty.
Of this latter, while Conscience teaches the obligation,
and Reason the expediency, Taste contents herself with
displaying the charms:—waging war upon Vice solely
on the ground of her deformity—her disproportion—her
animosity to the fitting, to the appropriate, to the har-
monious—in a word, to Beauty.

An immortal instinct, deep within the spirit of man, is thus, plainly, a sense of the Beautiful. This it is which administers to his delight in the manifold forms, and sounds, and odours, and sentiments amid which he exists. And just as the lily is repeated in the lake, or the eyes of Amaryllis in the mirror, so is the mere oral or written repetition of these forms, and sounds, and colours, and odours, and sentiments, a duplicate source of delight. But this mere repetition is not poetry. He who shall simply sing, with however glowing enthusiasm, or with however vivid a truth of description, of the sights, and sounds, and odours, and colours, and sentiments, which greet *him* in common with all mankind—he, I say, has yet failed to prove his divine title. There is still a something in the distance which he has been unable to attain. We have still a thirst unquenchable, to allay which he has not shown us the crystal springs. This thirst belongs to the immortality of Man. It is at once a consequence and an indication of his perennial existence. It is the desire of the moth for the star. It is no mere appreciation of the Beauty before us—but a wild effort to reach the Beauty above. Inspired by an ecstatic prescience of the glories beyond the grave, we struggle, by multiform combinations among the things and thoughts of Time, to attain a portion of that Loveliness whose very elements, perhaps, appertain to eternity alone. And thus when by Poetry—or when by Music, the most entrancing of the Poetic moods—we find ourselves melted into tears—we weep then—not as the Abbate Gravina supposes—through excess of pleasure, but through a certain, petulant, impatient sorrow at our inability to grasp *now,* wholly, here on earth, at once and for ever, those divine and rapturous joys, of which *through* the poem, or *through* the music, we attain to but brief and indeterminate glimpses.

The struggle to apprehend the supernal Loveliness —this struggle, on the part of souls fittingly constituted —has given to the world all *that* which it (the world) has ever been enabled at once to understand and *to feel* as poetic.

The Poetic Sentiment, of course, may develope itself in various modes—in Painting, in Sculpture, in Architecture, in the Dance—very especially in Music—and very peculiarly, and with a wide field, in the composition of the Landscape Garden. Our present theme, however, has regard only to its manifestation in words. And here let me speak briefly on the topic of rhythm. Contenting myself with the certainty that Music, in its various modes of metre, rhythm, and rhyme, is of so vast a moment in Poetry as never to be wisely rejected—is so vitally important an adjunct, that he is simply silly who declines its assistance, I will not now pause to maintain its absolute essentiality. It is in Music, perhaps, that the soul most nearly attains the great end for which, when inspired by the Poetic Sentiment, it struggles— the creation of supernal Beauty. It *may* be, indeed, that here this sublime end is, now and then, attained *in fact*. We are often made to feel, with a shivering delight, that from an earthly harp are stricken notes which *cannot* have been unfamiliar to the angels. And thus there can be little doubt that in the union of Poetry with Music in its popular sense, we shall find the widest field for the Poetic development. The old Bards and Minnesingers had advantages which we do not possess—and Thomas Moore, singing his own songs, was, in the most legitimate manner, perfecting them as poems.

To recapitulate, then:—I would define, in brief, the Poetry of words as *The Rhythmical Creation of Beauty*. Its sole arbiter is Taste. With the Intellect or with the Conscience, it has only collateral relations. Unless incidentally, it has no concern whatever either with Duty or with Truth.

A few words, however, in explanation. *That* pleasure which is at once the most pure, the most elevating, and the most intense, is derived, I maintain, from the contemplation of the Beautiful. In the contemplation of Beauty we alone find it possible to attain that pleasurable elevation, or excitement, *of the soul,* which we recognise as the Poetic Sentiment, and which is so easily distinguished from Truth, which is the satisfaction of the Reason, or from Passion, which is the excitement of the heart. I make Beauty, therefore—using the word as inclusive of the sublime—I make Beauty the province of the poem, simply because it is an obvious rule of Art that effects should be made to spring as directly as possible from their causes:—no one as yet having been weak enough to deny that the peculiar elevation in question is at least *most readily* attainable in the poem. It by no means follows, however, that the incitements of Passion, or the precepts of Duty, or even the lessons of Truth, may not be introduced into a poem, and with advantage; for they may subserve, incidentally, in various ways, the general purposes of the work:— but the true artist will always contrive to tone them down in proper subjection to that *Beauty* which is the atmosphere and the real essence of the poem. . . .

Thus, although in a very cursory and imperfect manner, I have endeavoured to convey to you my conception of the Poetic Principle. It has been my purpose to suggest that, while this Principle itself is, strictly and simply, the Human Aspiration for Supernal Beauty, the manifestation of the Principle is always found in *an elevating excitement of the Soul*—quite independent of that passion which is the intoxication of the Heart—or of that Truth which is the satisfaction of the Reason.

For, in regard to Passion, alas! its tendency is to degrade, rather than to elevate the Soul. Love, on the contrary—Love—the true, the divine Eros—the Uranian, as distinguished from the Dionæan Venus—is unquestionably the purest and truest of all poetical themes. And in regard to Truth—if, to be sure, through the attainment of a truth, we are led to perceive a harmony where none was apparent before, we experience, at once, the true poetical effect—but this effect is referable to the harmony alone, and not in the least degree to the truth which merely served to render the harmony manifest.

We shall reach, however, more immediately a distinct conception of what the true Poetry is, by mere reference to a few of the simple elements which induce in the Poet himself the true poetical effect. He recognises the ambrosia which nourishes his soul, in the bright orbs that shine in Heaven—in the volutes of the flower —in the clustering of low shrubberies—in the waving of the grain-fields—in the slanting of tall, Eastern trees —in the blue distance of mountains—in the grouping of clouds—in the twinkling of half-hidden brooks—in the gleaming of silver rivers—in the repose of sequestered lakes—in the star-mirroring depths of lonely wells. He perceives it in the songs of birds—in the harp of Æolus—in the sighing of the night-wind—in the repining voice of the forest—in the surf that complains to the shore—in the fresh breath of the woods—in the scent of the violet—in the voluptuous perfume of the hyacinth—in the suggestive odour that comes to him, at eventide, from far-distant, undiscovered islands, over dim oceans, illimitable and unexplored. He owns it in all noble thoughts—in all unworldly motives—in all holy impulses—in all chivalrous, generous, and self-sacrificing deeds. He feels it in the beauty of woman—

in the grace of her step—in the lustre of her eye—in the melody of her voice—in her soft laughter—in her sigh—in the harmony of the rustling of her robes. He deeply feels it in her winning endearments—in her burning enthusiasms—in her gentle charities—in her meek and devotional endurances—but above all—ah, far above all—he kneels to it—he worships it in the faith, in the purity, in the strength, in the altogether divine majesty—of her *love*.

ON POETS AND POETRY

(A Letter to B——)

IT HAS been said that a good critique on a poem may be written by one who is no poet himself. This, according to *your* idea and *mine* of poetry, I feel to be false—the less poetical the critic, the less just the critique, and the converse. On this account, and because there are but few B——'s in the world, I would be as much ashamed of the world's good opinion as proud of your own. Another than yourself might here observe, Shakespeare is in possession of the world's good opinion, and yet Shakespeare is the greatest of poets. It appears then that the world judge correctly, why should you be ashamed of their favorable judgment? The difficulty lies in the interpretation of the word "judgment" or "opinion." The opinion is the world's, truly, but it may be called theirs as a man would call a book his, having bought it; he did not write the book, but it is his; they did not originate the opinion, but it is theirs. A fool, for example, thinks Shakespeare a great poet— yet the fool has never read Shakespeare. But the fool's neighbor, who is a step higher on the Andes of the

mind, whose head (that is to say, his more exalted
thought) is too far above the fool to be seen or understood, but whose feet (by which I mean his every-day
actions) are sufficiently near to be discerned, and by
means of which that superiority is ascertained, which
but for them would never have been discovered—this
neighbor asserts that Shakespeare is a great poet—the
fool believes him, and it is henceforward his *opinion*.
This neighbor's opinion has, in like manner, been
adopted from one above *him,* and so, ascendingly, to a
few gifted individuals who kneel around the summit,
beholding, face to face, the master spirit who stands
upon the pinnacle. . . .

You are aware of the great barrier in the path of an
American writer. He is read, if at all, in preference to
the combined and established wit of the world. I say
established; for it is with literature as with law or empire—an established name is an estate in tenure, or
a throne in possession. Besides, one might suppose that
books, like their authors, improve by travel—their having crossed the sea is, with us, so great a distinction.
Our antiquaries abandon time for distance; our very
fops glance from the binding to the bottom of the title-
page, where the mystic characters which spell London,
Paris, or Genoa, are precisely so many letters of recom-
mendation. . . .

I mentioned just now a vulgar error as regards criticism. I think the notion that no poet can form a correct estimate of his own writings is another. I remarked
before, that in proportion to the poetical talent, would
be the justice of a critique upon poetry. Therefore, a
bad poet would, I grant, make a false critique, and his
self-love would infallibly bias his little judgment in his
favor; but a poet, who is indeed a poet, could not,
I think, fail of making a just critique. Whatever should

be deducted on the score of self-love, might be replaced on account of his intimate acquaintance with the subject; in short, we have more instances of false criticism than of just, where one's own writings are the test, simply because we have more bad poets than good. There are of course many objections to what I say: Milton is a great example of the contrary; but his opinion with respect to the *Paradise Regained,* is by no means fairly ascertained. By what trivial circumstances men are often led to assert what they do not really believe! Perhaps an inadvertent word has descended to posterity. But, in fact, the *Paradise Regained* is little, if at all, inferior to the *Paradise Lost,* and is only supposed so to be, because men do not like epics, whatever they may say to the contrary, and reading those of Milton in their natural order, are too much wearied with the first to derive any pleasure from the second.

I dare say Milton preferred *Comus* to either—if so —justly. . . .

As I am speaking of poetry, it will not be amiss to touch slightly upon the most singular heresy in its modern history—the heresy of what is called very foolishly, the Lake School. Some years ago I might have been induced, by an occasion like the present, to attempt a formal refutation of their doctrine; at present it would be a work of supererogation. The wise must bow to the wisdom of such men as Coleridge and Southey, but being wise, have laughed at poetical theories so prosaically exemplified.

Aristotle, with singular assurance, has declared poetry the most philosophical of all writings—but it required a Wordsworth to pronounce it the most metaphysical. He seems to think that the end of poetry is, or should be, instruction—yet it is a truism that the end of our existence is happiness; if so, the end of every separate part of our existence—every thing connected with our existence should be still happiness. Therefore the end of instruction should be happiness; and happiness is another name for pleasure;—therefore the end of instruction should be pleasure: yet we see the above mentioned opinion implies precisely the reverse.

To proceed: *ceteris paribus,* he who pleases, is of more importance to his fellow men than he who instructs, since utility is happiness, and pleasure is the end already obtained which instruction is merely the means of obtaining.

I see no reason, then, why our metaphysical poets should plume themselves so much on the utility of their works, unless indeed they refer to instruction with eternity in view; in which case, sincere respect for their piety would not allow me to express my contempt for their judgment; contempt which it would be difficult to conceal, since their writings are professedly to be understood by the few, and it is the many who stand in need of salvation. In such case I should no doubt be tempted to think of the devil in *Melmoth,* who labors indefatigably through three octavo volumes, to accomplish the destruction of one or two souls, while any common devil would have demolished one or two thousand. . . .

Against the subtleties which would make poetry a study—not a passion—it becomes the metaphysician to reason—but the poet to protest. Yet Wordsworth and Coleridge are men in years; the one imbued in contemplation from his childhood, the other a giant in intellect and learning. The diffidence, then, with which I venture to dispute their authority, would be overwhelming, did I not feel, from the bottom of my heart, that learning has little to do with the imagination— intellect with the passions—or age with poetry. . . .

Trifles, like straws, upon the surface flow,
He who would search for pearls must dive below,

are lines which have done much mischief. As regards
the greater truths, men oftener err by seeking them at
the bottom than at the top; the depth lies in the huge
abysses where wisdom is sought—not in the palpable
places where she is found. The ancients were not always right in hiding the goddess in a well: witness the
light which Bacon has thrown upon philosophy; witness the principles of our divine faith—that moral
mechanism by which the simplicity of a child may
overbalance the wisdom of a man.

We see an instance of Coleridge's liability to err, in
his *Biographia Literaria*—professedly his literary life
and opinions, but, in fact, a treatise *de omni scibili et
quibusdam aliis*. He goes wrong by reason of his very
profundity, and of his error we have a natural type in
the contemplation of a star. He who regards it directly
and intensely sees, it is true, the star, but it is the star
without a ray—while he who surveys it less inquisitively
is conscious of all for which the star is useful to us
below—its brilliancy and its beauty. . . .

As to Wordsworth, I have no faith in him. That he
had, in youth, the feelings of a poet I believe—for
there are glimpses of extreme delicacy in his writings
—(and delicacy is the poet's own kingdom—his *El
Dorado*)—but they have the appearance of a better
day recollected; and glimpses, at best, are little evidence of present poetic fire—we know that a few strag-
gling flowers spring up daily in the crevices of the
glacier.

He was to blame in wearing away his youth in contemplation with the end of poetizing in his manhood.
With the increase of his judgment the light which

should make it apparent has faded away. His judgment consequently is too correct. This may not be understood,—but the old Goths of Germany would have understood it, who used to debate matters of importance to their State twice, once when drunk, and once when sober—sober that they might not be deficient in formality—drunk lest they should be destitute of vigor.

The long wordy discussions by which he tries to reason us into admiration of his poetry, speak very little in his favor: they are full of such assertions as this—(I have opened one of his volumes at random) "Of genius the only proof is the act of doing well what is worthy to be done, and what was never done before" —indeed! then it follows that in doing what is *unworthy* to be done, or what *has* been done before, no genius can be evinced; yet the picking of pockets is an unworthy act, pockets have been picked time immemorial, and Barrington, the pick-pocket, in point of genius, would have thought hard of a comparison with William Wordsworth, the poet.

Again—in estimating the merit of certain poems, whether they be Ossian's or M'Pherson's, can surely be of little consequence, yet, in order to prove their worthlessness, Mr. W. has expended many pages in the controversy. *Tantæne animis?* Can great minds descend to such absurdity? But worse still: that he may bear down every argument in favor of these poems, he triumphantly drags forward a passage, in his abomination of which he expects the reader to sympathize. It is the beginning of the epic poem *"Temora."* "The blue waves of Ullin roll in light; the green hills are covered with day; trees shake their dusky heads in the breeze." And this—this gorgeous, yet simple imagery, where all is alive and panting with immortality—this, William Wordsworth, the author of "Peter Bell," has *selected* for his contempt.

We shall see what better he, in his own person, has to offer. Imprimis:

> *And now she 's at the pony's head,*
> *And now she 's at the pony's tail,*
> *On that side now, and now on this,*
> *And almost stifled her with bliss—*
> *A few sad tears does Betty shed,*
> *She pats the pony where or when*
> *She knows not: happy Betty Foy!*
> *O, Johnny! never mind the Doctor!*

Secondly:

The dew was falling fast, the—stars began to blink,
I heard a voice; it said—drink, pretty creature, drink;
And, looking o'er the hedge, be—fore me I espied
A snow-white mountain lamb, with a—maiden at its
*   side.*
No other sheep were near, the lamb was all alone,
And by a slender cord was—tether'd to a stone.

Now, we have no doubt this is all true; we *will* believe it, indeed, we will, Mr. W. Is it sympathy for the sheep you wish to excite? I love a sheep from the bottom of my heart. . . .

But there *are* occasions, dear B——, there are occasions when even Wordsworth is reasonable. Even Stamboul, it is said, shall have an end, and the most unlucky blunders must come to a conclusion. Here is an extract from his preface—

"Those who have been accustomed to the phraseology of modern writers, if they persist in reading this book to a conclusion (*impossible!*) will, no doubt, have to struggle with feelings of awkwardness; (ha! ha! ha!) they will look round for poetry (ha! ha! ha! ha!) and will be induced to inquire by what species of courtesy these attempts have been permitted to assume that title." Ha! ha! ha! ha! ha!

Yet let not Mr. W. despair; he has given immortality to a wagon, and the bee Sophocles has transmitted to eternity a sore toe, and dignified a tragedy with a chorus of turkeys. . . .

Of Coleridge I cannot speak but with reverence. His towering intellect! his gigantic power! He is one more evidence of the fact *"que la plupart des sectes ont raison dans une bonne partie de ce qu'elles avancent, mais non pas en ce qu'elles nient."* He has imprisoned his own conceptions by the barrier he has erected against those of others. It is lamentable to think that such a mind should be buried in metaphysics, and, like the Nyctanthes, waste its perfume upon the night alone. In reading his poetry, I tremble, like one who stands upon a volcano, conscious, from the very darkness bursting from the crater, of the fire and the light that are weltering below.

. . . .

What is Poetry?—Poetry! that Proteus-like idea, with as many appellations as the nine-titled Corcyra! Give me, I demanded of a scholar some time ago, give me a definition of poetry. *"Très-volontiers,"* and he proceeded to his library, brought me a Dr. Johnson, and overwhelmed me with a definition. Shade of the immortal Shakespeare! I imagine to myself the scowl of your spiritual eye upon the profanity of that scurrilous Ursa Major. Think of poetry, dear B——, think of poetry, and think of—Dr. Samuel Johnson! Think of all that is airy and fairy-like, and then of all that is hideous and unwieldy; think of his huge bulk, the Elephant! and then—and then think of *The Tempest*—*A Midsummer Night's Dream*—Prospero—Oberon—and Titania! . . .

A poem, in my opinion, is opposed to a work of science by having, for its *immediate* object, pleasure, not truth; to romance, by having for its object an *indefinite* instead of a *definite* pleasure, being a poem only so far as this object is attained; romance presenting perceptible images with definite, poetry with *in*definite sensations, to which end music is an *essential*, since the comprehension of sweet sound is our·most indefinite conception. Music, when combined with a pleasurable idea, is poetry; music without the idea is simply music; the idea without the music is prose from its very definitiveness.

What was meant by the invective against him who had no music in his soul? . . .

To sum up this long rigmarole, I have, dear B———, what you no doubt perceive, for the metaphysical poets, *as* poets, the most sovereign contempt. That they have followers proves nothing—

> *The Indian prince has to his palace*
> *More followers than a thief to the gallows.*

POEMS

EDITOR'S PREFACE

Although Poe left to the world only about fifty poems, he thought of himself primarily as a poet; in fact, he said in his preface to *The Raven and Other Poems*: "With me poetry has not been a purpose but a passion."

There were two periods when he was most actively devoted to the writing of poetry—in his youth before his marriage to Virginia and during the last five years of his life.

His poems are few in number and extraordinarily limited in range. In them, even more than in his stories, he was concerned almost exclusively with his inner self, with the object of his love, and above all with death, with the ending of things, and with the melancholy associated with loss and bereavement.

He wrote several definitions of poetry, but the one that applies best to his own work occurs in his "Letter to B———," which prefaced the *Poems of 1831*. There he said, paraphrasing Coleridge almost to the point of plagiarism:

A poem, in my opinion, is opposed to a work of science by having for its *immediate* object, pleasure, not truth; to romance, by having for its object an *indefinite* instead of a *definite* pleasure . . . romance presenting perceptible images with definite, poetry with *in*definite sensations, to which end music is an *essential*, since the comprehension of sweet sound is our most indefinite conception. Music, when combined with a pleasurable idea, is poetry; music without the idea is simply music; the idea without the music is prose from its very definiteness.

Poe carried out this principle in the writing of his poetry; sound plays an important part in his verse, sometimes to the exclusion of sense, as in "Ulalume." In this searching for tonal and associational significance he was far in advance of his time, for his contemporaries were writing conventional poetry in which the ideational content—feeble though it often was—was regarded as more important than anything else, and in which clear and easily understood imagery was considered essential. Poe's attempt to produce an effect upon the reader through the allusive value of his words, through their sounds and overtones, and their implication by context, marks him as one of the forerunners of modern poetry. He has more in common with T. S. Eliot than with Longfellow, and he is nearer to W. H. Auden than he was to the Literati of his own day. The French Symbolists carried his experiments many steps farther; it was through them that his work, with its emphasis on suggestion rather than on statement, has influenced twentieth-century poetry.

Despite its modernity of method, however, there is much that seems dated and even amusingly Victorian in his verse. As in most things he did, his poetry could be very good or very bad. Naturally only that part of it which this editor thought good—or at least biographically or historically important—has been included in this volume.

Two prose poems, "Shadow—a Parable" and "Silence —a Fable," are here arranged for the first time as free verse.

In addition to the poems contained in this section, three others will be found in the stories where Poe placed them. "To One in Paradise" appears in "The Assignation"; "The Conqueror Worm" in "Ligeia"; and

"The Haunted Palace" in "The Fall of the House of Usher."

The poem "Alone" is of doubtful origin, but so great an authority as the late Professor Killis Campbell said of it that "the case for Poe's authorship, in view of the internal evidence, seems to me to be strong." It was first printed in 1875 from a manuscript supposedly in Poe's handwriting. Certainly the poem sounds as though it had been written by Poe. In fact it is more "Poesque" than many of his acknowledged verses.

Prose Poems

SILENCE—A FABLE
[SIOPE]

"LISTEN to *me*," said the Demon,
As he placed his hand upon my head.
"The region of which I speak is a dreary region in Libya,
By the borders of the river Zäire.
And there is no quiet there, nor silence.

"The waters of the river have a saffron and sickly
    hue;
And they flow not onwards to the sea,
But palpitate forever and forever beneath the red eye
    of the sun
With a tumultuous and convulsive motion.
For many miles on either side of the river's oozy bed
Is a pale desert of gigantic water-lilies.
They sigh one unto the other in that solitude,

And stretch towards the heaven their long and ghastly
  necks,
And nod to and fro their everlasting heads.
And there is an indistinct murmur
Which cometh out from among them
Like the rushing of subterrene water.
And they sigh one unto the other.

"But there is a boundary to their realm—
The boundary of the dark, horrible, lofty forest.
There, like the waves about the Hebrides,
The low underwood is agitated continually.
But there is no wind throughout the heaven.
And the tall primeval trees rock eternally hither and
  thither
With a crashing and mighty sound.
And from their high summits, one by one,
Drop everlasting dews.
And at the roots
Strange poisonous flowers lie writhing in perturbed
  slumber.
And overhead, with a rustling and loud noise,
The gray clouds rush westwardly forever,
Until they roll, a cataract, over the fiery wall of the
  horizon.
But there is no wind throughout the heaven.
And by the shores of the river Zäire
There is neither quiet nor silence.

"It was night, and the rain fell;
And, falling, it was rain,
But, having fallen, it was blood.
And I stood in the morass among the tall lilies,
And the rain fell upon my head—
And the lilies sighed one unto the other

In the solemnity of their desolation.

   "And, all at once, the moon arose through the thin
      ghastly mist,
And was crimson in color.
And mine eyes fell upon a huge gray rock
Which stood by the shore of the river,
And was lighted by the light of the moon.
And the rock was gray, and ghastly, and tall,
—And the rock was gray.
Upon its front were characters engraven in the stone;
And I walked through the morass of water-lilies,
Until I came close unto the shore,
That I might read the characters upon the stone.
But I could not decypher them.
And I was going back into the morass,
When the moon shone with a fuller red,
And I turned and looked again upon the rock,
And upon the characters;
—And the characters were DESOLATION.

   "And I looked upwards,
And there stood a man upon the summit of the rock;
And I hid myself among the water-lilies
That I might discover the actions of the man.
And the man was tall and stately in form,
And was wrapped up
From his shoulders to his feet in the toga of old Rome.
And the outlines of his figure were indistinct—
But his features were the features of a deity;
For the mantle of the night,
And of the mist, and of the moon, and of the dew,
Had left uncovered the features of his face.
And his brow was lofty with thought,
And his eye wild with care;
And, in the few furrows upon his cheek

I read the fables of sorrow, and weariness, and disgust
    with mankind,
And a longing after solitude.

   "And the man sat upon the rock, and leaned his head
    upon his hand,
And looked out upon the desolation.
He looked down into the low unquiet shrubbery,
And up into the tall primeval trees,
And up higher at the rustling heaven,
And into the crimson moon.
And I lay close within shelter of the lilies,
And observed the actions of the man.
And the man trembled in the solitude;—
But the night waned,
And he sat upon the rock.

   "And the man turned his attention from the heaven,
And looked out upon the dreary river Zäire,
And upon the yellow ghastly waters,
And upon the pale legions of the water-lilies.
And the man listened to the sighs of the water-lilies,
And to the murmur that came up from among them.
And I lay close within my covert
And observed the actions of the man.
And the man trembled in the solitude;—
But the night waned, and he sat upon the rock.

   "Then I went down into the recesses of the morass,
And waded afar in among the wilderness of the lilies,
And called unto the hippopotami
Which dwelt among the fens
In the recesses of the morass.
And the hippopotami heard my call,
And came, with the behemoth, unto the foot of the rock,

And roared loudly and fearfully beneath the moon.
And I lay close within my covert
And observed the actions of the man.
And the man trembled in the solitude;—
But the night waned, and he sat upon the rock.

"Then I cursed the elements with the curse of tumult;
And a frightful tempest gathered in the heaven
Where, before, there had been no wind.
And the heaven became livid with the violence of the
       tempest—
And the rain beat upon the head of the man—
And the floods of the river came down—
And the river was tormented into foam—
And the water-lilies shrieked within their beds—
And the forest crumbled before the wind—
And the thunder rolled—
And the lightning fell—
And the rock rocked to its foundation.
And I lay close within my covert
And observed the actions of the man.
And the man trembled in the solitude;—
But the night waned, and he sat upon the rock.

"Then I grew angry and cursed,
With the curse of *silence*, the river, and the lilies, and
       the wind, and the forest,
And the heaven, and the thunder, and the sighs of the
       water-lilies.
And they became accursed, and *were still*.
And the moon ceased to totter up its pathway to
       heaven—
And the thunder died away—
And the lightning did not flash—

And the clouds hung motionless—
And the waters sunk to their level and remained—
And the trees ceased to rock—
And the water-lilies sighed no more—
And the murmur was heard no longer from among
them,
Nor any shadow of sound throughout the vast illimitable
desert.
And I looked upon the characters of the rock,
And they were changed;—
And the characters were SILENCE.

"And mine eyes fell upon the countenance of the man,
And his countenance was wan with terror.
And, hurriedly, he raised his head from his hand,
And stood forth upon the rock and listened.
But there was no voice throughout the vast illimitable
desert,
And the characters upon the rock were SILENCE.
And the man shuddered,
And turned his face away,
And fled afar off, in haste,
So that I beheld him no more."

◦   ◦   ◦

Now there are fine tales in the volumes of the Magi—
In the iron-bound, melancholy volumes of the Magi.
Therein, I say, are glorious histories of the Heaven,
And of the Earth, and of the mighty sea—
And of the Genii
That over-ruled the sea, and the earth, and the lofty
Heaven.
There was much lore too in the sayings which were said
by the Sybils;

*And holy, holy things were heard of old by the dim
     leaves that trembled around Dodona
But, as Allah liveth,
That fable which the Demon told me
As he sat by my side in the shadow of the tomb,
I hold to be the most wonderful of all!
And as the Demon made an end of his story,
He fell back within the cavity of the tomb
And laughed.
And I could not laugh with the Demon,
And he cursed me because I could not laugh.
And the lynx which dwelleth forever in the tomb,
Came out therefrom,
And lay down at the feet of the Demon,
And looked at him steadily in the face.*

SHADOW—A PARABLE

*Yea! though I walk through the valley of the Shadow
                              —Psalm of David*

YE who read are still among the living:
But I who write
Shall have long since gone my way
Into the region of shadows.
For indeed strange things shall happen,
And secret things be known,
And many centuries shall pass away,
Ere these memorials be seen of men.
And, when seen,
There will be some to disbelieve, and some to doubt,
And yet a few who will find much to ponder upon
In the characters here graven with a stylus of iron.

The year had been a year of terror,
And of feelings more intense than terror
For which there is no name upon the earth.
For many prodigies and signs had taken place,
And far and wide, over sea and land,
The black wings of the Pestilence were spread abroad.
To those, nevertheless, cunning in the stars,
It was not unknown that the heavens wore an aspect of
    ill;
And to me, the Greek Oinos, among others,
It was evident that now had arrived
The alternation of that seven hundred and ninety-
    fourth year
When, at the entrance of Aries,
The planet Jupiter is conjoined
With the red ring of the terrible Saturnus.
The peculiar spirit of the skies,
If I mistake not greatly, made itself manifest,
Not only in the physical orb of the earth,
But in the souls, imaginations, and meditations of man-
    kind.

Over some flasks of the red Chian wine,
Within the walls of a noble hall, in a dim city called
    Ptolemais,
We sat, at night, a company of seven.
And to our chamber
There was no entrance save by a lofty door of brass:
And the door was fashioned by the artizan Corinnos,
And, being of rare workmanship, was fastened from
    within.
Black draperies, likewise, in the gloomy room,
Shut out from our view
The moon, the lurid stars, and the peopleless streets

—But the boding and the memory of Evil, they would
    not be so excluded.
There were things around us and about
Of which I can render no distinct account—
Things material and spiritual—
Heaviness in the atmosphere—
A sense of suffocation—
Anxiety—and, above all, that terrible state of existence
Which the nervous experience when the senses are
    keenly living and awake,
And meanwhile the powers of thought lie dormant.
A dead weight hung upon us. It hung upon our limbs—
Upon the household furniture—upon the goblets from
    which we drank;
And all things were depressed, and borne down there-
    by—
All things save only the flames of the seven iron lamps
Which illumined our revel.
Uprearing themselves in tall slender lines of light,
They thus remained burning all pallid and motionless;
And in the mirror
Which their lustre formed upon the round table of
    ebony at which we sat,
Each of us there assembled
Beheld the pallor of his own countenance,
And the unquiet glare in the downcast eyes of his
    companions.
Yet we laughed and were merry in our proper way—
Which was hysterical;
And sang the songs of Anacreon—which are madness;
And drank deeply—although the purple wine reminded
    us of blood.
For there was yet another tenant of our chamber
In the person of young Zoilus.
Dead, and at full length he lay, enshrouded;

—The genius and the demon of the scene.
Alas! he bore no portion in our mirth,
Save that his countenance, distorted with the plague,
And his eyes in which Death had but half extinguished
      the fire of 'the pestilence,
Seemed to take such interest in our merriment
As the dead may haply take in the merriment of those
      who are to die.
But although I, Oinos,
Felt that the eyes of the departed were upon me,
Still I forced myself not to perceive the bitterness of
      their expression,
And, gazing down steadily into the depths of the ebony
      mirror,
Sang with a loud and sonorous voice the songs of the
      son of Teios.
But gradually my songs they ceased,
And their echoes, rolling afar off among the sable
      draperies of the chamber,
Became weak, and undistinguishable, and so faded
      away.

And lo! from among those sable draperies
Where the sounds of the song departed,
There came forth a dark and undefined shadow—
A shadow such as the moon, when low in heaven,
Might fashion from the figure of a man:
But it was the shadow neither of man,
Nor of God,
Nor of any familiar thing.
And, quivering awhile among the draperies of the room,
It at length rested in full view upon the surface of the
      door of brass.
But the shadow was vague, and formless, and indefi-
      nite,

And was the shadow neither of man, nor of God—
Neither God of Greece,
Nor God of Chaldæa,
Nor any Egyptian God.
And the shadow rested upon the brazen doorway,
And under the arch of the entablature of the door,
And moved not, nor spoke any word,
But there became stationary and remained.
And the door whereupon the shadow rested
Was, if I remember aright,
Over against the feet of the young Zoilus enshrouded.
But we, the seven there assembled,
Having seen the shadow as it came out from among
    the draperies,
Dared not steadily behold it, but cast down our eyes,
And gazed continually into the depths of the mirror
    of ebony.
And at length I, Oinos, speaking some low words,
Demanded of the shadow its dwelling and its appella-
    tion.
    And the shadow answered:
"I am SHADOW,
And my dwelling is near to the Catacombs of Ptolemais,
And hard by those dim plains of Helusion
Which border upon the foul Charonian canal."

    And then did we, the seven,
Start from our seats in horror,
And stand trembling, and shuddering, and aghast:
For the tones in the voice of the shadow were not the
    tones of any one being,
But of a multitude of beings,
And, varying in their cadences from syllable to syllable,
Fell duskily upon our ears
In the well remembered and familiar accents
Of many thousand departed friends.

Verse

A DREAM WITHIN A DREAM

TAKE this kiss upon the brow!
And, in parting from you now,
Thus much let me avow—
You are not wrong, who deem
That my days have been a dream;
Yet if hope has flown away
In a night, or in a day,
In a vision, or in none,
Is it therefore the less *gone?*
All that we see or seem
Is but a dream within a dream.

I stand amid the roar
Of a surf-tormented shore,
And I hold within my hand
Grains of the golden sand—
How few! yet how they creep
Through my fingers to the deep,
While I weep—while I weep!
O God! can I not grasp
Them with a tighter clasp?
O God! can I not save
One from the pitiless wave?
Is *all* that we see or seem
But a dream within a dream?

STANZAS

How often we forget all time, when lone
Admiring Nature's universal throne;
Her woods—her wilds—her mountains—the intense
Reply of HERS to our intelligence!
                    BYRON: *The Island.*

In youth have I known one with whom the Earth
In secret communing held—as he with it,
In daylight, and in beauty from his birth:
Whose fervid, flickering torch of life was lit
From the sun and stars, whence he had drawn forth
A passionate light—such for his spirit was fit—
And yet that spirit knew not, in the hour
Of its own fervour, what had o'er it power.

Perhaps it may be that my mind is wrought
To a fever by the moonbeam that hangs o'er,
But I will half believe that wild light fraught
With more of sovereignty than ancient lore
Hath ever told;—or is it of a thought
The unembodied essence, and no more,
That with a quickening spell doth o'er us pass
As dew of the night-time o'er the summer grass?

Doth o'er us pass, when, as th' expanding eye
To the loved object,—so the tear to the lid
Will start, which lately slept in apathy?
And yet it need not be—(that object) hid
From us in life—but common—which doth lie
Each hour before us—but *then* only, bid
With a strange sound, as of a harp-string broken,
To awake us—'T is a symbol and a token

Of what in other worlds shall be—and given
In beauty by our God, to those alone
Who otherwise would fall from life and Heaven
Drawn by their heart's passion, and that tone,
That high tone of the spirit which hath striven,
Tho' not with Faith—with godliness—whose throne
With desperate energy 't hath beaten down;
Wearing its own deep feeling as a crown.

"THE HAPPIEST DAY, THE HAPPIEST HOUR"

THE happiest day—the happiest hour
    My seared and blighted heart hath known,
The highest hope of pride and power,
    I feel hath flown.

Of power! said I? yes! such I ween;
    But they have vanish'd long, alas!
The visions of my youth have been—
    But let them pass.

And, pride, what have I now with thee?
    Another brow may even inherit
The venom thou hast pour'd on me—
    Be still, my spirit!

The happiest day—the happiest hour
    Mine eyes shall see—have ever seen,
The brightest glance of pride and power,
    I feel—have been:

But were that hope of pride and power
   Now offer'd, with the pain
Even *then* I felt—that brightest hour
   I would not live again:

For on its wing was dark alloy,
   And as it flutter'd—fell
An essence—powerful to destroy
   A soul that knew it well.

THE LAKE: TO—

In spring of youth it was my lot
To haunt of the wide world a spot
The which I could not love the less—
So lovely was the loneliness
Of a wild lake, with black rock bound,
And the tall pines that towered around.

But when the Night had thrown her pall
Upon that spot, as upon all,
And the mystic wind went by
Murmuring in melody—
Then—ah then I would awake
To the terror of the lone lake.

Yet the terror was not fright,
But a tremulous delight—
A feeling not the jewelled mine
Could teach or bribe me to define—
Nor Love—although the Love were thine.

Death was in that poisonous wave,
And in its gulf a fitting grave
For him who thence could solace bring
To his lone imagining—
Whose solitary soul could make
An Eden of that dim lake.

ROMANCE

ROMANCE, who loves to nod and sing,
With drowsy head and folded wing,
Among the green leaves as they shake
Far down within some shadowy lake,
To me a painted paroquet
Hath been—a most familiar bird—
Taught me my alphabet to say—
To lisp my very earliest word
While in the wild wood I did lie,
A child—with a most knowing eye.

Of late, eternal Condor years
So shake the very Heaven on high
With tumult as they thunder by,
I have no time for idle cares
Through gazing on the unquiet sky.
And when an hour with calmer wings
Its down upon my spirit flings—
That little time with lyre and rhyme
To while away—forbidden things!
My heart would feel to be a crime
Unless it trembled with the strings.

FAIRY-LAND

DIM vales—and shadowy floods—
And cloudy-looking woods,
Whose forms we can't discover
For the tears that drip all over.
Huge moons there wax and wane—
Again—again—again—
Every moment of the night—
Forever changing places—
And they put out the star-light
With the breath from their pale faces.
About twelve by the moon-dial
One more filmy than the rest
(A kind which, upon trial,
They have found to be the best)
Comes down—still down—and down
With its centre on the crown
Of a mountain's eminence,
While its wide circumference
In easy drapery falls
Over hamlets, over halls,
Wherever they may be—
O'er the strange woods—o'er the sea—
Over spirits on the wing—
Over every drowsy thing—
And buries them up quite
In a labyrinth of light—
And then, how deep!—O, deep!
Is the passion of their sleep.
In the morning they arise,
And their moony covering
Is soaring in the skies,
With the tempests as they toss,
Like——almost any thing—

Or a yellow Albatross.
They use that moon no more
For the same end as before—
Videlicet a tent—
Which I think extravagant:
Its atomies, however,
Into a shower dissever,
Of which those butterflies,
Of Earth, who seek the skies,
And so come down again
(Never-contented things!)
Have brought a specimen
Upon their quivering wings.

TO HELEN

HELEN, thy beauty is to me
   Like those Nicéan barks of yore,
That gently, o'er a perfumed sea,
   The weary, way-worn wanderer bore
   To his own native shore.

On desperate seas long wont to roam,
   Thy hyacinth hair, thy classic face,
Thy Naiad airs have brought me home
   To the glory that was Greece,
   And the grandeur that was Rome.

Lo! in yon brilliant window-niche
   How statue-like I see thee stand,
The agate lamp within thy hand!
   Ah, Psyche, from the regions which
   Are Holy-Land!

ISRAFEL

*And the angel Israfel, [whose heart-strings are a lute, and]
who has the sweetest voice of all God's creatures.*—KORAN.

IN Heaven a spirit doth dwell
  "Whose heart-strings are a lute;"
None sing so wildly well
As the angel Israfel,
And the giddy stars (so legends tell)
Ceasing their hymns, attend the spell
  Of his voice, all mute.

Tottering above
  In her highest noon,
  The enamoured moon
Blushes with love,
  While, to listen, the red levin
  (With the rapid Pleiads, even,
  Which were seven,)
  Pauses in Heaven.

And they say (the starry choir
  And the other listening things)
That Israfeli's fire
Is owing to that lyre
  By which he sits and sings—
The trembling living wire
Of those unusual strings.

But the skies that angel trod,
  Where deep thoughts are a duty—
Where Love's a grown-up God—
  Where the Houri glances are
Imbued with all the beauty
  Which we worship in a star.

Therefore, thou art not wrong,
  Israfeli, who despisest
An unimpassioned song;
To thee the laurels belong,
  Best bard, because the wisest!
Merrily live, and long!

The ecstasies above
  With thy burning measures suit—
Thy grief, thy joy, thy hate, thy love,
  With the fervour of thy lute—
  Well may the stars be mute!

Yes, Heaven is thine; but this
  Is a world of sweets and sours;
  Our flowers are merely—flowers,
And the shadow of thy perfect bliss
  Is the sunshine of ours.

If I could dwell
Where Israfel
  Hath dwelt, and he where I,
He might not sing so wildly well
  A mortal melody,
While a bolder note than this might swell
  From my lyre within the sky.

THE CITY IN THE SEA

Lo! Death has reared himself a throne
In a strange city lying alone
Far down within the dim West,

Where the good and the bad and the worst
    and the best
Have gone to their eternal rest.
There shrines and palaces and towers
(Time-eaten towers that tremble not!)
Resemble nothing that is ours.
Around, by lifting winds forgot,
Resignedly beneath the sky
The melancholy waters lie.

No rays from the holy heaven come down
On the long night-time of that town;
But light from out the lurid sea
Streams up the turrets silently—
Gleams up the pinnacles far and free—
Up domes—up spires—up kingly halls—
Up fanes—up Babylon-like walls—
Up shadowy long-forgotten bowers
Of sculptured ivy and stone flowers—
Up many and many a marvellous shrine
Whose wreathéd friezes intertwine
The viol, the violet, and the vine.
Resignedly beneath the sky
The melancholy waters lie.
So blend the turrets and shadows there
That all seem pendulous in air,
While from a proud tower in the town
Death looks gigantically down.

There open fanes and gaping graves
Yawn level with the luminous waves
But not the riches there that lie
In each idol's diamond eye—
Not the gaily-jewelled dead
Tempt the waters from their bed;

For no ripples curl, alas!
Along that wilderness of glass—
No swellings tell that winds may be
Upon some far-off happier sea—
No heavings hint that winds have been
On seas less hideously serene.

But lo, a stir is in the air!
The wave—there is a movement there!
As if the towers had thrust aside,
In slightly sinking, the dull tide—
As if their tops had feebly given
A void within the filmy Heaven.
The waves have now a redder glow—
The hours are breathing faint and low—
And when, amid no earthly moans,
Down, down that town shall settle hence,
Hell, rising from a thousand thrones,
Shall do it reverence.

THE SLEEPER

AT midnight, in the month of June,
I stand beneath the mystic moon.
An opiate vapour, dewy, dim,
Exhales from out her golden rim,
And, softly dripping, drop by drop,
Upon the quiet mountain top,
Steals drowsily and musically
Into the universal valley.
The rosemary nods upon the grave;
The lily lolls upon the wave;
Wrapping the fog about its breast,

The ruin moulders into rest;
Looking like Lethe, see! the lake
A conscious slumber seems to take,
And would not, for the world, awake.
All Beauty sleeps!—and lo! where lies
Irene, with her Destinies!

Oh, lady bright! can it be right—
This window open to the night?
The wanton airs, from the tree-top,
Laughingly through the lattice drop—
The bodiless airs, a wizard rout,
Flit through thy chamber in and out,
And wave the curtain canopy
So fitfully—so fearfully—
Above the closed and fringéd lid
'Neath which thy slumb'ring soul lies hid,
That, o'er the floor and down the wall,
Like ghosts the shadows rise and fall!
Oh, lady dear, hast thou no fear?
Why and what art thou dreaming here?
Sure thou art come o'er far-off seas,
A wonder to these garden trees!
Strange is thy pallor! strange thy dress!
Strange, above all, thy length of tress,
And this all solemn silentness!

The lady sleeps! Oh, may her sleep,
Which is enduring, so be deep!
Heaven have her in its sacred keep!
This chamber changed for one more holy,
This bed for one more melancholy,
I pray to God that she may lie
Forever with unopened eye,
While the pale sheeted ghosts go by!

My love, she sleeps! Oh, may her sleep,
As it is lasting, so be deep!
Soft may the worms about her creep!
Far in the forest, dim and old,
For her may some tall vault unfold—
Some vault that oft hath flung its black
And wingéd panels fluttering back,
Triumphant, o'er the crested palls,
Of her grand family funerals—
Some sepulchre, remote, alone,
Against whose portal she hath thrown,
In childhood, many an idle stone—
Some tomb from out whose sounding door
She ne'er shall force an echo more,
Thrilling to think, poor child of sin!
It was the dead who groaned within.

LENORE

AH, broken is the golden bowl! the spirit flown forever!
Let the bell toll!—a saintly soul floats on the Stygian
river;
And, Guy De Vere, hast *thou* no tear?—weep now or
never more!
See! on yon drear and rigid bier low lies thy love,
Lenore!
Come! let the burial rite be read—the funeral song be
sung!—
An anthem for the queenliest dead that ever died so
young—
A dirge for her the doubly dead in that she died so
young.

"Wretches! ye loved her for her wealth and hated her
for her pride,

"And when she fell in feeble health, ye blessed her
—that she died!

"How *shall* the ritual, then, be read?—the requiem
how be sung

"By you—by yours, the evil eye,—by yours, the slan-
derous tongue

"That did to death the innocence that died, and died so
young?"

Peccavimus; but rave not thus! and let a Sabbath song
Go up to God so solemnly the dead may feel no wrong!
The sweet Lenore hath "gone before," with Hope, that
flew beside,
Leaving thee wild for the dear child that should have
been thy bride—
For her, the fair and *debonair,* that now so lowly lies,
The life upon her yellow hair but not within her eyes—
The life still there, upon her hair—the death upon her
eyes.

"Avaunt!—avaunt! from fiends below, the indignant
ghost is riven—
"From Hell unto a high estate far up within the
Heaven—
"From grief and groan, to a golden throne, beside the
King of Heaven."
Let no bell toll then!—lest her soul, amid its hallowed
mirth,
Should catch the note as it doth float up from the
damnéd Earth!—
And I!—to-night my heart is light! No dirge will I up-
raise,
But waft the angel on her flight with a Pæan of old
days!

THE VALLEY OF UNREST

Once it smiled a silent dell
Where the people did not dwell;
They had gone unto the wars,
Trusting to the mild-eyed stars,
Nightly, from their azure towers,
To keep watch above the flowers,
In the midst of which all day
The red sun-light lazily lay.
Now each visiter shall confess
The sad valley's restlessness.
Nothing there is motionless—
Nothing save the airs that brood
Over the magic solitude.
Ah, by no wind are stirred those trees
That palpitate like the chill seas
Around the misty Hebrides!
Ah, by no wind those clouds are driven
That rustle through the unquiet Heaven
Uneasily, from morn till even,
Over the violets there that lie
In myriad types of the human eye—
Over the lilies three that wave
And weep above a nameless grave!
They wave:—from out their fragrant tops
Eternal dews come down in drops.
They weep:—from off their delicate stems
Perennial tears descend in gems.

THE COLISEUM

TYPE of the antique Rome! Rich reliquary
Of lofty contemplation left to Time

By buried centuries of pomp and power!
At length—at length—after so many days
Of weary pilgrimage and burning thirst,
(Thirst for the springs of lore that in thee lie,)
I kneel, an altered and an humble man,
Amid thy shadows, and so drink within
My very soul thy grandeur, gloom, and glory!

Vastness! and Age! and Memories of Eld!
Silence! and Desolation! and dim Night!
I feel ye now—I feel ye in your strength—
O spells more sure than e'er Judæan king
Taught in the gardens of Gethsemane!
O charms more potent than the rapt Chaldee
Ever drew down from out the quiet stars!

Here, where a hero fell, a column falls!
Here, where the mimic eagle glared in gold,
A midnight vigil holds the swarthy bat!
Here, where the dames of Rome their gilded hair
Waved to the wind, now wave the reed and thistle!
Here, where on golden throne the monarch lolled,
Glides, spectre-like, unto his marble home,
Lit by the wan light of the hornéd moon,
The swift and silent lizard of the stones!
But stay! these walls—these ivy-clad arcades—
These mouldering plinths—these sad and blackened
    shafts—
These vague entablatures—this crumbling frieze—
These shattered cornices—this wreck—this ruin—
These stones—alas! these gray stones—are they all—
All of the famed, and the colossal left
By the corrosive Hours to Fate and me?

"Not all"—the Echoes answer me—"not all!
"Prophetic sounds and loud, arise forever
"From us, and from all Ruin, unto the wise,
"As melody from Memnon to the Sun.
"We rule the hearts of mightiest men—we rule
"With a despotic sway all giant minds.
"We are not impotent—we pallid stones.
"Not all our power is gone—not all our fame—
"Not all the magic of our high renown—
"Not all the wonder that encircles us—
"Not all the mysteries that in us lie—
"Not all the memories that hang upon
"And cling around about us as a garment,
"Clothing us in a robe of more than glory."

SONNET—SILENCE

THERE are some qualities—some incorporate things,
    That have a double life, which thus is made
A type of that twin entity which springs
    From matter and light, evinced in solid and shade.
There is a two-fold *Silence*—sea and shore—
    Body and soul. One dwells in lonely places,
    Newly with grass o'ergrown; some solemn graces,
Some human memories and tearful lore,
Render him terrorless: his name's "No More."
He is the corporate Silence: dread him not!
    No power hath he of evil in himself;
But should some urgent fate (untimely lot!)
    Bring thee to meet his shadow (nameless elf,
That haunteth the lone regions where hath trod
No foot of man,) commend thyself to God!

DREAM-LAND

By a route obscure and lonely,
Haunted by ill angels only,
Where an Eidolon, named NIGHT,
On a black throne reigns upright,
I have reached these lands but newly
From an ultimate dim Thule—
From a wild weird clime that lieth, sublime,
    Out of SPACE—out of TIME.

Bottomless vales and boundless floods,
And chasms, and caves and Titan woods,
With forms that no man can discover
For the tears that drip all over;
Mountains toppling evermore
Into seas without a shore;
Seas that restlessly aspire,
Surging, unto skies of fire;
Lakes that endlessly outspread
Their lone waters—lone and dead,—
Their still waters—still and chilly
With the snows of the lolling lily.

By the lakes that thus outspread
Their lone waters, lone and dead,—
Their sad waters, sad and chilly
With the snows of the lolling lily,—
By the mountains—near the river
Murmuring lowly, murmuring ever,—
By the grey woods,—by the swamp
Where the toad and the newt encamp,—
By the dismal tarns and pools
    Where dwell the Ghouls,—
By each spot the most unholy—

In each nook most melancholy,—
There the traveller meets, aghast,
Sheeted Memories of the Past—
Shrouded forms that start and sigh
As they pass the wanderer by—
White-robed forms of friends long given,
In agony, to the Earth—and Heaven.

For the heart whose woes are legion
'T is a peaceful, soothing region—
For the spirit that walks in shadow
'T is—oh 't is an Eldorado!
But the traveller, travelling through it,
May not—dare not openly view it;
Never its mysteries are exposed
To the weak human eye unclosed;
So wills its King, who hath forbid
The uplifting of the fringéd lid;
And thus the sad Soul that here passes
Beholds it but through darkened glasses.

By a route obscure and lonely,
Haunted by ill angels only,
Where an Eidolon, named NIGHT,
On a black throne reigns upright,
I have wandered home but newly
From this ultimate dim Thule.

THE RAVEN

ONCE upon a midnight dreary, while I pondered, weak
and weary,
Over many a quaint and curious volume of forgotten
lore—

While I nodded, nearly napping, suddenly there came
   a tapping,
As of some one gently rapping, rapping at my chamber door.
"'T is some visiter," I muttered, "tapping at my
   chamber door—
            Only this and nothing more."

Ah, distinctly I remember it was in the bleak Decem-
   ber;
And each separate dying ember wrought its ghost upon
   the floor.
Eagerly I wished the morrow;—vainly I had sought to
   borrow
From my books surcease of sorrow—sorrow for the
   lost Lenore—
For the rare and radiant maiden whom the angels name
   Lenore—
            Nameless *here* for evermore.

And the silken, sad, uncertain rustling of each purple
   curtain
Thrilled me—filled me with fantastic terrors never felt
   before;
So that now, to still the beating of my heart, I stood
   repeating
" 'T is some visiter entreating entrance at my chamber
   door—
Some late visiter entreating entrance at my chamber
   door;—
            This it is and nothing more."

Presently my soul grew stronger; hesitating then no
   longer,

"Sir," said I, "or Madam, truly your forgiveness I implore;
But the fact is I was napping, and so gently you came
rapping,
And so faintly you came tapping, tapping at my chamber door,
That I scarce was sure I heard you"—here I opened
wide the door;——
             Darkness there and nothing more.

Deep into that darkness peering, long I stood there
wondering, fearing,
Doubting, dreaming dreams no mortal ever dared to
dream before;
But the silence was unbroken, and the stillness gave no
token,
And the only word there spoken was the whispered
word, "Lenore!"
This I whispered, and an echo murmured back the
word "Lenore!"
             Merely this and nothing more.

Back into the chamber turning, all my soul within me
burning,
Soon again I heard a tapping somewhat louder than
before.
"Surely," said I, "surely that is something at my window
lattice;
Let me see, then, what thereat is, and this mystery
explore—
Let my heart be still a moment and this mystery explore;—
             'T is the wind and nothing more!"

Open here I flung the shutter, when, with many a
    flirt and flutter
In there stepped a stately Raven of the saintly days of
    yore.
Not the least obeisance made he; not a minute stopped
    or stayed he;
But, with mien of lord or lady, perched above my
    chamber door—
Perched upon a bust of Pallas just above my chamber
    door—
              Perched, and sat, and nothing more.

Then this ebony bird beguiling my sad fancy into smil-
    ing,
By the grave and stern decorum of the countenance it
    wore,
"Though thy crest be shorn and shaven, thou," I said,
    "art sure no craven,
Ghastly grim and ancient Raven wandering from the
    Nightly shore—
Tell me what thy lordly name is on the Night's Plu-
    tonian shore!"
              Quoth the Raven, "Nevermore."

Much I marvelled this ungainly fowl to hear discourse
    so plainly,
Though its answer little meaning—little relevancy bore;
For we cannot help agreeing that no living human
    being
Ever yet was blessed with seeing bird above his cham-
    ber door—
Bird or beast upon the sculptured bust above his cham-
    ber door,
              With such name as "Nevermore."

But the Raven, sitting lonely on the placid bust, spoke
  only
That one word, as if his soul in that one word he did
  outpour.
Nothing farther then he uttered—not a feather then he
  fluttered—
Till I scarcely more than muttered "Other friends have
  flown before—
On the morrow *he* will leave me, as my hopes have
  flown before."
      Then the bird said "Nevermore."

Startled at the stillness broken by reply so aptly spoken,
"Doubtless," said I, "what it utters is its only stock and
  store
Caught from some unhappy master whom unmerciful
  Disaster
Followed fast and followed faster till his songs one
  burden bore—
Till the dirges of his Hope that melancholy burden bore
      Of 'Never—nevermore.' "

But the Raven still beguiling all my fancy into smiling,
Straight I wheeled a cushioned seat in front of bird,
  and bust and door;
Then, upon the velvet sinking, I betook myself to linking
Fancy unto fancy, thinking what this ominous bird of
  yore—
What this grim, ungainly, ghastly, gaunt, and ominous
  bird of yore
     Meant in croaking "Nevermore."

This I sat engaged in guessing, but no syllable expressing

To the fowl whose fiery eyes now burned into my
bosom's core;
This and more I sat divining, with my head at ease
reclining
On the cushion's velvet lining that the lamp-light gloated
o'er,
But whose velvet violet lining with the lamp-light
gloating o'er,
She shall press, ah, nevermore!

Then, methought, the air grew denser, perfumed from
an unseen censer
Swung by Seraphim whose foot-falls tinkled on the
tufted floor.
"Wretch," I cried, "thy God hath lent thee—by these
angels he hath sent thee
Respite—respite and nepenthe from thy memories of
Lenore;
Quaff, oh quaff this kind nepenthe and forget this lost
Lenore!"
Quoth the Raven "Nevermore."

"Prophet!" said I, "thing of evil! prophet still, if bird or
devil!—
Whether Tempter sent, or whether tempest tossed
thee here ashore,
Desolate yet all undaunted, on this desert land en-
chanted—
On this home by Horror haunted—tell me truly, I
implore—
Is there—*is* there balm in Gilead?—tell me—tell me,
I implore!"
Quoth the Raven "Nevermore."

"Prophet!" said I, "thing of evil!—prophet still, if bird
  or devil!
By that Heaven that bends above us—by that God
  we both adore—
Tell this soul with sorrow laden if, within the distant
  Aidenn,
It shall clasp a sainted maiden whom the angels name
  Lenore—
Clasp a rare and radiant maiden whom the angels
  name Lenore."
  Quoth the Raven "Nevermore."

"Be that word our sign of parting, bird or fiend!" I
  shrieked, upstarting—
"Get thee back into the tempest and the Night's Plutonian shore!
Leave no black plume as a token of that lie thy soul
  hath spoken!
Leave my loneliness unbroken!—quit the bust above my
  door!
Take thy beak from out my heart, and take thy form
  from off my door!"
  Quoth the Raven "Nevermore."

And the Raven, never flitting, still is sitting, *still* is
  sitting
On the pallid bust of Pallas just above my chamber
  door;
And his eyes have all the seeming of a demon's that is
  dreaming,
And the lamp-light o'er him streaming throws his
  shadow on the floor;
And my soul from out that shadow that lies floating on
  the floor
  Shall be lifted—nevermore!

A VALENTINE *

For her this rhyme is penned, whose luminous eyes,
    Brightly expressive as the twins of Leda,
Shall find her own sweet name, that, nestling lies
    Upon the page, enwrapped from every reader.
Search narrowly the lines!—they hold a treasure
    Divine—a talisman—an amulet
That must be worn *at heart*. Search well the measure—
    The words—the syllables! Do not forget
The trivialest point, or you may lose your labor!
    And yet there is in this no Gordian knot
Which one might not undo without a sabre,
    If one could merely comprehend the plot.
Enwritten upon the leaf where now are peering
    Eyes scintillating soul, there lie *perdus*
Three eloquent words oft uttered in the hearing
    Of poets, by poets—as the name is a poet's, too.
Its letters, although naturally lying
    Like the knight Pinto—Mendez Ferdinando—
Still form a synonym for Truth.—Cease trying!
    You will not read the riddle, though you do the best
      you *can* do.

ULALUME

The skies they were ashen and sober;
      The leaves they were crisped and sere—
      The leaves they were withering and sere;
It was night in the lonesome October
      Of my most immemorial year;

* This is an acrostic; by starting with the first letter and adding
one letter to the right on each successive line, the name FRANCES
SARGENT OSGOOD may be spelled out.

It was hard by the dim lake of Auber,
    In the misty mid region of Weir—
It was down by the dank tarn of Auber,
    In the ghoul-haunted woodland of Weir.

Here once, through an alley Titanic,
    Of cypress, I roamed with my Soul—
    Of cypress, with Psyche, my Soul.
These were days when my heart was volcanic
    As the scoriac rivers that roll—
    As the lavas that restlessly roll
Their sulphurous currents down Yaanek
    In the ultimate climes of the pole—
That groan as they roll down Mount Yaanek
    In the realms of the boreal pole.

Our talk had been serious and sober,
    But our thoughts they were palsied and sere—
    Our memories were treacherous and sere—
For we knew not the month was October,
    And we marked not the night of the year—
    (Ah, night of all nights in the year!)
We noted not the dim lake of Auber—
    (Though once we had journeyed down here)—
Remembered not the dank tarn of Auber,
    Nor the ghoul-haunted woodland of Weir.

And now, as the night was senescent
    And star-dials pointed to morn—
    As the star-dials hinted of morn—
At the end of our path a liquescent
    And nebulous lustre was born,
Out of which a miraculous crescent
    Arose with a duplicate horn—
Astarte's bediamonded crescent
    Distinct with its duplicate horn.

And I said—"She is warmer than Dian:
    She rolls through an ether of sighs—
    She revels in a region of sighs:
She has seen that the tears are not dry on
    These cheeks, where the worm never dies
And has come past the stars of the Lion
    To point us the path to the skies—
    To the Lethean peace of the skies—
Come up, in despite of the Lion,
    To shine on us with her bright eyes—
Come up through the lair of the Lion,
    With love in her luminous eyes."

But Psyche, uplifting her finger,
    Said—"Sadly this star I mistrust—
    Her pallor I strangely mistrust:—
Oh, hasten!—oh, let us not linger!
    Oh, fly!—let us fly!—for we must."
In terror she spoke, letting sink her
    Wings until they trailed in the dust—
In agony sobbed, letting sink her
    Plumes till they trailed in the dust—
    Till they sorrowfully trailed in the dust.

I replied—"This is nothing but dreaming:
    Let us on by this tremulous light!
    Let us bathe in this crystalline light!
Its Sibyllic splendor is beaming
    With Hope and in Beauty to-night:—
    See!—it flickers up the sky through the night!
Ah, we safely may trust to its gleaming,
    And be sure it will lead us aright—
We safely may trust to a gleaming
    That cannot but guide us aright,
    Since it flickers up to Heaven through the night."

Thus I pacified Psyche and kissed her,
    And tempted her out of her gloom—
    And conquered her scruples and gloom;
And we passed to the end of the vista,
    But were stopped by the door of a tomb—
    By the door of a legended tomb;
And I said—"What is written, sweet sister,
    On the door of this legended tomb?"
    She replied—"Ulalume—Ulalume—
    'T is the vault of thy lost Ulalume!"

Then my heart it grew ashen and sober
    As the leaves that were crisped and sere—
    As the leaves that were withering and sere,
And I cried—"It was surely October
    On *this* very night of last year
    That I journeyed—I journeyed down here—
    That I brought a dread burden down here—
    On this night of all nights in the year,
    Ah, what demon has tempted me here?
Well I know, now, this dim lake of Auber—
    This misty mid region of Weir—
Well I know, now, this dank tarn of Auber,
    This ghoul-haunted woodland of Weir."

TO———

NOT long ago, the writer of these lines,
In the mad pride of intellectuality,
Maintained "the power of words"—denied that ever
A thought arose within the human brain
Beyond the utterance of the human tongue:
And now, as if in mockery of that boast,

Two words—two foreign soft dissyllables—
Italian tones, made only to be murmured
By angels dreaming in the moonlit "dew
That hangs like chains of pearl on Hermon hill,"
Have stirred from out the abysses of his heart,
Unthought-like thoughts that are the souls of thought,
Richer, far wilder, far diviner visions
Than even the seraph harper, Israfel,
(Who has "the sweetest voice of all God's creatures,")
Could hope to utter. And I! my spells are broken.
The pen falls powerless from my shivering hand.
With thy dear name as text, though bidden by thee,
I cannot write—I cannot speak or think—
Alas, I cannot feel; for 't is not feeling,
This standing motionless upon the golden
Threshold of the wide-open gate of dreams,
Gazing, entranced, adown the gorgeous vista,
And thrilling as I see, upon the right,
Upon the left, and all the way along,
Amid empurpled vapors, far away
To where the prospect terminates—*thee only.*

FOR ANNIE

THANK Heaven! the crisis—
    The danger is past,
And the lingering illness
    Is over at last—
And the fever called "Living"
    Is conquered at last.

Sadly, I know
    I am shorn of my strength,

And no muscle I move
　As I lie at full length—
But no matter!—I feel
　I am better at length.

And I rest so composedly
　Now, in my bed,
That any beholder
　Might fancy me dead—
Might start at beholding me,
　Thinking me dead.

The moaning and groaning,
　The sighing and sobbing,
Are quieted now,
　With that horrible throbbing
At heart:—ah that horrible,
　Horrible throbbing!

The sickness—the nausea—
　The pitiless pain—
Have ceased with the fever
　That maddened my brain—
With the fever called "Living"
　That burned in my brain.

And oh! of all tortures
　That torture the worst
Has abated—the terrible
　Torture of thirst
For the napthaline river
　Of Passion accurst:—
I have drank of a water
　That quenches all thirst:—

Of a water that flows,
  With a lullaby sound,
From a spring but a very few
  Feet under ground—
From a cavern not very far
  Down under ground.

And ah! let it never
  Be foolishly said
That my room it is gloomy
  And narrow my bed;
For man never slept
  In a different bed—
And, to sleep, you must slumber
  In just such a bed.

My tantalized spirit
  Here blandly reposes,
Forgetting, or never
  Regretting, its roses—
Its old agitations
  Of myrtles and roses:

For now, while so quietly
  Lying, it fancies
A holier odor
  About it, of pansies—
A rosemary odor,
  Commingled with pansies—
With rue and the beautiful
  Puritan pansies.

And so it lies happily,
  Bathing in many
A dream of the truth

And the beauty of Annie—
Drowned in a bath
    Of the tresses of Annie.

She tenderly kissed me,
    She fondly caressed,
And then I fell gently
    To sleep on her breast—
Deeply to sleep
    From the heaven of her breast.

When the light was extinguished,
    She covered me warm,
And she prayed to the angels
    To keep me from harm—
To the queen of the angels
    To shield me from harm.

And I lie so composedly,
    Now, in my bed,
(Knowing her love)
    That you fancy me dead—
And I rest so contentedly,
    Now, in my bed,
(With her love at my breast)
    That you fancy me dead—
That you shudder to look at me,
    Thinking me dead:—

But my heart it is brighter
    Than all of the many
Stars of the sky,
    For it sparkles with Annie—
It glows with the light
    Of the love of my Annie—

With the thought of the light
Of the eyes of my Annie.

TO MY MOTHER

BECAUSE I feel that, in the Heavens above,
  The angels, whispering to one another,
Can find, among their burning terms of love,
  None so devotional as that of "Mother,"
Therefore by that dear name I long have called
    you—
  You who are more than mother unto me,
And fill my heart of hearts, where Death installed
    you,
  In setting my Virginia's spirit free.
My mother—my own mother, who died early,
  Was but the mother of myself; but you
Are mother to the one I loved so dearly,
  And thus are dearer than the mother I knew
By that infinity with which my wife
  Was dearer to my soul than its soul-life.

ANNABEL LEE

IT was many and many a year ago,
  In a kingdom by the sea
That a maiden there lived whom you may know
  By the name of ANNABEL LEE;
And this maiden she lived with no other thought
  Than to love and be loved by me.

I was a child and *she* was a child,
  In this kingdom by the sea,
But we loved with a love that was more than love—
  I and my ANNABEL LEE—
With a love that the winged seraphs of heaven
  Coveted her and me.

And this was the reason that, long ago,
  In this kingdom by the sea,
A wind blew out of a cloud, chilling
  My beautiful ANNABEL LEE;
So that her highborn kinsmen came
  And bore her away from me,
To shut her up in a sepulchre
  In this kingdom by the sea.

The angels, not half so happy in heaven,
  Went envying her and me—
Yes!—that was the reason (as all men know,
  In this kingdom by the sea)
That the wind came out of the cloud by night,
  Chilling and killing my ANNABEL LEE.

But our love it was stronger by far than the love
  Of those who were older than we—
  Of many far wiser than we—
And neither the angels in heaven above,
  Nor the demons down under the sea,
Can ever dissever my soul from the soul
  Of the beautiful ANNABEL LEE:

For the moon never beams, without bringing me dreams
  Of the beautiful ANNABEL LEE;
And the stars never rise, but I feel the bright eyes
  Of the beautiful ANNABEL LEE:

And so, all the night-tide, I lie down by the side
Of my darling—my darling—my life and my bride,
    In the sepulchre there by the sea—
    In her tomb by the sounding sea.

THE BELLS

I.

Hear the sledges with the bells—
        Silver bells!
What a world of merriment their melody foretells!
        How they tinkle, tinkle, tinkle,
            In the icy air of night!
        While the stars that oversprinkle
        All the heavens, seem to twinkle
            With a crystalline delight;
        Keeping time, time, time,
        In a sort of Runic rhyme,
To the tintinnabulation that so musically wells
        From the bells, bells, bells, bells,
            Bells, bells, bells—
From the jingling and the tinkling of the bells.

II.

        Hear the mellow wedding bells
                Golden bells!
What a world of happiness their harmony foretells!
        Through the balmy air of night
        How they ring out their delight!—
            From the molten-golden notes,
                And all in tune,
            What a liquid ditty floats

To the turtle-dove that listens, while she gloats
On the moon!
Oh, from out the sounding cells,
What a gush of euphony voluminously wells!
How it swells!
How it dwells
On the Future!—how it tells
Of the rapture that impels
To the swinging and the ringing
Of the bells, bells, bells—
Of the bells, bells, bells, bells,
Bells, bells, bells—
To the rhyming and the chiming of the bells!

III.

Hear the loud alarum bells—
Brazen bells!
What a tale of terror, now their turbulency tells!
In the startled ear of night
How they scream out their affright!
Too much horrified to speak,
They can only shriek, shriek,
Out of tune,
In a clamorous appealing to the mercy of the fire,
In a mad expostulation with the deaf and frantic fire,
Leaping higher, higher, higher,
With a desperate desire,
And a resolute endeavour
Now—now to sit, or never,
By the side of the pale-faced moon.
Oh, the bells, bells, bells!
What a tale their terror tells
Of Despair!
How they clang, and clash, and roar!
What a horror they outpour

On the bosom of the palpitating air!
Yet the ear, it fully knows,
By the twanging,
And the clanging,
How the danger ebbs and flows;
Yet the ear distinctly tells,
In the jangling,
And the wrangling,
How the danger sinks and swells,
By the sinking or the swelling in the anger of the bells—
Of the bells—
Of the bells, bells, bells, bells,
Bells, bells, bells—
In the clamor and the clanging of the bells!

IV.

Hear the tolling of the bells—
Iron bells!
What a world of solemn thought their monody compels!
In the silence of the night,
How we shiver with affright
At the melancholy menace of their tone!
For every sound that floats
From the rust within their throats
Is a groan.
And the people—ah, the people—
They that dwell up in the steeple,
All alone,
And who, tolling, tolling, tolling,
In that muffled monotone,
Feel a glory in so rolling
On the human heart a stone—
They are neither man nor woman—
They are neither brute nor human—
They are Ghouls:—

And their king is who tolls:—
And he rolls, rolls, rolls,
   Rolls
  A pæan from the bells!
And his merry bosom swells
  With the pæan of the bells!
And he dances, and he yells;
Keeping time, time, time,
In a sort of Runic rhyme,
  To the pæan of the bells:—
   Of the bells:
Keeping time, time, time
In a sort of Runic rhyme,
  To the throbbing of the bells—
Of the bells, bells, bells—
  To the sobbing of the bells:—
Keeping time, time, time,
  As he knells, knells, knells,
In a happy Runic rhyme,
  To the rolling of the bells—
Of the bells, bells, bells:—
  To the tolling of the bells—
Of the bells, bells, bells, bells,
  Bells, bells, bells—
To the moaning and the groaning of the bells.

ALONE

FROM childhood's hour I have not been
As others were—I have not seen
As others saw—I could not bring
My passions from a common spring—
From the same source I have not taken

My sorrow—I could not awaken
My heart to joy at the same tone—
And all I loved—*I* loved alone—
Then—in my childhood, in the dawn
Of a most stormy life—was drawn
From every depth of good and ill
The mystery which binds me still—
From the torrent, or the fountain—
From the red cliff of the mountain—
From the sun that round me rolled
In its autumn tint of gold—
From the lightning in the sky
As it pass'd me flying by—
From the thunder and the storm—
And the cloud that took the form
When the rest of Heaven was blue
Of a demon in my view.

OPINIONS

EDITOR'S PREFACE

Gathered together here are a number of short pieces which express Poe's views on a wide variety of subjects. Some of them have been excerpted from longer works, but many of them are complete just as Poe wrote them. He was fond of jotting down his ideas in this way, but he did not bury them in a notebook. He knew they were salable as fillers and in groups, so he disposed of them to various magazines, beginning with *The Southern Literary Messenger* in 1836, when he was on its editorial staff. Many of them also appeared during the late forties in *Graham's*, *Godey's*, *The Opal*, and *The Democratic Review*.

THE POET'S VISION

THAT poets (using the word comprehensively, as including artists in general) are a *genus irritabile*, is well understood; but the *why*, seems not to be commonly seen. An artist *is* an artist only by dint of his exquisite sense of Beauty—a sense affording him rapturous enjoyment, but at the same time implying, or involving, an equally exquisite sense of Deformity or disproportion. Thus a wrong—an injustice—done a poet who is really a poet, excites him to a degree which, to ordinary apprehension, appears disproportionate with the wrong. Poets *see* injustice—*never* where it does not

639

exist—but very often where the unpoetical see no injustice whatever. Thus the poetical irritability has no reference to "temper" in the vulgar sense, but merely to a more than usual clear-sightedness in respect to Wrong:—this clear-sightedness being nothing more than a corollary from the vivid perception of Right—of justice—of proportion—in a word, of τὸ χαλόν. But one thing is clear—that the man who is *not* "irritable," (to the ordinary apprehension,) is *no poet.*

GENIUS AND MADNESS

Let a man succeed ever so evidently—ever so demonstrably—in many different displays of *genius,* the envy of criticism will agree with the popular voice in denying him more than *talent* in any. Thus a poet who has achieved a great (by which I mean an effective) poem, should be cautious not to distinguish himself in any other walk of Letters. In especial—let him make no effort in Science—unless anonymously, or with the view of waiting patiently the judgment of posterity. Because universal or even versatile geniuses have rarely or never been known, *therefore,* thinks the world, none such can ever be. A "therefore" of this kind is, with the world, conclusive. But what is the *fact,* as taught us by analysis of mental power? Simply, that *highest* genius—that the genius which all men instantaneously acknowledge as such—which acts upon individuals, as well as upon the mass, by a species of magnetism incomprehensible but irresistible and *never resisted*—that this genius which demonstrates itself in the simplest gesture—or even by the absence of all—this genius which speaks without a voice and flashes from the unopened eye—

is but the result of generally large mental power existing in a state of *absolute proportion*—so that no one faculty has undue predominance. *That* factitious "genius"—that "genius" in the popular sense—which is but the manifestation of the abnormal predominance of some one faculty over all the others—and, of course, at the expense and to the detriment, of all the others—is a result of mental disease or rather, of organic malformation of mind:—it is this and nothing more. Not only will such "genius" fail, if turned aside from the path indicated by its predominant faculty; but, even when pursuing this path—when producing those works in which, certainly, it is *best* calculated to succeed—will give unmistakable indications of *unsoundness,* in respect to general intellect. Hence, indeed, arises the just idea that

> *Great wit to madness nearly is allied.*

I say "*just* idea;" for by "great wit," in this case, the poet intends precisely the pseudo-genius to which I refer. The true genius, on the other hand, is necessarily, if not universal in its manifestations, at least capable of universality; and if, attempting all things, it succeeds in one rather better than in another, this is merely on account of a certain bias by which *Taste* leads it with more earnestness in the one direction than in the other. With equal zeal, it would succeed equally in all.

To sum up our results in respect to this very simple, but much *vexata quæstio:*—

What the world calls "genius" is the state of mental disease arising from the undue predominance of some one of the faculties. The works of such genius are never sound in themselves and, in especial, always betray the general mental insanity.

The *proportion* of the mental faculties, in a case where the general mental power is *not* inordinate, gives that result which we distinguish as *talent:*—and the talent is greater or less, first, as the general mental power is greater or less; and, secondly, as the proportion of the faculties is more or less absolute.

The proportion of the faculties, in a case where the mental power is inordinately great, gives that result which *is* the true *genius* (but which, on account of the proportion and seeming simplicity of its works, is seldom acknowledged to *be* so;) and the genius is greater or less, first, as the general mental power is more or less inordinately great; and, secondly, as the proportion of the faculties is more or less absolute.

An objection will be made:—that the greatest excess of mental power, however proportionate, does not seem to satisfy our idea of genius, unless we have, in addition, sensibility, passion, energy. The reply is, that the "absolute proportion" spoken of, when applied to inordinate mental power, gives, as a result, the appreciation of Beauty and a horror of Deformity which we call sensibility, together with that intense vitality, which is implied when we speak of "Energy" or "Passion."

POETRY AND IMAGINATION

Who will deny that in regard to individual poems no definitive opinions can exist, so long as to Poetry in the abstract we attach no definitive idea? Yet it is a common thing to hear our critics, day after day, pronounce, with a positive air, laudatory or condemnatory sentences, *en masse*, upon material works of whose merits or demerits they have, in the first place, virtually confessed an utter ignorance, in confessing ignorance of all determinate principles by which to regulate a decision. Poetry has never been defined to the satisfaction of all parties. Perhaps, in the present condition of language it never will be. Words cannot hem it in. Its intangible and purely spiritual nature refuses to be bound down within the widest horizon of mere sounds. But it is not, therefore, misunderstood—at least, not by all men is it misunderstood. Very far from it. If, indeed, there be any one circle of thought distinctly and palpably marked out from amid the jarring and tumultuous chaos of human intelligence, it is that evergreen and radiant Paradise which the true poet knows, and knows alone, as the limited realm of his authority—as the circumscribed Eden of his dreams. But a definition is a thing of words—a conception of ideas. And thus while we readily believe that Poesy, the term, it will be troublesome, if not impossible to define—still, with its image vividly existing in the world, we apprehend no difficulty in so describing Poesy, the Sentiment, as to imbue even the most obtuse intellect with a comprehension of it sufficiently distinct for all the purposes of practical analysis.

To look upwards from any existence, material or immaterial, to its *design*, is, perhaps, the most direct, and the most unerring method of attaining a just notion of the nature of the existence itself. Nor is the principle at fault when we turn our eyes from Nature even to Nature's God. We find certain faculties, implanted within us, and arrive at a more plausible conception of the character and attributes of those faculties, by considering, with what finite judgment we possess, the *intention* of the Deity in so implanting them within us, than by any actual investigation of their powers, or any speculative deductions from their visible and material effects. Thus, for example, we discover in all men a disposition to look with reverence upon superiority, whether real or supposititious. In some, this disposition is to be recognized with difficulty, and, in very peculiar cases, we are occasionally even led to doubt its existence altogether, until circumstances beyond the common routine bring it accidentally into development. In others again it forms a prominent and distinctive feature of character, and is rendered palpably evident in its excesses. But in all human beings it is, in a greater or less degree, finally perceptible. It has been, therefore, justly considered a primitive sentiment. Phrenologists call it Veneration. It is, indeed, the instinct given to man by God as security for his own worship. And although, preserving its nature, it becomes perverted from its principal purpose, and although swerving from that purpose, it serves to modify the relations of human society —the relations of father and child, of master and slave, of the ruler and the ruled—its primitive essence is nevertheless the same, and by a reference to primal causes, may at any moment be determined.

Very nearly akin to this feeling, and liable to the same analysis, is the Faculty of Ideality—which is the sentiment of Poesy. This sentiment is the sense of the beautiful, of the sublime, and of the mystical.[1] Thence spring immediately admiration of the fair flowers, the fairer forests, the bright valleys and rivers and mountains of the Earth—and love of the gleaming stars and other burning glories of Heaven—and, mingled up inextricably with this love and this admiration of Heaven and of Earth, the unconquerable desire—*to know.* Poesy is the sentiment of Intellectual Happiness here,

[1] *We separate the sublime and the mystical—for, despite of high authorities, we are firmly convinced that the latter may exist, in the most vivid degree, without giving rise to the sense of the former.* [E.A.P.]

and the Hope of a higher Intellectual Happiness here-after.[1]

Imagination is its soul.[2] With the *passions* of man-kind—although it may modify them greatly—although it may exalt, or inflame, or purify, or control them—it would require little ingenuity to prove that it has no inevitable, and indeed no necessary co-existence. We have hitherto spoken of poetry in the abstract: we come now to speak of it in its every-day acceptation—that

[1] *The consciousness of this truth was possessed by no mortal more fully than by Shelley, although he has only once especially alluded to it. In his* Hymn to Intellectual Beauty *we find these lines.*

> While yet a boy I sought for ghosts, and sped
>> Through many a listening chamber, cave and ruin,
>> And starlight wood, with fearful steps pursuing
> Hopes of high talk with the departed dead:
> I called on poisonous names with which our youth is fed:
>> I was not heard: I saw them not.
>> When musing deeply on the lot
> Of life at that sweet time when birds are wooing
>> All vital things that wake to bring
>> News of buds and blossoming,
>> Sudden thy shadow fell on me—
> I shrieked and clasped my hands in ecstasy!
>
> I vow'd that I would dedicate my powers
>> To thee and thine: have I not kept the vow?
> With beating heart and streaming eyes, even now
> I call the phantoms of a thousand hours
> Each from his voiceless grave: they have in vision'd bowers
>> Of studious zeal or love's delight
>> Outwatch'd with me the envious night:
> They know that never joy illum'd my brow,
>> Unlink'd with hope that thou wouldst free,
>> This world from its dark slavery,
>> That thou, O awful Loveliness,
> Wouldst give whate'er these words cannot express.

[2] *Imagination is, possibly in man, a lesser degree of the creative power in God. What the Deity imagines, is, but was not before. What man imagines, is, but was also. The mind of man cannot imagine what is not. This latter point may be demonstrated.—See* Les Premiers Traits de L'Erudition Universelle, par M. Le Baron de Bielfield, *1767.* [E.A.P.]

is to say, of the practical result arising from the sentiment we have considered.

And now it appears evident, that since Poetry, in this new sense, *is* the practical result, expressed in language, of this Poetic Sentiment in certain individuals, the only proper method of testing the merits of a poem is by measuring its capabilities of exciting the Poetic Sentiments in others.

And to this end we have many aids—in observation, in experience, in ethical analysis, and in the dictates of common sense. Hence the *Poeta nascitur,* which is indisputably true if we consider the Poetic Sentiment, becomes the merest of absurdities when we regard it in reference to the practical result We do not hesitate to say that a man highly endowed with the powers of Causality—that is to say, a man of metaphysical acumen—will, even with a very deficient share of Ideality, compose a finer poem (if we test it, as we should, by its measure of exciting the Poetic Sentiment) than one who, without such metaphysical acumen, shall be gifted, in the most extraordinary degree, with the faculty of Ideality. For a poem is not the Poetic faculty, but the *means* of exciting it in mankind. Now these means the metaphysician may discover by analysis of their effects in other cases than his own, without even conceiving the nature of these effects—thus arriving at a result which the unaided Ideality of his competitor would be utterly unable, except by accident, to attain.

FANCY AND IMAGINATION

A new poem from Moore calls to mind that critical opinion respecting him which had its origin, we believe, in the dogmatism of Coleridge—we mean the opinion that he is essentially the poet of *fancy*—the term being employed in contradistinction to *imagination*. "The fancy," says the author of the "Ancient Mariner," in his *Biographia Literaria*, "the fancy combines, the imagination creates." And this was intended, and has been received, as a distinction. If so at all, it is one without a difference; without even a difference of *degree*. The fancy as nearly creates as the imagination; and neither creates in any respect. All novel conceptions are merely unusual combinations. The mind of man can *imagine* nothing which has not really existed; and this point is susceptible of the most positive demonstration—see the Baron de Bielfeld, in his *"Premiers Traits de L'Erudition Universelle,"* 1767. It will be said, perhaps, that we can imagine a *griffin*, and that a griffin does not exist. Not the griffin certainly, but its component parts. It is a mere compendium of known limbs and features—of known qualities. Thus with all which seems to be *new* —which appears to be a *creation* of intellect. It is resoluble into the old. The wildest and most vigorous effort of mind cannot stand the test of this analysis.

We might make a distinction, *of degree*, between the fancy and the imagination, in saying that the latter is the former *loftily employed*. But experience proves this distinction to be unsatisfactory. What we *feel* and *know* to be fancy, will be found still only *fanciful*, whatever be the theme which engages it. It retains its idiosyncrasy under all circumstances. No *subject* exalts it into the ideal. . . .

Many a schoolboy . . . admires the imagination displayed in Jack the Giant-Killer . . . is finally rejoiced at discovering his own imagination to surpass that of the author, since the monsters destroyed by Jack are only about forty feet in height, and he himself has no trouble in imagining some of one hundred and forty.

The fairy of Shelley is not a mere compound of incongruous natural objects, inartificially put together, and unaccompanied by any *moral* sentiment; but a being, in the illustration of whose nature some physical elements are used collaterally as adjuncts, while the main conception springs immediately, *or thus apparently springs,* from the brain of the poet, enveloped in the moral sentiments of grace, of colour, of motion—of the beautiful, of the *mystical,* of the august—in short, of the ideal.

The truth is that the just distinction between the fancy and the imagination (and which is still but a distinction *of degree*) is involved in the consideration of the *mystic.* We give this as an idea of our own, altogether. We have no authority for our opinion—but do not the less firmly hold it. The term *mystic* is here employed in the sense of Augustus William Schlegel, and of most other German critics. It is applied by them to that class of composition in which there lies beneath the transparent upper current of meaning an under or *suggestive* one. What we vaguely term the *moral* of any sentiment is its mystic or secondary expression. It has the vast force of an accompaniment in music. This vivifies the air; that spiritualizes the *fanciful* conception, and lifts it into the *ideal.*

This theory will bear, we think, the most rigorous tests which can be made applicable to it, and will be acknowledged as tenable by all who are themselves imaginative. If we carefully examine those poems, or portions of poems, or those prose romances, which mankind have been accustomed to designate as *imaginative* (for an instinctive feeling leads us to employ properly the term whose full import we have still never been able to define), it will be seen that all so designated are remarkable for the *suggestive* character which we have discussed. They are strongly *mystic*, in the proper sense of the word. We will here only call to the reader's mind, the "Prometheus Vinctus" of Æschylus; the *Inferno* of Dante; the "Destruction of Numantia" by Cervantes; the "Comus" of Milton; the "Ancient Mariner," the "Christabel," and the "Kubla Khan" of Coleridge; the "Nightingale" of Keats; and, most especially, the "Sensitive Plant" of Shelley, and the *Undine* of De La Motte Fouqué. These two latter poems (for we call them both such) are the finest possible examples of the purely *ideal*. There is little of fancy here, and everything of imagination. With each note of the lyre is heard a ghostly, and not always a distinct, but an august and soul-exalting *echo*. In every glimpse of beauty presented, we catch, through long and wild vistas, dim bewildering visions of a far more ethereal beauty *beyond*. But not so in poems which the world has always persisted in terming *fanciful*. Here the upper current is often exceedingly brilliant and beautiful; but then men *feel* that this upper current *is all*. No Naiad voice addresses them *from below*. The notes of the air of the song do not tremble with the according tones of the accompaniment.

CONVERSATION

To converse well, we need the cool tact of talent—to talk well the glowing *abandon* of genius. Men of *very* high genius, however, talk at one time *very* well, at another *very* ill:—well, when they have full time, full scope, and a sympathetic listener:—ill, when they fear interruption and are annoyed by the impossibility of exhausting the topic during that particular talk. The partial genius is flashy—scrappy. The true genius

shudders at incompleteness—imperfection—and usually
prefers silence to saying the something which is not
every thing that should be said. He is so filled with his
theme that he is dumb, first from not knowing how to
begin, where there seems eternally beginning behind
beginning, and secondly from perceiving his true end
at so infinite a distance. Sometimes, dashing into a subject, he blunders, hesitates, stops short, sticks fast, and,
because he has been overwhelmed by the rush and
multiplicity of his thoughts, his hearers sneer at his
inability to think. Such a man finds his proper element
in those "great occasions" which confound and prostrate
the general intellect.

Nevertheless, by his conversation, the influence of
the conversationist upon mankind in general, is more
decided than that of the talker by his talk:—the latter
invariably talks to best purpose with his pen. And good
conversationists are more rare than respectable talkers.
. . . Most people, in conversing, force us to curse our
stars that our lot was not cast among the African nation
mentioned by Eudoxus—the savages who, having no
mouths, never opened them, as a matter of course. And
yet, if denied mouth, some persons whom I have in my
eye would contrive to chatter on still—as they do now—
through the nose.

THE IMPOSSIBILITY OF
WRITING A TRUTHFUL
AUTOBIOGRAPHY

If any ambitious man have a fancy to revolutionize, at
one effort, the universal world of human thought, human
opinion, and human sentiment, the opportunity is his

own—the road to immortal renown lies straight, open, and unencumbered before him. All that he has to do is to write and publish a very little book. Its title should be simple—a few plain words—*My Heart Laid Bare*. But —this little book must be *true to its title*.

Now, is it not very singular that, with the rabid thirst for notoriety which distinguishes so many of mankind —so many, too, who care not a fig what is thought of them after death, there should not be found one man having sufficient hardihood to write this little book? To *write*, I say. There are ten thousand men who, if the book were once written, would laugh at the notion of being disturbed by its publication during their life, and who could not even conceive *why* they should object to its being published after their death. But to write it— *there* is the rub. No man dare write it. No man ever will dare write it. No man *could* write it, even if he dared. The paper would shrivel and blaze at every touch of the fiery pen.

HERO WORSHIP

No hero-worshipper can possess anything within himself. That man is no man who stands in awe of his fellow-man. Genius regards genius with respect—with even enthusiastic admiration—but there is nothing of worship in the admiration, for it springs from a thorough cognizance of the one admired—from a perfect *sympathy*, the result of the cognizance; and it is needless to say, that sympathy and worship are antagonistic. Your hero-worshippers, for example—what do they know about Shakspeare? They worship him—rant about him —lecture about him—about *him, him,* and nothing else —for no other reason than that he is utterly beyond their comprehension. They have arrived at an idea of his greatness from the pertinacity with which men have called him great. As for their own opinion about him— they really have none at all. In general the very smallest of mankind are the class of men-worshippers. *Not one* out of this class have ever accomplished anything beyond a very contemptible mediocrity.

THE DISTRIBUTION
OF VITAL ENERGY

There are few men of that peculiar sensibility which is at the root of genius, who, in early youth, have not expended much of their mental energy in *living too fast;* and, in later years, comes the unconquerable desire to goad the imagination up to that point which it would have attained in an ordinary, normal, or well-regulated life. The earnest longing for artificial excitement, which, unhappily, has characterized too many eminent men, may thus be regarded as a psychal want, or necessity, —an effort to regain the lost,—a struggle of the soul to assume the position which, under other circumstances, would have been its due.

MUSIC AND POETRY

The great variety of melodious expression which is given out from the keys of a piano, might be made, in proper hands, the basis of an excellent fairy-tale. Let the poet press his finger steadily upon each key, keeping it down, and imagine each prolonged series of undulations the history, of joy or of sorrow, related by a good or evil spirit imprisoned within. There are some of the notes which almost tell, of their own accord, true and intelligible histories.

LOGIC VS. TRUTH

A precise or *clear* man, in conversation or in composition, has a very important consequential advantage—more especially in matters of logic. As he proceeds with his argument, the person addressed, exactly comprehending, for that reason, and often for that reason only, agrees. Few minds, in fact, can immediately perceive the distinction between the comprehension of a proposition and an agreement of the reason with the thing proposed. Pleased at comprehending, we often are so excited as to take it for granted that we assent. Luminous writers may thus indulge, for a long time, in pure sophistry, without being detected. Macaulay is a remarkable instance of this species of mystification. We coincide with what he says, too frequently, because we so very distinctly understand what it is that he intends to say. His essay on Bacon has been long and deservedly admired; but its concluding portions (wherein he endeavors to depreciate the *Novum Organum*,) although logical *to a fault*, are irrational in the extreme. But not to confine myself to mere assertion. Let us refer to this great essayist's review of Ranke's *History of the Popes*. His strength is here put forth to account for the progress of Romanism, by maintaining that divinity is not a progressive science. "The enigmas," says he, in substance, "which perplex the natural theologian, are the same in all ages, while the Bible, where alone we are to seek revealed truth, has been always what it is." Here Mr. Macaulay confounds the nature of that proof from which we reason of the concerns of earth, considered as man's habitation, with the nature of that evidence from which we reason of the same earth, regarded as a unit of the universe. In the former case, the *data* being palpable, the proof is direct; in the latter it is purely *analogical*. Were the indications we derive from science, of the nature and designs of Deity, and thence, by inference, of man's destiny,—were these indications proof *direct*, it is then very true that no advance in science could strengthen them; for, as the essayist justly observes, "nothing can be added to the force of the argument which the mind finds in every beast, bird, and flower;" but, since these indications are rigidly analogical, every step in human knowledge, every astronomical discovery, in especial, throws additional light upon the august subject, *by extending the range of analogy.* That we know no more, to-day, of the nature of Deity, of its purposes, and thus of man himself, than we did even a dozen years ago, is a proposition disgracefully absurd. "If Natural Philosophy," says a greater than Macaulay, "should continue to be improved in its various branches, the bounds of moral philosophy would be enlarged also." These words of the prophetic Newton are felt to be true, and will be fulfilled.

ON INTUITION

There are few thinkers who will not be surprised to find, upon retrospect of the world of thought, how *very* frequently the first, or intuitive, impressions have been the true ones. A poem, for example, enraptures us in our childhood. In adolescence, we perceive it to be full of fault. In the first years of manhood, we utterly despise and condemn it; and it is not until mature age has given tone to our feelings, enlarged our knowledge, and perfected our understanding, that we recur to our original sentiment and primitive admiration, with the additional pleasure which is always deduced from knowing *how* it was that we once were pleased, and *why* it is that we still admire.

That the imagination has not been unjustly ranked as supreme among the mental faculties, appears from the intense consciousness, on the part of the imaginative man, that the faculty in question brings his soul often to a glimpse of things supernal and eternal—to the very verge of the *great secrets*. There are moments, indeed, in which he perceives the faint perfumes, and hears the melodies of a happier world. Some of the most profound knowledge—perhaps all *very* profound knowledge— has originated from a highly stimulated imagination. Great intellects *guess* well. The laws of Kepler were, professedly, *guesses*.

PLOT—A DEFINITION

An excellent magazine paper might be written upon the subject of the progressive steps by which any great work of art—especially of literary art—attained completion. How vast a dissimilarity always exists between the germ and the fruit—between the work and its original conception! Sometimes the original conception is abandoned, or left out of sight altogether. Most authors sit down to write with *no* fixed design, trusting to the inspiration of the moment; it is not, therefore, to be wondered at, that *most* books are valueless. Pen should never touch paper, until at least a well-digested *general* purpose be established. In fiction, the *dénouement*—in all other composition the intended *effect*, should be definitely considered and arranged, before writing the first word; and no word should be then written which does not tend, or form a part of a sentence which tends to the development of the *dénouement,* or to the strengthening of the effect. Where *plot* forms a portion of the contemplated interest, too much preconsideration cannot be had. *Plot* is very imperfectly understood, and has never been rightly defined. Many persons regard it as mere complexity of incident. In its most rigorous acceptation, it is *that from which no component atom can be removed, and in which none of the component atoms can be displaced, without ruin to the whole;* and although a sufficiently good plot may be constructed, without attention to the whole rigor of this definition, still it is the definition which the true artist should always keep in view, and always endeavor to consummate in his works.

THE THEATRICAL PROFESSION

There is no cant more contemptible than that which habitually decries the theatrical profession—a profession which, in itself, embraces all that can elevate and ennoble, and absolutely nothing to degrade. If some—if many—or if even nearly all of its members are dissolute, this is an evil arising not from the profession itself, but from the unhappy circumstances which surround it. . . . The theatre is ennobled by its high facilities for the development of genius—facilities not afforded elsewhere in equal degree. By the spirit of genius we say, it is ennobled—it is sanctified—beyond the sneer of the fool or the cant of the hypocrite. The actor of talent is poor at heart, indeed, if he does not look with contempt upon the mediocrity even of a king. The writer of this article is himself the son of an actress—has invariably made it his boast—and no earl was ever prouder of his earldom than he of the descent from a woman who, although well-born, hesitated not to consecrate to the drama her brief career of genius and of beauty.

BETWEEN WAKEFULNESS AND SLEEP

Some Frenchman—possibly Montaigne—says: "People talk about thinking, but for my part I never think, except when I sit down to write." It is this never thinking, unless when we sit down to write, which is the cause of so much indifferent composition. But perhaps there is something more involved in the Frenchman's observation than meets the eye. It is certain that the mere act of inditing, tends, in a great degree, to the logicalization of thought. Whenever, on account of its vagueness, I am dissatisfied with a conception of the brain, I resort forthwith to the pen, for the purpose of obtaining, through its aid, the necessary form, consequence and precision.

How very commonly we hear it remarked, that such and such thoughts are beyond the compass of words! I do not believe that any thought, properly so called, is out of the reach of language. I fancy, rather, that where difficulty in expression is experienced, there is, in the intellect which experiences it, a want either of deliberateness or of method. For my own part, I have never had a thought which I could not set down in words, with even more distinctness than that with which I conceived it:—as I have before observed, the thought is logicalized by the effort at (written) expression.

There is, however, a class of fancies, of exquisite delicacy, which are *not* thoughts, and to which, *as yet*, I have found it absolutely impossible to adapt language. I use the word *fancies* at random, and merely because I must use *some* word; but the idea commonly attached to the term is not even remotely applicable to the shadow of shadows in question. They seem to me rather psychal than intellectual. They arise in the soul (alas, how rarely!) only at its epochs of most intense tranquility—when the bodily and mental health are in perfection—and at those mere points of time where the confines of the waking world blend with those of the world of dreams. I am aware of these "fancies" only when I am upon the very brink of sleep, with the consciousness that I am so. I have satisfied myself that this condition exists but for an inappreciable *point* of time —yet it is crowded with these "shadows of shadows"; and for absolute *thought* there is demanded time's *endurance*.

These "fancies" have in them a pleasurable ecstasy as far beyond the most pleasurable of the world of wakefulness, or of dreams, as the Heaven of the Northman theology is beyond its Hell. I regard the visions, even as they arise, with an awe which, in some measure, moderates or tranquilizes the ecstasy—I so regard them, through a conviction (which seems a portion of the ecstasy itself) that this ecstasy, in itself, is of a character supernal to the Human Nature—is a glimpse of the spirit's outer world; and I arrive at this conclusion—if this term is at all applicable to instantaneous intuition— by a perception that the delight experienced has, as its element, but *the absoluteness of novelty*. I say the absoluteness—for in these fancies—let me now term them psychal impressions—there is really nothing even approximate in character to impressions ordinarily received. It is as if the five senses were supplanted by five myriad others alien to mortality.

Now, so entire is my faith in the *power of words*, that, at times, I have believed it possible to embody even the evanescence of fancies such as I have attempted to describe. In experiments with this end in view, I have proceeded so far as, first, to control (when the bodily and mental health are good) the existence of the condition: —that is to say, I can now (unless when ill) be sure that the condition will supervene, if I so wish it, at the point of time already described: of its supervention, until lately, I could never be certain, even under the most favorable circumstances. I mean to say, merely, that now I can be sure, when all circumstances are favorable, of the supervention of the condition, and feel even the capacity of inducing or compelling it:—the favorable circumstances, however are not the less rare—else had I compelled, already, the Heaven into the Earth.

I have proceeded so far, secondly, as to prevent the lapse from *the point* of which I speak—the point of blending between wakefulness and sleep—as to prevent at will, I say, the lapse from this border-ground into the dominion of sleep. Not that I can *continue* the condition —not that I can render the point more than a point— but that I can startle myself from the point into wakefulness—*and thus transfer the point itself into the realm of Memory*—convey its impressions, or more properly their recollections, to a situation where (although still for a very brief period) I can survey them with the eye of analysis.

For these reasons—that is to say, because I have been enabled to accomplish thus much—I do not altogether despair of embodying in words at least enough of the fancies in question to convey, to certain classes of intellect, a shadowy conception of their character.

In saying this I am not to be understood as supposing that the fancies, or psychal impressions, to which I allude, are confined to my individual self—are not, in a word, common to all mankind—for on this point it is quite impossible that I should form an opinion—but nothing can be more certain than that even a partial record of the impressions would startle the universal intellect of mankind, by the *supremeness of the novelty* of the material employed, and of its consequent suggestions. In a word—should I ever write a paper on this topic, the world will be compelled to acknowledge that, at last, I have done an original thing.

MAN AND SUPERMAN

I have sometimes amused myself by endeavoring to fancy what would be the fate of any individual gifted, or rather accursed, with an intellect *very* far superior to that of his race. Of course, he would be conscious of his superiority; nor could he (if otherwise constituted as man is) help manifesting his consciousness. Thus he would make himself enemies at all points. And since his opinions and speculations would widely differ from those of *all* mankind—that he would be considered a madman, is evident. How horribly painful such a condition! Hell could invent no greater torture than that of being charged with abnormal weakness on account of being abnormally strong.

In like manner, nothing can be clearer than that a *very* generous spirit—*truly* feeling what all merely profess—must inevitably find itself misconceived in every direction—its motives misinterpreted. Just as extremeness of intelligence would be thought fatuity, so excess of chivalry could not fail of being looked upon as meanness in its last degree:—and so on with other virtues. This subject is a painful one indeed. That individuals

have so soared above the plane of their race, is scarcely
to be questioned; but, in looking back through history
for traces of their existence, we should pass over all biographies of "the good and the great," while we search
carefully the slight records of wretches who died in
prison, in Bedlam, or upon the gallows.

THE SELF AND THE UNIVERSE
(From the conclusion to *Eureka*.)

We walk about, amid the destinies of our world-
existence, encompassed by dim but ever present *Memories* of a Destiny more vast—very distant in the bygone
time, and infinitely awful.

We live out a Youth peculiarly haunted by such
dreams; yet never mistaking them for dreams. As Memories we *know* them. *During our Youth* the distinction is
too clear to deceive us even for a moment.

So long as this Youth endures, the feeling *that we
exist,* is the most natural of all feelings. We understand
it *thoroughly.* That there was a period at which we did
not exist—or, that it might so have happened that we
never had existed at all—are the considerations, indeed,
which *during this youth,* we find difficulty in understanding. Why we should *not* exist, is, *up to the epoch
of our Manhood,* of all queries the most unanswerable.
Existence—self-existence—existence from all Time and
to all Eternity—seems, up to the epoch of Manhood,
a normal and unquestionable condition:—*seems, because it is.*

But now comes the period at which a conventional
World-Reason awakens us from the truth of our dream.
Doubt, Surprise and Incomprehensibility arrive at the
same moment. They say:—"You live and the time was

when you lived not. You have been created. An Intelligence exists greater than your own; and it is only through this Intelligence you live at all." These things we struggle to comprehend and cannot:—*cannot*, because these things, being untrue, are thus, of necessity, incomprehensible.

No thinking being lives who, at some luminous point of his life of thought, has not felt himself lost amid the surges of futile efforts at understanding, or believing, that anything exists *greater than his own soul*. The utter impossibility of any one's soul feeling itself inferior to another; the intense, overwhelming dissatisfaction and rebellion at the thought;—these, with the omniprevalent aspirations at perfection, are but the spiritual, coincident with the material, struggles towards the original Unity—are, to my mind at least, a species of proof far surpassing what Man terms demonstration, that no one soul *is* inferior to another—that nothing is, or can be, superior to any one soul—that each soul is, in part, its own God—its own Creator:—in a word, that God— the material *and* spiritual God—*now* exists solely in the diffused Matter and Spirit of the Universe; and that the regathering of this diffused Matter and Spirit will be but the re-constitution of the *purely* Spiritual and Individual God.

In this view, and in this view alone, we comprehend the riddles of Divine Injustice—of Inexorable Fate. In this view alone the existence of Evil becomes intelligible; but in this view it becomes more—it becomes endurable. Our souls no longer rebel at a *Sorrow* which we ourselves have imposed upon ourselves, in furtherance of our own purposes—with a view—if even with a futile view—to the extension of our own *Joy*.

I have spoken of *Memories* that haunt us during our youth. They sometimes pursue us even in our Manhood:

—assume gradually less and less indefinite shapes:—now and then speak to us with low voices, saying:

"There was an epoch in the Night of Time, when a still-existent Being existed—one of an absolutely infinite number of similar Beings that people the absolutely infinite domains of the absolutely infinite space. It was not and is not in the power of this Being—any more than it is in your own—to extend, by actual increase, the joy of his Existence; but just as it *is* in your power to expand or to concentrate your pleasures (the absolute amount of happiness remaining always the same) so did and does a similar capability appertain to this Divine Being, who thus passes his Eternity in perpetual variation of Concentrated Self and almost Infinite Self-Diffusion. What you call The Universe is but his present expansive existence. He now feels his life through an infinity of imperfect pleasures—the partial and pain-intertangled pleasures of those inconceivably numerous things which you designate as his creatures, but which are really but infinite individualizations of Himself. All these creatures—*all*—those which you term animate, as well as those to whom you deny life for no better reason than that you do not behold it in operation—*all* these creatures have, in a greater or less degree, a capacity for pleasure and for pain:—*but the general sum of their sensations is precisely that amount of Happiness which appertains by right to the Divine Being when concentrated within Himself.* These creatures are all too, more or less conscious Intelligences; conscious, first, of a proper identity; conscious, secondly and by faint indeterminate glimpses, of an identity with the Divine Being of whom we speak—of an identity with God. Of the two classes of consciousness, fancy that the former will grow weaker, the latter stronger, during the long succession of ages which must elapse before these myriads of individual Intelligences become blended—when the bright stars become blended—into One. Think that the sense of individual identity will be gradually merged in the general consciousness—that Man, for example, ceasing imperceptibly to feel himself Man, will at length attain that awfully triumphant epoch when he shall recognize his existence as that of Jehovah. In the meantime bear in mind that all is Life—Life—Life within Life—the less within the greater, and all within the *Spirit Divine.*

POE'S BOOKS
WITH THEIR FIRST PUBLICATION DATES

Tamerlane and Other Poems. By a Bostonian. Boston, 1827 *(1941)

El Aaraaf, Tamerlane, and Minor Poems. Baltimore, 1829 *(1933)

Poems. Second Edition. New York, 1831 *(1936)

The Narrative of Arthur Gordon Pym. New York, 1838

The Conchologist's First Book. Philadelphia, 1839

Tales of the Grotesque and Arabesque. 2 vols. Philadelphia, 1840

The Prose Romances of Edgar A. Poe. Philadelphia, 1843

The Raven and Other Poems. New York, 1845 *(1942)

Tales. New York, 1845

Eureka: a Prose Poem. New York, 1848

The Works of the Late Edgar Allan Poe, with a Memoir by Rufus Wilmot Griswold and Notices of His Life and Genius by Nathaniel Parker Willis and James Russell Lowell. 4 vols. New York, 1850-1856

Books which have been reproduced in facsimile are marked by an asterisk followed by the publication date of the reprint edition.

BIBLIOGRAPHY

THE TEXTS

The Complete Works of Edgar Allan Poe, edited by James A. Harrison (the Virginia or Monticello Edition, 17 vols., New York, 1902), has the most reliable text. It has been reprinted photographically. The Harvard University Press is preparing a new scholarly edition edited by Thomas Ollive Mabbott, the first volume of which (*Poems*) is to appear in 1968. *The Complete Poems and Stories of Edgar Allan Poe,* edited by Arthur Hobson Quinn and Edward H. O'Neill (2 vols., New York, 1946), contains the important writings.

The Letters of Edgar Allan Poe, edited by John Ward Ostrom (2 vols., Cambridge, Mass., and London, 1948), has been reissued as well as *The Poems of Edgar Allan Poe,* edited by Killis Campbell (Boston, 1917). A more recent collection of the poems has been edited by Floyd Stovall (Charlottesville, Va., 1965).

Biographies

Several appeared during the years after Poe's death, the most important of which was *Edgar Allan Poe, His Life, Letters, and Opinions* by John H. Ingram (2 vols., London, 1880), revised and reissued in one volume in 1884 and 1891. George E. Woodberry's *The Life of Edgar Allan Poe, Personal and Literary, with his Chief Correspondence with Men of Letters* (2 vols., Boston, 1909) was the first major study, although it was marred by its author's dependence upon Griswold and by his moralistic disapproval of Poe. Both Ingram and Woodberry have long been out of print.

Of the many Poe biographies published in the 1920s (by Hervey Allen, Mary E. Phillips, and Mary Newton Stanard among others) only Joseph Wood Krutch's psychoanalytical study is still available. Marie Bonaparte's *Edgar Poe, Étude Psychoanalitique* (2 vols., Paris, 1933) was translated into English by John Rodker and published in London in 1949. Her interpretation had Freud's approval.

The outstanding scholarly biography is Arthur Hobson Quinn's *Edgar Allan Poe, a Critical Biography* (New York, 1941; London, 1942), which has always been kept in print. A shorter popular work is Edward Wagenknecht's *Edgar Allan Poe, the Man Behind the Legend* (New York and London, 1963). *The Histrionic Mr. Poe* by N. B. Fagin (Baltimore, Md., and London, 1949, o.p.) emphasizes Poe's actor ancestry.

Criticism

Killis Campbell's *The Mind of Poe* (Cambridge, Mass., 1932; London, 1933) is a perceptive study that has been re-issued. *Literary Criticism of Edgar Allan Poe*, edited by Robert L. Hough (Lincoln, Neb., 1965), brings together a number of critical articles. *Poe, a Collection of Critical Essays*, edited by Robert Regan (Ann Arbor, Mich., 1967), contains modern pieces only. Other works of criticism are *Poe, a Critical Study* by Edward Hutchins Davidson (Cambridge, Mass., and London, 1957) and *The Recognition of Edgar A. Poe* by Eric W. Carlson (Ann Arbor, Mich., 1966).

Poe's European aspect has been widely covered. *The French Face of Edgar Allan Poe* by Patrick F. Quinn (Carbondale, Pa., 1957) has a list of books and articles about him in French. Out of print but useful when found are Célestin P. Cambiaire's *The Influence of Edgar Allan Poe in France* (New York, 1927) and Palmer Cobb's *The Influence of E. T. A. Hoffmann on the Tales of Edgar Allan Poe* (Chapel Hill, N.C., 1908). Baudelaire's three essays on Poe are in his *Histoires Extraordinaires*, edited by Y. G. Le Dantec (Paris, 1951).

Bibliographies

A Bibliography of the Writings of Edgar A. Poe by John W. Robertson (2 vols., San Francisco, Calif., 1934), although somewhat out of date, and out of print, is essential. *Literary History of the United States*, edited by Robert E. Spiller *et al.* (2 vols., New York, 1963; London, 1964, third edition), has a good list of books and magazine articles about Poe.